CLAY ST.
KEARNEY ST.
WASHINGTON ST.
MONTGOMERY ST.
B
B
B
B

Pale Truth

—~~—

Montgomery Street

Pale Truth

A NOVEL BY

DANIEL ALEF

To George Anderjack, a fellow Rotarian and lover of history... Enjoy!

Daniel Alef

maxit

Publishing, Inc.

maxit
Publishing, Inc.

1900 Avenue of the Stars, Suite 2410
Los Angeles, CA 90067
www.maxitpublishing.com

PALE TRUTH

Library of Congress Cataloging-in-Publication Data
Alef, Daniel, 1944-
Pale truth : a novel / by Daniel Alef.-- 1st ed.
p. cm.
ISBN 0-9700174-1-3 (alk. paper)
1. Price, Mary Ellen, 1825-1919--Fiction. 2. San Francisco (Calif.)--Fiction. 3. Women abolitionists--Fiction. 4. Afro-American women--Fiction. 5. Passing (Identity)--Fiction. 6. Freedmen--Fiction. I. Title.
PS3551.L3465 P35 2000
813'.54--dc21 00-009450

Printed in the United States
First Edition

Cover Design by LeVan Fisher Design
Text Design/production by Britt Menendez, B Designs/San Francisco

Dedication

Pale Truth is dedicated in loving memory to the following people who had a profound influence on my life:

To Genia for her wisdom *and* eternal love
To Zahava for teaching me the discipline *of the arts*
To Frank for the strength of his intellectual curiosity *and the love of books*
To David for his examples of devotion *and* loyalty
To Norman for his enduring patience.

If only you were here to share with me the
pride and joy of writing this book.

And to Aba for his defiance of time, age and mortality –
I hope to deliver a copy of this book on your 105th birthday.
Without all of you this book would have never been written.
Without you I would not have been. You are not to blame
for my failures, but you bear responsibility for my successes.

Celebration of Statehood

Contents

BOOK 2

1849 ~ 1851

Acknowledgments

I OWE A GREAT DEBT OF GRATITUDE TO A NUMBER OF PEOPLE WHOSE efforts helped make this novel a dream come true. First, thanks to my editor, Carol Lacy, who had little hesitation in cutting and shredding my work, with a view to keeping intact the rhythm of story-telling. A great editor, like a veteran guide, is indispensable; perhaps an author's best, or only, chance to stay the course. Kendra Arimoto also helped with editing and infusing new ideas where old ones seemed tarnished and feeble. I truly enjoyed our little coffee house chats and exchanges. My good friend Noah benShea's support and encouragement, coming no less from a best-selling author, were always inspirational. Others from MaxIt Publishing, from the top with CEO Jeffrey Little, to the troops in the trenches, were instrumental in making Pale Truth, my dream, a reality.

During the course of my research, an occupation in itself, others provided me with guidance, and information. Special thanks to the Bancroft

Library at the University of California, Berkeley, for their help. Not only is this facility an incredible repository of California history, the knowledgeable staff, and especially Susan Snyder, were always accommodating and eager to help. I received unexpected guidance from several sources. For example, Dr. Charles E. Nolan of the Archdiocese of New Orleans provided me with a copy of the curriculum for the Ursuline Convent in the 1840s. It was a small but pleasant surprise. I have the greatest admiration for W.C. Dover whose patience with my quest and endless tribulations has been, I am sure, sorely tested. I also wish to thank the staff at the UCLA Research Library, the UCSB Davidson Library, the Historical New Orleans Collection, the Louisiana State Museum, the San Francisco Maritime Museum, the Oakland Museum of California, the California Historical Society and the Museum of San Francisco for their kind help. I humbly bow to all of you and am awed by the depth of your knowledge, commitment and generosity.

And, of course, special thanks to my family, especially my wife, for reading so many seemingly endless drafts, countless editing sessions, and for giving me excellent counsel from a reader's point of view.

Daniel Alef

Preface

ON SEPTEMBER 9, 2000, CALIFORNIA CELEBRATED THE SESQUICENTENNIAL of its admission to the Union. One hundred and fifty years young, pulsating with life and vigor, equivalent in economic power to one of the top nations of this Earth, California thrives and trail-blazes into the twenty-first century. So it is hard to imagine what California was like when Congress voted to admit California as the thirty-first state in 1850.

The streets of San Francisco, the largest city at that time, were not paved with gold; they were not even paved. Montgomery Street, where the pyramid-like skyscraper now nestles in the middle of the city, surrounded by tall buildings, was the waterfront. This landmark actually sits in the shallows where waves lapped at the beach. Wharves extended into the cove, later to become streets as the people graded the hills, dumped the sand between the wharves and gradually reclaimed the bay. Tents and shanties littered the hills. Hundreds of deserted ships swayed idly with the tide, rigging in disarray, abandoned by passengers and crews, all bound for the gold hills. Some of these ships, like the *Niantic,* became land bound, sitting between clapboard buildings; one would think a strange and eerie sight, but not for the people of San Francisco.

It took one month for the news of statehood to reach California. And in the following decade California endured nearly every conceivable natural and man-made calamity, from destructive fires, civil unrest with vigilantes numbering in the thousands, public executions, earthquakes, squatter riots, corruption on an inconceivable scale, bank failures, and the flow of more gold and wealth than the world had ever seen.

Remarkable men and women came to this rugged land with dreams and secrets, with resolve and fear, with knowledge and ignorance. Leaving the past, living the present, lusting for the future, they struggled, survived, and ultimately had a profound effect on the course of California history. This is their story. This is the story of California.

Book One

1829–1849

Chapter One

Southern Belle

AUGUSTA, GEORGIA
1829 - 1836

February 23, 1829

My name is Delila, my name is Delila, SHE REPEATED OVER AND OVER in her mind as the pain gripped her abdomen, taking her breath away. She wanted to scream, to relieve some of the pain. Instead, she held her breath, clenched her teeth, and shut her eyes tightly.

After a minute the agony subsided and she gulped at the cool, fresh air. Opening her eyes she could barely make out the rough hew of the ceiling rafters through her burning tears. Her dress was drenched. Beads of perspiration trickled down her face and into her mouth. She licked her lips, tasting the salt. Enduring so much pain without uttering a sound, not even a muffled grunt, gave her some consolation, even strength. She had shown no sign of weakness.

Pleased with herself she slowly stood and walked unsteadily down the aisle between the straw-filled bedrolls that lined the slave quarters, focusing on the torn, stained linen curtains billowing in the gentle breeze. Sounds became distinct, too distinct—the breathing of the other slaves huddled quietly in small groups. They had not offered any help and now they were trying their best to appear inconspicuous. But even in the darkness their eyes reflected fear and loathing; the fear she anticipated, even intended. The loathing did not bother her. She simply shrugged it off.

She knew that her silence did not seem natural to them; that they were wondering how any person could endure so much pain over a prolonged period of time and remain totally silent, almost indifferent. She was certain that her silence confirmed what they had all suspected from the day she arrived at the plantation. Now, as she turned and walked back to her own bedroll, they shrank away.

Another violent contraction seized Delila in mid-stride. She slumped back to her knees, grasping her abdomen with her hands. But this time it was different. Instead of the sharp pains of the past two days and sleepless nights, it now felt as if the bones in her pelvis were ripping apart. She felt an inexorable urge to bear down and push, so she squatted and pushed with all her might, just as she had seen other women do. Still, she stifled the emerging grunt in her throat. She pushed and pushed hard in absolute silence.

It had been ten days since she last worked in the fields. Her pregnancy interfered with her ability to work and even the simplest task seemed too difficult. The overseer grudgingly allowed Delila to remain with the young children. Sitting uncomfortably on a rickety chair in front of the gray clapboard cottage, listening to the children crying, yelling, and laughing, reminded her of her own childhood. She thought of her mother, beautiful but distant, and the daddy she never knew. Now, between contractions, she pictured the father of her child, the English farmer who originally owned her, standing proudly, some would have called it arrogantly, watching her with those tiger-like golden eyes.

At first she had been frightened and reluctant, but later became an eager partner in his bed. He was a gentle lover who gave her much pleasure. Perhaps she should have known better, but she was a lusty woman and even now she imagined she could feel the heat of his body.

Chapter One

The crystal image of the man broke into brittle pieces and floated away as a sudden, forceful contraction stunned her. They were coming so quickly, one on top of the other, giving her little chance for respite. Delila was not sure that she could remain silent much longer. Again she squatted and bore down, pushing through the contraction and letting nature take its course. After a long minute she exhaled sharply, raised her head, took a deep breath, lowered her chin to her chest, and pushed again.

Suddenly something gave way, as if her skin were tearing. Unable to see over her belly she touched herself and felt something hard and realized it was the crown of her baby's head.

She exhaled again, tilted her head back, took another deep breath and pushed. The entire cottage was now silent, everyone frozen in place. Delila could feel the little head slowly turn as the body came out and slipped through her grasping hands to the ground. Like her mother the baby had not uttered a sound.

With trembling hands Delila picked up the baby and brushed off the small clods of dirt. She inspected the little girl and marveled at the new life, squirming and fidgeting as the air of the outside world caressed her tiny body. Despite the blood and yellow, cheese-like, substance that covered the baby's body, Delila could see that her features were fine, almost elegant. Hesitantly she brought her daughter to her breast. The dark nipple grazed the baby's soft cheek and the baby immediately turned her head until she could grasp the nipple in her mouth.

The other slaves watched in awe as Delila sat on the floor, blood dripping between her legs, the umbilical cord still attached to the baby and the afterbirth still in her womb. The women knew she had ripped badly, since the bright red blood was still flowing. Hot compresses applied before the birth would have made the tissue softer and less vulnerable to tearing, but no one dared to bring hot water or rags to Delila or to even suggest it.

They watched the baby suckling at her mother's breast and, for a brief moment, the women shared in Delila's motherly joy, forgetting all thoughts of her deviltry or mystical powers. But the men in the slave quarters did not feel anything for this woman or her child, certainly not sympathy and least of all empathy.

The baby sucked hard. A small contraction delivered the afterbirth and after a few minutes Delila severed the cord with her teeth.

The first rays of the morning sun filtered through the windows of the cottage. Delila shielded her baby's face from the light as she continued to nurse. Finally, content with her mother's milk, the baby relaxed and opened her eyes. Delila smiled at her baby but suddenly exhaled sharply, startled at the sight of her baby's eyes.

"*Flimani Koku!*" Delila gasped.

Everyone in the cottage heard her and gazed anxiously at the mother and child. Delila was staring at the strangest eyes she had ever seen in a baby or adult. One eye appeared to be green, the other blue or black.

—ᴡ—

NOT FAR FROM THE SLAVE QUARTERS THE HUGE PILLARED MANSION at Golden Oaks nestled in a grove of trees on a small hill overlooking the neat cotton and tobacco fields west of Augusta, Georgia. Sparkling white, with tall Ionic columns so popular among the more opulent gentry of the South, the plantation had been in the hands of the Saunders family for nearly three generations. Carlyle Saunders, a tall man in his early forties with hair prematurely white, and his wife Abigail, a stout but warm-hearted Kentuckian, were being served breakfast in the dining room. Carlyle had just finished his food and the servants quickly whisked the dishes away from the long, polished mahogany table and brought in the morning tea service. Carlyle adjusted his spectacles and picked up a newspaper at his side, then just as quickly dropped it on the table with contempt.

"Now that Jackson's been sworn into the presidency, it'd be nice, indeed, to know what he really stands for."

Abigail remained silent. Carlyle went on. "After all, he hasn't really made his position clear on any subject. I suppose he'll listen to his friends Isaac Hill and that Preston Blair—what are they calling them?" he looked at the paper and poked it with his finger, "There, his 'kitchen cabinet,' what a revolting term."

Chapter One

Abigail and Carlyle rarely discussed politics, but she knew his agitation did not have anything to do with Andrew Jackson. Something else was bothering him.

"He is very popular," she offered.

"Well, maybe. But if people really think he's for the common man they have a surprise coming, because he's really one of us. Has more slaves than we do. I prefer someone whose point of view is a bit more clear and certainly more predictable."

Carlyle was about to say something else when John Morrison, the overseer, came into the room carrying his hat under his arm.

"Well? What is it?" Carlyle demanded as he put down his cup of tea and wiped his lips with a linen napkin.

"I'm sorry for interrupting," Morrison began, "but I don't rightly know what has the slaves so upset, Mr. Saunders."

"What do you mean you don't know, John?" Carlyle's voice boomed across the dining room. "For three days everything's been in an uproar. We can feel the vibrations right here in this house." He tossed his napkin across the table. "I tell you I'm very uneasy about it."

"I know, Mr. Saunders," Morrison spoke hesitantly, "but I never saw anything quite like it. The slaves are terrified. But I don't know why. It don't make no sense."

Carlyle looked at Abigail who appeared a little distressed, though Carlyle imagined the motives for her anguish were entirely different from his.

"John, we've got to get to the bottom of this thing now! The longer it goes on the worse it's likely to become." Carlyle found himself more irritated by his inability to find out what was taking place right under his nose at Golden Oaks than by any fear of some impending disaster.

Morrison stood before the dining table, his self-assurance wavering. Carlyle noticed it immediately.

"Well? Come out with it, John. Let's have it," he demanded.

"I think it has something to do with that girl Delila, the one we got a few months back with Chauncey's slaves," Morrison said.

"She's the one having a baby?" Abigail asked, suddenly more interested in the conversation.

Slaves to Market

"Yes ma'am. That's the one," Morrison replied politely.

"Are you telling me that what's going on here has something to do with one girl? One simple girl?" Carlyle asked incredulously.

Morrison hesitated. "Well, it seems like the others are afraid of her. Something to do with voodoo . . . " Morrison trailed off and realized just how absurd it sounded.

"Bah!" Carlyle scoffed. "Just stupid tribal superstition. That's all."

"But she has been a handful of trouble," Morrison said.

"I know. I know." Carlyle recalled how Delila arrived with several other slaves in payment of a debt owed to them by their neighbor, Hiram Chauncey. Delila had been morose and difficult from the first day.

Morrison, a knowledgeable and reliable overseer, one of the best Carlyle had ever known, did not like the girl from the start. He pressed Carlyle to get rid of her but Carlyle refused, claiming she should be given a chance. Delila did not change. She remained testy, obstinate, and completely uncooperative.

Carlyle looked at Morrison. "Should've got rid of her when you first suggested it."

"I understand, Mr. Saunders." Morrison was contrite.

Abigail now leaned forward, her face intent. Carlyle noticed it and understood her sudden interest, but continued, "If it turns out she's somehow involved get rid of her. I don't care what you do. Sell her. Give her away. It's almost time to plant and we can't afford this disruption."

"Darling," Abigail interrupted,"how can you even think of sending her away when she's about to have a baby?"

Carlyle instantly recognized her expression. "I don't intend to do anything to harm her, Abbie. I want her off our hands, that's all. We can't allow one slave to cause trouble. Think of the precedent it'd set. Why, the other slaves would get the idea they can make trouble and get away with it. And then where will we be?"

Carlyle could see that Abigail was not mollified. He smiled wearily at his wife, then turned to Morrison. "But first make sure you find out if she is involved with the problem."

The Saunders lived a pleasant and easy life. They were sociable and highly regarded by their neighbors. They treated their slaves relatively well and, unlike many of the other owners, Carlyle refused to take advantage of the young women he owned. Even after all these years he loved Abigail intensely and found no reason or desire to go beyond her bed. But they both suffered deeply, each carrying the burden in their own quiet way.

More than ten years had passed since their infant daughter, Eleanor, had passed away. Her lungs had not completely formed, their neighbor and good friend, Dr. Vernon, gently informed them as he laid the little body in Abigail's lap for her last fleeting moment with her daughter.

Carlyle and Abigail never fully recovered, and after nearly a year had passed they decided to have another baby. They tried desperately to have children, but so far had failed. And they knew time was passing them by.

Carlyle submerged his depression and feelings of inadequacy as a man by working harder to make Golden Oaks the best, most productive and prosperous plantation in the South. He did not blame his wife; it would have been unchivalrous of him. Instead he made his people work harder, but not under oppressive conditions.

Carlyle believed in efficiency and productivity. They represented the entire sum of his philosophy. He had the ability to get the most out of his slaves and out of his land without cudgel or cruelty. It was not necessary. His slaves were well fed, well clothed, and the children relatively well cared for, but not because Carlyle considered them as anything other than property. He loved his land and loved his slaves in the same way—as highly prized chattels. They belonged to him and he had a responsibility to make the most of them. When he treated his land well it produced more and better crops. The same applied to his slaves. They were indispensable to the success of the plantation.

Unlike Carlyle, Abigail did not think of the slaves entirely as property. She thought of them more as children, children who were incapable of taking care of themselves and needed strong parental authority mixed with kindness to survive. Like many Southern women of her station, she did not engage in political discussions or express her political views on the issue of slavery. Slavery was a given and accepted. It was as much a part of her and Carlyle's life as the plantation itself. But unlike many other whites she did not see the slaves as animals. Her views, subtly crafted, moved an unsuspecting Carlyle to more humane treatment of the slaves. Those who refused to work or did not work to his expectations were sold or traded, not mistreated. He kept corporal punishment to a minimum. However, those transgressions that merited punishment were dealt with harshly, and even Abigail did not dare intercede.

Abigail empathized with new mothers of young children. She appealed to her husband to give the mothers better care and less onerous conditions.

His love for Abigail made it impossible for Carlyle to refuse her entreaties, even though in many cases they made no economic sense to him. She would visit the women and check the children for disease or malnutrition. At Christmastime Abigail would bestow all manner of gifts upon them. At times, to Carlyle's dismay, she invited the mothers with their children into the main house, usually at some holiday or festival. And this was the only reason Delila had not been shipped out earlier.

—~—

MORRISON LEFT THE MANSION, MOUNTED HIS HORSE, AND RODE quickly to the back section of the plantation where a recent flood had sent water roiling through the weeping willows alongside the usually placid stream, washing out one of the roads. Moses Jackson, his trustee, and his crew were repairing and grading the road. Maybe old Moses could shed more light, though Morrison was not optimistic. No one, not even Moses, had been forthcoming, but he would now apply more pressure, just as the Saunders were pressuring him.

As for Delila, he could not stand her. Something about her made him uneasy, and he reasoned that she must be at the root of the problem.

As he rode through the verdant land he mulled the slaves' unprecedented behavior. He would get rid of Delila no matter what, but he knew Carlyle and Abigail and he would have to deal carefully with Delila.

The men were listlessly filling in a large washout on the dirt road when Morrison arrived and leaped off his horse. Moses had been cajoling the men to work harder, to little avail. He put down his shovel and approached Morrison, taking his hat off in respect to the overseer. What could he tell Morrison? The white man did not understand these things.

Delila was a voodoo queen. Every slave knew it. She had power. She had come from Santa Domingo and was the daughter of the island's most celebrated voodoo queen. Slaves who arrived with her kept away from her and related hair-raising stories of her prowess.

Delila was headstrong and ornery and made everyone's life more difficult by threatening spells, performing exotic liturgies, and generally staying to herself, her face locked into a cruel and arrogant expression. She intimidated all of them, though Moses suspected much of it was done for show. Still, he had seen too many strange things in his life and had no intention of testing her powers. He was too old and too wise to do that.

The expected birth of her baby made everyone more nervous. If anything happened to the baby what would Delila do? Would she blame them? Would she cast a spell on the plantation?

As her pregnancy matured and the expected delivery neared, the fear and tension reached a debilitating state, where the slaves simply went through the motions of working and accomplished nothing. Word had already gotten to Moses that the baby was fine and some of the anxiety was ebbing away. No word of the baby's eyes had yet filtered down to the men in the field.

"Have you found out anything, Moses?" Morrison asked.

"No, Suh," Moses shook his head in reply, but kept his head lowered more for fear of having his eyes give him away than from a sign of respect.

"God damn it, Moses! I told you to find out. If you can't find out what's going on I'll just have to get someone else to replace you." Morrison, known for his stolid demeanor, was shouting.

The other men edged slowly away, frightened by Morrison's outburst. Even his horse, ears twitching and head bobbing, started to shy away. Morrison immediately grabbed the halter, pressing his forearm along the horse's rippling neck, using his elbow for leverage, and continued to rail at Moses. The horse became more agitated and started to back away from the men.

Moses moved to the other side of the horse speaking gently and trying to caress its head. Morrison held on firmly, also speaking softly to the animal. But despite their combined efforts the horse became more aroused. Suddenly the horse reared and knocked old Moses to the ground. Morrison, afraid the horse might trample Moses, pushed the horse away, but lost his grip on the halter. Facing the wheeling horse he yelled and waved his hands to force the horse backward.

The horse, now in complete confusion and blinded by fear, circled around until its hind quarters were directly in front of Morrison, then kicked as it bucked. One hoof hit Morrison flush on his forehead with such force it actually snapped his head back, sending his body flying backwards. He landed on his back with a dull thud, dead before he hit the ground, his neck broken and the front of his head caved in.

The men rushed towards him but dared not touch the body.

The horse broke away at a gallop, bucking at some unseen specter.

Moses got to his feet unsteadily, wiped the dust from his clothes, and bent over Morrison, whose lifeless eyes stared straight into the sky. Moses crossed himself and gently closed Morrison's eyes. He and the men had no doubt who was responsible for this calamity, but they simply looked at each other in silence, each one seeing a mirror reflection of his own fear. Moses quietly thanked the Lord it was not him.

Delila had power, more power than he could imagine. He looked down at poor Morrison; a sad testament to her wickedness. Whether or not Delila caused this accident did not matter. Not to him. The deed was done and Moses understood how it would be interpreted by all the slaves. No one would ever dare to question or cross Delila or the product of her union with the devil.

—ɱ—

As the days passed, life at Golden Oaks slowly returned to normal. Delila, who had not yet thought of a name, decided to call her child Mary Ellen. She had once heard the name and liked it.

When no calamity befell the other slaves, they returned to work, grateful to escape her company. She remained with her baby and did not go back to the fields.

Carlyle and Abigail never learned what caused all the agitation, though they grieved at Morrison's death. He had been a competent and loyal employee.

Shortly after learning of the baby's arrival, Abigail went to the small wood-frame shack where the women and young children lived. She found Delila in one corner, the baby suckling contentedly.

Abigail knew only that Delila had been acquired in payment of a debt, and that Carlyle did not like her attitude. She was taller than the others with raven-black skin. She gave Abigail an imperious look.

Abigail was surprised to see how the other women kept their distance. Normally a new mother would be surrounded, the other women helping both mother and child, giving comfort and lending a hand; that was the custom. Its notable absence was disquieting.

As Abigail approached, Delila's obsidian eyes flared and flashed defiance. Undaunted, Abigail sought out the tiny new life. Without a word she knelt next to Delila and confidently opened the edge of the soiled cloth in which the child was wrapped. She caught her breath. Instead of finding a replica of the mother, Abigail was staring into the strangest eyes she had ever seen in a baby. Each eye was slightly different in ways she could not be sure of in the shadows. Perhaps it was the color, or the shape, or the way the baby peered out at the strange world into which she was born. Also, the baby's skin was light golden amber. Abigail was intrigued.

"What a lovely baby you have, Delila." Abigail smiled warmly at the taciturn woman. "Have you decided upon a name yet?" She asked, a little less certain in view of Delila's muted belligerence.

Delila looked sternly at Abigail but did not respond. She did not want this foolish white woman meddling with her baby.

Abigail, however, would not be deterred. "Delila, I am going to arrange for some things for you and the baby. We want the baby to have a good, healthy start in life, don't we?" Abigail stood up. "I'll be back soon." She smiled thinly and left. Delila, her expression unaltered, watched her go.

Ignoring Delila's overt hostility, or what Abigail felt was truculence, Abigail frequently visited mother and child.

After several weeks Delila's mood changed from hostile defiance to bland indifference, nothing more. Abigail could see that the other slaves were terrified of mother and child. It was not just Delila's attitude. There was something else, something she could not understand and no one else would explain to her.

As tiny Mary Ellen grew, the difference in her eyes became quite pronounced. One eye was green, the other brown. Abigail felt a deep sorrow for the lonely child. Mary Ellen was obviously bright, perhaps precocious, and Abigail, ever ready to empathize with the forlorn, found herself spending more and more time with the unusual slave child.

Delila was a strict and harsh mother. She loved her daughter but did not know how to show it. Easily frustrated she would push and prod Mary Ellen to behave perfectly, sometimes shouting and sometimes striking out at the little girl. None of the slaves dared to intercede.

Gradually little Mary Ellen built a wall between herself and her mother. Starved for love, she tried to get close to her mother, but Delila never touched her gently or hugged her the way other mothers did their children. And Mary Ellen had no friends. The older children gave her a wide berth or ran away if she approached.

Unable to express her love to Mary Ellen, Delila became more protective of her daughter, almost as if by such actions she could make Mary Ellen understand just how much she cared. But Delila, heeding the lessons wrought by her own mother and the history of her tribe passed down orally through the generations, knew that she had a mission to accomplish—to pass on to Mary Ellen knowledge of the mysticism and power she was blessed with. Delila did not have the slightest interest in having Mary Ellen be like the other children. She was different; she was better; and she had to be stronger and tougher.

One day, after a particularly harsh admonishment ministered by Delila with a resounding slap to the face, Mary Ellen rushed outside and slumped against the trunk of her favorite tree, a huge old oak near the mansion. Abigail, who was strolling through the garden, found her sitting dejectedly, clutching her knees to her bosom, tears leaving long wet tracks down her beautiful bronze face.

"What's the matter, darling?" Abigail asked softly and knelt next to the child.

Mary Ellen did not stir. She continued to stare straight ahead.

Abigail sidled closer to Mary Ellen, put her arm around the girl's small shoulders and held her. Surprisingly, Mary Ellen turned, placed both her arms around Abigail, put her face on the older woman's shoulder and, clutching tightly, started to sob a deep, melancholy cry, which soon had both of them weeping. No words were exchanged as they held on to each other under the massive boughs of the majestic oak.

After a while Mary Ellen stopped crying, but kept her arms around Abigail and her head on Abigail's shoulder. Abigail gently stroked the child's head and felt Mary Ellen's body slowly rise and fall with the rhythm of her breathing. She had never felt so close to a child. Strange thoughts of her own girlhood and little Eleanor were interwoven with the physical reality of Mary Ellen nestled in her arms.

From this point on Abigail became more and more involved with Mary Ellen. In many ways Mary Ellen became the child Abigail never had and could never have. The two would be found together often, singing children's rhymes, playing the piano, painting, or sewing.

Mary Ellen looked forward to seeing Abigail and would squeal in laughter at her sight. Abigail found a happiness in her life that made her eagerly look forward to the rising sun each day.

Delila's jealousy, which she either could not contain or did not bother to hide, manifested itself in many ways, but chiefly in creating an even greater gulf between mother and child.

Not surprisingly, the other slaves kept their thoughts to themselves. They went about their business, working long days except for a brief respite on Sunday mornings. The slaves paid little attention to Delila and Mary Ellen since they were too preoccupied with surviving and trying to live as comfortably as their bleak circumstances would allow. Mother and child were shunned, something Delila found acceptable but Mary Ellen barely endured.

Carlyle tolerated the company of the little girl. He noted the happiness she brought to the mansion and to Abigail, and let things be. But deep inside he was troubled. Mary Ellen was Delila's daughter, and Delila was evil.

Chapter Two

The Power

GOLDEN OAKS, GEORGIA
MARCH 1836

A DREARY GRAY MANTLE OF THICK CLOUD BLOCKED THE SUN'S RAYS. For over two weeks it had rained almost every day, drenching those who ventured outside. The saturated earth had its fill of water, and the rain simply created larger puddles, more mud and torrential runoffs. Roads were impassable and, with little to do, Carlyle and Abigail remained cooped up inside their house, reading books and trying to keep themselves occupied. Dry logs hissed and snapped in the fireplaces, throwing off light and heat, while the wind outside howled fiercely.

Late Thursday afternoon, just before dark, Carlyle and Abigail were sitting in the parlor having tea. Carlyle could tell that Abigail was agitated, but attributed her moodiness to the weather. Several times she seemed on the verge of saying something, then stopped, set her mouth firmly and gazed into the fire. He waited patiently.

"Carlyle, honey," she said softly, "what do you think about Mary Ellen?"

Carlyle mulled this over in his mind, wondering where this conversation would lead.

"She seems to be a nice girl. A little strange, wouldn't you say?"

Abigail smiled wanly. "Yes, she is different from the others. But you do think she is nice," she asked rhetorically.

Carlyle answered anyway. "Yes, darling. I just said she is nice."

"Have you noticed how bright she is?" Abigail asked. But her eyes were far away.

"Yes, Abbie, I suppose she is," Carlyle admitted. He had never really thought much about it, but he could recall several instances when the child displayed an uncanny intelligence and an obvious inquisitiveness that he found curious, not so much because she was a slave, but such inquisitiveness was not really something he attributed to girls. At times her inquisitiveness could be irritating. She went into everything. She examined objects with meticulous care and wonderment. Mary Ellen already knew the alphabet and could recognize some words in the books Abigail read to her. Even the most mundane objects could attract Mary Ellen's interminable attention. A moth fluttering against a closed window, seeking the light outside, or against a lamp, would become a source of considerable interest. Then she might capture it carefully and examine the insect as if she could somehow pry from it the secrets of life.

"What's this all about, Abigail?" he asked, puzzled by Abigail's remarks.

Abigail looked brightly at her husband. "I've been giving this a lot of thought, dear." She paused. "You know, she has no playmates among the others."

Carlyle understood "others" to mean the slaves, but he remained mute.

"It seems as if there's a curtain between Mary Ellen and the others, and I still haven't been able to discover its origin."

"Well, it's probably that impossible mother of hers," Carlyle scoffed. "I don't think I'd want my children playing with Delila's progeny," he said lightheartedly, and laughed.

A cloud formed over Abigail's face. "We don't have any children, Carlyle."

"I'm terribly sorry, Abigail." Carlyle wished he could take back the words. "I didn't mean it the way it came out."

Abigail remained silent for a while and sighed. "I know that. And I'm not sure you'll understand what I'm about to ask, but you do know that I'm very fond of Mary Ellen."

Carlyle tensed up. "Yes," he said.

"I'd like to give Mary Ellen a proper education." Abigail looked directly at him.

"What do you mean by 'a proper education'?" he asked, not certain what his wife meant.

"You know. She should learn to be a proper girl, to be raised properly, to learn to read and write and do all the things a young lady should do."

Carlyle looked at his wife as if she were insane. He sat down on the silk settee next to Abigail and tenderly cupped her hand between his. "We can't do that, Abigail," he said pleadingly. "She's a slave. She's a Negress."

"I don't know . . . " Abigail started to say, but Carlyle cut her off.

"You know damned well that she's a Negress. My god, woman, you were there shortly after the baby was born."

"I know that." Abigail seemed flustered. "But look at her skin. Look at her eyes. Her father must have been white."

"So what?" Carlyle's voice boomed across the room, as he became more agitated. "She's still a slave. She's still a Negress. The color of her father's skin has nothing to do with it. Delila is as black as she is moody and irritable. And her daughter is her product. Nothing more."

They remained quiet, neither one looking at the other, but Carlyle's face had darkened and Abigail knew that Carlyle had to be struggling with his temper.

Carlyle's struggle ended. "I don't know what's gotten into you, Abigail. You're speaking rubbish. And it's unlawful. How could we do what you're asking? How?"

Abigail looked at her husband, her eyes intense and her brow knitted into deep furrows. "You don't understand, Carlyle."

"Of course I do," he responded tersely. "She could never be accepted in our society and she'll never be accepted among her own, where she belongs. You'd destroy the girl, not to mention becoming the laughingstock of Georgia, if they didn't put you in jail."

Abigail Saunders

Abigail inhaled sharply and clasped her hands, squeezing her fingers together until they turned white. Obviously Carlyle did not understand, and she could not blame him. What she proposed ran against everything both she and Carlyle had been taught to believe in. But Abigail's feelings for Mary Ellen had blossomed, so she had steeled herself for Carlyle's reaction. A power she could not understand compelled her to act.

"Carlyle, this girl will never be accepted by her own people, whether or not she's educated. I don't know why. I've tried to find out. I don't expect her to be accepted by our folk. But she has a wonderful mind, a brilliant mind. She absorbs everything and is always eager to learn more. She doesn't speak like the others. Just by listening to us she has learned syntax and her grammar is surprisingly good. We should free her mind. Let it wander where it may. There is a greatness in her which I can feel in the bottom of my heart."

Abigail's plea bordered on heresy and Carlyle was becoming uneasy and more than a trifle alarmed. Suddenly he turned to face Abigail and snarled: "She is not your daughter! She is not my daughter!" He turned away, trying to compose himself.

"Perhaps you should see Dr. Vernon," he said harshly, then stood and started to walk away. Abigail had never seen him look so angry or be so intolerant and unaccommodating. She started to say something, but decided to remain silent. Instead she looked down at her lap and started to cry. Carlyle heard the sobbing and stopped at the door. They rarely argued and he prided himself on his ability to control the entire plantation without having to resort to shouting, something he found repugnant. He had never spoken to Abigail so roughly, especially in reference to their daughter, but he was confused and scared. He could tolerate Mary Ellen, all right, but she was his property, not his daughter. He did not have a daughter, or a son. His thoughts twisted like a knife through his abdomen. He sighed wearily and made a determined effort to let his anger subside. He stood by the door and watched his wife's shoulders shake.

Abigail was special. She was his best friend and his most trusted counselor. She was always there for him when he needed her. She never turned him away, no matter how ill behaved or irrational he may have been. She never raised her voice, or chided him for being rude or churlish. Her advice had always been reasonably offered and well considered. It was usually to the point—a quality he did not expect to find in a woman. Carlyle valued her judgment, but the notion of teaching Mary Ellen was ludicrous. He could not understand how Abigail could even make such an idiotic suggestion.

Finally, she looked up at him and the pain in her face forced him to stifle any other harsh comments he was about to make. "Look, Abbie," he lamented and walked back towards her, "if you insist on this course of action, one which I'm completely opposed to, and intend to pursue without my concurrence or support, at least don't mislead yourself. I honestly don't know what good it could do to teach her to read and write, either for you or for her. On the contrary, I believe it represents a very dangerous precedent for us and for them. And if you are bent on teaching her, do it quietly and without fanfare. Just don't ask me to approve."

Abigail smiled halfheartedly. This was as much as she had any right to expect. Pressing Carlyle further would only aggravate matters and make things worse.

"Thank you, darling," she said gratefully. "Believe me I understand how you feel, but it's something that I have to do. I'm not sure I can even explain it. I promise not to allow this to become public knowledge. Perhaps we should have a separate room here . . . " she hesitated briefly as she noticed Carlyle's expression darkening, "but only to give her a place to study and for her books." She reached for his hand pleadingly and touched it tenderly.

Carlyle exhaled deeply. It was no use. He felt as if Abigail was manipulating him; but he could not order her to forget such a horrid move, one that could destroy Golden Oaks. Still, he was the man of the house and would have the last say. "Alright, Abbie. Alright. Teach her as you will. Just don't be too obvious about it and, please, I beseech you, keep it to yourself. God knows the slaves will probably know about it soon enough. Let's just hope that our people don't get wind of it." He paused and looked in Abigail's face. "Teaching a slave to read and write." He shook his head ruefully, hardly believing his own words. Then he pointed his finger at Abigail. "But nothing more, I tell you!"

Abigail jumped up and gave him a peck on his cheek, then turned and called for their servant.

"Jacob. Please go fetch Mary Ellen and bring her here right away."

Jacob, his white hair standing out against his black skin, left the house and slowly walked to the cottage where he found Delila speaking softly to Mary Ellen. Mary Ellen smiled at Jacob, but Delila glared at him.

"Misses Abigail wanna see Mary Ellen," he said timidly.

"Wha' fo'?" Delila demanded.

"I dunno, Delila." Jacob looked nervously at his feet, perspiration beading on his face.

Delila had an uncanny ability to read people and instantly knew he was lying. She stood slowly, rubbed her palms on her flimsy dress, and walked towards Jacob. He backed up as if pushed by an invisible force.

"Ah ain' gwine ax agin. Wh' fo' dey wan' her?" She moved closer to Jacob, her eyes blazing malevolently.

Chapter Two

Jacob nervously rubbed at the sweat on his forehead and face. His eyes burned with sweat and tears, clouding his vision of Delila. Delila saw his hands shake and knew that he did not want a confrontation with her; he appeared to be on the verge of bolting, eager to get back to the house with the girl.

"I don' wan' no trouble, Delila. I'll tell you w'at I heard." He tried to speak calmly and appear confident, but the nervous timbre in his voice gave him away.

Delila did not react. Not a muscle in her taut body moved or flexed. Instead she continued to glare. Shaken, he continued, "Misses Abigail wanna teach yo' child readin' 'n writin'. Give 'er proper ejicashun. Misses wanna special room inna house jes' fo' 'er." He had overheard the entire conversation between Carlyle and Abigail.

"An' de Massa? Wha' he wan'?" Delila spit the words out at him, and the purpose of the question was eminently clear to him.

"Nothin'. You know he never take no colored women." This was true, but there were men who liked children, though Carlyle had never exhibited such tendencies. So Jacob just shook his head back and forth. "Massa don' wan' Mary Ellen," he concluded.

Delila screwed her face into a questioning look as if she could not understand what Jacob was alluding to. Then suddenly, as if inspired by some divine intervention, everything became crystal clear. Abigail treated Mary Ellen like her own child and Delila resented it silently, mostly out of jealousy and partly because she knew how much Mary Ellen enjoyed it. Yet Delila believed Mary Ellen was unique and had special powers. Perhaps this was the fruit of Mary Ellen's powers and would one day make her even more powerful—by learning what the white people knew, for they also had power, a different power, maybe even greater than voodoo she grudgingly acknowledged to herself. Delila turned back to Mary Ellen, ignoring Jacob who had worked his way back toward the door to wait.

Delila spoke softly. "Yo' lissen chile, heah? Wha' yo' wan' from dem w'ite foke?" Delila watched Mary Ellen closely, trying to fathom how much Mary Ellen knew or expected about what Jacob had just revealed.

But Mary Ellen just looked innocently at her, not knowing how to respond to the question. If she knew something it did not show. Delila could not prepare Mary Ellen for this new situation. What she knew about the Saunders was limited to bits and pieces of conversation overheard in the slave quarters. Delila had never set foot in the big house. She had always treated Abigail with so much disdain that she expected no kindness in return. If anything she expected reciprocity. But, unaccountably, Abigail never reacted or retaliated in kind.

Having never been educated, Delila did not understand how reading or writing worked. She thought of it as a mysterious ritual, not unlike one of her own. But it seemed to be a complete waste of time. She knew that white folk put a great deal of stock into it and maybe Mary Ellen would find it useful in the future, though she doubted it.

Delila, worried that Mary Ellen would lose her special gifts and powers by spending too much time in the rich house, eating rich food, and being around people who were completely ignorant of her real potential. Mary Ellen would never be white and if she spent all her effort to be something impossible, she could lose forever some of her unique qualities. On the other hand, Delila had to admit to herself that with all her own powers she still remained a slave, without friends, and with little control over her own destiny. Maybe Mary Ellen would fare better.

"Lissen chile," she said as she grasped Mary Ellen by her upper arms, squeezing hard for effect. Mary Ellen was startled as those vice-like fingers gripped her tightly. She could not budge and watched her mother warily. "We done come from a long line of queens. Yo's a voodoo princess. Yo' unnerstan'? Yo' got de power. Looka dese people!" She waved insolently at the other slaves who kept their distance. "Dey's all afraid o' yo'." She shook her child gently for effect. "Dey's afraid 'cause yo' got de power. Use it chile."

For a brief moment Mary Ellen saw a softness in her mother. She wondered what her mother meant. If she had any power she certainly did not feel it. If she had so much power why could she not make the other children play with her? Something she wanted so badly and missed so much. She noticed the fear with which the other slaves regarded her. At times, when she was particularly cross, she would make a face at one of them, the way her mother did, and that person would start signing the cross and get out of her way. She always assumed it was her eyes that did it. She hated her eyes. Why could she not be born normal, like everyone else? Why had the Lord been so mean to her and made her so different? If she really had power she could make her eyes dark brown like all the other slaves had.

As if reading her thoughts, Delila continued. "Don' nevva fo'git, chile. Yo' diff'nt. Yo' betta. Yo' got voodoo power. Use it!"

Mary Ellen had seen her mother conduct small rituals and build unusual objects. Delila made her participate, but never explained the meaning of the rituals. They spoke about coiled serpents and waking the dead. It terrified the slaves, and at times Mary Ellen wanted to laugh at their reaction because she did not see why they should be so scared. She knew her mama must have some kind of power, but she did not know what it was, where it was kept, or how her mother got it. Stories of life in the islands and a continuous reference to "voodoo" and the rituals had a romantic attraction for the inquisitive child. Somehow members of her family, particularly the women, were imbued with this power and people were terrified of it. Ostensibly she had it as well. Mary Ellen found it mysterious, oftentimes mystical, and usually amusing. But if Delila caught her with so much as a smirk, she would deliver a blow to Mary Ellen's face with her open hand, leaving a stinging pain, humiliation, and a clear message. Mary Ellen kept the humor to herself.

Mary Ellen looked at her mother. "Mama. Who was my daddy?" she asked nervously. They never spoke about this. It was a forbidden subject. Delila either did not respond or harshly told the child not to ask. A few times Delila hit Mary Ellen when the question came up, but the headstrong little girl would not give up. Mary Ellen felt as if this was the right time to ask again.

Delila laughed abruptly then glared at Mary Ellen. She sighed heavily and looked away. "Yo' daddy was a w'ite man. Big 'n pow'ful. I kin see his golden eyes and wild red hair now," she smiled to herself.

"Where is he?" Mary Ellen prodded gently.

"Dead," Delila said softly. "Kilt in a fight." Delila turned glistening eyes to Mary Ellen and cupped her chin in her hand. "Som'time yo' look jes' like 'im chile." Then Delila did the strangest, most unexpected thing. She softly nuzzled Mary Ellen's hair and tears welled up in her eyes. She looked gently at her daughter. " 'Member, hon. Yo's a voodoo princess."

"You always tell me that, mama," Mary Ellen said uncertainly. "But I really don't understand it."

Delila looked lovingly at her daughter. She liked her spirit and quick mind. "Yo'll see one day. T'ings is jumble up now. But yo'll see."

"Mama, will you teach me?" Mary Ellen still did not know what she would learn, but she had never felt this close to her mother and whatever she could say or do to keep the closeness and the warmth, she would.

However, Delila's mood, like a tornado, changed abruptly. "Git chile. Go to the w'ite foke. Dey's callin' fo' yo'."

Chapter Three

Strange Encounter

AUGUSTA, GEORGIA
JULY 1842

THE RICH COTTON FIELDS SPREAD BEFORE HER LIKE A WHITE CARPET patterned in green. Mary Ellen perched on her favorite rock, a large granite boulder on top of the hillock overlooking the rich farmland, absorbing the warmth generated by the golden rays of sun. It was a beautiful day in late May—the humid days of summer late arriving—and the first buds of Spring burst from their dormancy. For the first time in months the pall of depression that had enveloped her lifted as she gazed at the world about her. The only dark place left was her concern for Abigail.

After any slight exertion, Abigail would be exhausted. Going up a single flight of stairs would leave her short of breath and gripping the balustrade so tightly that her knuckles turned white. Looking back over the past year Mary Ellen realized that there had been little telltale signs that Abigail was physically deteriorating. However, Mary Ellen had not been unduly alarmed until the day she discovered Abigail lying at the foot of the bed, clutching her abdomen and moaning in pain. Drawn by Mary

Ellen's anguished cries for help Carlyle rushed to his wife and realized, for the first time, just how seriously ill she was. Looking at her wan, pallid face he felt a terrible sense of foreboding.

Mary Ellen spent more and more time at Abigail's side, bringing food, reading to her, gently massaging her worn muscles while trying to cheer her up and make her more comfortable. Dr. Vernon's orders for everyone to keep away from Abigail, to allow her to rest and recuperate, did not apply to Mary Ellen. If Dr. Vernon and Carlyle were reluctant to give Mary Ellen full access to Abigail, their dilemma was resolved by Abigail's insistence on having Mary Ellen attend to her needs. Whenever Abigail woke up from a long slumber she would immediately summon Mary Ellen. Dr. Vernon cautioned Carlyle that a healthy mind and positive attitude were perhaps the strongest of elixirs.

Despite Mary Ellen's care Abigail's condition worsened. Mary Ellen felt the burden of an overwhelming grief, a sense of despair that comes from the looming darkness of an imminent loss. This morning, Dr. Vernon arrived at Golden Oaks to examine his patient. He recognized how stressed and exhausted Mary Ellen was and gently told her to get some rest; thus was Mary Ellen by herself, sitting on her rock well above the fields. She marveled at the glorious vista, yet wondered why God elected to inflict so much pain on someone like Abigail, someone so decent and loving.

Mary Ellen tried to relax and take in the sunshine, but her mind jumped from thought to thought: from Abigail's condition, to their relationship, to her status at Golden Oaks. No matter how well she had been treated by the Saunders, she was still a slave. Nothing would ever change that.

The whole notion of slavery seemed so inconsistent with everything she had been taught by Abigail and in her readings of the Bible. It made little sense to her that an omniscient being would create so much splendor, yet allow so many of his children to be mistreated, particularly if the tone of their skin did not match the loveliness of the pale cotton fields before her. She could see the slaves working in the fields and she felt a pang of guilt. Her life certainly was not very trying. She had been selected for different treatment and she did not have a single clue as to why. She once overheard one of the slaves tell some others that she had used her voodoo powers to enchant the Saunders. Infuriated, she was about to tell them how stupid they were, that she had no powers and if she did she certainly had not enchanted anyone, but when they saw her approaching they hurriedly disbanded and silently walked away.

Mary Ellen felt guilty for another reason. She had not really given her own mother much thought in the last few months. Their relationship had always been somewhat strained, not at all like that of a mother and daughter, but more like teacher and student. Delila rarely smiled and either did not know how or could not show her feelings toward Mary Ellen. They never touched. There were no hugs or kisses or soft maternal caresses children crave, or the closeness between mother and child that offered solace and security. They spent most of their time together talking about voodoo, Delila delivering a lecture, a soliloquy about their powers, and Mary Ellen listening raptly to her mother's intense discourse. All of Delila's efforts were directed at passing on to Mary Ellen generations of acquired knowledge. These lessons focused on mysticism and sacred rites, most of which Mary Ellen found amusing. But to her mother these subjects were sacrosanct and to be treated in deadly earnest.

Delila's death came unexpectedly. One moment she was fine, telling Mary Ellen what Mary Ellen had heard so many times before, how voodoo could be used to heal the sick, inflict pain—or worse—on their enemies, or instill enough fear to scare others into total submission and subservience. Then Delila sat down wearily and massaged her temples roughly with her long bony fingers. Softly, without her usual rancor or coarseness, she complained about having a severe headache, leaned back and collapsed to the floor. Mary Ellen saw her falling and rushed to her side but Delila was already dead.

The slaves at Golden Oaks were relieved and their upbeat mood stood in stark contrast to Mary Ellen's pain and sense of loss. She struggled with her feelings quietly, alone for the most part, sustained entirely by Abigail's warmth and love. During the year following her mother's death Mary Ellen discovered the benefit of one of the rituals she learned from her mother. She put herself into a dream-like state, where her very being would spread out beyond her body and become a part of her surroundings. Focusing on abstractions, such as a single color, the sound of the wind, or even the rhythmic pounding of her heart, while banishing unrelated thoughts, Mary Ellen would enter into what she felt was a spiritual reawakening. As the year progressed she found herself patiently looking forward to these bouts of solitude. The sessions became longer and, when she would snap out of her inner self, she would feel strangely tranquil and totally at peace.

But Abigail's unexpected illness, coming so soon after Delila's death, covered Mary Ellen with a smothering burden and left her with few opportunities to be alone, to escape from her burdens or her increasing dread of the future. Now, here alone, sitting on that smooth granite boulder, she closed her eyes, blocked all further thoughts and forced herself to focus on her breathing. Instantly the warmth spread inside her body. She could feel her heart rate slow and the enveloping serenity, but in the background she sensed some disturbance. She tried to reject it by thinking of a single color, green, something that usually helped her reach the desired state, but she could not succeed as the sound grew louder and louder. Slowly the distraction materialized and she immediately recognized the pounding hoofbeats of a horse riding hard on the road.

She opened her eyes and focused on a man riding on a beautiful roan stallion, almost the same dark red and brown of the winding dirt path. The image shimmered in opaque waves of heat rising from the road. The horse projected a primal power, the man a controlled and graceful figure. Yet both man and beast were synchronized into one blurry motion as they roared towards Mary Ellen. She stood and the man abruptly reined his horse and stopped abreast of Mary Ellen, drawing a cloud of enveloping dust. The rider was in his mid-twenties or early thirties and elegantly dressed.

"Is this Golden Oaks?" he asked, as his horse excitedly flared its nostrils and chomped down on the bit, its mouth soaked in lather from the hard ride, its sweaty body glistening.

Mary Ellen found herself staring into the clearest light blue eyes she had ever seen. "Yes it is," she answered.

Chapter Three

"How do I get to the Saunders' home?" His intense gaze penetrated her inner soul. She was at once both frightened and exhilarated.

He leaned forward over the animal's neck and patted it affectionately.

"Just keep on riding that way to the end," Mary Ellen pointed down the road, "then take the right fork. If you take the left fork it will take you to the road to Augusta."

"How far to the fork?" he asked.

"Oh, I suppose about a mile." Mary Ellen really did not have any sense of distance, but it did not seem too far off.

The man spun his powerful horse around in a complete circle, almost like a dance, with the magnificent animal proudly rearing its head, raring to go. It was the most beautiful horse Mary Ellen had ever seen. The rider pulled back on the reins, causing the horse to take a few reluctant steps backward. He looked at Mary Ellen curiously.

"What's your name?" he asked.

"Mary Ellen, sir," she responded hesitantly, his question catching her off guard.

He stiffened noticeably and appeared surprised. "How old are you?" he asked.

"Thirteen, last May."

The rider paused for a moment, as if uncertain what to say next.

"Do you have any family?" He watched her intently.

It was a strange question and she did not know if she should answer it. It really was none of his business. But as she made eye contact with him she felt something almost hauntingly intriguing, and found her reluctance to answer him slipping away.

"No, sir. My mama died last year and I have no family connections," she finally said.

"Where did you learn to speak like this, girl?" He smiled and his tone was both pleasing and reassuring, as if he had a desire to converse with her.

Mary Ellen felt enormous pride. For the first time she understood the benefit of Abigail's well directed efforts to teach her to speak properly.

"Mrs. Saunders, sir. She's been my teacher."

"Ah. Abigail Saunders." He stared at her thoughtfully for a moment, somewhat lost in thought, then remarked: "Good. She's a fine teacher. Thank you." He saluted her with his riding crop and spurred his horse into a run, trailing a long, billowing, reddish dust cloud behind him.

—∞—

ABIGAIL LAY IN HER CEDAR FOUR-POSTER BED, DRAPED WITH EXQUISITE Irish linen. Sunlight pierced through the large windows and flooded the room. Dr. Vernon sat on the bed, examining Abigail, listening to her breathing and probing her abdomen, feeling the lumps and tissue that he wished were not there. Her liver was nearly twice its normal size.

"Does it hurt when I press your abdomen?" he asked gently.

"A little," she answered hesitantly, "but I can take it." Her wan, haggard face painfully forced a smile.

Tiny beads of perspiration dotted her pale forehead like droplets of morning dew on a wilted rose. She squinted, causing the lashes to dampen. Gray, slightly pursed lips curled around clenched teeth as she fought the pain. Satisfied he could do nothing more, Dr. Vernon covered Abigail with her nightgown and raised the sheet just over her chest.

"Are you comfortable now, dear?" he asked.

"Tolerably so." She looked away.

Dr. Vernon stood up, cupping Abigail's soft and frail hand in his. "I'm going to let you rest now."

Abigail nodded and he laid her hand back on the bed. For a brief moment he thought she would ask him the inevitable question.

"Just do as I said before, Abigail. Take one spoonful of this laudanum in the morning, once after you dine at noon, and again before you go to sleep. It' ll make you more comfortable."

Abigail's smile had been reduced to a slight twitching of her lips. Dr. Vernon felt terribly upset watching his close friend, someone he had known since childhood, wasting away. He felt so helpless to retard the progress of the disease. Something was destroying her liver and now attacked other organs. Thirty pounds disappeared within weeks, leaving her wafer thin. He

Slaves in Cotton Field

had seen many cases of life and death, yet he could not predict how much time Abigail had left. The pain increased day by day and he knew would eventually become unbearable. If he medicated the pain sufficiently she would rest in a semi-comatose stupor. That was not living. He shook his head in dismay and sadness. He estimated three months, maybe six months; he did not believe in miracles despite witnessing several unexpected recoveries. She was resting comfortably now, her eyes shut and her face peaceful.

He went downstairs to the parlor where Carlyle cradled a crystal tumbler filled with golden bourbon. Carlyle had never been much of a drinker and it was too early in the day even for a veteran drinker, but Dr. Vernon understood. Carlyle, for all his efforts on Golden Oaks, really cared about only one thing—Abigail. Carlyle knew. He knew his wife would be taken from him and he now resorted to the only thing he thought would drive the demons away—bourbon.

"Sit down, Carlyle, and let's talk," Dr. Vernon beckoned him over. Carlyle exhaled and sat down wearily. His hands were trembling. Dr. Vernon watched him carefully.

"Abigail's liver continues to enlarge, and whatever she has is now spreading throughout her body." Carlyle's jaw quivered and his bloodshot eyes moistened. Despite his effort to retain some composure, he looked terribly depressed, and as vulnerable as a child.

"I have left medication for her. Try to get her to eat. I know most of the time she doesn't want to, but try. Sometimes she will keep it and sometimes not. But she needs nourishment."

"She's dying, isn't she?" Carlyle moaned as if delivering a desperate plea for Dr. Vernon to contradict what he knew to be fate.

"We are all dying, Carlyle," Dr. Vernon sighed.

"You know what I mean, Bill. How much more time does she have?" Carlyle demanded.

"It's hard to say . . . " Carlyle was about to remonstrate, but Dr. Vernon held him off with a wave of his hand.

"Listen to me, Carlyle. I've seen miracles . . . " Carlyle started to protest again, but Dr. Vernon continued. "And I've seen people go in one month. I would say Abigail has three, maybe six months left. But I can't be sure."

Carlyle felt as if he had been struck in the chest with a sledgehammer. He leaned forward and covered his eyes. His body began to tremble. "I can't live without her, Bill. What will I do?"

"She isn't dead yet," Dr. Vernon remonstrated brusquely. "Right now instead of feeling sorry for yourself you might just think about what you can do to make things more comfortable for Abigail." Dr. Vernon spoke more harshly than he felt, but sometimes the shock of hard words helped get someone like Carlyle back on track, to refocus his efforts, at least for the time being

"You're right. Of course you're right." Carlyle used a handkerchief to wipe his face, took one more swig from his glass and pushed it roughly aside. Just then the two men heard a cough, looked up, and saw Abigail leaning on the banister at top of the stairs watching them intently. Her frail body stood erect, supported by thin legs that showed through her nightgown.

Chapter Three

"Why, honey, we didn't know you were standing there." Carlyle tried to sound cheerful. "You should be in bed."

"I know you didn't," she said evenly.

Her knees gave way causing her to sway before catching herself with the banister. The men rushed up and helped Abigail back to bed.

"I'm fine, I'm fine. We need to talk, now."

Dr. Vernon excused himself and Carlyle sat beside Abigail, taking her hand.

"Darling," Carlyle started the conversation, "Dr. Vernon and I were just talking about various possibilities, nothing certain, you understand?"

"Carlyle, Carlyle. You dear foolish man. You're the one who doesn't understand." She smiled and gently squeezed his hand. "I don't have 'various possibilities.' I'm dying and I've accepted my fate."

Carlyle started to object, but she squeezed his hand again and gazed into his eyes. He looked away feeling uncomfortable and dejected.

"At first," she continued, "I was angry. Why did it happen to me, to us? It didn't seem fair. But I've had a wonderful life and if the good Lord has decided to take me, I must accept it. I admit I don't understand how He works or how He chooses, but He has his reasons and I won't argue with them. My only fear is for you. Carlyle, I don't mean to be unkind, I say this with both love and sadness, but you're the one I'm worried about. In this way you are so," she paused, searching for the right word, but finding none, continued, "you are weak, my darling, and I worry about how you will survive."

Carlyle stood up and walked to the window overlooking the massive oaks lining the drive to the manor. He saw his beautiful plantation, the stately trees, and lush green fields, but felt only a vast emptiness. Abigail gathered her strength and tried again to get out of bed. Carlyle turned and rushed to her, embracing her. He continued to hold her. He wanted to lean down between the billowed shadows to steal her pain and relieve her of the burden. He wanted to take her hand, the way she did his the time his mother passed away. Abigail wrapped her arms around him. She began to sob and buried her face deep in his neck and chest. Her tears moistened his collar. She embraced him with all her might. Flashes of old times, as newlyweds, flooded her mind. Her grip tightened and she felt like a child, almost ashamed. Suddenly she realized she was not the one shaking. His grip loosened and chest quivered. The sounds leaving his mouth were not baritone and strong, but feeble and scared. She took his hands, then his arms, and finally held him, squeezing his head against her own and smoothing his damp hair. His palms spread the tears across his flushed face like a child. His hand groped for hers. After awhile Abigail closed her eyes and lapsed into a light sleep. Carlyle covered her with clean sheets and walked out quietly to continue the discussion with Dr. Vernon.

Dr. Vernon stood when Carlyle entered the living room. "How is she?"

"She's sleeping."

"I'm so sorry, Carlyle. I wish I knew how . . ."

A knock at the door brought Dr. Vernon's words to a halt. Jacob, who had just appeared with silver service of coffee and biscuits, went to the door.

"Mr. Americus Price of Price's Landing," Jacob announced and presented Mr. Price's card to Carlyle. Carlyle glared at the finely engraved piece and handed it over to Dr. Vernon who dissected each word.

The Price family was well known throughout the South, particularly in Mississippi and Missouri where they owned large tracts of land. Most of what Carlyle knew about the Price family had actually come from bits and pieces of conversation with Abigail, who had been a neighbor of the Prices in her early years, or from talk among their friends. Americus had a mixed reputation because of his misanthropic, almost rebellious ways, yet was regarded as one of the most eligible men in the South.

Carlyle, torn apart by his emotions, grunted wearily. He was in no mood for visitors but Southern hospitality could not be refused, not even in this difficult time.

"Please show him in, Jacob," Carlyle said gruffly.

Americus entered the room. Carlyle and Dr. Vernon instantly recognized by the cut of his riding clothes why this young man was so actively pursued by the parents of every daughter of marriageable age. His double-breasted coat of emerald green was exquisite. The off-white pantaloons of finest cotton and soft leather boots punctuated his elegance.

Chapter Three

The men introduced themselves.

"I am terribly sorry to barge in so rudely without any advance notice," he said. "Please accept my apologies." He bowed slightly.

"Please do come in. Have a seat Mr. Price," Carlyle pointed to the settee. "Would you care for something to drink. You look quite . . ."

"Quite dusty, I'm sure." Americus smiled warmly, as his eyes surveyed the room. "A glass of water would be greatly appreciated. Thank you."

Dr. Vernon moved aside to give Americus room, and Carlyle sat next to them in a chair. Jacob served the fresh brewed coffee to Dr. Vernon and Carlyle, pouring it into fine bone china cups. Then he gave Americus a tall glass of water with a slice of lemon in it, which Americus eagerly gulped down. Americus had already observed the somber expression on the men's faces and how Carlyle appeared rumpled and weary, as if he had not slept for several days.

"What can we do for you, Mr. Price?" Carlyle asked once Americus sat down.

"I have come to pay Mrs. Saunders a visit," Americus replied somewhat hesitantly.

Dr. Vernon and Carlyle looked at each other in surprise.

"And what would be the purpose of your visit, Mr. Price?" Carlyle asked, a harsh edge to his voice.

"Actually I came at her request," he responded diffidently.

"You came at my wife's request?" Carlyle's astonishment registered immediately. "I'm not sure I follow you, Mr. Price, but that can't possibly be."

"Mr. Saunders, I assure you I have come at her request. She sent me a letter which I received only last week." He produced a letter from his dusty coat. "You see, I've been away for some time, so I couldn't come earlier."

"May I see that letter?" Carlyle demanded.

Americus hesitated, then replaced the letter back in his jacket. "I'm terribly sorry, but I cannot show it to you." Americus's discomfiture was quite noticeable. He squirmed in his seat.

Dr. Vernon placed a hand on Carlyle's arm. "Perhaps you might tell Mr. Saunders the nature of your visit, then," he suggested politely, though nonplused by Americus's behavior.

"I'm sorry, but I can't," Americus looked terribly uncomfortable.

"How dare you, sir?" Carlyle erupted. "You come uninvited into my house, demand to speak with my wife, and furthermore have the gall to refuse me an explanation? Please leave now. Get out of my house at once! Now!" He pushed Dr. Vernon's hand aside, stood up and prepared to eject the visitor from his house.

"Please, Carlyle," Dr. Vernon interceded. "Let Mr. Price explain himself. I'm sure there must be some reasonable explanation for his statement." As implausible as it might be, he thought to himself.

Carlyle, who had nearly knocked his chair backwards when he stood up, reluctantly sat down.

"I'm very sorry," Americus said faintly, "but I'm only following the instructions of your wife, Mr. Saunders. I was told not to discuss the purpose of my visit or to reveal the contents of the letter with anyone, so I cannot breach the confidentiality unless she permits me to do so."

Carlyle and Dr. Vernon looked at each other in bewilderment. "Are you telling me," Carlyle said uncertainly, "that Abigail . . . Mrs. Saunders invited you to come here on some confidential business and that you were not to reveal the nature of your visit to anyone, including her husband?" Carlyle looked at the ceiling in amazement as if this lunatic's sole purpose was to drive him mad. "Why, I can't believe it. Surely she would have told me." He looked incredulously at Dr. Vernon.

"Mr. Saunders, your wife wrote to me and asked me to visit with her on a very delicate matter as soon as possible. I arrived as fast as I could. I don't know if you are aware that my family has known Mrs. Saunders for many years. I really don't know what else I can tell you. But please accept my apology for any pain my visit has caused. Believe me it was not my intention and I'm certain that if I were in your shoes I would be just as angry and upset as you are. But Mrs. Saunders can, I'm sure, clear up this matter for all of us." Americus looked at Carlyle who was not certain what to do or how to proceed.

"But you aren't in my shoes," Carlyle cut back harshly and reached for his drink.

Dr. Vernon simply settled back in his chair, dumbfounded.

Chapter Three

Abigail, in great pain, watched the men below. The sound of hoofbeats approaching the manor had aroused her from her light sleep. Slowly, and with great difficulty, she had gotten out of her bed and returned to the top of the landing where she had overheard the entire conversation, but did not interrupt.

"Mr. Price. I don't know what business you have with my wife, but your visit has come at a very inopportune time. We have critical family matters to discuss and perhaps we could have you come back at some other time. With some notice, I might add." Carlyle remained agitated and angry. He considered Americus's actions completely unacceptable; a stranger daring to come to his house, even if invited by his wife, and refusing to tell him what it was all about.

Amidst the tension, Jacob entered with freshly brewed coffee for Carlyle and Dr. Vernon, and a pitcher of water. He refilled Americus's glass and started to refill the coffee cups. Jacob's hand trembled and he spilled some coffee while pouring it into Dr. Vernon's cup. Jacob muttered something to himself, wiped the table and saucer dry, then retired as quickly as he could.

Americus paused, uncertain what to do next, and swallowed a gulp of water. He was about to say something when Abigail spoke. "Carlyle, please don't be rude to Americus. He is our guest at my invitation."

Startled, everyone looked up. "You should be in bed, Abigail," Dr. Vernon exclaimed.

Abigail ignored him. "This is very important, Carlyle. Please do come upstairs now and help me down." She spoke with such intensity and determination that her manner clearly suggested she did not expect to be defied.

Dr. Vernon, followed by Carlyle, ascended the stairs and helped Abigail down to the drawing room. If she were in pain she did not show it. Dr. Vernon marveled at his friend's strength and courage.

"Americus, how have you been?" She gave Americus her hand to be kissed, then sat down.

"I'm fine Abigail." He was about to ask her the same question, but realized how hollow and mendacious it would sound. "You look tired,

Abigail. Perhaps it would be better if you were to follow Dr. Vernon's advice. I can always come back another day."

"No!" Abigail responded strongly, then repeated more calmly: "No. But thank you for your concern, Americus. How are your parents? I trust all is well with them?"

"They're fine. Getting older of course. My father broke his hip falling off his horse last month and is unable to get around. Mother is fine. She sends her regards."

"I'm terribly sorry to hear about your father. He has always been such a vigorous man. It must be very upsetting and depressing for him to be incapacitated." Abigail looked saddened.

"He is now, but I'm sure he'll recover," Americus said.

Dr. Vernon and Carlyle remained mute, Carlyle biting his lower lip in frustration.

"Perhaps we should discuss your visit, Americus," she suggested.

Americus looked at the two men and Abigail understood.

"It's all right. I've known Dr. Vernon almost as long as I've known you. He's a dear friend and can be trusted. Carlyle is obviously very upset by your visit and if we speak openly he will understand that it wasn't meant to hide anything from him." She gave Carlyle her best smile, then turned to Americus and continued. "I wrote to you because I knew I was desperately ill. I did not mention it in the letter but I am sure you noted the urgency of my request?"

"Yes, I did. I'm truly sorry to hear that you're ill and I hope you'll recover quickly," Americus said softly. Her wasted frame, drawn face, and protruding cheekbones, along with Carlyle's behavior, suggested otherwise, that his old friend had little time left; he felt a deep sadness.

"No, Americus, I won't recover, as these men know all too well. That's why you're here," she said this with emphasis and a clear indication that she did not seek any response.

"I wrote to you about Mary Ellen, the girl," she began and saw Americus's face light up.

"I believe I met her on the way over here. Quite fortuitous you might say. She is exactly as you described her, except those strange eyes."

Chapter Three

Abigail smiled. "Yes, she has very unusual eyes. And she is a most unusual girl."

Carlyle could not believe what he was hearing. Abigail, nearly on her death bed, and Americus Price, someone he had never met, were sitting in his house discussing Mary Ellen.

"Is Mr. Price here for some reason other than a discussion about Mary Ellen?" Carlyle interjected in bafflement. "Because I can't believe he came here at your invitation to discuss . . ." he was about to say "slaves," but knew it would offend Abigail, so he said, "this girl. This is preposterous."

Dr. Vernon was very uncomfortable. He knew how much Mary Ellen meant to Abigail, so her interest or concern in Mary Ellen, especially at this stage of her life, seemed reasonable to him. Still, something about the course of this conversation unsettled him.

"Carlyle, you know Mary Ellen is very important to me. I care dearly for that girl. I've made a proposition to Americus which I think you will find quite to your satisfaction." She spoke bluntly and with resolve. Carlyle shook his head, but remained quiet.

"As I told you in the letter, Mary Ellen is a slave here at Golden Oaks." Abigail's face suddenly tightened as a spasm of pain gripped her. Dr. Vernon started to rise but Abigail waved him away. She wiped her mouth with a small linen cloth. She recovered her composure and continued resolutely. "I want to make arrangements for her after I'm gone. I know how you feel about things, so I asked you here to meet her and decide if you would take her."

Carlyle nearly dropped his coffee cup. He looked at it and took a swallow, wiping his mouth with his forearm, all thoughts of manners and courtesy set aside.

"I can't believe what I'm hearing. You're arranging for Mary Ellen to be taken by Mr. Price? And you didn't even ask me?" His voice kept rising and his face had turned a shade of crimson. "You're not acting rationally. I will not permit this discussion to continue." He rose.

Americus looked at Carlyle in surprise. "I'm confused, Mr. Saunders," he said. "Aren't you interested in this girl's future welfare?"

"Of course I am." Carlyle became indignant. "She's one of my slaves!"

Abigail recoiled. "This is precisely why I asked Americus to come, Carlyle. To you Mary Ellen is nothing more than a slave." She stopped to regain her breath. "You've never seen it, you don't understand it, and you'll never do anything about it. She has to have a future and I can't be certain you would do what I require."

Now Americus was equally confused. "Then I still don't understand. Aren't you an Abolitionist, Mr. Saunders?"

Dr. Vernon and Carlyle both flinched noticeably, as if struck by an insulting accusation. Carlyle stood suddenly nearly tipping over the tray and coffee service. He slowly advanced towards Americus, his face filling with black rage. "How dare you, sir!" Carlyle shouted. "How dare you make such a scurrilous charge? I won't have it. I am shocked by your utter lack of civility. Now get out!"

Abigail, unable to speak because of a stabbing pain in her side, looked beseechingly at Carlyle, hoping he would not continue with his threat until she recovered her voice. But Carlyle, his voice cracking, paid her no attention.

Dr. Vernon intervened and placed himself between the two men, facing Carlyle.

"Carlyle, please," Dr. Vernon pleaded. "Don't get so upset. Sit down. I'll handle this." Carlyle stopped, but did not sit down. Dr. Vernon turned to Americus.

"Stop it!" the order came from Abigail who managed to stand up, holding to the back of the settee for support.

Abigail's voice had an immediate effect on Carlyle. Like a little child he went to her and gently helped her to sit. She took his hand and made him sit next to her.

"Perhaps I should leave," Dr. Vernon suggested uncertainly. The discussion about Mary Ellen's future had sedition written all over it and he did not want to have anything further to do with it. The less he knew, the better.

"You'll do no such thing. We . . . I need you here."

Reluctantly Dr. Vernon also sat down. He had warned both Carlyle and Abigail on many occasions that educating any of the slaves could be regarded by their neighbors as acts attributable to someone with abolitionist tendencies and, in the least, they would be absolutely shunned by their community. This subject was not discussed by the genteel families in Georgia or elsewhere in the South. It was treasonous to their way of life. He did not even want to consider what the worst case might be. But Abigail held firm, denying any interest in freeing slaves or engaging in abolitionist activities. Carlyle, Dr. Vernon knew, agreed with him, but could never go against his wife's wishes.

Abigail leaned towards Carlyle. "Darling. He didn't mean this with disrespect." She turned back to a very confused Americus. "This discussion has nothing to do with the abolitionist movement. It simply concerns one girl, one very unusual and promising girl. Someone I happen to love as my own child."

Carlyle looked down at his feet and said nothing.

Abigail winced as pain wracked her body again, then collected herself and smiled at Americus; a disarming and genuine smile of warmth. She turned to Carlyle.

"Dear, why don't you take Dr. Vernon and show him how well your new project is doing." Abigail was referring to the birth of a new colt from the lines of an English race horse which they had purchased the previous year and set out to stud with their prize mares. The colt had the most beautiful configuration and was admired by everyone. Carlyle acted like a proud father.

Carlyle understood this request, as did Dr. Vernon, though neither seemed certain whether to leave Abigail.

"Go ahead, you two. I'll be fine. If I need you I'll send Jacob." She made her best effort to appear lighthearted and smiled charmingly at the two men. The two men walked out disconsolately.

Abigail regarded Americus. "No, my dear Americus, Carlyle is not an Abolitionist. Far from it."

"I'm dreadfully sorry, Abigail. I didn't know."

"Well, you didn't have any way of knowing about Carlyle. Perhaps I should have said something in my letter, but I didn't expect to go down hill so quickly." She looked into Americus's pale blue eyes. "I know about your sympathies, your involvement . . . " Her piercing look made it clear to Americus that she knew much more about him than he realized. "But Carlyle and Dr. Vernon don't share your views." She paused.

Americus remained silent but Abigail could see the wheels of his mind spinning wildly. People in Georgia did not speak about this subject openly, and Americus had become somewhat alarmed by Abigail's revelation of her husband's viewpoint. He had clearly misunderstood the nature of Abigail's letter about Mary Ellen, reading much more into it, perhaps because he wanted to believe Abigail shared his sympathies. If Abigail had such sympathies she had not made them evident.

"I care about Mary Ellen," Abigail continued. "I want her to have a future. That's why I asked you to come. I wanted you to meet her and, if you agreed with me, to listen to my proposition. That's all. This is not part of some grander scheme. It's all about one girl, but a very special girl."

Americus thought about the dusty road and the thirteen-year- old girl looking at him with those incredible eyes. "Frankly, I was completely taken off guard by Mary Ellen," he admitted. "She's obviously very precocious and you've done a grand job of educating her."

"Thank you, Americus."

Abigail's feelings for Mary Ellen were so genuine, so apparent that Americus felt free to discuss his impressions of the child. The fortuitous meeting with Mary Ellen and something about her presence struck a strong sympathetic chord in his mind. He was completely opposed to slavery and secretly transferred funds through European channels for use by the abolitionist movement in Boston. To his knowledge few in the South outside of his family had the slightest suspicion of his views. But Abigail's work with Mary Ellen symbolized what could be done, what could be achieved.

"Now, Americus, please let me tell you what I want." Her smile faded and she paused, seeing Jacob standing nervously by the door. "Jacob, please bring Mr. Price some more water," she said.

"Abigail . . . " Americus began, then stopped as Jacob entered, refilled Americus's glass and removed the coffee service tray. His expression remained impassive.

Chapter Three

"When I saw her I felt that there was something unique about her. . . almost mystical." He noticed Abigail's head tilt askance and her eyes soften.

"Americus, Mary Ellen is so precious, so very dear to me. I love her with all my heart. Carlyle cares for her, but mostly at my instigation. No one has ever shown much interest in her, only fear. Her development should be encouraged, but it won't happen if I'm not here. Carlyle is a dear man, but his standing in the community is more important to him than Mary Ellen's future. He would probably retain her as a house servant without any onerous duties. But no further education. He has warned me for years how teaching Mary Ellen to read and write could be ruinous. But he is the love of my life and has acceded to my wishes. Now, I am asking you to continue with the work I started."

"Abigail," Americus paused, and looked into her honest open face, "I am, at heart, an Abolitionist. It is exactly because of people like Mary Ellen that things have to change here in the South. And whether people want it to or not, change it will. But perhaps too late for Mary Ellen."

"Exactly." Abigail's gaze hardened. "I want to give Mary Ellen to you with the following understanding. You will continue with her education, and when she is eighteen, you will give her her freedom. Make appropriate arrangements for her, help her get out of the South and establish a new life elsewhere. Of course, to satisfy Carlyle you will purchase Mary Ellen. I will give you the money, $1,000, to do so. Carlyle will feel relieved, and the payment of $1,000 will make him feel he has not lost his property. I will also give you another $2,500 which you will hold in trust for her. Invest it wisely, Americus." She stopped and gently dabbed away some tears with her lace handkerchief. "Americus, I obviously can't do this in writing, so I have to trust your word. Please promise me that if you agree to take her, you will fulfill all my requests and conditions." Abigail's eyes locked into the deepest reaches of Americus's conscience.

"I'll do as you ask Abigail," he said softly. "I'll do it because you've asked me to, and my family has always respected you. And I'll also do it for Mary Ellen. After all, it's her life we are talking about. Finally, I'll do it because it's the right thing to do. So I promise to fulfill all you've asked of me to the best of my ability."

"No, Americus. I want you to promise me absolutely, unconditionally. No limits. Not even your ability. Do you understand?"

Americus nodded, though he could not see how he could promise something which might be beyond his ability.

"Come sit next to me," Abigail implored. She took his hands as if she could feel his innermost thoughts by touching them. "Promise me, Americus," she pleaded.

"I promise," he said. "Let's talk about her education. What would you suggest?" he asked.

"I would send her to a convent. You have a house in New Orleans, don't you?"

"Yes.

"I would suggest the Ursaline Convent."

"That's a good idea. It's not far from my house, on 24 Chartres Street."

"Good. Then she could go to the Ursaline Convent there for three years. When she has learned everything they can teach her, then give her tutors. Let her learn all she can from teachers and tutors. The rest she'll learn on her own. I know one day she'll become a great success. I feel it in my bones, in my heart, and above all in my soul." Abigail started to cry softly, smiling at the same time.

Many of the finest families of New Orleans sent their daughters to the Ursaline Convent to be educated. But Mary Ellen did not come from one of these families.

"The question, Abigail, is how we can do it? Who is she? Where is her family? They won't take slaves." Americus pursed his lips.

Abigail's expression seemed to brighten considerably and she gripped his hands more tightly. "I have an idea."

—᠁—

AS ABIGAIL SUSPECTED, IT DID NOT TAKE MUCH TO CONVINCE CARLYLE to sell Mary Ellen to Americus Price. Not that he did not like the girl. He did. The price and terms were unimportant to him. Although he felt something for Mary Ellen, it really had never developed beyond a simple fondness, and Americus's fortuitous arrival and offer to purchase Mary Ellen had been just what he needed to remove this last impediment to a normal plantation.

Since the inception of Abigail's illness, Mary Ellen spent more and more time with Abigail. In part this was good since it made Abigail more comfortable and offered her the company she sorely needed. But at the same time Carlyle felt as if Mary Ellen's presence prevented him from spending whatever precious time remained with Abigail. If Mary Ellen could be removed, and removed with Abigail's blessing, it would be best for everyone concerned, though he did not necessarily share Abigail's approval of Americus, and certainly not his politics. And Carlyle, unlike Abigail, considered Mary Ellen in somebody else's hands to be fair game for Americus. After all, men will always be men, and Abigail simply did not understand it.

Abigail's and Carlyle's discussion in the week following Americus's unexpected visit ended up being devoted to the matter of logistics more than anything else. Although Carlyle could not imagine what would be so difficult about sending Mary Ellen away, Abigail faced a frightful dilemma: how to break the news to Mary Ellen. She would have to tell Mary Ellen about her illness and anticipated death, though she sensed Mary Ellen knew. This alone would cause Mary Ellen great pain. But removing Mary Ellen from Golden Oaks, the only home she had known since birth, would exacerbate the already difficult situation.

One evening Mary Ellen was invited to dine with the Saunders. Seated at the long mahogany dining table, Abigail looked frail and pallid. She seemed extremely depressed and Carlyle's attempts to lighten her spirits with humorous anecdotes and local gossip failed. Carlyle looked nervously at Mary Ellen. His attempts to maintain some semblance of normalcy were unsuccessful. The conversation was strained. Mary Ellen could sense Abigail's desire to discuss something, but Carlyle did not like to discuss any business at the table. After Jacob cleared the table the Saunders asked Mary Ellen to sit down with them in the parlor.

Abigail made it, but with some difficulty. Simply moving to the parlor left her exhausted and drained. But she was determined.

"Darling," Abigail said softly, "as you know, I'm not well." She looked away for a moment, then continued. "I don't think you know just how ill I am. I'm very ill."

"You'll get better," Mary Ellen said uncertainly.

"No, Mary Ellen, I will not get better," Abigail said this with a clear and strong voice. "Unfortunately, my dearest, I will be meeting my maker soon enough."

"You can't. You can't!" Mary Ellen suddenly cried out, her small hands balled into fists. "You'll get better. You have to."

Abigail looked at Mary Ellen and held out her arms. Mary Ellen ran to her and embraced her with all her might, dropping her head on Abigail's lap and wailing disconsolately.

Abigail patiently stroked Mary Ellen's hair and softly caressed her face. Mary Ellen gripped Abigail afraid to let go. Carlyle turned away from his wife and the girl's intimacy. He felt emotionally drained. "Mary Ellen," he said, "you must listen to what Mrs. Saunders wishes to tell you. This is very important."

Mary Ellen raised her head, looked at Carlyle as if seeing him for the first time. Only then did she notice just how haggard and spent he appeared.

Mary Ellen dried her eyes with her hands and looked at Abigail with love and adoration.

"Mary Ellen, I wish there could be some other way. Life hasn't been very fair to you, has it? Between your mother's unfortunate departure, and with me about to join her."

Carlyle frowned, the notion of his wife and that crazy Delila being in the same place in the hereafter, seemed idiotic and totally unacceptable.

Mary Ellen started to cry again, but this time under control.

"But God also blessed you with a wonderful, fertile mind. What will happen to you, dear child, when I'm gone?" Tears started to fall from Abigail's sunken eyes.

Carlyle interceded. "Mary Ellen, my wife and I have made arrangements for your future." Mary Ellen looked at him as if he were speaking some incomprehensible foreign language. Frustrated, he blurted out,

Chapter Three

"Don't look at me that way, Mary Ellen. This is for your own good."

Abigail grasped Mary Ellen's hands and held them tightly. "Mary Ellen, the arrangements we have made are for your own good. We have arranged for you to study at the Ursaline Convent in New Orleans. They will continue with your instructions."

Mary Ellen started to protest, but Abigail squeezed her hands and continued. "You will be under the care and protection of Americus Price."

Mary Ellen's face registered no recognition.

"He's the man you saw on the road last week, the one riding the horse."

Mary Ellen gasped slightly. Carlyle missed the gesture, but Abigail almost anticipated it. "Mr. Price will keep you until you're eighteen years old. Then he will give you your freedom." Abigail smiled, but Mary Ellen sat frozen. Carlyle shook his head in disbelief. They had argued about that part of the covenant for nearly a week and finally Carlyle decided not to question what he really could not control. After all, Mary Ellen was Americus Price's property and what he chose to do with her was his business, although it was not only a foolish business but a very dangerous one.

"I know you might not see things clearly now, my dear, but when you are an adult you will appreciate just how important this is to me, as it will be to you. And you will better understand why we are doing this." Abigail started to cough, and the coughing fit turned into a very painful episode as Abigail's insides felt like they were being stabbed with a knife. She bent over and Carlyle ran to her.

"You better get back into bed. This is too much for you to handle right now." But Abigail resisted. Pushing him away she made it clear she wanted to speak.

"Just one more moment." She took a small box on the table next to her chair and gave it to Mary Ellen. "This is yours," Abigail said. "I hope you like it and cherish it. My mother gave it to me when I was your age. You've been like my own child. I love you as my own. I could not have had a more wonderful child. You'll do well. I can feel it in my heart. Be a good person and care for others. And above all, don't give up learning. That will be your salvation. I can see it so clearly."

Conflicting emotions flooded through Mary Ellen. She also felt the same way toward Abigail. But too many things were happening at one time for a thirteen-year-old girl to absorb so quickly. She was confused, scared, depressed, and exhilarated—all at the same time.

Abigail started to lean over as if she were falling and Carlyle helped her up and carried her frail body up the stairs to the bedroom.

Mary Ellen watched sadly and whispered, "I love you." Neither Abigail nor Carlyle heard it.

—~—

STANDING NEAR THE PARLOR DOOR, JACOB HAD BEEN ASTONISHED TO overhear the entire discussion about Mary Ellen's freedom. He nearly gasped out loud. To Jacob and the other slaves the dream of freedom was something they knew they would never realize. Although it was a dream that every slave held, it was never discussed. Those who dared to violate this rule were given harsher work, sold to another plantation, or even whipped. So when Jacob regaled the slaves with the remarkable tale of Mary Ellen he was too afraid to mention anything about her gaining her freedom. Still, what they all heard was something so unusual and unheard of in those times that word spread quickly in the slave quarters and again confirmed what they had known all along—Mary Ellen had the power.

The day after her final dinner with the Saunders, Mary Ellen was given a muslin dress and round-toed slippers tied with ribbons about her ankles. Then she was sent by coach to the home of Americus Price in New Orleans. Abigail, heavily sedated and in a semi-comatose state, was unaware of Mary Ellen's departure. Despite Mary Ellen's tearful pleas, she had not been allowed to see Abigail or to say good-bye. Carlyle, terribly depressed, had looked at Mary Ellen with sunken eyes, and simply waved her away without a word. His haggard appearance had a sobering effect on Mary Ellen as she rode the coach to New Orleans.

CHAPTER FOUR

The Ursalines

NEW ORLEANS

1842-1846

HAVING NEVER SET FOOT BEYOND GOLDEN OAKS, MARY ELLEN FOUND the trip to New Orleans to be incomprehensible and frightening, yet disturbingly exciting. She arrived in New Orleans confused and emotionally drained, torn between pathos and apprehension, bewilderment and excitement. Her mind clung to her past, never straying too far from brooding thoughts of Golden Oaks, Abigail, or her mother—the sum total of her universe. Still a spark of interest had been aroused, awakened by the intoxicating new world around her. The late summer months were turning into the flaming oranges and brilliant reds of fall as Mary Ellen arrived in New Orleans to meet with Americus Price.

Everything around her was new and different. Sycamore and cypress trees lined the cobbled streets the coach traveled on; strange odors and the clamorous noises flooded her senses. She could feel the pulse of a city, the first city she had ever seen, with a multitude of people, houses, horses, carriages, streets, and shops. She was fascinated with the broad streets,

The Ursuline Convent

one-room Creole cottages with palmetto-leaf roofs. Through exquisite grilled gateways in high walls she glimpsed other houses as large or even larger than Golden Oaks with pink-red tiled roofs, broad balconies and verandas railed with intricate wrought iron.

Americus Price's house, on 24 Chartres Street, was in the heart of the Vieux Carre. The plaster-faced brick building had wide balconies on the second floor, supported by Ionic columns with large windows framed by batten. The house reflected strength and gentility. Mary Ellen was ushered through a courtyard with a gated entry. Two massive doors opened into a house filled with beautiful furniture and works of art.

She was taken directly to her room. Exhausted by the long, arduous trip and overwhelmed by all she had seen, she paid little attention to the room as she removed her dusty clothes and fell into the large four-poster bed with its soft bedding and pillows. She had a deep but fitful sleep, haunted by strange bewildering dreams where Delila and Abigail appeared together, Delila speaking precise and dignified English, while Abigail shrieked and raved in some mystical voodoo chant. They were surrounded by an exotic land unlike anything Mary Ellen had ever seen before; it did not resemble Louisiana, Alabama, or Georgia, the route she had just taken. Rather there were many hills, higher than any she had ever seen, some brown and barren, others flush with thick green forests surrounded by a huge expanse of water. Grimy men with hairy faces, all dressed identically in red but sporting a wide assortment of hats, were the sole inhabitants. Other than Abigail and Delila, no women were present in this foreign land or in this curious dream.

The next day, after bathing the caked dust from her body, and donning clean clothes, she breakfasted with Americus in the dining room, a long, airy room surrounded on three sides by large bay windows facing a lush garden. Americus, dressed elegantly in a waistcoat of brown broadcloth with a high stand-up collar, politely inquired about her trip and encouraged her to eat. Mary Ellen was famished and quickly consumed poached eggs, sausages, and coffee, taking additional servings and allowing Americus to do all the talking while she heaped spoonful after spoonful of the tasty food into an already crowded mouth.

"As you know, you will soon be admitted to the Ursaline Convent to begin your studies," he said as he dabbed his mouth with a napkin. "This is the arrangement that Abigail, I mean Mrs. Saunders and I made."

Sorrow and grief shown in Mary Ellen's eyes, so Americus hesitated for a moment and let Mary Ellen compose herself. He cleared his throat and continued. "Do you know anything about the Ursalines?" he asked.

"No," she admitted.

Americus picked up a small book and opened it to a page marked with a short leather strap. Mary Ellen saw the date 1841 printed on the cover in large bold letters. "I have this Catholic Almanac which describes the education at the Ursalines and what is expected of you." He glanced at the marked pages and smiled. "They are really quite advanced, you know. Look at page 155." He handed her the book. "Go ahead, read it."

Mary Ellen wiped her hands before taking the book. Then she looked at the page Americus had opened and read it carefully. When she finished she returned the book to Americus who proceeded to read it aloud. "The system of instruction embraces the following subjects: English and French, Writing, Arithmetic, Geography, the use of the Globes, History (ancient and modern), Mythology, Chronology, English and French Literature, Astronomy, Needle-Work. Elements of Philosophy, Botany and Chemistry will be taught to those young ladies whose parents desire it."

Americus stopped and regarded Mary Ellen with a pleased expression. "So you see, they have quite a curriculum, perhaps the best in the south. And I will allow you to study philosophy, botany and chemistry, if you wish."

Americus looked at the book and laughed. "They even teach music and dancing."

Mary Ellen blushed and looked away. The thought of dancing seemed exciting and somewhat dangerous to her. She had never seen Abigail or Carlyle dance, but the slaves danced, and at times her mother engaged in rituals where she danced as if possessed.

Mary Ellen had not really known what to expect of the convent; actually she had given it little thought. The courses Americus had mentioned were intriguing. She had never learned anything about the stars and was not really sure what botany, chemistry, or philosophy were, but they sounded fascinating all the same.

"Yes. They have an amazing program," Americus continued. "I suggest that you read the Almanac carefully." He closed the book and handed it back to Mary Ellen.

"We must also discuss other quite important issues." He cleared his throat again. "You are owned by me, but it's a nominal ownership, a temporary legal requirement."

Americus paused when he realized, from Mary Ellen's quizzical expression, that she did not understand what he had just said.

"You were left in my charge, Mary Ellen, and I have obligations to meet. I'll provide for your education, room, and board. When you're eighteen I'll give you papers which will confirm your freedom; you'll no longer be a slave. This is what I promised Mrs. Saunders. I'll keep my word, which I also now give to you."

Mary Ellen remained silent, then reached for another slice of freshly baked bread. Americus continued. "The Ursaline Convent provides girls of your age with a wonderful opportunity to become educated adults, which is what I think Mrs. Saunders had in mind for you—to become an educated, free adult."

Mary Ellen remained quiescent, unsure of the direction he was taking.

"Many of the girls of Creole families are sent there."

"What does 'Creole' mean?" Mary Ellen asked, her mouth full of that delicious bread.

"Creole means people of French or Spanish descent. You may not know, but this land, Louisiana, and certainly New Orleans, was once a French possession, populated by French subjects."

"I know a little about it," Mary Ellen said uncertainly.

"Well, their descendants are the Creoles, and the more fortunate girls are sent to the Ursaline Convent for their education."

Mary Ellen looked out the window then turned back to Americus. "I've never known any . . . Creole girls. I've never really known any girls around my age, not even at Golden Oaks."

Americus understood her reference to mean slave girls, not white girls.

"Well, you'll meet such girls at the Ursalines," Americus said.

"How will they treat me?" Mary Ellen asked openly, and Americus responded instantly.

"They'll treat you like any other girl."

"But I'm not like one of them," she said, suddenly alarmed. "they'll avoid me, like the children at Golden Oaks."

"What do you mean avoid you?"

"The children wouldn't play with me. No one was allowed to play with me."

"Not allowed to play with you? You mean you were shunned? At Golden Oaks?" Americus seemed genuinely puzzled. Abigail had never mentioned any incidents of Mary Ellen being shunned by anyone.

"I don't know. The other children never played with me. I never had any friends. Abigail was my only friend." And here Mary Ellen lowered her eyes as if by looking at the table Americus would not notice her eyes and realize that they were responsible for her being shunned.

"Well, I don't know the whats or whys of things at Golden Oaks, but here you'll not be shunned. You'll be treated as one of them."

"But they won't want to play with me," Mary Ellen balled her hands into fists and bit her lower lip. "I'm just a . . . a slave girl. I just don't understand." Mary Ellen started to cry softly.

Americus got up from his seat across the table and sat in the chair next to Mary Ellen. He spoke softly. "Mary Ellen, no one will know anything about you being a slave. You'll pass as a white girl."

"How can I?" Mary Ellen protested. "I couldn't pass as a white girl. That's impossible. I am not white. I am a slave."

"No. As far as I'm concerned you are not a slave. And that's what really matters. Look at your skin. It's only slightly darker, and no darker than many Spanish girls, Creole girls. If I'm not mistaken, I think you're partly white." Americus said this carefully and gently.

Mary Ellen continued to cry, and her lament, Americus admitted, was a reasonable one. The veil of white, the specter of trying to be passed off as a white girl, could be so easily ripped away if Mary Ellen did not act the part with some degree of composure and confidence. In the little time they had left, he would have to train and prepare her for this deception. She would leave for the convent in a week, but Americus felt confident that this would be sufficient time.

In the course of the following week Mary Ellen and Americus engaged in extensive discussions about what might be expected of her. As they spoke of her experiences at Golden Oaks, Mary Ellen realized that she did know how white people lived and behaved, at least adult white people. She had been equally at home in the slave quarters, with Delila, and at the Saunders mansion, essentially living a white existence. She knew how to act around white adults. Most importantly, Americus explained, her ability to speak so well disguised all traces of her birth.

"It's remarkable how the ears, upon hearing a well-spoken word, will confirm the opposite of what the eyes might see," Americus told her. "In fact, the ears will deceive the eyes into seeing something which may not even be there. So, you see, Mary Ellen, Mrs. Saunders prepared you quite well indeed for this journey. You'll be doing this not only for yourself, but to achieve her dream."

Chapter Four

Thoughts of Abigail flooded Mary Ellen's mind. She wanted to know how Abigail was faring, whether her condition had worsened, but she was afraid to ask, afraid to find out what she already knew deep in her heart—that Abigail had died. She missed Abigail's tenderness, the love she gave so completely, so unselfishly, and their conversations that ranged over a wide variety of subjects and interests.

As if Americus could read her thoughts, he said: "There's no greater honor you could bestow on that decent, kind, and gentle woman, than to fulfill her dreams for you. Educate yourself, and do something worthwhile with your life."

Mary Ellen listened intently as they continued their conversations about the Ursaline Convent. Mary Ellen still could not shake the nagging fear that she would somehow slip up and be found out.

"Most of the nuns are sympathetic," he said, "not necessarily to the abolitionist cause, though I suspect many of them are supportive, but opposed to the terrible cruelty arising from the subjugation of other human beings. So even if you were to be, shall we say, discovered, such a discovery would not result in any significant problem."

Mary Ellen regarded this comment with some suspicion, and Americus noted her look. "I've been told that some girls at the convent are or were slaves," he remarked. "Although they're schooled, I believe, at a different location from the Creole girls, the convent is already doing what's unheard of—educating slaves. I also understand that there's one ordained nun who was a former slave."

Americus placed his hands on Mary Ellen's shoulder, his strong fingers holding her tightly. "Still, it would be best if you don't discuss your background with anyone unless absolutely necessary! No matter how sympathetic they appear."

She nodded and looked into his serious face. "But sometimes they'll ask me questions about where I came from, where I was born. I can't ignore them. What would I say?" Mary Ellen asked.

"You'll tell the identical story to every one who inquires. You're an orphan, that's true. You lost your parents when very young, and didn't really know them. That's also true. You're a distant relative of mine. This is true."

Mary Ellen looked at Americus disbelievingly, as if she had misheard him. "How can that be?" she asked.

"It's true, Mary Ellen. We're all Adam and Eve's progeny. We're all God's children. So we're related in some distant fashion. You ended up living with me under my trusteeship. This again is true. The more truths we have, the better. Of course we'll slightly shade the truth with minor details which may be more easily understood and accepted by others and lead to fewer questions. But, keep in mind that the less you say the better. Don't embellish. The more you say the greater the possibility that someone will find inconsistencies in your story, or situations where you could be required to produce facts that you don't have."

They spent much of the time discussing Americus's family and fleshing out the story of her orphanage, her ancestry, and her history. Mary Ellen committed this information to memory, absorbing as many facts as her limited time with Americus allowed. Still the apprehension remained, and as she would later discover, this apprehension never fully abated throughout her time at the convent or during her life.

As the week lapsed, Americus found himself more and more drawn to the enigmatic and precocious young girl in his charge. Tall and mature for her age, her mind worked brilliantly, much like that of an intelligent adult, yet her vulnerability and innocence were just as remarkable. And those eyes, which required some getting accustomed to, were beautiful but, like their owner, seemed to have their origin in two different and conflicting worlds. Mary Ellen possessed some innate power, a magnetic allure that enthralled him; a power she did not seem to know she had. On the contrary, everything she did or said came out modestly with a genuine impulse, an apparent innocence, not driven by ulterior motives. Nevertheless, the power was there, and Americus at times felt enslaved by his own slave.

—∾—

MARY ELLEN ARRIVED AT THE URSALINE CONVENT UNCERTAIN AND with a lingering sense of dread. She was greeted correctly by the mother superior who gave her a tour of the premises that would serve as her home for the next three years.

"This is a very special, very holy place, Mary Ellen," the nun told her. "In 1727 the first nuns of our order arrived from France. They came here to heal the sick and care for the less fortunate, the orphans. Ten years later this building was built." The nun had a proud look and a beatific smile. "It is the oldest building in Louisiana." Then she turned to Mary Ellen. "And through God's intervention, this is the only building to survive two horrible fires that completely gutted all of New Orleans."

Mary Ellen followed the nun along floors of wide cypress boards, worn deep over the years by the nuns, and up a gently curved staircase to the second story, guarded by a black balustrade with intricate hand-hammered ironwork. She felt the strength of the beams and rafters of hand-hewn cypress logs. Not a single nail had been used in building the convent; it was held together by wooden pegs. Outside, a high-walled garden provided Mary Ellen with her only opportunity to commune with nature, for she would not leave the convent under any circumstances, even when the other girls took their one week of summer break or the two weeks allotted at the end of December.

After her tour she was introduced to several nuns who served as her tutors, as they sometimes called themselves.

One of the nuns, who clearly presided over the others, said, "We have pupils of all denominations, here. But members of our community are strictly Catholic and everyone is expected to attend Divine Worship. We will adorn your mind with useful knowledge and you will be accustomed to habits of order, cleanliness, and polite manners. The girls are never allowed to go beyond the superintendence of our Ladies, who will secure the preservation of your morals and the willing observance of our rules."

Mary Ellen listened halfheartedly as her mind roiled with her new surroundings, especially the library, stocked with an inexhaustible store of books, from theological tomes and catechisms to books on etiquette, geography, art, music, astronomy, philosophy, and literature. These reflected the Ursaline desire to provide their charges with the best education possible. The library at Golden Oaks reflected Abigail's interests and

Carlyle's determination to have a showplace. But the Ursaline library had such an extensive collection of rare and modern works that Mary Ellen could hardly wait to delve into them and discover the store of knowledge.

"As we informed Mr. Price," the nun continued, "you are not expected to wear any particular dress for class days, but on Sundays and Thursdays during winter you have to wear a blue merino dress with a black belt; and in the summer a white frock with a blue belt, and the cape tied in front with a blue ribband."

Mary Ellen arrived well prepared with twelve changes of linen, twelve pocket handkerchiefs, twelve pairs of stockings, six muslin and six cambric capes, two black silk aprons, napkins, towels and a large mattress; all provided by Americus.

Mary Ellen fell into a routine very quickly. Between her classes and her chores—from washing floors, laundering linen, and running errands—she huddled in the corner of her small cubicle and read her precious books by dim oil or candlelight late into the night. She practiced writing, making sure her penmanship met her own exacting goal of perfection. Other young women from some of the wealthiest families of New Orleans studied French and history, but they were more drawn to the arts, music, and the more important elements of appropriate and fashionable behavior. Mary Ellen had no interest in learning about social accomplishments. She felt awkward and could not understand how such behavior would ever be of any benefit to her. But in her zeal to please the nuns, or Ladies, as they were also called, she excelled in every subject, including etiquette.

The nuns, though impressed by Mary Ellen's acuity and perseverance, never indicated any concern about her being sent to them for an education. If they suspected anything about Mary Ellen's background, they did so in silence; not so much on account of any vows but because of the munificent gift Americus Price made to the convent, and also because they genuinely liked Mary Ellen.

The nuns, however, did wonder why this brilliant girl kept so much to herself, rarely responding to friendship or companionship from the other girls. She remained solitary by her own choice. She never felt comfortable with the other girls; she did not know what to talk about. She and

Chapter Four

Americus had never taken into consideration what she had not learned at Golden Oaks: how white girls interacted with one another. Despite the presence of so many girls at the convent, many her own age, she never formed any close friendships.

Mary Ellen would curl up into a ball at night, lying quietly in her bed, thinking about the wide green open spaces of Golden Oaks, the vast cotton fields, the freedom to roam, and the feeling of home.

One afternoon, while Mary Ellen was completely engrossed in *The Iliad,* a couple of girls scurried into the library. Mary Ellen was annoyed for she enjoyed the solitude and always went where she could be alone. The couple whispered together in the corner where Geology became Geometry. Their desire for secrecy was conspicuous. Mary Ellen thought that the blonde looked like a squirrel, gnawing on her fingernails and glancing toward the sister who was filing books and paying no attention to them. The other girl, a redhead, resembled a parrot.

Mary Ellen, despising their camaraderie and scoffing at their immature silliness, stood to leave. As she drew closer to the pair the words "voodoo" and "laveau" reached her ears. Suddenly the girls burst out giggling, then desperately slapped their hands over their mouths and slipped out of the library. Mary Ellen followed them out the door, feeling an overwhelming excitement.

"Excuse me, I couldn't help but overhear—" Mary Ellen said softly.

"You didn't hear anything," squawked the parrot.

"But I—"

"No, you didn't."

"I heard you talking about voodoo and Marie Laveau."

"So what's it to you?" the squirrel chattered.

"I'm familiar with voodoo."

The parrot challenged, "Prove it. How did you become so familiar?"

"Well, I, uh. I knew a voodoo princess. Yes, she worked on the plantation where I used to live," Mary Ellen stopped. She remembered Americus's warning not to embellish her superficial history with lies.

"Really? Do something she did." The squirrel's eyes lit up as she bit the skin around her thumbnail and tore it off.

Mary Ellen probed her maternal lessons and exclaimed, "*Flimani Koku!*"

The squirrel's eyes widened but the parrot scoffed. "Anyone can make that up. What does it mean?"

"When you see Marie Laveau ask her. She'll tell you." Mary Ellen turned to leave.

"Hey," called the parrot, "which plantation did you say your princess lived at?"

Before Mary Ellen could answer the squirrel turned to the parrot and exclaimed, "We should take her with us."

The parrot nodded her head then clapped. "So, Mary Ellen, want to go to town with us? We're going to see one of Marie Laveau's voodoo ceremonies. Obviously you've heard of her, you being so familiar with voodoo and all."

Mary Ellen noticed the sarcastic tone in her voice. "We aren't allowed to go into town," Mary Ellen said flatly.

"Oh, we know," murmured the squirrel nervously, "believe me, we know." She began attacking the remaining fingernails.

"But who can come to New Orleans and not see the voodoo magic?" The parrot flapped her arms and taunted the squirrel and then Mary Ellen. "You aren't scared, are you?"

Though completely shocked by their offer and profoundly intrigued by the idea, Mary Ellen found herself declining. "No." She turned to leave.

"Wait," the parrot demanded. "We know your kind."

Mary Ellen stiffened. The book slipped from her hand and pounded the floor. She bent over to fetch it. "Excuse me," she murmured and turned again to escape. She feared she had said too much.

"We have you all figured out."

Mary Ellen's mind leaped back through time and settled slowly onto her mother and then onto Abigail. She could hear Americus's voice telling her to make Abigail proud. Abigail was telling her to understand. Delila kept murmuring over and over about Mary Ellen's power. Her eyes danced from the redhead to the blonde. She felt her pulse quicken and heat filled her chest and stomach. She almost lost the book again but caught it with her other hand.

"I have no idea what you're talking about. There's nothing to know."

Chapter Four

"See!" The blonde turned to her comrade. "See, I told you so. She thinks she's so high and mighty. She thinks she's above everyone else because she learns everything so fast." Turning to Mary Ellen she went on, "My brother's just like you. He went off to school and when he came home he wouldn't talk to any of us. He wouldn't even go riding with our little brother. He said he couldn't 'risk tainting his superior intellectual state.' Ha! Fine, we don't want your kind with us. Come on, let's go have fun without this princess."

Mary Ellen wanted to laugh. She wanted to laugh so hard that her stomach hurt and her eyes teared. She wanted to reach out and hug those girls. "No, wait, I'm sorry. I didn't mean to . . . I mean, I'll go. I will go."

"What? Are you sure?"

"Yes."

Mary Ellen hurried to her room. She had not opened her trunk since the day she had arrived. She had no need for town clothes whatsoever. She fumbled through her few belongings and decided her good summer Sunday frock would just have to do. She would be sure to hide her dark hair inside her bonnet as usual.

It had been dark for an hour by the time the girls crept from their quarters and down the long corridor. They remained silent as they scurried along the stairwell like mice in a cat-infested home. The parrot led the way while Mary Ellen followed. Their hearts raced. As they neared the main door, the giddy squirrel giggled.

"Hush!" said the parrot. "Do you want to get us all caught?" Mary Ellen was chosen to open the door. Her arms throbbed as the blood pulsed violently throughout her body. She slowly pushed the heavy door, careful not to make it creak. Inch by inch moonlight slipped through the increasing gap and the cracks between the hinges.

"Oh come on!" The impatient parrot forced the door open in one quick motion letting out a loud bang as it slammed against the wall. The girls flew out the door like disturbed bats from a cave.

"Halt!"

The girls froze. Their shoulders sank as they slowly spun around to face their doom.

"What are you doing?"

Mary Ellen looked at the others, prepared to explain the truth when suddenly the two girls burst into tears. Between sobs they cried, "We didn't want to go. We didn't want to break the rules, sister. But she threatened us with her voodoo. We are so sorry, sister. Please forgive us. We didn't want to go, honest."

Mary Ellen could not believe what she was witnessing.

"Well, Mary Ellen," The sister shone the lamp in her face. "What do you have to say for yourself."

Mary Ellen remained silent.

"Mary Ellen? It is much wiser to confess your sins."

Mary Ellen remained silent.

"Is it true that you know about voodoo?"

"Yes," said Mary Ellen, lowering her head.

"Girls, go up to your rooms and wash your faces and go to bed. Mary Ellen, come with me."

Sister Jean Marie always took that extra step when helping Mary Ellen with her studies. She especially enjoyed working with the girl on that forbidding subject: mathematics, which both secretly enjoyed. They also found themselves toying with Aristotelian logic late into the nights.

"Frankly, I'm appalled. I would have expected this sort of thing from some of the others, but not you. How could you do this to us, to me? What is this talk of voodoo?"

"I told them I was familiar with it."

"Since when have you begun to practice black magic. This is the Lord's house and we will not tolerate anything other than a faith in Him."

"I haven't been practicing. I just know about it."

"How do you know about it?"

"There was a voodoo princess at a plantation where I used to live."

"I see. Mary Ellen, you don't want to end up like those types of people do you? That isn't the kind of life to strive for, is it?"

"No, ma'am." Mary Ellen's answer was heartfelt and sincere.

"More importantly, we've been so good to you. Why would you want to leave?"

"Sister, I don't. I don't want to leave."

Chapter Four

Mary Ellen did not want to leave. Yet how could she explain the feeling? How could she begin to describe her loneliness, an existence founded at birth and something she suppressed but always loathed? Also, how could she tell Sister Jean Marie that at the convent the regime was much more strict then she was accustomed? She found herself having to abide by a set of complex rules for the first time in her life. At first she chafed at the limitations, but realized early on that any impulsive action on her part, any attempt to disregard or violate the rules, might lead to greater scrutiny and increase the risk of discovery. At times Mary Ellen felt as if she were in prison, partly created by her attempt to pass as white, partly by the strict rules and limited mobility. Any offering of friendship, a momentary feeling of camaraderie consumed her senses like a glass of water after trekking through dust and heat. It was her breath of fresh air. It had felt so good.

"I don't know. I don't know."

"Don't know what, Mary Ellen?"

Mary Ellen just stared at Sister Jean Marie. The sister became more and more irritated, clutching her rosary and glaring at Mary Ellen, feeling betrayed.

"I'm sorry, you leave me no choice but to punish you. But for heaven's sake child, if you haven't been in the wrong then speak up."

—~—

THE ATTEMPTED LARK SLOWLY FADED TO THE RECESSES OF THE CONVENT'S mind. Mary Ellen went about her extra chores with resignation. In time the sisters' faith in Mary Ellen was rebuilt and she and Sister Jean Marie reconciled. By the time Mary Ellen reached the age of sixteen the Ladies had exhausted their ability to teach her anything more. She could read and write as well as the best of them, though Sister Jean Marie could still solve problems that Mary Ellen found too complex.

Upon learning of Mary Ellen's remarkable progress, Americus was faced with a dilemma. It would be more appropriate for Mary Ellen to remain in the Convent until her eighteenth birthday when she could leave fully emancipated, but he instinctively felt the environment would arrest further development at a critical time in her life. Finally, after wrestling with the alternatives for weeks and finding no solution, Americus made a crucial decision based on his intuition.

—∞—

DURING HER ENTIRE STAY AT THE URSALINE CONVENT MARY ELLEN never left the grounds and never really saw New Orleans although she heard many stories about the city and its diverse populace. While other girls went home at vacation time, Mary Ellen remained alone, feeling abandoned. She could not understand why Americus did not invite her to his home; why she spent New Year's evening alone, or with the Ladies.

During the year she would listen as the other girls sat at night and exchanged experiences, many of which Mary Ellen suspected were grossly exaggerated, as if the girls could impress each other with such tall tales, but these stories only served to give New Orleans an even greater sense of mystery and excitement.

On several occasions the girls talked about voodoo, and Mary Ellen would listen intently to their prattle, especially when they mentioned Marie Laveau. The girls laughed and made lewd comments about Laveau; ridiculed the notion that Laveau could control New Orleans or had unprecedented power, but they were clearly terrified of the woman and their laughter had a hard edge which Mary Ellen found amusing. With each tale Marie Laveau grew in size and Mary Ellen became intrigued by the stories, some of which made more sense to her than to the girls. She would lie idly on her mattress during the rest periods and imagine herself meeting Marie Laveau. She decided that one day she would meet the Voodoo Queen of New Orleans.

There were moments, especially during vacations, when time passed so slowly, when Mary Ellen felt that the walls around her growing taller and more confining; but most of the time she was preoccupied by her studies, plunging into her books with a relish, devouring them as fast as she could so that she was not aware of the passage of time. Then she received a letter from Americus informing her that she would be leaving the Ursalines.

Chapter Four

As the day for her departure approached, Mary Ellen once again found herself buffeted by mixed emotions. The Ursaline Convent had been her home for three years, and although she had chafed at the restrictions imposed by the order and the limitations on her movements, she had developed a fondness for many of the Ladies who had to live by the same canons and limitations, and she discovered a sense of security, if not serenity. But Mary Ellen's longing to see the outside world exceeded all other feelings. Where she had used her imagination to soar to foreign lands, to listen to great thinkers, and engage in mental conversations with mythical characters, perhaps now she would have the opportunity to really experience what she had learned.

After a tearful departure Mary Ellen left the Ursaline Convent to be reunited with Americus, and this made her nervous, though she really did not know why. She had spent one busy week with Americus years earlier and now realized how little she knew of the man. After her sudden departure from Golden Oaks, and the week of intensive preparations for the Ursaline Convent, Mary Ellen had not really paid much attention to Americus and that week seemed very remote and distant as she now moved slowly down the cobblestone lane toward his house.

Their communications during the years at the convent were limited. Americus wrote infrequently, short notes expressing his satisfaction with her progress and encouraging her to continue to work hard. Still, the picture of him on his steed, dressed magnificently in his forest green jacket, was forever imprinted in her mind. She was excited at the prospect of seeing him again, but remained troubled and anxious about his intentions after so many years; whether he would keep his promise to set her free.

Back in Americus's house, Mary Ellen smelled the odor of burning wood, the stale breath of furniture, and the moldering garden, all familiar smells which made the years gone by vanish, as if she had never left for the Ursaline Convent. She was brought into a large room where she had never been. It was furnished in the style of Louis XIV with an ornate desk in the middle of the room. Americus was busy writing, his face locked in concentration.

"Miss Mary Ellen," the butler announced. Mary Ellen entered the room, trying her best to walk as she had been taught at the Convent. Americus looked up, smiled warmly, then motioned for her to wait a minute by wagging his index finger and returned to his writing where he scribbled a few more words, punctuated his sentence with a flourish and set the quill down.

"Well, well," he said as he got up, rubbed his hands together and came around the desk to greet her, his eyes blazing with intensity, but tinged with a twinkle. He clasped her hands warmly in his.

"I see the sisters did a wonderful job." He held her at arm's length, almost as if they were dancing, and appraised her. "Of course they did have a marvelous subject to work with."

Mary Ellen felt her face redden. Americus smiled and led her to one of the chairs facing his desk. He returned to his seat and placed his elbows on the desk, forming a little steeple with his long, slender fingers and propping his chin on his finger tips. It reminded Mary Ellen of a man at prayer.

"Mary Ellen, the reports I've received from the sisters suggest that you are quite an ardent student. I'm quite satisfied that you acquitted yourself well. How did you enjoy your stay at the convent?" he asked.

Mary Ellen felt uncomfortable. She did not want to say anything negative or unkind, not after the efforts Americus and the Ladies had undertaken to give her an education. She looked down at the floor while working out her answer, but nothing came out.

"Mary Ellen, are you all right?" Americus looked at her intensely and Mary Ellen snapped out of her daze.

"Oh, I'm sorry, Mr. Price. I was just thinking how to answer your question. I learned a great deal. They were very kind to me, and they had a most wonderful library." Her face brightened up. "I'll miss them and the library, I'm afraid." She paused briefly. "But I'm ever so grateful for the opportunity you gave me," she responded, selecting her words carefully.

Americus was intrigued by the tall, soft-spoken girl who carried herself with such deportment; one confident and comfortable with herself, though somewhat distant and reflective. She had changed a great deal during the three years. Where once there had been a girl, he now faced a lovely, intelligent young woman. Obviously he had made the right decision to bring her back; his instincts about Mary Ellen, even from their first encounter on the dusty road, had not led him astray.

The reports from the nuns described a precocious but solitary girl who shied away from any social intercourse. She had a dark, golden complexion and could not really give a suitable explanation of her upbringing, at least not one that could withstand close scrutiny. And then there were those strange haunting eyes. Even if no one discovered her real origins, the lack of suitable history could raise suspicions. Americus had no doubt that Mary Ellen would have a future, but not in the South.

Americus remained silent as he thought about Mary Ellen. She was turning into a beautiful woman. He could see how her young breasts were already filling her dress, and felt his pulse quicken, but he immediately crushed all such thoughts. He was embarrassed and angry with himself for even allowing such feelings to enter his mind.

Mary Ellen could sense some sort of struggle within Americus. She also felt as if he looked at her with some intensity and felt something in her stomach turn; a pleasant but frightening feeling. He remained quiet, lost in thought, and Mary Ellen misread it as if he were displeased with her for some reason. She became more nervous.

Finally he spoke, as if a heavy burden had been lifted. "I'm going to send you to my plantation in Missouri, at Price's Landing. I think the farther we move you north the better it will be. I've arranged further tutoring for you and you'll continue with your education."

Americus stood and walked around the desk to stand before Mary Ellen. "I must tell you that I fully intend to honor my commitment as a gentleman to Mrs. Saunders and give you your freedom when you turn eighteen. However, I counsel you not to discuss this with anyone. We will modify your story of being an orphan under my protection. The story in Missouri, where they know my immediate relatives, must be different. You will say, only when asked mind you, that your father died many years ago and, more recently, your mother who is a distant relation of mine. I have decided to provide you with care and support until you are eighteen years old. At that time you will be sent to Boston and be on your own. That's the story. And that's what will happen."

He moved back around the desk and picked up a sheet of parchment. "Here is a letter that explains your history in greater detail. Memorize the details and destroy this document. We were successful at the Ursaline Convent, and we will be equally successful at my home at Price's Landing."

Americus then sealed the letter with wax and handed it to Mary Ellen.

His warmth had now changed into a brusque, businesslike demeanor. But no matter how hard he tried, there was a tinge of something unsettling in his mind, and it terrified the hell out of him. He would have to keep his distance from Mary Ellen. She had a strange and unclear effect on him, a strong and powerful pull, not unlike the one he felt on the road to Augusta. But he convinced himself that he would remain true to his commitment and not allow any thoughts to impede his plans for Mary Ellen's future.

CHAPTER FIVE

Americus

PRICE'S LANDING, MISSOURI

1846–1847

THE SHRILL SOUND OF THE STEAM WHISTLE ON THE *BELLE CREOLE* boomed across the broad muddy river as the white paddle steamer wound its way along the Mississippi. Mary Ellen stood at the railing, her dress caressed by the gentle breeze, and watched the large boat negotiate the point as they neared Price's Landing. Currents and eddies in the turbid water formed swirling shapes and figures that reminded Mary Ellen of cumulus clouds, but they marked shifting sand banks and shoals which made the approach to Price's Landing treacherous. The river bottom had claimed several ships that had their bottoms torn, or were snagged, or ended with exploding boilers. The captain kept a sharp lookout.

The trip from New Orleans had been a mind-opening experience. Virtually all of Mary Ellen's life had been spent at two places, Golden Oaks and the Ursaline Convent. Each was sheltered from the glare of the outside world, giving its occupants a skewed, if not provincial, view of life. Now, as she floated on the mighty Mississippi, passing one small village or

Mississippi River ~ 1847

farm after another, she could see life as it really was. Her image of whites was formed by her association with the Saunders, Americus, and the girls and nuns at the Convent. She assumed that all whites were rich, powerful, and lived in plush surroundings. The notion that some whites were not rich but were very poor had been unimaginable. But the poor whites were quite visible from the steamboat.

The second dissonant sound of the whistle heralded their arrival at Price's Landing, and she could see before her, on the left, a small wharf along a straight patch of sand towards which the *Belle Creole* now headed. The enormous paddle wheel slowly reversed the direction of its revolutions, then stopped to allow the boat to drift sideways. The boat swayed gently as it nudged the side of the wharf. Large ropes were thrown to a man standing on the wharf who quickly secured them to posts. As the port side of the boat came to rest next to the wharf two sailors from the boat leaped on the dock and secured other lines, making the boat steadfast. A narrow wooden gangway was hurriedly pushed over the side and extended to the wharf. It lay nearly flat because of the low tide and the *Belle Creole*'s low waterline.

Mary Ellen went ashore as supplies and merchandise for the plantation were unloaded and bales of cotton piled along the wharf, as well as other goods, were taken on board. She watched as the steamboat paddle wheel started churning again, turning the water into a boiling cauldron of white foam. Large plumes of steam billowed from the dual smoke stacks, the lines were released, and the boat slid from the dock, heading slowly downstream towards the middle of the wide river. She felt a sense of sadness that this part of her life was ended.

The supplies were stowed on the same wagon that would carry Mary Ellen to the plantation. Riding along the wide road lined with mature oaks, whose boughs reached across and touched, forming a spectacular entry, she realized that the plantation was ornate and meticulously maintained. The tall-pilloried mansion had been in the Price family for nearly half a century.

She was shown to the comfortable guest room and no one questioned her presence. All members of the staff deferred to her. If the slaves at the plantation had any knowledge of her background, or any suspicion, it did not register and was not discussed openly. Americus had warned Mary Ellen not to get involved or spend any time with the slaves since it would only serve to undermine her ability to pass. With this in mind, Mary Ellen remained largely to herself; but she hungered for companionship, even though she had lived in her own shell for much of her life.

Americus's parents had passed away some years earlier and Mary Ellen's only contacts were with the household servants and her tutors.

One servant, Adelina de Boisrouge, an older Creole woman from New Orleans, had been in charge of the kitchen at Price's Landing for as long as anyone could remember. Mary Ellen's first contacts with Adelina were neither friendly nor hostile. Adelina never rushed into anything. She liked to take her time, ruminating and mulling things over carefully before judging anyone. She wanted to see for herself why Americus had brought this mysterious young girl to Price's Landing. She never asked Mary Ellen about her past, and whatever she suspected she kept to herself.

Adelina was a marvelous cook. Equally at home with Creole, French, and other European cuisine, she prepared different foods to whet Mary Ellen's appetite. The two laughed at Mary Ellen's capacity to consume enormous quantities of Adelina's fine cooking and still remain slim and grow more beautiful by the day. Soon Adelina had Mary Ellen in the kitchen, donning an apron and working side by side, learning how to prepare exquisite meals. During her time at Price's Landing Mary Ellen evolved into an excellent chef for which Adelina proudly took all credit.

Mary Ellen's tutors, who continued with her education and refinement, were astonished to be assigned by Americus Price to instruct and educate this girl whose relationship to Americus remained a mystery. They were captivated by her beauty, though they found it difficult to look into her eyes, not knowing which eye to focus on, almost as if one eye was blind. If they suspected a certain liaison with Americus, it was dispelled quite early by his conspicuous absence.

Mary Ellen's capacity to learn astonished her tutors. She was bright, inquisitive, with a keen mind and a rapier-like logic. Instead of becoming a boring chore, Mary Ellen became an intellectual challenge and more often than not the tutors came out second best in their spirited scholarly duels.

"This man is ingenious!" Mary Ellen proclaimed after closing her book.

"Who, my dear? Which genius are we discussing today?" inquired Tutor Garrison.

"This Montaigne. His strategies for power and leadership are quite profound and seem to be extremely effective. He argues that as a leader it is better to be feared than regaled and loved. Respect stems from fear, and power from respect. Quite true is it not?"

Garrison chuckled. "Ah, but Mary Ellen, you are overlooking the ultimate question. Is it better to be feared and powerful or loved and happy? Is fear essential to obtain true power and what is any occupation, or life for that matter, without love?"

"Hmmm. Well, fear is just the catalyst for power. From power comes position, status, wealth, and many followers. I would think this would leave one rather happy."

"But love, my dear, what about true love?"

"Oh, bah! Have you ever met a king who never weds?"

"I have never met a king. In fact, I believe that is why we came to America; to avoid the monarchy."

"Well, Garrison, true love, eh? Are impoverished people happy? No. But the rich are always smiling, dancing, eating, laughing. It is a gay and warm life with power and wealth. Besides, if I were the epitome of Montaigne's formula for a prince, I could buy myself twenty handsome fellows and pay them to love me!"

"Oh, dear, Mary Ellen. Who is your tutor?"

"An idyllic English fellow who wastes away the days reading literature, spinning his philosophies, arguing with his young students, and picking daisies while dreaming of a romantic existence in which ignorant bliss has stolen the place of wealth and power in man's list of priorities." The two fell into a fit of laughter. "In other words, an unrealistic dissolute."

These were some of Mary Ellen's finest days and yet incomprehensible, almost surreal. Time passed quickly. She sensed a freedom unlike anything she had ever experienced before, more open, unstructured, and unencumbered than even during her childhood at Golden Oaks. She did as she pleased, except to travel any distance from the plantation, the one rule imposed by Americus. Now, as she neared her eighteenth birthday, Mary Ellen found herself counting the days. She would lie on her four-poster bed with the windows thrown open to the sultry breezes and try to imagine what she would do as a free woman. Such flights of fancy were mixed with her desire to see Americus. But he never came. Mary Ellen learned that Americus's absence from Price's Landing was quite normal. He rarely spent any time there, preferring to travel, usually spending his summers in Europe or on the East Coast.

Mary Ellen devoted her time and energy to learning. She studied the classics and even engaged her tutors in discussions of commerce, a subject not deemed suitable for a woman, though by the time such discussions were entertained her tutors had ceased to regard her from a gender standpoint. She was smart with an iron-clad mind and remarkable memory.

She also loved history. She learned as much as she could about the colonization of America, although her real underlying interest in this subject related to her curiosity about slavery. Her tutors were reluctant to discuss emancipation, slavery, and, above all, abolitionism. She did not press, but in the course of their discussions, particularly those centered on the Missouri Compromise, she learned how the northern states had enacted emancipation legislation and were pushing for the prohibition of slavery in the west. Mary Ellen managed to draw her tutors into discussion of Benjamin Lindy, the mild-spoken Southern abolitionist, but they refused to discuss the more aggressive northern movements. Of course, as Americus had cautioned, she could not even give the slightest hint of her underlying interest to her tutors, not even a subtle one.

Mary Ellen also became fascinated with America's expansion. She consumed everything written about the Oregon Territory and California. At times she would take a picnic, spread a blanket under a massive oak tree, and imagine she were in the wilderness, riding on a beautiful horse, meeting exotic Indians and Mexicans dressed in colorful serapes. Her view of the frontier, she knew, was romantic and probably unrealistic. After all, other than from some engravings, she had never seen an Indian or Mexican and did not have the foggiest notion of what their habiliments looked like. Indians were notoriously fierce and dangerous and, she suspected, fought the white man for freedom at every turn. She wondered if the Indians and Californios, as they were called, bore any similarities to her people. But she felt an inner shame watching the slaves accept their lot without a whimper while the Indians in the west continued their bitter fight against the settlers and blue coats.

—⁓—

IN FEBRUARY 1847, MARY ELLEN RECEIVED A LETTER FROM AMERICUS. He was in New Orleans and intended to return to Price's Landing and remain through the Spring, possibly into early Summer. He also anticipated celebrating her eighteenth birthday with her. Mary Ellen was thrilled by the news. She had not seen Americus for nearly two years. At times she would lie awake at night and see his image on that roan horse, galloping down the dirt road at Golden Oaks. Somehow this one defining moment of time was incandescently imprinted in her mind.

His reference to her birthday made her smile. Abigail and Americus promised that she would be given her freedom when she turned eighteen. Although her mother, Delila, was unsure of the date of her birth, Abigail remembered the day. It was February 24, 1829. Delila refused to acknowledge that date, probably more out of spite for the blossoming relationship between Abigail and Mary Ellen than for any other reason, so no one really celebrated her birthday until after Delila's death. Then Abigail insisted on observing February 24 as Mary Ellen's formal birthday. Abigail invited all the children at Golden Oaks to attend. They did, but what should have been a fun-filled day with games and songs turned out to be a somber and subdued occasion. The children were reluctant guests, forced to attend and too frightened to interact with Mary Ellen.

Americus arrived on Sunday, February 21, by paddle steamer. Mary Ellen waited anxiously at the wharf until the boat docked. Americus leapt from the slow moving boat to the dock, rushed to Mary Ellen and swept her off her feet with a bear-like hug. She was too stunned to respond. His show of affection was completely unexpected. She blushed as he put her down and looked appraisingly at her.

"You're even more beautiful than I remember," he said sweetly.

A servant interrupted them to inquire about Americus's baggage, breaking the spell.

When Americus concluded giving instructions for his baggage and other large boxes that were unloaded by deckhands, he took her hand and walked to his carriage.

"I've heard some very impressive reports about your studies," he said. "It seems that you have extended your tutors to their limits." He laughed, his blue eyes twinkling. "I suppose the only thing left for you to do now is to go to Harvard College." He laughed again.

Mary Ellen could not tell whether he was laughing at the absurd notion of her going to college, or whether he genuinely admired her educational achievements. As they walked towards the carriage he continued to hold her hand and became thoughtful.

"You know, Mary Ellen. We have to think very carefully about your future. I truly want you to have a wonderful and productive life." He looked downcast as he said this and Mary Ellen wondered why. Then, as if snapping out of some meditative state, he said, "Anyway, let's start with your birthday. You'll be eighteen and you know what that means."

She smiled demurely. She hesitated to raise the subject that occupied her thoughts nearly every moment of every day. Mary Ellen could not shed the mantle of fear that somehow Abigail's and Americus's promise of freedom had been forgotten. She was afraid to say the word "freedom," as if its utterance would shatter what was in reality an illusion. Regardless of how she had been treated, or how well she had been educated, legally she was a slave without a single legal right; and no oral promise of freedom, regardless of how well intentioned or given, could ever be enforced in any court of law. She would have to wait and see and hope that the promise would be fulfilled.

"You're very quiet," he said, knitting his brows, "I hope I haven't offended you in some way?" He stopped at the carriage and looked at her searchingly, hesitantly.

"No. I'm just glad that you finally came," she said earnestly. "Welcome home, Mr. Price."

"Please. Call me Americus. After all you are family and a friend."

"I'm just not used to calling you by anything other than your family name," she said defensively. "It doesn't sound right."

"Of course it sounds right. 'Mr.' sounds too formal, too forbidding." He laughed, but it sounded a trifle forced to her.

He helped Mary Ellen into the carriage and sat down beside her. "In three days you'll be eighteen. I've already had my attorney in Boston prepare the necessary papers for your emancipation. This was my promise. If you have any doubts about my intentions, let me dispel them right now."

Americus noticed the immediate effect this statement had on Mary Ellen. Her whole face brightened considerably as if the clouds had just parted allowing the sun to spotlight her skin. Even her body seemed to settle more relaxed into her seat. She sighed audibly, and clasped his hands tightly in hers. Then she looked shyly at the floor as if deciding what to do. Suddenly she turned to him and kissed him on his cheek. Americus, strangely stirred by this simple gesture, felt himself flushing. He did not understand his own reaction and this surprised him. In fact during the last two weeks he was strangely excited by the prospects of returning to Price's Landing, and he knew it was not the plantation that brought this agitation about. Mary Ellen, he told himself, was his protégée, who with his help might one day help her people out of slavery. He always suppressed other thoughts. Still, Mary Ellen's kiss had been a pleasant surprise and extremely disconcerting. They rode quietly back to the manor, each lost deep in their own thoughts, and both of them quite unsettled.

During the next two days Mary Ellen saw little of Americus. On the twenty-fourth she walked into the kitchen where Adelina was preparing dinner. Adelina turned around, holding a large plate, and noticed Mary Ellen by the door. Adelina put the dish down, looked furtively around then rushed to Mary Ellen.

"Shoo," she waved a towel at Mary Ellen as if a mouse had just invaded the kitchen.

"Get out of here right now," she said warmly. "Don't let anyone see you in here. Mr. Price told me to prepare something special. For your birthday." She explained. "It's a surprise, so get out before you see what it is." Adelina gently pushed Mary Ellen back through the door.

"Have you seen Ame . . . Mr. Price?" Mary Ellen tried to correct herself, but Adelina, too busy with the preparation of the birthday dinner, hardly paid any attention, and Mary Ellen was grateful.

"He left for St. Louis early yesterday. But he's expected back later this afternoon. Now don't come back into this kitchen! You hear? Or you'll spoil everything." Adelina started to close the door behind her. As Mary Ellen turned to walk away, Adelina's head popped around the door. "I think he has something special planned for you. Hadn't seen him act like this ever." Before Mary Ellen could say anything Adelina's head popped back behind the door and she was gone.

Mary Ellen felt the excitement build. She went back to her room and lay down on the bed. She picked up the new novel Americus had brought to her from New Orleans, Herman Melville's *Typee: A Peep at Polynesian Life,* and started to read. She did not recall falling asleep, but a soft knocking on her door startled her. She opened her eyes. It was already dark outside. Again the soft knocking and then one of the servants, Martin, asked if he could come in. Mary Ellen, still trying to clear the cobwebs told him to enter.

Martin walked in carrying a large shiny red box which he placed on the small round table in the corner.

"What is it?" Mary Ellen asked.

"I don't rightly know, Miss Mary Ellen," Martin replied slowly, then walked out of the room.

Mary Ellen stood and went to the table. She opened the envelope on the box. The note was from Americus.

"My dearest Mary Ellen. I thought you should have some nice clothes for your birthday celebration, so I took the liberty of obtaining something for you while I was in St. Louis. Shall we meet for dinner in the dining room at 8:30? With warm regards, your good friend, Americus."

Mary Ellen opened the container and found a beautiful emerald green silk dress with open sleeves flaring widely below the elbow and embroidered with black accent. Another box, under the dress, held new shoes, elaborate black satin and white kid pumps with chain stitch embroidery, cut steel beads, and an intricate bow of green ribbon centered about a silver buckle. Americus also included fashionable gloves of black silk. She tried on her new clothes and surprisingly they fit her perfectly, as if designed for her. She wondered how Americus had managed to make sure the dress and shoes would fit so well. She went to the mirror and admired the person she saw. She slowly turned from side to side and saw in her reflection a woman who seemed much older, more sophisticated and certainly more beautiful than she felt.

At 8:30 sharp Mary Ellen descended the stairs and found Americus waiting for her. He was dressed in a green brocade broadcoat with a striped black satin floral design. His well-cut black trousers extended to his square-toed shoes which appeared to be new. He leaned on a cane with a silver handle, but straightened noticeably as Mary Ellen came down the steps. He held out his hand to her and helped her down the final steps. He looked at her approvingly and smiled.

"You look so beautiful, I could hardly have imagined it."

"Thank you Americus," she replied. "You look quite nice too."

Americus led her to the dining room. A beautiful array of flowers set in a silver bowl rested in the center of the elegant long table. The table was set exquisitely for two, with the finest china and silverware. Two flames of candles on the table flickered mischievously, throwing lights and shadows around the room. Americus held out a chair and allowed Mary Ellen to gather in her billowing dress. Several servants in white jackets stood along the wall.

As soon as Americus took his seat opposite Mary Ellen the servants poured champagne into two elongated crystal goblets. Americus lifted his glass in salute. The pale platinum color of the champagne sparkled like jewels in the candlelight.

"Mary Ellen, tonight, on the twenty-fourth day of February, 1847, we are here to celebrate the most important birthday of your life. You are eighteen-years-young tonight. I propose this toast to honor this day and to honor a very beautiful lady," Americus paused as he looked searchingly at Mary Ellen, "and one of the most intelligent I have ever had the privilege of knowing."

Americus stopped and waited. Mary Ellen was not certain what to do but Americus nodded his head toward the glass of champagne in front of her and Mary Ellen hesitantly picked up the glass.

"Happy Birthday!" he exclaimed and took a sip of the champagne. Mary Ellen followed his lead and took a sip. The champagne tickled her tongue, but she found it to be a pleasing sensation. No sooner had she placed the glass down on the table when a servant, standing inconspicuously behind her, topped off her glass.

"Let's have dinner first, then we can truly celebrate your birthday properly." He picked up a small bell next to the table and rang it. Adeline, carrying a large covered silver dish immediately came through the door followed by two servants, each carrying several smaller dishes. The plates were placed on the table and Adeline brought the large dish to Mary Ellen. Their eyes met and Adeline looked knowingly at Mary Ellen, but did not say a word. Mary Ellen looked at the dish and exclaimed. "Why, duck a l'orange, my favorite." She turned to Americus. "Thank you. You've been so thoughtful, I can't thank you enough."

"You should thank Adeline for the food. I only asked her to cook what she thought you would like the most. Otherwise I had nothing to do with that."

Adeline shot him a quick look of rebuke, shook her head, and served Americus. The other servants now produced the remaining courses.

They ate silently for the most part, exchanging simple pleasantries. Americus described his recent trip to St. Louis and compared it to the older cities in the East. He described Cincinnati, Boston, New York, and Philadelphia giving Mary Ellen a glimpse into a world she did not know and did not yet understand.

After they finished dinner and the dishes were cleared, Americus lit a cigar, inhaled deeply, then took a small valise which had been set next to his chair and walked towards Mary Ellen. He pulled out a chair and sat next to her. Mary Ellen felt warm, strangely calm, and somewhat light-headed. She wanted to laugh but managed to stifle it.

Americus pulled out several documents and looked at Mary Ellen. They stared at each other for what seemed, to Mary Ellen, to be an eternity. Her mind cautioned against staring and such boldness, but she did not seem to be able to follow her mind's prudent commands.

Americus ordered the servants to leave. Then he picked up one leaf of the parchment paper. "This document, which I have already signed and which has already been witnessed by my lawyers, is your complete emancipation and confirms that as of today's date you are a free woman. I had three copies made with original signatures. One remains with my attorneys, whose names and address are shown on the document. I will retain one of the copies and this one," he passed over the document, "is yours. Guard it as you would guard your life. If you lose it, contact me or the attorneys and they will swear an affidavit of duplication and provide you with a conformed copy. Or," he paused again and regarded Mary Ellen pensively, "you can always obtain another original from me."

Mary Ellen tried to listen to Americus attentively but the words sounded muddled, as if he were speaking through a pillow. She understood that Americus meant that she was free, but her mind was somewhat fuzzy. She tried to read the document but found it difficult to focus and concentrate on the indenture. She giggled.

"I have two more things for you," Americus said softly as he reached for another document and signed it gingerly before her. Then he passed the document to Mary Ellen. It was a bank draft for $2,500. Before she could say anything Americus moved closer to her and said, "Being free is the most important thing we can have. But being completely poor is a form of slavery and subjugation. It forces you to do things you wouldn't want to do. Abigail placed these funds in trust for you. You've earned interest and you now have much more, but this will give you a head start with your freedom. Use it wisely, use it discreetly and, above all else, judiciously. Since I have been given the responsibility of giving you your freedom, I want to insure that you will truly be free!"

As Americus said this their legs barely touched, just his calf next to her shin, but the feeling was like a jolt of lightning. Her first impulse was to draw away, but she liked the feeling, the warmth that emanated from her leg throughout her body, so she kept it there and hoped he would not draw his away. He did not, but he did not seem to be affected by it.

"I also have this present for you." He reached into his valise and took out a small wooden box with delicate and intricate carvings on it. She noticed the name Mary Ellen Price engraved on the cover. Slowly she opened it and found a beautiful necklace with a string of sparkling pearls. She inspected the pearls with curiosity. Each one was perfectly spherical. She really did not know what to say, in part because she still felt the electric touch of his leg against hers and because she also did not know how to respond. She sensed that this necklace had to be extremely valuable, but she did not know whether to accept it or how or why she would reject it.

Americus looked at her. "May I put it on you?" he whispered.

Mary Ellen lowered her head and Americus placed the necklace around her neck. To reach her he leaned closer and his leg pressed against her thigh. She felt a strange sense of pleasure deep inside her body, but her mind mingled with strange and uncertain thoughts.

"Please don't misunderstand me, Mary Ellen," she heard him say, but the voice seemed so far away. "I'm giving this to you because you are someone very special and I care very much for you. But don't feel that you have to give anything in return. This is a *gift* and I hope you understand what I'm saying to you."

Mary Ellen turned to him and took his hand. She put his hand in her lap and leaned to him and kissed him on the lips. At first Americus hesitated, but then their lips pressed harder and her mouth opened to his. He pulled her closer to him and the wonderful feeling of it made her groan inwardly. She took his hand and placed it on her breast. She could feel him rise and touched him softly. The heat of their bodies nearly exploded in her, but suddenly she felt him pulling away, pushing her shoulders back.

"Mary Ellen," he blurted. "I think you had too much to drink and I am too much of a gentleman to take advantage of you. God knows I have enjoyed your kiss more than anything in this world, but I will not allow the drink to give me some undue and inappropriate advantage." He stood up abruptly and walked to the door where he turned around. "I will send Adelina to help you get to bed." He noticed the tears in Mary Ellen's eyes. He looked at her then mouthed softly, "I love you." And he turned away leaving Mary Ellen shaking with emotions, many of which were new to her.

The next morning Mary Ellen woke up late. It was a cool, brisk day and the sun, already at its apex in the cloudless sky, sent shafts of bright rays through the breaks in the closed curtains. Mary Ellen opened her eyes and found it difficult to focus. She felt slightly dizzy. The room seemed to be turning slowly, almost floating, making her nauseous. She tried to lift her head off the pillow and her efforts were instantly greeted with a stabbing pain in the back of her head. She closed her eyes and lay still. Finally, screwing up her courage she tried again. The room continued to swim about her, but the effect had diminished. She rubbed her temples and slowly the room remained still long enough to come into focus. Mary Ellen forced herself to sit up. As she did so, small snippets of memory of the previous evening fell into place, though she could not distinguish between her dreams and reality. She recalled kissing Americus passionately, with a longing desire. She assured herself that it must have been a dream.

Chapter Five

Mary Ellen drew back the soft blankets, put her legs over the side of the bed and carefully stood up. She could not trust herself not to fall. She managed a few unsteady steps to the wash basin, filled it with water from a pitcher, and washed her face vigorously. The cold water made her skin feel alive and seemed to reawaken her very being. She let her bedclothes slip off her shoulders, unable to recall ever putting them on when she went to bed. She could barely recall going to bed. Memories of the previous night were blurred images streaked across a tattered canvas.

She desperately tried to collect her scattered fragments of thought and mend them back together. Using a small washcloth Mary Ellen wet her neck and dabbed some water on her chest between her breasts. As she touched her nipples the feelings of the previous night returned. She forced herself to think hard, to unclog her mind and remember everything that happened at dinner. Then she remembered the paper. For a brief moment she was gripped by panic. She frantically looked about the room and found it resting on top of the bureau. She rushed to it, nearly tripping over the carpet, finding that her body rebelled at the most elementary and simple physical commands.

The piece of paper, really a short document, meant she was now a completely free person. She found it especially hard to understand how one piece of paper could accomplish such a miracle. This one thin piece of parchment represented the difference between day and night, heaven and hell, slavery and freedom and, at times, life and death. She picked it up, holding it gingerly as if the mere touch of her hands could somehow erase its contents and jeopardize her freedom. Sitting on the edge of her bed, her hands trembling, she read it several times, first with a mix of uncertainty, foreboding, and suspicion which slowly dissipated. Subliminally memorizing its contents, each reading lessened her apprehension. The words "free" and "emancipated" made her feel warm deep inside her soul. Placing the document into the top drawer of her bureau she noted the small box and remembered the necklace. This, too, seemed to have been part of a dream, but there it was, just as she had remembered it. She opened the box and beheld the dazzling pearls with some misgivings. It was beautiful and she could never have imagined owning anything like it. But she could not imagine why Americus would get her such an ostentatious and expensive gift. Such things, she believed, only happened in the cheap romantic novels she devoured.

Her feelings about Americus were in utter and hopeless confusion, uncertain whether they rose from gratitude, love, or passion. It was unimaginable to her that he could have any romantic inclination toward her, yet she recalled his last words to her. Struggling to understand and failing, Mary Ellen finally shrugged her shoulders and decided to let things happen without trying to decipher their meaning. Her willingness to give herself to Americus had been made abundantly clear to him. Likewise, she knew he wanted her. Still, he had the strength and self-possession to behave with the utmost propriety. She would not have resisted his advances. On the contrary, she would have been a willing partner. She smiled at her unashamed thoughts and wondered how her reaction even this morning would have been received by the Ursaline sisters.

The champagne may have contributed to the disregard of all inhibitions. However, it was not a satisfactory explanation or excuse. She had never touched any liquor before, but she knew what it did to others. She had seen it often enough. Mary Ellen did not blame the drink. She learned one thing about herself: down deep in her heart, in her spirit, she lusted and enjoyed every single minute of it. The champagne did not create or induce it. Perhaps the champagne served as the mechanism that allowed these deeper feelings to surface.

During the subsequent weeks Americus seemed uncertain how to treat Mary Ellen. He took great pains to avoid any discussion of their dinner. Not only did Americus not mention the dinner, he assiduously avoided even the most innocent physical contact between them. Americus seemed bent on acting properly and not succumbing to his own desires. But Mary Ellen knew the spark between them had not been extinguished.

—~—

ON MAY 1, 1847, MARY ELLEN JOINED AMERICUS FOR A PICNIC IN AN old grove of majestic oaks next to a small stream, one of the many tributaries that fed the hungry Mississippi. God seemed to bless the land with many colors as Spring ushered in new blooms, light green ripening buds and pink, white, and yellow flowering trees. They went on horseback and, although Mary Ellen still did not feel comfortable riding, the exhilaration of moving so quickly through impenetrable woods, fording streams, and easily crossing endless fields, overcame her apprehension. Finally they came to their destination, a small but exquisite stream where Americus and his father had fished when he was a small boy. They spread a blanket on one of the sandy banks, near languid pools of crystal-clear water.

Adelina had packed freshly baked bread, assorted cheeses, some Cajun sausages, bright red tomatoes, and large ruby grapes. They hardly spoke as they ate, each basking in the shade of the large verdant trees and absorbing the rich beauty all about them. The scent of honeysuckle permeated the woods. Americus passed the food to Mary Ellen, and as he did so she noted a slight shadow cross his brow. When they had finished eating Mary Ellen lay back and looked at the patches of blue sky through the leafy boughs above. Americus remained seated and watched Mary Ellen intently.

"It's beautiful here, isn't it?" he asked.

"It is absolutely glorious. How did you ever find this spot?" she asked.

"My daddy and I used to hunt in these woods. One day we were stalking this large beautiful stag. We followed him slowly, trying to keep close, but not letting him pick up our scent or sound. Then he simply vanished. We lost sight of him as if he were some apparition. While we searched we came across this stream with these deep wading pools and some fish, and this became our secret fishing hole. This is where I learned to swim. Sometimes I would flounder and end up drinking the water. It's so sweet it must come from a fresh underground spring not far from here."

Mary Ellen sighed. This spot was as close to heaven as she could imagine, and obviously Americus felt the same way.

Americus leaned closer to Mary Ellen. A few sharp rays of sunlight directly behind Americus penetrated the forest. Facing the sun Mary Ellen could not see his face, so she used her hand as a visor. Americus had become very serious.

"Mary Ellen," he said, "you know that I've grown quite fond of you." He stopped, hesitantly searching for the right words. "Perhaps more fond than I had thought possible." He looked up at the woods and inhaled sharply.

"I wanted you to know that I am terribly sorry about what happened at your birthday dinner. We haven't spoken about it and I've delayed the subject long enough. I need to get it off my chest." He paused and pursed his lips. "Please believe me that I hadn't planned on what happened between us. I was entrusted to be your guardian. Then on the day of your emancipation, the most important day of your life, I completely lost all sight of my responsibilities, if not my senses. But I want to assure you that my feelings were genuine, that I was not trying to take advantage of you." Again he sighed heavily.

Mary Ellen touched his face gently. Americus started to take her hand in his but suddenly tensed, his entire body rising, as if it had rebelled against any sign of tenderness.

"Please, Mary Ellen. You have to help me. You may have greater strength and more control than I. Don't you see that if I allow my feelings to intervene with my responsibilities and my promises, I will be a failure; unable to discharge my obligations to Abigail, to you, and to God. Without honor I am nothing." He looked pleadingly into Mary Ellen's eyes.

"I don't understand any of this," Mary Ellen replied wearily. "You're giving me too much credit. All I know is that I want . . . " she faltered as she searched for the right words, but finding none, she continued, "to . . . to be with you as much as I think you want me."

Americus reacted as if he had been slapped. "Surely you can't mean that." He looked away.

"Why?" Mary Ellen prodded. "Why can't I have feelings? Why can't I express them to you? And if not to you, to whom?"

"You don't know what you're saying. You are confused. Perhaps it has something to do with your, er, liberation. You were sent to the Ursaline Convent for a purpose. To learn right from wrong, to understand virtue and order. To learn not to succumb to temptations. To develop a sense of decorum. You just can't talk about such things, and certainly not with anyone of the opposite sex." Americus looked more pained than angry.

"You're right. I don't understand." Mary Ellen found her temper rising. "Let's pretend this never happened. Let's pretend it doesn't exist. Is that what you want?"

Americus looked sullenly at the blanket like a small child but said nothing.

Mary Ellen continued, "Isn't such pretending a lie? And isn't it sinful to lie?"

Americus looked up and sighed. "I don't wish to discuss this any more. I've given you my apology and I thought you would understand how I have responsibilities and obligations which I cannot ignore."

"Am I a free woman, or not?" Mary Ellen nearly shouted.

"Of course you're a free woman," Americus answered, puzzled by her outburst as much as by the question.

"Then if I'm free I'll decide what's right for me. What I should say. What I should do. I have my honor and I know the difference between right and wrong. You and I did nothing wrong. Nothing! I'm beginning to suspect that there is something else behind your reactions. After all, I'm not really white. Isn't that really it? If I were white you would not act like this! Admit it!" Mary Ellen broke into tears.

Americus wanted to put his arms around her, to comfort her, but he did not.

He spoke in hushed tones. "You're completely wrong about that. I do love you. You're special. Your, um, heritage is irrelevant to me. You're a free, beautiful, and intelligent woman. That's all I see. I love you as much or more than anything else in this world. For once in my life I cannot, will not, get what I truly want more than life itself. But that's where it has to stop. If I allow us to continue it would be my end, the end of everything I've stood for. I gave you your liberty, not to subsequently subjugate or ensnare you. Any relationship between us is completely out of the question, not because of color, but because I've given my word and will not break it under any circumstances. I can endure pain, not dishonor. And you, Mary Ellen. You can't be certain what you feel for me. It could well be gratitude for your freedom, and in short order you might find yourself feeling oppressed by your own feelings. Ultimately you would blame me and hate me for it. Perhaps one day you'll understand this." Americus rose and walked to the water's edge. Mary Ellen wept.

"You've been described as a distant relative of mine to folks around here. Don't you see that any relationship, even the most innocent one, might be suspicious and raise unwanted questions. I think it would be safest for you to go east. My good friends in Cincinnati, Mr. and Mrs. Louis Alexander Williams, are childless and strongly involved in the abolitionist movement. I'll make arrangements for you to go there. You can live with them until you're established and can provide for yourself."

Mary Ellen stopped crying. "And what will you do, Americus?" she asked wearily.

"I'm not sure. I have to go to Europe to meet with some of our major customers. I need to negotiate some new cotton supply contracts. Maybe now would be a good time to go."

Mary Ellen stood and reached for the straw basket and blanket. She missed Americus's expression, one of sheer misery and wanting. As they rode silently back to the plantation she noted the set jaw and almost fatalistic look in his eyes. Freedom was glorious, but it was not freedom from pain or affliction.

Chapter Six

The Abolitionist

CINCINNATI, OHIO
JUNE 1847

In June of 1847 Cincinnati had already grown into a town consisting of seven long streets, each ending at the bank of the Ohio River. Etched out of a thick forest, the hamlet teemed with commerce. Situated close to the confluence of the Ohio and Miami Rivers, Cincinnati was midway between Pittsburgh and Cairo, Illinois, on the Mississippi River. It was also one of the southernmost towns of the northern states, sitting across the water from Kentucky.

The influx of Germans in the early part of the decade provided the spark for growth. Vineyards in the surrounding hills supplied the succulent grapes for these Prussian wine makers. A rich history, the development of a municipal university nearly thirty years earlier, and a bustling port created a potpourri of an old-town atmosphere mixed with the excitement of new development. Many of the original trees from the forest which filled the basin, making it difficult for the earliest settlers to create enough space for a town, remained. Neat red and brown brick buildings lined the streets with towering trees providing much needed shade in the sultry summers.

Mary Ellen found lodging at the Williams residence on 48 Fifth Street. Hardly distinguishable from neighboring homes, the two-story house had a formal entrance, framed by two large white columns, and an eclectic mixture of older furniture which Sarah Williams brought from her home on Nantucket Island. Louis Alexander Williams, a large flaccid man, welcomed Mary Ellen heartily and introduced her to his wife Sarah, a doughty woman with a kindly face. The letter of introduction of Miss Mary Ellen Price, which Americus had sent only a month earlier, had been received warmly. The Williams arranged for Mary Ellen to have a small room on the ground floor, in the back near the garden. Spartanly furnished and tidy, Mary Ellen found the room airy and delightful. She would seek a job, perhaps working for Mr. Williams in his store, and start her new life as a free woman. Although her education included many subjects and areas, she wanted to learn more about commerce and to understand how a business enterprise operated. Working for Williams afforded the perfect opportunity to learn this first hand.

Americus had cautioned her again and again not to reveal any of her background to anyone, no matter how sympathetic they were or appeared to be. Any deviation from her role as Miss Price, he told her, or any hint of her former status would only result in someone taking some advantage of her. Her emancipation could never be revoked, he stressed, but if anyone suspected anything it would be most detrimental to her chances for success in her new life. She must continue to pass as white for the time being, though Mary Ellen did not have the faintest notion of what "time being" meant.

Prior to her departure from Price's Landing Americus wore a long and heavy face. They hardly spoke to each other. Mary Ellen remained silent, afraid of losing the last vestiges of self-control. Her emotions were smoldering in a cauldron filled with fear, desire, excitement about the future, and sense of personal loss. She did not want to leave Americus, but he left her with no choice. Americus, acting out of some higher sense of duty, did not give Mary Ellen so much as a cousinly kiss or friendly hug. She could see him, standing stiffly on the dock, waving his hand mechanically in a

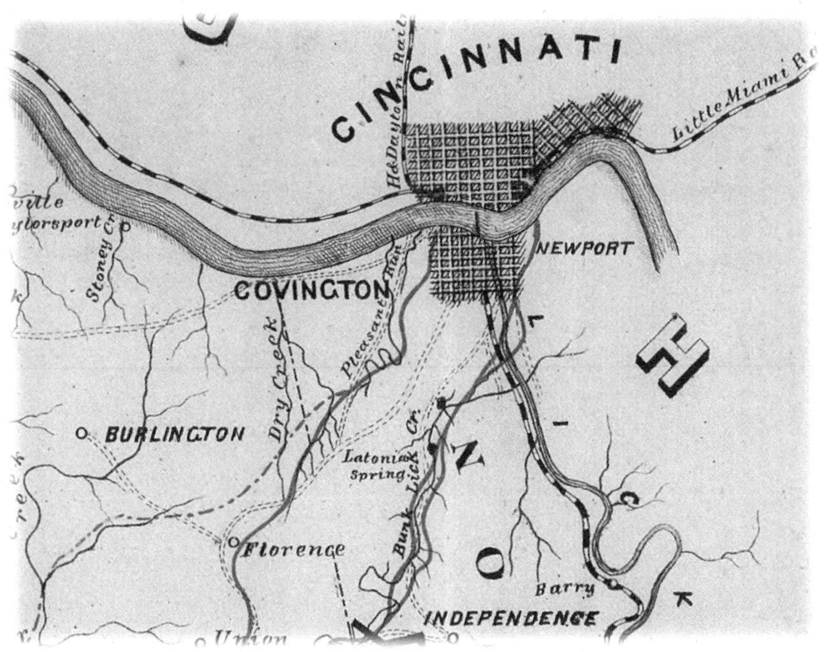

Cincinnati Environs

listless manner, receding into her past, as the boat made its way down the river toward Cairo. Her last image of Americus was one of melancholy and despair. Tears streaked down her cheeks and she waved back to Americus, uncertain whether he could see her and wondering whether he felt the same about her as she did about him.

The Williams met her at the dock in Cincinnati. They were warm and appeared to be genuinely interested in her welfare. Williams, to his surprise and delight, found Mary Ellen to be a quick learner. His company, L.A. Williams & Co., on Main Street, sold dry goods, groceries, farm produce, men's and women's ready-to-wear, and served as commission and forwarding merchant for wool, which came down the Miami River in keelboats or flatboats. These boats, which Williams owned, remained stocked when the supply stores were full until they could be off-loaded and transshipped up the Ohio River to Pittsburgh.

At first Mary Ellen learned to stock the goods, making sure the items were maintained on the shelf and properly displayed. Whatever reluctance Williams may have had at the beginning to give such responsibility to Mary Ellen quickly dissipated as she peppered him with questions, some of which he had never before considered, but upon reflection realized were important. Soon he had her performing physical inventory, making sure his books and records accurately reflected what goods were available, which items should be ordered, and what had been sold.

Mary Ellen took to commerce as a duck takes to water. She had a natural flair and in short order could see areas where Williams could improve his business. Instead of telling him what he should do, she formed suggestions in his mind by asking Aristotelian questions. If he knew he was being manipulated he never let on. At home he would tell Sarah how much he wished he had a son with half the brains and talent of Miss Price and how fortunate some young man would be to catch her. But if Mary Ellen had any interest in the young men who now came more frequently to browse through Williams's store, walking down the aisles and inspecting things in which they had little or no apparent interest, she did not show it. Instead, she spent so much time at work that Williams had to lay down the law: Mary Ellen could not work any time from Friday afternoon until Monday morning.

One afternoon Mary Ellen was in the store by herself, rearranging some goods on one of the shelves, when a thin, nervous man came in. He looked around, peering down one end of the store to the other, and, dissatisfied, walked up to Mary Ellen.

"Have you seen Mr. Williams?" he asked in an agitated state.

"He went out before noon and I am not sure whether he will return," she replied.

The man looked around as if Williams might be hiding somewhere.

"Will you be seeing him before eight o'clock tonight?" he asked.

"Yes. I imagine I will see him at home for the evening meal." She could not fathom why the man seemed so nervous and edgy.

"Good. Please tell him Mr. Steimle was here. Tell him we will meet at Frank Brockmeyer's house at eight tonight." He bobbed his head in a shallow bow and was gone.

Chapter Six

Williams, who had been out at some of the outlying vineyards buying a few barrels of wine on his own account, which he intended to sell on his own label in the east, returned home in time for supper. Mary Ellen informed him about Mr. Steimle and noted the exchange of knowing glances between Sarah and her husband. Mary Ellen, whose incredible culinary knowledge had become the talk of Cincinnati, helped clean the dishes from the table when Sarah asked her to come and sit down with them for a small talk.

Mary Ellen cleaned her hands on her apron and settled down at the chair.

Williams began. "Mary Ellen. Mr. Price told us that you were quite sympathetic with his views on slavery. If I am in error please let me know."

"I do believe Mr. Price and I agree completely on slavery," Mary Ellen responded shakily, uncertain where this conversation would lead and thinking that perhaps her past had somehow been discovered.

Sarah noticed Mary Ellen's hesitation and fear.

"Now, now, Mary Ellen. Please don't be disturbed on our account." She looked questioningly at her husband who nodded for her to continue. "We also share deeply in Mr. Price's views. So you are among friends." She smiled kindly at Mary Ellen who still wasn't certain what Sarah meant.

Fortunately, Williams, who had a genuine fondness for Mary Ellen, made it clear. "My dear girl," he said, "what my wife is telling you is that we are abolitionists. So you needn't concern yourself about your political viewpoint with us. I'm quite certain one could not be so open back at Price's Landing, but we are not in the South, or in Missouri for that matter." And he spit the word Missouri with some hostility. "We are in Ohio, a good Northern state where our laws prohibit slavery and the indignity visited upon our less fortunate Negro brothers by Southern malcontents."

During Williams's entire discourse Mary Ellen had kept so still and had clutched her hands so firmly that she now felt the same prickling in her hands that she got when her feet fell asleep. She tried to relax but her attempts to smile seemed so artificial and obvious. But Mr.

Williams continued, satisfied from Mary Ellen's silence that she did share their views.

"Tonight is a very special night, Mary Ellen." He leaned forward conspiratorially and spoked softly as if someone might overhear him. "we're holding a meeting among our friends. We have some very special people who'll be attending this meeting. Perhaps you'd like to join us." He looked at her triumphantly, as if his invitation would make her feel special and important.

But Mary Ellen felt queasy and faint. She did not want to draw any special attention to herself. Yet she could not refuse. Her refusal might make the Williams think she did not share their viewpoint and cause some friction which would be to her detriment. And she did believe in the abolitionist movement. Irritated with herself for her fears and what she could only consider a form of selfishness or cowardice, she immediately decided to go.

"Of course I would like to come," she said. "But I have never attended one of these meetings. I'd like to go to one just for the sake of listening and learning. If that'd be agreeable?" she asked demurely.

Sarah took her hand. "Of course, dear. You will be with me. I don't engage in any of the discussions myself. I do what Louis asks of me. So we could all sit together and listen. How does that sound?"

THE MEETING WAS HELD IN FRANK BROCKMEYER'S HOUSE A SHORT block from the Williams. About twenty people were there when Mary Ellen arrived with the Williams. They were already engaged in a spirited discussion, so she sat down next to Sarah and away from the principal debaters where she could better see and avoid being seen.

One man, yelling above the others, brandished a newspaper which he waved above his head. "Mr. Garrison says it right here in *The Liberator*. He has become an anticleric and is completely against organized religion. That's going too far. That's what I think. We're all good Christian folk and we should be thankful for that."

Williams had made his way to the center of these men and said. "That's humbug. I don't believe Lloyd Garrison is really against organized religion per se as he is against those feeble religious leaders who fail to see the suffering and refuse to acknowledge the sinful nature of slavery and those who support it. I, too, am a Christian. But I believe Jesus wouldn't tolerate slavery or, what's more, those who fail to speak against it."

The others immediately took up the argument about religion, giving Mary Ellen a chance to look around again. Most of those attending the meeting were men. A few women were there, mostly sitting quietly, some knitting, others watching the spectacle intently. One woman, however, noticed Mary Ellen and smiled at her. She did not seem at all perturbed by the men's heated discussion. Dressed with a bonnet in the manner of Quakers, and with a calm, self-assurance, she interjected. "Gentlemen. Gentlemen. Perhaps we could get on with our meeting. It seems we have several items on our agenda and we should proceed accordingly."

Those who were standing and arguing now took their seats and a hush descended on the congregants.

"If the Reverend Schoenhoff would please start our meeting with a prayer, perhaps one calling for all of us to come together and unite for peace and freedom." The woman spoke confidently as if she were in complete control.

"Thank you, Mrs. Mott." Reverend Schoenhoff, who had been somewhat dismayed by the anticlerical remarks attributed to Garrison, began. "Thank you, Lord, for bringing us together today. Lord, we pray for the deliverance of all those who have been taken from their families, from their homes and have been made into mere possessions, human chattels, by those who have lost sight of your wisdom and direction. Lord, let us pray that your light shall shine on them and bring them out of this Egypt and out of slavery. Lord, may we succeed in our humble effort to do what is right and what is good. Please give us the strength and help us end the misery which we all have come to know and which can never be tolerated by right-thinking Christians. Lord, we are all in your hands and in your mercy. Amen."

Everyone responded with "amen" and Reverend Schoenhoff sat down, turning to Mrs. Mott. Mary Ellen was surprised to see the deference which the entire congregation gave to this woman who acted as if she were accustomed to it.

"Who is that woman?" Mary Ellen whispered to Sarah.

"That's Lucretia Coffin Mott," Sarah whispered back.

"First, I would like to thank all of you for coming tonight. Thank you Mr. Brockmeyer for the use of your home." Lucretia Mott smiled to Brockmeyer. "And thank you Mr. Steimle for helping us arrange this meeting."

Steimle still looked quite nervous to Mary Ellen. He simply looked down at his own feet. Lucretia Mott continued. "I have come here all the way from Massachusetts to discuss with you the need to rid our nation of the festering disease called slavery, not only for those unfortunate beings found in the homes and plantations throughout the Southern states of our great nation, but for those less conspicuously enslaved: The women."

Some of the audience groaned and some of the men frowned, but Mott remained unvexed and continued as if she had not heard a word. Mary Ellen had never seen any woman, with the exception of Abigail, take such an active role in the company of men, though Abigail did it with élan and never directly or conspicuously. Mary Ellen was mesmerized by Lucretia Mott, more by her obvious strength than by the content of her talk.

As Mary Ellen looked around she noticed one man, heavy set, with floppy jowls, and a large head, leering at her with cold brown beady eyes. A few wisps of hair had been plastered to his pate in an obvious effort to hide his baldness, but its effect was amusing and almost caused Mary Ellen to laugh. But his expression did not change and it made her uneasy as he continued to stare at her unabashedly. She avoided eye contact and looked away.

Another man now spoke. He was slim, wiry, and dark, with a remarkable firmness expressed in his face. His gray eyes were penetrating and steady, lending him the aura of a magician as he spoke energetically, gesticulating at times to punctuate his remarks. All around him listened intently.

"We must have immediate, complete, and uncompensated emancipation of all slaves. There is no room for debate, discussion, negotiation, or any other form of equivocation. And this must take place throughout our great nation. Slavery must end in the South, and all forms of segregation or other methods of enslaving free people must end in the North. However, I cannot join in with those of you who espouse violence. I grew up in this fine state. For the last three years I have lived in Akron. I can assure you that the people there are as determined as you are here to rid this nation of this moral transgression. But we don't need violence. We can and must accomplish our goals without it. If we resort to violence are we any better than the savages who subjugate others violently?"

"I completely disagree with you, Mr. Brown," the fat, florid man said heatedly with a thick German accent. "With all due respect for our Quaker friends," he turned to Lucretia Mott and her husband James and nodded his acknowledgment of their presence, "but this pacific attitude is as stifling as it is revolting. We have accomplished nothing. There is slavery in Missouri. There is slavery in the South. If additional territory is admitted to the Union we will find more slavery. I'm sorry, but if violence is the only method of achieving our goal, so be it. Let's embrace it, not shun it. Those who shun it are cowards." He sat down and wiped his brow from his exertion. He turned to Mary Ellen and smiled at her.

Mary Ellen shivered as if a cold gust of icy wind had embraced her. There was something so sinister about this man's smile that Mary Ellen immediately turned away.

"Herr Vogt, you certainly aren't suggesting John Brown is a coward, are you?" one of the men asked incredulously.

The fat man stood up and waved his hand deprecatingly. "No, no. Please don't misunderstand. Of course I know Mr. Brown is a man of great personal courage. Perhaps I am slightly confused because I know Mr. Brown is hardly a stranger to violence." He sat down heavily and looked over toward Mary Ellen again.

Mary Ellen looked back at Mr. Brown, lost in thought and paying little attention to the discussion which now swirled all about her. The man called Brown smiled benignly at Herr Vogt. He finished speaking and was being heartily congratulated by the others for a fine speech. Mary Ellen had not really followed all the discussions, finding many hollow phrases and slogans, but nothing concrete or significant. Lucretia Mott spoke mostly of the need to emancipate women, and suggested a convention be held for women, a concept Mary Ellen could see was clearly unacceptable to most of the men in the crowd.

Mary Ellen was clearly disappointed. This had been her first abolitionist meeting. Other than Abigail, Americus, and the Williams she had never really known anyone who spoke openly of ending slavery. After her arrival in Cincinnati she had seen Garrison's newspaper, *The Liberator,* and read it avariciously. And she came to her first abolitionist meeting with greater expectations, only to find each person harboring his or her own agenda. There were plenty of platitudes, and everyone seemed to be in favor of ending slavery, though none had really provided any concrete suggestion. It was all hollow talk. It made her feel guilty and weary with a sense of oppression. The road to freedom for her people did not really exist and would be a long time in coming.

Slowly the people left the room, but the Williams remained together with John Brown, Steimle, and the Brockmeyers. Vogt sidled up to Mary Ellen and was introduced by Louis Williams, although Mary Ellen felt some friction between the two men. She held out her hand which he took into his fleshy paws.

"I couldn't help notice a stranger in our midst. It is my pleasure and honor to meet you, Miss Price." He wheezed as he spoke and looked quizzically at her, as if trying to unfathom some deep mystery. He still held her hand in his fleshy hands until Mary Ellen pulled away. Vogt clearly wanted to remain next to Mary Ellen, but Williams took him by his elbow and led him to the door where he whispered in his ear. Vogt shook his head in acknowledgment and understanding and looked back at Mary Ellen. She pretended not to notice, but his gaze bore through her. Finally he left.

When Brockmeyer was satisfied that everyone else had left, he bolted the door and asked everyone to follow him. They went through the back, Steimle looking furtively around for any signs of detection. They went down a short trail and to a stone house surrounded by a copse. Steimle knocked. Three sharp taps on the door. It opened and someone peered out, then let them in. As soon as Mary Ellen came in, the door closed behind her and was locked. The room was dimly lit by a single candle. No one spoke, but Steimle went to some crates in one corner and removed the top crate. Only then did Mary Ellen realize that they weren't crates, but a blind for hiding things. Steimle whispered and two black men emerged, sweating profusely, their eyes wide with fear.

Mary Ellen watched in astonishment.

John Brown spoke. "These men are slaves who escaped from a plantation near Tunica, Mississippi." He walked up and put his arm around one of the men who was so startled by John Brown's intimacy, he nearly tripped backwards.

"I understand," Brown spoke to the two men. "Let me assure you. We are not returning you. We'll arrange for your safe passage to Boston and make arrangements to help you once you get there. You'll be leaving tonight."

The two slaves looked at each other. They were terribly frightened. Obviously someone had provided them with clean clothes that did not fit too well but were probably considerably better than the clothes they wore where they came from. Mary Ellen could see that neither man believed he was safe and certainly not free.

"Until you move farther north there is no guarantee that someone hunting you will not find you. The farther north you go, the better your chances." John Brown did not have to tell them what would happen if they were caught. After his business debacle in Northern Ohio and the loss of his business, Brown knew that there were no guarantees in life. There was not much he could do for these two miserable men because they did not know how to be anything else but slaves. It would be difficult to pass them off even in Boston as freemen. But they had to try and hope that if they were caught they would end up with some sympathetic judge, something they could never find in the South.

Brown, Williams, Steimle, and Brockmeyer huddled and made their preparations to spirit the dispirited men onward. Mary Ellen approached one of the men. He immediately noticed her eyes and for some reason he became more frightened and agitated.

Mary Ellen tried to calm him down. "These men are doing everything they can for you. Please don't worry, you will be all right." She said this without much conviction in her voice. But the man just continued to stare at her eyes.

"Steimle, go ahead to the canoe and make sure everything is clear," Williams ordered. "We will row them to the keelboat which will be leaving this morning. I know the crew. They were hand-picked by me and can be trusted."

All the men headed down another trail leaving Sarah and Mary Ellen to return to their home. They walked slowly down the now deserted roads. It was a sultry evening, extremely hot and humid. Mary Ellen did not want to go inside or to sleep so she told Sarah she would walk for a while before turning in. Sarah said goodnight and went inside the house leaving Mary Ellen with her thoughts. She headed up the street feeling quite relieved and thankful that she did not have to share in the experience of those two blacks. How would they survive in Boston or anywhere else? They were not skilled. They could not speak well. They really weren't prepared. Still, they were out of bondage for whatever limited time they had. The same sense of relief also brought a sense of guilt. Here she was free. She could pass as white and work in the white world without any qualms. Why did God bless her and not the others?

Lost deep in her own thoughts Mary Ellen did not notice the man walking up behind her trying to catch up with her. A hand touched her shoulder. It was so unexpected and sudden she felt her heart jump and the blood course through her body from intense fear unlike any she had ever suffered. She gasped as she wheeled around only to find herself nearly face to face with a sweaty and wheezing Vogt. He was breathing heavily and grinning at her.

"I'm sorry. I must have startled you," he said in a manner that Mary Ellen immediately understood to mean that he really was not sorry at all.

"What are you doing out here?" she mumbled.

"That's exactly what I was going to ask you?" he said and looked around.

Mary Ellen followed his gaze and realized she had walked to the end of the road near the river. There were no houses and only a few storage sheds nearby. She became alarmed.

"I think I better get back to my house. Mr. Williams doesn't like me to be out too late and will come looking for me."

Vogt found this amusing. "I'm surprised he let you go out so late at night if he's so concerned."

Mary Ellen started to turn and go back, but Vogt moved quickly for such a large man and blocked her way.

"I'd be happy to walk you back," he said. "But perhaps you could help me shed some light on something which I find puzzling," he mused.

Mary Ellen remained silent.

"You are not from around here," he said knowingly. "You are too beautiful and I would have noticed you before."

"I'm from Missouri," she said, her mind reeling, wondering what she should do and how she should react.

"Ah huh. That must be it," he said and stroked his chin as if in deep contemplation.

"Miss Price. Not a relation to the Price family of Missouri, are you?"

"Why, yes. Exactly. I am a third cousin of Americus Price."

Vogt laughed heartily. "I know the Price family. They are all so creamy white and yet you are of a darker complexion. I would have thought you were . . . " he paused for a moment, again as if in deep thought, and then his face lit up as if by some mystical inspiration, "perhaps Creole. No. But that couldn't be it. It would hardly qualify you as a member of the Price family."

Mary Ellen felt bile climbing up her throat, but at the same time his manner of speaking down to her also rankled her.

"Mr. Vogt. I'm not really interested in what you think. If you are so interested perhaps you should ask Mr. Williams or write to Mr. Price. Anyhow, it's none of your business."

She started to walk around him but he grabbed her arm crudely and pulled her close to him. Now she smelled the whiskey on his breath and noticed the flushing of his face.

"I don't know who you are, Miss Price, and frankly, I don't care," he smirked, then ogled her openly, his eyes running up and down her body. It made her flesh crawl. "I just thought we could have a good time together," he said. "You are a very handsome woman."

She tried to pull her arm away, but his grip was like a vise.

"Let me go!" she demanded. She started to scream but he slapped her back and forth across the face, knocking her to the ground semi-conscious. She felt herself dragged by her arm on the ground toward some bushes. She tried to resist and managed to kick him in the leg. He countered with a second crushing blow to her face. She could feel her eye closing and something warm streaming down the side of her face. She fought not to lose consciousness trying to blink away the enveloping darkness.

He threw her into a small clearing behind the bushes.

"If you scream I'll kill you," he whispered menacingly and she knew he meant it. "When this is all over we could blame it on those two escaped slaves that you were all hiding at Brockmeyer's. "If you try to tell them I did it, I will deny it. They'll believe me because I've lived here for many years. This is a German community. You are new to these parts. You are not German. Nobody will believe the slaves if they deny it. And frankly I think there's something you want to keep hidden. So shut up. You might even enjoy yourself."

He started to rip at her clothes. He grabbed her breasts. She started to fight again, clawing at his face and managing to rip a gash across his cheek. He touched his face, felt the blood, and became enraged. He started to slap her face back and forth.

"You stupid bitch," he kept saying over and over as he flailed at her. But even in his rage he became tired and finally stopped to catch his breath.

"Well, now. You aren't going to be so pretty after all." He admired the carnage. He unbuckled his pants and pulled them down. Then he reached for her. "I have something for . . . " Mary Ellen closed her eyes. But she did not feel anything. He never finished the sentence. Instead she heard a loud crack and opened her eyes.

Vogt's face registered complete and total shock. The second crack sounded through the night like an explosion and Mary Ellen could see a large slat whip through the air and connect with the side of Vogt's face. He fell to the ground as if his legs had been cut away and blood spurted from several deep gashes on his face. The large slat continued to rain blow after blow on Vogt who tried to fend off the attack with his arms, and pleaded for mercy, but the blows continued unabated. They were so powerful that one of Vogt's arms simply broke as if it had been a piece of rotten wood, the crack echoing through the stillness of the night.

"You goddamn bastard." Mary Ellen heard a man's voice, a familiar voice, but she could not place it. "You are the devil. Prepare to meet your maker." The blows continued, one after another. "You are the worst of all sinners." The voice thundered as the blows rained. After a while Vogt ceased to make any noise or any movement. He lay still in the clearing which now hung with complete silence. Vogt did not have any form or any features to him. He appeared to be a large lump of flesh, covered with a shiny black coat which reflected in the moon.

Then Mary Ellen noticed Vogt's body being dragged towards the river. She heard a grunt, followed by a splash, and then footsteps returning. One of her eyes was completely closed. She tried to squint with her other eye and could barely make out the man's features. She felt the man lift her up and speak gently to her.

"You don't have to fear him ever again. He's gone. You'll be all right." He gently carried her up the street. She knew it was John Brown.

Chapter Seven

Queen of New Orleans

NEW ORLEANS
1848-1849

Sarah Williams attended to Mary Ellen's wounds, applying cool compresses to the damaged areas, and fighting the onset of infection. The blows had been severe but no bones were broken, and the swelling on her cheekbone gradually receded. At first Mary Ellen's face was hideously misshapen and covered by a patchwork of black and blue welts over a crimson background. Fortunately, the cuts were superficial and not expected to leave any scars. Best of all, a fear that Sarah and Dr. Benjamin shared, Mary Ellen would suffer no permanent damage to her eyesight.

John Brown duly reported everything as it had happened, dispensing the facts as if he had been an objective onlooker, not a participant. He told the coroner's inquest that he had just turned down Second Street when he saw Mary Ellen walking alone. Then he saw Vogt stalking the girl. There was no mistaking his furtive actions—an animal tracking its prey in the dark, lurking quietly nearby, waiting for the victim's most vulnerable moment, then pouncing and rendering the prey inert. Mary Ellen was completely innocent of any wrongdoing. If Vogt had been left alone, Brown asserted, Mary Ellen, an innocent young girl, would have been raped and possibly killed.

Vogt's body was found downriver, entangled in the limbs of a dead tree that lay in the shallows. By the time the body was discovered the rushing waters had washed all the blood away, leaving only a multitude of bruises. Brown's attorney claimed the bruises could have been the result of a boat passing over Vogt. Or else the swiftly moving current could have thrust or snagged the body on the smoke stack, hoist, or pilot's cabin of a sunken ship, a common enough occurrence. Only the previous Spring the *Perillot* collided with another boat, causing its boiler to explode. The vessel sank in less than ten minutes. Pilots who navigated the Ohio steered clear of the site. Vogt's body was found about a mile downstream from the *Perillot.*

After extensive discussions and arguments, some of which nearly erupted into fistfights, and the lack of witnesses who could testify against Brown, Vogt's death was finally attributed to drowning since his lungs were filled with water. Still the debate on whether to charge John Brown with aggravated assault or other criminal violation raged for nearly a week. The anti-Abolitionists jumped on the bandwagon claiming that Brown once again demonstrated the violent tendencies of the abolitionist movement. They claimed that Brown killed Vogt to keep him from disclosing the whereabouts of escaped slaves. Although Ohio opposed slavery, its laws did not extend to protecting those who aided slaves; many still regarded helping runaways as a form of receiving stolen goods.

Those in this German community who maintained that Mary Ellen must have seduced Vogt began to question Williams about her background. What did he really know? Where did she really come from? Americus Price was away in Europe, so no one could certify Mary Ellen's character or history. Letters written by several Ursaline nuns were rejected as prejudicial and not subject to cross examination. Ultimately, Williams himself began to question Mary Ellen's character and convinced himself that she had beguiled poor Vogt into this predicament.

Even though Mary Ellen's physical scars healed, the psychological damage of the attempted rape, and the haunting memory of Vogt standing over her, short of breath, face contorted with rage when she defied him, threatening that the community would believe his story over hers, did not recover so quickly. And it was exacerbated by Williams's slowly changing attitude.

Williams cowered at the attention drawn to him and his family. His business suffered. When Mary Ellen was physically fit and able to return to work, some members of the community refused to shop at Williams & Co., others declined any form of business relationship with Williams as long as he harbored Mary Ellen. Williams's anger increased in direct proportion to the economic and social losses he suffered. Ultimately he concluded that Mary Ellen had been guilty of every conceivable allegation made against her, from whoring, to baiting Vogt, and ultimately to being an accessory to murder.

He summarily dismissed her, intending to get her completely out of his life. Sarah's intercession saved Mary Ellen. When Williams told Sarah he wanted Mary Ellen to move out, Sarah scolded him, asking him how in good conscience he could even suggest something like that. Taking Mary Ellen's side she eloquently pleaded her case and, when it became clear that her husband refused to hear anything antithetical to his viewpoint, she simply bore down and laid down the law. Mary Ellen would remain. If he did not like it he could leave. Louis Williams had never seen his wife so irate and so uncompromising. She held firmly and he yielded. Mary Ellen, conscious of the hostility directed toward her, withdrew more and more.

As often happens, the public's outcry diminished with time. People went about their business, dealing with new problems and finding new stories and new causes with which to agitate themselves. No charges were ever brought against Brown. Even if charges had been brought, John Brown left for the East Coast shortly after the inquest where he intended to set up a new business as an expediter and agent for wool merchants of northern Ohio. He had no immediate plans to return to Cincinnati.

But Mary Ellen did not have the luxury of moving. Her life turned dark and foreboding. Always concerned that someone would dig into her past and discover her background, coupled with Louis Williams's open hostility, she became increasingly depressed and withdrawn. Most of the Germans in the community shunned her, flooding her with memories of the way the slaves and their children treated her at Golden Oaks.

Only Sarah's friendship and support sustained Mary Ellen through these trying times. Sarah became Mary Ellen's confidante and tried to allay the fears and depression that Mary Ellen obviously suffered. Mary Ellen spent much of her time in her room, reading books and newspapers. To earn a living she did odd jobs, ran errands, mended clothes, and, due to her extraordinary talents as a cook, was occasionally hired to help prepare food for important dinners, large gatherings, or special events. But her life had changed unalterably. Instead of hope and promise Mary Ellen found despair. The sense of freedom and exhilaration she felt upon her arrival in Cincinnati vanished.

Sarah realized how desperately Mary Ellen needed to recover and get on with her life. She embarked on a mission that she knew might help Mary Ellen crawl out of the deep hole and back into the light of day. She sent several letters to Price's Landing and to New Orleans in an effort to locate Americus to seek his aid and advice. Although Americus had written several letters shortly after Mary Ellen's arrival, the correspondence became infrequent, then stopped. Mary Ellen attributed the lack of communication to his travels, and suggested to Sarah that Americus was probably still traveling through Europe.

It had not taken long for Sarah to discern Mary Ellen's feelings for Americus. The sad and lonely girl was clearly in love with him. Her affections for Americus were so strong that she had placed him on a pedestal. But Sarah believed that no human being was so richly deserving of such lofty status unless he were a piece of sculptured marble. Mary Ellen could not find a single fault in Americus. Sarah understood these feelings. Everyone had a first love, and this was Mary Ellen's. She smiled to herself as she recalled her first love, the passions she harbored silently and remembered so vividly to this very day. She was only fourteen years old. Stephan Voorhies, who was eighteen, seemed to be perfect. Only later, when she really got to know him, did he turn into an ordinary man with the usual blend of strengths and weaknesses, not the perfect hero of her heart.

Mrs. Muriel Hussey owned a thriving store dealing in goods not unlike those which could be found at Williams, though she tended to have a greater variety of things that appealed to women, from bolts of silk and muslin to ribbons and other accessories. A Quaker, and known in the town affectionately as "Grandma," Mrs. Hussey and Sarah had been close friends since childhood. Grandma Hussey believed Mary Ellen's and John Brown's version of the Vogt incident, had seen the physical trauma Mary Ellen suffered as a result of the attempted rape, and agreed to help. She hired Mary Ellen to do exactly the kind of work she did at the Williams's store. Mary Ellen plunged into her work with an intensity that caught everyone but Sarah by surprise. Mary Ellen's hard and enterprising work was just the balm she needed to heal her emotional wounds. If it did not completely mend the grief it allowed Mary Ellen to reestablish some order in her life, though not with the same degree of happiness or excitement she had felt before. As the days passed into weeks, and weeks turned into months, life generally returned to normal. Even Louis Williams softened up a bit. He could see how diligently Mary Ellen worked and applied herself, how properly she conducted her affairs at all times. Finally he had to admit that Sarah had been right; his original hypothesis that Mary Ellen had somehow lured old Vogt, in retrospect, seemed preposterous. He had been mistaken and felt quite guilty.

On the morning of July 23, 1848, Mary Ellen was rearranging bolts of cloth at Grandma Hussey's store when three men came in. One of them yelled excitedly: "Grandma. Did you hear about this?" The man waved a newspaper at Grandma Hussey, who was making some bookkeeping entries in a journal.

Grandma removed her glasses, placing them carefully next to the journal and stood, "Hear about what? What are you shouting about, Jasper?"

"It's all right here. They've found gold in California!"

"What's that you say?"

The man holding the paper read: " '*People are running all over the country and picking it out of the earth here and there, just as 1,000 hogs, let loose in a forest, would root up ground-nuts.*' "

He looked up, his eyes wide with excitement. "Can you beat that?" he asked, then continued. " '*As to the quantity which the diggers get, take a few facts as evidence. I know seven men who worked seven weeks and two days, Sundays excepted, on the*

Feather River; they employed on an average fifty Indians, and got out in these seven weeks and two days 275 pounds of pure gold. I know the men, and have seen the gold.'"

"Ain't that somethin'?" the third man said. "Just imagin' walkin' round and pickin' up gold that's jist layin' there. Read to Grandma about them ten men."

The reader eagerly proceeded. "'*I know ten other men who worked ten days in company, employed no Indians, and averaged in these ten days $1,500 each.*'" He stopped reading and looked at the others in amazement, trying to imagine $1,500 worth of gold; and for only ten days work! Although they had already read and reread the entire story of the discovery of Gold in California, they weren't satisfied.

"$1,500 in ten days! Wouldn't take long to get filthy rich."

"I'd work one year. Could probably get . . . " The second man counted to himself and finding it too difficult, guessed: "$25,000!"

"Go on, don't stop readin'," Jasper prodded. He did not like the interruptions.

"Okay, don't push me, Jasper. I'm gettin' there. Well, it says: '*I know another man who got out of a rock basin, not larger than a washbowl, two and a half pounds of gold in fifteen minutes. Anyone can get eight to ten ounces of gold per day and even the least active man can get one or two.*'" He looked up and repeated: "Can you beat that?"

Mary Ellen had not thought about California, that magical land of her dreams, for some time. She knew about the Treaty of Guadalupe Hidalgo and how California had become a territory of the United States. The papers closely followed the events in California as the United States rode the wave of Manifest Destiny toward the Pacific Ocean. She remembered how often she would lie in her room, or out in the green fields and imagine life in California, in that exotic land where everyone was free, food plentiful, and the elements friendly. She knew her pastoral dream was wishful thinking and a fairly naive impression. Who knew what the conditions were really like in California? She did not believe the newspaper report for one moment. Gold may have been found in California, but not in such quantities and easy pickings as claimed. Innately conservative in many respects, Mary Ellen felt the article belonged in one of two categories: It was either a complete hoax or a gross exaggeration.

With unabated excitement the men continued to discuss gold and

California among themselves as they slowly walked out of the store and sought someone else who might respond more enthusiastically and share in their rapture. They were undaunted by Grandma Hussey's direct and practical questions which were at odds with their views. They could not answer many of the questions, so they simply ignored her reaction and left.

"What do you make of all of this?" Grandma Hussey asked Mary Ellen.

"I always longed to visit California. I used to dream about it. But not for gold," Mary Ellen confessed.

Grandma Hussey placed her arm around Mary Ellen. "I've lived in Cincinnati most of my life. My folks came out here when this was the frontier. They had grand visions of a bright future, not the bleak life they had in Boston. In some ways their dreams came true. Life certainly wasn't easy for them. On the contrary, making a home, getting enough food, surviving hostile Indians and just eking out an existence was anything but easy. Still, they did find a respite from the smelly, overcrowded city with soot-encrusted and grimy brick buildings they despised. They told me over and over that if they had to do it all over again they would, and were thankful for the opportunity."

"Then you were very fortunate," Mary Ellen said, thinking of her own childhood and her mother.

Grandma Hussey went on: "Yes. They gave me a better life here than I would've had back in Boston. But I've got to tell you, Mary Ellen, when I hear about California it stirs up my blood some, and reminds me how much I would've enjoyed trailblazing and starting a new life in a new world. Now I'm too danged old." She paused in contemplation, then added. "That's our lot, isn't it?"

Grandma Hussey went back to her table to finish her journal entries. As she sat down she looked up at Mary Ellen. "I agree with you about the gold. Had I been younger I might've gone, but not in search of gold. It would've been in search of a new and exciting life." Wistfully she returned to her work, leaving Mary Ellen to wander in her own imagination.

Crushing news came less than a week later. The Williams received a letter from Americus Price. As soon as Sarah read it she rushed over to Grandma Hussey's store, found Mary Ellen, and took her aside. Grandma Hussey noted the commotion, immediately felt Sarah's discomfiture and decided to step outside for a few moments to give the two women some time alone.

"Louis and I just received this letter from Americus," Sarah said softly. "I think you better read it." Mary Ellen could tell it was bad news from Sarah's demeanor, though she could not imagine what it might be. As she took the letter out of the envelope an empty feeling settled in her stomach and she found it difficult to breathe. Biting her lower lip she read the letter. As she did so, tears welled up in her eyes and ran down her face, and she started to tremble. Finally, she let the letter drop to the dusty floor and rushed out of the store, brushing against Sarah on her way out. Sarah retrieved the letter and read it again. It had been posted in Paris, France, and dated May 3, 1848.

> My dearest Louis and Sarah,
>
> I trust this letter finds you all well. I have some wonderful news for you. I married Catherine Hunter in Geneva last week. Her father, Robert Hunter, whom I am sure you have heard about, is currently serving as the American Ambassador to the throne of France. Our wedding at Notre Dame Cathedral was attended by the French royal family as well as many other notables from other European countries. I wish you could have been here. It was like a dream. Catherine and I plan to travel through Europe this summer and then to return to her home in Sikeston and finally back to Price's Landing. We are very happy and look forward to many years together. I must write to many of my friends so please excuse the brevity of this letter. I look forward to seeing you some time in the future. Until then my best wishes to you all. Also, please extend my greetings and salutations to Mary Ellen.
>
> With kind regards I remain, your faithful friend,
>
> Americus

Sarah also cried. When she picked up the letter at the post office earlier in the day she rushed directly to her husband's store. They read the letter together. Louis had no inclination of Mary Ellen's feelings for Americus and so he just found the letter interesting and somewhat amusing.

He told Sarah about the Hunter family and laughed about old Joseph Hunter, Catherine's grandfather, who kept a coffin under his bed at his plantation on an island between Little Nigger Wool Swamp and Big Nigger Wool Swamp. Joseph was considered to be rather odd. Every so often he would get his manservant to pull the coffin out and help him climb into it. If he fit in the coffin, everything was fine. If he did not he knew it was time to fast and reduce his food intake. Louis Williams seemed genuinely happy for Americus.

But Sarah knew better. Although Mary Ellen never told anyone about her feelings for Americus, she shared with Sarah many things during her recovery from Vogt's beating. Sarah, in her soft, quiet way, put all the bits together and deduced a clear picture of Mary Ellen's infatuation. She realized how devastating the letter would be for Mary Ellen, especially now that Mary Ellen had managed to put her life back into some semblance of order and to rebuild some much needed confidence.

Mary Ellen did not remember the exact moment of her decision. She could not remain in Cincinnati any longer. All her memories and experiences in Ohio were tainted with sadness. She really could not get over the shock of learning about Americus's wedding. Deep depression and the feeling of total isolation returned. She could barely work and hardly ate any food. Looking wasted and wan, Mary Ellen went through the motions of living. Sarah became alarmed and discussed this with Grandma Hussey. Both women were sympathetic and after many tortured discussions decided it would be in Mary Ellen's best interest if she could get away and go somewhere else where she could regain her health and her spirit.

At first, Grandma Hussey urged Mary Ellen not to leave. She believed that the problem was in Mary Ellen's mind and wherever Mary Ellen went, the problems, images, and fears would follow. Sarah disagreed, and ultimately her view prevailed. She agreed with Grandma Hussey that people should not run away from their problems, but there were times where a changed environment, one filled with a whole slew of new and different problems, created enough diversion to allow healing of old wounds to take place.

Mary Ellen felt the same way. All the ill will she encountered following the Vogt affair returned to her mind. Cincinnati, the Ohio River, the straight roads leading to the surrounding hills were now hostile and terribly confining. Going back to any of the Southern states was out of the question. The same held true for Missouri, although the reasons were entirely different. At first she considered heading up to Pittsburgh, or Philadelphia, or maybe even Boston. Perhaps she could even contact John Brown who would surely help her find a job. Then a new idea germinated, fuzzy at first, but rapidly growing—why not California? She could really start a new life there, one without any of the worries about her past, or about slavery, or about Americus. The more she thought about California the better it sounded and the more confidence she gained.

Sarah noted the change and when she discovered the reason she and Grandma Hussey encouraged her to do it, although they were very concerned about the many real risks young Mary Ellen would encounter. They were also a trifle uncertain whether the conditions in California, on the frontier, were appropriate for a young woman. With rough miners seeking gold and who knows what else, wild Indians, surly Mexicans who had been displaced by the victorious Americans, bears, lions, and other unimaginables, Mary Ellen would face great danger. But Mary Ellen had made her decision and they all helped her prepare for her trip.

First she would go to New Orleans. From there she would take a ship to Panama, cross Panama and head up the Pacific to California. It seemed somewhat simple, although the women thought they understood how dangerous such a trip would be.

Mary Ellen also had some confidence from a different source. She had built up quite a nest egg between her own savings and the fund entrusted for her care by Abigail. She had nearly $6,000, and reckoned that would give her a solid start in the new land. She did not share this with either Sarah or Grandma Hussey, deciding to keep her own financial position to herself.

The chance to go back to New Orleans provided Mary Ellen with an opportunity to do something she had not considered doing before. It did not require any immediate action; she could make the decision en route prior to her arrival in New Orleans. She did not mention this idea to either Sarah or Grandma Hussey.

As a going-away gift the two women purchased the tickets for Mary Ellen's journey. First-cabin fares were too expensive, so they purchased second cabin on the *Benson* from New Orleans to Chagres and then on the *California* from Panama to San Francisco. Louis Williams, acting as if he had never turned against Mary Ellen, regaled her with his views on how she should conduct herself and gave her $500. He felt a genuine fondness for Mary Ellen and was really sad to see her leave. He knew something had happened, something that persuaded Mary Ellen to leave, but Sarah would not tell him anything.

On the trip down the Mississippi River Mary Ellen found herself invigorated and thrilled almost as much as she had been on her first journey to Price's Landing. Now everything seemed different, as if she were looking at a different world from a different set of eyes. The river was filled with floating logs, most of which drifted closer to shore. Gray moss hung in streamers from the branches of cypress trees, and wild vines and shrubbery covered the shore. Only as they approached New Orleans did the scenery really change. Fields of sugarcane and corn replaced the receding forest. Large homes, many two or more stories with cool balconies, were ensconced in orange trees and acacias. The rich blossoms of the crepe myrtle reminded Mary Ellen of some of Sarah's watercolor paintings where light strokes of pink would highlight the work.

Mary Ellen had plenty of time to think and consider what she would do in New Orleans. The *Benson* would not be departing for Chagres on the Isthmus of Panama until the following week, giving her nearly seven days to visit the Ursaline Convent, confirm her travel arrangements to San Francisco

Marie Laveau

and, if she could muster the courage, seek out Marie Laveau. She really did not make up her mind until the paddle steamer had docked. It should not have been such a difficult decision but it made her nervous anyhow.

—∞—

THE BEATING CONGA WAS INCESSANT AND THE SOUND ENGULFED THE night. Goose bumps covered Mary Ellen's flesh and the back of her spine tingled as the steady, rhythmic cadence gnawed on her nerves. She watched the dark bodies, glistening from sweat, twisting and pulsating in strange, erotic, and haunting movements. The men and women were propelled around the grassy knoll as if drawn by unseen forces attracting and repelling the bodies without any sense or order. Their loins were covered with red handkerchiefs, their feet encased in sandals. They seemed oblivious to the smoke and haze that surrounded them, their dilated black pupils unfocused and unblinking.

Gradually the tempo increased, faster and faster. The dancers, some alone, others paired up but oblivious to one another, jerked and convulsed. Mary Ellen found the movements at once repulsive and intimate, haunting but desirable. The drums reached a climax of strident dissonance, earsplitting and unearthly, then suddenly stopped, leaving a hollow silence, broken only by the crackling and hissing of sodden wood on the fire.

The grassy knoll on the shores of Lake Ponchartrain was covered with a thin sheet of fog that extended over the black and satin surface of the water. A man and a woman were seated near the drums, distinguishable from the others by a blue cord around each of their waists. At their feet, within a large circle drawn in the grass, rested a simple box with glass sides covered by a large, flat, metal pan. Inside the box a large Copperhead hissed, its muscular brown and bronze body tightly coiled, its erect head shifting back and forth. A small forked tongue darted ceaselessly into the night air as if it could capture the vibrations and heat from the bodies of the exhausted dancers. A small package, similar to those Mary Ellen had helped her mother make years ago, containing herbs, horsehair, broken bits of horn, peppers and cloves of garlic lay next to the alter.

The man whispered over and over, "Come closuh. Come closuh." Slowly the congregation gathered toward the circle, their eyes focused on the serpent, the fire casting fickle shadows across their intense faces. "De powah o' de Serpen' is heah. Ah can feel de powah. It be gitten' stronger an' stronger. De Sperit comin'. De Sperit comin' heah." His voice grew stronger and suddenly, with remarkable agility, he leaped toward the alter, placed his large black hand on the metal pan and peered at the congregation. "De Sperit is heah, now!" he said slowly and with confidence, his eyes wide and a large knowing smile across his face.

He was tall, almond colored, broad shouldered, and muscular, with a thin waist and long powerful legs. The subdued light of the fire enhanced the silhouette of his body making him appear even more powerful. His nose flared as he looked at the nearly naked men and women standing around the alter. In a daze, heaving from their exertions and trying to catch their breath, they stared at the snake. The man bent down, stalked around the dancers as a lion stalks its prey, going from man to woman. He stared at their faces and their eyes as if he were silently questioning them; his head slowly tilting from shoulder to shoulder, back and forth. When he completed the circuit, having inspected every man and woman, he returned in the same stalking manner to the woman who had remained seated motionless and oblivious to all before her. He whispered to her.

Slowly she stood, her face frozen into a grotesque expression and her eyes unblinking. She walked to the box and nimbly climbed on top of the metal plate. The Copperhead bobbed back and forth, the interminable tongue seeking its prey, prepared to strike. Nonplused the woman looked around and suddenly pointed at a man, her face turning into rage.

She shrieked, "Is dere sumpin' wrong wid' 'im?" The young stocky black man looked terrified. She repeated, "Is dere sumpin' wrong wid' 'im?" Her eyes closed, her head fell back, and she began speaking in a deep guttural voice: "I see 'im! Hit's all jumble' and mess' up." The others started to hum in a soft monotone but their voices grew louder as if to ward off evil spells. "W'at yo' willin' to do to take 'im in?" she looked at the frightened man. He fell and prostrated himself before her. She raked him with her blazing eyes, then stepped back off the box and picked up the small package next to the alter. She approached the man who was now lying prone on the ground, bent over and thrust it into his hand.

"W'ateva yo' wan'!" he mumbled, his face pressed against the grass.

The woman returned to the alter, picked up a bottle of dark puce liquid and drank it, letting some of it spill over her mouth, giving it a macabre bloody appearance. No one stirred. No one dared to breathe as if breathing alone might draw her attention and bring her wrath upon them. She filled her mouth once more with the liquid and spit it over the prostrated man. He remained completely inert; not a muscle budged. After a moment she took his hand and pulled him up. With his eyes focused on the ground he meekly stood, his body shuddering uncontrollably. She thrust the bottle into his hand and forced it to his mouth, making him drink from it.

The tall husky man with the blue cord walked up to the woman and handed her a shapeless piece of black wax. She took it and started kneading it in exaggerated movements, grunting with each effort looking about her triumphantly. "Drop of de man's blood," she said, chanting it like a mantra, over and over, as the shapeless mass slowly gained shape—arms, legs, and finally a head. She lifted the waxen figure above her head for everyone to see, and as she did so the drums again began a soft and slow beat. The tall man raised a knife in the air and plunged it into the breast of the little figurine. The assembly now took up a chant, feet patting a beat on the grass.

As the rhythm of the chanting and the drums picked up, the woman took the waxen shape and placed it on a large smooth stone near the center of the fire and wax figure melted into a dark pool of liquid. The woman began to shout, "Mary, Jesus, Joseph . . . " and continued through the Act of Contrition, following the Catholic rite, as if at Sunday mass. Immediately the throng broke into loud shouts of "Maron! Maron!" repeating it over and over, while the man brought out a large statute of St. Anthony which he placed on a small tablecloth beside the woman. She then shouted "Done set de table, St. Maron now. W'at yo' gonna do?" The phrase was picked up by the crowd and became the new chant.

Suddenly she shrieked, the unearthly sound penetrating the night.

Everyone became silent. She walked around the statute of St. Anthony hideously wailing, "W'at yo' gonna do? Oh, W'at yo' gonna do? Oh, Maron, oh, Saint Maron, W'at yo' gonna do?" Then she looked up to the black sky. "Yo' answer me, Maron! W'at yo' gonna do?" She stamped her foot and spat on the image, whereupon the wailing from the others commenced and rose higher and higher. Curses, screams, epithets were hurled at the statue. She drank from the bottle again, spat on the image's head, and fell on the ground, beating the grass with her fists in a frenzy, yelling, "Answer me, Maron!"

One of the congregants ran over with a handful of salt which he sprinkled over her writhing body and shouted, "She done possess! Saint Maron done answer 'er!" The tall muscular man shouted in ecstasy above the din, "De Sperit done come strong on 'er!" The crowd suddenly broke up into laughter and gaiety as if some mystical spell had just been lifted.

Mary Ellen, sitting under a large Cypress tree watched the ceremony with fascination, her mind in an uproar, assimilating everything she could from Marie Laveau, the Voodoo Queen, who was now cleaning the salt off her lithe body. Mary Ellen was also affected sexually by the erotic movements of the tall muscular man, Laveau's "king" and lover, Christophe Glapion. She felt heat in her loins as she watched his muscles rippling and gleaming in the firelight, his body thrusting in blatant rhythmic gestures. But when his eyes met hers she consciously and with great effort forced herself to turn away and resist any temptation. She was there on a mission and nothing, not even Christophe's animal appeal, would divert her attention. Nothing. Still, there was no denying she was aroused, and wanted Christophe to herself; but he was Marie Laveau's man and Mary Ellen was worried that Marie had noticed her inner feelings.

The girls at the Ursaline Convent had piqued Mary Ellen's interest in Marie Laveau. When she was at Price's Landing Adelina talked about voodoo frequently. Her grandfather had been a distant relative of Marie Laveau's beau and Adelina knew him well. She told Mary Ellen that she should meet Marie Laveau if she ever got to New Orleans. Adelina had seen the awesome powers of the Voodoo Queen and at each telling the powers became greater and greater.

Chapter Seven

Mary Ellen knew Adelina had exaggerated the stories because some of the tales were so ridiculous and improbable, Mary Ellen could only laugh. Adelina would then immediately leave the room crossing herself repeatedly. She warned Mary Ellen not to laugh or she might one day suffer some horrible pain or affliction. Other than Adelina's ramblings about voodoo, Mary Ellen did not think about voodoo until the night Vogt attacked her. As he hammered on her with his fists, she became incoherent. She envisioned her mother's warnings as well as Adelina's forewarning. As she recovered from the beating she wondered if she was attacked because she had laughed at her mother and at Adelina's injunction about voodoo.

Marie Laveau's power in New Orleans, with both Negroes and whites, was well known and, if not highly respected, greatly feared. This fear, not unlike the terror Mary Ellen seemed to inspire among the slaves at the Golden Oaks, was a powerful tool, a potent weapon which Mary Ellen might find useful one day, particularly among the blacks and especially in the unknown lands of California. Marie Laveau presented a wonderful opportunity to unravel some of the mystery and magic behind Voodoo.

Once she had decided to go to California Mary Ellen became very resolute, highly ambitious, and determined to succeed. A woman, even a free one, had little chance of succeeding anywhere. To succeed in the west, Mary Ellen reasoned, a woman would have to employ every ounce of intelligence, use every wile and gift in her possession, to overcome the mantle of discrimination. Already considerably more educated than most woman, knowledgeable about commerce, equally refined, she could still be at a tremendous disadvantage in any society that looked to the color of her skin and not to her abilities. Being educated and refined had its benefits, so did luck; however, one could not rely on luck.

Watching Marie Laveau, Mary Ellen realized how little she recalled of her mother's lessons. She had not been completely schooled in the art of voodoo—interpreting its mysteries or conducting its rituals and religious ceremonies.

Marie Laveau obtained valuable confidential information through a successful network of spies and informants throughout New Orleans.

She either sold this information or extorted large funds from blackmail. Her spies were slaves—houseboys, cooks, and maids—who worked on the plantations and in the homes of the aristocracy of New Orleans. Her informants were carefully selected and clandestinely trained. They were taught how to listen to discussions about finance, politics, property, or just plain gossip and report everything back to her. In many cases the slaves did not understand the discussion, but they learned to memorize as much as possible. Very few could do it well, but some seemed to have nearly photographic memories. Mary Laveau explained what to look for, how they could tell when meetings were convened behind closed door, conversation in muted tones, or anything else that seemed unusual or extraordinary. Strangely, the white community, so careful to keep their conversations private, assumed that their black servants were either disinterested or completely ignorant and unable to follow such discussions. They could not have been more wrong.

None of the slaves dared to refuse Marie Laveau's instructions to spy on their masters or her requests for information; or to reveal to anyone what she was doing. The penalty for failure or for displeasing Marie, they were certain, would be worse than hell. After all, she was the Voodoo Queen. Many of the wealthiest whites in the community were afraid of antagonizing this Voodoo Queen who held potent information about them.

Mary Ellen intended to learn as much about voodoo as she could—how Laveau controlled blacks and whites, how information was processed, and how the network functioned. She made every effort to be nonthreatening to Marie—feigning weakness, diminishing her strength and ardor, always lowering her eyes timidly and glancing at the ground when Marie spoke to her or looked at her searchingly. This caution included staying away from Laveau's man, Christophe Glapion.

Mary Ellen had contacted Adelina about meeting the Voodoo Queen. Adelina introduced her to Christophe, Chrisophe took her to Marie. Mary Ellen and Marie liked each other from the start.

"Did you enjoy your first initiation ceremony?" Marie asked, dropping her accent and speaking with an almost aristocratic mien; she was fluent in French and Spanish as well.

Chapter Seven

"It was fascinating," Mary Ellen replied.

"The man who was initiated tonight works for John Lambert, one of New Orleans's greatest lawyers, and a scion of one of the first non-French families to settle here. He will be an excellent source of highly confidential information," Marie spoke confidently.

"I noticed that you mingled some Catholic rites into the ceremony," Mary Ellen said demurely.

"Yes. Most of the slaves receive Catholic instruction and I thought, rather than fight Christianity, to embrace it as if it were a part of voodoo. It doesn't matter what the priest says, we simply use and magnify the fears the church instills. When we're finished, they're all scared to death." She laughed, her large white teeth shining in the darkness, and her eyes dancing in merriment.

"Do white people ever come to these ceremonies?" Mary Ellen asked.

"Oh, yes. Quite often." Marie Laveau made a mischievous and lurid twisting motion with her hips. "Young men really like the erotic nature of the dancing and the nubile women," she laughed again.

"Do they become initiates?" Mary Ellen was puzzled.

"No! Never!" Marie became serious. "In fact, when they come, we change the ceremony and focus on the dancing to excite them. Later, if they want a black woman, that can be fixed." Then Marie smiled ruefully. "After that they're in my power."

Christophe Glapion, after arranging for the ceremonial items to be taken away, now joined them, dressed, handsome, and smiling. They walked back to a small house commonly known as "Maison Blanche," where Marie arranged for trysts and assignations with sumptuous feasts, succulent food and the best champagnes. Appointments had to be made in advance and she served only those in the white community whom she considered useful. Her clients included many men in high places. She was cunning yet generous, treacherous yet benevolent, but above all diabolical; Mary Ellen intended to be even more powerful.

As they slept the few hours remaining before daylight, Mary Ellen had strange dreams where her body was entwined with Christophe, his arms locked around her, bodies moving together to the rhythm of the drums, beads of perspiration flowing between their smooth bodies, her nipples erect, their craving getting stronger and more violent. Suddenly he turned into a huge hissing serpent, but the serpent's head was the head of Marie, with blood all over her mouth, staring and shrieking in laughter. She woke with a start. Everyone else was sound asleep. She crept out of the house and walked to the edge of the lake where thin slivers of silver reflected off the placid water and patches of fog crowned the lake with tufts of white cotton. *I better leave for California soon,* she thought. *I got what I wanted but if I stay I may want more, and I cannot afford it.* She lay back on the grass and envisioned Christophe's bronzed body, something she would never have.

As a parting gift Marie Laveau arranged for Mary Ellen's tickets to be upgraded to first cabin on her Atlantic sojourn on the Benson and her Pacific leg on the *California.* Mary Ellen did not learn of this until she boarded the packet and the captain personally escorted her to her well-appointed cabin, reserved in the name of Mary Ellen Christophe. If Marie knew of Mary Ellen's innermost feelings she never let on and her parting had been most gracious, friendly, and cheerful.

As the ship sailed out of New Orleans, gliding on a wide current of brown water with forests of willow and cypress on one side and swamps on the other, Mary Ellen breathed a sigh, relief for the start of her adventure and regret for unrequited love.

Book Two

1849–1851

Chapter Eight

The Panama Crossing

CHAGRES, PANAMA
JANUARY 11, 1849

THE RHYTHMIC POUNDING OF THE SIDE-PADDLE AND THE GENTLE pitching of the *Benson* over the rolling waves were the only sensation of movement. A thick gray fog enveloped the ship, limiting visibility to less than a hundred feet. Neither bow nor stern could be seen while standing amidship, only fleeting glimpses of water gliding by.

Despite the dreary day, and despite the suffocating humidity, passengers on the *Benson,* a wooden side wheeler with three masts, round stern with sharp tuck and billet head, gathered on the main deck, happy to end their voyage. Animated voices filled the sultry air as the men and women craned their necks, staring intently, willing the fog to suddenly lift and reveal the exotic jungles of Panama. But they were still nearly two miles offshore. Currents and shifting sandbanks made it impossible for any ship to get closer.

Suddenly a shudder vibrated through the ship, the side-paddle reversed, and the *Benson* came to a halt. Large chains and anchors splashed into the placid water. The piercing blast of the steam whistle heralded the end of the Atlantic passage and nearly two hundred passengers broke into a chorus of shouting and applause.

Colbraith O'Brien stood alone on the forecastle deck, showing little sign of festiveness, and regarded the passengers with some measure of scorn; his reserved and intense demeanor did not invite conversation, which was just fine with him. A ruddy beard hid most of his features, except his steely blue eyes. Tall and broad-shouldered, he had few illusions about the difficult journey ahead—crossing the Isthmus of Panama, a region of pestilent jungles and impassable mountains.

Most of the passengers, lulled into a sense of security by the relatively calm and uneventful trip from New York to Chagres via New Orleans, had gradually shed their fears of the unknown. As far as Colbraith was concerned, they had become unduly optimistic and totally unrealistic about the remainder of the voyage and the treasure awaiting them in California. Unlike the others, Colbraith was not relying on glowing narratives of gold discovery; these were fairy tales. Instead, before departing New York he set out to learn as much as he could about crossing the Isthmus and plying the Pacific Ocean from Panama to California. Even aboard the *Benson* he painstakingly grilled Captain Morse about the next leg of the trip. What he learned was disconcerting: Panama fever and cholera were endemic, occasionally rampant; if one survived illnesses there were crocodiles, poisonous snakes and frogs, and gangs of bandits who preyed on unwary travelers. The remainder of the crossing would be difficult and dangerous.

However, the other passengers did not want to hear this. As the ship plodded towards Panama, passengers, initially strangers, quickly formed friendships. Sitting together day and night confined to two small decks, they took every opportunity to excitedly discuss their plans. During meals, between meals, late at night or early in the morning before breakfast was served, they broke into small clusters and spewed their brand of optimism until they had reinforced one another's unwarranted dreams. They were all going to strike it rich and return to their homes in the lap of luxury. The risks, if any, were completely ignored. None of them knew anything about California.

Chapter Eight

Colbraith did not express his opinion. He listened idly to their dreams but kept his own to himself as he overheard passengers paint rosy pictures of arriving in California, walking into nearby hills, plucking rocks of pure gold lying on the open ground, and becoming instantly rich. This view, instilled by headlines in New York papers—such as "Gold Found in Lumps of 16 and 25 Pounds," or "Gold to an Immense Amount Obtained by Digging and Washing" was common. Horace Greely augmented this view when he published his prediction, in December of 1848, that California would produce a billion dollars of gold in four years; a number so staggeringly large at the time it was incomprehensible. A billion dollars just sitting on the ground, ripe for picking.

Few of the gold-seekers had any knowledge of mining or gold, or even what it looked like in its natural state. Colbraith was amazed that some of the more naïve passengers believed they would find gold in the streets of San Francisco. Many carried expensive gear, purchased in the East, that would soon be lost, stolen, or simply discarded. Colbraith believed some members of this cheerful crowd would perish before reaching California; a few would succeed in finding gold; one or two might even attain their dreams and strike it rich. The majority, however, were doomed to a hard, dangerous life of bare subsistence. It was a one-way trip; most of them would never see their families or their homes again. They would die and be buried in a strange land, lost forever.

Pragmatic all his life, the dangers ahead were obvious to Colbraith. Even before the tragic accident that killed his brother, Colbraith was never lulled into a false sense of security or swayed by fanciful prophesies. Tammany Hall had taken out the last vestige of his hopes and dreams. Colbraith tightened his jaw and gritted his teeth as he thought about New York and the two-timing bastards. He would have vengeance. The success or failure of his current plans depended solely on his efforts, hard work, and dedication; not by the beckon of some sparkling ore or ignorant vision. Let the fools fight each other for the pickings. He had different dreams. He wanted power. Nothing more.

Another shrill blast of the Klaxon, a signal to disembark, stirred the passengers into action. They rushed to get their portmanteaus, boxes, packages, and other gear to the deck. Several lighters, small craft of different sizes, some with sails, some hauled by men with oars, a few with small steam engines, materialized out of the fog, drawn to the *Benson* as vultures to carrion.

Slowly, but with much commotion, the passengers disembarked, boarded the rickety lighters, and headed for the small wharf on the white beach at Chagres where the sun was penetrating the mist, making the heat oppressive and unbearable.

Chagres, an old neglected, rundown fortification, its battlements decaying and turning back to sand, overlooked the small bay and entrance to the Chagres River. It hardly looked like a port or a town. A few wretched native huts dotted the shoreline. It was now engorged with people, mostly American, destined for California.

Colbraith jumped on the weather-beaten boards of the wharf and supervised the removal of his luggage. Locals, offering various services, wares, fruit, and other unrecognizable foods descended on the passengers. It was a scene directly out of Dante's Inferno, a bedlam of pushing, shoving, shouting passengers trying to get their baggage ashore while competing with buzzing insects, and roaring vendors.

One man, clothed only in tan-colored coarsely woven cotton pants, approached Colbraith. He was shoeless and hatless. His small, dark, wiry frame and thick, black hair glistened with perspiration. "Señor! You wish to go to Panama?" he inquired politely.

Colbraith barely acknowledged the man as he inspected the unattractive town.

"I take you to Panama," the man persisted. "I have four people, can take one more."

"How do you go? By Cruces?" Colbraith asked as he looked down at the short man. There were alternate routes: Cruces, farther up the river but closer to Panama City or Gorgona and a longer trek by mule. Each had an advantage, but at this time of the year Colbraith had been warned to stick with Gorgona since the roads from Cruces were more likely to wash out in heavy rains.

The Panamanian regarded Colbraith more thoughtfully. "No, Señor. I go on river to Gorgona and take mule to Panama."

Chapter Eight

Colbraith looked at him but said nothing.

The man continued, "I do everything—food, boat, mule—everything!" He smiled. Colbraith appraised him and wondered if he should look around and get his bearings before selecting a guide. But he saw the large throng massing near the wharf, all competing for the services of a few legitimate guides and those who called themselves guides. Captain Morse had warned Colbraith that unscrupulous peons, seeing so many rich Yankees seeking passage across the Isthmus, would claim to be guides. And desert their charges at the first opportunity. Colbraith liked this imperturbable little man. The Panamanian's expression did not falter or waver from Colbraith's harsh gaze.

"How much?" Colbraith asked blandly.

The Panamanian looked at Colbraith's baggage. "This yours?"

"Yes," Colbraith replied.

"The bongo, $60. Two mules from Gorgona, one you ride, one for this." He pointed to Colbraith's trunks. "Mule cost $25 and food more $15.

"$25 for both mules?"

"No, Señor," he looked at Colbraith as if Colbraith were trying to rob him. "$25 each."

Captain Morse had admonished Colbraith and other passengers to bargain with the natives in Panama. He warned that anyone who did not bargain would be robbed from one side of the isthmus to the other. "Like having the scarlet letter "F" for fool imprinted on your forehead for the remainder of your crossing!" Morse laughed.

"I'll give you $45 for everything," Colbraith said, "half now and half when we arrive in Panama City."

The man blinked, shook his head as if he had not really heard what Colbraith had just said, and pleaded with a pained expression. "Señor, is impossible. I have four children. Must buy food." He held up four fingers, pointing to each one for emphasis. He then appeared to count on his fingers and said, "Okay. $100! $100 everything! I take you."

Colbraith's expression remained impassive. Although he knew he was probably paying too much, he offered, "$65. That's it. Half now, half later."

The small man grinned, his weather-beaten face crinkling into a multitude of furrows, revealing large and surprisingly white teeth. Five customers paying from $65 to $100 each, for one week's worth of work was more money than he had ever earned or could imagine earning in his life. This was his third crossing in the last six weeks. Silently he blessed the saints then whistled towards a small crowd of locals squatting under a tall palm. An exact replica of the Panamanian, only younger, came running up. The older man introduced him as "Alberto. My son." Alberto, dressed exactly as his father, dragged Colbraith's trunks towards the river with considerable effort. Colbraith paid $44 in Spanish doubloons and followed Alberto to the river. The Panamanian turned to Colbraith, grinning, and said, "I am Jose Ignacio."

Colbraith responded, "I'm O'Brien. Where did you learn to speak English?"

Ignacio beamed, "I work on ship. Must speak English or very bad for me." Colbraith understood. "Bad" was probably an understatement. Ignacio must have had a rough time being the lowest rung on the ladder on some English or American vessel; probably the subject of considerable abuse. But Jose survived; a survivor like himself. Colbraith warmed to the little man, certain he had made the right decision.

"Señor. Is good you not stay here more." Ignacio waved his arm at the settlement. "Very bad. Many people. Many sick and die." He crossed himself and proceeded to the river without further explanation.

Ignacio's bongo, a twenty-five-foot-long, three-foot-wide flat-bottomed boat, looked old and worn. A palm leaf awning set on top of four poles, like a pole barn, provided the only shelter. Three men and one woman were already on board, sitting in the shade of the palm leaves, fanning themselves with their hats and swatting at the persistent mosquitoes; their baggage stored haphazardly towards the bow, making the bongo look top heavy and unseaworthy. As Colbraith boarded, the others squeezed closer to one another, trying to make room for him. Colbraith offered to sit near his trunk where he could jury-rig some cover, suggesting the other men rotate every six hours. No one objected. The woman watched Colbraith carefully, but did not speak. The bongo now sat only a few inches above the water line.

Chapter Eight

Bongo on the Chagres River

Alberto and Ignacio stood at the rear of the craft and proceeded to push the bongo into the Chagres River with long poles. Occasionally a pole would stick to the muddy bottom, pulling one of the men into the water.

Colbraith watched the two men working side by side, nimbly and coordinated, pushing the bongo against the current through the rotting vegetation. At Chagres the river was quite broad, but as they proceeded northwest they encountered narrows with churning rapids. The passengers disembarked and helped Ignacio and Alberto pull the bongo with coarse ropes. As much as possible they steered the boat close to banks, in the shallows. But sometimes the channel was too deep to pole through. Then Ignacio and Alberto slid into the water and kicked the bongo ahead. Progress was slow but steady.

Colbraith, who had never imagined life in a tropical jungle, devoted himself to extinguishing every mosquito within sight or sound. The large, engorged mosquitoes were easy targets, but messy; their smaller cousins were pesky and incessantly buzzed in his ears. Between the fierce heat and unremitting insects, none of Ignacio's passengers had energy or desire enough to converse.

As the sun descended that evening a light breeze from the mountains provided the first relief from the heat, but not the mosquitoes. Colbraith was lying under his makeshift cover, using a jacket for protection, when one of the men approached and told him it was his turn in the shelter. Colbraith thanked him and carefully made his way under the awning, trying not to tip the already overloaded bongo into the water. It was nearing dinnertime and Colbraith realized that he was ravenous, not having eaten since he left the *Benson* that morning. He wondered if his fellow passengers, those still at Chagres or the ones fortunate to be floating on bongos, were still as exhilarated about their voyage as they had been aboard ship.

Ignacio pushed the bongo to a small sandy cove near the village of Gatun, announcing that they would camp on the riverbank. When they had all piled out of the bongo, Alberto started a small fire and put coffee water on while the others put up hammocks for the night. Ignacio set up a small canvas lean-to for the woman. The group huddled around the fire, not for warmth, since the temperature was still in the low nineties and humid, but because it seemed to discourage mosquito attacks.

One of the men who had been closely scrutinizing Colbraith asked, "Say, aren't you O'Brien?"

The man was young, probably under twenty, short, with a mop of reddish blond hair and freckles. Colbraith tried to recall if he had ever seen him before, but drew a blank.

Colbraith did not answer, but the young man was not deterred. "You don't know me, but I worked on your campaign."

This remark caught the others' attention and made Colbraith uncomfortable.

"My name's Mike Donnelly," the young man said as he stood and extended his hand. Colbraith had little choice but to shake it.

If young Donnelly had been involved in Colbraith's run for office, he must have been a Tammany man, which excluded him from qualifying as an innocent. Donnelly plowed ahead, "Yeah." Turning to the others he said, "He would've been a congressman today, if it hadn't been for them bosses from Albany, especially Charles Hayford."

This last statement evoked images that Colbraith had tried hard to suppress for nearly three years, images of his zeal and expectations as a raw twenty-six-year old, and the repercussions to his campaign when the Tammany aristocrats decided to make an example of him. He could neither forgive nor forget the election nor the rich Albany power brokers. After the fiasco Colbraith understood that he could never again run for office in New York, under any party's banner. His catastrophic run for office buried his political future so deep it could never be resurrected. The only silver lining of the loss is that it helped him focus on California. And here he was, out on a bongo in the middle of the Chagres River, encountering someone who must have been a shuffler, buying votes in some New York City ward, and involved in his campaign. The world was small and shrinking rapidly and these chance meetings were likely to occur even in places as far away from New York as Panama.

But the unexpected encounter and recollection of his painful experience only served to reinforce Colbraith's intense feelings: regardless of cost, and by any means possible, he would achieve his goals in California, just so the bastards from Albany and New York City would have to acknowledge his power and pay him back.

Donnelly was still speaking, the others listening intently, especially the mysterious woman who had hardly said a word. "I heard you busted the jaw of Big Red," and turning to the two men by way of explanation, "Red was the foreman of Engine Company 41, who said he didn't trust anyone who didn't drink, or somethin' like that. And Big Red was just that. *Big*. A brawler. Well, Mr. O'Brien here just walked up to him, cool and collected, as if he were at church on a Sunday morning, and slammed Big Red with his fist. Knocked Big Red out cold. So I hear." Donnelly kind of shrugged his shoulders as if that was the end of the story. The others, except the woman, looked at Donnelly and then more carefully at Colbraith. The woman just shook her head and looked away.

Colbraith pursed his lips. "Look, that was a long time ago. Let it rest. Right now I'd rather think about the future, not the past."

Donnelly looked crestfallen, almost as if he had been slapped by his best friend. Colbraith did not want to embarrass the lad; one never knew when someone might be useful or needed in the future, and someone like Donnelly who obviously held him in high esteem could become useful.

Colbraith smiled expansively and asked Donnelly, "Why are you heading to California?"

Donnelly brightened up considerably but looked puzzled by the question. "Why I suppose just like everybody else. Headin' out to get my share of the gold."

"Do you know anything about gold? Or about mining?" Colbraith inquired.

"Well, no, but . . . but I know its there. Why, everyone knows it's there. I'll get me a pick and dig it up. I hear tell there's so much gold the hardest part is how to store it." He laughed.

Colbraith laughed too, but inwardly sighed. "Well, good luck to you."

"You too, Mr. O'Brien. Say, if you need someone to work your claims you just let me know."

"I'll do just that."

One of the other men introduced himself. "I'm Lowell Sandlin from Ohio, and this here is my little brother, John." At the mention of Ohio the woman whirled around and just as quickly stopped. No one except Colbraith saw her reaction. Lowell was nearly bald with a few wisps of stringy blond hair and a plain open and honest face; if he concealed any thing it was certainly not apparent. Probably a farmer, Colbraith mused. John was quiet, almost too subdued and Colbraith thought he looked ill. John simply produced an insipid smile and promptly leaned back against one of the boxes as if the exertion of holding himself up was too much. There was a dull glow in his eyes that disturbed Colbraith and made him very uncomfortable. Everyone now turned expectedly to the woman. She wore a bonnet and most of her face was covered. "I'm Mary Ellen Price of Missouri," she said, then turned shyly away. Donnelly made a face and raised his eyebrows suggestively, but Colbraith ignored him. Lowell and his brother politely said their hellos.

The conversation was interrupted by Ignacio who brought and served them tropical fruit unlike anything Colbraith had ever tasted, something called papaya. Then he surprised all of them with a cut of beef that he cooked slowly over the fire. For the coup de grace he produced a loaf of dark bread. Everyone was amazed, expecting the usual fare of dried beef, boiled ham, sea biscuits, or sardines. They were so hungry they hardly talked during dinner.

After dinner Donnelly produced a small silver flask of brandy, took a swig, coughed as the burning liquid drained down his throat and passed it on. John Sandlin was now fast asleep. Colbraith politely declined the invitation. Lowell helped himself and handed the flask back to Donnelly. He offered it to Mary Ellen, but she declined. Colbraith noticed something strange about her eyes but before he could determine what it was she turned away.

Contentedly lying there, their stomachs filled, a little fog settling into their minds, Lowell and Donnelly started a pleasant relaxed conversation. John remained asleep while sweat poured from his brow. Mary Ellen remained to herself.

Lowell explained how he and John had originally outfitted themselves to cross the continent along the Platte on the Oregon and California Trail. But when they read the advertisements for the comfortable accommodations on the ships, the safety, and how much faster they could get to California, they sold their equipment, headed by train to New York, and booked passage on the *Allegro,* which had arrived at Chagres a week before the *Benson.* Lowell, who appeared to be in his thirties, told them the decision to come to California was a difficult one, but made by the whole family. He and his brother had left their wives and kids, Lowell had four, John two, with their parents on a farm near Lexington, Kentucky. Their plan was to return to Ohio in two years, provide their children and wives with all the things they never had, acquire more land,

and live comfortably for the rest of their lives. But he was worried about his younger brother who seemed to have caught a fever during the week they were stuck in Chagres, trying to find an agent to take them across the Isthmus. They had been warned by their captain to deal only with recognized agents, all of whom were gone when they arrived. Fortunately they hired Ignacio just before the *Benson's* arrival. Otherwise they might have been stuck in Chagres even longer.

That night the men slept ashore in their hammocks and Mary Ellen behind her canvas partition; but Colbraith decided to sleep next to his trunks with revolvers loaded and primed. He slept soundly until a party of macaws started a dissonant screech in the woods, the call taken up by monkeys, completely waking up everyone. Ignacio prepared a quick breakfast of coffee and eggs and the same papaya fruit. By 4:30 they were back on the river heading towards Gorgona.

After four days on the river, fighting the current and an occasional alligator, watching John's health deteriorate and Lowell become more despondent, they reached Gorgona. Ignacio, true to his word, had a string of mules ready for the passage across the mountains to Panama City using the old but paved Spanish Road used by Spain to transport Aztec and Mayan gold for shipment to Spain. Ignacio acquired some mules and began preparations for the next leg of their journey.

John Sandlin had been delirious for the past twenty-four hours. He was taken to a small clinic operated by American missionaries. Colbraith, Donnelly, and Mary Ellen refrained from pressing Ignacio to proceed, although Donnelly clearly showed some impatience, but deferred to Colbraith. For Ignacio each lost day meant lost profits, but this was in God's hands and Ignacio did not wish to upset the God who had smiled upon him so benevolently.

Due to its higher altitude Gorgona offered the first respite from the miserable heat. Quietly the three men and Mary Ellen whiled the time away, waiting for word about John's condition before resuming the final leg of the crossing. Ignacio arranged accommodations at a small hotel that they found surprisingly clean and comfortable; in fact everything about Gorgona seemed to be the antithesis of Chagres.

But, like Chagres, the town was bloated with Americans, many having been abandoned by unreliable or crooked agents. One desperate middle-aged couple, completely unsuited for the rough crossing, the climate, or even the life they could expect in California, were trying to sell the equipment they purchased at outrageous prices in New York to raise funds to hire another agent to take them to Panama City. But the Americans in Gorgona were not interested buyers and the locals were only willing to steal it, legally if they could, illegally if they could not.

In some cases the mules promised at Gorgona did not materialize and the agents exclaimed they were cheated by someone else, so additional money had to be paid by the naive Americans to contract new mules, which were in extremely short supply. As a result, clothing, gear, and trunks were often abandoned or left in the care of agents as the people proceeded to Panama City, either by foot, or on the few animals available. The decision to continue with their journey across the Isthmus and board a vessel headed for San Francisco prevailed over remaining with equipment and waiting for additional animals. The "agents" were milking these Norte Americanos for everything they could.

Later that night Colbraith, Donnelly, and Ignacio were seated on the veranda of the Pension Gorgona, engaged in small talk, mostly about the effect the American intrusion had on the isthmus, while Mary Ellen sipped tea at another table. Lowell approached, having just returned from the clinic. His eyes were red-rimmed and his clothes disheveled. Colbraith knew the bad news from Lowell's walk, but Donnelly looked up, smiled and asked Lowell how John was doing.

"John's dead." Lowell sat on the stoop and buried his face in his hands. "What am I going to tell Ma and Pa? What am I going to tell his wife?" He paused and the silence was intense. "It's all my fault." He started to rock back and forth. "It was my idea to go to California. How can I go back and tell them?" Now he turned and looked at Colbraith. "What am I going to do?" He heaved a sigh and buried his head back in his hands. Suddenly he stood, looked up at the black sky and yelled. "Why, God? Why John? He was good. A good father. Why him? Goddamn it, why him?"

Colbraith stood and grabbed Lowell by the shoulders and spun him around. "I'll tell you what you're going to do. You're going to do what any decent brother would do. You're going to go back there and take care of yours and his. My brother died when he was seventeen. I thought it was my fault. Maybe it was. Unlike you I couldn't make up for it. If you don't go back and face it and take care of your responsibilities, then the hell with you." Colbraith let go of his shoulders and sagged wearily on the stoop.

Lowell had tensed up, almost as if he were about to explode; but it slowly passed and he sat next to Colbraith and looked at his feet. In a resigned voice he said, "You're right, of course. It's my responsibility. But I don't know if I'm strong enough to take care of both families."

"No one ever knows," Colbraith responded more softly.

"I hope my folks will forgive me. I hope God will forgive me." Lowell started to sob quietly, his face buried in his hands again. After a few minutes the sobbing subsided and he looked up, wiped his eyes and nose on his sleeve with a broad sweep of his arm, and spoke into the night. "I'll do it. I'll go back and take care of things. It's only right." He stood and turned towards Colbraith. "Thank you, Mr. O'Brien. It must have been painful to lose a seventeen-year-old brother. God bless you."

As Lowell walked up the veranda, toward the entrance to the hotel, Mary Ellen joined him. She placed her arm around his shoulder and said something to him. He began to cry again as they departed letting the hotel door swing back and forth. The others fell into silence.

Colbraith thought about Richard. He died trying in vain to save some kids from getting killed. John's death was different. Panama fever claimed another American son, father, and husband. How many have died and how many more will die on this effort to find gold at the end of the rainbow? Colbraith shook his head said good night to Donnelly and Ignacio and turned in for the night.

The next morning, services were held at the church, attended by Ignacio and his family, Colbraith, Donnelly, Mary Ellen, and the middle-aged couple they met the previous day. Lowell sat quietly with a measure of self-control and dignity. After the service Lowell arranged to have John buried next to the clinic—so far away from Ohio and in a place neither of John's offspring were ever likely to visit.

—᠁—

THE RICH, VERDANT JUNGLE CANOPY DID LITTLE TO KEEP THE SHEETS of rain from falling through the green leaves and foliage, inundating the six people and their weary mules. The roar of the rain was so deafening, so overwhelming, that conversation between the riders was impossible. The road was steep; on one side the jungle rose up a sheer incline and disappeared into the mist; the other side fell precipitously into an impenetrable abyss. All the riders wore wide-brimmed hats, pulled low across their faces, and were covered with brown, well-worn oilskins; only their cracked and mud-soaked boots remained exposed. They hunched deep into their saddles, their heads bowed forward, shoulders raised to protect their necks from the incessant rain. The mules they rode slogged through the mud and water, their heads lowered, looking as dejected as the humans.

Ignacio, oblivious to the monsoon, walked ahead of the pack leading a string of seven pack mules, each laden with boxes, trunks and bags secured by manila hemp tied and cross-tied to prevent slippage. The pack mules were tethered to each other in single file, nose to tail, and were moving slowly. At Colbraith's urging, and with some financial support from Mary Ellen that surprised Colbraith, Ignacio agreed to take the American couple to Panama City in place of Lowell and John. Lowell would wait for Ignacio's return from Panama City and head back to Chagres with Ignacio and Alberto on the bongo. From there he would take the first ship back to New Orleans and then a steamer up the Mississippi, the fastest way back to Kentucky.

The road was less than ten feet wide, but in some places the jungle encroached, narrowing the corridor even more. Rivulets and small streams of brown water cascaded across their path. The ancient cobblestone road, worn smooth over the years by man and nature, had been allowed to languish and stagnate for over a century. It was nearly impassable during the rainy season.

As suddenly as the rain had started it stopped. Clouds quickly dissipated, revealing a resplendent azure sky, beaming sun, and hot, sultry air swirling into pools of mist. A brief moment of absolute silence shook the men out of their lethargy only to be replaced by a cacophony of birds, monkeys, and buzzing insects. The riders removed their oilskins, shook them vigorously and stuffed them into saddlebags. Now they sat straight in their saddles and looked around as if discovering their whereabouts for the first time.

"Ignacio! How much farther?" Colbraith asked. Ignacio kept his pace but turned his shoulder and yelled: "Only two, maybe three more hours, Señor!" Satisfied, Colbraith settled back in his saddle as the mule maintained an even pace, its feet striking the cobblestones like the ticking of a metronome. He let his mind drift back to New York and Catherine, which seemed not only far away, but long ago.

Just before noon on January 16, 1849, after traveling more than seventy-five miles by bongo and mule through the unforgiving jungle, Ignacio led the travelers down the last slope and they got their first glimpse of Panama City. Panama City had, for centuries, been the great center of Spanish trade and the oldest European metropolis in the Western Hemisphere, dating back to its founding in 1519. In more recent years the city had been neglected into a general state of dilapidation. The port, bordered by a rough sea wall, was located conspicuously on a tiny peninsula that protruded into a calm bay, dotted with frond-covered isles.

Ignacio led them through the arched Gorgona Gate, with its ancient bells, and into the cobble-stoned city. Many red-tiled towers on oyster shell plastered churches competed with two- and three-story buildings of whitewashed stone or adobe along the narrow streets. Taller buildings, some reaching six stories, were on main streets, two of which intersected the city's main plaza. Long lines of balconies and sheltering verandas extended over the streets, nearly meeting in the center. Little sunshine squeezed through onto streets below, rendering them narrower than they really were. Curtains of moss and creeping vines traversed cracking walls, giving much of the city a dingy and ragged appearance as the jungle reclaimed its rightful prominence and checked the ascendancy of Spanish civilization. But the onslaught of nearly two thousand Americans, caught

Panama City

between the grip of necessity and the vise of opportunity, were spending freely at prices no Panamanian would have dreamed of. The transient Americans gave the city the appearance of a thriving metropolis.

Stores, gambling houses, an occasional stable, and restaurants occupied the lower stories. Upper floors served as living quarters and offices. In the afternoon, residents of the city sought refuge in the shelter of balconies where soft westerly breezes lessened the oppressive heat.

Ignacio led them straight into the large, open, earthen plaza. The square was filled with people and pack animals. One of his sons appeared, hitched the mules to rails, and proceeded to unpack the assorted trunks, boxes, and bags, which were in generally good order despite the rough journey across the isthmus. Colbraith withdrew a small pouch, poured out $35 in doubloons and handed them to Ignacio.

"Here's $35. You did a good job!" Colbraith never felt comfortable tipping anyone, but he liked Ignacio and Ignacio had taken good care of them. He deserved it.

"Thank you, Señor Colbraith." Ignacio then turned to Mary Ellen. "Do you know where to stay?"

"No," she acknowledged.

Colbraith remained standing nearby listening to the conversation.

"You need hotel. Too many people, Señora Price and Señor Colbraith. Is better I get hotel for you."

Ignacio walked over to a group of men squatting under one of the trees on the edge of the plaza, spoke quickly, and two of the men got up, dusted themselves and returned with Ignacio.

"These men take you to hotel. I know manager. He give you rooms."

Before Colbraith could reply, one man picked up Colbraith's baggage and the other started dragging Mary Ellen's portmanteau down Calle Esperanza. The two Americans followed them to the San Elmo Hotel, a small three-story building filled with people, mostly Americans headed for California. The manager listened to Ignacio's man, nodded his head, and told Mary Ellen and Colbraith to follow him.

Colbraith felt fortunate to find space, vacated shortly before his arrival, as he subsequently discovered, by an Argonaut who left Panama

City prematurely, his gold fever replaced suddenly by a mortal case of Panama fever. His quarters were furnished with one worn cot covered by a stained, grass-filled mattress. Privacy consisted of a single sheet of dirty linen hanging from the ceiling and separating his cot from the other twenty cots in the room. At this time, late afternoon, only a few men lay disconsolately in their cots, probably beset with some fever or another. Colbraith had second thoughts about staying in these crowded conditions, but heeded Ignacio's warning to get a room for the night and stay inside to avoid the night's *mal aria,* or bad air.

Mary Ellen fared little better. She found herself in a room with a dozen cots, each separated from the others by a canvas. She was too exhausted from the trip across the Isthmus to look carefully at the facilities. Instead she lay down and quickly fell asleep.

After securing his trunk under his cot Colbraith set out to arrange his passage from Panama City to San Francisco by the first available ship. The proprietor of the San Elmo directed Colbraith to Mr. Joshua Nelson of Messrs. Zachrisson, Nelson & Co., agents for Howland & Aspinwall, the company associated with Pacific Mail and controlling all shipping along the route from Panama City to San Francisco.

Colbraith followed the directions back to the plaza and down Avenida Real on the left for about a hundred yards. A large wooden sign with the words "ZACHRISSON, NELSON, Shipping Agents and Banking," painted in dark green over white background, was prominently displayed over the entrance to a large three-story stone building. A large American flag, draped over the railings of the second-floor balcony, wavered listlessly in the soft afternoon breeze. Inside, to the right of the entryway, a staircase led to the second floor. A smaller sign with an arrow pointing up, read: "Shipping Agents - Bank - Second Floor." Immediately to his left, through an open door, was a smoke-filled room with four tables and benches filled to capacity by several boisterous men and a few women. He stepped in, looked around and was immediately greeted by the strident sounds of different languages. The men, dressed in a rich mixture of strange clothes in styles he had never seen before, were playing Monte, each gambling with different forms of exchange, from Spanish doubloons, to gold nuggets; a scale sitting prominently at each table measured the value of the gold.

Colbraith went up the stairs to a small foyer with a long bar and several chairs. A dozen men, sweating profusely from the heat and lack of circulating air, were standing at the counter, arguing loudly.

"Mr. Nelson, we were told there would be no problem procuring tickets from here to San Francisco," said a tall, elegantly dressed man, shaking his fist violently at the man behind the counter, his face flushed in rage.

"I'm sorry, gentlemen," Mr. Nelson replied. "There is absolutely nothing I can do. You do realize there are nearly two thousand people here in the city who want to go on. Tickets were sold on a first-come, first-served basis."

This didn't satisfy the tall, silver-haired man. "The *California* arrived on Wednesday. What were those Peruvians doing on board?" he asked heatedly.

"Captain Forbes didn't have any idea so many people would be here and took them on in Peru as paying passengers."

"The hell you say. They're not even god-fearing Americans."

"Captain Forbes will move them on deck and we will make room for another three hundred passengers, but no more. As it is, we are already overbooked and overloaded," Mr. Nelson declared wearily, mopping his brow with a large white handkerchief.

"Well I'm not satisfied. This is absolutely ridiculous. Mr. Nelson, you're both U.S. Counsel and the U.S. and Pacific Mail agent, are you not?"

"I am."

"Isn't it your responsibility to take care of our passage?"

Mr. Nelson sighed, "As I said before, Mr. Gwin, we are doing the very best we can."

"And as I've said before, that's not good enough," Gwin replied acidly and turned to the other men. "I'm calling a meeting at the American Hotel for eight o'clock tonight. Gentlemen, spread the word and let's see what we need to do to resolve this matter." He turned about abruptly and stormed out of the office with the others following.

Colbraith walked up to the counter and introduced himself. "I have a letter from Howland & Aspinwall instructing you to provide me with a ticket on the *California*." He withdrew a crinkled letter from his breast pocket and handed it to Nelson. Nelson placed a pair of spectacles near the tip of his nose and read the letter. When he finished he glanced over the glasses at Colbraith, exhaled sharply and shook his head as if to say "what can I do?" and handed the letter back to Colbraith.

"Mr. O'Brien, I can't count the number of people who have letters such as yours. But my hands are tied. I just don't have enough ships at this moment, though more are expected soon."

Colbraith kept his intense look, riveting Nelson to the point of discomfort. "Are you an agent for Howland & Aspinwall?"

"Yes, I am, but . . . "

Colbraith cut him off curtly. "When I booked passage on the Benson I was assured of passage on the *California.* I was also told the ticket for first-cabin passage to San Francisco should be purchased in Panama City for $200." Then raising his voice, "And I was assured of priority over anyone from any other ship." He stopped for a long moment, but kept his gaze. "I didn't ask you if you could get me a ticket. I didn't even ask if you had space available on any other ship. Here is the $200." Colbraith removed his pouch and poured the contents on the counter.

Nelson did not move. He had received many threats in the course of the past few weeks. He kept a loaded pistol under the counter, but something about Colbraith made him uneasy, not just his size, but his menacing cold, blue eyes. Nelson had a few tickets in the office safe for very important persons, usually government officials and others, and he managed this little cache artfully, with great subtlety to line his pockets.

"Mr. O'Brien, if I may explain . . . " Colbraith waved his hand in dismissal, but Nelson continued, "We have several ships arriving shortly, the packet *Philadelphia* will offload coal next week and take on all who are unable to get aboard the *California.* If that would be acceptable . . . "

Colbraith exploded. "It's not! I don't intend to get on any sailing vessel and tack back and forth across the Pacific, ending up in Hawaii and hoping for enough wind to get me back to California. I want a steamer and only the *California* is acceptable. I'm being gouged, paying $50 per night for a miserable cot. And for what? For the opportunity of picking up Panama fever or cholera? Mr. Nelson, I'm not going to ask you again. Give me the ticket now!" The last words were barely audible, spoken in a growl.

Nelson decided to deal with Colbraith. "I may be able to get you a ticket from one of the passengers who wishes to wait for some companions arriving from Chagres, but the going rate is $1,000. Are you prepared to pay that?"

With lightning fast movement, Colbraith grabbed Nelson by the lapels of his jacket, pulled him over the counter as if he were a rag doll, his feet dangling in the air, and brought his face within inches of his own. Nelson's face registered shock. He did not struggle, but his eyes were wide open and his jaw flapping.

"$200 is all you get. Not more, not less. Is that clear?" Colbraith gently placed Nelson back on his feet. "And don't reach for the gun you have under the counter. If you do I'll shove it so far down your throat nobody will ever be able to extract it."

Nelson quickly and silently complied; nervously walking back to his desk, slowly opening his drawer, making sure his hands were clearly visible at all times, and trying his best not to provoke this man. He removed a small gray metal cash box and withdrew a ticket. He immediately placed the box back in his desk, countersigned the ticket, and handed it to Colbraith who carefully inspected the ticket, then regarded Nelson as if in the cutting silence he could read Nelson's mind.

"Is this the correct departure date?" he asked Nelson.

"Yes, she leaves tomorrow afternoon at three o'clock." Beads of perspiration gathered on Nelson's brow.

"Thank you, Mr. Nelson," Colbraith said in a perfunctory manner, then turned around and walked out.

His hands shaking uncontrollably, Nelson immediately reached for a bottle of rye under the counter, next to the worthless gun, and barely managed to uncork it.

—∞—

MARY ELLEN STIRRED FROM HER SLEEP. AS SHE OPENED HER EYES THE smell assaulted her like a tidal wave. She couldn't identify it, but it made her bile rise; she had to get out of the stuffy room. Even though it was still dark outside she had little interest in returning to her cot. She decided to find someplace to get dinner. She was grateful that she only had to stay one night in Panama City; the *California* was due to depart the following day. She had a ticket for the *California* and the personal assurance of Marie Laveau that she would have no difficulty getting on board once she arrived in Panama City. She had little doubt about Marie's promise. Mary Ellen stepped outside and was surprised by the number of Americans milling in the street. She overheard some talk of the American Hotel and decided to see if she could get a decent meal there.

The lobby of the old hotel, formerly known as the Hotel Rio Negre, now inhabited by a horde of transient Americans, was so crowded that a noisy throng—more than two hundred—were standing shoulder to shoulder outside on the cobblestone street. The men were clearly enraged. Mary Ellen realized that it could turn into a mob. The men were tense; flustered by their inability to get out of Panama City. A few women were in the crowd so Mary Ellen did not feel afraid. Rather, she realized that the men were preoccupied with getting to California. Stuck in this godforsaken land, facing exorbitant prices, a rising tide of new arrivals, and virulent diseases would have been enough to set off most men. But it sounded as if they were afraid that the gold might run out before they had their chance at it. Mary Ellen sensed that these men would fight to get aboard a ship bound for California. Suddenly she was gripped by a new fear: maybe she would not get on board the *California*

Shortly after 8:00 P.M. several men appeared at the hotel entry and moved out onto the veranda. One of the men stood on a box and yelled, "Let me have your attention! This here is his Honor W.P. Bryant, chief justice of Oregon. He's been elected president of our committee and wants to say a few words to you."

An older gentleman, tall and gaunt, took to the makeshift podium, hands held high as if by this simple action he could calm the crowd.

"General Persifor Smith is here. Like us he's on his way to San Francisco to assume command of the Pacific Division. That means California. And like us he's incensed that seventy or more Peruvians have been accommodated on the *California* in place of Americans. He has just prepared the following letter to Mr. Nelson, the Aspinwall agent, who also happens to be the acting U.S. Counsel."

Taking out some spectacles and focusing on a rumpled piece of paper he commenced to read to the crowd: "Sir: The laws of the United States inflict the penalty of fine and imprisonment on trespassers on the public lands. As nothing can be more unreasonable or unjust, than the conduct pursued by persons not citizens of the United States, who are flocking from all parts to search for and carry off gold belonging to the United States in California; and as such conduct is in direct violation of law, it will become my duty, immediately on my arrival there, to put these laws in force, to prevent their infraction in the future, by punishing with the penalties prescribed by law, on those who offend. Your cooperation is demanded!"

There was a general murmur of agreement in the crowd and some shouts to dump the Peruvians off the ship. But Bryant again called for silence and continued. "This letter was delivered to Mr. Nelson and he now assures me that everyone here will be placed on either the *California,* that departs tomorrow, or on the *Philadelphia* that will be leaving the following day."

Mary Ellen remembered Colbraith's remarks about getting on any vessel other than the *California.*

Bryant waited for the jeers and catcalls to subside, then continued. "The Peruvians have paid for their passage . . . "

Again, he was interrupted by derisive hoots and insults.

"But, Captain Forbes has notified me that they will be placed on deck and room made available in steerage for three hundred additional passengers."

This time the jeers turned to hoorays and general bedlam, some in the crowd actually started dancing and singing. As Bryant started to get off the box someone called out and asked: "How will they decide who goes on the *California* and who goes on the *Philadelphia*?" But this question and the interrogator were drowned in a raucous sea of voices expressing relief and excitement.

Mary Ellen noticed Colbraith standing at the outer fringe of the crowd, simply watching the proceedings, appearing almost disinterested. What Mary Ellen could not tell is that Colbraith did not suffer from lack of interest; on the contrary he found this event very illustrative. As a political animal he never missed an opportunity to size up a crowd or a situation, learning all that he could about the collective mentality of the men who would become the majority of Californians, his future constituency. They were very much of the same mold as the voters he dealt with in New York, particularly the low, hardworking class of semi-illiterates, who could easily be maneuvered, by money or by platitudes, into supporting his form of political order. Suddenly he burst out laughing, actually surprising some of the people who were standing next to him, and himself, when he realized how he had become just as excited at the prospects of getting to San Francisco—but for entirely different reasons.

Chapter Nine

The California

PANAMA CITY
FEBRUARY 1849

COLBRAITH, DRESSED IN LIGHT COTTON LINEN PANTS AND SHIRT, placed some cash into a belt that he tucked around his waist underneath his shirt, and armed himself with a revolver, the handle visible and easily accessible. He walked across the plaza under an overcast sky and headed toward the seawall that surrounded a small promontory lined with palm trees. Even at dawn, the coolest part of the day, the sticky air and sweltering heat made him perspire.

He gazed at the calm ocean and out to the small islands that dotted the horizon. No ships were visible. The tides in Panama Bay were treacherous and ships made the run toward the shore only at high tide. Then they would ride at anchor about three miles offshore, unable to get any closer because of rocks and shoals.

Despite the early hour people were already gathering at the bluff overlooking the Bay of Panama in anticipation of the California's arrival. It's owner, the Pacific Mail Steamship Company, extolled the two-hundred-foot wooden side-wheel steamer with two decks and two masts as the most efficient, safe, and expedient mode of transportation to San Francisco. The *California* had actually arrived the previous evening, but moored at the verdant island of Taboga, about twelve miles from Panama City, to restock its supply of coal and to fill its barrels with sweet spring water.

Colbraith wondered whether Nelson really intended to allow so many people to board the *California* and the *Philadelphia.* It did not seem possible that these two ships could indulge the desire of so many Americans to leave Panama City when there were over two thousand of them in town. Colbraith harbored no illusions about an orderly or safe boarding. Even with the endorsed ticket in his pocket, he would not rest until he was safely on board and well ensconced in his berth. Those left in Panama after the departure of these two ships were unlikely to reach California for some time to come and would be exposed, in the meantime, to disease and corrupt officials.

By eleven o'clock the tide started to turn, the clouds burned off, and the blue waters of the Pacific lapped at the sea wall, rising rapidly. By now nearly a thousand people had assembled, Mary Ellen among them, anxiously waiting for the ship's arrival.

A sharp blast of cannonade from a shore battery just north of town announced the ship's arrival and stunned the throng into a short-lived silence. Mary Ellen could see the *California* emerge from behind the leeward islands and turn toward the coast. Black puffs of smoke billowed from the tall black stacks amidship and dispersed into the azure sky. A large American flag fluttered from the stern. Colorful naval pennants and signal flags hung from the rigging. The event had all the noise, color, and pageantry of a Fourth of July parade. Plying rapidly through the blue waters, trailing a white foam wake the *California* drew nearer. Then she hove to and dropped anchors as the multitude on shore cheered.

Joshua Nelson paid no attention to the ship. Instead he and his employees nervously set up small kiosks and tables to handle the huge number of passengers and coordinate all boarding chores, from arranging a suitable number of lighters and tenders, mostly bongos, to baggage handlers and

Chapter Nine

The "California"

ticket clerks. The captain's gig brought Captain Forbes ashore, dressed smartly in his pressed white naval uniform with polished brass buttons and embroidered gold insignias and stripes. He saluted Nelson who responded with a simple nod. They sat at one of the tables and engaged in some heated discussion, their voices rising and falling like waves on the ocean. Both men looked agitated and strained.

Finally Nelson stood up, followed by Captain Forbes, and addressed the milling crowd. "Gentlemen and ladies," he coughed to clear his throat. "If I could have your attention. We must have your cooperation if the passengers are to board in a timely and orderly fashion. Boarding will commence at 2:00 P.M. sharp." Nelson's voice cracked and he stopped to mop his brow with his sopping handkerchief. "First, each ticketed passenger must present his ticket at the designated tables behind me. The tickets will be checked and, when duly confirmed, will be countersigned and dated by me. No one will be permitted to board without my countersignature. The first passengers to board will be those who hold first-cabin vouchers. Then we will board second. Steerage will be last." Nelson paused, and cleared his throat again. "Let's proceed."

People immediately started to press forward and Captain Forbes whispered urgently in Nelson's ear. Nelson called out, "Just one moment. Please. Captain Forbes has an important announcement to make!"

Captain Forbes stepped up on a small crate as if he were ascending a throne and spoke in a commanding voice: "Although the *California* was designed to carry a maximum of two hundred passengers, I've made arrangements through the good offices of Mr. Nelson to take aboard four hundred, double what we expected. Those who cannot be accommodated on this ship will leave tomorrow on the *Philadelphia* which is being converted and provisioned in Taboga as I speak."

One voice in the crowd yelled, "We didn't get this far just to go to Hawaii!"

The previous night Mary Ellen had learned that the *Philadelphia* was a schooner and she silently thanked Colbraith for his timely admonition about traveling by sailing ship to California. Like all sailboats, the *Philadelphia* could not draw a straight bead to California. Instead she would have to tack west for a considerable distance before tacking back east, so far west in fact that many boats simply continued on to Hawaii, took on new provisions, traded goods, booked additional passengers and cargo, before running with the wind back to California. It was not a short or comfortable trip. That is why Pacific Mail purchased steamers for the Panama-California route.

Captain Forbes, his face crimson, gritted his teeth in anger. "Unfortunately we can't always have all the things we want when we want them. Our company is going out of its way to satisfy you people." Nelson winced as Forbes continued at full throttle, "even those of you who didn't come here on our line and didn't purchase tickets for the onward passage in advance. We do not have to do anything more. If you are dissatisfied then make your own arrangements." Captain Forbes looked at Nelson who simply shrugged his shoulders in complete resignation. Captain Forbes, his temper still in command, looked back at the unruly throng. "Let me warn you. Anyone caught trying to board my ship without the required signatures will be subjected to immediate expulsion! You will be thrown overboard wherever we are , even if we're a hundred miles offshore. I trust that is clear!" He turned and, stout body erect, proceeded in military fashion back to his gig. He would supervise everything from the deck of the ship where no one dared to question his authority—a law unto himself.

Instantly the crowd surged forward, everyone attempting to get to the tables first. Panama City officials were also there in force to help maintain order. But the swell of people simply brushed aside the few soldiers dressed in ragged uniforms and carrying rusty weapons. The small band of troops eyed the huge gathering furtively and with apparent fear. No one wanted to interfere with so many heavily armed and distraught Americans pressing forward in an effort to get aboard. General bedlam reigned.

Colbraith had already arranged for his own lighter, stowed his trunk on board, and had it ready to take him to the *California* once boarding commenced. A countersigned ticket might assure him the right to board, but he did not want to get stuck on shore, unable to find any means of conveyance to the ship. Colbraith did not doubt for a minute that Captain Forbes would sail away at the set departure time, even if not all passengers had boarded.

Colbraith also sensed that the overcrowded and frenzied conditions on shore were ripe for a riot. He wanted to board as quickly as possible, so he elbowed and pushed his way through the crowd, using his size and brute strength, earning insults, a few threats, but above all enough room to maneuver.

Long lines had already formed and Colbraith took his place in the first cabin line close to the table. He noticed Mary Ellen standing just ahead of him. She nodded to him and he returned the salutation. Nelson's staff carefully and thoroughly inspected Mary Ellen's ticket. They checked and double-checked her name against the ship's manifest and the passenger list. Then they handed the ticket to Nelson who immediately countersigned. Mary Ellen noticed Nelson's disquietude. She looked in the direction of his gaze and saw that he was furtively looking at Colbraith. When Colbraith glared at Nelson the agent quickly and with some apprehension etched on his face quickly looked away. Nelson instructed Mary Ellen to proceed directly to the boat, not at two o'clock as publicly announced. As she stood there trying to figure out what to do next she felt a soft tap on her shoulder.

"I've chartered a lighter, Miss Price," Colbraith offered in a stiff, almost formal demeanor. "Even with the countersigned ticket there is no assurance you'll get to the ship. There's room on my lighter."

Mary Ellen hesitated for a moment and Colbraith took her delay as a rejection of his offer. He nodded his head and quickly stepped away.

Frightened, Mary Ellen called out: "Mr. O'Brien, wait please."

Colbraith stopped and turned, his face inscrutable.

"If that offer still stands I would be most thankful if I could get my portmanteau on your lighter."

"Get your baggage and I'll meet you here in thirty minutes. If you're not here at that time I'll leave."

Mary Ellen had little doubt he would be true to his word and quickly hired a man at an outrageous price to carry her trunk. She returned in time to find Colbraith anxiously waiting. His baggage had already been stowed so she proceeded to get on his lighter and together they headed for the *California*.

—~—

ONCE MARY ELLEN AND COLBRAITH WERE ON BOARD, MEMBERS OF the crew directed them past the deckhouse where the officers' quarters and galley were located. They squeezed through a narrow companionway to the first deck where the first and second cabins, stretching along the entire deck from bow to stern, were located. Staterooms along either side of the deck opened into the dining salon and other public rooms that extended down the middle of the ship. Colbraith found his cabin and entered with barely a shrug to Mary Ellen who continued along the deck until she found her cabin. There were three narrow berths in Colbraith's cabin, one above another, together with a cushioned locker that accommodated a fourth passenger. The room had a mirror, toilet stand, washbowl, water bottles and glasses. A carpet covered the floor and the berths were screened with outer damask curtains, extending from top to bottom, and inner cambric curtains.

Second-class accommodations were not apart from first cabin, but Mary Ellen noticed that the staterooms contained ten or more open berths, the only privacy being afforded by curtains between the berths.

First- and second-cabin passengers sat for meals at long tables just outside their staterooms. Between meals the passengers used these tables to socialize or for writing and reading. Long "railroad seats," with reversible backs, were fixed along either side of the tables, with racks for glasses above them.

Colbraith made himself at home. As the first passenger in the stateroom he selected and occupied the lowest berth. On the trip from New York to Chagres he discovered, to his dismay, that when the ship pitched unexpectedly, the unfortunate soul who occupied the top bunk could find himself hurled roughly to the floor—usually while asleep. He found some fresh bedding and conscripted it for himself. There were not enough sheets and pillows or blankets to go around.

Shortly after 2:00 P.M. Captain Forbes received the ship's manifest listing 364 paid passengers and a crew of thirty-six. The ship was not designed to accommodate so many passengers cramped together for three to four weeks, armed and impatient to get to California. Captain Forbes glanced at the passenger list. It included some very important persons: General Persifor Smith and his wife, heading to California to assume command of the territory; General Adair with his wife and six children, all sharing one cabin; and, Captain James Kearney. Others were notable for different reasons. Senor Villanul had boarded with fifteen Peruvians, a very unpopular group with the Americans. And there were ministers, judges, thieves, gamblers, whores, and perhaps worst of all, lawyers.

The shrill blast of the ship's whistle announced the departure. The passengers milled along the gunwales on the two decks and watched the tenders rise and fall with the waves, many still filled with frenetic individuals demanding passage, some pleading, others threatening, while the crew prevented boarding by anyone not on the manifest. A single gunshot fired at the ship by a lone disgruntled man sent some of the passengers ducking and others scurrying for cover. This man immediately earned the scorn of the others on his tender. They shoved him into the water. He rose to the surface thrashing wildly and yelling that he could not swim.

Captain Forbes called for the anchors as the steam powered engine built up pressure and the side-paddle started turning. Mary Ellen watched the scene with a mixture of dread and excitement. She could still hear snatches of jeering and yelling from the shore, borne with each gust of wind, but the voices faded as the *California* headed out of the bay and started the final leg of the journey.

Slowly the green carpet of Panama dissolved from sight, leaving only Mount Darien in view. Colbraith, like Mary Ellen, joined the first- and second-cabin passengers at the starboard rails and watched the mountains recede slowly and disappear behind the horizon. He remained at the rail, looking at the deep blue water. For the first time in many months Colbraith felt invigorated. The gentle wind and salty spray lapped at his face. Also, for the first time in many months, Colbraith dared to think that California might help him recover from his memories, though, he knew, nothing could quench his thirst for vengeance.

Feeling weary and relaxed Colbraith returned to his stateroom, lay down on the lower berth and fell into a deep sleep.

As Mary Ellen returned to her cabin she passed Colbraith's room, where the door was slightly ajar. Several men were engaged in excited conversation and Mary Ellen's curiosity got the better of her. She sat at one of the long tables next to Colbraith's room, ordered coffee from the steward, opened a book that she had in a small valise and pretended to read, but her attention was riveted to the conversation.

Colbraith stirred in his cot as voices, first disparate and dreamlike, became coherent; conversation about books and ships, laws, London, and Parks. He thought about how good it felt to sleep, but the voices persisted, more distinct and louder. Slowly he realized that they were coming from inside his cabin. He opened his eyes and saw a small man with an oversized head, leaning against the cabin door, gesticulating wildly as he talked.

Chapter Nine

"I'll never go to Europe. This is the greatest adventure on earth. Why go anywhere else?"

The other man sat on the top bunk so Colbraith could only see two legs swinging back and forth like a little child on a swing. But the man had a rich and melodious voice.

"After Harvard I needed a break. I didn't know what to do. My brother wrote some articles for the *Democratic Review* about Oregon. He also learned a great deal about California. After the Mexican War he said that if he were a young man he would go to San Francisco. He thought San Francisco had the only good harbor and would one day become a great city. He offered to pay for my trip here."

"How generous," the shorter man said.

"Yes, but I didn't follow his advice. This was three years ago; when Colonel Stevenson formed the First Regiment of New York Volunteers. My brother suggested I join them. I declined."

"You didn't miss anything. I understand that his regiments never got to fight. They've disbanded. So what did you do?"

"I went to Europe instead. To see, to feel its culture. I ended up staying in Paris and falling in love with every woman I met. I would've stayed there forever, but my father cut me off and told me to earn a living. One day I was reading the *New York Herald* in Galignani's New Room in Paris. I read President Polk's speech about the discovery of gold in California. My brother's views on San Francisco flashed into my mind and I decided to go to California. And here I am."

"So you came for the gold?" The shorter man seemed puzzled. "I thought you weren't interested in gold."

"I'm not. Gold is the lure. It'll become the focus of everything. One day California will be a major center of commerce. There'll be incredible opportunities. I want to be there right from the start. What about you?"

"You're a very lucky man. I had to go to work for my uncle, a book publisher, when I was fifteen. I've been his principal book salesman for the last three years. After Mason's report on the gold I told my uncle there would be a great market for books in California and he sent me off." The small man looked up at the upper bunk with small eyes, covered with bushy eyebrows.

"There. Exactly what I mean. You bring books. Other commodities will be required. Houses will be built. Streets will be paved. Businesses will start; the beginning of great commerce. That, my friend, is why we are so lucky. Everyone wants gold. But those who provide services and goods will prosper."

"Well, I almost lost it all before I started," the small man laughed. "Nearly lost my books at Chagres. Some native tried to take my portmanteau, found it too heavy because it was laden with books, and pushed it over accidentally spilling the books all over the wharf. I damn near fell into the water trying to save the books."

"So what are your plans in California?" the rich and melodious voice asked.

"I'll sell the books. Everyone is so preoccupied with gold, I doubt anybody has thought of reading. People always need something to read. I'll have a monopoly. I'll sell these books at high prices. If I'm successful my uncle will let me open my own publishing house."

The steward's whistle announced meal service. The man jumped from the bunk and landed in front of Colbraith. He was tall and slim, with dark curly hair and a smooth shaven, almost baby-like, face.

"Well, shall we?" he asked the small man.

"After you," he responded.

Mary Ellen watched two men exit Colbraith's room. One was short, with a large round head. The other man had a carefree expression on a thin face, but there was something arrogant about him. They headed to a table nearby and were soon engaged in more animated conversation. Mary Ellen decided not to risk anything by further eavesdropping on their conversation so she returned to her cabin to meet her new cabin mates.

Colbraith got up slowly, his legs slightly wobbly and his stomach a bit queasy. He filled the washbasin and washed his face. He was definitely not hungry. He decided to tour the *California*; he was curious about conditions down in steerage. He descended to the lower deck. It extended the entire length of the boat on both sides of the huge side-lever engine. The rank smell of bile, sickness, and sweat assailed his nose even before he reached the poorly ventilated deck. There were no rooms just hundreds of berths—each berth he estimated to be about six by one and one-half feet—in three vertical tiers, one atop the other and three across; the person having the middle berth would have to climb over his neighbors to get to his berth. The sick and healthy were packed closely together; men and women, nearly three hundred in all, crushed like sardines, in many cases two to a cot. He could not imagine this. *How could they sleep?* he wondered. He supposed they had to sleep in shifts, taking turns, one sleeping while the other stayed elsewhere on the deck; but the deck was already packed to the railing. And if two were in the cot at the same time they would be unable to change positions, unless they were contortionists. Three weeks of hell. Colbraith shook his head at the sight of so many people without a shred of privacy, many probably too seasick to get to the ship's rails. It was hell! The more he looked at the crowded deck the more he was sure about his intuition that life in California would not be easy or comfortable. He did not empathize with these people since he attributed their willingness to endure such miserable conditions to greed—the lust for gold. These people, and so many others like them, all streaming into California as fast as their dreams and money would allow, in his view, were ripe for manipulation—and would be the underpinnings of his success.

Revolted by the conditions, Colbraith returned to the less congested and more airy upper deck as quickly as his feet could move, but the image of steerage would remain in his mind forever. He sat at one of the long tables and asked a steward for a slice of dark brown bread and hot black coffee. He pondered how life could change so drastically in a moment of time and how much hardship people would tolerate just to pursue a dream. Colbraith went back to his cabin and found it fully occupied. The others introduced themselves.

The short, affable man spoke first. "I'm Henry Croft," he said. "And this is Stephen Field."

"How do you do?" Field extended his hand in a friendly, but reserved manner.

"Colbraith O'Brien," Colbraith said and shook each man's hand.

Upon hearing Colbraith's name Field's eyes narrowed a bit, giving him a snake-like appearance.

"Didn't you run for Congress in New York?" he inquired.

"Yes, I did," Colbraith answered reluctantly.

"I voted for you," Field continued. "Damn shame you lost. What a sham."

Colbraith's tension eased a bit.

"A good friend of my family, Colonel J.D. Stevenson, suggested we vote for you. He said you would make an excellent congressman."

"Ah, yes. Colonel Stevenson," Colbraith mused. "A good friend. He's in San Francisco now."

"That's what I heard," Field said. "After the First Regiment disbanded he moved from Santa Barbara to San Francisco. He wrote a letter to my brother telling him San Francisco is the place to be."

"He's the first person I intend to contact when I arrive," Colbraith said. One of his officers returned to New York with a message from Colonel Stevenson describing California and San Francisco in glowing terms. A clear and unmistakable message for Colbraith.

"Do you have his address by any chance?" Field inquired.

"In fact I do," Colbraith said.

"Good. If you wouldn't mind giving it to me. I plan to pay him a visit as well," Field said.

"It's a small, strange world we live in," Croft interjected. "I'm eagerly looking forward to our arrival."

Colbraith removed a small packet of notes from his portmanteau and found Stevenson's address. Field copied the address and Colbraith noticed his fluid handwriting. Field obviously came from an advantaged, upper-class background with an exceedingly good education. His dress, his manner, his writing, all spelled wealth, and a sense of confidence that came from wealth. A different type of self-assurance from the one Colbraith had painstakingly developed. If Field had a care in the world it did not show. In contrast, Colbraith almost felt naked, as if his doubts and uncertainties were transparent and obvious.

How strange, Colbraith thought, that neither of his two cabin mates were bound for California by the lure or lust for gold. Croft, open and plain, had one goal in life—to start a publishing company. Field was different, more complex, and certainly not as friendly and talkative as he appeared. In some ways Field reminded Colbraith of the aristocracy in Albany. The man was as slippery as an eel.

A third man, who had been lying in the cushioned locker during this conversation, got up and tried to straighten his crumpled and sweat-stained clothes.

"I'm Alister Frost." He spoke with an English accent. The others introduced themselves, but Frost did not seem to be interested in engaging in any further conversation. He simply shook hands with the others, his grip limp and his hand drenched in a cold damp sweat. Perhaps the most notable feature, Colbraith thought, was Frost's inability or unwillingness to make eye contact, as he tugged and brushed at his clothing. Colbraith could not tell if Frost was shy and introverted or simply unfriendly; he made little effort to converse with the others and answered the few questions directed at him with simple, brief responses, then returned to his berth. Colbraith, Croft, and Field exchanged questioning glances.

Colbraith turned in with his revolver tucked under the pillow. He lay facing the open porthole. A gentle breeze cleared the small cubicle of all odors, particularly the smell of the mildewed carpet. The ship's paddle-wheel kept a steady cadence. Outside, on deck, someone played a guitar and sang a romantic and melodious ballad. Unable to sleep, Colbraith thought about San Francisco, but his thoughts were interrupted by images of New York and Catherine. If he had one regret in his life other than the loss of his brother, it was his inability to tell her how sorry he was, how his own best friend had double-crossed him and worked behind his back to keep them apart. He shivered, unable to dispel the dark and turbulent thoughts that pressed on his mind.

The next few days were sanguine. The ship winged through a glassy sea with crystal clear blue water. Porpoises frolicked alongside, displaying phenomenal speed and agility, and seemed to be laughing at the plodding, noisy, ungainly ship. The tranquil ocean had a soothing effect on the passengers as the chaotic days of Panama, like the land itself, receded. People became congenial and relaxed, and shipboard friendships sprouted with ease.

Despite ever-present rumors of illness and mutiny from the crammed passengers in steerage, no major problems arose. They slept on deck, attaching hammocks to the rigging or simply found space between spars and ropes. Only those still too ill remained confined in their cots. Most of the passengers who had been seasick at the start of the voyage thanked the placid waters that made it possible for them to recover. A cautious optimism prevailed throughout the ship.

The *California* kept within sight of land, a green strip along the starboard horizon. Mary Ellen passed her time on the upper deck, most often reading, or simply whiling the time away, lost in thought about the people who had influenced her life, especially Americus, Abigail, and her mother. She noted how others engaged in philosophical and political debates, oftentimes pitting northerners against those who originated in the South. She listened to the songs and music of one impromptu trio, made up of a three-stringed guitar, an accordion, and an old fiddle; the songs a mixture of the old and new, including many new ditties about California and gold. Though congenial, she kept pretty much to herself. She did not join in extended conversations. She watched some of the bolder women as they joined in song and dance with men on deck, but she had nothing in common with these women. Instead she simply remained standing or sitting near the railing, watching the others.

Passengers formed groups or associations, Mary Ellen noted, for a variety of reasons and engaged in different activities, from Bible study to formulating the rules that would govern passenger behavior. One group, concerned with profanity aboard, circulated a petition more out of boredom than of interest in the subject matter:

> Ship *California*, 1849
>
> Feeling that profane and indecent language is both wrong and ungentlemanly, without excuse and deserving no indulgence and alike contrary to the precepts of morality and good breeding; and believing also that from association or concert of action comes strength of resistance against pernicious habits, therefore,
>
> We, the undersigned do *agree* as gentlemen, that during the

> present voyage to California, we will not on any pretext whatsoever, indulge in profanity or vulgarity; and that furthermore should we at any time be found so far forgetful of ourselves and what is due to us as gentlemen, as to use any of the interdicted expressions, we will not take offense when called upon to answer by any one of the undersigned.

A lawyer drafted the paper and thirty-three male passengers, including Colbraith, signed it. Mary Ellen never learned why the resolution excluded female passengers.

—~—

THE PASSENGERS GREETED CAPTAIN FORBES'S ANNOUNCEMENT THAT the *California* would pay a call to the port of Acapulco in three days with great enthusiasm. The ship needed to replenish its depleted supply of provisions, including coal and water. The passengers needed a brief respite from the crowded ship. Unlike the majority of his shipmates, Colbraith did not care. He would have preferred to continue without any interruption. By now everyone had fallen into a daily routine. When the captain made his announcement, Colbraith was sitting at his usual seat at the long railroad table, reading a book. He heard a commotion not too far away. Turning around he saw a small crowd of passengers surrounding and besieging the first mate. They spoke animatedly and gesticulated wildly.

"It's been stolen, I tell you," one man said indignantly. "I had the wallet in my cabin, in my portmanteau."

Another passenger exclaimed heatedly, "That's right. I'm missing some of my money. Just like I told Captain Forbes yesterday."

"You will have to file a formal complaint, as I explained," the first mate responded.

"We don't need formal complaints. We need you to do something," the man lamented. "I need that money for San Francisco!"

"You'll have to take that up with Captain Forbes," the first mate repeated, then told a sailor to get the captain.

The crowd continued to grow surly and a few minutes later Captain Forbes made his way through the throng. He listened to the heated complaints. Several passengers had been robbed of valuable possessions, usually small items of considerable value, like a wallet containing expensive jewels, or money or gold.

"Look," the captain yelled, "let's all calm down. I can't listen to all of you speaking at once."

But the irate passengers demanded immediate action and exhorted Captain Forbes to find and punish the thief.

Colbraith noticed a thin man with flaxen hair and light blue eyes, dressed in well-tailored clothes, pushing his way through the crowd toward Captain Forbes.

"Captain, I'm Thomas Brand," the man spoke with a Scottish brogue. "You must do something! My doubloons have been stolen. There's a bloody degenerate among us. I want my valuables back. Do whatever is required. Search everyone. Let's find the bugger."

Captain Forbes looked at Brand with some annoyance and astonishment. "Sir, are you suggesting that the ship's crew search every passenger on board this ship?"

"Yes, I am," he answered heatedly. "If that's what it takes."

"And this would include a search of each person's baggage as well?" Forbes mercurial temper went up one more notch.

"Yes," Brand answered, but with less assurance in the face of Forbes's glare.

"And you would be able to tell your doubloons from someone else's doubloons?" The captain exploded.

Brand did not answer.

"Well," the captain scoffed, "that's preposterous. Out of the question. It's a physical impossibility. My god, men," Forbes looked at the crowd imperiously, "don't you realize that there're nearly four hundred passengers on board. And there is the small matter of operating this ship to insure your safe passage. Even if we searched everyone on board there's no assurance the stolen items could be recovered, even if they are identified. And if the thief is so clever, he will have stowed his cache somewhere."

Chapter Nine

As Captain Forbes addressed the crowd Colbraith noticed Mary Ellen push her way toward Forbes.

Forbes continued, "So I suggest that it's the responsibility of each of you to protect your own possessions."

Mary Ellen smiled at the captain and said, "That won't be necessary, captain."

Her statement caused a stir, like the buzz of a beehive. Colbraith noticed that Forbes seemed reluctant to look directly at her. Perhaps, Colbraith thought, it was her eyes. He also noticed for the first time how her delicate features were complemented by a confident bearing and a dusky, almost exotic, complexion. *Strange,* he thought, *it hasn't occurred to me before. She's uncommonly beautiful.*

"And you are?" Forbes asked.

"Mary Ellen Price," she answered.

"Ah, yes, Miss Price. What light can you shed on this?" the captain asked dubiously.

"I saw a man emerge from one of the cabins yesterday . . . "

The captain interrupted her in mid-sentence: "I don't see what that has to do with anything."

She smiled benignly and said: "If you would please allow me to finish you might see much better." The captain clenched his jaws, waited for some catcalls to subside, and glared at Mary Ellen.

"The man came out of one cabin yesterday looking furtive," she continued unfazed. "Today I saw the same man emerge from two different cabins, again with the same devious look. When he saw me he quickly turned away and headed for the opposite companionway."

"That's hardly any reason to suspect him. He could have been visiting other people," the captain countered.

"No. I know he's your man."

"How can you be so certain, Miss Price?" the captain asked doubtfully.

"Woman's intuition, captain," she said evenly.

"Bah! You expect me to confront someone merely on a woman's intuition?" he asked incredulously.

The crowd pressed in and a murmur rose. "She's right!" one man insisted. "Her suggestion is better than no action," another yelled. "Let's find the culprit." "The woman's right!" The crowd picked up the chorus.

Captain Forbes raised his hands to quiet them and addressed Mary Ellen. "Well, now suppose you're right, could you identify the man?" he inquired, his voice dripping with sarcasm.

"Yes!" she answered evenly, smiling at the captain.

"Madame, since you appear so certain of yourself, where would you suggest we start?" the captain asked in a patronizing tone. "Would you like to go through steerage first? Perhaps our robber is on cabin deck, lying on his cot in a first class cabin. I'll send along one of the crew to assist you."

Mary Ellen's eyes blazed for a brief moment and Colbraith held his breath, expecting her to respond to Captain Forbes's rudeness. But like a panther sheathing her powerful claws, Mary Ellen quickly masked her anger and again smiled benignly.

"No, captain, that won't be necessary. You see, his clothing, quite expensive I would think, would suggest you start with the cabins first. If you want my help, do let me know. I'm in cabin 12." She smiled, this time clearly disingenuously at the captain, abruptly wheeled around and walked through the silent crowd.

Thomas Brand broke the spell, his anger obvious. "Captain, we are holding you and this shipping line responsible. If that lady is correct, and could identify the culprit, but you choose to ignore this matter, then, sir, you will pay."

Captain Forbes's ruddy face turned crimson. Other members of the crowd clearly supported Brand's comments and soon Captain Forbes found himself besieged on his own ship. He turned to Brand, as if he were the catalyst for the mob, brought his face close to Brand's and hissed. "This is my ship, sir! I am the captain! You will do as I say, not the other way around! And I suggest you watch your tongue!" He spun around took a few steps, stopped and turned abruptly toward Brand again. "And if you lost something, you go find it. You find the culprit and bring him to me. And if you do, then I will take appropriate action." Without another word Forbes thrust his way through the crowd, which parted like the Red Sea.

Chapter Nine

Brand, fighting for self-control, held his tongue, but his eyes blazed hatred at the retreating captain. Some of the other victims immediately surrounded Brand and soon the group headed, as Colbraith suspected, to cabin 12. He followed out of curiosity.

Brand knocked on the door and Mary Ellen opened the door slightly. "I'm sorry to disturb you, Madam," he said. "But it appears our captain is too busy to take any interest in his passengers' welfare."

"Yes," she said.

"Would you mind coming with us. We will escort you through the deck. We will go into each cabin until we find this man. If you identify him and we catch him you will have done a great service to all aboard this ship."

"All right, I'll help you," she said hesitantly. Colbraith noted how Thomas Brand regarded Mary Ellen as if she had placed him under a spell. Colbraith understood. Under different circumstances and different times he might have been willing to place himself under her spell as well, but after Catherine he vowed never to let his emotions interfere with his future, at least not until he achieved his goals.

Thomas Brand stepped aside as Mary Ellen stepped out of her cabin.

"My name is Thomas Brand," he said.

"A pleasure to meet you," she said and looked directly into the Scot's gleaming blue eyes.

The others stood behind Brand, not quite certain how to deal with this enigmatic woman. But Thomas Brand took her arm and escorted her towards cabin 1.

At this point Colbraith decided to retire to his cabin. He doubted that anything would come out of their efforts to locate the thief. When Colbraith tried to open the door to his stateroom, it seemed to be locked or wedged. He knocked several times, but heard no response. Finally, he put his weight against the door and pushed hard. It gave way. As he stepped inside he found Frost leaning over the locker, closing one of his bags quickly and sliding it deep into the locker. Frost's forehead glistened from perspiration and his shirt, under his arms, was sopping wet. Frost mopped his brow with a stained handkerchief, nodded to Colbraith in a perfunctory manner and lay down in the locker facing the wall. Colbraith looked at the door and noticed a small jam on the floor.

Colbraith watched Frost, breathing heavily, his body rising and falling rapidly, as if he had just performed some difficult physical work. Even the position of Frost's body seemed unnatural and too rigid for someone lying on his side. Finally, Colbraith stretched out on his berth with his hands folded under his head and stared at the cot above him; but he did not feel tired anymore.

A few minutes later someone knocked loudly on the door. Frost made no move to answer, so Colbraith got up and opened the door. Brand stepped in followed by Mary Ellen. Mary Ellen recognized Colbraith and smiled. "I'm very sorry to bother you, Mr. O'Brien, but we have a small emergency."

"Yes. I heard," Colbraith replied and noticed Mary Ellen staring at Frost, who had his back to her. She tensed, then looked at Brand who noticed her expression.

"That's him?" Brand whispered incredulously.

"Yes," she replied.

"But how can you be sure? You haven't seen his face!"

Frost had not moved a muscle and still faced away from them.

"I can tell. It's definitely him!" She spoke with conviction and authority.

Brand tapped Frost on the shoulder. "May we talk to you, sir?" Frost did not budge. Brand shook Frost's shoulder. Frost leaped out of his locker with surprising speed and agility and stabbed Brand in the chest with a dagger he held in his right hand. Brand had turned aside at the last second, but the knife cut deep, nearly to the hilt. Colbraith, without a second's hesitation, grabbed Frost's arm and twisted it roughly. Frost grunted and released the knife which remained imbedded in Brand's chest. Frost threw a punch at Colbraith, but Colbraith deflected his arm and grabbed Frost's fist in midair. Colbraith now held Frost's arms in a tight grip. Frost kicked viciously, missing Colbraith's groin but catching Colbraith in the shin. The pain shot through Colbraith's body like lightning. Frost pulled his fist free and tried to punch Colbraith again.

The others standing in the doorway sounded the alarm, calling for the ship's crew. The close quarters of the cabin made it impossible for anyone else to enter or intercede. Brand had collapsed to the floor clutching the knife in his chest and staring at it with bewilderment. Mary Ellen immediately bent over him. Colbraith gritted his teeth to steel against the pain and roughly turned Frost around and grabbed him by the hair. Frost twisted and fought as if he were twice his size. Colbraith could barely hold him.

Noticing the metal washbowl on the toilet stand next to him, Colbraith let go of Frost's hair and grabbed the washbowl. Frost spun around but Colbraith slammed the bowl in his face, then continued to hit Frost in the face with the bowl, putting as much force as he could into the blows, until Frost stumbled down. Colbraith dropped the bowl but Frost came up roaring again, his face bloody and torn, his eyes crazed. He rushed at Colbraith. Colbraith lowered his shoulder and thrust it hard into Frost's midsection. Frost doubled up, bent over Colbraith's shoulder like a sack. Colbraith rammed Frost against an adjoining ship post. The crushing blow knocked the wind out of Frost's lungs and he crumpled to the floor like a shapeless heap of clothing.

Colbraith stood over Frost, waiting to see if he would get up again. Colbraith looked over at Brand. "Get the ship's doctor here now!" Colbraith yelled.

"Take him to my cabin," Mary Ellen insisted, "and I'll care for his wound until the doctor arrives."

They carried Brand, a senseless and stunned look on his face, his lips curled in shock, face ashen, to cabin 12.

Colbraith ordered several men to hold Frost, then pulled out the bag from Frost's locker, the one he saw Frost conceal. He emptied the contents over the cot, and watched in amazement as jewels, gold, coins, and other valuable objects, a treasure trove of wealth, spilled out. *What a moronic animal,* Colbraith thought, as he looked at Frost. Being a thief was bad enough, but to stab someone without any opportunity of escaping exhibited either mindless violence or mind-boggling stupidity.

Captain Forbes entered the room with two armed crew members. Without a word two sailors hog-bound Frost by his legs and hands, hoisted him up, and removed him from the cabin. His eyes were wild, and spittle mixed with blood covered his mouth.

"Thank you, Mr. O'Brien," the captain said. "Mr. Nelson told me about you. I think the thief selected the wrong cabin mate."

"Perhaps you should thank Miss Price for identifying the sodden thief," Colbraith suggested.

Captain Forbes grinned. "Perhaps, Mr. O'Brien, perhaps." Then he ordered another crew member to clean up the blood and help rearrange everything, after which he was to bring all of Mr. Frosts possessions to the forecastle.

Before Captain Forbes left, Colbraith asked him, "What will you do with Frost? He attempted to murder Mr. Brand."

"We don't have a brig on board, so I'll drop him off shortly before we arrive in Acapulco."

"And how shortly would that be?" Colbraith inquired.

"Probably ten miles short," Captain Forbes smiled maliciously. "Not a bad swim. He might even make it, but he'll have another problem."

"What's that?" Colbraith asked.

"Those are shark infested waters, Mr. O'Brien." Captain Forbes's grin faded as he walked out.

THE *CALIFORNIA*'S DOCTOR RUSHED FROM THE FORECASTLE TO THE upper deck and found the door to cabin 12 ajar with several people peering into the small compartment. He pressed his way through and found Thomas Brand lying on a berth with Mary Ellen nursing his wound, carefully washing the area around the hilt of a knife jutting out of Brand's chest. She moved aside and let the doctor examine the injury.

"It's a nasty one," he said to her.

The doctor spoke quietly to one of the sailors who immediately departed. The doctor turned to the woman. "I suggest you step outside."

"No. I prefer to remain here. I've seen much worse," she lied.

The doctor called upon another sailor to hold Brand's arms, then he grasped the hilt of the knife and pulled it out slowly, as if he were repairing the wound by removing the knife. Brand groaned, then screamed.

Mary Ellen felt the bile rising in her throat, but kept her eye on Brand.

Blood started to ooze out of the wound and the doctor immediately wiped it away with a bloody rag. "I see no evidence that any major blood vessels are affected, but there could be considerable internal bleeding," he said.

"Could it have penetrated his lungs?" she asked.

"It's doubtful. If it had we would see more signs of the damage. He seems to be breathing all right. But the blade might have penetrated his abdominal cavity and damaged some internal organs. My greatest concern is internal bleeding and infection."

The doctor probed the wound as Brand groaned loudly in pain.

"Get him something strong to drink," the doctor ordered.

A passenger standing at the door immediately drew a small flask from his jacket and handed it Mary Ellen. She carefully raised Brand's head and poured some of the drink into his mouth.

"Not too much," the doctor cautioned her.

Mary Ellen helped Brand sip some more whiskey as the doctor continued with his examination.

The doctor called for a heated iron and a sailor returned shortly with an iron, its tip red hot. The doctor worked quickly. He called another sailor to help hold Brand down, then he applied the iron to the wound and cauterized it. The smell of burning flesh permeated the room, causing some of those who remained standing at the doorway to gag and depart. Mary Ellen remained still and watchful.

"His abdominal muscle is cut but it doesn't seem to go any deeper, though it's nearly impossible to tell for sure. He should be kept very quiet and someone has to watch out for any signs of fever." He dressed the wound carefully and closed his bag. He handed a bottle of laudanum to Mary Ellen and said, "I prefer not to move him right now. You seem to have some nursing experience. Until we can arrange for a change of quarters for you perhaps you could care for him. I'll come back to see him this afternoon to change his dressing. Give him one tablespoon of this every four hours." The doctor looked at his patient who now exhibited the first effects from the alcohol.

As the doctor left he asked the other passengers to let the patient rest. Begrudgingly they closed the door, leaving Thomas Brand and Mary Ellen alone.

She looked at Brand, his blue eyes dancing but unfocused. He tried to sit up but gasped at the pain. He tried to laugh but began to cough harshly. He almost doubled up as the pain shot through his abdomen. "Oh," he groaned. "That hurts!" Mary Ellen sat next to him and wiped perspiration from his brow. He smiled and said: "Say, you're, you're a beau . . . beautiful lass . . . ," he slurred the words, which accentuated his Scottish brogue. He tried again, "You're quite love . . . very lovely." He smiled at his success.

Mary Ellen ignored his comment. She would care for him but had no interest whatsoever in getting involved with him or anyone else. She heard him repeating the word "beautiful" but each time it came out softer and finally a faint whisper. Brand was sound asleep, his face calm. She wondered why she had brought so much attention to herself—a foolish thing to do. Now she had obligated herself to care for someone she did not know and did not really care much about.

—~—

BY LATE EVENING PERSPIRATION SOAKED BRAND'S BODY, HIS FOREHEAD burned and he spoke incoherently in delirium. The infection had set in quickly and the doctor expressed concern about Brand's ability to recover. Mary Ellen made arrangements to have Brand remain in the room with her, which she understood would be the source of considerable gossip, regardless of the circumstances. The captain arranged for the other women in her compartment to exchange a cabin with three men who agreed to sleep in hammocks on deck for the night. But it turned out to be three nights. Mary Ellen remained on watch, changing Brand's dressing, giving him the medication prescribed by the doctor, and placing cold compresses on his forehead to fight the fever. Even Captain Forbes expressed his appreciation for the manner in which Mary Ellen committed herself and worked ceaselessly to nurse Brand back to health. Captain Forbes made it clear to her that he did not think all that highly of Brand. When Captain Forbes looked at her with what she regarded as a curious expression she wondered whether he thought the same thing she did: why did she do it?

Approximately three hours before the *California* arrived in Acapulco, Alister Frost, pinioned between two swarthy sailors, was brought on deck kicking, spitting, and haranguing passengers, crew, and everyone or everything else he could think of. The burly sailors placed him upright on the rail. He tried to balance himself and leaned backward to avoid falling overboard, but at Captain Forbes's command, the sailors pressed a long pole into the small of Frost's back and hurled him into the drink. The passengers who lined the ship's rails returned Frost's invective, jeering and commending him for his willingness to swim with the sharks. Some pundits claimed that Captain Forbes only threw him overboard to kill the sharks who would feast on his poisonous and filthy body. Frost's head, bobbing up and down in the roiling waves, slowly disappeared from view as the hulk of the *California* pressed on toward Acapulco.

In port, as provisions were loaded aboard, the passengers were given the day ashore as respite from the now monotonous cruise. Preoccupied with their excursion ashore the passengers quickly forgot about Mary Ellen, Brand, and Frost, and concentrated on exploring this small Mexican outpost. The short respite in Acapulco, and one more day ashore at Mazatlan, were the last days of leave before taking the long and final leg directly to San Francisco.

As they proceeded north the weather slowly but inexorably changed from the heat of Panama, to the mild semi-tropical climate of Baja California, and finally to the winter cold and rains of California. The passengers settled themselves in the shelter of the decks as the rough seas and seasonal monsoons struck with a fury. Thomas Brand lingered near death for nearly two days before the fever broke. Twice he woke from his comatose state, smiled wanly at Mary Ellen, muttered a few words about her beauty, then lapsed back into the depth of his delirium. Mary Ellen, exhausted beyond normal limits of endurance, remained by his side, aided from time to time by the ship's doctor, and slowly nursed him back to health. On the fourth day he moved back into his cabin and Mary Ellen inherited her two female roommates who came back wearing curiosity on their smiling faces.

It took Brand nearly another whole week to regain enough strength to move around the first deck. Mary Ellen did not visit him and made a concerted effort to avoid any further contact with him. She slept for two days without a meal. When she woke up she felt renewed. Her impromptu conduct, she realized, brought her too much attention. She decided that it would be best if she were not seen in public for the remainder of the voyage, as if this could somehow erase any notoriety she may have achieved by her precipitous action. She paid a steward some money and arranged to have her meals brought into her cabin. The women who shared her cabin did not protest, though she could tell they were very curious about everything she did.

The other passengers were now so preoccupied with their arrival in California, they paid Mary Ellen little heed and seemed to have forgotten the incident; everyone, that is, except Thomas Brand. He continued with his efforts to see her and to talk to her.

On the twenty-fourth of February the *California* rounded the south point of the Monterey headlands. The first mate notified Captain Forbes that they did not have enough coal to reach San Francisco. Captain Forbes decided to make an unscheduled stop at Monterey, which for years had served as the principal Mexican outpost in California.

When the passengers learned of this unexpected stop the excitement built up to a pitch fever as they scrambled and tripped over each other in a mad rush to see California. Every part of the *California* from which a view of the golden land could be seen was crowded with excited passengers curious to see the California of their dreams for the first time. Colbraith, standing at the congested forecastle deck, found the scene reminiscent of Chagres, only this time he too felt the thrilling moment as the ship approached the green shore dotted with white adobe structures.

The *California* skimmed into the bay and approached the rocky shore. Cheers and excited shouts went up from the deck at the sight of the

American flag, visible through the dim mist, fluttering from a tall pole on shore. Then a bright orange flash, followed by a small cloud of smoke and the roar of a cannon, boomed across the waters. This sequence was repeated over and over as the shore batteries provided the ship with a welcoming eighteen gun salute. Men, women, and children on shore ran to the wharf waving their arms, and watched the ship's arrival. Sailors and passengers on a brig anchored nearby, showing Peruvian colors, also waved and cheered wildly.

On signal from Captain Forbes, the *California*'s engine stopped and the side-wheel stopped turning, allowing the ship to drift towards the wharf on its own momentum. A hush fell over the ship as the passengers watched until the anchors were lowered and set. Occasionally they heard the jubilation from the shore, carried by the wind. The *California*'s passengers spontaneously returned the acclamation with an orchestrated cheer. The people ashore and those on the Peruvian brig responded in kind. The cheers went skipping back and forth across the waters nine times and everyone participated, even Colbraith's deep-throated voice joined in the din.

When they docked, one of the town officials informed Captain Forbes that a delivery of coal was not expected for another week and the coal hampers were empty. Captain Forbes immediately ordered his crew to cut between twenty-five to thirty cords from the oak woodlands nearby. Some of the passengers, mostly young men with little baggage and impatient to get to the gold fields, received permission to disembark. They immediately set off for Sutter's Fort, impervious to everything around them and thinking only of gold. If someone had fallen overboard these men would not have noticed it and, if they had, would not have done a thing about it. Gold fever, Colbraith mused, was aptly named and just as likely to kill you as any other fever, perhaps even more so.

As soon as the crew completed loading the wood on board, the ringing of the bell and steam whistle reminded the passengers still on shore to reboard. While piling the wood next to the boiler the bosun's mate looked under a tarp and found an additional supply of coal—enough to get the ship to San Francisco. Captain Forbes fumed at the time lost in making the unnecessary call to port. Colbraith noticed a change in the crew's attitude and behavior. They became more insolent and less responsive. Even Captain Forbes had a difficult time controlling the recalcitrant crew. As the ship steamed north of Monterey the crew evidently could think of only one thing—gold. They acted furtively and ignored their duties.

An alarmed Captain Forbes warned the crew. All of them had signed up for a two-year hitch and were essential to the proper operation and maintenance of the ship and its equipment. The Pacific Mail company chose most of them and trained them at great expense in their respective fields of specialization in the new ship's operations and procedures. They were irreplaceable. If any of them jumped ship, Captain Forbes remonstrated, he would have them arrested for breach of their papers and cast in irons on the return to Panama.

Confusion and apprehension reigned among passengers and crew. Colbraith watched black rain clouds forming far on the horizon and moving rapidly toward the *California.* He wondered if they were a sign of trouble when the ship reached San Francisco.

Chapter Ten

The Arrival

SAN FRANCISCO
FEBRUARY 25, 1849

Dawn broke over menacing dark clouds and an angry black sea. The *California*'s bow plunged into the rifts between large rolling waves, then surged upward only to cleave through the foaming crests and descend again. The side-lever engine, immune to the elements, pulsated as the ship fought the surge, the swells, and the powerful gusts. Wave after wave pounded the ship as if the gods were intent on preventing more people from flooding into California and looting the earth's treasures. Staggering and pitching, the *California* stubbornly forged ahead, rounding Clark's Point and bearing for Golden Gate, the narrow entrance to the bay of San Francisco.

After so many weeks at sea the passengers paid little attention to the ship's struggle. The closer they got to their destination the more impatient they became. The men, and the few women, packed their gear—gold mining equipment, retorts, crucibles, pickaxes, shovels, and tin-pans—in separate bags then filed along crowded companionways to the deck, like a

San Francisco in 1849

long line of ants. They wanted their equipment accessible, so as to be first to go ashore, as if the loss of a few minutes could impinge on their success. With few jaded exceptions, everyone expected to find lots of gold and find it quickly.

The decks of the *California* resembled an arsenal. Published reports of Indian raids, wild beasts—especially the huge bears—and gold thieves compelled many to equip themselves with every available means of defense. Guns, pistols, rifles, clubs, Bowie-knives, powder flasks, and assorted swords, either resting among pieces of baggage or carried openly by the excited passengers, bore a clear and unmistakable message: don't tread on me.

Mary Ellen packed her trunk and paid one of the sailors to bring it up to the gunwales. She watched, both fascinated and horrified as the land swept slowly by. The turbulent gray ocean reflected the dark nimbus clouds lying low over the bay and completely obscuring the surrounding hills. Hundreds of horses and cattle fed on the gentle, treeless slopes, an austere and forbidding landscape, unlike any coastline Mary Ellen had ever seen or expected to see.

As the ship passed through the Golden Gate, Mary Ellen overheard Generals Persifor Smith and Adair discuss the U.S. Naval squadron that lay near the shore at Sausalito: the *Ohio, Portsmouth, St. Mary Crane, Dale* and *Warren.* General Smith expected Commodore Jones to order a general salute from the vessels. As if on cue the cannons of the warships fired simultaneously, rolling like thunder across the open water, echoing seconds later off the distant mountains. The ear-shattering power of so many cannon firing at one time was chilling.

With the Golden Gate now behind them, the pounding waves gave way to a light chop whipped into small white crests by the blowing wind. Several islands dotted the bay. A thick forest covered the largest one, on the port side. The closer island looked like a large rock dumped haphazardly by whatever sea god inhabited these uninviting waters.

The ship slowed to a few knots. San Francisco appeared on the starboard side, perched on a long mud flat reaching from the shore to the heights above. A small flotilla of ships lay near the distant shore, almost on the beach, their masts swaying gently.

Captain Forbes let the *California* drift with the tide and ordered the boatswain to lower the anchors. The ship slipped alee as it tugged against the chains.

Unlike picturesque Monterey with quaint white adobe and red tiled cottages, the ramshackle shacks and tents that littered the hills of San Francisco were drab and unsightly. The people lining the shore of Yerba Buena Cove, waiting to greet the ship, reflected the same disagreeable quality. They did not cheer. They did not wave. They watched the ship with grim, appraising faces. This reception had an immediate and sobering effect on the passengers. For the first time during the voyage they seemed uncertain and apprehensive. Strained faces gazed at the reality of what had been their dream for months; San Francisco did not resemble anything they had expected. They drifted closer to the nearly thirty vessels that lay next to the shore, their tall masts and rigging in disarray, without canvas or soul in sight. Word spread quickly that these ghost ships had been deserted by both passengers and crew scrambling over each other in their haste to reach the gold fields. Some of the ships were only a few feet from the sandy shore.

His white uniform and gold buttons shining like a beacon of light in stark contrast to the grey all around, Captain Forbes stood on the bridge, picked up a megaphone and bellowed: "Ladies and Gentlemen. Welcome to San Francisco."

The passengers craned their heads toward him. Although he stood military erect, he grinned. "This calls for a celebration. I've asked the cook to break out some of our special delicacies." Like a dying ember brought back to life by a fresh wind, the spark of excitement returned to the passengers.

"We'll be disembarking shortly, after the Pacific Mail Agent arrives," the captain explained. Some people started to protest, but Captain Forbes pointed to boats putting out from the beach and heading to meet the *California*. "As you see they will arrive shortly." Meanwhile little sugar cakes were passed around and the passengers ate them absent-mindedly while they waited. Captain Forbes's ebullience did not last long; four hundred passengers fighting to disembark and only a few boats were arriving from shore. He turned to his first mate and said, "Employ the lifeboats." Even with all the lifeboats making several trips, it would be evening before all the passengers landed; assuming the crew did not abandon the ship and bolt for the hills.

Many of the boats nearing the *California* had only one operator. The crew quickly set about to help secure these small vessels to the side of the ship, allowing their occupants to board. One man stood on his rolling boat, legs apart for balance, and held up a sign,"Blake's Auction House." He yelled: "Captain, what's the merchandise aboard?"

"Come aboard and see for yourself," Captain Forbes replied

The passengers had assumed these men were porters for their baggage. They were not. Some were merchants, others were employers seeking carpenters, blacksmiths, clerks, cooks, waiters, and offering to pay what seemed to be outrageous prices for day labor. A day's wages in San Francisco equaled one week or even one month's salary in New York.

Chapter Ten

Others coming aboard were commission merchants trying to purchase whatever merchandise the *California* carried. Soon the stunned passengers found themselves besieged by buyers offering to buy almost anything of value. Loud and rancorous negotiations took place between merchants representing the shippers and merchants acting for their own account. One merchant held an impromptu auction for his merchandise, completing the auction in less than a minute and selling the goods to other insatiable merchants without ever having taken delivery. Transactions were consummated on a handshake, though the terms, conditions, and prices proved as incomprehensible as a foreign language to the Argonauts.

As deals were struck the merchants immediately arranged to offload their cargo. One merchant cornered one of the sailors and offered to pay him twenty dollars to help unload some boxes to the merchant's boat. The sailor looked hesitantly over his shoulder, then quietly pocketed the money.

The passengers soon realized that these boats were not for them. Only one or two boatmen, who either had sold their merchandise on board or had failed to purchase anything, offered to take the passengers ashore, but their prices seemed indecent. Only Generals Smith and Adair, and other military personnel aboard, had assured portage. They patiently waited to be retrieved by boats from the naval squadron. Captain Forbes, having commanded his crew to man the lifeboats, read from the ship's manifest, and assigned the passengers to the boats. First cabin was given precedence, then second cabin, and finally steerage. Mary Ellen felt fortunate to be one of the first ashore along with Colbraith, Field, and Croft.

As soon as Mary Ellen stepped from the boat, dozens of voices attacked her, momentarily overwhelming and jumbling her senses. She followed about ten feet behind Colbraith who proceeded with the nonchalance common to confident men. She planned to follow his lead. One passenger disembarked with a bunch of pineapples tied together and thrown over his shoulder. A tall gaunt man who looked like a scarecrow, accosted him. "Do you want to sell them?" the tall man asked in a high-pitched voice and pointed at the fruit.

"Well, maybe," the surprised passenger responded uncertainly.

"How much do you want for them?" the tall man asked.

"Well," the passenger hesitated. "I'll let you have them for, ah . . . ten dollars." Mary Ellen guessed he had only paid a few cents for each fruit in Panama City.

"Can I see them?" the tall man asked.

The passenger laid the six pineapples on the ground as a small crowd gathered. The tall man inspected them carefully. Then, without hesitation, he handed the passenger some Spanish doubloons in the amount of ten dollars and took the fruit. The shocked passenger stood with his mouth open looking at the doubloons in his hand. Another man, on seeing the pineapples, immediately asked whether they were for sale. "How many in the bunch?" he asked.

"Six," the tall man replied.

"Want to sell 'em all?" the man asked.

"No," the tall man replied.

"How about selling me three?" the man persisted.

"I might."

"How much?"

"Fifteen Dollars!" the tall man replied unabashedly.

"I'll take them." And the transaction was completed to the passengers' astonishment, Colbraith's amusement, and Mary Ellen's amazement. The tall man left without another word, pocketing a profit of five dollars and carrying three pineapples. The passenger who brought the fruit from Panama City remained standing in stunned silence. This instant glimpse into the economic reality of the region gave Mary Ellen her first insight into what she could expect in this alien land. One had to maintain a level, quick thinking head to survive in San Francisco.

"Carry your trunks?" A small man approached Colbraith and the others, his clothes wet and disheveled, his face filthy. Mary Ellen listened to their negotiation and watched them head into the makeshift town.

Mary Ellen suddenly felt utterly isolated, as if she had been deserted, left alone in a forbidding land. The *California* had become her home, providing her with a sense of security. Her decks, cabins, companionways, the ocean spray, the black smoke, even the passengers, had become prosaic, familiar to the point of being comfortable. In the bowels of the ship she felt secure. On shore she was alone, as alone as she had ever been.

Mary Ellen clutched her trunk, fingernails digging into the palms of her hands. Bodies, tents, horses, mud, carriages, became blurred images painted carelessly upon a dirt canvas.

"Does anyone know how to cook?" a middle-aged man, dressed in his Sunday best, yelled as the passengers slowly made their way across the muddy road.

His question brought Mary Ellen out of her reverie. She glanced at the hills dotted with tents and it dawned on her that lodging would be scarce and very expensive. She walked up to the man who continued calling out: "I need a cook."

"How much will you pay?" she asked.

He appraised her carefully, like a farmer inspecting a horse before purchasing it. "Do you know how to cook?" he finally asked.

"Yes. I'm an excellent cook," she replied diffidently.

"Well . . . I can pay $100, maybe $120 per month," he said hesitantly.

It was a lot of money but Mary Ellen had seen the commotion on board the *California* and had already concluded that prices in San Francisco were completely unrelated to anything she had seen in Cincinnati or New Orleans. At Williams's store she learned that prices were higher for goods in demand, while merchandise the customers rejected ended up at lower prices. San Francisco merchants demanded everything. And prices reflected this crazed demand. She decided to take a risk and bargain.

"I'm sorry I wasted your time," she said and walked away.

"Wait! Wait!" He ran after her, his feet squishing in the mud. "I can pay more if you're as good a cook as you claim."

"I already told you I'm not just a good cook," she said haughtily. "I'm an excellent cook."

"Well . . . "The man chewed on a fingernail. "Well, I can pay you $200 per month," he doubled the offer and scratched his temple nervously.

"Do you provide accommodation?" Mary Ellen asked, intentionally ignoring his offer.

"Yes! Of course!" he beamed. "Our boarding house is the best in town!"

"How many boarders?" she asked.

"Ten, including my associate and me."

"If you provide lodging and $300 per month, I'll cook for you and serve as your housekeeper," she countered.

The man looked stunned. "Well . . . that's impossible. I think it's out . . ."

Mary Ellen shrugged her shoulders with a disinterest she did not at all feel. "Good day, sir." She turned and started to walk in the direction Colbraith had gone, without any idea of where she could go. Her heart pounded and her stomach tightened. Perhaps she had overplayed her hand. Soon other passengers from second cabin and steerage would be landing.

The man hesitated for a second before he rushed to her. "Look, if you're really as good as you say, it's a deal." He offered his hand and she shook it. It was then that he first noticed her amber skin and unusual eyes.

"I'm Mary Ellen Price."

"Good. Well, Miss Price, my name is Charles Case. Our establishment is the Excellent House, on Washington Street. Here, let me help you with your portmanteau." Case lifted the heavy trunk. "Unfortunately, as you can see, we are all a little short on help. But it's not too far. Please follow me. I know my associate, Mr. Heiser, will be pleased."

MARY ELLEN HAD NEVER SEEN SUCH A BLEAK, UNINVITING LANDSCAPE. It started to rain as she and Case headed toward the boarding house, pausing occasionally to let Case rest. Soon a cold, strong wind blew sheets of rain horizontally, drenching both of them. The muddy streets—no sidewalks, no planking, no stonework—were a congealed mess of brown from end to end. Everywhere else was gray in the rain. The bay and Montgomery street, which served as the coastal road, were indistinguishable. Even the grassy hills with rude structures of every sort were gray. Some of these were complete buildings, others in various stages of construction; but most were canvas sheds.

The Excellent House was a crude two-story clapboard building erected in great haste, with little attention to detail. The interior reflected rough men's tastes and lack of care for their surroundings. Mary Ellen's room was

Chapter Ten

Muddy Streets

small but neat. She had barely managed to unpack and dry herself off when Case asked her to accompany him for some shopping. He wanted Mary Ellen to become familiar with their suppliers as soon as possible.

Outside, huddled against the rain, Mary Ellen was both disappointed and exhilarated. Though she had warned herself not to romanticize the Pacific coast, especially San Francisco, she never imagined such an uninviting view. Yet it was a mysterious place with unquestionable vigor.

The voices of men shouting came through the clamor of the rain. They were trying to pull a horse out of the rain-soaked mud. The braying horse, mired up to its belly, thrust its head forward, jerking to break loose. But the mud sucked at its legs, holding it tightly. One merchant began dumping large crates into the mud for the men to stand on as they feverishly worked to free the sodden horse. Mary Ellen read on one crate: "Haymarket Ltd. Fine India Tea."

"Did you see that?" Mary Ellen gaped incredulously as the merchant hurled each wooden box a little farther, creating a haphazard and unsteady walkway. "Those crates can't be filled with tea. They must be empty."

"They're full, and tea sells for a dollar a glass," Case, who was enjoying Mary Ellen's wide-eyed amazement, told her.

Mary Ellen and Case walked down Clay Street along the plaza, Case called it the heart of the city, toward Kearney Street. On one corner a building displayed a large sign: "Jonathan D. Stevenson, Gold Dust Bought and Sold Here." Case stopped.

"I need to attend to some matters here," he told Mary Ellen. "Why don't you come in out of the rain?"

Drenched, Mary Ellen was amenable. The name of the establishment sounded familiar.

"Well, come on, Miss Price."

The store was filled with customers. Case was immediately intercepted by a couple of acquaintances, leaving Mary Ellen lingering next to the door. The rain was lessening and people were beginning to emerge from stores and restaurants. She started to step outside but hesitated when she saw Colbraith and Field coming up the walk. She moved back from the doorway.

"You know, this isn't even a small village, let alone a town," Colbraith said as he and Field entered the building. Colbraith saw Mary Ellen and nodded his recognition, then returned his attention to Field. "The only advantage is that everything seems to be near the plaza, which is fortunate enough for us. I wouldn't want to risk my life crossing these damned streets and drowning in this sludge."

"I thought San Francisco was larger. But first impressions can be misleading. We haven't seen much of the town yet. It may be small and provincial, but the prices are certainly not," Field mused.

Field impressed Mary Ellen as a young, pompous man from a wealthy family who could glide comfortably through any situation without concern. He was always bantering and grinning, though to Mary Ellen his smile seemed a bit disingenuous. Colbraith, on the other hand, was always serious and intense; he seemed uncomfortable in Field's presence.

They walked toward a man standing behind a small counter weighing gold dust on a scale. If he heard Colbraith and Field, he did not acknowledge it. As he deposited the small pile of dust into a leather pouch, Colbraith and Field removed their soaking hats and approached the counter.

The man looked up and surprise registered immediately. "Well, I'll be!" he said. "Mr. Field and Mr. O'Brien." He tied the pouch, then walked from behind the small bar and shook each man's hand vigorously. Colonel J.D. Stevenson was tall and lanky, with black hair turning silver.

"Nice to see you, Colonel," Colbraith said as he surveyed the narrow, deep office, dimly lit by candles along the walls.

"A pleasure, Colonel," Field remarked, but his eyes strayed to the pouch and the gold.

Colonel Stevenson! That's it! Mary Ellen remembered overhearing the discussion outside Colbraith's cabin aboard the *California.*

"I'm not surprised either of you came here, though I didn't know you were acquainted with each other," the Colonel said bemused, his eyebrows arching high.

"We were shipmates," Field declared. "Never met each other before."

"What a coincidence. Well, it's about time you boys came here. This is a glorious country. Don't let the elements fool you." Stevenson smiled expansively. "It hardly ever rains here. By April we'll be completely dry with the best weather you've ever seen. No snow. Not even frost. And in the summer," he shook his head, "in the summer, it doesn't get hot or humid. Simply amazing."

Mary Ellen felt uncomfortable standing alone. Case was engaged in animated conversation and looked in her direction as if she were a bird who might fly away.

Stevenson noticed that the men were drenched. "Here, let me have those oilskins." Colbraith and Field handed their outer clothes to Stevenson and hung their hats on a hat rack. Stevenson placed their coats near a small wood-burning stove to dry and invited the men to sit next to the stove, the only source of heat for the premises. Stevenson reached for two cups and a pot of coffee brewing on the stove. The coffee smelled delicious and Mary Ellen would have liked some. But no one, other than Case, seemed to even notice her presence.

"First, let me say how sorry I am about your brother, Colbraith. It must have been a dreadful blow for such a young man to die so needlessly. He was a hero, saving those children. I know you were very close to each other."

"Thank you," Colbraith's voice was strained. He was clearly uncomfortable.

"God has mysterious ways which we don't understand," the colonel added.

"I'm sorry, Colonel," Colbraith flashed, "but it had nothing to do with God. Just plain bad luck." Colbraith quickly reined in his emotions. He did not believe in a supreme deity manipulating things according to some grander scheme. Richard died because he tried to diffuse a bomb that some children had found; Richard, his only remaining kin on earth, happened to be in the wrong place at the right time. Now Colbraith was completely alone.

Stevenson changed the subject. "I was also sorry to hear about the congressional election, Colbraith. Unfortunately my efforts on your behalf went for naught. Under the best of circumstances I don't think Tammany was prepared to support you for higher office. In this matter I feel that I have failed you."

"It wasn't your fault. I don't think anyone could have changed the outcome. I would be lying if I said I wasn't disappointed. I was a loyal Tammany Democrat, I devoted my life to them. To set up another Democratic congressional candidate to run against me and allow the Whig to win was unconscionable." He shook his head, pursed his lips, and glared at the reflection of flames dancing on the floor. When he looked up his eyes burned with anger. "But I tell you, Colonel, those bastards in Tammany will have to reckon with me some day. In their own backyard."

Stevenson noted Colbraith's reluctance to say more and turned to

Field. "Your brother Dudley really thought you would come out with my First Regiment of New York Volunteers in 1847."

Mary Ellen noticed that Field seemed a bit uncomfortable, hesitant, but he squirmed out of it.

"I almost did," he said, "but I had planned to go to Europe and I had to get it out of my system. Of course, had I known gold would be discovered, I might have come sooner."

"Indeed I'm happy to see both of you here," Stevenson remarked. "Ever since my regiment disbanded I've been involved in assaying and in some land transactions." He leaned forward, almost conspiratorially, and continued. Mary Ellen leaned forward as well.

"Let me tell you," he spoke slowly, "this is really the land of golden opportunity. You made the right decision." He leaned back, clasped his hands together, then leaned forward again, looking around as if his words might be overheard. He saw Mary Ellen and said softly, "Oh, hello, Miss. Can I help you?"

It took Mary Ellen a moment to realize that the Colonel was addressing her. Colbraith again looked at her searchingly, but said nothing. "Oh! Oh, no. Actually I'm just waiting for Mr. Case."

"Well, miss, there's a chair near the door if you would like to sit down."

Mary Ellen knew their conversation would not continue in her presence, so she smiled gracefully and took the seat near the door.

Colbraith watched Mary Ellen appraisingly, then returned his attention to Stevenson. Stevenson, apparently satisfied, continued.

"In the short time since I arrived in San Francisco I have made a fortune." He paused, letting his words sink in. "Nearly two hundred thousand dollars in six months. I'm rich and there are great fortunes to be made here." He leaned back, placed his hands behind his head and watched their reaction.

Mary Ellen strained to hear every syllable of the conversation. She realized that the idea of extreme wealth did not have the same effect on Colbraith as it did other men. His eyes were not gleaming as if he were holding a chest of gold at that very moment. Field appeared bemused by

Stevenson's remarks. Mary Ellen suddenly realized that she had completely forgotten about Case. She searched the room but did not see him. Just as she was about to stand and make her way back to the boarding house, Case appeared.

Stevenson meanwhile began walking Colbraith and Field to the door. He said, "The office of alcalde is a creation of Mexican law. It's like a mayor, but more powerful. It actually combines the roles of justice of the peace, mayor, and whatever other powers the elected official can muster, such as recorder and collector. Build up your power base in San Francisco, Colbraith. When the time is right you'll waltz into that office."

Mary Ellen could not help but wonder whose office and what power?

Chapter Eleven

The Hounds

SAN FRANCISCO
MAY-JUNE 1849

COLBRAITH AND HIS PARTNER, FREDERICK H. KOHLER, RAISED THE crude stone crucible from the furnace by two long wooden handlebars and carefully carried it to the adjacent table. Several flat empty castings rested on the table. Kohler, as large as Colbraith, his reddish hair plastered to his forehead by sweat, strained and grunted as they moved the crucible. Their faces gleamed from the flames and glistened with perspiration. They slowly poured the molten liquid into the castings, letting little of the fiery liquid wash over the side. Any spillage would simply be collected from the stone surface after hardening and reused later. The heat of the magma-like substance washed their faces like the caress of a desert wind. They returned the empty receptacle to a wooden stand set on another long table between neatly stacked gold and silver bars.

Kohler and Colbraith worked together with the ease and comfort that comes only from a shared experience. They were silent. They had both done this so many times during the previous two months that each knew what the other would do without any prompting. They watched as the golden liquid in the castings congealed. Then they extracted the newly formed bars and began the laborious process of rolling the warm gold into strips of uniform thickness and quality. Kohler fed the thin bars into the rollers while Colbraith turned the cogwheel. Colbraith handed the finished strips back to Kohler who measured them carefully. Then Kohler and Colbraith inserted the strips into a press, which punched out circular gold disks called planchets. Each disk had to have a uniform thickness and weight. Again the duty fell upon Kohler to measure them and he did it with a scale and calipers. The men hardly paid any attention to the stifling conditions in the room. The air was still and rank. The small window set high on one wall provided little ventilation. Fresh air could not penetrate the musky conditions in which the men worked. Outside, the scent of late Spring and the sweetness of the early Summer foliage lay in ambush, unable to gain the smallest foothold. The two men inside did not have the luxury or time to smell the fresh air, let alone think about it.

Several of the planchets were too thick, so Kohler filed them down at the edges, working over a chamois on the clear part of the table. The filings were valuable. One day's remnants represented many ounces of nearly pure gold mixed with silver alloy. Every speck would be collected at the end of the day and reused later. Kohler constantly weighed the filed planchets until their weight met his exacting measurements. A few of the planchets were too light and Kohler simply tossed them back into the crucible. They would be remelted and recast.

Kohler then passed the acceptable planchets to Colbraith who rolled the rims to make them slightly higher than the surface of the disks. Already these rolled and rimmed planchets resembled the final product—gold coins, but faceless ones. The two partners working side by side struck the disks with dies to form the impression of the final coins—"K&O" at the top, "$5" in the middle and "S.M.V. 1849," standard mint value and the year, at the bottom. Both sides bore the same impression. They placed the gleaming coins into small neat piles and got them ready for the final stage. Colbraith polished each coin to a fine buff and handed the coin to Kohler who inspected the finished specie with an eyepiece. Kohler weighed the coin one final time. Satisfied with his work, Kohler stamped the set with a three-digit number which he then recorded in a log. The code had been Colbraith's idea. It allowed them to track every coin, from the date of its minting to the buyer who acquired it. Colbraith asserted that such a code would provide some security against others trying to flood the market with identical coins or counterfeit bearing less gold content. Merchants were encouraged to check with K&O if they were suspicious of any coins.

Colbraith rolled the coins into blue paper bearing their logo and the value of the roll—"K&O Gold Coins: $100 - Twenty $5 Coins." Earlier in the day they minted five hundred ten-dollar coins, the day's full allotment, which had been rolled into yellow dyed paper and placed into the safe.

Colbraith returned to the stone table where he collected the tailings which spilled over from the castings and placed them in a separate sack with the remnant filings. Finally, after placing the newly minted rolls of coins into their safe, the exhausted men, each carrying a separate key, locked it. By agreement Stevenson held a duplicate set of keys if anything were to happen to either of the two men.

They had worked with few breaks for nearly ten long hours. During this time they had minted 500 ten-dollar and 750 five-dollar coins. Their gross profit from the day's mintage would be $1,750, one dollar for each five-dollar coin, and two dollars for each ten-dollar coin. The merchants who purchased the coins paid Kohler and Colbraith in gold dust. They accepted the gold dust at a value of $15 per ounce, and transferred it to Stevenson for storage. Most merchants valued gold dust at $16 per ounce, so Colbraith and Kohler were really getting another dollar per ounce. They were making a remarkable four dollars for each fifteen dollars of coins minted and sold. Working with hundreds of ounces daily they were each netting well over a thousand dollars per day.

Kohler sat down wearily on a stool, wiped his brow with a rag and ladled a glass of tepid water from a large ewer. The heat from the furnace and the intense work was enervating. They had been working like this now for more than two months and they wondered, alone and in silence, how much longer their bodies would be able to sustain the demanding work.

But they were slowly and inexorably becoming rich, even by the standards of San Francisco. Unlike gold mining, with all of its attendant risks, they only had a few risks. The end of import duties on Americans or the end of hoarding gold coins by the military authorities were the principal risks. In either case legal gold coins would find their way back into circulation. Colbraith suspected that others would soon be minting coins and the competition would force everyone to place more gold and less alloy into the coins, restricting profits dramatically.

Colbraith and Kohler both knew these risk would materialize one day, probably sooner than later. They decided to limit their inventory to not more than a thousand ten-dollar and a thousand five-dollar coins. If the bottom of the market fell out for any reason and their coins were no longer accepted, they would melt the coins down, extract the gold, and suffer a minimal loss.

As Stevenson predicted, their newly minted coins were now readily accepted throughout San Francisco as the most convenient means of exchange. At first the merchants only took small quantities. Although the coins had all the hallmarks of professional minting, they were not legal tender. The merchants found the concept of using the coins in lieu of gold dust appealing. Coins were a lot easier to handle, store, or deal with. But the merchants were uncertain whether the coins would be found acceptable in general commerce.

Kohler, as Colbraith quickly discovered, possessed a genius for making things. His blend of skill and art allowed him to build or mint just about anything with precision and a high degree of professionalism; he had golden hands. The quality and appearance of their coins helped gain acceptability.

Several of the more prominent merchants only agreed to a consignment of the coins on Stevenson's recommendation. They had the coins assayed. The assayers reported that each and every coin tested contained exactly the same quantity of gold, just as represented by Kohler and O'Brien's new company, K&O Bullion. Within a few weeks the coins had gained the trust of all the principal merchants, even those who were known for being staunchly conservative in their fiscal dealings. Now K&O

faced the daunting task of continuing to mint enough coins to satisfy the hungry and growing demand.

Colbraith also helped himself to some of the water, then he checked his timepiece. "It's already past five o'clock," he said with some urgency. He quickly washed his hands and face in a small basin and grabbed his hat.

Kohler placed his hands on his knees and started to rise. "I guess we better get going." He stood up and tried to stand upright, but felt the stiffness setting in. His muscles and joints groaned in rebellion.

They closed and locked their shop then hurried down to Kearny Street. San Francisco had changed dramatically in the months since Colbraith arrived on the *California.* Nearly a thousand new folks were arriving every week. Canvas and ramshackle frame structures littered the hills, erected hastily with whatever materials could be found. People filled the streets, dressed in red and blue flannel shirts, sporting an array of hats as if individuality could be best expressed by the style of hat and the manner in which it was worn. People representing every corner of the earth mixed together, dressed dissimilarly in their colorful native costumes. Newcomers, their faces upbeat and uncertain, rubbed shoulders with old-timers, downbeat and certain. Many of the San Franciscans who left for the mines in 1848 and early 1849 now returned, some rich, some broke, and all glad to be back in town, in "civilization."

It had not rained in San Francisco for nearly two weeks. The muddy streets which were so perilous only a month earlier had disappeared, replaced by a less dangerous but equally irritating dust. Away from the streets the warm air was fresh, golden and blessed. But in the streets the dust came in swirls and eddies, prompted by the smallest disturbance: a gentle puff of wind or the hoof beats of a horse. Even the footsteps of one person would raise a fine powder that covered everything. The grit clung to clothes, to skin, in shoes, between toes, and in every other crevice imaginable. It chafed hands, rubbed skin raw, shriveled lips into lizard-like worms, clogged up nasal passages like blocked adobe pipes, and inflamed already red and sore eyes.

Colbraith and Kohler headed directly for a large tent on Kearny Street, next to the City Hotel. A large sign on top of the entry announced

"Tammany Hall." Recently set up by several New Yorkers from Stevenson's First Regiment, Tammany Hall had become a gathering hole for many New Yorkers. Boasting ten gaming tables and a complete bar imported all the way from New York, Tammany Hall stayed open twenty-four hours a day, seven days a week. Colbraith could not help feel a strange dread at the thought of entering Tammany Hall, though the large canvas tent that loomed before him hardly aspired to the same lofty pretense as the wigwam back home. Stevenson had set up a meeting for Colbraith to meet John Pullis, sheriff of San Francisco, and Jack Patterson, one of the officers in Stevenson's volunteers. San Francisco had a large enclave of New Yorkers. Sheriff Pullis and Patterson, Stevenson told Colbraith, knew most of them. They made it their business to know and could be helpful with organizing support if Colbraith eventually embarked on his quest for political power. Kohler had already agreed to help Colbraith get started, offering both his financial and personal support, which Colbraith gratefully accepted.

As they stepped into the noisy tent, three men, all bearing guns in their belts, confronted them. All three were huge. "This is a private tent, gentlemen," the biggest man said. He towered menacingly over both Colbraith and Kohler. Almost six feet seven inches tall, sporting a full dark brown beard that reached his massive barrel chest, with arms the size of small tree trunks, the man glared at Colbraith and Kohler through small mirthless eyes.

"That's all right, Sam. They are my guests," Sheriff Pullis called out. Sam did not budge for a second or two as if to remind everyone that he had control—no one entered or left the premises without his permission. Then he grudgingly stepped aside and with a flourish of his arm waved Colbraith and Kohler in.

"This way, gentlemen," he growled, but his words sounded hollow and completely disingenuous.

Colbraith and Kohler went to Sheriff Pullis's table. Colbraith turned to find Sam still looking intently at him, then turning back to confront some other people who now entered the tent.

"Mr. O'Brien and Mr. Kohler. Please sit here," Pullis pointed needlessly to the only two chairs not occupied. "Let me introduce you to my associates. This is Jack Patterson." A tall, pleasant looking man, with bright eyes under bushy eyebrows and a thick mop of black hair, saluted Colbraith. "That bushwhacker over there is Charles "Dutch" Duane. We call him Dutch Charlie, but he is usually called by whatever name he wants." Colbraith understood. Dutch Charlie was another huge man, about the same size as Sam. Unlike Sam who resembled a grizzly bear, Dutch Charlie had a clean-shaven, square-jawed face, chiseled like marble, with pale eyes equally cold. He nodded to Colbraith and Kohler. "And this here is C.R. Lee." Lee, a man of middle stature with no remarkable features smiled and offered his hand. They shook hands and sat down.

"I didn't realize Tammany Hall wasn't open to the public," Colbraith said as he glanced quickly around the other tables to see if he knew anyone or if someone looked familiar. But no one did.

"Well, we've had some trouble recently," Sheriff Pullis said uncomfortably. "Some of our city's residents are in favor of allowing criminals to go unpunished. They don't like the work we do here because, I suppose, they're threatened by it. Of course if they didn't commit crimes they shouldn't be in such a snit. We don't want any troublemakers coming in here. We keep the riffraff out."

"We've always welcomed the public," Patterson said with a deep resonant voice. "However, the growth of San Francisco, like the growth of any other area, brings with it an undesirable element. As you undoubtedly know we've organized and we need to make more secure arrangements."

Kohler and Colbraith exchanged looks. They had been working hard from the first day they met. They did not socialize. They did not have any time. Up at the dawn of each day, they dined after work and retired spent and exhausted to their hotel rooms. In these circumstances they had not kept abreast of local news. What they knew they learned from Stevenson whenever they brought gold dust to his business for storage. They did not have a clue about Patterson's or Pullis's organization. Stevenson only mentioned a group of New Yorkers working together. Fortunately Patterson helped them out.

"When we first formed The Hounds, we did it for social reasons. You know, a chance to get together. After all we were all from New York. We had something in common. So we organized. I purchased this tent. We decided to call it Tammany Hall, like the one in New York. A place to meet. Then Sheriff Pullis, who is our steward, retained us to collect judgements that were turned over to him from the court. We also serve the city by patrolling the streets and letting would-be thieves and murderers know that they have us to contend with. We don't ask much for return."

"It's all very legal," Pullis interjected.

Some voices rose near the entrance and the men turned in time to see big Sam lift a disheveled man off the ground by the scruff of his shirt and toss him out as if he was emptying a pail of water.

"Who is he?" Colbraith asked.

"Ah, that's our military leader, Samuel Roberts. Almost as big as Dutch Charlie here," Lee told them. Dutch remained immutable. Colbraith marveled at the size of the two men. Sam Roberts and Dutch Charlie dwarfed him and he was nearly 230 pounds and six-foot-two-inches. They would make pretty decent shoulder-strikers, he reasoned.

"What would you like to drink?" Sheriff Pullis asked.

"Coffee would be fine," Colbraith's answer surprised the men.

"Have something stronger?" Patterson persisted.

"No. We've had a long day. Something stronger would put me out," Colbraith said genially. He knew that his failure to drink could be regarded by these men as a sign of unfriendliness, or worse, weakness. He had not touched a drop of liquor since the day he destroyed his three taverns in New York, wielding an axe like some berserk murderer in a blind rage. Colbraith swore he would refrain from drinking until the day the leaders of Tammany paid homage to him.

"I'll have a whiskey," Kohler said. He knew Colbraith did not drink, and although he did not feel like drinking he ordered the whiskey to deflect attention away from Colbraith. Dutch had a crooked smile on his lips and seemed on the verge of saying something. Pullis scratched his head then leaned forward toward Colbraith. "I've always wanted to know something. How did you knock Yankee Sullivan out? I heard so many different versions. You carry anything in your fist? Brass knuckles?"

"No," Colbraith said casually. "Hit him once and he fell. Nothing to tell really." Colbraith recalled that night, his first night with Walsh's firemen. They met at Gossling's Restaurant to confront one of Walsh's political opponents, who was protected by his shoulder-strikers and their leader, Yankee Sullivan, a world champion boxer.

The smile on Dutch's face disappeared as if a light had been extinguished. He suddenly seemed very interested in Colbraith. "You the guy who dropped Yankee?" he asked, genuinely surprised.

"Colbraith's the one," Kohler took the banner. "Slammed him with his ham fist so hard Yankee went to sleep before he hit the ground."

"Were you there too?" Dutch asked and looked impressed.

"No. But Yankee told me all about it."

Colbraith smiled involuntarily. The story was told often, but it lacked the poignant truths: it was blind luck and he broke his arm in the melee.

"I always imagined it was somebody bigger than me," Dutch confided. "I fought him once and he nearly broke my jaw." Dutch rubbed his jaw as if the pain had returned in the telling.

Lee brought the drinks and the conversation turned slowly to politics. Colbraith listened politely. These New Yorkers were unsophisticated. They knew nothing about politics or the political machinery needed to run a city like San Francisco. Sam Roberts and Dutch Charlie were rough men who would understand only the street part of shoulder-striking and intimidation. They and others like them would be useful in the trenches, but certainly could not be relied upon to help formulate the political infrastructure upon which elections were won or lost. Lee, a merchant, and Pullis were only slightly better. Colbraith did not know how Pullis managed to get the job of sheriff, though he intended to find out. They were followers, not leaders. Jack Patterson was different. He could speak well. Patterson had a gift for gab. He could talk swiftly and sell his wares. Someone who could be bought and sold easily. Patterson would be loyal to money and power, no one and nothing else. Patterson could win some local election if the proper machine were put into place.

Colbraith realized just how much he missed people like his old mentor from New York, George Wilkes, someone who knew and understood elections and politics from every phase, every angle; someone whose insightful advice was always on the mark. The talk of Yankee Sullivan and the stirring of old recollections gave Colbraith pause. He wondered whether he could induce Wilkes and Yankee to come to San Francisco. Yankee's fame and the camaraderie these big fellows would develop would be helpful. He also wanted Yankee's views—always on target and very practical. Few others understood just how bright and clever Yankee Sullivan really was. And Yankee had become his ally.

—m—

MARY ELLEN WALKED HURRIEDLY TOWARD THE PARKER HOTEL. CHARLES Case had asked her to drop in on the manager and find out where they laundered their sheets and table cloths. The cost of laundry had skyrocketed. People found it less expensive to wear a shirt until it became dirty, then throw it out and buy a new shirt. The laundering facilities at the Excellent, the Case & Heiser boarding house, were not large enough to handle their needs, at least not with so many people boarding. They desperately needed to make better arrangements. Mary Ellen's work as the housekeeper kept her very busy. She arranged three meals each day for fourteen boarders, mostly men who worked for Case & Heiser's company. Two people helped her with her duties. One, a boy only fifteen years old and not very bright, helped with all cleaning chores and cooking duties. The other, almost fifty, very old by San Francisco standards, kept the frame building in running order. Unfortunately both men shared the same luckless fate—dullness. Even such simple things as polishing brass lamps seemed too much for them. Mary Ellen had to show them, over and over, just how it should be done. But the lamps always appeared tarnished and old instead of new and shiny. Getting away from the Excellent House was one of Mary Ellen's obsessions. Shopping, buying produce, anything to get into the streets of the city, served as a catalyst for excitement and hope.

She enjoyed strolling along the roads, marveling at the spectacle of seeing people from so many countries milling on the streets, especially around

The Parker Hotel

the plaza. A polyglot of so many races, languages, customs and dress, all intriguing and so different from anything she had ever seen back home. She found the oriental races most fascinating, with pale yellow complexion, strange, slanting eyes, all dressed alike in dark blue and sporting pig-tails. They jabbered in curious lilting voices, making unfathomable sounds. The South Americans or Chilenos, as the Americans called them, came from many different countries, but mostly from Chile, Peru, and Mexico. They were dark-eyed and wore dark cloaks or colorful serapes with vivid stripes of orange, green, red, and blue. New Zealanders, proud and stocky, bore intricate tattoos that were visible on every exposed part of their bodies.

Handsome, tanned Sandwich Islanders or Kanakas, as they were known, roamed in groups. Some of the men were huge, but they always seemed cheerful and friendly. Malaysians, Abyssinians, and polite Spaniards, the latter goat-chinned and fair-skinned, mixed with Americans from every part of the land. The English, Germans, Italians, and French were well represented in large numbers. There were few women in San Francisco and even fewer native blacks. Occasionally she saw a black person, usually unarmed, dressed neatly with a white shirt, and walking with the peculiar gate of someone perpetually frightened, as if expecting to be beaten at any moment of time. On a rare occasion Mary Ellen would encounter some rough looking black man, dressed either like a miner or someone fresh from the frontier, thrusting his head forward belligerently, as if daring anyone to tangle with him. But such men were a rare sight.

As she approached the Parker Hotel she saw a band of men strolling toward her, some carrying fife and drum and making a racket. A few of the men carried banners proclaiming them to be the Hounds. There were about a dozen of them, some singing, others shouting at each other. All were well armed. Three of the men were drinking from shining green bottles and walking unsteadily. Then she noticed the solitary black man walking in front of the Hounds, his head downcast, not really aware of or paying any attention to the commotion behind him. The black man turned to enter the Parker Hotel and his elbow accidentally touched the leader of the Hounds who had snuck up behind him, making faces and carrying on with the antics of some little school boy. The black man muttered an apology, but then looked up, saw the angry, hate-filled face, and became very frightened.

"This Nigger touched me!" the Hound screamed at his friends and pretended to rub his skin as if he had just been infected with a massive dose of poison oak.

The black man cowered and backed away saying, "Sorry master. Sorry."

The Hounds quickly encircled their quarry.

"You black bastard! You touched me!" the leader continued to bellow, his eyes blazing with fury. "Who's your owner? Where is he? I demand compensation! Damn it!"

Chapter Eleven

The black man shrugged his shoulders in resignation. A small crowd gathered. Mary Ellen watched, stunned at the anger the Hound displayed for no apparent reason. The black man could not avoid touching the Hound because the Hound had come up to within inches of the man. *Why is he provoking the incident,* she wanted to yell, but remained frozen, unable to even move. Thoughts of the violence in Cincinnati filled her with terror. Not unlike a terrible nightmare.

All the Hounds joined in the chorus, howling incoherently at the frightened man. Others in the crowd also yelled, some in support of the Hounds, others in opposition. One man coming out of the Parker Hotel noticed the fracas and made an immediate about-face going back through the front entrance.

"I ain't going to say it again," the leader of the Hounds shouted, his spittle flying from his foaming mouth. Where's your goddamn owner? I want compensation. I want it now!"

"I don't have an owner. I'm a freeman," the black man said weakly.

"Don't you go about telling no lies, Nigger. I ain't going to ask again. Whose going to pay me?"

The black man did not know what to say or do so he said nothing and looked down at the ground.

"Ain't you got ears?" the Hound yelled. "What's them big things for?" he walked up to the black man and grabbed one of his ears. With thumb and forefinger holding tightly to the ear lobe the Hound yanked hard and the black man groaned loudly in pain. Someone in the crowd yelled, "Let go of his ear. He ain't done nothing to you."

The Hound's eyes opened wider in disbelief. "Who says he ain't done nothing?" The Hound looked at the crowd, trying to identify the speaker. Then he turned to his prey and said, "He touched me. That's bad enough. I'll get some disease."

"Go back where you came from!" someone else yelled, but it was unclear whether the subject of the taunt was the Hound or the black man.

"Let him go!" someone else called out.

The offended Hound went into a rage. "So you want me to let go of his ears. Okay!" And without another word he whipped out his Bowie knife and with one rapid stroke cut the black man's ear completely off. The man screamed and grabbed the side of his head where his ear had been. Blood poured out of the gaping wound and through his bunched fingers.

"Here. I'll let go of his ear," the Hound hurled the ear into the crowd. "Satisfied? You asked for it!" The other Hounds started to laugh, hoot and jeer. A few in the crowd joined them, but most of the crowd remained silent, stunned by the cruel action. The Hound returned to his victim. "Next time you better listen better, nigger. You only got one left. You don't want to lose it too!" The Hound feigned another attack with the bloody knife. The man fell down to his knees cowering, one bloody hand clutching the side of his head, the other up to defend his remaining ear. He pleaded for mercy. But the attack ended almost as swiftly as it had begun. The Hound merely shrugged as if he had lost any further interest in his quarry. He brushed by the shaken man without further thought, wiped the blade clean on his pants, and went back to the other Hounds who started to march down the street, singing their songs, as if nothing had happened.

Mary Ellen rushed to the black man, took out a cotton handkerchief and applied it to the ear. A few others in the crowd offered some kindly words of support, directed more at the deplorable act of the Hounds then at the man's bloody fate. Instead, they simply dispersed leaving Mary Ellen holding the now bloody handkerchief against the crying man's head. Only two men remained and helped the wounded man stand up.

"Please help him," she pleaded. Then turned to the man who continued to sob. "Come with me," she said gently. He looked up at her uncertainly. "Come with me," she repeated. I'll wash that wound and get a doctor."

—᠁—

"WHAT'S YOUR NAME?" MARY ELLEN ASKED AS SHE WATCHED THE doctor cauterize the raw wound to staunch the bleeding.

"Samuel," he answered groggily, the whiskey taking effect.

"Don't move!" the doctor commanded as he bandaged Samuel's head.

They were all gathered in the kitchen of the Excellent House on

Washington Street. Charles Case walked back and forth nervously like a caged animal.

"I can't believe those animals," he said. "How could they do something like this?" he asked rhetorically.

"Unfortunately you are right, Case. They are animals. They think they can do as they please in this city," the doctor replied as he wrapped the white dressing one more time around Samuel's head.

The room fell into silence as the doctor finished. A small dark brown stain on the head dressing marked the area where Samuel's ear had been.

"Why don't we get the sheriff to arrest them?" Mary Ellen asked innocently.

The doctor packed his instruments into a small black bag. His solemn face made his mustache droop, both ends pointing to the ground. He looked at Case then at Mary Ellen, but decided to say nothing.

"Change his dressing as I suggested. I'll be back to check on him in two days." He walked out.

Two other men who had witnessed the maiming and had brought Samuel crying and stumbling, exchanged glances, then tipped their hats to Mary Ellen and left. Mary Ellen looked at Case.

"I don't understand. Why can't we have those men arrested?" she asked vehemently.

"The sheriff is one of them. They think they're acting under color of law. No one can do anything," Case responded.

Samuel looked up, his eyes barely focusing, and smiled at Mary Ellen. Then he started to sing, but his words were slurred and the melody seemed lost in a fog.

"It isn't right. What they did was so cruel, so heartless. Can't anything be done?" she asked perplexed and frustrated.

"Not on account of this," Case responded diffidently.

Mary Ellen understood instantly. Samuel had few rights, even if he were a free man. No one would come to his aid, certainly not in the face of such violence. Case, she knew, had a decent heart. He simply expressed his honest view, something which she respected. She retreated for some water and handed the glass to Samuel. He continued to look at her with a foolish grin and sloshed the water as he tried to drink it. She steadied his hand and let him drink a few gulps.

"Thank you," he said and his head started to roll around as if his neck were a swivel.

"Where do you live, Samuel?" she asked.

He simply hummed some unfathomable song, but did not reply. He looked groggy and his head started to fall forward to his chest.

"Can I leave him in the store room for the night, Mr. Case?" she asked uncertainly.

Case thought for a moment. "Yes. But just for this night. We can't take in every man down on his luck. We don't have the room and we don't have the resources to be so charitable. But just this one night."

"Thank you," she said and the two of them picked Samuel up and helped him shuffle to the store room. Mary Ellen took one blanket which she placed on the ground and Samuel lay down and was sound asleep instantly.

As they returned to the kitchen Case said, "These Hounds are a law unto themselves. They're getting bolder every day. Sooner or later they'll cross the line. Right now they're too powerful. Sheriff Pullis is with them. We don't really have any other law. There are over a hundred of those mangy dogs. They're dangerous. Hounds . . . bah! They're nothing but rabid dogs!"

"I was told they changed their name to 'Regulators,'" mentioned Mary Ellen.

"So I heard. If the folk in this town get the mind to do something, there'll be some hangings. It can't go on like this." He shook his head ruefully. "Did you find out about the laundry?" He asked, trying to turn the conversation back to business.

"No. Never got the chance. But the cost of washing is so much that many people are simply throwing away their old clothes."

"I know, I know," he said dejectedly. "Keep looking for some facilities. I leave it in you hands. Find a laundry and make a reasonable contract for us." Case trusted Mary Ellen implicitly. Her talents and brightness, especially in business, were conspicuous. Case trusted her instincts as well as her skills. Even her competence in the culinary arts turned out to be better than she had claimed.

Mary Ellen's skills did not go unnoticed by others. Heiser and Case had occasional guests at the Excellent House, mostly for business, and word of her inspired meals spread throughout the community. Case's closest friend and neighbor, Selim Woodworth, one of the stalwarts in the community had already asked Case for permission to have Mary Ellen cook at a large party he intended to host the following month at his home. The most important people in San Francisco were expected to attend and Selim wanted to impress them with the perfect party, which meant the finest food. Case had not mentioned this to Mary Ellen, yet. He trusted Selim implicitly and knew that his friend would not try to lure Mary Ellen away by offering her higher paid employment. But there were many in San Francisco who would not hesitate to offer her obscene amounts of money to change jobs. And Case did not know how Mary Ellen would react. He treated her well, and with respect. But Case did not trust the influence of money.

Mary Ellen found Charles Case and David Heiser to be perfect gentlemen and employers. They treated her with the utmost respect and delegated to her all the responsibility of running their boarding house. They did not interfere, even if they disagreed. They expressed their viewpoint but left the ultimate decisions to her. They were busy with their mercantile business, which was growing rapidly, and were delighted to have someone so competent run their other affairs. The boarders, did not complain. Even those who made passes at Mary Ellen, were rejected smoothly and without remonstration. Mary Ellen was comfortable and respected at the Excellent House but she had loftier ambition. The whole episode of the laundry rekindled an idea which she now chose to follow up.

CHAPTER TWELVE

The Regulators Unleashed

SAN FRANCISCO
JULY 1849

SAM BRANNAN, SHORT AND STOCKY, CAME OUT OF HIS NEW STORE ON Montgomery Street, between Sacramento and California, with his partner John Osborne. He squinted at the bright sunlight. Impassive to the sparkling day under a cloudless cobalt blue sky, the two men inspected the merchandise near the entry and moved items around to display them better. They stacked shovels, picks, pans, blankets and other gold-mining equipment in neat piles outside the store. Brannan had a reputation for buying huge quantities of merchandise, always trying to corner the market. He would outbid other merchants for goods whenever a ship arrived in the bay. As a result Brannan, at various times, cornered such diverse commodities as beans, coffee, and wheat, forcing prices to skyrocket. He could purchase large quantities because he had ample space to store the merchandise with three stores in the gold country near Stockton and an existing large store in San Francisco. The new store on Montgomery Street was his pride and joy. He purchased the land from E. Mickle & Company, paying $9,000 in gold

San Francisco Metropolis

dust. Somewhat careless and always in a rush he did not even bother to get a receipt from Mickle's clerk. He simply left the gold with the young man and told him to give it to Mickle. That is the way business was conducted in San Francisco—by a simple handshake. Brannan, working with two employees and other laborers, managed to build the store in only one week, but it cost him a hefty $10,000 for supplies and wages.

Two customers were inside the store and one customer loitered in the front, looking carefully at the shovels. Finally he selected one shovel and went inside to pay the clerk.

"I sure hope we can move this merchandise quickly," a jittery Osborne said. "We may have a real problem with title if Mickle's clerk pocketed the money." Brannan and Osborne had learned that morning that Mickle's clerk snuck out of town a few nights earlier without letting anyone know his intended destination. He was last seen riding south on the Mission trail, but for all practical purposes he had disappeared. Mickle claimed that he never saw Brannan's $9,000.

"Don't fret so much, John," Brannan replied in his usual gregarious manner. "We bought the land fair and square. I paid Mickle's agent. If he skipped town with the money, that's their problem, not ours. This is our land. This is our store. Nobody's going to take it away. We're going to make a fortune here. Hell, we've got a gold mine just in tea alone."

Two days earlier Brannan attended an auction. A shipment of Oolong and Young Hyson tea consisting of five hundred cases came up for bidding in fifty case lots. Brannan, perched on a box, a long cheroot in his mouth, whittled on a pine branch as he watched the price climb up steadily to sixty cents per pound. He had not said a word. The bidding stopped and just as the auctioneer prepared to close the sale Brannan bid sixty-one cents. Other merchants, knowing of Brannan's penchant for getting a good price, took immediate notice, but were unprepared to match Brannan's sudden bid. The auctioneer closed the sale at sixty-one cents and then asked Brannan how many cases he wanted at that price. Brannan, as the successful bidder, had the right to choose the number of lots he wanted. To everybody's surprise Brannan decided to take all ten lots—five hundred cases. Even Talbot Greene, one of his major competitors, and close friend, appeared stunned.

He protested that his store also wanted some of the tea, and Brannan, boasting a wry smile, told Greene he could buy all the tea he wanted, but at his price, which was now $1.25 per pound. Talbot laughed good naturedly at his friend's offer and politely declined. But now, only two days later, Brannan believed he could sell the tea for up to $5.00 per pound. Enough to offset the entire cost of his store.

Brannan had arrived in Yerba Buena with a group of Mormons in 1847. They were bound for Brigham Young's capital in Deseret, Utah. But upon arrival at Yerba Buena Cove, Brannan decided to stay put. He could not explain his interest in the area. After all, only a few hundred people lived a quiet life in fairly squalid conditions. But Brannan had a vision of a bustling community, a vision not shared by any of the Mormons in his company. They wanted him to lead them on to Utah as he had promised. He told them they could go on their own or stay with him. Using the printing press and money he took from the Mormons, some claimed without their consent, and which were destined for Brigham Young, he started the first newspaper and embarked on several business ventures. Despite the protestations of the Mormons in his company, or by the elders in Salt Lake, and despite several lawsuits filed against him by disgruntled Mormons who claimed he had stolen their money, by 1849 Brannan had become one of the richest men in San Francisco. Brannan possessed a boundless energy and his newfound wealth did not soften him up one bit. He still had the bulldog's indomitable spirit. In July 1849, Brannan's taste for life and desire for power had not abated. He had not come close to achieving his goals.

Brannan and Osborne finished fussing about with the merchandise, moving a score of shovels farther from the door until they were satisfied with the display. They were suddenly distracted by some boisterous laughter. A group of men had just turned the corner and Brannan's stomach turned. The Hounds, or Regulators, as they now called themselves were headed directly for his store. The men milled around and began to sullenly and roughly rifle through the merchandise. Some men picked up shovels and pretended to engage in a sword fight.

"Hold on, hold on!" Brannan yelled as he and Osborne made a futile effort to keep the men from handling the goods or disrupting the display. Brashly the Regulators grabbed everything they could.

"Look here, Red," one disheveled man pointed to the neatly stacked blankets.

"Just what we've been talking about." A large redheaded and massively bearded man suddenly clutched a handful of blankets and started to walk away casually without paying. As he did this, the others followed suit, one seizing some shovels, others a stack of pans or picks, and all headed in different directions.

"Get the shovels!" Brannan ordered Osborne. Then Brannan took off after the man with the blankets.

"Stop! Goddamn you! I said stop!" Brannan caught up with the man who turned pugnaciously to face Brannan.

"Give me the blankets!" Brannan commanded. "You've got to pay just like everyone else!"

"The hell I do! We work for the city. Give the bill to the alcalde."

"No, you don't. You don't work for this city." Brannan became enraged. "Pay now or give it back."

A small crowd of onlookers watched silently but at a cautious distance. The man ignored Brannan and casually ambled away. Brannan placed a hand on the thief's shoulder and seized his coat. The man whirled around and struck Brannan a solid blow right between the eyes. Brannan released his grasp and staggered back partially blinded. The thief looked around menacingly, then walked off as if he did not have a single care in the world. Osborne, who had been equally unsuccessful with his assailants, some who threatened to kill him with the new shovels, found Brannan walking back unsteadily holding his bloody face in his hands.

"Are you all right?" Osborne inquired.

"Yes," Brannan replied tersely.

A throng of people gathered around the store as Brannan and Osborne walked in. Brannan went to a small wash basin and washed his face. He looked into a small mirror and saw the angry swelling and gash across the bridge of his nose. Brannan wiped his face dry and threw the small bloody towel across the room in disgust.

"I'm going to file charges," he told Osborne.

"Who are you going to file charges with?" Osborne asked lamely.

"I'm going to Sheriff Pullis. It's his job to arrest these men. Those thieves should be in jail. We've got plenty of witnesses."

Osborne simply shook his head in dismay. "Pullis won't do it, Sam. Why waste your time?" But Brannan ignored his partner and left the store.

He headed to Sheriff Pullis's office. Pullis listened politely to Brannan's tale. "I want those Hounds arrested," Brannan told the sheriff when the story was finished.

"Arrest them?" Sheriff Pullis asked skeptically. "Not me. Why those men have more political, not to mention fire power, than anyone else in this city. You go arrest them, if you want to. Bring them in and I'll bind them over for trial."

"You yellow son-of-a-bitch! I know you're in cahoots with them," Brannan fumed, his face turning a shade redder but not enough to mask the angry bruise on his nose. "I know this and so does everyone else in this town."

Sheriff Pullis stood up abruptly and faced Brannan. "Blow it out your ear, Sam. I ain't got time to listen to your shit. Get the hell out of here."

Brannan did not budge. The two men stared at each other, neither giving an inch. Suddenly Brannan grabbed Sheriff Pullis's jacket with his fist and said, "Pullis, so help me God I'm going to do something about this. When I get through you better be out of this territory."

"Don't threaten me, Brannan," Pullis yanked his jacket out of Brannan's hand. "You open your yap one more time and you're going to find yourself behind bars." Sheriff Pullis hissed, the blood vessel in his forehead expanded and pulsated like a caterpillar working its way into a cocoon.

"Yeah! Sure!" Brannan laughed and walked out. "You don't even have a jail. And you wouldn't know what to do with it if you had one." At the doorway Brannan stopped and yelled, "Remember, I warned you. Better hightail it out of town, sheriff. Just like them Hounds, your neck is on the line. And it's a mighty tight fit." Brannan strolled away casually, but inside he was livid.

Chapter Twelve

He decided to pay a visit to Edward Kemble, editor of the *Alta California,* San Francisco's leading newspaper. Kemble once worked for Brannan and Brannan had sold him his printing press and paper in 1848 for only $800. Brannan's magnanimous gesture gave Kemble the break he needed, and they remained close friends and allies.

Kemble, dressed with a printer's apron, was busy typesetting when Brannan came into the office of the *Alta California.* Kemble's hands were covered with grease and ink, so he did not offer his hand to Brannan. He noticed Brannan's heavy expression and lacerated nose and knew something was amiss.

"Sam, what brings you here?" he asked.

"The Hounds just stole some of our merchandise," Brannan said.

"How do you know it was the Hounds?" Kemble became very attentive.

"They just did it an hour ago. In broad daylight. In front of a score of witnesses." Brannan told Kemble the whole story. Kemble found a pen and started to write some notes as Brannan raged at the incident.

"You didn't really expect the sheriff to do anything, did you?" Kemble asked.

"No. I was really so angry I thought maybe if they acted so openly, so overtly, he would be forced to take some action. But he laughed at me. Told me if I wanted them arrested, I should do it myself."

Kemble set his pen down and looked thoughtfully at Brannan. "Maybe that's not such a bad idea. Maybe it's time the people took some action to get rid of these biters."

"How are the people going to do that?" Brannan scoffed. "There's over a hundred of them. They're armed. They were soldiers. The citizens wouldn't stand a chance."

"I don't agree. The Hounds are ordinary, lazy criminals. As long as people act scared witless they will continue to strut and throw their weight around. But they are not fighting for their homes, or to protect their families. Just for money. Once people realize they have to fight to protect themselves, their property, and their families, they'll go to the end of this earth to expel the rotten lot. Get the public angry enough and they could become a force to be reckoned with." Kemble walked back to the case of type.

"Did you hear about the Parker Hotel?" Kemble asked.

"No. What about it?"

"Seems that Samuel Roberts brought about thirty Hounds for dinner, sat down and ordered the best food. When they finished they simply walked off without paying. When the maitre d' asked them to pay, Roberts told them to send the bill to the alcalde. The maitre d' insisted on immediate payment and Roberts started to throw dishes and glasses around. His men followed suit and nearly destroyed the place. When the maitre d' tried to stop the carnage they beat the hell out of him. Then they left."

"They've gone too far!" Brannan said. "We've got to take some action. I'm sick and tired of this. We need some law and order. I wonder if Alcalde Leavenworth is in with them. They keep throwing his name around. They told me the same thing today—the city will pay."

"I don't know if Leavenworth is one of them. But I'm going to write an article on the Hounds for tomorrow's edition. I'm going to call on the public to get rid of them. Let's get this out in the open."

"That could be dangerous," Brannan warned.

"You know, Sam, that's part of this business. I intend to write what I want. That's the only way I know to publish a paper."

Brannan knew Kemble was not someone easily intimidated or put off. "I'll back you up, Ed. Whatever it takes," Brannan offered.

—~—

KEMBLE SAT AT HIS DESK COMPOSING A FEATURE ARTICLE ON THE PACIFIC Mail Company and its ships when the door to his office burst open at the hinges and came crashing down to the floor. Startled, Kemble rose as Samuel Roberts and several men entered. They were all armed. Roberts strode past the counter and headed for Kemble. Kemble tried to appear unfazed, but Roberts had a crazed look in his eyes.

Roberts surveyed Kemble's office and noticed the type set in large frames on a table. He swept the frames to the floor with a massive swing of his arm. The small lead letters exploded and spread all over the floor like hail falling from a raging thunderstorm. Then he upended each table and desk and sent them tumbling over, spilling their contents of papers, ink, pens and other supplies on the floor. He approached Kemble and took out a rumpled page from his pocket.

"What's this?" he asked as he waved a page of the newspaper in front of Kemble's face.

"It's a newspaper," Kemble answered benignly.

Roberts was not sure whether Kemble was playing with him. He glared down at Kemble who remained outwardly impassive.

"Listen smart ass. You ever write something like this here about the Society of Regulators again and you won't have a newspaper to print. In fact, there won't be anyone to print it. Do you get my drift?"

"I'm one person, that's all," Kemble spoke defiantly. "I know you can shut me up. Shoot me in the back some dark night. I know your ways. But the whole town is up in arms. You've gone too far. They're sick and tired of you and your henchmen. Kill me and the people will come for you. They'll hang you. And you know it."

Roberts edged closer. "We agree about one thing. The people are sick and tired. They won't lift a finger. They're scared. And if you had more brains you'd be, too. Cause I ain't going to warn you again. Lay off our society."

"What 'society'?" Kemble's voice trembled with emotion. "You're just plain criminals."

Roberts lifted his fist, "Why you rotten son-of-a-bitch, I ought to . . . "

"Go ahead. Hit me! Kill me," Kemble remained defiant, daring Roberts. "As sure as the sun comes up tomorrow you'll hang."

Roberts inhaled slowly, sucking the air loudly through his teeth. He looked just like a Grizzly bear, only less predictable, perhaps even more dangerous. Suddenly he smiled at Kemble. "You've got us all wrong. We're a law-abiding society.

"What society? The Hounds?" Kemble scoffed.

"No. We're part of the Supreme Order of the Star-Spangled Banner."

"Never heard of the Star-Spangled whatever it is," Kemble said.

"Well, mister editor. Seems you learned folk don't know everything. It's a large society in the East, and we've formed the Western branch."

"Who're we?" Kemble asked, puzzled.

"Anyone who believes in God. Anyone who was born in these United States and ain't a member of the Catholic Church," Roberts recited. "We are pledged to America for Americans."

Kemble was speechless for a moment. Then he said softly, "I don't find such a society in keeping with anything American. Now, if you'll please leave. I've got a paper to publish."

Roberts bent his massive frame and brought his mouth close to Kemble's ear. Kemble automatically flinched, not knowing what to expect. He could smell Robert's stale breath and it made him queasy.

"Don't mention the Hounds or the Regulators or the Supreme Order, unless you wish to say something kind. No more warnings Kemble. Publish one more piece of trash like this and no one will recognize your face, even if they find the body," Roberts whispered hoarsely and motioned for his men to withdraw. Roberts waited until his men had left. "Remember, not a word." Roberts placed his forefinger to his thick lips to signify quiet, then turned around and violently kicked aside some of the furniture as he made his way out of the premises.

—~—

COLBRAITH AND KOHLER PLACED THE LAST BAGS OF GOLD DUST IN Stevenson's huge safe. Stevenson signed a receipt which Kohler placed in the pocket of his frock coat. He planned to attend a fancy-dress ball and masquerade at the Parker House. He paid fifty dollars for his ticket and would soon join other hot-headed young men, flush with money and drinks, mingling with scantily dressed women who knew how to please their men while extracting their gold with greater ease and more success than the most successful miners in California.

"Don't lose that paper," Colbraith warned Kohler. "The Colonel would develop a sudden case of amnesia and keep our gold."

"I would never do something like that," Stevenson gleamed. "Of course I already forgot how much gold you deposited with me today. So as Colbraith says, watch that receipt. And whatever you do, don't let some sweet damsel pilfer it as she massages your weary body."

Kohler looked aghast. "Massage my body? You mean such things happen at these balls?" They all laughed.

"Knowing the charming ladies you are about to meet, forget the receipt, just hold on to your balls," Dutch Charlie Duane chimed in.

Duane and Patterson were in Stevenson's office when Colbraith and Kohler arrived with the gold. They were engaged in some serious discussion, Colbraith noted, which he and Kohler had accidentally interrupted by their unscheduled arrival.

Kohler sidled up to Colbraith and spoke under his breath, "Something's afoot. They're pretty intense. Stick around and see what this is about. I suspect it's important." Then Kohler bid his adieu and rushed out into the night.

Colbraith had come to the same conclusion. His curiosity had been piqued as well.

"Colbraith," Stevenson called out, "before you go perhaps we could have a word with you."

Colbraith joined the three men in Stevenson's office. Colbraith sat on the small divan. Dutch Charlie sat straight-backed on a chair which appeared to strain under his enormous weight. Patterson, as usual, seemed very friendly and affable, though Colbraith sensed an underlying tension.

Stevenson, with his military flair, got right to the point. "Colbraith, what's your view of the Hounds?" The three men looked at him intently.

Colbraith felt uncomfortable responding to the question since Patterson and Duane were members, Patterson an officer of the group.

"They are pretty well organized," came the noncommital answer.

Stevenson reacted instantly. "No. No. Please, don't give me a political response. I, that is we," and he looked at Patterson and Duane for approval, "want your real view. Please."

"The Hounds are out of control," he said warily, and noted the exchange of glances between the three men.

"What do you mean out of control?" Stevenson leaned forward, a serious cloud on his face.

"I've heard people speaking about some of their actions. The Hounds have lost their way. Instead of working toward some political position, a political organization, they have become an armed group acting in a manner that has turned the general population against them. What I hear isn't good."

"But don't you think we need such an organization to keep law and order?" Patterson asked.

"Of course we need law and order, but it has to be official and politically sound. No, the Hounds have lost all perspective on law and order. And that fellow Roberts is an egomaniac. I've had some conversations with him and it always comes back to America for Americans. He's a dangerous man."

"I've noticed that you don't come around very much," Dutch Charlie said. "Why? You're a New Yorker."

"This has nothing to do with New York. I'll not allow myself to get trampled in San Francisco by associating with a group that will ultimately be expelled. I'll tell you, and maybe I shouldn't say this, but you asked, it won't take long before the people do something. When they do, anyone associated with the Hounds, regardless of their intentions, good or bad, will go down with them." Colbraith turned to Patterson. "John, you have a political future, here. But if you stay with the Hounds, you'll have nothing."

Dutch Charlie sat impassively. But Patterson listened intently.

"I agree with Colbraith," Stevenson sat back and folded his hands behind his head. "If they persist in acting as they have during the last month I can assure you I'll be the first one to have them arrested and expelled from this territory. I know most of those men. They were in my regiment. Most of them are good men. Well trained. But Roberts has turned them into a lawless bunch. They don't fit in with San Francisco's future."

"But Sheriff Pullis is a Hound. Alcalde Leavenworth works with them. How will the people fight such a strong force?" Patterson asked.

Colbraith noted that Patterson referred to the Hounds as "them," not "us."

"Pullis is nothing. He couldn't be a sheriff of vacant land. Leavenworth will side with whichever group has the best possibility of succeeding. He's a political animal. Let me tell you, San Francisco isn't populated by a bunch of *dilletantes*."

Dutch Charlie looked puzzled.

Chapter Twelve

"I mean there are a lot of tough men in San Francisco. The population of this town is very unusual. The men of this town risked their lives to come out here. They endured great hardships. They're not cowards, gentlemen. When they're pushed too far, they'll beat the hell out of the Hounds. It won't even be a contest."

Patterson and Duane regarded each other knowingly. Finally Patterson said, "Colonel, as you know Dutch and I've been talking. The Hounds are fixing for a fight. I intend to distance myself from them. I've signed a letter of resignation, which I dated last week. I've placed it in safe keeping so that I'm not drawn down by Roberts if the Hounds lose. Dutch, I suggest you do the same thing."

Dutch looked at the ground and rubbed his fists together. "I don't like Roberts. Never did. He's the self-anointed supreme leader. There ain't enough room for him and me. I don't know if the people have the guts to go against Sam and the boys. But I don't intend to be a part of anything planned by Roberts. I'll stay out."

"That may or may not work," Colbraith offered. "If you don't make a clean break now you may still be drawn in."

"I'll take my chances," Dutch Charlie Duane replied.

Sunday, July 15

"SHERIFF, I NEED YOUR HELP," GEORGE FRANK RAPPED HIS KNUCKLES ON Pullis's door on Sunday morning. Sheriff Pullis opened the door slightly and recognized the merchant.

"What do you want, George? This is Sunday. What's the emergency?"

"I've got to see you about collecting Cueto's debt."

"Can't this wait until tomorrow? This is a day of rest and I intend to take it easy," Pullis groaned.

"No, it can't. Let me in, sheriff," George pressed.

Sheriff Pullis opened the door and let George into his room. "What's so goddamn urgent it can't wait?"

"I was told Pedro Cueto may leave town."

"So what?" Sheriff Pullis glared at the man as if he were insane. "I can't help you. I told you yesterday. Pedro said he didn't owe you the money. He refused to pay me."

"Sheriff, I've got a judgment against him for five hundred dollars." George took some rumpled papers and handed them to the sheriff. "He's got to pay."

Sheriff Pullis looked at the papers. "I can't do anything on Sunday." He handed the papers back to George.

"But if he skips town I'm out the money. He already sold the land he bought from me."

"I don't care about your money. I don't collect on Sundays. That's final." Pullis stood by the door waiting for George to leave it.

George did not move. "Look, sheriff. I'll give you half of anything you collect."

Pullis drew on his chin in contemplation of the offer. He could not get Cueto to pay, but if he gave the job to Sam Roberts, Pedro would pay it. Nobody could collect debts like Roberts. He always convinced debtors to pay up.

"Get out of here. I'll see what I can do. I keep half, that's our deal. So don't forget it. But don't bother me again on Sunday, you hear?" Pullis shoved George out the door.

Later that morning, after breakfasting at the Parker Hotel, Sheriff Pullis met with Roberts at Tammany Hall and asked him if he would collect a debt in exchange for keeping one quarter of all he collected. When Pullis mentioned Pedro Cueto, Roberts's eyes lit up like a blazing furnace.

"Another damned Chileno?" Roberts asked.

"Yes. Can you do it today?"

"With pleasure. I'll take some of the boys tonight," Roberts responded confidently. "But we won't do it for a quarter split. It ain't enough money. Give us half."

Sheriff Pullis anticipated the negotiation. "I'll give you one-third. That's plenty of money for such a small job." Pullis had already calculated that Roberts would keep $167 while he would get $83 without having to lift a finger or spend any time. Then he noticed the look on Roberts's face. "Don't use unnecessary force Sam. We don't need no trouble. Just get the money."

That night at Tammany Hall, Roberts waited until his men had consumed enough fiery liquid to soften their inhibitions. He jumped on a table as if it were a small box and roared for silence. All games and revelry at Tammany Hall ceased instantly. Cards, bottles, and glasses were placed on the tables, next to bags of gold dust and gold coins. Everyone's attention was riveted to Roberts.

"Boys, the alcalde asked us to go and collect a debt from Pedro Cueto tonight," he stormed.

"How much money?" someone asked.

"Owes five hundred dollars," Roberts responded and looked around.

The men stirred uneasily. Someone yelled, "What's the big deal, Sam? Five hundred ain't worth beans."

Sam smiled. The speaker had no interest in collecting such a small debt on a Sunday evening, not when a game of faro or monte could provide more excitement, more money, and plenty of spirits. Roberts did not expect anyone to be interested in leaving the bosom of Tammany Hall for such a small sum.

"Pedro Cueto is a goddamn greaser. A Chileno," he explained.

"Come on Sam. What's this all about?" another man called out.

Roberts pulled out his pistol and fired it into the ground. The sharp crack thundered through the tent. Everyone stood still. A pall of complete silence descended and embraced the heated tent like a thick ground fog.

Roberts glared, his eyes red and his face screwed up in a rage. He yelled, "I'll tell you what this is about. Like I've said before it's time for America for Americans. When the Chilenos killed Beatty no one did anything about it. Now's our chance. We're acting in an official capacity, for the alcalde. I say let's whip and drive out every damned Chileno in town. Are you with me?"

The tent exploded as the Hounds screamed and roared their approval. Bottles were raised to cheers and the fiery liquid flowed rapidly over the lips and down bear-like chins. The frenzy of men yelling and whooping themselves into a violent rage brought a smile to Roberts's grizzled face. He anticipated their reaction. Some yelled "Remember Beatty!" Beatty, a mean-spirited, small-minded man, had attacked a Chileno while trying to collect a debt. He was killed when the Chileno defended his home and accidentally shot his attacker. Sheriff Pullis seized all the Chileno's assets and sold them to the highest bidder. But the Hounds were not satisfied. They wanted more. They wanted blood. The brazen act of a Chileno killing an American, regardless of the circumstances, was unacceptable. Sheriff Pullis held them at bay, but now Roberts was about to unleash the dogs.

Armed with pistols, knives, and clubs nearly forty men poured out of Tammany Hall and headed silently for the foot of Telegraph Hill where the community of Chilenos lived. Most of the Hounds were on foot, though a few were mounted. They arrived quietly in the small valley where dozens of tents were spread out, all occupied by groups of men and a few families. Smoke rose from small fires next to the tents and the light of the flames danced in shadows across the canvas. Many of the dwellers had lamps inside the tents and shadows of the inhabitants reflected against the thin canvas sheets. In one tent a man with a wonderful tenor voice sang a soft melancholy song to the accompaniment of a guitar. From another tent came the wail of children.

Roberts looked around at his men. Satisfied he raised his pistol and fired a single shot into the black sky. His signal was instantly followed by gunfire which split the silence in the valley. The Hounds rushed forward violently tearing down tents and clubbing anyone who dared to oppose them. Going from tent to tent they plundered everything of value and destroyed what they could not or did not want to carry. Two men entered one tent and grabbed a young girl. A young man tried to defend her, but was shot in the knee, as the young girl screamed in horror. Roberts, his pistol in one hand and a Bowie knife in the other, entered a darkened tent. An elderly man with curly gray hair stood near the entrance, just behind the flap. The startled man looked up at the huge dark hulk in front of him as if he had just seen an apparition from the netherworld. He shrank back in terror but Roberts simply slashed him across the face with the knife. The man fell down holding his face and moaning. Two other men in the tent instantly crawled under the loose canvas and fled as Roberts fired his gun indiscriminately through the canvas at where he supposed they were, heedless of whom he might have

The Hounds Attack

shot. Terrified men and shrieking women grabbed their children and ran out of the tents, heading up Telegraph Hill. The mounted Hounds immediately gave chase shooting and clubbing the fleeing swarm. Several Chilenos fell as the blows rained down on them and bullets pierced their flesh. What had been a quiet, sultry night now erupted into earsplitting cacophony of shots being fired, men yelling, women screaming, and children crying.

Within a few minutes only a few tents remained standing. The Hounds, exhausted and spent from their predations, roamed and stalked the encampment paying no attention to the groans of wounded men lying on the ground. About twenty men entered the tent of Domingo Cruz. One of them noticed some bottles and demanded a drink as if he were speaking to a bartender. Cruz could not tell if the man was toying with him, so he did not respond quickly enough. This insult riled the men into another frenzy and they started to break everything in sight, while two of their comrades started to club Cruz with the broken legs of a table.

"Why are you doing this?" Cruz pleaded as he collapsed to the ground, nearly senseless.

"We are here at the orders of the alcalde," one of the men responded as he set fire to the tent. The Hounds walked out as Cruz struggled to crawl out of the burning inferno. Smoke and red circles swirled into the air. In the tent of Domingo Alegria the Hounds found and confiscated several thousand dollars in doubloons. No one looked for Pedro Cueto. All thoughts of collecting the debt were forgotten. Instead the Hounds broke into two groups of twenty each and continued their forage into the remaining tents, looting, beating, raping, and torching.

Roberts found one young girl, wearing a thin cotton nightgown. He grabbed her. The girl's father tried to protect her, but Roberts backhanded the man, sending him flying across the tent. The man lay motionless in a heap. Roberts ripped the clothes off the girl and grabbed her breasts. She screamed and he punched her in the face breaking her nose and knocking her out. Blood came pouring out of her nose and mouth. Roberts kicked her. Then he shot the man who remained motionless and headed for the next tent. Most of the tents were on fire and the reflection of the flames added to the macabre scene of darkened men, casting hideous and contorted shadows, running from tent to tent, chasing men, women, and children.

As the night wore on the sound of yelling and screaming subsided. The Hounds, weary from chasing and beating the Chilenos lost their lust. As the fires slowly snuffed themselves out an eerie quiet returned to the small smoke-filled valley at the foot of Telegraph Hill. Broken, battered, and bloodied bodies lay awkwardly among the charred ashes and ruins of the tents. The survivors appeared dazed by the suddenness and ferocity of the attack. A chorus of soft melancholy sobbing of men cradling their raped women, and women gently rocking their terrified children or beaten men, rose and fell through the quiet of the night.

Chapter Thirteen

Leashing the Hounds

SAN FRANCISCO
JULY 1849

Monday, July 16

THE DROWSY BOARDERS OF THE EXCELLENT HOUSE MADE THEIR WAY into the dining room for breakfast. Shuffling feet, early morning grumbling, and stale breath heralded their arrival. The men scratched themselves like mangy dogs, though they tried to do so politely when Mary Ellen walked in. Their appearance reminded her in some ways of participants in voodoo ceremonies—bloodshot, unfocused eyes, shirttails hanging languidly over their partially buttoned pants; hair plastered with oil or left standing awkwardly in different directions after a fitful night's sleep. A few cups of coffee and a stomach full of food would revitalize the men and send them off to work considerably more alert and with a lighter step.

Mary Ellen had already arranged the table with a fresh linen tablecloth, clean dishes, and silverware. She insisted, from the inception, that a well-set table, coupled with a good home-cooked meal, would provide their lodgers with a taste of domestic influence. They would be more comfortable and better tenants she told Case. He acquiesced. Her prophecy materialized in a short time. Case could see the changed, upbeat mood of the boarders. Civil conversation and neat, if not always clean, attire replaced short tempers, fiery tirades, and slovenly manners. Mary Ellen, in some ways, had become their surrogate mother or sister, listening patiently to their stories of loneliness, learning about broken families back home, from Ohio and Kentucky, to New York and South Carolina. These men shared their joys and sorrows with her. They even shared their most prized possessions next to gold—their letters. She cried with them, laughed and rejoiced on those rare occasions when good news arrived. She listened attentively, offered her shoulder or a gentle rebuke when warranted, always mindful of the need to remain nonjudgmental. The men responded. They found in Mary Ellen the ideal confessional, and they trusted her absolutely. Domestic tranquility infused the Excellent House to the delight of Case and Heiser.

In the middle of the table she set a large basket filled with freshly baked bread which Joseph had purchased earlier that morning from the new German bakery on Kearney Street. The dark grainy bread's sweet aroma drifted through the dining room. Mary Ellen poured coffee, silently preferring to listen to the men talk and not to herself. She recalled Marie Laveau's injunction. "Listen and learn! Never give in to the desire to befriend or impress," Marie cautioned. "It's an easy trap to fall into. Too many people like to hear the sound of their own voice. It may be rich and melodious but they learn nothing. It just makes them all the more ignorant." Mary Ellen heeded this advice and noted how well it served her. Usually, after a cup or two of steaming coffee, a lubricant that loosened morning tongues, the men would engage animatedly in business conversations. Most of them worked for Case & Heiser. Mary Ellen listened attentively to these conversations. The men, accustomed to her company, paid no heed to her presence, even when the discussions focused on very sensitive and confidential matters. She paid particularly solicitous care to the discussions between Case, Heiser and their business associates, especially the Woodworth brothers, Selim and Fred, and the new shipping agent, Minturn, though she could not recall his first name. They were all regulars at dinner. Mary Ellen garnered a fairly clear picture of the commercial and social life of San Francisco. She learned first hand how business was conducted in the city, who the major players were, where the money went, who would succeed and who would fail. Economic and commercial forecasts were favorite pastimes, a preoccupation for just about everyone in the city. Everybody dabbled in it. Their predictions changed daily with each incoming wave of gold from the mines or people from distant shores. But this morning, perhaps because it was Monday, the men appeared somewhat subdued and reserved.

After breakfast, as Joseph and the mindless boy were clearing the table, Kanaka Davis burst into the dining room, startling everyone. Out of breath and drenched in perspiration, he stopped next to the table, slumped over and placed his hands on his knees, appearing exhausted. Mary Ellen and Case rushed over to him.

"What's wrong? Are you all right?" Case asked as he placed his arm around the hunched figure.

Kanaka straightened up, his ponderous body shaking, and unfastened his damp collar as if such an act would release the words lodged in his constricted throat. "Did you hear what happened last night?" he gasped, the words wavering, each syllable punctuated with pauses as his lungs sought purchase. Kanaka's manner startled Mary Ellen and the men. Like others from the Sandwich Isles, he was known for his composure and equanimity. But the man standing before them in the dining room this morning bore no resemblance to the placid man. Instead, Kanaka Davis appeared haggard, bewildered, nearly hysterical.

"What are you talking about? What's the matter?" Case probed, the concern registering on his face. Kanaka, with jet black hair, handsome though slightly bulbous nose, allowed himself to be led to the table where he sat wearily. His gentle black eyes and fleshy face belied an intelligent and stirring mind. He lived next door, a resident of San Francisco from the times before the gold rush. He now owned large tracts of land, some of which he had purchased almost by accident for a few dollars before Marshall's discovery. Kanaka went to the gold fields but never found gold.

He was not suited for the harsh environment, the terrible winters, the constant dampness and physically demanding work. He returned to San Francisco weary and broke, only to find himself rich beyond his wildest dreams. In his absence his worthless land had turned into gold. Although a large man by any measure, the cause of his ever-spreading girth could be laid directly in the delicate hands of Mary Ellen. Her savory dishes induced Kanaka Davis to attend meals at the Excellent House as a frequent guest. But this Monday morning, Kanaka's visit and manner alarmed Mary Ellen. Everyone at the table remained silent and waited anxiously.

Slowly gaining composure, Kanaka inhaled and spoke. "A terrible thing happened last night," he stammered. "They sacked the entire village of Chilenos at Telegraph Hill."

"Who did?" Case asked uncertainly.

"The Hounds! The Hounds!" Kanaka's brief composure broke like a crumbling dam and he buried his massive face in his hands as if to shield his eyes from the sights in his mind.

Mary Ellen stood behind him and gently placed her hands on his shoulders and soothingly kneaded the tense muscles. Kanaka looked up and spoke so softly everyone craned their necks and strained to listen. "Last night they attacked the Chilenos at Telegraph Hill. Killed two men. Many women were . . . " Kanaka looked at Mary Ellen uncertainly " . . . violated. They burned their homes, beat the men and women viciously. Some were shot. Not a single one was untouched, it's all ruins," his voice grew more shrill. "Oh my goodness it was terrible. Just terrible." His ever-gentle eyes were moist. "I've taken one family of four into my house. Others are trying to help. William Howard has taken about eight Chilenos into his home. Telegraph Hill looks like a scorched battlefield."

William Howard was another old-timer who settled in California in 1838. He purchased the Hudson Bay Company facilities in 1847 and became a successful merchant, perhaps one of the most highly respected members of the community. Mary Ellen really liked the self-assured but gentle man who always found the time to give of himself. That he had taken in eight refugees under his roof did not surprise her.

Samuel, who had just walked into the room overheard Kanaka's tale and reached for his ear, as if someone were about to cut it off again. He stood there trembling.

"Who else knows about this?" Case asked.

"Word is spreading like wildfire. By now it must be common knowledge. I heard Brannan is up in arms. Kemble woke him up at dawn and told him what happened. The Hounds stole from Brannan's store, you know."

"Yeah, I heard about that," Case said.

"Brannan and Captain Bezer Simmons went to Alcalde Leavenworth's office. They will demand that he arrest the Hounds responsible for this incident. They don't expect much help from Leavenworth. Brannan also called for a meeting at Howard's place on Montgomery and Clay at ten o'clock this morning. He'll bring us up to date and tell us what the alcalde said."

The men were visibly appalled. Mary Ellen could feel the tension and the anger, like the tingling of the skin when lightning is about to strike.

"Well, we must do something about them," Case said and threw his napkin angrily on the table. "This is the final straw. If we don't act now, who will be next? Nothing is safe from these animals. They're taking over the town. We can't let them." He stood up. "You men," he turned to the others sitting silently at the table, their food untouched, "let's put some money into a pot and start a relief fund."

Case seized the bread basket, spilled the bread onto the table and the men quickly emptied the contents of their pockets into it. "Let's find out what Brannan is up to." All the men were now up and following Case. Mary Ellen stood by uncertainly. Case turned to her. "We may need to provide some shelter for some of the victims. See what we can rustle up. Blankets, clothes, anything."

"Be very careful, Mr. Case," Mary Ellen cautioned.

Case looked at her with an appreciative smile. "Now don't you go worrying yourself none, Mary Ellen. After today the only ones who'll be worrying are the Hounds—as their necks stretch and they face their maker."

Case wiped his mouth with the napkin. Clutching the basket filled with nuggets, coins, and a few bags of gold dust, he walked out with determination, followed by the other boarders and Kanaka Davis, despair still etched into his fleshy face.

Samuel remained still, unable and unwilling to move.

"It's all right, Samuel," Mary Ellen said gently, taking his hand in hers and leading him back into the kitchen. "You have nothing more to fear from that rabble. Mr. Case and the others will put a stop to this business. This lawlessness." Her own words sounded hollow and the pit of her stomach burned with uncertainty and fear.

—~—

OUTSIDE THE EXCELLENT HOUSE BEDLAM REIGNED. PEOPLE WERE rushing toward Clay Street, their faces grim and wrathful. Selim Woodworth pushed his way roughly through the throng. Nearly a head taller than all those around him he quickly spied Case.

"Can you believe this?" Woodworth asked, his long curly black beard unkempt with a few scraps of food still entangled near his lips. "Why, its sheer madness."

Case noticed that his tall friend had two pistols tucked into his belt next to a knife. They turned down Clay Street and found the street full of people. They pushed their way through the throng until they found Brannan, Kemble, and Howard, all engaged in a spirited discussion.

"He can go to hell," Brannan spat the words out. "Won't lift a finger."

Howard placed his hand on Brannan's shoulder. "This is the final straw. He's lost the respect of this community."

"If he ever had it in the first place," Kemble joined.

"I'm going to tell the people of San Francisco exactly where Alcalde Leavenworth stands. They won't be happy." Brannan pursed his lips and his jawbones seemed to pulsate slowly. He pulled his silver watch from his fob pocket. "Well, it's time, gentlemen."

The entire intersection of Clay and Montgomery was completely blocked off, choked with hundreds of angry, seething San Franciscans. Brannan started to speak, "Last night . . . "

"We can't see you!" someone yelled from the crowd. Others called for Brannan to step closer. Then Brannan spotted a large oak barrel, so he mounted it. Now he could see just over the heads of those milling in front. A huge throng had converged. People were jammed shoulder to shoulder like sardines. He looked around, saw many familiar faces, but he also saw a few men who glared at him with open hostility. Nearly everyone in the crowd was armed.

"By now you all know what happened last night," his voice carried over the uplifted faces. "Wanton murder, rape, assault, arson and every conceivable crime committed under the shade of darkness. A whole village of men, women, and children, killed, injured and now left indigent and helpless. How long are you going to stand for this?" His voice trembled. A loud grumble echoed from the crowd. "Hounds? How aptly named. Animals! Curs! They think they can do as they please. But they're mistaken. Gravely mistaken. They've stolen from me. They ransacked the Parker House. And they'll steal from you. They'll come after you, I tell you. Have any of them been arrested?" He paused as the crowd returned a chorus of, "No!" "That's right—no, not a single one. And we all know why. Because the sheriff, Pullis, is one of them. He has the same smell and the same fleas. And let's not forget our alcalde, Leavenworth."

The crowd stirred as the men shouted epithets at the mention of each name, calling for the execution of Pullis and sending the alcalde out of town with tar and feathers. Brannan noticed that a few men had now taken their pistols out of their belts. They looked at him with hostile expressions; a few smiled menacingly every time he mentioned the previous night's predations.

"This morning Captain Bezer Simmons and I met with the alcalde in his office. We asked him to arrest the perpetrators. Do you know what he said?"

Again, many in the crowd shouted no and Brannan lifted his hands to still them.

"He said: 'We have no proof against anyone.' Can you imagine that? No proof? Broken and smashed bodies lying everywhere. People without homes. Graves being dug. Children left parentless." Brannan arched his brow. "No proof?" he said mockingly.

The crowd roared. But there were too many people packed in the narrow intersection. More people were arriving, drawn by the noise. But the narrow street forced them to stand at some distance from Brannan. The crowd had spilled over to Montgomery Street where many were standing in the wet sand, just a few feet from the lapping water's edge. Brannan noticed the bulging population, people streaming like rivers into an already overfilled lake. The damn would burst soon.

"It's too crowded here. Let's move to the plaza!" he shouted.

As word spread outward, like the circles formed by a pebble dropped into water, the crowd started to make its way westward up the hill to Portsmouth Square. Brannan, Kemble, Case, Woodworth, Davis, and Howard walked hurriedly together.

"I think the Hounds are here," Brannan said to Howard.

"I saw them. You better be careful, Sam."

"You don't think they would dare attack you in front of this mob, do you?" Woodworth asked.

"Who knows what they'd do. They're crazy. Especially Roberts," Case said.

As they neared the plaza, Howard turned to Brannan. "Where do you want to stand?"

Brannan smiled. "I've got an idea."

COLBRAITH AND KOHLER WERE INSIDE STEVENSON'S OFFICE DISCUSSING the previous night's debacle.

"It wasn't a question of whether they would make some calamitous move. The question was when. And now we know the answer. What a bunch of idiots. And some of them were my men. I brought them to these shores and I feel the weight of responsibility." Stevenson paced back and forth, his brows knitted so closely together that his forehead looked like a plowed field ready for planting.

"Can't blame yourself," Colbraith tried to placate the agitated man. "You predicted it all along. In the absence of any real law and order or the institutions needed to prevent this sort of thing violence is bound to happen."

They heard a deep resonant sound outside, growing louder, like a swarm of grumbling bees.

Chapter Thirteen

Colbraith continued as Fred Kohler went to the window. "I find it remarkable that a city like San Francisco, with a permanent population in the thousands and doubling in size every month, allows such lawlessness. Ostensibly there's a city council and an alcalde. Just remarkable."

"Come look at this," Kohler called out.

Stevenson and Colbraith rushed to the window. Below them they could see a mass of people moving together in a snakelike procession toward the plaza.

Stevenson turned to Colbraith, "Something big is taking place at the plaza. I suspect it has to do with the Hounds."

"Looks like the entire population of San Francisco is headed that way," Kohler remarked to no one in particular.

"Well, I'd like to find out what's going on," Colbraith declared.

Kohler rushed to his chair, grabbed his hat, and the three men went outside where they were engulfed by the mob. In seconds they found themselves being carried away by the crunch of humanity unable to do anything except to hang on for fear of falling and getting trampled.

—m—

ALCALDE LEAVENWORTH'S OFFICE ON CLAY STREET, AT THE REAR OF the City Hotel, faced Portsmouth Square. Brannan climbed up the side-stairs of the hotel, made his way to the roof of the alcalde's house and perched precariously near the edge, with his legs wide apart, waiting for the crowd to settle in. He looked down from his roost and was instantly seen by the masses who pressed in closer to the alcalde's building.

Brannan could see more men in the crowd inching their way forward with guns drawn. He took a deep breath and continued. "A few days ago some Hounds stole from my store. When I asked our sheriff to arrest them, the goddamned lily-livered yellow son-of-a-bitch told me that he didn't have the power. He said if I wanted them arrested I should do it myself. And that's why I've called you all here."

William Howard tugged at Case's elbow. "I'm afraid there are a lot of Hounds mixed into this crowd. I've seen some of them. I heard them threaten Sam. One said that his family would be in danger. I don't know if he should continue like this."

"I see them, Bill," Case replied. "We need to get the word to Sam." Case turned around and noticed Talbot Greene standing nearby. He quietly moved to Greene's side and whispered in his ear. Greene, his face remaining impassive except for a slight wrinkling of his brow, nodded his head and quickly moved away through the crowd.

Brannan paused for a moment and looked at the aroused crowd.

"What should we do, Sam?" someone yelled.

"How do we stop them?" another voice blared.

Soon the entire assembly stirred with cries of assent. One man, standing near the front looked at Brannan with a malevolent glare and mouthed the words, "We're going to kill you."

Brannan raised his arms again to calm the crowd. Then he glared at the man with a blazing intensity until the man looked away uncomfortably. Suddenly he heard footsteps on the roof and Talbot Greene appeared. He handed Brannan a small piece of paper. Brannan read it, gritted his teeth, hatred flashing in his eyes. Talbot Greene retreated a few steps and knelt down. Brannan's erect body loomed alone over the masses as they silently waited for him to speak.

"My friends, this city is in jeopardy. The rotten Hounds are getting bolder and bolder. Last night they killed and pillaged. Who will be next? What will stop them from destroying everything? What little government we have is helpless, if not worthless. There is no one to protect our women and children. We have to do it ourselves. And by god we will do it."

A loud groundswell of voices reverberated through the plaza like a tumultuous wave slowly rising only to break on the shore, as the people vented their deep-seated agreement with Brannan.

He continued, "We must take immediate action. Not tomorrow, but today. Now who's with me?"

A chaotic roar greeted this question as hundreds of angry protesters pressed forward as if being closer to Brannan gave them absolution. Among the throng, in scattered groups, some of the Hounds grasped their weapons. One man, near the front, removed his pistol and the glint of sunlight caught Brannan's eye. He paused briefly and inhaled.

"I've been told that there are a few mongrels among us." Brannan raised the paper as if to read it. "And they are now threatening me. They say if I don't shut up they will kill me or my wife and child, or burn down my house." He stopped, his eyes blazing and his face turning a dark shade of red. Then he slowly unbuttoned his shirt from the collar down baring his massive chest. "Well, go ahead, shoot, you miserable bastards!" He looked down at the man with the gun.

A pall fell over the crowd. "I said, go ahead and shoot, you miserable cowards!" Brannan challenged them again.

This time the crowd stirred into action, like a giant dragon woken from an infernal sleep as men turned and faced the Hounds in their midst. The frightened Hounds started a mass retreat, their hands on their weapons, but the weapons concealed. Brannan cast his glare at the man below. The man in the front of the crowd looked uncertainly at his gun but was instantly grabbed and thrown roughly to the ground by some of the bystanders. Like someone possessed, he punched and kicked at those near him who in equal frenzy returned his gesture with a flurry of punches and kicks. His pistol pitched out of his hand. But with a sudden paroxysm he managed to free himself from the grasping hands, some clutching tufts of his hair. The terrified man bolted screaming through the crowd in a mad effort to escape, his bloody face contorted with fear and panic; large portions of his scalp were missing.

Brannan confidently buttoned his shirt. "You are a bunch of dirty, rotten, worthless trash. Scum. You don't have the guts to kill me or anyone else anymore, cause you know you'll hang. We're coming after you! We're going to beat the living hell out of you! Then we're going to hang you! You're finished! You hear? You're finished for good." The crowd, in one voice, vented its rage in complete agreement.

Talbot Greene edged closer to Brannan who stood panting and handed him another note. Brannan looked surprised for a brief moment, then broke into a broad grin and waved the note in the air as if to bid the departing Hounds a fond adieu.

"Alcalde Leavenworth, our esteemed leader, has just issued a proclamation for an indignation meeting right here in the plaza at three o'clock this afternoon. We need to have the entire population of this city present. Friends and neighbors, we are finally going to take some official and immediate action. There are thousands of us, only a hundred of them. Let's expel them once and for all. Let's bring the criminals to justice. We will reconvene and organize in the plaza at three o'clock this afternoon."

Brannan came down from the roof with Greene. Woodworth and Howard both had their guns drawn and held at their sides.

"You are in some danger, Sam. I suggest that you stay under guard until we finish with this business," Woodworth cautioned. Brannan patted his friend on the shoulder.

"I'm not worried," he said, his voice raspy and raw.

"What are you going to propose?" Howard asked.

"It's very simple. Let's organize a large force of armed men to serve as a police force, arrest the dregs, try them if need be, and hang them, just as Sheriff Pullis suggested. The Regulators need regulating." The men laughed uneasily.

Woodworth, Howard, Davis, Kemble and a few other men formed a secure cordon around Brannan and quickly escorted him back to his home. Case excused himself and returned to the Excellent House.

Colbraith, standing nearby, regarded Brannan with a mixture of admiration and dismay. Clearly Brannan had a fiery demeanor and a faculty for leadership. He had a huge mob ready to do whatever he suggested. Colbraith wondered whether Brannan could keep his temper in check. Bearing his breast and daring the Hounds to shoot was brilliant, but only because they had not done so. Colbraith understood how differently it could have ended for Brannan, though he suspected that the Hounds would end up the same whether Brannan lived or died. Again, he found it remarkable that a city with a purported municipal government would allow a mob to decide how to redress grievances committed by a lawless element in its midst. In his view the existing government, such as it was, had left a void in leadership, a void large enough to swallow the Island of Alcatraz. But it also offered a magnificent opportunity. In just a few minutes many of his views and ideas had crystallized with absolute clarity; although he felt that the Hounds and their use of the Tammany name may have tainted those immigrants from New York, especially those with real Tammany Hall experience.

"I'm coming back at three o'clock," he announced to Stevenson and Kohler. "Wouldn't miss it for the world."

Stevenson and Kohler were taken aback, not so much by what Colbraith had said, but because he smiled, a rare and genuinely novel event.

—m—

MARY ELLEN HAD RUMMAGED THROUGH THE BOARDING HOUSE AND found some old unused blankets. She also filled a box with some discarded clothing, mostly dirty, but usable. Case and Mary Ellen went to the Case & Heiser warehouse where Heiser was already busy putting together some packages of sundry items for the victims, from clothes and food to tools. No customers came to their store while they worked. Commerce, the moving force of San Francisco, had come to an abrupt ending; something the forces of nature—rain, wind, or biting dust—could not accomplish. The saloons were filled to the brim, but few patronized the gaming tables. Instead, everyone was engrossed with the Hounds. Generous libations greased their liquid tongues.

Shortly before three o'clock, Mary Ellen, Case, Heiser and some of the other men from the boarding house made their way to Portsmouth Square to attend the indignation meeting. Alcalde Leavenworth had arranged for several tables to be set up at the highest point near the City Hotel.

Mary Ellen turned to Case. "This is the largest crowd I have ever seen here for any occasion."

Case agreed. There were, in his opinion, well over two thousand San Franciscans. They were all armed and grim-faced. Noticeably absent from the crowd were the Hounds. Not a single Hound had dared to show his face. And more people were arriving and pressing into the already crowded area.

At precisely three o'clock Alcalde Leavenworth, who had been continuously looking at the silver watch in his hand as if it might run away from him, finally stood atop one of the tables and brought the meeting to order.

City Hotel

"The first business is to elect a chairman and secretary for this meeting. We must do it right."

A few hecklers let Leavenworth know that they did not hold him in the highest regard, but the majority quickly silenced the few gadflies. William Howard, perhaps the most popular man in San Francisco, and running unopposed, quickly received a robust and unanimous acclamation from the crowd. Howard took over as official chairman of the meeting.

Woodworth turned to Brannan. "This is the largest assembly I've ever seen in this city." Woodworth, who had come to California as an ensign on a U.S. warship in 1848, had been in San Francisco almost as long as Brannan had.

"You bet!" Brannan replied tersely.

Howard, slowly made his way to stand in front of the central table and looked at the astonishing crowd. His deer-like brown eyes, usually soft and warm, were intense and steely hard. He, too, marveled at the size of the gathering, recalling his first arrival in California in 1838, as the first American to settle in the area. Where only a few huts existed in 1838, he now beheld a burgeoning city with a rapidly growing population.

In measured Bostonian Brogue, with his prominent cleft chin thrusting out aggressively, Howard raised his hands to silence the crowd.

"We must elect a secretary to record these proceedings," he declared. "I want every decision we make at this meeting duly inscribed, for I believe we are finally taking that crucial step of securing the citizens of our fair city from wanton criminal activity. I propose the election of Dr. Fouregard as secretary."

"I second the motion," Woodworth yelled instantly.

"All in favor?" Howard called out.

A thunderous chorus of ayes descended from the undulating mass of people.

"All opposed?"

The crowd quieted down with a few jeers from some staggering drunks.

"I declare Dr. Fouregard elected."

Dr. Fouregard sat down at the head table and produced a sheaf of papers, a pen and inkwell and immediately began writing.

Colbraith, Stevenson, and Kohler pressed their way forward earning a few ungrateful remarks, until they stood directly before the tables.

"We should be up at the front to register our support," Stevenson had suggested a few minutes earlier when they entered the plaza to find it occupied to capacity, and overflowing to the side streets. "This could be a watershed for those of us who emigrated from New York," he turned to Colbraith, "and for anyone aspiring to office."

Colbraith agreed so they plunged into the crowd like boats heading out to sea through incoming waves. Colbraith did not need any prodding. Having formulated his new plans, success depended on his ability to work well with all the prominent leaders in the city. Virtually all the important people were present. He could not afford to straddle the fence or remain anonymous. He had to act.

The crowd started to chant Brannan's name. The refrain picked up by hundreds of throats. "Brannan. Brannan. Brannan." Howard smiled genuinely and turned to Brannan, who stood expectantly by him.

"You better address them or we'll be hung before the Hounds."

Brannan mounted the table next to him and began slowly. But his expression confirmed to Colbraith that the zeal shown earlier remained unaltered.

"We are gathered here to take immediate action on a matter of the greatest urgency for this city. You all know the group calling themselves the Regulators or the Hounds. You know of their actions, their depredations. They have stolen food and destroyed the premises of Rousson's," he hesitated, "not once but twice. They stole from my store. They stole from old Frenchman. We are not talking about petty thievery or larceny. We are talking about thirty-five to forty rogues helping themselves to someone's property, like eating all the food in a restaurant, then destroying the premises if their demands are not met quickly enough. Isaac Bluxome erected a store on Montgomery at considerable expense. The Hounds confronted him before he had his first customer and tried to steal his merchandise. They stole shoes, blankets, clothes, mining equipment—all in the name of law and order." Here Brannan paused briefly, turned and looked evenly at Alcalde Leavenworth who kept his gaze solidly on the ground inspecting every grain of sand within a few inches of his toes.

"They have beaten innocent people, claiming they were collecting legal debts for the sheriff, who is one of them." Brannan now looked for Sheriff Pullis, but his absence was conspicuous. "These incidents now pale before the heinous conduct directed at the Chilenos of our city. And if they do it to the Chilenos without fear or recrimination, without accountability, who is next? Of course it is us—you!" Brannan pointed at someone in the crowd. "And you!" Pointing at another. "Your families. Me. None of us is safe any longer. Not in our place of business. Not in our homes. Certainly not in the streets of this city. So I am proposing this!" Brannan gestured with his finger as if to make an exclamation point. "We form a police force now, right this minute. This constabulary will be given instructions to immediately arrest those responsible for the killing and the mayhem. I say roust the rest of the rabble out of their den and send them off packing."

The crowd roared its approval, the noise blasting the warm day like a sudden winter squall.

Brannan raised his hands and waved for silence. "But first we must think of all those injured and ruined by the perversions committed last night. Men, women and children desperately need shelter and food. I want every man and woman here to dig into your pockets right now and take out some gold. Dr. Fouregard will collect the money which will be dispensed to those wretched victims."

Howard handed Dr. Fouregard a large basket. Dr. Fouregard quickly wound his way through the crowd imploring people to provide aid. Soon other baskets were brought forward and filled with bags of gold dust, nuggets, coins and anything else of value. The brimming baskets were retrieved and placed on one of the tables. Woodworth, Howard, and a few other men immediately placed themselves around the table, conspicuously displaying their weapons. Dr. Fouregard assigned several men to take a count of the contents and account for all the contributions.

Brannan continued. "Now let's organize—we need a real police force. Who will volunteer?"

A pressing wall of armed men instantly surged forward toward the tables, nearly toppling them over and crushing those standing nearby. Colbraith braced himself from being trampled and joined one of the lines. Likewise Stevenson and Kohler queued up. Dr. Fouregard called for more paper and ink. They materialized from behind him and the enlistment began in earnest with long lines winding their way across the plaza.

"Brannan, do you want to lead these men?" Howard asked.

"No. Let's get someone competent. Who has strong military experience?" Howard asked Woodworth.

"Why don't you place Willard Spofford in charge?" Woodworth offered and looked at the long lines of volunteers. "Ah, there's Stevenson," he pointed.

Brannan's eyes narrowed. "Most of the Hounds came with him. Can we really trust him?"

"He's always been a good leader. Came with what he had, Sam. You know his reputation. Can't fault him for how these men have acted. He has nothing to do with them," Woodworth responded.

"I see he's got those other New Yorkers with him, O'Brien and Kohler," Howard remarked. "I've seen O'Brien go into Tammany Hall."

Talbot Greene interceded. "I suppose every New Yorker at one time or another has gone in there. But their reputation in the coinage is excellent. I buy from them and so do you, Bill."

Howard nodded his head in agreement.

"I also use their coins," Woodworth said as he brushed his beard with his hands. "They're okay, though it's hard to read O'Brien. He may be stone cold, but he ain't no criminal."

"Okay, let's see if Stevenson will agree to lead a company," Howard continued to look at the long lines.

"There's Wadleigh, Simmons," Woodworth hesitated.

Howard added: "I see Smith, Gillespie, Hughes . . . "

"Hold on, Bill. That's enough. Too many chefs or is it chiefs," Brannan chortled.

"Hey, Willard, come over here," Howard called out. "Why don't you sit with Selim and get things organized?"

While Spofford and Selim Woodworth set about to organize the new constabulary, Howard turned to the restive crowd. "Our job is not done yet. Please. Can I have your attention!"

As the people settled down and became attentive Howard continued.

"We must do everything by the book. We will need to have trials . . . "

The crowd started to rumble.

"We don't need no trials. Just hang the bastards," someone yelled and soon others joined.

"Can't trust no judges or lawyers. It don't work. Hang them."

Brannan jumped up next to Howard. "Bill is right. No one here is any more eager than I am to hang those devils. But let's do it the legal way."

"You be the judge, Sam!" one man yelled and soon the entire contingent started to chant, "Brannan, Brannan, Brannan," again.

Brannan shook his head back and forth. "No sirree. Not me. They

Chapter Thirteen

Portsmouth Square

robbed me. I'm biased. Let's get the right people. Bill, why not appoint lawyers and judges we trust to do this."

Howard held his hands up again to silence the crowd. "Sam's right. I suggest we appoint two prosecutors, two defenders, and two new judges to help the alcalde here, people we can trust to try the rascals."

Like a wave rising and crashing on the shore, then receding only to come back again, the throng murmured and the jeers died down.

"I suggest we appoint Hal McAllister and Horace Hawes to represent us and prosecute the animals. What say you?"

The roar of approval came as one voice.

"And for defense lawyers . . . "

"They don't need lawyers . . . " someone interrupted.

"Yes they do. I suggest Peter Barry and Myron Norton."

Barry and Norton, who were standing close to each other looked as if they had swallowed a horse. Barry looked at Howard, his face in complete shock. Norton spoke to him quietly, but Barry's expression barely changed.

Howard understood. "Look men. The job of defending these thugs is the toughest of all. You know Norton and Barry. If there is any problem with either of these fine gentlemen, let's hear it now."

The crowd continued to murmur, but not a single objection was raised.

"Finally, we need two judges. Men whose integrity and judgment are beyond question."

Brannan spoke. "Many of you do not know this, but we have among us a very distinguished gentleman, William Gwin. He has been a U.S. Marshal, a Commissioner of Public Works in New Orleans, and a congressman from Mississippi. No one, but no one in this city is more qualified to serve as an impartial judge. Mr. Gwin, would you please come here so that everyone can see you?"

A tall, elegantly dressed man walked up to the table, ramrod straight, his face shaven and his short graying hair combed back revealing an aquiline nose with a small wart on the side. Brannan thought to himself how Gwin carried himself so well, strong but not hostile, friendly but not endearing. He looked like presidential material. Brannan was one of the few people who knew of Gwin's intention to become a senator from California.

The man looked vaguely familiar to Colbraith. He had seen him before but could not place him. Gwin reminded Colbraith of portraits of Andrew Jackson. The tall Southerner looked confident and comfortable in front of the people. He turned and faced the crowd. He waved to them as if he were running for office.

Howard stepped up to him and shook his hand.

Gwin stepped back and Howard spoke: "I share Sam's enthusiasm for Mr. Gwin. I also suggest the appointment of Howard Hawes as the other judge."

Brannan could tell the crowd was becoming restless and had tired of all the appointments. "Just hold on for a few more minutes, folks. I know you want action. And we will have it shortly, as soon as the troops are mustered. But we need your approval of these appointments. It's your indignation meeting."

The crowd came back to life. "Aye, Aye, Aye," they yelled.

Howard took this opportunity and shouted, "All in favor?"

The ayes continued.

"All opposed?"

The din ended.

"You now have your prosecutors, defenders, and judges. Are there any other motions?"

Howard looked around. "I declare this meeting adjourned. Let's get the bastards!"

Willard Spofford set about to organize the new police force. He formed six companies, headed by Stevenson and the others. One of the largest merchants in the city, Hiram Webb, owner of Webb & Harris contributed sixty new muskets. By five o'clock in the afternoon San Francisco's new police force was fully armed, organized and ready for action.

—∾—

THE UNPAINTED ADOBE BUILDING ON BROADWAY AND POWELL HAD ONE heavy oak door entrance and two small windows facing the street. Isaac Bluxome, Jr., leading twenty new constables stationed five men under each window, dispersed five men to the middle of the intersection with a good view in all directions and positioned the remaining force at the front door.

Bluxome pounded the door with the hasp of his Bowie knife. "Roberts! You're under arrest. Come on out slowly and with your hands up."

The edgy volunteers pointed their muskets at the building, their fingers reflexively feeling for the trigger. Bluxome pounded again.

"Roberts. This is your last warning. Come out or we're coming in after you."

Shutters on the windows across the street slammed shut causing a few of the policemen to wheel around as if they were about to be attacked from behind.

"All right, men. Break the door down!"

Two of the largest constables immediately set about the task and simultaneously heaved their broad shoulders against the door. It barely budged.

"Again!" Bluxome commanded.

The men grunted as they slammed into the door again. It gave in a bit. The other constables had their guns ready and aimed at the door, though their fellow police occupied most of the space.

After the fourth try, the sweaty men managed to break the door down, with one of the men stumbling in on all fours. The rest of the newly appointed police rushed past. Bluxome waited anxiously outside. Finally one of his men came running out.

"No one inside."

"Damn," Bluxome muttered under his breath. This is where Roberts resided.

"Let's head over to Tammany! On the double. He must have been warned."

The squad ran down Broadway where they encountered another company of men lead by Stevenson.

"Roberts is gone. He isn't at his house, though we had good information that he was there," Bluxome told Stevenson. "So we're heading for Tammany."

"There is at least one company already surrounding Tammany," Stevenson advised. "They aren't letting anyone out."

"But if Roberts is in there they'll make a stand," Bluxome warned.

Stevenson put his hand on Bluxome's shoulder in a paternal way. "No, Isaac, he won't. Roberts won't fight. I know. He came with my volunteers. He's one of those who musters courage only when he physically overmatches his adversaries. I suspect he's hiding somewhere, scared shitless."

The two companies fell together and headed for Tammany. They turned right on Kearney and headed for the massive tent situated just past the plaza. When they arrived there were more than fifty men surrounding the canvas shelter of the Hounds. These men were lead by Hal McAllister.

"What's going on, Hal?" Stevenson asked.

"We're about to go in and arrest any Hounds we find in there. We've been negotiating with some people inside for the last five minutes. They claim there are no Hounds there."

Chapter Thirteen

"Well, hell's bells. Hal, you can't lawyer this thing. All negotiations are over. Let me handle this," Stevenson said. He walked toward the entrance to the tent.

"Men. This is Colonel Stevenson. We're coming in and taking the Hounds."

"Colonel, there ain't no Hounds in here," a voice called back.

"That you Lawson? You goddamned rot-sucking pig. You're one of them. Now let's not have any firing, cause we are coming in and if anyone lays a hand on us we are going to set a torch to the tent and burn the lot of you. You hear me?"

The last words caused a stir and commotion inside with some voices arguing.

"All right, Colonel," a different voice answered. "We're coming out. Don't shoot."

The tent flaps lifted and several men came out with their arms in the air and were immediately surrounded by McAllister's men. Soon others came filtering out, walking slowly and carefully, many with their shoulders hunched in resignation, others walking as softly as if they were treading on slippery ground, trying to be as inconspicuous as possible.

"That's one of them Hounds!" one of the constables shouted and pointed at a man who edged back to the tent. Soon other Hounds were spotted and were immediately set upon. Within minutes seventeen Hounds had been arrested without offering any resistance. Roberts was not there.

"The rest of you better get back to your homes!" Bluxome advised. "Cause someone may mistake you for these miserable wretches and shoot you on sight. Now get on."

The rest of the crowd dispersed leaving the Hounds ringed by police.

"Where are we going to place this scum?" McAllister asked.

San Francisco, relatively crime free during the initial rush to the gold fields, did not have a jail.

Stevenson answered. "The *U.S.S. Warren* is lying at the harbor. They have a brig. Let's take them and see if the navy will accommodate us during their trials."

"Hal, mind if I have a word with one of them?" Stevenson offered.

"Go right ahead, Colonel. They're not going anywhere right now."

"Lawson, get your rear over here on the double!" Stevenson commanded.

John Lawson, tall and thin, a shock of black hair sprouting straight up as if struck by lightning, bolted as if he were still under Stevenson's command.

Stevenson grabbed the lapel of Lawson's dirty jacket, roughly pulled him over to the side, and forced him to sit on a barrel. Stevenson hovered menacingly over the cowering man.

"Where's Roberts?"

"I don't know, Colonel," Lawson stuttered, and looked away.

Stevenson grabbed Lawson's chin and made him gaze directly into his eyes. "John, I'm not going to ask again. Let's just say a good word from me might be the greatest and healthiest thing that ever happened to you. Or your neck."

Stevenson let the words fall slowly and kept his grip on Lawson's chin, holding the dirt-encrusted face a few inches from his own as he glared malevolently at the man.

"Now, for the last time, where is Roberts."

"He's going to kill me, Colonel."

"No, he won't. He's going to be the first to hang."

Stevenson let go of Lawson's face and Lawson wiped the perspiration from his forehead with his forearm, spreading the grime into a new pattern.

"He's on the schooner *Mary* bound for Sacramento. Says he'll lay low for a short time then come back and take his revenge on Brannan and the others." Lawson blew his nose and then looked pleadingly at Stevenson. "Please don't let anyone know I told you."

Stevenson regarded his former volunteer with a bemused smile and shook his head.

"Son, it don't matter. I told you, Roberts is history. Get back with the others."

Lawson dawdled for a moment, his eyes cast down in hangdog fashion, and slowly ambled back to the other prisoners, flanked by two sentries.

Stevenson turned to McAllister. "Hal, you know where the *Mary* is docked?"

"Yes. Leaves for Sacramento tonight."

"Well, Roberts is on board."

McAllister smiled. "I'll go fetch him."

—~—

THE CREW OF THE *MARY*, A TWO-MASTED SCHOONER, WAS PREPARING to hoist the sails on the fore and aft rigs. The ship captain's commands cracked like a whip and the decks exploded into action. Hal McAllister and nearly thirty men reached the small wharf at the end of Broadway just as the hawsers were being untied.

"Captain," Hal McAllister shouted, "hold this ship. You're not to leave this wharf!"

The *Mary's* captain wheeled around, his face a shade of purple and his cheeks puffed.

"How dare you, sir . . . " he stopped and noted the armed men level their rifles at the ship's deck. "Under whose authority are you acting?" he demanded, though the edge in the timbre of his voice had passed.

"Captain, I am Hal McAllister. We are San Francisco police acting directly under the orders of Alcalde Leavenworth."

"Well, what has that got to do with the *Mary*?"

"Sir, we believe that one or more of the men we are searching for are hiding aboard your ship. May we come aboard?"

"No, you may not," the captain cut McAllister off indignantly.

During this rapid exchange the sailors had floundered and when confronted with all the guns trained on them, had completely ceased all movement.

"Back to your stations, men, and let's have the sheets," the captain exhorted his crew.

"Captain, if this boat attempts to leave the dock I will order my men to open fire. Is that clear?" McAllister barked so loudly he surprised himself. "Men, if this ship moves one inch from this dock open fire!"

The captain was about to respond but watched the nervous men on the dock train their guns on the crew. "Hold steady and make the sheets tight. All you men, he turned around to face his crew, stand clear. We are being boarded." He glared back at McAllister.

McAllister positioned a dozen men on the wharf with instructions to detain anyone trying to leave the boat and to watch the water around the wharf for anyone taking a midnight swim. He boarded with the rest of his men, stationed another half dozen men on the deck and began searching the ship. The ship's captain refused to cooperate. He claimed that no one matching Roberts's description was on board. Suddenly three shots rang out in rapid succession, followed by yelling and shouting below deck. Soon the hatch over the hold swung open and three men were led out, one clutching his bleeding ear, another hopping on one foot, the third bent over and covered with blood. They were surrounded by some of McAllister's men who prodded them forward roughly with the ends of the muskets. McAllister recognized the Hounds.

"Take them to the Clay Street Wharf. A doctor can look at them when they're on the *Warren*.

One constable ran to McAllister and reported: "Roberts is hiding down there. We know he's in there." McAllister looked at the ship's captain who seemed to have lost whatever fight remained and sedulously avoided eye contact.

McAllister walked over to the hatch and peered down into the darkness. As his eyes adjusted, he noted that his men were formed in a tight circle facing outward in all directions, facing stacks of boxes and crates.

"Come on out, Roberts, or we're going to fire!" McAllister yelled.

"Don't fire! I'm coming," Robert's grating voice boomed instantly. "Don't fire!"

The large hulk came out from behind some crates overlain with tarps. He appeared timorous, defeated, his shoulders bowed and his face pale.

—ꟽ—

ALCALDE LEAVENWORTH PRESIDED OVER THE TRIALS OF THE HOUNDS, not as a judge or prosecutor, but as a chess master moving his pieces across the board to gain an advantage, a political advantage. Mary Ellen, like most of San Francisco's populace, followed the trials with eager anticipation. Case let her take one morning off to attend the trials. She found herself pressed into a small galley in Leavenworth's office mesmerized over the proceedings and the powerful people meting out justice to the men in irons. The Hounds no longer posed a threat to San Francisco. Instead those sitting in their makeshift courtroom, their legs bound in irons, appeared deflated and scared. They no longer resembled powerful wolves, working in clever concert to bring down their prey. Tails between their legs, de-fanged, de-clawed, they looked like mangy dogs, more accustomed to being kicked than kicking.

Mary Ellen knew many of the spectators, but her attention was drawn to the hulking and brooding figure of Colbraith. She doubted that he noticed her because he was entirely preoccupied with the conduct of the judges, especially Gwin. Even when the lawyer examined witnesses Colbraith's dark, impenetrable gaze remained fixed on Gwin. How strange, she thought, and felt as if these two men were entwined in some mysterious and powerful embrace, but not one of admiration or friendship.

She also noticed the presence of Thomas Brand, making her a bit uncomfortable and self-conscious. Thomas smiled and tipped his hat to her. She simply nodded in acknowledgment and with some effort returned her attention to the proceedings. The jury returned with a guilty verdict for every defendant and the dejected prisoners were led out and taken to the *Warren*. Meanwhile officials could determine how and where the men would serve their sentences.

Despite all the rough talk of hangings and long prison sentences, in the end, the defendants, including Roberts, were banished for other lands under a threat of immediate execution if they ever returned to California. Mary Ellen did not follow the throng that surrounded the Hounds. She could see Brand trying to make his way toward her, so she simply fled back to the Excellent House. She did not understand how killers in irons could be set free while others in bondage, guilty of no crime other than being born with a different color, would never be set free and were pursued by their masters when they managed to escape, regardless of distance or time. If men like Roberts were set free, she, too, would do all that she could to help innocent people gain their freedom and remain free.

Chapter Fourteen

State or Independence

SAN FRANCISCO
AUGUST 1849–JANUARY 1850

Mary Ellen watched the black hansom approach, the spokes of the large wheels whirring counterclockwise, backwards, something she found mysterious and baffling. The driver, sitting behind the passenger's compartment, leaned back and drew the reins in tightly. The white steed immediately arched its powerful neck, sweat glistening in the early afternoon sun, and came to an abrupt stop, sending a long trail of dust behind the hansom dancing with the afternoon breeze.

The sole occupant, Colonel J.D. Stevenson, quickly alighted, spoke a few words to the driver, and approached Mary Ellen, his tall lanky body erect in a military posture. Dressed impeccably and sporting a wide Panama hat to ward off the afternoon sun, he was precisely on time for their meeting. Since she was the only person standing in this desolate portion of land, he could hardly miss her.

"Good day," he greeted her warmly, briefly removing his hat, his ruddy bald head gleaming in the sun. "I presume you are Miss Price," he smiled, then looked at her inquisitively. "Have we met before?"

Mary Ellen recalled her first day in San Francisco when she spent some minutes in Stevenson's office while he met with Colbraith and Field. "No, I don't believe we have," she replied.

Stevenson continued. "I see that you found the right location." Colonel Stevenson studied her with appraising eyes.

"Yes, Kanaka's directions were quite precise."

Stevenson looked back to the city, "Kanaka is a remarkable man. Owns almost as much land as I do." He smiled at her again, and Mary Ellen could see that Colonel Stevenson regarded himself highly.

"Of course this land," he waved his hand at the surrounding open fields and scattering of tents and board structures in the distance, "may not look like much now, but I assure you that it will be part of the city in less than three months. You can see the incredible growth all around."

Mary Ellen was standing in a flat area south of the city at the intersection of two new lanes, Jessie and Ecker Streets. Although the streets were on plat maps, there was little evidence of them on the ground. Fortunately she knew how far the intersection was supposed to be from Market Street.

"You are only a few blocks from Montgomery and quite close to the shore," Stevenson continued. He turned to her and again looked at her as if trying to divine something about her. "May I inquire what you intend to do with the land?" he asked.

"I haven't really decided yet," she answered uncertainly, unwilling to reveal her plans to him. If Colonel Stevenson did not believe her, he did not show it.

"Well, this is a fifty-vara lot which I recently acquired from Judge Colton." Stevenson walked the dimensions of the lot, counting one vara with each elongated step, until he had a rough measure of the parcel. "That's the approximate size and location," he said.

"Kanaka told me you were asking fifteen hundred for it. Is that correct?"

"Why yes. That's my price. Of course it's firm, nonnegotiable."

"I was hoping for something less," she said and waited for his reaction.

"Less?" he laughed heartily. "Why, fifty-vara lots near the plaza are now selling as high as twenty thousand."

Chapter Fourteen

"Then why is this property priced so low?" she inquired.

Colonel Stevenson offered his arm, "Shall we take a walk toward the beach? I can explain it very clearly."

Mary Ellen accepted his arm and they walked along a narrow path between small sand mounds toward the water. The wind whipped up the water into small white caps that dotted the bay like tiny, wispy clouds. Closer to the shore a score of lighters moved from ship to shore bringing passengers and merchandise to the city. To the north, carts and porters milled with hundreds of disembarked passengers and stacks of cargo, goods, and baggage.

"Isn't this remarkable?" Colonel Stevenson marveled. "I never tire of watching this great city grow. There is so much energy. Who would have believed, even six months ago, that we would have so many people?"

Mary Ellen felt the same vibrancy and sense of exhilaration at the city's irrepressible growth, like a massive, powerful, out of control lion running loose. In February of 1849, when she arrived, San Francisco boasted a population of nearly two thousand. Six months later, according to Case, the population had grown to nearly twenty thousand.

As if reading her thoughts, Colonel Stevenson said: "I think we now have something in the order of ten thousand people coming into San Francisco every month. Many will head straight for the gold fields. Others will remain in the city or return when they discover that gold mining is not an easy vocation. So you can see why I think this is a good location. The population of San Francisco will spread rapidly and simply overrun this place in a matter of months."

"You were going to tell me why the price was so low," Mary Ellen reminded him.

"Oh, yes. I'm sorry." Colonel Stevenson stopped and turned to Mary Ellen, his manner somewhat conspiratorial. "Do you know who Justice Colton is?"

Mary Ellen frowned. She knew that her boarders, Case and Heiser, neither liked nor trusted the justice of the peace.

"I've heard of him," Mary Ellen acknowledged.

"Well, Horace Hawes, who was recently elected to the office of

Prefect for San Francisco, instructed Judge Colton to sell some municipal land to raise sorely needed funds for the city." He paused as if to see whether Mary Ellen could follow his explanation. "Do you know of any of this?" he finally inquired.

Mary Ellen knew quite well what had taken place. Horace Hawes was a well-respected lawyer. General Riley, the military governor who replaced the officious imbecile Persifor Smith, had issued a proclamation in June calling for the election of a city government and an assembly to draw a state constitution. Case, Heiser and their friends were in general agreement that Riley was genuinely interested in California's future and sought to establish a civil government pending admission of California into the Union. In the San Francisco election John Geary was elected as alcalde, a new town council or ayuntamiento had been seated, and Hawes received most of the votes for Prefect. No one was certain what the Prefect's functions were to be, but Hawes had subsumed an autocratic rule, similar to that of mayor or governor. No one knew how that reconciled with Alcalde Geary's role or that of the town council.

"A little," Mary Ellen decided not to reveal the extent of her knowledge of the city's affairs or politics.

Stevenson continued. "Under Mexican law a town can sell its land. As I understand it, Mexican rule of law still applies since California has not been formally admitted to the Union. Anyway, that's probably too much for you to comprehend at one time," he smiled condescendingly, and Mary Ellen returned a discreet, though less than frank smile.

"I'm not sure I understand," she said disingenuously. "Colonel, are you saying that Mr. Hawes, who is an eminent lawyer, has sold you this land?"

Stevenson chortled, "No, no. As prefect he has the right to sell the land for the city. He told Justice Colton to sell the land. I purchased twenty lots from Colton at a most favorable price, I must tell you, and I intend to sell these lots quickly to recover my capital." He winked at her as if he were confiding a secret. "You see I intend to open a bank. And banks need funds. The price I'm offering to you will give me a handsome profit. Perhaps in a short time I could get more, but I want to sell quickly. I assure you that at these prices I'll have these lots sold in no time."

Chapter Fourteen

Mary Ellen knew this was not an idle threat. When she first approached Kanaka Davis with her idea of purchasing some land and building a laundry he did not take her seriously. He counseled her to remain where she was. Mary Ellen could not be certain why Kanaka reacted as he did. Was he apprehensive that he would miss her fine cooking at the Excellent House, or had he simply balked at the notion that a woman wanted to engage in a commercial enterprise? Undeterred, she slowly brought Kanaka around, especially after explaining that she had no intention of leaving Case & Heiser. She intended to hire workers to operate the laundry. She had the funds, though she would never reveal to anyone the trust fund Abigail had established years ago. Finally, Kanaka relented and gave his tepid approval. But he cautioned her that a woman was unable to effectively negotiate with the young, aggressive, and collectively invincible men of San Francisco. He suggested that she employ Colonel Stevenson as a realty agent. Stevenson, he told her, could be trusted. He knew as much about real estate in San Francisco as anyone. His reputation was impeccable. He moved in the best circles. Also, he had already accumulated considerable wealth and would be less likely to take advantage of a woman.

Colonel Stevenson struck Mary Ellen as vainglorious and conceited; but he also seemed to be frank and direct.

"How can I be certain about the legality of this grant, Colonel?" she asked. "After all I'm sure there might be some confusion about what laws apply and who has the right to make laws."

Colonel Stevenson laughed again and patted her on the back gently. "Why, Miss Price, that's a very intelligent question." He did not add "for a lady," though Mary Ellen was certain that was exactly what he meant. "There is great confusion. But as far as Colton's lots are concerned, I think just about every lawyer in this town has obtained some from him. Now they wouldn't do something like that if they thought the grants were invalid, would they?" He seemed pleased with himself. "I suggest you go to any lawyer of your choice and ask him. I'm certain you'll get the same opinion."

"Thank you, Colonel Stevenson," she offered her hand. "I'll have the funds for you by tomorrow. If you would be so kind as to arrange for the papers to be drawn up, I'll have them reviewed by an attorney. There is one condition, however."

Colonel Stevenson's eyes narrowed and he seemed to brace himself, but he remained silent.

"I wish to keep this matter very private and absolutely confidential," she said as she noted a sense of relief in Stevenson's manner. "No one is to know about it."

"I pledge to you my word as a gentleman that all our dealings will remain in the strictest confidence." Colonel Stevenson spoke as if he were swearing an oath of office. "However, you'll have to have some name on the deed, a name you can trust and prove. You'd best speak to counsel about that."

They shook hands and Colonel Stevenson offered to give her a ride back to the Excellent House in his hansom. Mary Ellen graciously declined. She did not want to raise any questions by being seen in the company of Colonel Stevenson. If Stevenson had any qualms about her ability to pay, he did not mention it, and they parted in good spirits. She instinctively trusted Colonel Stevenson and hoped that the trust was merited. She returned to the Excellent House feeling giddy about her plans. Six months earlier she thought of owning some land, now it had become a reality, a first step.

The notion that a laundry could be commercially viable in San Francisco was obvious to Mary Ellen. One of her most pressing problems in running the Excellent House, was the dearth of laundry establishments to handle the bedding and linen. People were literally throwing money away; it was cheaper to discard soiled clothes and buy new ones than to find a laundry and pay the exorbitant cost of cleaning the garments. She intended to charge ten dollars per load, each load representing about one week of worn clothing. She hoped to hire the unemployable, former slaves who were now arriving in California in increasing numbers. In return for providing jobs for those who could not get work from other sources she would secure her employees' loyalty, and benefit handsomely from the lower wages she would pay.

She had complete confidence that a new laundry would be viable. Mary Ellen also reasoned that the investment in the land could pay off

Chapter Fourteen

Bay View of San Francisco

quite well. The difficulties, she knew, revolved around the implementation of her plan. The high prices for goods and services put a crimp on profits. Interest on borrowed capital hovered at about ten percent per month, an exorbitant cost she was unwilling to bear. Fortunately she had the funds to buy land and construct a building. However, with land prices and the cost of other commodities swirling upwards to inconceivable heights, she could not afford any of the land in the city proper. Instead she had to look to the city's outskirts. Finally, Stevenson recommended, through Kanaka Davis, that given her limited budget she should explore the new area south of Market Street.

Feeling heady from the exhilarating prospect of opening a new chapter in her life, she walked up Sansome Street, watched the milling throngs and imagined how many customers she would have when the business opened. At the intersection of Sansome and California Street she noticed a man staring at her intently. She ignored him and continued nervously around the corner when she felt someone touch her shoulder. It startled her and she whirled around. The man had taken his hat off and with an apologetic manner stammered, "I'm sorry to bother you madam, but may I have a word with you." He appeared docile and compliant, but he continued to stare intently at her. He had warm brown eyes, the color of a mountain pond, set on two huge white saucers surrounded by a thin face the color of a walnut shell. His straight black hair was plastered with heavy grease. The way he stared at her filled her with a mixture of anxiety, apprehension, and curiosity.

"Can I help you?" she asked gruffly.

"I'm sorry to disturb you," he said, rubbing his hands on his pants. "I know who you are," he looked almost frightened by what he said. He held his hands together twisting his fingers and gazed nervously around.

"I don't know what you're talking about," Mary Ellen exclaimed with feigned indignation. An enormous sense of foreboding entered her soul as she watched this small man, who appeared to be in his mid thirties, fidget like a frightened mouse.

"I'm sorry," he repeated and started to back away. His way of walking back struck her with the force of a sledge hammer. She immediately knew and understood. He did not look like a former slave. He did not sound like one. He did not look black. But the way he backed up, as if the force of the whip were about to descend upon him, and the intimidated look, led her to an instant, haunting realization. It was as if they belonged to an arcane society, shared a common secret and signed themselves with body language. She glared at him for a moment, angry at the intrusion and frightened by the knowledge that they shared a secret, yet he knew and she wanted to know how. For the first time in many months, if not years, the dread and uncertainty that she thought she had left behind, thousands of miles away in a different land and a different time, returned with a vengeance. This revelation startled her to the core.

"Just a minute," she said a bit too harshly and looked around uncertainly. There were no loiterers in the streets. She forced herself to remain calm and spoke softly, trying her best to appear relaxed. "I'd like to hear what you have to say, but not here. Follow me."

Chapter Fourteen

She walked down Montgomery and back to the less crowded southern beaches. Mary Ellen stifled the urge to turn around to see if the man was following her. She wished he was a figment of imagination, or would disappear in a puff of smoke, but she knew better. This was real—and it brought about the one primal fear she could never shed, not in her entire life—the fear of being discovered.

At the beach she casually walked near the water's edge. Inside she felt stiff as a ramrod and her hands quivered uncontrollably. She clutched her dress to stop the shaking. She planned to walk far enough from the crowds so as to speak more openly, but stay within sight of other people. He came up slowly behind her, avoiding any eye contact. Mary Ellen regarded him with a cool glare, but her body screamed in disquietude. She felt the panic, the bile rising in her throat, and gritted her teeth to control herself.

"What is it you wish to tell me?" she asked.

Again he wrung his hands. "I'm sure you don't remember me. You were too young, but I once lived at Golden Oaks."

Her body jerked involuntarily. She continued to glare at the man, feeling nauseated. But she remained silent.

"You are Mary Ellen, aren't you?" he faltered.

"That's my name, but I don't know anything about Golden Elms or Oaks, or whatever," she said derisively. "Perhaps you've mistaken me for someone else." She wanted to leave, but her feet remained rooted in place.

Her words struck him like a blow and he winced and backed off again. "I'm really sorry. I don't mean to intrude or to upset you. But I thought I could be of some service to you." He spoke softly and respectfully. Mary Ellen continued to glare at him but said nothing.

He wilted under her glare.

"How, pray tell, could you help me?" she finally said, her voice tinged with scorn.

"Please, Miss Mary, I won't say a word, as God is my gospel. I'll keep quiet." He looked at her pleadingly. "I'm not ashamed to admit that I'm really afraid."

"Well, how could you help me?" she asked again, but this time with less edge to her voice.

"If you come back to the hotel where I work I'll show you."

Mary Ellen's mouth dropped. "I beg your pardon?"

"Oh, no. Please don't get me wrong. I have something I want to show you. I think you will find it useful."

Mary Ellen calmed a little but her mind remained in a turmoil. Someone from her hidden past had recognized her so readily, and this recognition formed a bridge to those days she had worked so diligently to destroy. All her work, all her plans, could be undone so easily by one simple revelation. She would lose her job at the Excellent House. She could forget owning land or running a business. It would be catastrophic.

"What's your name?" she asked more kindly, hoping that sugar would reap a greater harvest than vinegar.

"George Gordon. But that wasn't my name then. I was at Golden Oaks for only three months, but I've never forgotten you. You were some child. Kept to yourself mostly, but you had all the slaves so scared. Me too. Still am." He smiled, but Mary Ellen's face remained impassive. His smile vanished, replaced by fear again.

"I gather Golden Oaks is some plantation in the south and you were a slave. But you don't speak at all like one," Mary Ellen remarked candidly.

"I know. I spent many years in the north. It's a long story," he stammered and his face twitched.

"And you certainly don't look like a slave. If you were, how did you gain your freedom?" She could not help herself.

Gordon paused, shifted uneasily and Mary Ellen immediately knew the answer. This knowledge served as a salve for some of her trepidation. If Gordon was not a free man, there could be no assurance of what would become of him. He was passing himself as a white man and did a fairly decent job of it. But if he were caught, the result would be devastating to him.

"Mr. Gordon, obviously I can't come to the hotel with you. It wouldn't be proper. You can show me what you have outside."

"No, Miss Mary, you wouldn't want me to show it outside. Someone else might see it. I haven't let anyone see it, not ever."

Mary Ellen made her decision instantly. "Okay, Mr. Gordon. Come to the Excellent House. Do you know where it is?" He nodded. "Good. I'll appear to interview you for a job. We will be alone and you can show me what you have. But from now on you will call me Miss Price, is that clear?"

"Yes, Miss Price."

"And let me assure you, Mr. Gordon, if you dare to utter one word of slander about me I'll make your life on this earth a living hell! And you can take my word on St. Maron for that." Her eyes bore into Gordon's soul and he quickly crossed himself and bowed to her.

"Don't do that in public!" she exclaimed quietly but with urgency. She did not want anyone to observe his action.

"Yes. Miss Price. I won't do that again." The tick returned.

"Good. Come this evening at seven o'clock. Most of the boarders will be out on the town and you can give me a show of whatever you have. But heed my warning!" She tersely walked away from him, her stomach convulsing.

Mary Ellen returned to the Excellent House completely ruffled. If Case or Heiser noted her frayed nerves or her inability to focus on the simplest duties, they did not make a comment. She made herself generally unavailable, delegating her normal duties to Samuel who had now been accepted as an indispensable part of the boarding house.

At seven o'clock sharp George Gordon arrived carrying a small satchel. Mary Ellen ran to the front door and ushered him in. She had already explained to Charles Case that she needed more help at the boarding house and would interview a candidate for the job that evening. She led Gordon to a small windowless supply room and closed the door behind them. They sat on separate crates in the dimly lit room. One solitary candle flickered as they spoke. He held the small brown satchel close to him.

"Well, Mr. Gordon, what is it you wish to say to me," she asked as her eyes were drawn to the satchel.

Gordon hesitated for a moment as if to gather his thoughts. He told her how he had been sold to a Virginia plantation where the treatment of slaves could best be described as cruel and inhumane. He had been whipped so many times for the slightest transgressions he finally decided to run away. Light skinned, he thought he would be able to pass as white if only he could speak as they did. So he listened attentively and studied the manner in which the white folks spoke. Late at night he would whisper the words to himself and engage in imaginary conversations.

By the time he ran away Gordon felt he could get by. Sometimes people looked at him questioningly, but no one confronted him. He made his way to Pennsylvania, then up to Rhode Island. He worked at odd jobs, always keeping a low profile. When he heard about California, and how people from all over the world were rushing there for the gold, he decided that the new land would offer him greater protection. He reasoned, rightly as it turned out, that there would be so many different shades and races of people, he could blend in more easily. As a runaway he was always in danger of discovery, especially by his previous owners, who would work him to death if they ever found him.

Mary Ellen was intrigued by his story which was not too dissimilar from hers. But she had the legal papers to prove her freedom; he did not. This placed Gordon in her hands, though this particular sword had one sharp edge and one blunt one, for he could also wreak havoc on her life, but only by forfeiting his own. This they tacitly understood. San Francisco was rife with tales of southern aristocrats coming to California for the express purpose of hunting down former slaves. After all, runaway slaves were valuable property and were regarded no differently than stolen merchandise. The penalties were severe.

"I don't understand something," she said. "Why did you seek me out? Why not simply remain anonymous?" she asked, bewildered by his actions. She would have avoided such contact at all cost.

"It wasn't easy for me. My first instinct cried a terrible warning. I avoid socializing. I stay to myself. I have no friends. But I'm afraid. With no one here who knows me I could be picked up at any time and sent back. I saw you. The way you dress, the way you walk, with so much confidence . . ." he trailed off. "I thought you could be my friend. That maybe you were trying to hide the way I am."

It sounded so childish it almost made Mary Ellen laugh. But Gordon's open face and his apparent fear brought her to her senses. She decided to set the ground rules.

Chapter Fourteen

"First," she said, "our conditions are different. I am a free woman. My owner emancipated me years ago. I have the papers to prove it.

"I would give anything to have such papers." As he spoke Mary Ellen detected tears in his eyes.

Mary Ellen continued: "To protect myself I lodged duplicates with legal affidavits at several law firms on the eastern seaboard. They can vouch for me and can arrange for the courts in those states to issue whatever documents I would require. You, on the other hand, are on the run. Your freedom depends on your ability to remain hidden behind white skin. How can I help you?"

"I'm not sure. But I feel better just knowing someone I can share my thoughts with. You can't imagine the torture of keeping something like this inside and always living with fear."

Mary Ellen did not respond. She knew such fear.

"Anyway, you might be able to use me to your advantage," he offered. "For example, I brought some things with me. You might find them useful." He opened his satchel and removed several jars. "This is a bleach I learned to make. I combine it with powder and milkweed and spread it on my skin, especially my face. It makes me look even lighter."

Gordon offered to demonstrate its efficacy. Mary Ellen reluctantly exposed her shoulder and allowed him to apply the lotion on a small area, an area normally hidden by her clothing.

"You'll see how this makes your skin white enough to pass without leaving any telltale signs."

He then removed another jar. "And this is a pomade which I also make. It makes the hair straight. Look at mine."

Mary Ellen had noted his straight black hair. Not a single riffle appeared. Her hair tended to curl slightly and she usually hid her hair with bonnets; she had tried different emollients, but none worked very well.

"This is very impressive, Mr. Gordon," she said.

"I brought these for you. You can keep them."

Mary Ellen regarded Gordon with a new sense of respect. He was bright and creative. He could read. Perhaps, she thought, Gordon could be someone she should employ to run the laundry or do other important work for her.

"I may have something for you," she finally said.

"Miss Price," he said, "I'm not very brave and not very strong. But I can work hard and I learn quickly. I'm sure you would find me useful."

They continued to talk for nearly an hour. She explained some of her plans for the future and then she ushered him out cordially. After Gordon left she bumped into Case who inquired about her interview.

"He won't do," she said simply and walked away smiling inwardly.

—∾—

"GENTLEMEN, I PROPOSE A TOAST," CASE STOOD UP HOLDING A CRYSTAL goblet by the stem. The rich mauve color of the wine reflected beams of golden light from the gas lanterns hanging on the walls and the array of candles set on the long table. "Here's to a new California. Here's to a new constitution. And here's to the men who will represent San Francisco in the Convention."

The dinner guests at the Excellent House stood up and saluted each other then saluted their hosts, Case and Heiser, each now standing at the opposite ends of the table. Mary Ellen had set the table for ten additional guests with the finest European linen, elegant bone china, and a new set of silver cutlery recently imported from England. William Gwin, Bill Stuart, Joe Hoborn, Sam Brannan, and Colonel Stevenson sat next to Case while Tom Larkin, the old U.S. counsel from Monterey, Selim Woodworth, W.D.M. Howard, Ed Gilbert, and A.J. Ellis sat next to Heiser. All except Brannan, Woodworth, Stevenson and Howard, had recently been elected as San Francisco's delegates to the State Convention that General Riley had proclaimed would be held on the first of September to allow the people of California to prepare their own constitution and laws. General Riley had confided with several people that he hoped his action, the adoption of a state constitution, would be the impetus for Congress to act more decisively and admit California into the Union. He thought this action would bypass the usual interregnum of administering the area as a territory. By late August 1849 California had not received territorial status, nor had Congress taken any decision on the future of California. And no decision appeared likely in the near future. Although General Riley ostensibly led a military rule, he understood that Californians would oppose military rule. Instead, he made it abundantly clear that he would serve only as a temporary civil administrator.

San Francisco, as early as 1848, had embarked on creating its own government and conducting elections without waiting for official sanction or recognition. After all, people needed some form of civil government in a growing metropolis and they wanted one in which they were represented. San Francisco adopted the Mexican form of ayuntamiento and elected an alcalde instead of creating an American style municipal form of government found in most American cities. Now Riley pressed for a change. He expected the people of California to adopt an American form of government, based on American constitutional principals and precedents.

After the toasts were completed and Gwin had made a short speech, the men settled down to a sumptuous feast which Mary Ellen had spent the better part of two days preparing. As she passed Selim Woodworth he grasped her hand and said: "I do believe you're the best hostess and best cook in all of San Francisco." Those around him who heard his remarks immediately uttered their wholehearted agreement. Mary Ellen thanked Woodworth and continued to supervise the evening's gala celebration. Attentive to every detail, she still made it a point to hover around the table and listen to the conversations, especially those of Gwin, Brannan, and Stevenson.

Mary Ellen was thankful that Stevenson did not say a word to her or even acknowledge her presence. Woodworth and Howard were frequent guests at the Excellent House. Gwin and Brannan were not, but they were highly respected. Brannan, an old-timer by San Francisco standards, was well-known. He was powerful and rich although some said he drank too much. Gwin had been in California nearly six months, which by Case's and Heiser's reckoning, made him one of the earlier settlers of San Francisco. His aristocratic mien and political experience propelled him into the limelight. He was already touted as one of the leading candidates for the senatorship as soon as Congress admitted California into the Union.

"Commodore Jones has kindly arranged for the brig *Fremont* to pick us up and take us to Monterey," Gwin explained to Case. "Seems as if Thomas Butler King arranged everything. He told the Commodore to have the sloop *Edith* pick up all the southern delegates from Santa Barbara to San Diego."

"Is Butler a delegate?" Case asked referring to the President's special envoy, and the man many in Washington expected to become California's senator.

"No, he's just interested in the senatorship," Bill Stuart responded. Gwin shifted uneasily in his chair.

"Bill, you don't really think King has any chance of being elected as a senator. Why that man is a buffoon." Hoborn looked appalled.

"I can't rule out anything, Joe. Why, we don't even know how senators will be selected or elected. Maybe the final provision will favor him. Who knows?" Stuart replied.

"I'm hopeful we'll use other state constitutions as a model for ours," Gwin suggested. "It makes more sense. Most likely the legislature will elect the two senators." Gwin wiped his mouth with his napkin.

"We'll know in a few days, hopefully," Stuart offered noncommittally.

Stuart constantly needled Gwin and Gwin showed little sense of humor in his responses. One of Mary Ellen's primary interests was in divining how the delegates felt about slaves. She felt reasonably certain California would oppose the institution of slavery, but she wanted to know how the state would treat freed slaves or even runaways. Gwin was a southern aristocrat, someone who had either owned slaves in the past or still owned slaves. Most likely, Mary Ellen thought, Gwin would support slavery, a dangerous man for her if he were to ascend California's political ladder, a likely possibility.

Mary Ellen went into the kitchen briefly to check on the apple pies still in the oven. The crusts were turning golden brown just at the right time. Satisfied she returned in time to hear a loud altercation. Sam Brannan pounded the table. "Tom, with all due respects to you, I'm telling you that if we aren't a state soon, the hell with the Union. Let's declare independence. We've waited long enough for those imbeciles back in Washington to decide. If they don't want us, then I say let's go our own way."

Chapter Fourteen

"You know damn well these things take time. There's a serious issue about slavery. They don't want to upset the balance between free states and slave states. Congress will come around soon enough. We're much better off being part of the United States. If we could barely defend ourselves against the Hounds, how do you propose we defend ourselves against some belligerent nation? What about an army? What about a navy? You can't even get enough sailors to man the four hundred ships rotting in San Francisco bay. Being independent is utter nonsense, Sam. And you know it." Larkin leaned back in his chair, his easy demeanor and lanky six-foot frame, completely relaxed.

Brannan was not mollified. "We don't need anyone else to protect us. We can do it ourselves. The problem, Tom, is that you've been here too long. You've been so chummy with the U.S. military you've lost your objectivity."

Larkin remained unruffled. "Sam, your problem is that you never had it in the first place. Stop being so bombastic for once. You don't run your business this way, do you?" Larkin regarded Brannan with a steely look.

Brannan's face turned crimson and the vein in his temple pulsated as if it were about to burst.

Case interceded in the nick of time. "Gentlemen! Gentlemen! We're here to celebrate what I suspect we all really want. California is moving inexorably toward statehood. I agree with Sam that Congress has moved too slowly. Seems as if their roads toward decision are impassable much of the year." Case turned to Brannan. "But Sam you know that the Union needs us as much as we need them. My god, all this gold, all this wealth. Would you let it out of your control for even a split second?" He immediately answered his own question. "Why of course not. And the United States won't either. Tom is right. All this wealth could whet the appetite of some greedy nation if they believed for one brief moment that we were truly independent. It'll never happen."

Samuel, apparently unaware or heedless of the quarrel, entered the dining room carrying a large silver tray with three baked pies. The heady aroma instantly filled the room and seemed to act as a salve to the heated emotions, because Larkin and Brannan lapsed into silence. Samuel set the tray down next to Mary Ellen and she proceeded to cut the pie and dole out the slices into plates for Samuel to serve.

Brannan sat down wearily and a bit unsteadily. Mary Ellen suspected that Brannan had imbibed too much. Brannan sipped some more wine and said: "You're right, Case. I'm sorry, Tom. I suppose that's why I didn't want to be a delegate to the Convention in the first place. The people voted me in, but I told them I couldn't be a delegate because of pressing business. The truth is I'll never have the patience for politics. Those fellows in Washington just get me so damned riled up. They talk a subject to death and never reach a conclusion. Seems that their only concern is slavery. And we all know this won't be a slave state. So why talk so much? Just decide, goddamn it. We'll never have slavery here."

Everyone turned involuntarily to Gwin. Even Mary Ellen stopped cutting the pie.

Gwin placed both his hands on the table as if he were about to stand up, but remained seated. "Let me suggest one thing to you gentlemen," he said slowly, choosing his words carefully, "the real issue is California's boundary. That's the thorny question. I don't think slavery or involuntary servitude is necessary in California. If the price of white labor is too high we have other choices—there are others we can turn to. The principal question is just how much territory California will occupy—where its boundaries will lie. How far east and how far north? Do we go as far as Salt Lake? Do we involve the Oregon Territory? But let's not quarrel now. Tonight we are here to celebrate, not to engage in dispute. There will be ample opportunity to debate all these complex issues in Monterey in a few weeks."

He picked up his wine glass and stood. "I'd like to propose a toast. Here's to Mr. Case and Mr. Heiser for giving us such a pleasant evening and a most sumptuous meal." Everyone raised their glasses and toasted the hosts while Case pointed his glass toward Mary Ellen and winked. Mary Ellen flushed at the overt recognition, and received immediate acknowledgment from Woodworth and Stevenson who also raved about the wonderful food.

Mary Ellen could see how Gwin had ascended to prominence so quickly. He was smooth and clever. She found Gwin's stand on slavery both surprising and encouraging. Virtually every southerner sought to have California become a slave state. But Gwin, an aristocratic southerner, did not seem at all perturbed by Brannan's remarks. Nor did Gwin seem at all interested in the slavery issue. However, the discussion had been so general. Several issues remained unclear to Mary Ellen. How would the new constitution deal with freed slaves? What about runaways? Nearly everyone at the table, with the exception of Brannan, felt fairly confident that a new constitution would be in place within a month. Mary Ellen knew she did not have long to wait for her answers.

MARY ELLEN POURED THE POMADE INTO HER PALM. SHE SLID THE bristles of her brush down the smooth oily tendrils of coarse hair. As she combed, the strokes became quicker and harder. She began to violently beat and pull at it and smashed it against her head. Tears formed in her eyes as she tried to rub the natural bend and wave out. Then she hurled the brush against the mirror. The shattered glass remained in place, a spider's web shimmering with morning dew. Her arms fell to her sides and her sleeve slipped off her shoulder, baring the spot on which Gordon had applied his potion. She looked down upon the flawed skin. It looked like a drop of milk in a bowl of honey. A tear fell upon the spot and chased after her sleeve. She looked up at the mirror. Five sets of abnormal eyes and five marred shoulders were thrown back at her. A cruel reminder of truth, of reality. She gathered her hair and swept it up into a bun and fastened her bonnet. Then Mary Ellen rubbed her shoulder dry of tears. Her finger ran along the bleached spot and lingered on the natural sandstone color. She returned the sleeve to its proper place and stooped to pick up the broken handle of her brush.

CHAPTER FIFTEEN

The Election

SAN FRANCISCO
1850

San Francisco, January 8, 1850

RAW WIND AND INTERMITTENT FREEZING RAIN HAD NOT DETERRED most of the citizens of San Francisco from voting. Bundled in thick coats and oilskins, people filled the streets, many wading through the deep mud.

This was Mary Ellen's first opportunity to see an election, and she was excited at the prospect. She knew that her enthusiasm was stimulated, in part, by the colorful parades with bands playing and banners blazing all over town the past few days. She had pleaded with Case to take her to the polls despite his remonstration that voting is not a woman's business. Mary Ellen sensed that Case did not believe women had the brains to vote but had the good sense not to mention it. Women had never voted in any election in California, nor would they be entitled to vote in San Francisco's first valid election. The California Constitution, adopted in Monterey and approved in a special statewide election in November of 1849, created suffrage only for white male citizens of the United States and white male citizens of Mexico who had elected to become American citizens.

Case argued that it would be inappropriate for a woman to be seen at the polls. Of the few women living in San Francisco, he reminded her, many were engaged in questionable or immoral activities. Mary Ellen told him she would go by herself if he did not escort her. So now the two of them trudged through muddy streets toward the poll at Crockford's corner of Clay and Kearney Streets.

A wariness overcame her as they approached. No other women were around. Roughly dressed men nearly blocked their way, shoving tickets listing a slate of candidates into their hands or making suggestive comments to Mary Ellen.

"Here's for Geary, and the old council!" one man thrust the paper in Case's face.

Case frowned and ignored the man.

"Geary and the old council forever!" another yelled.

"Forever is a long day," one man countered, spittle from his mouth mixing with the light rain. "Rotation in office, is my doctrine!"

Mary Ellen and Case continued toward Crockford's, weaving through the human obstacles.

A man stuck his face directly in front of Mary Ellen. "Hey lady, the old council has made enough money. Let's give a new one a chance at the crib."

"Don't waste your time Wiley. She don't vote," another man said.

"But she's a looker, ain't she?" the first man ogled her, his gaping smile revealing only a few teeth, brown and rotten like burnt kernels on a charred corn cob.

"No time for that now, we've gotta work," his friend yelled and soon they were lost in the crowd, thrusting their tickets into unwanting hands, and yelling their candidate's platform.

Mary Ellen brushed another man aside just as a tall man, with a good portion of his body dripping in mud said: "I go for a new council. They'll

Chapter Fifteen

San Francisco, 1850

give us sidewalks and clean streets!" He shook himself like a wet dog, mud sticking stubbornly to his clothes.

A small boy in a red shirt and tarpaulin hat yelled, "We want another yuntermenter."

A thick Irishman waded through the mud to the boy. "So it's a gutterminty that ye want? Here, take it, and good luck till ye!" He picked up the helpless boy and sent him flying into the mud face first. "I'm thinkin' ye won't want another gutterminty, least not soon!" The man glared at the boy, then roared in laughter. The startled boy looked up, half his face hidden behind a mask of dark muck. He stood, wiped his face with small hands and walked away slowly. Suddenly he turned and called out in a high-pitched voice, his face red: "We want another yuntermenter!" and scrambled away quickly before the brawny Irishman could react.

Mary Ellen, standing next to Case, waited in line as it slowly wound its way to the polling table. In front of them a heavyset, good-looking dark-skinned man, with straight, jet black hair, who appeared to Mary Ellen to be a Pacific Islander, listened attentively to a small, red-haired, disheveled man next to him. When the two men reached the desk the Islander presented a green ticket, which had Frank Turk, as alcalde, and Turk's slate of candidates.

Case turned to Mary Ellen and pointed to several men standing nearby. "They're the election judges and inspectors." he whispered. "Each one, I'm sure, has been bought by one or more of the candidates. Watch them carefully. The trick," he laughed, "is to get the ballot into the ballot box. Never let them handle it for you. They can switch tickets faster than a Mississippi gambler can turn a card from the bottom of a deck."

Mary Ellen noticed that Case grasped his ticket, supporting Geary's candidates, more tightly.

"I challenge that man!" one of the inspectors declared when he noticed the heavy-set man in front of Mary Ellen.

"Then we must swear him in," the judge sitting at the desk responded and took the man aside.

The judge produced a Bible and indicated for the Islander to put his hand on it. The Islander looked at his associate uncertainly and the red-headed man grabbed the Islander's huge hand and put it on the Bible.

"Do you swear that what you tell me is the whole truth, so help you God?"

"Huh," the Islander responded loudly, and the judge accepted this grunt as an affirmative response

A small crowd of onlookers had gathered around the men.

"Where were you born?"

"New York."

"Where you from?"

"New York."

"In what street did you live?"

Chapter Fifteen

"New York?"

"Do you know where New York is?"

"New York."

The first inspector to raise an objection interceded. "Turn him out, he's a Kanaka!"

"Get him out of here," the chief judge barked and several men quickly arrived to lead the man away while his redheaded associate complained futilely to each of the judges.

Mary Ellen reached the desk. The boarded ballot box with one slit on the top sat at the center of the table. Several piles of different colored ballot tickets were stacked next to the ballot box.

"What can we do for you?" the judge demanded.

Surprised by the question directed to her, Mary Ellen impulsively replied, "I'm here to vote."

Case was stunned speechless. The judge leaned back as if struck. Everyone within hearing distance tuned toward them.

"Ain't no women allowed to vote in this election," the judge finally recovered and turned to Case.

Mary Ellen was prepared to challenge the judge, to ask what law applied to prevent her from voting, but she decided to remain quiet and not create a spectacle.

"Joseph, she works for me," Case remarked uncertainly. "Wasn't sure whether she could vote."

"Oh, Mr. Case, I didn't see you," the judge said. "But you know as well as I do that we can't let women vote. Even the new constitution don't allow it. If we let women vote, then what?" He shook his head demonstratively. "Why, we'd have children, foreigners, even Africans, asking to vote. We'd go to hell in a handbasket," he suddenly remembered that Mary Ellen stood there. "Sorry, Miss, nothing personal. May I have your ballot, Mr. Case?"

Case placed the ballot directly into the box. Mary Ellen got a frosty look from the judge, who quickly turned his attention to the people behind her and Case.

"What in the world were you thinking?" Case asked angrily as they walked back through the tumultuous crowd. "I knew it was a mistake to bring you here. I don't know how you talked me into it."

Mary Ellen looked downcast and after a few moments of being pummeled and jostled by the unruly crowd, Case's dark mood changed.

"I suppose no real harm done. Let's get out of here," he said. As they returned to The Excellent House, the rain abating, Mary Ellen watched all the men in the streets and made a special vow to herself, a vow she had every intention of fulfilling come what may.

CHAPTER SIXTEEN

The Elaborate Plan

SAN FRANCISCO
1850

MARY ELLEN LOOKED AT THE TWO-STORY FRAME BUILDING ON CLARA Street with pride. Sitting on a fifty-vara lot in an empty block, surrounded by wind-blown brush and small sandy knolls, her second laundry stood as a silent sentinel to her hard work. Already producing a large stream of income, Mary Ellen projected that it would return her investment within two months. The white exterior boarding and green grillwork, painted during the few intermittent sunny days, seemed impervious to the pounding of the incessant and depressing rain.

But Mary Ellen did not have time to gloat or to be smug. She was worried because so much depended on Charles Minturn's steamship line. Minturn, one of the River Kings, whose burgeoning steamship line now included the *Senator,* the newest steamship plying the river between Sacramento and San Francisco, was looking for laundry facilities. If she could get his business it would confirm her success.

Her musing was interrupted by the arrival of a hansom. A man leaped from the cab and approached her.

"Good day, sir," Mary Ellen said, looking to see if Minturn was also in the hansom.

"Good day, I'm Richard Pettigrew, Charles Minturn's agent. I've been sent to inspect the facilities and evaluate the operations so Mr. Minturn might come to a final decision."

"I see." Mary Ellen tried to conceal her disappointment. She hoped Minturn would join them. She knew him as a frequent visitor to the Excellent House, but of course a man of his status and wealth would not waste his time running petty inspections. "My name is Miss Price, let me show you around.

"Ah, Miss Price, Selim Woodworth speaks highly of you."

Mary Ellen could not hide her smile. Woodworth was one of the few men in whom she could confide, and who was aware of her involvement in the laundry business. He advised her after purchasing a third parcel from Colonel Stevenson that despite the steep price, its location was superb. It was closer to the wharf and therefore would enable Mary Ellen to provide Minturn and other shipping lines and hotels with a convenient location for their laundry business.

Mary Ellen forewarned George Gordon, who now worked for her, about the importance of winning Minturn over. He knew the contract to launder all of the shipping line's linen was crucial to the new laundry's success. Gordon operated both of her laundries as well as her new livery stable on the corner of Sansome and Washington streets. In order to impress Minturn with a well-staffed and efficient operation he brought in a group of Ecker Street Laundry employees along with loads of its laundry.

Mary Ellen and Pettigrew walked into the premises and were instantly assaulted by the heat and humidity. He tried his very best to appear detached, if not completely apathetic. She clenched her fist. Pettigrew pulled on his collar while small beads of perspiration broke out on his forehead and temples. The laundry operations were maintained downstairs, where the clothes and linen were placed in large shallow vats and hand washed with soap and water. The washed clothes were rinsed in other vats and finally hung up on lines to dry indoors where several wood stoves blazed with constantly kindled fires, stoked by one employee.

Pettigrew did not say a word. He watched without expression, occasionally wiping his face with a soggy handkerchief, and listened to Mary Ellen's explanation. They went up a flight of stairs to the second floor where the dried goods were ironed and folded. One of the women folding some linen smiled at them and Mary Ellen noticed how Pettigrew straightened his back imperceptibly and nearly returned the smile. The woman, Ann Phoebe Smith, had almond colored skin, large brown eyes, and perfect ivory-white teeth. Ann had just arrived from Boston. A former slave, she escaped from Louisiana through the Underground Railroad. George Gordon brought her to Mary Ellen's attention and Mary Ellen instantly hired the beautiful girl who now lived in one of the rooms on the second floor.

As they headed back to the stairway Ann approached them along the narrow hallway. They passed each other and Ann brushed lightly against Pettigrew. She smiled at the startled man who managed a nervous smile and instantly seemed to regret it. A stern expression instantly replaced the short-lived smile. He could do little to hide his interest, however, because his eyes, Mary Ellen noted, followed Ann as she continued down the passageway. Pettigrew started to walk onward but accidentally bumped into Mary Ellen. She gritted her teeth as a sharp pang grabbed her ankle where Pettigrew's toe struck a nerve, but she tried not to react. Pettigrew instantly removed his hat and apologized profusely, stammering almost incomprehensibly.

After they finished touring the premises they walked outside where the cold air seemed most agreeable. A blanket of gray sky stretched from horizon to horizon, cutting off the peaks of the hills surrounding San Francisco.

"So, what do you think of our little operation?" Mary Ellen asked affably, trying not to show her nervousness.

"Well, I don't know," he said hesitantly. "We have a great deal of laundry and I'm not sure this facility can handle the job."

"But I've explained to you that we have another facility on Ecker Street,

View from Telegraph Hill

and the third one will be completed by the end of the month. Surely three laundries are more than enough to meet your requirements," she suggested.

"That's true. But you've been in business only a short time. How could we be assured that you'd be . . . " He searched for the right words. " . . . be available in the future?"

"You mean, how can you be sure I'll still be in business, don't you?" She smiled disarmingly.

"Well, yes, I suppose that really is it," he said.

"Mr. Pettigrew," she said, "how long have you been in San Francisco?"

"One week," he quipped. "I'm not sure that has anything to do with it," he added.

"I think it does. You see, nobody's been here very long. The same question could be asked of just about every business in this city. But I've been here a year, and that makes me an old-timer," She smiled. "I've outlasted most of the people here, and I'm sure Mr. Woodworth would tell Mr. Minturn how reliable I am, and how good my word is."

She noticed that Pettigrew seemed a bit uncomfortable at her mention of his boss's name. "Of course you'd have to come here from time to time," she suggested, "to inspect the facility to make sure it lives up to your and Mr. Minturn's standards."

Pettigrew furtively looked up at the second floor of the building. "I suppose that's right," he said a bit too quickly, and Mary Ellen knew she had Minturn's agent. "I'd have to come here to review the conditions," he said, then added, "of course, only until we could be certain that your operations are as successful as you believe they will be."

"We could make our arrangement provisional," Mary Ellen smiled charmingly. "Provisional on your being satisfied and comfortable with our operations."

Pettigrew simply nodded in agreement. Mary Ellen noted that the beads of perspiration had reappeared as if Pettigrew were standing next to one of the hot stoves downstairs.

"Perhaps you could have the papers drawn to your satisfaction, Mr. Pettigrew, and we could commence as soon as you're available."

Pettigrew hesitated for only a second. "All right. I'll do it right away. But our arrangement is only provisional," he insisted.

"Of course," Mary Ellen demurred. "I wouldn't have it any other way. Now, if you will excuse me I have to return inside to review some matters with my staff."

She bid him adieu and noticed that he was almost reluctant to leave, occasionally staring at the second floor.

Back inside Mary Ellen counseled with Gordon. When the first laundry arrived from Minturn's ships he was to give that order his immediate attention. All of Minturn's business, she told the entire staff, had to be given priority. Anyone who failed to follow her directions would be fired summarily. Mary Ellen then went upstairs. She found Ann in her room.

"Well done, Ann," Mary Ellen said. "But next time a bit more subtle. Do you understand what I'm saying?"

"Yes, ma'am," Ann answered, but Mary Ellen was doubtful.

"Don't be so obvious. Smile, but don't smile too much. Do you understand, Ann?"

"Yes, ma'am," Ann smiled attentively.

"Now, this man, his name is Pettigrew, will come here from time to time. You are to be accommodating, but don't be reckless. If you scare him away, it could ruin some of my business. Be nice to him, but not too nice. Do you understand?" Mary Ellen took the beautiful girl's chin in her hands.

"Yes, ma'am," Ann answered and looked down. "I promise not to do somethin' that could hurt you."

"Good girl, Ann. Now I've seen you with that sailor, what's his name?"

Ann brightened up. "Oh, Philippe? He's from Madagascar."

"Be very careful, Ann. He has a good family. They've helped me. But Philippe is wild." She did not add "crazy" which most people thought.

Ann smiled at the thought. Mary Ellen raised Ann's chin again.

"I mean he might be dangerous, girl. Be careful."

"Yes, ma'am."

—ɯ—

MARY ELLEN DEPOSITED THE MONEY AT HER BANK, PAGE, BACON & CO., on Clay Street, then stepped outside. She wore a bonnet and carried a parasol and handbag. The street was flooded with bright sunshine but large formless shadows floated across the partially planked road and sidewalk. She looked at the sky just as a gust of wind tugged at her bonnet. Billowing clouds chased each other across the blue expanse, but there was little likelihood of rain. She walked up Clay, crowded with pedestrians, and checked her handbag to make sure that the receipt for her deposit was well secured, then fastened the clasp shut. She was not paying attention and accidentally collided with someone so hard that her parasol and handbag sprawled to the ground.

She immediately knelt to retrieve her possessions while uttering "I'm sorry, I wasn't paying attention." The person she had bumped into had also crouched to help her and Mary Ellen flinched when she recognized the familiar light blue eyes.

"It's not your fault," Thomas Brand smiled, his Scottish brogue intriguing, his eyes dancing. "How are you, Miss Price?"

"Fine, thank you." She straightened nervously, wondering why she felt so confused.

He was dressed well, more like an Eastern banker than a San Francisco merchant.

"I saw you at Roberts's trial," he said warmly. "I wanted to talk to you, but you left early."

"Yes," she replied awkwardly, "I had to get back to work." She tugged at her dress to straighten the folds, trying to decipher her welling emotions.

"Well, you didn't miss much. What a travesty. After all that work they simply sent the Hounds on their way. Roberts and his cohorts should have been swinging from a yardarm." Thomas's blue eyes flared with intensity for a brief moment. Then like snuffing out a candle the intensity was replaced by a twinkle and warmth.

"I'm sorry. How rude of me, no more politics. We haven't spoken to each other since the *California*. I tried to find you so many times after we landed," he said without any hint of anger or censure. "But no one seemed to know your whereabouts. I was sorry we couldn't get together," he remarked ruefully. He had a long, gentle face with bushy sideburns flush to his chin line.

"How are you faring?" Mary Ellen asked, trying to appear neither too interested nor too brusque.

"If you mean my knife wound, it's completely healed." He tapped his chest. "As good as new. Of course I have a wonderful scar to remind me of the incident. It's not as if I can forget it," he laughed.

She could not understand her desire to leave, to escape, as if Thomas Brand somehow represented a threat. His smile and easy manner were disarming as they were alarming.

"I'm sorry you had to go through something like that. You nearly died," she said.

"Now that would have been terrible, wouldn't it?" he laughed. "But having survived, I'm almost glad it happened."

"Glad?" she asked incredulously.

"Well, maybe glad is a trifle strong. Shall we say, gratified." She noticed the little laugh lines around his eyes. She had not noticed them before.

"Perhaps I'm missing something, but gratified that you were nearly killed?"

He looked benignly at Mary Ellen. "If you have a few minutes, I'd like to explain to you. May I buy you a coffee at Woodward's?" he asked.

Mary Ellen was about to say no, but the pleading look in his eyes made it impossible.

"Where is Woodward's?" she asked. "I've never heard of it."

"It's on Pike Street, not too far from Selover's place. It's just a minute or two from here. Would you care to join me?"

He offered his arm and after juggling her parasol and handbag Mary Ellen accepted it. He chatted amiably the three blocks to Pike Street, one block before Stockton. An uneasy feeling disturbed Mary Ellen. She could not fathom why she felt so anxious. She had saved his life. His presence, his ability to walk, to talk, to think, were all attributable to her care on the *California*. They both knew that. She had held the most precious commodity he owned, his life, in her hands, willing away an inevitable death. On board the rocking steamer she had made every effort to avoid him. She did not know why. Perhaps she had not trusted herself and did not want to be encumbered with any liaison or relationship. But over the days, then weeks and months, the small current of curiosity grew. At times, when she was alone at night, thinking of the past and the future, images of Thomas Brand, lying helpless in her berth, hovering in the twilight of death, intruded unexpectedly. She had given him life.

They sat at a small table in the back of Woodward's Coffee House, recently established by William Woodward of Boston. The smell of Java and Turkish coffee and other blends permeated the small, charming room. Delicate lace tablecloths, fine colorful crockery, and a delightful selection of tortes made it particularly attractive. A small fire burned in the fireplace giving the already warm room a nice golden glow. Most of the tables were empty at this hour in the afternoon.

Thomas stared questionably at Mary Ellen. It made her very uncomfortable and he immediately sensed her distress.

"I'm sorry. I didn't mean to stare so rudely," he apologized, "but you're uncommonly beautiful and it is very hard for me to take my eyes off you. But I really don't mean to be such a philistine." He let his hand glide over hers as if to reassure her.

Chapter Sixteen

Mary Ellen found his touch surprisingly appealing, raising small goose bumps on her skin. She retracted her hand.

"Mr. Brand, I shouldn't be here. I am glad to see that all is well with you." She stood to leave.

"Well, yes, it is." He took hold of her hand and gently pulled her down to her chair. "You saved my life and San Francisco has been more than kind to this Scotsman."

She liked the lilt of his brogue.

"And what are you doing these days?" he asked, a warm smile on his face.

"I manage Case & Heiser's boarding house," she said.

"Ah, Case & Heiser. That's the Excellent House on Washington Street. Quite properly named, I hear. They entertain quite lavishly. Many prominent people dine there, I'm told, though I have not had the privilege of being invited."

"Yes, Mr. Case and Mr. Heiser take pride and joy in their lavish parties," she said demurely.

"Ah, I can see that you're quite modest. For I've also heard," he tilted his head, "that a woman is in charge of their entertainment; someone who doubles as a great cook whom many consider to be San Francisco's finest. That would be you, would it not?"

"I think that's exaggerated, Mr. Brand," Mary Ellen said. "Are you fully recovered from the stabbing?" she changed the subject.

"Yes. Feel like a new person. Even the time I spent in the gold mines, during the last months of the winter season, didn't affect me too much, though at the beginning the muscles were quite tender."

"How did you like being up at the mines?" she asked.

"I really did very little mining on my own. I'm part of a consortium that owns the New Almadén mine. Have you heard of it?"

"No, I don't think so," Mary Ellen racked her mind but the name did not ring a bell. "So you own the mine?"

"Oh no, not at all. I work for the people who own it. I do have an interest but it's a minor one," he said. "I must be boring you, this talk of business."

"Actually, I enjoy learning about business. I hear many things at our dinners and I think I'm getting quite an education."

Thomas regarded her silently, appraisingly. Then he went on. "My associates are Eustace Barron, the Bolton family, and Alexander Forbes. Have you heard of them?"

Mary Ellen tried to suppress her recognition. These were, indeed, important and powerful men. She heard them mentioned quite often at the dinner table.

Thomas continued. "In fact I was just returning from a meeting with our attorney Henry Halleck, of Halleck, Peachy & Billings when we bumped each other."

"I know of the Halleck who is involved in politics. Is he the one?"

"He is, but I suspect his law firm is earning a substantial amount of money, perhaps too much to allow him to become more involved in politics."

"A visit to a lawyer," she smiled. "I hope your associates are not in some legal difficulties."

"No, nothing out of the ordinary. The usual questions. Mostly revolving around title. Oh, and Mr. Barron just purchased an island off the coast of Santa Barbara called Santa Cruz Island. He bought it from Andres Castillero who received it from Governor Alvarado in 1838. We want to insure that the titles to both the island and New Almadén are confirmed. Mr. Halleck has been engaged to do this for us." Thomas stopped. "I'm sorry Miss Price, but this must be boring to you. I don't seem to know how to act around women any longer, it's been so long since I've had the pleasure of speaking to a decent woman. All I do day in and day out is talk of business. I'm sorry."

"No, please go on. It's fascinating. I was thinking of buying some land myself," she said. "Are questions of title really serious?"

"Oh yes!" he leaned forward. "Critical! Outside of San Francisco the real question is whether Mexican titles will be confirmed when California becomes a state. Then there's the question of whether Mr. Sutter's claims and all those who claim under him will be confirmed. And in San Francisco," he stopped, looked around, and lowered his voice, "virtually every lot and parcel may be in question."

"I beg your pardon?" Mary Ellen sputtered, startled by this comment. "You must be joking?"

"Oh, no. I kid you not. You see there's a question of who has the right to convey titles. Now that we have a state government, though we don't have a state, how will they deal with all these water lots which were recently auctioned? And who had authority to sell lots during General Riley's administration, and before him, during Governor Mason's?" Again he looked around the room and in hushed, almost conspiratorial tones, which Mary Ellen found amusing. "Mr. Halleck tells me that the biggest problem he foresees in San Francisco arises from land known as the Colton Grants. He says title to these lands will be in question for years to come. He thinks the Colton grant issue will erupt any day."

His comments struck Mary Ellen with the force of a sledge hammer. She tried to remain calm, but it felt as if her heart had stopped beating. Suddenly the room started to spin around. She felt light-headed and nauseous.

"Are you all right?" Thomas asked anxiously.

"Yes, just some water," she cleared her throat.

"Bring us some water!" Thomas yelled at the proprietor who rushed forward with a full glass. Mary Ellen sipped the cool water slowly, not looking at Thomas.

"Are you sure you're all right?" he asked again.

Mary Ellen took a few more sips, dabbed her chin dry and straightened her back. "Yes, I am. I just felt flushed for a moment. I don't know what got into me." She tried to avoid eye contact, but it was impossible.

He examined her face. Uncomfortable in his gaze she tried to move away, but could not summon the energy to do it. She felt weak and uncertain.

"Do you want me to summon a doctor?" he asked.

"No. It's not necessary." Mary Ellen gripped the water glass with shaking hands and sipped water. "I must go now," she started to stand, but the walls began to spin again. She sat still and tried to relax, the way her mother taught her so many years earlier, the way she used to do on the Georgia fields. Slowly her heart stopped racing and the walls came into focus.

"I'll be all right in a few minutes. I was just dizzy," she said quietly.

Thomas regarded her intently and said: "If you are in some trouble, I'm sure I can help you."

"That's quite all right. I'll be fine."

But Thomas would not be put off. "Mary Ellen," he stopped. "May I call you Mary Ellen?"

She nodded, hardly paying attention.

"I know I'm a stranger," he continued, "and perhaps it's inappropriate for me to delve into your private affairs. But you once saved my life. You didn't have to. Don't you see that I owe you a great deal more than I can ever repay—I owe you my life. If you have a problem, you can confide in me. At the mere mention of the Colton grants you looked like you saw a ghost. Are you by any chance connected with Colton?"

"No," she took off her bonnet and straightened her hair. She felt hot and light-headed.

"But you have something to do with a Colton grant?" he pressed on. They both realized that his hand was cupping hers and Thomas hesitated for a moment than removed it. Mary Ellen took a handkerchief out of her bag and dabbed at her face. She sighed audibly.

"Yes," she said quietly. "I have a piece of land which I purchased from someone who bought it from Mr. Colton." Mary Ellen felt a chilling tingle in her spine. Losing the land on Ecker would disrupt her laundry business, cause a severe financial strain, and probably lead to the loss of Minturn's contract. What seemed so secure and promising only a few hours earlier, had suddenly become vulnerable and uncertain.

"Don't you worry. I think I can fix this for you. Please trust me. Tell me all about it."

"I'm sorry, I must go." Mary Ellen feared she had already said too much.

"Come now, Mary Ellen. I told you. I *owe* you my *life*. Please let me help you."

"I don't believe I said I was in trouble."

Thomas leaned back in his chair and began rotating his mug between his index finger and thumb. "I just assumed there was . . ."

"Well *don't* assume. You have no right to assume anything!" Mary Ellen felt a torrent of emotion rising within her. It was more confusion than anger or fear. She looked into the black whirlpool inside her coffee cup. She felt her resolve weakening, pulled by an urge to trust Thomas Brand.

Thomas just stared at her. He cradled her image in his eyes; at that moment he realized that their meeting could not have been serendipitous.

Thomas searched her face, her peculiar eyes, a portraiture of grace, beauty, and strength. He wished he were a painter. When she turned towards the window, ribbons of afternoon light danced about her face, and he wished he were the sun. But when she smoothed the skirt of her dress and crossed her arms at her slender waist, he wished he were her lover.

"Look, I know that my telling you to trust me may sound hollow; after all they're only words. But you'll see. I think you and I can help each other." As he tipped the mug to his lips some coffee spilled onto the table.

"I don't even know you." She felt herself slipping.

Thomas produced a handkerchief from his pocket and nervously dabbed the small puddle of coffee. "Of course you do. I refuse to believe we happened to find each other by chance." His words caused Mary Ellen to shift her arms and her elbow nudged her own mug. She winced as it tumbled off the table and shattered on the floor like a spilt jigsaw puzzle. Thomas ignored the cup. The proprietor rushed over to clean the mess.

"All right. I'm trusting you, Mr. Brand." And Mary Ellen could not explain why. She then simply explained the purchase.

"And that's all?" He asked.

She remembered how during Abigail Saunder's illness the doctor would ask the same questions over and over. He never believed her initial reply and persisted until he got an answer he felt closer to the truth. Mary Ellen felt that she was being prodded and pressured, as if she was Thomas's patient. And like Abigail, Mary Ellen had suppressed the truth and pain for so long. In a brief hour Thomas had managed to scale the fortress that Mary Ellen took a year to construct about her heart, soul, and ambition. She related all her transactions, the laundries and the livery stable. As she talked, Thomas's expression changed like a child's ripping apart the packaging of a gift. His businesslike nod transformed into disbelief and amazement. His mouth formed a tiny "o"; he was entranced with her every word.

"This is remarkable," he said in amazement. "Does anyone else know of this?"

"No. You're the only one. Mr. Woodworth knows a little as does Colonel

Stevenson and Kanaka Davis. But you're the only one who knows *all* my affairs." She looked at him pleadingly, stunned by what she had just said.

Thomas cupped her hands in his. "Your story is safe with me," he said kindly, as if to answer her question. "But you are right not to divulge too much to anyone. No offense, but women are not supposed to engage in business like men. Certainly not in this city. Most men here would either resent it or try to take advantage of you."

Mary Ellen was not sure why she should think he would not.

Thomas continued. "Things may change when more women migrate to the west. For now, you're wise to be so careful. I have some ideas I'd like you to think about. In the meantime I'll see what I can do about your Ecker property. Colonel Stevenson is right. Most lawyers in this town own Colton grants. I'll discuss it with Halleck. Shall we meet here tomorrow at the same time?"

His hands felt cool and smooth and his voice reassuring. After being so careful for so many years and keeping her activities so private, she felt ashamed of herself for being so weak and telling so much of her affairs to a complete stranger. It felt as if she had been swept into a raging river and was being carried away by a swift and powerful current. Unable to swim to either shore she would have to be content with drifting as far as the current would take her, come what may.

—~—

A FEW DAYS LATER A COURIER DELIVERED A PACKAGE TO MARY ELLEN at the Excellent House. She signed the receipt and noted that it had come from the law firm of Halleck, Peachy and Billings. The small package contained a letter from Halleck, marked private and confidential, which expressed in some detail his opinion that her title to the Ecker property had been properly and legally acquired, that the chain of title could not be effectively challenged, and that Colonel Stevenson had agreed to pay for any title defense required in the future. Halleck also included an official government document, executed by General Riley, and bearing the seal of the United States, which confirmed Colonel Stevenson's title to that particular lot.

Chapter Sixteen

Mary Ellen did not fully understand the legal arguments, but the gist of the letter was clear and unmistakable. Although the letter did not remove all of Mary Ellen's doubts, since each piece of her financial world revolved around her land, it did serve another equally important, purpose: Thomas had been true to his word. She shook the package hoping for a more personal note from Thomas himself. But it was empty. She shook her head at the thought and chuckling put the documents away.

After completing her chores at the Excellent House Mary Ellen went to her laundry at Carla Street. When she entered the building she found herself in the midst of a raging argument between George Gordon and a brawny seaman. She recognized the sailor, Philippe. In the beginning of their relationship, Ann Phoebe Smith had found Philippe exciting and arousing. But her infatuation soon turned to dread as she discovered his violent tendencies. She tried to avoid him but the man stalked her like a wounded lion.

"She does not wish to see you. This is a business establishment. You must leave." Gordon was firm.

"I ain't leaving' till I see her," Philippe bellowed, his jugular vein was swollen and looked like a serpent. He towered threateningly over Gordon who tried to maintain his authority.

"What's going on here?" Mary Ellen interceded, placing herself between the two men. Gordon seemed relieved, but Philippe remained unmoved, his mouth sneering and his eyes on the stairs.

"This is my building. If you can't control yourself get out."

Philippe turned slowly to face her and glared malevolently. Mary Ellen shuddered involuntarily. She had seen such a cold, hard look only once in her life, back in Cincinnati. Philippe's bloodshot eyes had the same, vacant look. She drew her breath in deeply.

"Please get out or I will call the police."

Philippe laughed mirthlessly. "How are you goin' to get the police here? Eh?"

He was right. It would take some time to get back to the center of town, even with her hack waiting outside. Who could tell what this man would do during her absence?

"I know your family," Mary Ellen tried a different tack. "I don't think they would appreciate your action."

He smiled, a sinister smile, "I don't give a damn about my family. But if you want me out of here so badly, I must first see Ann. Then I go."

"You will go if I bring Ann down to see you?"

"Yes. I want to tell her one thing. Then I go."

"I have your word?" Mary Ellen said.

Philippe frowned and yelled. "I've told you I'll go!"

Mary Ellen went upstairs and found Ann lying on her bed in a fetal position, crying hysterically.

"He'll leave as soon as he sees you. He wants to tell you something," Mary Ellen said.

"I'm so afraid of him, Miss Price, please don't make me go downstairs," Ann sobbed.

Mary Ellen understood, and caressed Ann's hair. "We'll be with you, so you don't have to worry."

"But you don't know him. He's crazy," Ann wailed.

"He won't do anything. Gordon has a gun next to the desk. Let's go downstairs. Stay behind me. See Philippe for a moment. Don't say anything, just shake your head as if you agree with whatever he says. Then he'll leave. Just come down for a moment so we can get rid of him."

Ann, her shoulders hunched in total fear, and her body shuddering, followed her down the narrow stairs.

Philippe stood like a statue, glaring intensely at Ann.

"Would you like some water, Philippe?" Mary Ellen tried to diffuse the tense situation. She motioned to Gordon toward the desk. Gordon understood and moved closer to the desk. Suddenly, without a word, Philippe sprang like a panther, shoved Mary Ellen aside roughly, whipped out a knife and grabbed Ann by the hair. She screamed. Philip twirled her around, pulled her toward him and with one massive stroke slit her throat. Ann's eyes widened in total disbelief and a gurgling sound rose from her mouth. Blood poured copiously over Philippe, then he let her sink to the floor surrounded by a crimson pool of her own blood.

Gordon pulled out the gun and fired it at Philippe, but missed. The spent bullet ricocheted through the ceiling. Philippe turned toward Gordon who fumbled with the trigger. Mary Ellen, moving quickly, jumped on Philippe's back, her arms encircling his muscular neck. Philippe simply grinned and started to slash at Mary Ellen. A guttural scream broke from Gordon as he ferociously rushed at Philippe, swinging the gun like a club. He caught Philippe on the temple with a wild blow. Philippe dropped the knife, clutched his head, and fell to his knees while Gordon continued to swing the gun up and down wildly, screaming maniacally at the fallen man.

Another blow laid Philippe out on his stomach, groaning, spittle and blood oozing out of the corner of his mouth. Now some of the other laundry workers rushed forward and helped Gordon pin down the semi-conscious Philippe. Gordon brought some rope with which he roughly hog-tied Philippe, who lay moaning on the floor. Mary Ellen rushed to Ann. Her lifeless eyes were already glassy and Mary Ellen knew Ann was dead.

"Gordon, have someone get the sheriff immediately. Use my rig. Don't tell anyone I was here." She turned to the other employees who had gathered around Ann's body. "You haven't seen me. Is that clear?" Mary Ellen realized that she needed to frighten them to insure their silence. She knelt next to Philippe and spit in his face, and yelled: "I'll see that you hang, you goddamned beast. And I'll see you in hell!" She started chanting a voodoo incantation, working herself into a frenzy and calling for St. Maron.

—~—

THE *ALTA CALIFORNIA,* SAN FRANCISCO'S LEADING PAPER, REPORTED THE violent death of Ann Phoebe Smith at the hands of her lover, Philippe, the subsequent battle and his arrest. Although the prisoner either could not recall the incident or refused to discuss it, witnesses at the laundry described the scene in macabre detail. Each witness tried to best the others until the violent incident took on a demonic cast of unprecedented proportions.

According to the sheriff the traumatic event had affected Philippe's memory and his silence, even in the face of physical interrogation, made it impossible for anyone to eke out anything about his motive. His trial and subsequent execution followed quickly, without delay, to a relieved court, sheriff and most of all, Mary Ellen.

She fretted about the incident, unable to sleep at night, wondering what would be said about her and by whom. Any revelation of her involvement in this incident would bring to light her commercial activities and get her fired by Case and Heiser. Any connection between the murder and her would destroy all her carefully laid plans. It affected her so much that even Case, who was not the most observant individual, mentioned that she appeared to have lost weight. She prayed every night, seeking the Lord's help in avoiding attention. As if her prayers were heard, and much to her relief, no one mentioned her, not during the investigation, not at the trial, and not at the execution, which she did not attend.

None of her employees mentioned her presence at the murder and the authorities were content to let this dark incident pass without any real investigation. Surprisingly, Gordon was even more afraid of discovery than Mary Ellen was. She tired to allay his fears, but Thomas's good advice helped. Thomas counseled Mary Ellen to pay off the family. He explained how she could best insure that Phillippe's family would remain silent and not subject her to blackmail in the future, something she had not thought of. The carrot, the monies to be paid to them over a period of years, and the stick, a threat of imminent harm and loss of funds if they raised any cain, worked well. In fact Philippe's family seemed delighted by this newfound wealth and relieved as everyone else to be rid of his explosive tirades and violent episodes. It was an open and shut case—the trial and execution took less than a month, partly because so many people witnessed the violent act.

Gordon, and strangely, Thomas, were the only people in whom she could confide her fears, although she did not tell Thomas of her background or of her heredity. She described what happened with Ann Phoebe Smith as it happened but did not tell Thomas how she had arranged to bring Ann to San Francisco, or how she had become more involved in funding the activities of the Underground Railroad. She had written to John Brown who responded and placed her in touch with more people in Boston. Mary Ellen wanted to bring as many slaves to San Francisco as possible. Ann Phoebe Smith had been the first one. Now she was dead.

After the execution Mary Ellen received an unexpected invitation to meet Thomas on Eustace Barron's new ship the *Eustace.* They had been meeting quite often at Woodward's Coffee House or at her two laundries. They tried to be circumspect, selecting times when few people were likely to show up at the coffee house. And Mary Ellen did not want to be seen with Thomas too often by her own employees. Each time they met Mary Ellen found herself more closely drawn to him. She could tell he had a crush on her, but remained a gentleman at all times. Occasionally they would touch accidentally and Mary Ellen could feel the heat of the moment and a great desire. The proprietor, if he noticed their meetings, or how they related to each other, acted with the greatest sensibility and prudence.

Mary Ellen felt that Thomas could be trusted with her innermost secrets and aspirations. They spoke intimately and animatedly, sometimes indifferent to their location, at other times with great care and deliberation. At first Thomas counseled Mary Ellen on her business arrangements. But it did not take long for a transposition of their roles as Mary Ellen, employing her quick and incisive mind, found answers, solutions, and recommendations for Thomas's business problems. Her ideas were always refreshing and presented Thomas with a new insight which he appreciated. At their last meeting he brought her some flowers and a beautiful pendent. She thanked him and kissed him gently on his cheek. She could feel his desire and they stood for a brief moment completely unaware of their surroundings. But at that moment Selim Woodworth entered the coffee house. Mary Ellen saw him first. She immediately stepped away from Thomas who also recognized Selim, though Selim did not notice them at first. They exchanged perfunctory greetings and Mary Ellen thought Woodworth looked inquisitively at them, though she could have imagined it. This dangerous encounter brought them back to their senses. They decided, that afternoon, that they could no longer meet in public places.

She read the invitation again.

Dear Miss Price,

Could you please attend a meeting on Mr. Barron's ship, the *Eustace,* to discuss some important matters relating to a function which Mr. Barron would like to hold aboard his ship. This meeting will be at 10 o'clock sharp on Friday morning. The *Eustace* is moored at Long Wharf. I think this meeting is quite important for your future. If you are unable to attend for any reason, please let me know by return note.

Yours faithfully, Thomas Brand

Mary Ellen was intrigued by the reference to her future and wondered what Thomas had in mind. She also felt heat surge throughout her body. It felt as if she had stepped from the cool shelter of the building into the raging afternoon heat. Her face was flushed the color of blush roses in full bloom. The note itself was innocuous. Anyone else reading it would have thought nothing more about it. However, Mary Ellen knew Thomas. This invitation was not an ordinary one. Not at all. It piqued her interest and the allure escalated as Friday approached.

On Friday, at exactly ten o'clock, she boarded the *Eustace* where Thomas awaited her on deck. It was a beautiful ship, its hull painted a royal blue with white trim, meticulous teak decks, polished mahogany, shiny brass fittings; every detail attended to. The ship appeared deserted. Not a single sailor was on deck.

"Welcome aboard." Thomas extended his hand to Mary Ellen who looked up at the tall masts and the new rigging, everything new, clean and elegant. How different, she thought, from her experience on the crowded voyages from New Orleans and from Panama City.

"What a lovely ship," she said and let Thomas lead her across the deck and through a door. "Where is everybody? It appears abandoned," she said.

Thomas smiled. "It is, at least until this afternoon."

She looked at him in puzzlement.

"Come on," he continued to lead her through a maze of inner passageways into a large cabin, sumptuously fitted with damask curtains, a large silk covered divan, rich Chinese and Persian carpets. A Louis XIV desk and chairs occupied one corner. Two large portholes with burnished brass frames were open and Mary Ellen could see Telegraph Hill in the distance with its tower of signal flags on top. The blue Pacific water seemed to match perfectly the brown and tan hues of the cabin.

"I've never seen such a beautifully appointed room," she commented as she walked around, trailing her hand softly on the different textures. "I certainly never thought such a room could exist on a ship."

Thomas said nothing. He continued to grin amiably.

"What are you smiling about," she laughed. "You look like you've just made a major gold discovery."

"I have," he said and pointed to the divan. "Please sit down."

She did as instructed, crossing her legs and feeling the incredible smoothness of the silk. Thomas sat next to her and took her hands in his. He looked at them.

"I had to meet with you alone. There is so much I want to tell you and so much we need to talk about. Fortunately, today Mr. Barron has the entire crew on a trip to Benecia. He left two guards. I told them I would be here and gave them the time off. So we have the ship to ourselves for at least four hours."

"You sly devil," Mary Ellen smiled. "Are you trying to seduce me?" she laughed. But Thomas actually appeared hurt by the remark. She instantly regretted making light of something which seemed so important to him. She took his hands and raised them to her lips. "I'm sorry, Thomas. It's just so wonderfully surprising, so different. Please accept my apology. I didn't mean to be so puerile. Please."

Thomas looked at Mary Ellen with his brilliant and translucent eyes.

"Mary Ellen, you know how much I care for you? I've been attracted to you, no, those words don't even begin to explain how strongly I feel. I've been drawn to you like the tide is drawn by the moon since we were on the

California. Not because you saved my life. It's much more, much deeper. Something I have no human control over. I've found someone I think of as a soul-mate."

He stood up abruptly and began pacing back and forth, nervously rubbing his flaxen hair.

"I don't even know if what I'm saying makes much sense. I want to say it properly, but it's impossible to put into words." He hesitated a moment. "I want you to care about me as a person, care about me as much as I care about you. I know you have some feelings for me, but I'm afraid you don't share the same feelings I have. I just want to tell you that I didn't bring you here to seduce you. I don't want to scare you away. I have something else in mind." He resumed sitting next to her.

"Then why this ship? Why go to such great lengths to get me to come here? Certainly not to talk about business," she said, still uncertain about his intentions.

"But that's exactly what I want to talk about. What I want to propose is something we need to discuss in the greatest secrecy. I wanted to impress you with the ship, but not in the manner you might think. Its purpose will become self evident."

For some reason Mary Ellen felt a tinge of disappointment but she remained silent and listened to his proposal. Thomas spoke with great intensity, clarity, and deadly earnestness. He had obviously given his plan a great deal of thought. She was fascinated by his vision and his knowledge. What she had found most interesting was how his plans tracked hers so closely and so well.

"So you see," he said, "I have excellent contacts, from the Rothschilds, the Barrons, Alexander Forbes, and others. These associations provide me with access to virtually every part of society. I know very little about your background. You're obviously well-educated, much more so than most women." He noticed her wry expression and smiled. "And, of course, most men. But you never talk about your childhood, so I haven't presumed to inquire. It's quite clear to me that there are things which you wish to keep dormant. And I can live with that. But I'm sure you see the advantages our association can have. You have an incredible mind and fantastic ideas. I don't know how you get your information, and I don't need to know. Whatever your sources are, they're excellent. I was prepared to hold on to my interest in Dillingham & Spears. When you told me they were about to fold I found it hard to believe. I checked but found nothing to substantiate your news. But I placed my trust in you and sold my shares. Less than twenty-four hours later they had left San Francisco and are still being chased by their creditors. You're truly amazing."

Thomas continued laying out his views and plans. When he finished he regarded Mary Ellen with expectation tinged with weariness, as if an artist was doomed to have his painting critiqued. Mary Ellen waited for a moment, composing her thoughts.

"Your plan hinges on you being the front for our partnership, and I understand that. It's an excellent idea. I would provide you with the information on which you would act. It gives us access that I wouldn't have on my own. But how do I know that you'll share equally with me?" she asked. "How do I know you won't simply take all the profits, which will be in your name only, and leave me penniless some day."

"Oh, dear Mary Ellen. You don't understand, do you? My god, I owe you my life. Do you think I'd be able to live with myself if I didn't share everything with you? We can have a grand life together. And of course you know that I'm in love with you."

Mary Ellen felt herself stumbling over her words. She tripped over her instinct to return his sentiments and instead sounded dry and impersonal, much to her regret. "I want to keep business and personal feelings apart," she said. "I need to have some legal assurance that my rights are secured. Would you do that for me?"

Thomas sank into his shoes as she swept his feelings aside, disposing of them so quickly.

"Of course. We can go to Halleck or whoever you suggest and have the necessary papers drawn up. I'll give you whatever security and assurance you wish."

"Thank you, Thomas. I understand that you're very fond of me, but these feelings could change. I know you mean well, but who knows about the future," she said gently.

"You're wrong, Mary Ellen," he said with ardor and conviction. "For me this is a lifetime decision, not just a run-of-the-mill, maudlin knee-jerk reaction. I've thought about you for what now seems to be a better part of my life, and you've shown me so much more in the past months. Your aptitude and my connections," he suddenly laughed, "makes for one incredible partnership that we'll keep for a lifetime. You'll see."

Mary Ellen leaned over and kissed him on his cheek, then on his lips. He hesitated for a moment then pulled her closer to him, his lips brushing softly against hers. She could feel his heat, his rising hardness pressing tightly against her and suddenly she wanted him as much as she could tell he needed her. He started to undress her slowly, his gentle hands caressing her breasts, his finger tips lingering near her nipples without touching them, then sliding down her chest to her stomach. Her skin tingled as goose bumps flared under the touch of his fingers and down her legs. She felt so alive, and so happy to be alive. Every sense in her body seemed heightened. She listened to his breathing become more rapid and intense in symmetry with her desire. As he undressed she could smell his animalism, his freshly laundered clothes, and the salty air of the bay. So alive, so glorious, that she did not want it to ever end. She closed her eyes and let herself go to his rhythm, rising and falling, as the ocean waves drift slowly toward the shore, getting stronger, more powerful, then rising one final time to crash and spread softly on the warm, tawny sand.

Chapter Seventeen

Statehood, Sisterhood

SAN FRANCISCO
OCTOBER-DECEMBER 1850

Friday, October 18, 1850

THE MUTED RUMBLING OF A CANNON ROLLED OVER THE HILLS LIKE distant thunder, startling the men gathered in Colbraith's office.

"It must be steamer day," Colbraith muttered, and continued to read the document aloud. The other men, leaders of Empire One, shifted restlessly, but remained seated at the long table listening to Colbraith.

Empire One was now well established as San Francisco's first volunteer fire company. It resembled its New York antecedents in every respect. It fought fires, an omnipresent danger to the tinder box buildings of San Francisco. It was a civic-minded social club among ex-New Yorkers. Most importantly for Colbraith, it served as his political arm, through which he could organize elections, buy votes and intimidate opponents and their followers.

The men gathered in Colbraith's office were known as shoulder-strikers, or Colbraith's b'hoys, men who could fight fires or political opponents with equal zeal. They employed naked muscle to achieve political aims. Their loyalty to Colbraith was absolute.

A second report, slightly louder, was soon followed by a third blast. The men sprang to the windows and looked out at the bay. Nothing out of the ordinary appeared on the dark blue water. Hundreds of ships moored in the bay or along the wharves seemed at rest. A few schooners scudded with the wind, trailing white frothing wakes, but bore no warning flags or tell-tale tufts of gray smoke belching from a fired cannon. The cannonade continued and soon the streets below were filled with people gesticulating wildly, cheering, and running toward the wharves.

"Look there!" Yankee Sullivan pointed to Telegraph Hill. Early settlers had erected a tall wooden tower on Telegraph Hill, a site commanding a view from the Pacific Ocean through Golden Gate. Each day an attendant perched atop the tower, like an old salt, searching the horizon with a brass telescope. Upon spying an inbound ship he would seek its identity from national or signal flags and bunting, then hoist the appropriate pennants or flags that identified the ship and, occasionally, its cargo. He would then clamber down the tower and fire a small cannon at the base of the tower to announce the ship's arrival. These signals drew hundreds, sometimes thousands, of people to the beach, and later to the wharves, depending on which ship had arrived and the cargo or passengers it carried.

Colbraith gasped at the red, white, and blue pennants hanging from the tower alongside the banner of the mail steamer *Oregon*, all fluttering in the strong wind—the long-anticipated signal flags for statehood. Telegraph Hill's cannon, like a brazen bell, continued its call.

"I think that's the signal we've been waiting for," George Wilkes commented excitedly. "California is the thirty-first state!"

The b'hoys pummeled one another and embraced as pandemonium exploded all around them, in other rooms and in the streets below. Yankee Sullivan hugged his old nemesis Dutch Charlie in an embrace that would have suffocated a normal-sized man. Colbraith raised one of the windows and the shrill clamor of the screaming crowds burst into the room. Gunfire erupted as firearms were discharged into the air, sounding like thousands of firecrackers. People engulfed the streets of the city, rushing by

Chapter Seventeen

Telegraph Hill

Empire One like a huge wave of water brought about by a sudden storm.

"Where will the *Oregon* dock?" Colbraith bellowed to make himself heard over the earsplitting din.

"I don't know. Might be Central Wharf," Wilkes yelled back. "Hell, I'd beach the steamer for all its worth. I wouldn't mind going down there to watch the spectacle. What an amazing sight."

Colbraith looked toward Central Wharf. "The wharf is clear," he announced. "That's where they'll dock."

Colbraith and the men rushed out of the building and plunged into the crush flowing swiftly down the road. The crowd bore them away like a riptide. People were gushing out of every building, heading toward Montgomery and Sansome Streets. Already hundreds of people dotted the surrounding rooftops, trying to gain a better vantage point. Many had telescopes focused toward Clark's Point. The sound was thunderous: people railing and shouting, guns firing, and the signal gun proclaiming the *Oregon's* arrival continuing its methodical beat. Colbraith caught a glimpse of Brannan hustling down the street, swallowed by the crowd. All past animosity was forgotten as Brannan saw Colbraith and waved excitedly.

As the *Oregon* appeared around Clark's Point the roar of the crowd abated for an instant, then erupted with renewed vigor—a maelstrom of voices magnified and echoing against countless walls and buildings. The *Oregon* presented herself proudly to the city. Her masts, from taffrail to main top, were covered with gallants, pennants, and flags. All the colors of the rainbow, blues, greens, reds, and yellows, glittered in the shimmering sun. One huge flag fluttering from the mainmast bore the inscription "California is a State." The roll of several large cannon from the plaza greeted the arriving ship.

Yankee tried to speak to Colbraith, but his voice was drowned by the ear-splitting clamor of the crowd. Yankee grabbed Colbraith's shoulder and motioned him to the side as they neared Central Wharf. Yankee and Dutch formed a wedge with Colbraith following closely. Yankee placed his stubby fingers into cracks in the wall of a warehouse next to the wharf, slowly clambered up the sheer wall, slid over the top, and disappeared. Colbraith and the others followed and perched precariously on a roof overlooking Central Wharf. They had an unimpeded view.

The mail steamer veered from its course, heading toward Sausalito and away from the wharves. The crowd now jeered its disapproval, wondering why the *Oregon* was bound for Sausalito instead of the wharf. Wilkes suggested that the ship's captain probably carried some important communiqué for the naval squadron based there. After a few minutes, small puffs of gray and black smoke emitted from the sides of the naval ships. A few seconds later the roar of naval cannon rumbled over the city.

As the firing continued, the *Oregon* turned back toward the city and the crowd surged forward. Colbraith looked around and could not believe what he saw. Thousands of people had congregated near the water's edge, thick as bees on a hive, maneuvering and jostling for a better glimpse of the approaching ship. The naval squadron kept up a blasting cadence with a score or more of guns. Other ships in the bay hoisted their national flags adding to the festive regalia. Hardly a mast, of the thousands of masts swaying gently in the bay, remained undressed as a multitude of bunting, flags, and pennants now dotted the flotilla and sprinkled their brilliance like precious gems.

The *Oregon* slowly hove-to abeam Central Wharf. Hawsers and lines were thrown from the ship and made taut. Nimble sailors lowered gangplanks. A steady stream of excited passengers and crew disembarked from the ship and were engulfed by the swelling crowd. Unseen hands threw bundles of newspapers to armed sailors on the dock. The sailors formed a cordon around the newspapers, preventing the crowd from tearing the bundles apart. Colbraith's old bunkmate, Croft, along with other men, began arranging the papers into neat stacks and distributing them to newsboys, who pushed through the mob selling the papers. Colbraith called down to one boy who came close to the warehouse, but the boy either could not hear or was too busy selling papers. His high pitched voice sounded above the din: "California is a state! Read all about it! $5 a paper! Special edition! Read all about it!"

—∞—

THE FEVERISH CITY CONTINUED TO CELEBRATE THROUGHOUT THE DAY and well into the night. Mary Ellen had spent most of the day with Heiser. Captain Patterson, commander of the *Oregon* and a personal friend of Heiser, arranged for Heiser to accompany him as he presented Mayor Geary with the news of California's admission into the union. Mary Ellen tagged along, feeling a sense of freedom not too dissimilar from the feelings she had when she gained her own freedom from Americus Price. She felt a kinship, a sisterhood with the state, a state that finally prevailed against the powerful forces in Congress, forces supporting slavery. California was free at last, and prospering. She was free, and prospering.

Keeping up with Heiser and Captain Patterson was not easy. Mary Ellen had to keep a close eye on the two men who plunged headlong into the crowd. Like dolphins leaping ahead of a ship, word of Captain Patterson's presence spread ahead in the crowd. People parted for the captain. Heiser and Mary Ellen made a desperate effort to stay right behind him. One or two steps away Patterson would disappear behind a solid wall of humanity. The mob jostled Mary Ellen, a rough and jarring ride. She received a beating from thrown elbows, rough shoulders, and hard knees. People stepped on her worn feet, but she managed to hold on, to remain upright and to keep on the trail of Heiser and Patterson.

They found Geary at the plaza. He represented the city, not the state, so a formal ceremony could not take place. Instead, a semi-formal announcement was made near Geary's office, not far from the smoking cannons. As Geary spoke, Mary Ellen's gaze wandered to the American flag rippling on the tall flagpole. It had thirty stars, not thirty-one stars. Nearby, the driver of Crandall's stage, the mail stage bound for San José, mounted his box behind six mustangs and lashed them to a gallop, crying "California is admitted!" A ringing cheer rose from the crowds as the stage flew by.

After the *Oregon's* arrival, many of the boarders at the Excellent House returned to place red, white, and blue crepe paper on the building. Inside, they moved the furniture aside in preparation for the celebration. Heiser instructed Mary Ellen to prepare a great feast for the evening. He did not know how many people would show up, but told her to plan for twice the usual diners. Mary Ellen warned him that she might not have enough provisions to make a grand feast, and even if she could find the necessary provisions, would not have enough time to put it all together. Heiser dismissed her concerns with a cheery wave of the hand, reminding her that it was a special occasion, a special day in their lifetimes. So she promised to do the best she could, and this was enough for Heiser. After Geary's speech, Mary Ellen excused herself and returned to the boarding house. Heiser went off to visit the *Oregon* with Captain Patterson.

The sun sank below the hills of San Francisco, and a moonless starry night replaced the fleeting twilight. Hardly a soul in San Francisco noticed. Every restaurant, all the saloons and hotels, each public facility, blazed in bright lights and with festive people. Fireworks hastily assembled by merchants roared into the night sky. The deep thumps of cannon fire continued. People congregated in the streets, dancing, laughing, and listening to hastily convened bands playing patriotic music.

With the exception of saloons and some restaurants, all business activity had ceased and all stores had shut down after the *Oregon's* arrival. Even mother nature, with her devastating fire of Christmas 1849, or torrential rains of that winter, could not bring commerce in San Francisco to such an abrupt standstill. But statehood, which nearly everyone in the city had sought from Congress for several anxious years, had finally arrived. People greeted the news and each other with jubilation, warmth, and affection; all disputes, disagreements, and conflicts were set aside. Parties and balls erupted extemporaneously with little or no planning. There was no time to issue formal invitations. Strangers invaded parties they could never attend under normal circumstances. The rich mixed with the poor, the young with the old, and this heady intoxicating joy over statehood affected everyone. Processions, formed by the revelers, wound their way through the streets. Bonfires burned incandescently from the hills and in the middle of streets.

Mary Ellen worked at a frenzied pace, trying to make order out of absolute chaos. When the large number of guests became obvious, Mary Ellen suggested to Heiser that they set up a buffet. They did not have enough help on October 18 with such short notice to provide full service to all the company and lodgers who now reveled at the Excellent House. People came and went in such numbers Mary Ellen could not keep track. Nearly seventy-five people had shown up for dinner. Some had been drinking all day and could barely stand or sit. Others were so engrossed in the day's events they barely touched their food. Mary Ellen did not care. She just wanted to get the work done and go to sleep. She rushed Samuel and the boy to clear the dishes while she and Joseph brought out dishes of roasted duck.

As she carried a tray from the kitchen, uncharacteristically paying little attention to the guests, she heard a familiar burr, a cheerful voice that startled her. The tray in her hand dipped and she nearly lost the duck at the unexpected sight of Thomas Brand.

They never met at the Excellent House. This rule had never been questioned or broken, so that Thomas's arrival made her apprehensive at first. But no one paid either of them any attention; every person in San Francisco had only one topic on their mind—statehood. The realization that for once

The Niantic

they could be together in public, in her own territory, with Case, Heiser, and so many other notables present, brought a fleeting smile to her face. Complete strangers embraced on this day, so that anyone seeing them together would assume they were simply celebrating the day's events. He beckoned her with a shrug of his head. Mary Ellen deposited the duck on the serving table, arranged the trimmings and condiments, then quickly returned to the kitchen. Gordon, brought in by Mary Ellen earlier that afternoon to supervise the kitchen and service noticed Mary Ellen's expression.

"George, I'll be stepping out for a while. Can you manage without me?"

"Of course," he said, his voice dripping with false censure. "I don't see what the difficulty would be. Only seventy or maybe a hundred guests."

Mary Ellen thanked him as if she had not heard the sarcasm. "I'll be back in about an hour."

She found Thomas standing near the front entry, the door thrown wide open to the street. She heard, even before she saw, the milling throngs outside.

"Let's take a walk," he offered his arm. "How long do you have?"

Chapter Seventeen

"I should be back in an hour or less," she held on tightly, feeling the warmth of his body and inhaling his scent.

"Good. Let's go down to the shore. It's a beautiful night."

They walked arm-in-arm, in silence, down to Montgomery and toward the wharves, skirting every conceivable obstacle, and there were many. The night around them erupted in merriment and noise, bells ringing, rockets whining up into the darkness, exploding and raining iridescent sparkles. Bands played, men and women cheered, quartets made of complete strangers sang, some in harmony, most not, but all in fun.

"It's amazing the entire city doesn't catch fire," Thomas said as they detoured around a massive bonfire.

"Could you ever have imagined a scene like this?" Mary Ellen could not believe the spectacle before her eyes. "An incredible day."

"Yes, my love, it's an incredibly happy day for us," he said.

Suddenly Mary Ellen halted. They were at the foot of Clay Street. She stood in front of the hulk of a dark wooden ship and gazed in wonder. Her stomach somersaulted, palms moistened, and breath sucked from her lungs. Her mouth gaped wide open and her hand struck her chest as it rose and fell with each thrust of her heart.

"I've never seen this before," she marveled.

"It's been here some time," Thomas seemed puzzled. He looked at her with concern. "Are you al—"

"Maybe I've never paid any attention, but isn't this remarkable?"

Thomas gazed at the forlorn ship. As far as he was concerned this weather-beaten and tattered relic of the sea was anything but remarkable. In fact, he could not believe it had not been chopped into wood for fuel. "That's the *Niantic*," he said. "What's so remarkable about it?"

"What's so remarkable? Don't you see, Thomas? Have you ever seen a ship on a street before? Ever in your life?" To Mary Ellen this ship was a black pearl nestled in the flesh of a San Franciscan oyster.

Thomas mulled this over. "No, I guess not," he said.

"Exactly. This is the most beautiful thing I have ever seen. It . . . " Mary Ellen tried to find the right words.

They walked closer to the brooding hulk sitting alone in darkness. A sign in front of the ship offered storage facilities, secure from rain or fire, for a dollar per month per barrel of 196 pounds or ten dollars per month per ton of 40 cubic feet. It was signed by Whitehead, Ward & Co.

"That company, I know of it," Mary Ellen said fervently. "Kanaka Davis is a partner. I know him."

"What's it to you, Mary Ellen? You're so excited," Thomas was puzzled by her intense interest.

Thomas flinched when she spoke.

"Thomas! Do you trust my judgment?" She turned to him.

"Of course I do. Why do you ask?"

"I have a great idea for this ship," she remarked, her eyes gleaming. "I want to buy it. Build a hotel right on its deck. It would make a lot more money as a hotel than for simple storage. What do you think?"

Thomas looked up and tried to imagine what Mary Ellen had in mind. It sounded interesting, though he really could not appreciate its economics. Mary Ellen was pragmatic. She did not wallow in unrealistic dreams. This notion of converting an old hulk into a hotel was intriguing, but caught him by surprise.

"Doesn't it depend on the price, assuming it were for sale?"

"Dear Thomas," she kissed his cheek. "Everything in this city is for sale."

"Well, let's not dwell on this tonight," he held her close to him. "We can check on it in the next day or two. From its appearance," he smiled, his eyes twinkling, "it isn't going anywhere. One thing's for sure, it'll have to be painted."

Mary Ellen frowned and examined the brown paint, "The paint still looks fresh."

"I know, but the brown. It just wouldn't be very inviting. Perhaps if it were white."

Mary Ellen felt tears push at her eyelids and turned away from Thomas pretending to shade her eyes from the lamp. "No, the hotel can be white but the ship stays brown."

"Whatever you wish." He placed his arm round her shoulder.

They both laughed but Mary Ellen could not get the *Niantic* out of her mind. She would own the ship come hell or high water.

Chapter Seventeen

Thomas Brand and Mary Ellen returned to the Excellent House an hour later. He made her promise to join him the following evening, when she would be free for the night. She kissed him quickly then pushed him away and ran into the boarding house wide awake and excited. In the hallway she bumped into Charles Case.

"Where have you been?" he asked. "I've been looking for you."

"I stepped outside for a few moments to get some fresh air," she replied, hoping her glow would not be noticeable.

Case stood with Captain Patterson and two other people, a man and a woman. The man was dressed elegantly, but his clothes better suited to a colder climate, not San Francisco. He had a cold, arrogant smile. A thick cigar jutted from the corner of his mouth. The stunning woman next to him had an angelic face, beautiful blond hair, large light green eyes, and the most perfect lips Mary Ellen had ever seen. Unlike the man, she did not seem to have any airs about her, just a friendly, approachable, face.

"This is Mr. Bushnall and Miss Catherine Hayes," Case introduced them. Bushnall bowed pedantically. Mary Ellen thought he looked like a pompous jackass.

Catherine Hayes smiled demurely, but with an innocent and fresh expression. "It's a pleasure to meet you, Miss Price," she said.

"Yes," Bushnall agreed. "Mr. Case has been regaling us with your exploits in cuisine. It appears your reputation is well deserved."

Bushnall had a slight foreign accent, not unlike some of the Germans in San Francisco. But there the resemblance ended, for the San Francisco Germans were genuinely cordial and hard working. Bushnall, Mary Ellen thought, had probably never done an honest day's work in his life.

"Mr. Bushnall and Miss Hayes arrived on the *Oregon* today," Case explained. "They are Captain Patterson's guests."

Captain Patterson smiled, and Mary Ellen knew the smile. It insinuated so much about the captain, but so little about her. She returned a frosty smile.

"Miss Hayes is a famous singer from New York and Europe," Patterson explained. "She'll be singing here in San Francisco. How fortunate you are."

"Miss Hayes will be staying with us for a few nights until adequate accommodations can be arranged for her at the Oriental Hotel," Case

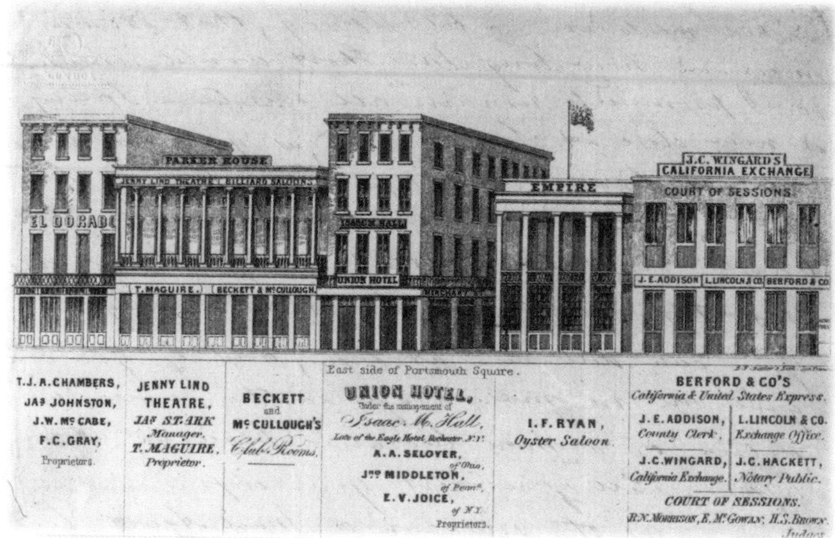

The Jenny Lind Theatre

advised Mary Ellen. Mary Ellen was about to remonstrate that they did not have any open rooms, but Case explained that he would leave his room temporarily and move in with Mr. Heiser. "Mr. Bushnall will stay with Mr. Woodworth."

"I do hope you'll come to my concert," Catherine Hayes told Mary Ellen.

"Yes, absolutely," Mr. Bushnall quickly interjected. "And of course you'll come as our guest."

"Well, we must be off," Captain Patterson remarked. "I promised to show them the town tonight."

"Perhaps you could show me some things in San Francisco from a woman's point of view," Catherine said to Mary Ellen. "It seems like such a romantic place."

"I'd be delighted to," Mary Ellen responded dubiously, wondering whether anyone could really call San Francisco romantic. It had a beautiful bay, and majestic views. The city itself did not offer much scenic beauty, though it was improving day by day, with more planked streets and sidewalks, nicer and more permanent buildings, many with masonry and brick exteriors. But she had never thought of the city as romantic. Then her thoughts swirled to Thomas Brand and a slight twinge tugged at her stomach.

Bushnall, Patterson, and Hayes bid their adieus and left. Mary Ellen called upon Samuel to rearrange Case's room for Hayes. Mary Ellen thought Hayes to be one of the loveliest women she had ever seen. Hayes's skin was so beautiful and soft; white as the buds of spring flowers. Then Mary Ellen wondered how Thomas would regard Catherine Hayes. Suddenly she felt scared, chilled by an inner wind, as thoughts of Thomas discovering her background swirled in her mind. She shuddered and felt terribly alone.

—~—

THOMAS MCGUIRE HAD MANY THINGS IN COMMON WITH COLBRAITH. An Irishman, he had owned a saloon in New York, the City Hall Palace, a meeting place for Tammany politicians. McGuire had also owned an interest in the Park Theatre, which featured some of the more popular melodramas of the time intermingled with such conventional fare as Shakespeare.

Colbraith never learned what prompted McGuire to sell his saloon and move to San Francisco with his dowdy and unattractive wife. Upon arrival in San Francisco McGuire opened a large saloon and gambling hall. It was reasonably successful, as were all saloons of that period. He joined Empire One and became one of Colbraith's most trusted supporters.

Several days after the *Oregon*'s arrival, McGuire called upon Colbraith and invited him to visit his saloon on Kearny. Colbraith accompanied McGuire the short distance on Kearny, but instead of walking into the saloon, McGuire led Colbraith through a side entrance, up a flight of stairs and into a huge loft.

"This is where I want to start a new theater," McGuire said excitedly, his passion readily apparent. "I plan to call it the Jenny Lind Theatre. The stage will go there," he pointed to the dimly lit end of the cavernous room. "I'll put in settees capable of holding five hundred persons with ease. I'll paint the walls and ceilings in fresco."

Colbraith tried to envision a theater, the full production with actors and singers dressed in colorful costumes, and a large crowd watching in rapt silence. "Tom, you know more about the theater business than I do. If you think it'll happen, make it happen."

"Oh, I know it could work. We have the population. The Atheneum Saloon has done well. Dr. Collyer sells tickets for $1 each. I could turn this place into a major drama center, and bring in some of the greatest plays, actors and singers of our time."

Colbraith listened to McGuire and found his enthusiasm infectious. They discussed McGuire's dreams and ambitions. "I'll have this place finished and an opening night on Monday, October 28th."

"That's the night before the city's celebration of statehood," Colbraith cocked his head.

"Right. People are getting all excited about the Grand Celebration on Tuesday. So I decided to open on Monday night. We're already preparing. No one will be working on Monday night. I'm certain I'll have a full house with people waiting in line. My timing couldn't be better."

"Do you have an opening act or play?" Colbraith asked.

"Of course! I've arranged for Madam Korsinsky to open that night. She's from Naples, you know, and is considered one of the greatest vocalists of our time. There'll be singers, magicians—why, it'll be grand!"

Colbraith had never heard of Korsinsky, but that did not mean anything. He looked up at the lofty ceilings. "Can you sustain such a large theater?"

"Yes, but only if I can produce great shows and bring in world-class talent. In fact I've already retained my big show, which will start the following weekend. On Friday. It'll have the town salivating on the planked streets. But I need your help."

"How can I help you?"

"We can do it the way we did it in New York. I'll set up one special box with four seats which we can put up for auction. The auction will dazzle the public, especially if the competition is among the volunteer fire companies. You could have Empire One start the bidding. If Empire One wins, I'll pay you back the winning bid and give you the box for nothing. How about it?"

"Sounds interesting. It'd be good for the city and create a spirit of healthy competition. I'd go for that. But I wouldn't take the money. Give the money to some charity, regardless of who wins. What kind of show do you have planned for Friday? Is it a play?"

McGuire smiled conspiratorially. "No. I've got the hottest singer from New York. She is great. This city will fall madly in love with her."

"Well, who is it, Tom? Or is it such a great secret you can't tell me?"

"It's the Swan of Erin," McGuire replied, then noting the puzzled look on Colbraith's face. "Haven't you ever heard of the Swan of Erin? Or the Irish Linnet?"

Colbraith still didn't know who McGuire was talking about.

McGuire shook his head in disbelief. "My god, man, where on earth have you been? It's Catherine Hayes. She arrived Friday aboard the *Oregon*."

—~—

COLBRAITH REELED UNDER THE STUNNING NEWS. HE COULDN'T EVEN recall leaving McGuire or how he managed to return home. At the mention of Catherine's name his heart pounded, his hands began to tremble and he heard a rushing sound in his ears, almost as if he were standing next to a waterfall. He realized he had not taken a breath. He steadied himself. If he or McGuire said anything after that shocking revelation he did not recall it. All he could think about was Catherine, and this thought brought back burning memories of New York, his dead brother, the aborted election for Congress, and Catherine's mystifying departure. Now she had mysteriously reappeared, and he did not know if this was a wonderful dream, a vicious nightmare, an omen, or some unfathomable game God was playing with him.

After a sleepless and tormented night, Colbraith went to his office at sunrise. After making a few inquiries he discovered that Catherine had rented a room at the Oriental Hotel, with a gentleman named Bushnall taking the adjacent room. Restless and irritable, Colbraith waited until late in the morning to pay Catherine a visit. His dark resolve and edgy temper sent those around him scurrying for cover.

Finally, as the clock struck eleven o'clock Colbraith inspected his attire, made sure everything about him looked neat and presentable, then headed for the Oriental.

The small two-story hotel looked much older than it was, though by San Francisco standards it was one of the older buildings, having survived the Christmas fire. If the porter at the tired lobby had any reservations about giving Catherine's room number to Colbraith, it quickly dissipated under Colbraith's intense glare. Colbraith thanked the porter and climbed the rickety stairs to the second floor. A worn green carpet with a red and yellow floral design muffled his footsteps. A musty smell permeated the hallway. He stood for a long moment before the olive green door, the number "6" painted in black, and hesitated. Finally he tapped loudly on the door. It opened ajar and Catherine's face came into view. At first she just stared blindly, then put her hand in front of her mouth, a look of complete astonishment blanking her face. They stared at each other, then Catherine slowly opened the door, and Colbraith entered. She offered her hand to Colbraith. He held her delicate hand gently and pressed her fingers to his lips. Catherine pulled her hand away.

"I'm sorry to startle you in this manner. I should have sent an announcement of my intention to visit you," Colbraith found his voice dying, "but I just found out you were here."

"Colbraith," she said flatly and with little inflection. "I heard you went west, but I didn't know what had become of you." She looked at him uncertainly. "Won't you please sit down?"

She moved some of her clothing aside and quickly tidied up her bed. Two large black double-end trunks occupied one wall. One of the trunks was ajar, revealing fancy evening dresses which, Colbraith assumed, were for her performances. Another dress was draped over the solitary chair in her room and Catherine whisked it away quickly as she motioned for Colbraith to sit down.

"You haven't changed a bit," Colbraith tried to make conversation, but he felt lugubrious and his words stilted.

"I'm not sure if that's a compliment or not," Catherine said as a fleeting smile crossed her face.

"Oh, no, its definitely a compliment," Colbraith leaned forward. "You are still just as beautiful," his eyes caught hers, but she averted his look.

"You look more mature, Colbraith. It seems as if California has been good to you," she looked at his tailored clothes.

Colbraith followed her eyes. "I've been fortunate. You know, being at the right place at the right time."

"Tell me about California," her face lit up. "I've heard so many wonderful, incredible stories, its hard to tell what is true, how much is exaggerated and what is pure fiction."

"California is all of those, and more. I would be. . ."

The door to Catherine's room opened and a well-dressed man, wearing a tall hat and cape, entered without knocking. Colbraith recognized Professor Heinholz instantly. His clothes had changed, now well cut and made of the finest material. He had put on some weight and appeared more confident, more arrogant. But his face, and that bitter, almost sneering expression were exactly as Colbraith remembered.

"Well, Mr. O'Brien," Heinholz smiled benignly, but his voice seeped with derision. "Fancy seeing you here."

"Thank you Professor Heinholz," Colbraith returned the greeting with false cordiality, "but the pleasure is certainly all mine."

At the mention of his name, the professor seemed unsettled. Catherine intervened.

"Colbraith, Professor Heinholz changed his name," she looked at Bushnall uncertainly, "for professional reasons. He's now James Bushnall. He has been my manager now for years." She didn't offer any further explanation of the name change.

Bushnall tipped his hat to Colbraith, his mirthless smile at once cold and hostile.

"Ah, Mr. Bushnall, is it? So sorry. You reminded me of someone in my past who is best long forgotten and buried."

Bushnall's eyes flickered briefly with hatred, which even Colbraith found surprising. Bushnall turned to Catherine. "We're scheduled to dine with Mayor Geary. We're due to leave in five minutes. Please don't be tardy. It wouldn't set a good precedent. I'd like to make a good impression on this frontier town's potentates. Good day, Mr. O'Brien." Bushnall closed the door behind him without waiting for any reply.

"I have to go, Colbraith. I'm sorry." She was about to say something else, but stopped and kept her lips pursed, as if they would reveal some inner secret which she wanted to keep under lock and key.

"I didn't mean to interfere, Catherine. Perhaps I could see you soon. I'd be delighted to show you San Francisco. It really is an incredible city. We are planning a huge commemoration of California's admission to statehood next Tuesday, the 29th. I would like you to join me, if you can. I think you would love this city."

She turned away from Colbraith. "I don't know if it's such a good idea for us to be together," she said. "I'm not certain I could take it."

Colbraith wanted to go to her and put his arms around her, to bury his face in her neck and inhale her very essence, with her beautiful hair caressing his face. Instead, he said: "I understand, Catherine. Of course I will be busy in planning the celebration, but I'll call on you in a few days, if you should change your mind."

Catherine remained facing away from him. He walked to the door and closed it gently behind him.

—∾—

Tuesday, October 29, 1850

THE GRAND MARSHALL OF THE DAY, COLONEL J.D. STEVENSON, SAT with military bearing on a sleek black stallion and looked across the plaza with a keen eye. He wore a white scarf with gold trimmings and a blue sash that announced his status. As the master of the most complicated and biggest event ever undertaken, perhaps anywhere west of the Mississippi, Stevenson had the right to fret and be nervous. Instead he remained strangely calm as he surveyed the incredible scene. A detachment of Company M of the Third U.S. Artillery, under the command of Lieutenant Gibson, prepared a row of one hundred cannons for the commemoration. Thousands of banners and American flags hung from balconies, out of windows, and in every stall. The ships in the harbor, at Colonel Stevenson's request, hoisted their national flags from royal truck to the flying gib-boom ends, and flaunted ensigns, jacks, and signals, like fields of wild flowers in the midst of a royal blue ocean.

The streets were filling with excited spectators dressed in their Sunday best. Stevenson ordered the military to fire one blast of a cannon at sunrise, which served as a wake-up signal for the people of San Francisco. A second blast of cannon from the plaza at ten o'clock in the morning alerted the parade participants to assemble in formation. The enormous cortege, scheduled to begin an hour later included nearly every organization and every important person in the city, if not the state. Getting so many men, carriages, and horses in place, organized and ready to move at the appointed time, required a fair amount of planning, extraordinary organizational skill, a load of iron-hard patience, and a barrel full of luck. The final signal, a blast of two cannons, would order the procession to move, guided by appointed marshals and aides who were now streaking back and forth on splendid horses, making sure all the carriages, floats, and riders were present and in position to move. The trunk of the main column had formed on Montgomery Street while various branches, divisions of the procession, had formed on Sacramento, Commercial, and Clay Streets ready to amalgamate with the main force.

Colbraith sat astride a slightly smaller horse, considerably less comfortable on the horse than Stevenson. He had assisted Stevenson for long hours in organizing the entire parade. Although Stevenson would lead the parade as chief marshal, Colbraith accepted the role of marshal of all firemen and would lead the Fifth Division consisting of the firemen and watermen of the port. They would follow Mayor Geary's Fourth Division of aldermen and other city officials.

As the cavalcade headed up Montgomery to Kearny and Kearny to Clay, the divisions on the other streets would join at their appointed intervals. The parade would continue up Clay to Stockton, through Stockton to Washington, down Washington to Montgomery, and up Clay again to the plaza where it would form a huge square in front of the orator's stand.

The double clap of thunder rumbling through the city startled the spectators; the signal guns had just fired. Stevenson smiled as Colbraith wished him luck. Colbraith then spurred his horse forward on Montgomery Street followed by his aides wearing blue scarfs with silver trimmings.

The formation began to move like a lazy giant snake uncoiling and stretching. Without another word Colbraith and his aides turned and rode in the opposite direction. He passed a company of mounted Californians, dressed in their traditional Mexican riding garb, with wide sombreros, silver rigging, and proud horses bearing equally proud men. General Pico, his back stiff, his head erect, led the riders. He carried a large blue satin banner with thirty-one silver stars and the inscription "California—E. Pluribus Unum" in gold letters. A large band followed, playing "Hail Columbia." The Society of Pioneers was next, bearing a large gold-fringed white satin banner with a picture of a pioneer just landed on the shores of California.

Colbraith overtook another band, then the California Guards, the Washington Guards, officers of the U.S. Army, sailors, and former volunteers, including those who served under Colonel Stevenson in 1847.

A division of foreigners marched behind the military—Englishmen carrying the Cross of St. George, Italians, Spaniards, Frenchmen, and Germans, each bearing his national flag.

The next group of marchers the largest, about fifty Chinese dressed in black pants, pleated vests, and strange conical hats, were preparing to move. They too carried a large banner with Chinese characters and the inscription in English "China Boys."

Mary Ellen, standing near the beginning of the parade, recognized their leader, Norman Ah-sing, one of the smartest men she had met in San Francisco. Although Norman seemed overly modest and difficult to read behind his omnipresent smile, she sensed he wielded almost tyrannical authority in his community. Through one of her employees she had learned that Colbraith wanted Norman as an ally. Norman offered him the use of his restaurant for sensitive meetings, but otherwise gave no hint of his inclination or intention.

The triumphal car, drawn by six white horses, followed the China

Boys. The carriage carried thirty little boys dressed in white shirts, black pants, and liberty caps. Their parents nervously walked beside them, making sure all the boys remained in place. Each boy carried a shield bearing the name of one state. A beautiful little girl sat calmly in the center of the wagon, dressed in white, with a garland of dark red roses ringing her blond hair. She held a pole, bracketed to the floor of the wagon, bearing a large white satin banner trimmed with gold proclaiming "California—The Union, it must be preserved." The crushing crowd on both sides of Montgomery cheered loudly as the carriage load of bright-eyed children jerked forward toward Kearney. Simultaneously the guns in the plaza began pounding the air with round after round of cannonade.

Colbraith, meanwhile, was still riding against the parade. He waved to his friend Mayor Geary on a beautiful white Arabian. This part of the procession remained in position waiting for those ahead to move. Geary smiled cordially and waved back. The city's aldermen and other heads of the various city departments sat impatiently on their horses.

The San Francisco Police Department headed by Marshal Malachi Fallon followed the city's officials. At the corner of Sacramento, Colbraith found the firemen's division. The foremen of the various fire companies, together with the other fire marshals and their aides, came to meet him.

Empire One, its fire carriage glistening in the bright sun, was the first fire company in the procession. Hundreds who were marching today wore Empire One's distinctive fire hats and new sparkling white uniforms. American flags fluttered from Empire One's fire wagon, and hose and suction carriages. Each row of Empire One firemen carried a flag. The carriages had trimmings of red and white flowers. Red, white, and blue ribbons trailed from ropes and ladders on the second wagon. The St. Francis Hook and Ladder Company came next, followed by Empire One's chief rival, the Howard Hook and Ladder Company, which had two engines and six carriages, due mainly to the munificence of W. D. M. Howard, their wealthy patron. All the new fire companies were represented in the parade, including California No. 4, Monumental, and Knickerbocker No. 5. Sansome Hook and Ladder brought up the rear.

Mary Ellen joined the crowd following the parade toward the plaza. She found the noise, the crowds, the colors, the floats, and the sheer magnitude of the procession numbing. It overwhelmed the senses. She longed to have Thomas at her side, caressing her hand and giving her a sense of order, strength. She felt like a leaf dancing in step with a powerful wind, having surrendered all control or direction to her partner. She walked along mechanically.

At the plaza a large gallery behind the speaker's stand held an unusual number of women in a city where women numbered less than one percent of the population. More women stared from the windows of adjacent buildings. Thousands of people packed the area in front of the platform. Mary Ellen barely heard the speeches and orations, lost in her thoughts and overwrought by the spectacle.

Once more the band played "Hail Columbia" at the conclusion of which Colonel Stevenson declared the procession over and turned to Reverend Huddart to deliver a prayer.

"Oh Lord, our Governor, the High and Mighty ruler of the Universe, who dost from Thy Throne behold all the dwellers . . . "

—~—

A DEAFENING EXPLOSION NEARLY KNOCKED MARY ELLEN SENSELESS. Pieces of metal and wood shot through the air and sprayed across the wharf as if hurled by a tornado. People screamed. Men and the few women loitering nearby scattered in fear like wild horses bolting from a range fire.

Mary Ellen had left the festivities at the plaza and was waiting for Thomas at the foot of the wharf. She looked up just in time to see a black funnel, completely intact, somersault toward the sky and then loop back down into the water. A spout of water shot up and the funnel disappeared, swallowed by the calm sea. Only a few men stood resolutely, almost calmly, and surveyed the scene.

"What the hell was that?" Mary Ellen heard Colonel Stevenson's voice over the din.

Chapter Seventeen

Colbraith, standing with Colonel Stevenson, shouted, "That steamer just blew up!" He pointed to where the ship had just been, the wreckage on the water bearing little impression to a sea-going steamer. Colbraith dashed to the edge of the wharf. Most of the terrified people were scrambling away from the wharf fearing a second explosion.

Mary Ellen remained rooted to the ground, allowing the river of people to flow around her. She watched as Colbraith took command.

"We need some boats here right away!" Colbraith called out. "Anything that floats. If anyone survived the blast they'll need medical attention as quickly as possible. Colonel, maybe you could go and find some doctors," Colbraith suggested. Even in these circumstances he felt uncomfortable giving orders to Colonel Stevenson. Stevenson, still wearing his blue sash and white scarf, nodded and hurriedly set off toward the city.

Someone remarked "I doubt anyone in the city has paid any attention to that explosion. It probably sounded like another cannon or someone hailing the day with black powder. People are going to assume its simply part of the day's celebration."

Smoke and steam rose from smoldering flotsam. An eerie silence like a thick fog bank hung over the water. It lasted less than a minute when the wind brought the first muffled sounds of yelling from the water, then wrenching screams.

"People are alive out there!" Colbraith yelled. Colbraith climbed down a rope ladder and into a small row boat tied to the wharf. One white and one black man, both dressed in a sailor's uniforms, offered to go with him, but Colbraith asked the first to stay on the wharf and help organize the volunteers and rescue efforts. He also wanted to make as much room for any survivors they could fish out of the water. He turned and searched the crowd. His eyes fell upon Mary Ellen.

"Miss Price! Stay here and help, please!" He called out then leaped into the boat.

"I'll row, you direct me," Colbraith commanded as he picked up the oars, stabbed the water with powerful strokes, and headed for the wreckage. The short, stout black man looked at the wreckage and gave Colbraith bearings. Loaders, lighters, scows, and other boats, some lowered from dozens of ships nearby, slowly converged on the scene. Colbraith carefully approached one man in the water who called out for help. He was dressed in a captain's uniform. A large gash spread across his forehead and his left arm floated at an awkward angle. They pulled the injured man into the boat with great difficulty. Colbraith underestimated the strength required to pull a body out of the water and into the skiff. A bone protruded from the injured man's arm. Blood flowed copiously from several puncture wounds and his white uniform was now a damp pink streaked with red rivulets. A foot-long spike was lodged in his thigh. When they pulled it out blood spurted nearly a foot into the air. They rushed him to the wharf where Mary Ellen jumped into the skiff and fell at his side.

"Get something to tie around his leg," she ordered while pressing her hand directly on the torn artery. Colbraith found a piece of rope which he tied around the thigh. He then used the spike as a lever to tighten the rope until the bleeding stopped.

"We need to get this man to a doctor or he'll die," she said.

The man gritted his teeth in pain and grabbed Colbraith's jacket with his good arm. "No! Don't!" his teeth chattered uncontrollably. "I'm Captain Cole of the *Sagamore.* The boiler must have blown. Go back. There are others in the water. Go save them."

Several men brought Captain Cole to the pier. Without a word Colbraith took up the oars and headed to the debris while Mary Ellen and other onlookers attended to the Captain. Bodies and body parts, and a small doll, benches, trunks, clothes, a headless torso floated by. An elderly man paddled through the water staring blankly at them without a word. They pulled him on board. He was completely unmarked but Colbraith noted a large knot on the back of his head. Colbraith waved his hand in front of the man's eyes but the elderly man did not blink or speak. Colbraith could not tell if the man was blind. More bodies floated by. One man swam by them heading for shore. When they offered to pick him up he told them in a clipped English accent to save room for the injured. Another boat nearby pulled several people from the water, including the limp body of a small girl who appeared to have lost a leg.

Chapter Seventeen

Colbraith had never been in a war, but imagined that the scene around him resembled a battlefield.

They rescued five people and headed back to the wharf. Captain Cole told Colbraith he had approximately 175 people on board, though he had not had a chance to see the final manifest. They had been bound for Stockton. "The boiler was nearly new," he lamented. "The port's boiler inspector told me it was the best boiler in the port."

"Hush," said Mary Ellen in a soothing voice while sponging his forehead with a torn piece of the sailor's damp shirt.

A bewildered crowd had gathered at the wharf. The wounded were carried off to the hospital by ambulances and any other wagons that could be mustered. Other injured passengers and sailors were taken aboard adjacent ships for medical treatment. Several U.S. naval ships sent their surgeons to help treat the more severely wounded, especially those requiring amputations and treatment for injuries that resembled combat wounds.

Mary Ellen tended to victim after victim. She held men as they took their last breaths, held weeping children unable to find their parents. She tried to comfort the tortured living who lay moaning and screaming.

The surgeons quickly and skillfully removed arms and legs. They sewed stumps and cauterized wounds. The stench was unbearable.

Finally, after the last few living were removed from the dock and the dead covered and blessed, Mary Ellen tried to wipe the crusted blood from underneath her fingernails. In a daze she sauntered to the edge of the wharf and realized Colbraith was still searching for life, his focus intense as he plunged oars into the dark water.

She had seen him return to the wreckage several times that afternoon and into the night, picking up survivors, some holding desperately onto large floating remnants of the *Sagamore;* others treading water alone or in small clusters. Exhausted physically and emotionally, Colbraith worked late, constantly exploring the murky and dreary darkness under torchlight for more survivors. More than forty dead bodies had already been recovered.

Fireworks throughout the city rocketed skyward from the plaza, lit up the blackness, heedless of the devastating disaster that had taken place in the bay. The festivities continued unabated amid the raucousness of staccato-like firecrackers and deep throated cannon. Only in the dim lagoon, its raven black waters reflecting the colorful burst of rockets and carrying debris of the wreckage ashore, was the *Sagamore*'s tragedy apparent. Pieces of wood and metal, remnants of tattered clothing, and parts of human beings, drifted quietly to the strand.

Mary Ellen watched Colbraith encircle the harbor one last time. This man bore no resemblance to the cold, indifferent, businesslike man she'd observed so many times before. She admired him. Since her arrival she had been entranced by this enigmatic character.

He leaped upon the dock and scanned the crimson waves. As he approached her he kneaded his shoulder and rubbed his haggard face. He stopped alongside her. "Thank you," he sighed wearily.

"You're welcome," she replied.

Colbraith hesitated for a moment as if he wanted to say something, then nodded to Mary Ellen and continued on into the night.

—∞—

JOHN DOLAND HAD BEEN A MEMBER OF CALIFORNIA FOUR, ONE OF SAN Francisco's volunteer fire companies, since its inception. A regular member who dutifully attended all meetings, training sessions and participated with his fellow firemen in social functions, Doland appeared to eat, live and breathe California Four. But Doland had another life, and this one belonged to Colbraith; he was trained and paid for by Colbraith. The public never saw Doland with Colbraith. Only firefighting functions led to brief and trivial encounters. Wilkes had set up an ingenious means of communication between Colbraith and Doland, always conducted through the good offices of Norman Ah-sing. A note in the *Alta California* using a predetermined signal would set up the time and place of each meeting. Doland would have a meal, either lunch or dinner, at the Red Dragon, a Chinese restaurant infrequently visited by anyone outside of the Chinese community. Doland would take his usual seat at a small corner table and Ah-sing would meet with him to deliver Colbraith's messages or to retrieve from Doland advice or urgent messages relating to California Four's plans, especially those that related to political action.

On this cheerful, sunny Saturday Doland arrived at California Four's Sacramento street building early in the morning and went about his business of polishing the fire engine. The location of the fire engine placed him right next to the entry. Anyone entering or leaving the premises had to walk by Doland. He waited until one of the foreman's closest friends arrived. They exchanged greetings.

"Did you hear about Empire One and the singer?" Doland asked nonchalantly as he polished one part of the engine's fender. If anyone had watched carefully they would have noted that this particular fender had now been polished a dozen or more times. If there had been a spot or some grease marring the perfect shine it would have been removed long ago.

"No. What about Empire One," the man stopped and asked. Anytime anyone mentioned Empire One the discussion instantly became the center of attention.

"I heard," and Doland looked around as if someone might leap out and prevent him from speaking, then continued in a lowered voice, "Empire One is planning to bid for the box on a new singer from New York. They have a special deal with McGuire of the Jenny Lind Theatre to win the raffle with a low bid."

The man looked at Doland suspiciously. "How do you know this?"

Doland spotted another imaginary spot of dirt that drew his attention. "I have a friend who works at Jenny Lind. He overheard a conversation between Scannell and McGuire."

"Does Billy know about this?" the man asked, referring to the foreman of California Four.

"I don't think so," Doland replied truthfully. "I haven't seen him since I heard."

"Well, let's go get him. I think he would be interested in this. Who is this singer? What's so special about her?"

Doland related the story he had been told, and this story was repeated to the foreman who scratched his head. He asked Doland how much they planned to bid. Doland said $250 was their limit, and the foreman whistled. "That's quite a bit for four tickets, but I think we could come in with an opening bid of $300 and suck it right from under them while they wonder what to do and what happened." He smiled to himself at the thought of Empire One, O'Brien, Kohler, Scannell and so many others losing face. He asked Doland to find out more about Catherine Hayes. Doland agreed to do so.

The same story spread through St. Francisco Hook and Ladder, Sansome Hook and Ladder, Knickerbocker Five, and the Howard Engine Company, as Colbraith's insiders spread inconsistent stories about Empire One's intentions. Colbraith wanted every fire company to actively bid for the box, but with some preexisting notions about Empire One's limits. The arrangement which he had worked with McGuire—to raffle a box to the highest bidder whenever a new act came into town—now took on an entirely new meaning. He fully intended to have the box for himself; he wanted to display to Catherine Hayes his power and his generosity. Above all he wanted to see her, and to have her see him, under better circumstances.

The auction went off as planned. Word had spread throughout the city about an impending battle between the fire companies. This made tickets for the opening of Catherine's show highly prized and in great demand. All the city's luminaries had appealed to McGuire for tickets and soon tickets were selling at double and triple their cost. McGuire selected Selover as the auctioneer. Selover, McGuire, and Colbraith developed their strategy and laid out their plans for the auction.

On the day of the auction, attended by hundreds of firemen and interested onlookers, Selover gave a resounding speech about Catherine Hayes, her enchanting voice, and her foreign acclamations, including one from Paris at the Theatre de la Gaîté. He started the bidding at a paltry $100, but California Four quickly upped the bidding to $500. Their cheers faded instantly as other fire companies remained in the bidding war. At $750 for a single box of four seats for an unknown act, the enthusiastic bidding waned. The sober delegates of the fire companies discovered that their information about the bidding was inaccurate; they were no longer reckless in their effort to prevail.

Empire One had actually remained completely out of the bidding until the last bid of $800. Captain Scannell of Empire One stood up. "I bid $1,000!" he said and nodded to Selover.

The Howard Fire Company remained undaunted. It responded with $1,025. Empire One came back with $1,050. The bidding went back and forth and William Howard, who stood aside and let his captain bid, signaled for the captain to refrain from bidding any higher. He had the money, plenty of it. At other times and in contests with other people he would have enjoyed bidding higher just to find out what game was being played. But it was apparent to him that Colbraith, for some reason, wanted the box, and he knew about McGuire's friendship with Colbraith. Howard quickly reasoned that an arrangement had been concluded by them in advance, and he decided this was not a suitable time and certainly not a good reason to antagonize Colbraith.

"The last bid is $1,125! Going once, going twice, sold to Empire One! Congratulations, gentlemen."

The incredulous crowd erupted in cheers. The firemen in the audience, many wearing their hats, sent the hats flying through the air.

"Ladies and Gentlemen, may I have your attention?" Selover tried to subdue the chaotic crowd. "I am informed that Mr. O'Brien has purchased twenty dress-circle seats at three hundred dollars apiece provided the money is contributed by the Jenny Lind Theater to the hospital. Mr. McGuire has agreed to this. I am also happy to report that I, too, will be attending Friday night's concert."

ON SATURDAY NIGHT THE ENTIRE FORCE OF EMPIRE ONE, IN FULL dress and regalia, and following a large brass band, marched to the Oriental Hotel. Crowds of gawkers quickly jammed the planked sidewalks and watched the spectacle. A carriage stopped and Colbraith, dressed elegantly in a newly tailored broadcloth jacket, pressed pants and a black silk top hat, alighted. He waited anxiously and, as prearranged by McGuire, Catherine and Bushnall came out and stepped into the coach. He had not spoken to Catherine in more than a week. At times he felt as if she were about to warm up to him as she once had, but usually she remained friendly but distant.

The brass band picked up its music and the entourage continued to the Jenny Lind Theatre. Colbraith and Catherine exchanged a few pleasantries, but Colbraith felt ill at ease in the company of Bushnall. Catherine appeared nervous, and Colbraith attributed it to pre-performance jitters. Bushnall was polite, not cordial, but Colbraith could see and feel a mixture of malevolence and fear in the man's eyes. At the theater they were met by California Governor Burnett, dressed nearly the same as Colbraith, and Lieutenant Governor McDougall, wearing his usual ruffled shirt, buff vest and blue coat with brass buttons. Colbraith introduced them to Catherine and Bushnall. The two state leaders and Bushnall were his personal guests for the box. They entered the theater while McGuire escorted Catherine back stage. Kohler, Stevenson, Wilkes, Sullivan, and Scannell had already found their seats in the dress circle immediately adjacent to the box, while other guests of Empire One slowly found their way in the large auditorium. Other Empire One firemen had an entire section of the theater set off to themselves.

Colbraith sat down and waited for what seemed to be hours, but had probably been no more than thirty minutes. He let Burnett and McDougall pump Bushnall for the latest gossip in New York, and Bushnall used the opportunity to impress his important box-mates with discreet stories of many well-known New Yorkers. The stories fascinated Burnett and McDougall, but Colbraith silently wondered how much Bushnall knew personally, and how much of what he related he had heard from others. Bushnall was a good talker and this relieved Colbraith of having to say much. Finally the lights dimmed and the curtain rose. Catherine stood alone on the large stage, her beauty nearly overwhelming Colbraith with grief. As if the crowd agreed with him, there was a stunned silence. She began to sing. Her first song, "The Irish Immigrant's Lament," struck an emotional note with many members of the audience. Colbraith, too, felt it and knew that many of his firemen were from Irish homes where their fathers and mothers had been immigrants; some of the men were Irish immigrants themselves. When she finished the crowd exploded in applause and cheers. Several bouquets of flowers, some prearranged by Colbraith, flew onto the stage.

Catherine ignored the flowers and continued to sing. With each song the assembly became more boisterous. Men had tears running down their cheeks. In a town overwhelmingly populated by males, the sight of such a striking and beautiful woman, almost angelic in appearance, tugged at the men's heartstrings. But the combination of her looks and voice really rattled the audience. They cried, yelled, shouted and displayed an enormous amount of love for the slight figure standing alone on the huge stage, but sending her lilting voice ringing through the rafters. She delivered a rendition of "Savourneed Deelish" which made Colbraith's skin crawl with goose-bumps, and ended with a new song which had not made its appearance in California, "Kathleen Mavourneen." The audience went wild. Hats were thrown into the air, men stood on their seats. Dozens of bouquets were thrown to the stage creating a ring of flowers, made up mostly of roses, around Catherine. She smiled and blew kisses to the spectators. Then something strange took place, something Colbraith had never seen before. Gold coins began to descend on the stage, thrown by the audience; a rain of gold coins cascading softly around Catherine, but aimed so as not to hurt the source of their affection. Bushnall, who knew that "Kathleen Mavourneen" would be her last song, excused himself and went back up the aisle. Colbraith watched him stop near the exit, light a cigar and puff a blue cloud into the air. He grinned with satisfaction, but without mirth, and Colbraith wanted to kill him.

Men from Empire One rushed to the stage and lifted a frightened Catherine off the floor. They carried her to the carriage outside. Before Burnett, McDougall, or Colbraith could get out of the theater, the band suddenly regrouped and at Bushnall's prodding headed back to the Oriental Hotel. The Empire One volunteers carried torches and provided escort for the carriage unaware that their leader had not been able to get into the carriage for the ride. The parade made its way back to Catherine's hotel. Bushnall thanked the men and suggested that they ought to retire and let Catherine get some sleep. The crowd dispersed just as Colbraith arrived. Bushnall met Colbraith at the lobby.

"Sorry you missed the ride back," he said. "Your men insisted on getting Catherine back to the hotel."

"I'd like to talk to her," Colbraith said.

"I'm dreadfully sorry," Bushnall said, but his eyes danced and glittered. "Catherine is exhausted. I'm sure you understand. She has asked that she not be disturbed. Of course you can see her in a few days, after she has rested."

Colbraith was not sure how to respond, but he did not want to create a scene, especially not on the night of Catherine's triumph.

"I'll be back," Colbraith said and turned to leave.

Bushnall grinned. "This is an incredible city. I think we might stay here awhile."

The last words caught Colbraith by surprise.

"Good night, Mr. Bushnall," Colbraith said coldly and walked out.

"The pleasure has been mine, Mr. O'Brien," Bushnall's laughter followed Colbraith into the street.

Chapter Eighteen

The Niantic

SAN FRANCISCO
1850-1851

Mary Ellen grabbed Thomas by the wrist, pulled him inside, and closed the door. She tossed his hat onto the bed, removed his jacket, and began unbuttoning the top four buttons of his shirt. She pressed her cheek next to his chest then looked up at him.

"So? How did it go? What did Kanaka have to say?" She kissed his chest.

Thomas, enjoying the control, toyed with her. "Kanaka? Kanaka who? I haven't a clue what you're talking about." He pushed her off. "By the way madam, who are you?"

"Oh, Thomas!" She slapped him playfully. "Be serious. Tell me, is the *Niantic* ours or not?" Her mismatched eyes danced.

"The *Niantic*? And I thought you were content with me and me alone. I guess I should've known better." He smiled and pulled her back into his arms. "Well, I did as you said. After some small talk I brought up the *Niantic*, told him I was interested in it. And made an offer."

"And? Did he take it?"

"Well . . . no."

"What?" Mary Ellen stepped back, her eyes no longer gleaming. The intensity of her reaction surprised Thomas and quickly dashed his reverie. He had never seen Mary Ellen so obsessed with anything.

"Well, he responded courteously. It seems someone else has already made an offer. Kanaka said he'd have to think about it. This other man offered less but has more social and political clout than I do. Kanaka said he'd have to think about it."

"Who? Who wants the *Niantic* ?"

"He already owns plots on either side of the *Niantic*. It's just right that he buy it. He'll probably take the old ship down and merge the three."

"No! We've got to have her, Thomas. I'll go to Kanaka myself."

"You know that isn't possible."

Mary Ellen ignored him. "Perhaps the Colonel or Mr. Woodworth can put in a good word for us. They're important people."

"That may work. I don't know, dear, he didn't promise anything."

"There must be more to it. He didn't mention who made the offer?"

"He . . ."

Mary Ellen cut him off. "Thomas, offer Kanaka more."

"That's ludicrous! Mary Ellen, I don't understand your infatuation with this ship. We already own enough land. This plot doesn't compare with what we own. And we don't have enough cash right now. We've agreed not to go into debt, not with such ridiculous interest rates."

"Don't worry about the money. Thomas, you said you trusted me. Now, please," she breathed the words into his ear, inching closer. Her lips brushed his cheek and caressed his chin. "Offer him whatever it takes. Trust me."

Thomas agreed to try but shook his head, "Kanaka won't refuse O'Brien. He just won't, no one does."

Those words sent Mary Ellen backing up again. "You never said it was O'Brien who made the offer!" She was relieved and stopped to think. "It'll be fine."

"Excuse me, we both know O'Brien won't budge on anything he wants."

"Oh, my dear Thomas, I've seen him. Despite his appearance I believe he really is a compassionate man. I'm sure he'll understand. Wonderful! Simply perfect! Now, go on. Make the offer and we'll settle this. Won't it be marvelous! The *Niantic*, ours." She smiled dreamily.

Mary Ellen returned to her room at the Excellent House. Though she made light of Thomas's pointed remarks about insufficient funds, her mind reeled with apprehension. The lack of cash posed a serious problem. She would not borrow money, not so much because of high interest rates, but because she viewed it as a subtle form of slavery. She sat on her bed and thought long and hard about doing what had been inconceivable in the past. She went to her bureau and unlocked the small jewelry case. She fingered the pearl necklace, and regarded it with a mixture of pain and awe. Tears welled in her eyes as she thought about Americus and her eighteenth birthday. She vowed, years ago, to keep the pearls for life in memory of a special moment and a wonderful man. She seldom took them out and never wore them. Now she touched the smooth pearls, lustrous even in the shaded room, the curtains drawn tight. Suddenly she clutched the necklace, squeezing it with all her might, and watched her fingers turn white, almost the color of the pearls. Then she sighed and thought about the *Niantic*. After a moment she got up, put the necklace in her purse and left her room.

—m—

"KANAKA, I WON'T HAVE IT! I CANNOT BELIEVE WHAT I'M HEARING! WE had a deal. We agreed."

"You made an offer, Mr. O'Brien, and I told you I would think it over . . . let's just talk about . . . "

"Don't give me that rubbish, Kanaka. I want that lot."

Thomas scratched his forehead, sighed, and interjected. "Mr. O'Brien, I made him a better offer, and this is California. It's about the money."

Colbraith pounded his fist on the table. Both men flinched and leaned back out of Colbraith's reach.

"I don't know what else to say," said Kanaka. "Mr. Brand and I already

The Grand Plaza

wrote the papers up. It's final. Perhaps you can purchase the land from him somewhere down the line."

Colbraith was livid. His eyes were bloodshot and the bags under them pulsed in time with each deep breath.

"Kanaka, we'll deal with this later. I have a meeting. As for you, Mr. Brand, you're going to wish you never crossed paths with me. Nobody crosses me, not when it comes to this city's land. I own it. I'll own you. Good day, gentlemen."

THOMAS DID NOT RELATE COLBRAITH'S REMARKS OR REACTION TO Mary Ellen or the fear they instilled in him. She was too excited by the news to be burdened by some politician's hysteria. Mary Ellen and Thomas immediately set about converting the *Niantic* into a hotel. They tore down the masts and constructed a two-story wooden building right on the main deck. Every room boasted pane glass windows. A large sign on the roof heralded "Niantic Hotel." One of the original masts was placed on top of the roof where an oversized American flag fluttered with the wind. Potential lodgers in the crowded and ever-growing city found the hotel enticing.

Mary Ellen spent the last days of construction in one of the rooms. She wanted to be sure everything went perfectly. One afternoon she emerged from the hotel and walked out onto the street to admire their creation. Mary Ellen wanted to catch a glimpse of her lady as she endured the final makeover. The painters were giving the ship an extra coat of paint.

"Oh my God!" Mary Ellen gasped. She almost lost her footing. She scrambled forward and attacked one of the painters. "What are you doing!"she screamed. "What's going on!"

The shocked painter put both hands in the air to defend himself, gaped at her as if she were mad, and muttered, "I'm painting like I was told, ma'am."

"No, no! The color! You're painting her white! Only the hotel should be white. The hull must be a dark brown! Dark Brown!"

"But, but," the boy had a confused look on his face, "Mr. Brand told me he changed his mind and the whole thing should be white."

"No, when?"

"Just a half hour ago, during our lunch. So I told everyone else and we set to it. It's been an awful hassle, ma'am," he stuttered, "the black shows through until about the fourth layer."

"You must be mistaken, Mr. Brand would never do that . . . " She was about to add "without consulting me" but checked herself in time.

"Well, Mr. Brand is the owner. We're following his instructions."

Mary Ellen was at a loss for words. For reasons she could not really explain, the *Niantic's* hull could not be white even though the adjoining buildings were. She was also angered by Brand's failure to discuss this matter with her. She anticipated his explanation. The color of the ship is insignificant, he would say, and not something he felt any compulsion to discuss with her. Mary Ellen knew he would be right. Still, she would not permit the *Niantic's* hull to be painted white.

Mary Ellen turned and set out to find Thomas so they could work it out.

CHAPTER NINETEEN

San Francisco Underground

SAN FRANCISCO
1850–1851

SELIM WOODWORTH COULD BARELY CONTAIN HIS ANGER. "I'M DISGUSTED with Justice Bennett's decision," he exclaimed.

His brother Frederick and Charles Case nodded in agreement. They had just finished dinner. Mary Ellen poured the three men coffee from a new silver ewer and then sat down to join them. They did not pay any attention to her. Although Case clearly appreciated Mary Ellen's talents, and placed the successful operation of the Excellent House entirely in her hands, he did not display much fellowship. Frederick and Selim, on the other hand, seemed to have a palpable fondness for Mary Ellen. They openly expressed their admiration for her wit and charm, as much as for her eclectic talents, particularly cooking. Such rapport with Frederick and Selim usually brought an invitation for Mary Ellen to join them after dinner. Not this evening. She had never seen Selim, his thick black shaggy beard unkempt, look so dark and sullen, and so distant. Yet Selim's outburst about the loss of titles, and his reference to Colton,

Lombard, North Point & Greenwich Docks

prompted Mary Ellen to sit at the table and listen to their discussion.

"I can't understand the reasoning," Selim roared and slammed his fist on the table. The delicate china cups rattled and tiny waves of coffee spilled over the lips, like ships tossed by an angry sea. Mary Ellen quickly attended to the spattered table cloth. Selim continued the maelstrom without so much as a glance at Mary Ellen.

"How can they declare all grants by the alcalde and the ayuntamiento insufficient to give title to land? This makes no sense to me."

"I don't know what to say," Case appeared stunned by the decision. "What else did Atwill claim?"

"Nothing else!" Selim fumed. "He claims he bought the property from Colton in December 1849 and then developed his land. He told the court that I don't have title."

"But you did get a deed, didn't you?" Case asked uncertainly.

"Of course he did," Frederick intervened. "Edwin Bryant was the chief magistrate and alcalde in 1847. He conveyed the 100-square-vara lot to Selim. Selim went ahead and staked out the lot, built a fence, and began construction of a building pad."

"But didn't the old grants require occupation?" Case probed.

"Yes, they did," Selim responded, "but in 1848 the ayuntamiento passed an ordinance that held that the failure to fence or build on lots couldn't result in forfeiture of title."

Mary Ellen held her breath. At least the court held that a Colton grant was valid. She remembered Colonel Stevenson's injunction—so many lawyers in town own Colton grants; it is unlikely any court will hold them invalid.

"The idea that scarcely a man in this city has a valid title seems too preposterous and monstrous to contemplate," Case concluded.

Selim agreed wholeheartedly. "I devoted myself to this land and this country. I was commanding a U.S. naval ship when the war with Mexico ended. Commodore Stockton himself declared me a citizen of California and a resident of San Francisco. Now Justice Bennett comes along with his fine eastern schooling, takes my rights and throws them away as if they meant nothing. It isn't fair and it isn't right."

"What'll you do now?" Case asked.

Selim stroked his beard in contemplation. "This matter isn't over. They'll argue it again. Justice Hastings dissented and his opinion favored my position. The Colton grants are invalid, and eventually the courts will acknowledge it. In fact, Folsom has a similar case before the Court of First Instance. He thinks he'll win. He never gave up possession, but Colton still sold Folsom's lot to Root."

Mary Ellen felt uneasy, but tried not to show it. John Folsom was one of the richest men in San Francisco, purported to be worth about $1 million, second only to the mysterious James Lick. Folsom did things methodically, without fanfare, but always with a successful result. Under different circumstances Mary Ellen might have been less apprehensive since the court's decision favored the Colton grant. Folsom's involvement raised the possibility that the Colton grant issue had not been finally settled. Mary Ellen continued to listen intently, while pouring more coffee and attending to the nettled men's needs.

Case lit his pipe and sent small clouds of bluish smoke into the air. "It's ironic that while this decision annulling titles from alcaldes hangs over our heads the aldermen have the nerve to call for another sale of city lots."

"It isn't ironic and it has nothing to do with nerve," Frederick responded gruffly. "It's sheer madness. This city is hellbent on ruination. We have an enormous debt. Do you know how much interest is accruing on the scrip they issued?" Frederick asked rhetorically. "Three percent per month! Why, they'll never be able to redeem that paper."

"That's their excuse for selling more city lots—to get the funds to pay off the debt," Selim offered, appearing less interested in this topic than on his own case.

Mary Ellen listened to the men grumble about the council's creation of a sinking fund, run by three commissioners notorious for their inability to reduce this deficit from the nascent city's books. Instead they now contemplated a new loan of $750,000, still bearing interest at three percent per month. The city had been gutted financially by men more interested in their own aggrandizement than by any public altruism. The city council and the sinking fund commissioners planked streets and sidewalks where they owned land, or graded and provided other improvements where they or their friends could benefit.

Fortunately for Mary Ellen, her small coterie of well-placed servants, maids, bootblacks, and cooks, employed in the better boarding houses, hotels, homes, and restaurants, fed her with fairly sensitive information. Coupled with what she or Thomas Brand could glean directly from their own sources Mary Ellen had a remarkably accurate portrait of the city and its prospects. And she acted promptly on sensitive information. When she learned that the city planned to make improvements in the area fronting Central and Long Wharf, and two separate sources confirmed this intelligence, she had Thomas purchase a large block of shares of stock in both the Long Wharf and Central Wharf Associations. The stock tripled in less than six months. Based on similar information she purchased more land next to areas destined to receive the city's largesse.

Chapter Nineteen

The value of these lots also appreciated rapidly in a short time, a steeper rise than the booming real estate market overall. Lots and buildings with planked sidewalks sold for more than identical lots fronting dirt roads or winter wash gullies. Graded streets offered more business and more convenience than rutted and steep streets. Mary Ellen had a deft hand and an almost uncanny ability to spot a good deal.

Now the Woodworth decision in the supreme court gave her pause. Many of their lots had been granted originally either by an alcalde, Colton, or by the ayuntamiento. There were few other sources of land grants. What if she and Thomas did not have good title to some of these lots? What then? She needed Thomas's sage counsel, especially his contacts with his lawyers Halleck, Billings and Peachy, but Thomas was somewhere between Panama and Mexico City.

She brought the men large crystal decanters of cognac that sparkled brilliantly in the lamplight with a rich amber hue. Frederick took out a long Havana cigar, ran it back and forth under his nose, bit off the end and lit it. He leaned back and puffed several times until the end glowed an angry red and a diaphanous swirl of smoke rose. Mary Ellen did not like the smell of cigars, but Frederick seemed to relax a bit. She left the men and went to her room, her mind in a turmoil.

She had not seen Thomas for nearly three weeks. He had left for Mexico City to visit one of his principals, Eustace Barron, who now owned the island of Santa Cruz, a few miles off the coast of Santa Barbara. At the urging of Senators Gwin and Fremont, Congress created a land commission to review all Mexican land grants. Barron wanted Thomas to present his land title to the island to the land commissioners. Barron purchased the island from Andres Castillero, who obtained a grant for the island from Mexican governor Alvarado in 1838. Thomas hoped this grant would not cause much controversy. Unlike other Mexican grants, its boundaries were well-defined and beyond the average squatter's ability to occupy. Still, his concerns were based on Halleck's comments about the hidden agenda—Congress's underlying objective of undermining as many Mexican land grants as possible, using the land commission as the first step in a lengthy process of condemnation. This course would remove the land from the original grantees and revert it to the United States. Millions of acres were at stake. Millions of dollars. Claim submission was not optional; it was mandatory. The only way anyone holding a land grant could retain it was to have the land commission confirm it.

Thomas worked closely with the law firm of Halleck, Billings and Peachy. He retained them originally to submit a claim to the land commission for Barron and his partner Alexander Forbes, for the New Almadén quicksilver mine and adjacent lands in the Pueblo Hills of San José. It was a formidable law firm in any matter related to San Francisco land. Peachy had been San Francisco's city attorney and authored a highly respected report on the power of the ayuntamiento to grant and sell lands. The legal community regarded Peachy as a top expert on the question of land titles.

On the way to Mexico City Thomas had taken a detour to Panama where he traded exchange drafts for gold from California for silver, at a favorable rate of exchange. Despite all his banking experience and his financial contacts, the idea of this exchange had been Mary Ellen's. How she discovered this unusual imbalance in the rate between gold in California and silver in Panama was a mystery to him. Mary Ellen only laughed when he asked, and suggested that he confer with the good offices of the Rothschild family if he thought her information was inaccurate. Nevertheless, upon his arrival in Panama with the gold drafts drawn on Adams & Company, he found the exchange rate for silver to be even more favorable than Mary Ellen had anticipated. Moreover, the bank and express company she recommended turned out to offer the best rates of all.

Mary Ellen waited impatiently for Thomas to return. He could best protect their property interests and ferret out what the lawyers really thought. She also missed his company, his soft eyes looking deeply into hers, the soft touch of his hands on her body. She put her hand on her breast and closed her eyes, thinking of Thomas, his gentleness and his long, lanky body. They fit so well together. A slight shiver crept up her spine. She opened her eyes and exhaled deeply. The spell was broken as more mundane problems flooded her mind.

Chapter Nineteen

Unlike most people who find additional responsibilities and activities burdensome, if not overwhelming, Mary Ellen had unbounded energy for new projects and new opportunities, as if they gave her a source of inspiration, making her stronger and happier. She managed the Excellent House, her three laundries that now laundered the linen of several major shipping companies, the livery stables, and her favorite, the *Niantic*.

To Mary Ellen the *Niantic* was something special. It did not belong. A dark-hulled ship stranded in the middle of a street, surrounded by white and grey clapboard buildings, bullheaded and determined to stay where it was. Unwilling to accept the way things were. Other structures looked alike but the *Niantic* was different. It refused to be relegated to the bay where it would fit so much better with the hundreds of ships at anchor. It would succeed, alone if necessary, where others failed. She was determined to make the *Niantic* a solid, well-entrenched institution in this emerging city despite the odds against it.

Mary Ellen had another impulse, one that she did not wish to share with Thomas, at least not yet: helping more Negroes escape from the South and enter a new life in California. This compulsion had grown over the last year. She could bring slaves, smuggled out of the South on the underground railroad, to San Francisco, where jobs were plentiful. She laughed at the thought of how Southerners would howl with indignation when slaves were smuggled out of their plantations at night and disappeared to some faraway shore. A bit of perverted justice, Mary Ellen thought, for people who could not appreciate the indignation and rage of the families in Africa after slave-traders invaded their villages and smuggled the very same people to the far-off shores of America in the first place.

She could bring more smuggled slaves to California, give them jobs and a better future. In moments of clear reflection and honesty Mary Ellen had to admit to herself that her interest, in part, emanated from the need for cheap labor in her business ventures. The ex-slaves, malleable and frightened people, would be bound to her as to their freedom. However, intervening events and her own success allowed her views to germinate into a greater moral action. Mary Ellen did not know when the lines crossed and her desire to help had overtaken her own economic interests. Perhaps it had been at the incitement of George Gordon when Mary Ellen opened her third laundry at the intersection of Geneva and San José Streets.

Gordon, normally placid and well natured, seemed terribly anxious and more moody than usual. When Mary Ellen asked him why he was so agitated, Gordon lapsed into a soliloquy which foretold of a bleak future for Negroes in California. News of the passing of the Fugitive Slave Law of 1850 by Congress, as part of the Compromise of 1850, reached San Francisco. Aimed at ending the sectional divisions that threatened the nation, Henry Clay proposed a series of acts designed to satisfy the North and the South. One of the acts, the Fugitive Slave Law, provided for the return of escaped slaves to their owners. As an escaped slave, Gordon had good reason to be afraid. This was not the first time legislators had enacted such laws, but the laws had never been enforced and many states had adopted legislation prohibiting state officials from cooperating with slave owners or handing fugitive slaves to their legal owners. Still, such action seemed extremely unlikely in California.

Gordon pointed to California's demographics, nearly all male, white, young, with many hailing from the South, as an ominous portent. But his real concern arose from the antics of California's first governor. In his first address to the legislature, Governor Peter Burnett urged the legislators not to show misplaced mercy for Negroes or to hesitate to adopt measures by which the legislators would enjoin Negroes from moving into California or testifying in court against whites. His blatant injunctions that the migration of Negroes, "darkies" he called them when not speaking publically, into California spelled disaster, fell on sympathetic ears. Burnett recommended a course of action designed to make California less appealing to freedmen of Negro descent. Give them no legal rights, Burnett said, or the specter of living as whites would create a black tide of immigration, with a ruinous effect. Burnett favored any legislation that would eliminate such incentives.

The legislature responded, Gordon explained sadly. It adopted new laws that prohibited Negroes from serving as witnesses or testifying in court cases involving whites. New bills flooded the senate and assembly. One pernicious act called for the suspension of all immigration of Negroes into California. Mary Ellen had not heard of that law, but Gordon explained how it passed the assembly only to be mysteriously postponed by some political maneuvering in the senate where it died without a vote when the legislature adjourned. These laws, the constant and uninterrupted haranguing of the large population of southerners in California to allow the institution of slavery in the state, and the possibility of forcibly being sent back to the South, terrorized Gordon. It made Mary Ellen sick and angry.

Gordon's fears festered and Mary Ellen found herself so disturbed by the legislative actions that she wrote to John Brown at an address provided to her by her newest acquaintance, Mifflin W. Gibbs, a tall black man who emigrated from Philadelphia to California in early 1850. Born as a freeman, Gibbs was active in civic affairs back east and had worked in the Underground Railroad. When he arrived in California he tried to work as a carpenter, but white construction crews resented his presence and he soon found himself without a job. A chance encounter between Gibbs and Gordon on the streets of San Francisco, resulted in a close friendship between the two men. Gordon told Gibbs he knew a white woman who might help him. Gordon brought Gibbs to Mary Ellen and she advised him to open a small boot blacking stand where he could wait on customers during the day and clean boots left overnight. If Gibbs suspected anything about Mary Ellen's background, he kept it to himself. Like Mary Ellen, Gibbs spoke well, an educated man. Mary Ellen sent customers to him and helped with his business.

Gibbs asked Mary Ellen what she wanted from him. A man not given to levity, always clothed in a serious mien, Gibbs actually laughed when Mary Ellen told him. She asked him to listen carefully to his white customers, and to report any sensitive commercial information or other delicate indiscretions, since men tended to talk while their boots were being polished. "So you want me to be your spy," he grinned and shook his head in disbelief as if to say "what a crazy woman." His laughter ended just as suddenly when Mary Ellen asked him to get John Brown's address.

Gibbs, his strong, chiseled face, with a thin, straight nose and high cheekbones, worked hard and made his business grow. Unfortunately for Mary Ellen, Gibbs did not meet her criteria as a malleable Negro. He was grateful to Mary Ellen for helping him get his start in San Francisco. Yet he sent her little useful information. Whether he never heard anything worth repeating or simply found the act of eavesdropping demeaning, Mary Ellen never found out. Gibbs always took the moral high ground. He had strong opinions about everything, but particularly the difficult life Negroes encountered in San Francisco and California. Mary Ellen countered that Negroes had better opportunities in California than in most of the other thirty states of the Union. Gibbs did not agree. He cited the same legislative action that vexed Gordon.

Gibbs told Mary Ellen that he would dedicate his life to the cause of his people, much as he had back in the Atlantic states. He would work to overturn the sinful legislation. They had many provocative arguments about the best course of action. Mary Ellen liked the more subtle approach: placing people in jobs, showing the community how Negroes could do the same work as whites. Gibbs countered that such action might even cause more resentment and antagonism as Negroes took away jobs. Mary Ellen would become angry with Gibbs intransigence. "Don't you see that California will grow, this city and others will grow, and there will be lots of jobs for everyone?" Gibbs wouldn't budge. Mary Ellen had little doubt that he would draw a great deal of attention to himself. So she pressed no further, preferring to keep all contacts and communications with Gibbs at a comfortable distance, preferably through Gordon.

Gibbs did help Mary Ellen with John Brown. He knew an address in New York where mail could be sent to abolitionists. He felt reasonably certain that any letter sent to Brown at that address would reach him eventually. Mary Ellen crafted a carefully worded letter to John Brown that she sent to Boston. Six months elapsed and Mary Ellen forgot all about it when she went to the post office and found a letter addressed to her in John Brown's bold strokes. His views had not changed, though his words were harsher and his intensity even more singularly directed.

She sent money to William Lloyd Garrison and to John Brown. They helped her start a new branch of the Underground Railroad, taking escaped slaves from the east coast to California. A trickle, at best, the slaves made their way via Panama, though the risk of stopping at any southern ports made this mode of transportation more risky. Others ventured the overland route in wagons drawn by eight mule teams or six oxen. They arrived in small groups, usually accompanying some white family so as not to draw too much attention to themselves. Mary Ellen gave them lodging after carefully indoctrinating them to their new land, warning them about the many southerners who inhabited the land. She placed them into jobs where they could earn a living and provide her with more valuable information.

Mary Ellen learned that Gibbs, together with another man by the name of Townsend, had started an organization they called the "Franchise League," a clumsy attempt to force the California state legislature into giving resident Negroes the right to vote. She felt that their efforts, no matter how laudable, were not only premature, but could lead to the passage of even harsher laws. As expected, Gibbs and Townsend made no headway, and Mary Ellen tried to remain as far removed from them and their efforts as possible. She rebuffed all efforts by Gibbs for direct aid and support. Instead she gave Gordon small amounts of money for the two men, but with a clear fiat to keep her name out of it. She intended to remain anonymous. She told Gordon to say whatever he needed to say to discourage Gibbs from making any more appeals to her. A silent distance developed between her and Gibbs for which she was thankful.

Mary Ellen directed all her efforts to improve her business ventures and provide the growing community with more servants, cooks, and handymen. She had no intention of establishing a fifth column amid the huge and evolving white population, recognizing the futility of any such effort. Having good inside, confidential information for her own business prospects, helping Garrison and Brown in the east coast by providing money and jobs, and giving those unfortunate enough to have been enslaved from birth a taste of freedom, sufficed for now. By the end of 1850 Gordon, still uneasy but completely committed to Mary Ellen's efforts, triumphantly told her that based on what he knew there were nearly 250 Negroes in San Francisco, and more arriving every day, some destined for jobs set up by Mary Ellen and her growing enterprises.

—~—

THE BROWN BAROUCHE, LINED WITH LIGHT-BLUE SATIN, WITH YELLOW wheels and drawn by two magnificent black horses with a Negro groom in livery sitting in the smart rear tiger seat, drew up to the Excellent House. The driver, a huge man, so large the carriage looked unaccountably undersized, reined the proud horses. Mary Ellen, kneeling in the rose-bed next to the gate, her hands scratched from pruning the struggling bushes, watched Case alight and thank the driver. The giant acknowledged Case with a slight nod and spurred his horses onward. Fortunately the road had been planked, depriving Mary Ellen and the Excellent House of the usual coat of fine, choking dust.

Case walked up the path and tipped his hat to Mary Ellen.

"Good day, Mary Ellen," he said in a jocular vein. "Taking care of the roses, I see."

Mary Ellen noticed a slight quiver at the corner of his mouth. "Good day to you, Mr. Case. That was quite a carriage. I've never seen one so . . . "

"You mean so pretentious?" Case smiled knowingly. "So gaudy?" he forced a high-pitched laugh, which he seemed to instantly regret. "That belongs to Mrs. Milton Latham. It's the first one of its kind in San Francisco. It's roomy, comfortable, and garish." Case paused and his face became serious. "Mary Ellen, perhaps you and I could have a few words," he beckoned her.

"All right. Just let me clean my hands," she wiped her hands on a white apron and followed Case into the house. He took a crystal tumbler and poured himself a drink while Mary Ellen went into the kitchen and washed the soil from her hands.

Case paced back and forth, looking into his glass in contemplation, as if it were a crystal ball with profound revelations. When Mary Ellen returned he said, "Please sit down, Mary Ellen." He continued walking to and fro. "I have something important to tell you."

Mary Ellen sat down on the emerald green damask settee and waited for the news. She could tell Case felt uncomfortable, and it made her skin crawl with goose bumps.

"Mary Ellen," he said, "Mr. Heiser and I have done quite well in San Francisco. We've decided to return to the east coast for an extended visit with our families. Our agents will continue to run the mercantile business, but we decided not to continue with the Excellent House." He let the news fall and waited for Mary Ellen to recover.

Mary Ellen sat in stunned silence, stunned in part by the news, but even more by her failure to learn about Case and Heiser's plans or intentions. She had not gotten the slightest wind of this despite maintaining one of the city's finest information-gathering operation. She chastised herself. After all, this information must have been known to some around the Excellent House.

"We've sold the Excellent House to Mr. Latham."

Another lapse of information, and the surprise registered on her face. She might have been willing to purchase the boarding house through Thomas, if she had any idea it was for sale.

"But why?" she asked, her voice sounding a bit shrill. "I could have run it for you, just as others can take care of your other business operations?"

Case looked at the floor for a moment, then up at the highest point on the ceiling, as if he could look directly into heaven. She could see the small balding spot on the back of his head which he tried to cover with nearly every conceivable mask, including boot black. He cleared his throat and looked directly at Mary Ellen. "We don't believe boarding houses have any future, not with all the hotel construction now taking place in San Francisco—the Union, Oriental, Bryant, St. Francis. Why, someone has even built a hotel on top of the old *Niantic*."

Mary Ellen gasped audibly and Case looked at her in surprise. "Oh, I didn't believe it either until I saw it going on top of that old bark or schooner or whatever it is. The funny thing is that Mr. Heiser thinks it's a great idea. I think it reflects the lunacy of our times. Anyhow," he coughed to clear his throat, "the point is that hotels will take all the business away and this building isn't really large enough to serve as a hotel. So we sold it." He looked at Mary Ellen and she noted a look of sorrow cross his face. "Of course, we'll pay you a substantial bonus—a portion of the proceeds of the sale. After all, if it hadn't been for you I don't know how we would have kept it this long. So we're treating you like one of our partners."

Mary Ellen's jaw slackened and she just stared at Case. He misread her look.

"Oh, please Mary Ellen, don't take it so hard. I don't know what Mr. Latham plans to do with it, but if he keeps the boarding house I'm sure he would wish to have you stay. I know Selim Woodworth would like to retain you to run his household. He'll pay you handsomely and provide you with room and board. I dare say he'll probably pay you more than we ever did, and you'll have less work to do. There, doesn't that sound good to you?" he implored.

Mary Ellen smiled benignly. Case was a fairly simple and obvious man. His mention of the *Niantic*, though, catching her off guard, did not imply that he knew anything about her involvement. If it had been anyone else, Mary Ellen would have been concerned, but not with Case. On the contrary, Case now presented her with a solution to a burgeoning dilemma. The time required to run and manage the Excellent House cut too deeply into her more lucrative commercial interests. There was not enough time in the day to do all that she wanted to do. She remained with Case and Heiser out of loyalty and because it drew the added dividend of granting her access to some of the city's most important people when they dined at the boarding house, though of lately such affairs had become a rarity. If she had prayed for deliverance it could not have come at a more opportune time or at a better price. Case and Heiser always treated her fairly, but she never expected them to give her a share of the proceeds upon sale of their boarding house. Such largesse surprised her. Beset with mixed emotions, Mary Ellen sensed that one stage of her life in San Francisco was about to end, another to begin.

She understood, for the first time, just how much the Excellent House meant to her, not so much in economic terms, but as a bastion of support, with a solid roof over her head, food on the table, and dependable and caring persons around her. A small current of sadness undercut the stirring excitement of her next step in the journey of life.

Chapter Nineteen

The opportunity to work for Selim Woodworth appealed to her. The money was not so important. Selim loved to entertain, to throw gala dinner parties, to fete the upper crust of San Francisco and Monterey society. Her culinary skills were in great demand. On several occasions she cooked for Selim's parties and helped with the dinner service. Selim spared no expense at these lavish soirees and his invitations were highly sought after. She would enjoy working with Selim. But best of all, she would now have the time to devote to her own interests. Mary Ellen felt overwhelmed by conflicting emotions.

"I'm truly happy for you, Mr. Case," Mary Ellen said fondly, "because I know how much you've wanted to see your family. We've talked about them so often that I feel I know them. Still, I'll miss both you and Mr. Heiser very much. I do appreciate the kindness you've shown me and all that you've done for me."

Case's eyes moistened but he appeared relieved. "Good! I'm glad you understand. I dreaded telling you because I know how much this place means to you." He grasped her hand and held it tightly. "Mr. Heiser and I have always valued your judgment. I know you'll be successful with whatever you do."

"How long before the transfer takes place?" she asked.

Case pursed his lips. "Unfortunately, Mr. Latham will be taking possession at the end of this week. Of course I could ask him to let you stay until you find suitable accommodations."

"No, thank you. That won't be necessary. I'd prefer to work with Mr. Woodworth."

"Ah, he'll be so delighted to hear that," Case clapped his hands. "Whatever you choose, you'll have sufficient funds from your share of the sale to take up lodgings almost anywhere in the city."

A fleeting thought of staying at the *Niantic* flashed through her mind, but she quickly stifled the notion. Somehow living on the *Niantic* would take some of the mystique and romance out of it. She did not want to spoil her feelings for the project and she had another alternative in mind: the Tehama House, a new hotel recently renovated from the old Jones Hotel on the corner of Sansome and California Streets.

Case was right. Several new hotels had already been built and others were in various stages of construction. She toyed with the idea of taking a room in the elegant Union Hotel. The huge four-story brick building on Kearny and Clay offered outstanding accommodations in a fire-proof building and claimed to be the first of the premiere hotels in the city. But Mary Ellen never completely trusted one of its owners, Selover, a close ally of Colbraith's, despite the reports that he had spent more than $250,000 to build and furbish the hotel to the highest standards found in any American city. Likewise she quickly rejected any thoughts of lodging at the St. Francis Hotel on Dupont and Clay, although the idea made her smile involuntarily. The city's elite congregated at this fashionable hotel, but the rooms were separated by the thinnest board partitions without any lathe or plaster. Anyone whispering too loudly could be heard in adjacent chambers, and Mary Ellen had a small clique of servants eavesdropping on private and interesting conversations.

The Tehama House, a three-story affair with tall windows and building-length verandas supported by square columns, mimicked the architectural style of George Washington's Mount Vernon, only larger, more modern and lavishly appointed. The hotel offered its lodgers meals at Alden's Branch, an excellent restaurant on the ground floor. Thomas maintained a room there and, upon returning from Mexico City, would be stunned to find Mary Ellen living in the same hotel. She felt a mild uncertainty about his reaction. Undoubtedly he would be caught off guard. She could see his light blue eyes dancing merrily and his Scottish brogue becoming more pronounced as it usually did when he could not contain his ardor. Mary Ellen smiled inwardly at the prospects of being so close to him and sharing a greater intimacy.

The next evening she went to visit Selim at home, the first house built on a water lot. People proclaimed the notion of building a house on a water lot madness. Anyone other than Selim, people scoffed, would have been institutionalized with dementia. But Selim had a reputation as a strong, level-headed, man. Still, a house on water? People laughed, but now his house occupied solid ground at an ideal location and many others had followed suit. Although Selim now lived nearly full time in San Francisco, he

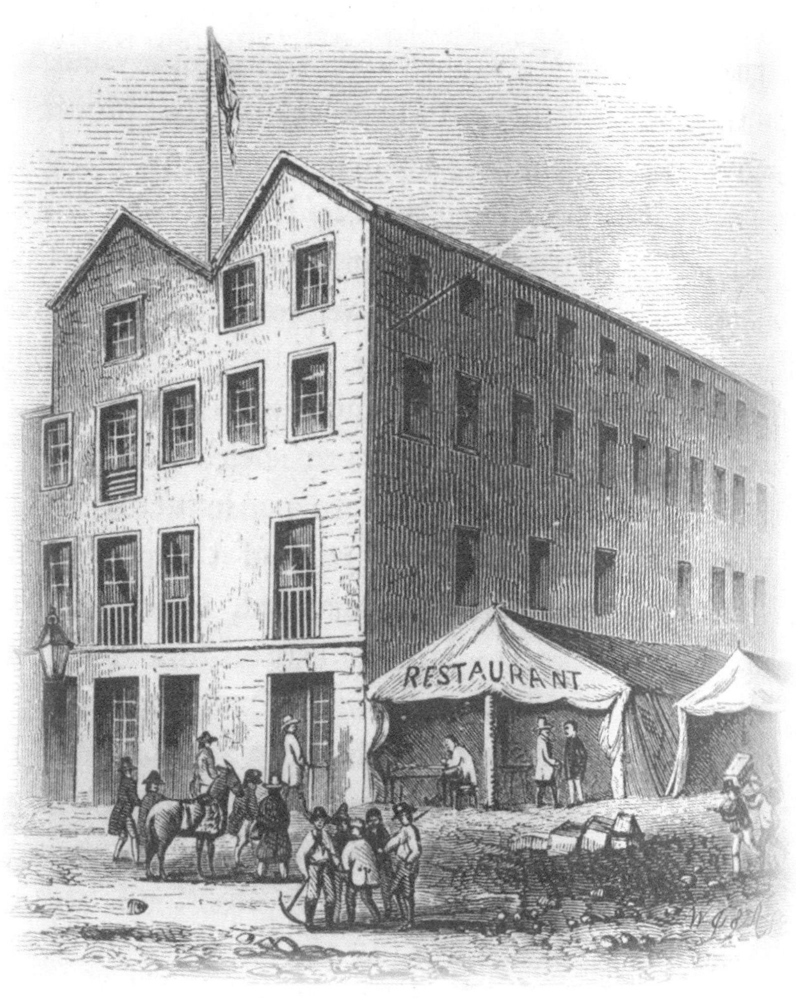

The St. Francis Hotel

had been elected in 1850 to the 1851 state legislature, as a senator from Monterey. This meant that for the first six months of 1851 he would spend his time in three cities: his home city of San Francisco, Monterey where his constituency resided, and San José where the legislature would convene.

A young black girl, one of Mary Ellen's recent placements, nervously greeted Mary Ellen at the door. She barely masked her fear of Mary Ellen, and quickly ushered her to Selim's study. Selim seemed like his old self, gracious and jovial, markedly different from the gloomy and angry man berating the injustice of Justice Bennett's decision a few weeks earlier. Selim explained his circumstances and seemed preoccupied with the opening session of the legislature. They discussed Mary Ellen's employment and after a few minutes struck a deal. Mary Ellen would manage his house, all the servants, and prepare meals on Friday and Saturday evenings when he entertained. She declined a room, preferring to take her residence at the Tehama House. Selim agreed to a salary of five hundred per month for what was essentially part-time employment, an exorbitant sum of money for the work. Selim appeared to be delighted by her acceptance and expressed his gratitude that she would be joining his household. He immediately described his plans for the next opulent affair.

—∞—

STEAMER DAY OCCURRED ROUGHLY EVERY FORTNIGHT, USUALLY AROUND the first and the middle of the month. The regular service between San Francisco and Panama, like the rhythmic heartbeat of a living being, created a lifeline between the Atlantic states and California. Regular service meant continuous, not precise or timely service. Weather and equipment played the most prominent and most wearying roles affecting schedules. Occasionally a ship would go down. More often a sudden and raging Pacific storm would either drive the hapless boat into safe harbor or retard its progress by days or a week. So if the mail steamers did not arrive on time, the people understood. The important thing was that the service remained regular and more frequent as more ships went on line.

The Telegraph Hill cannon and pennant display would herald the arrival of the *California* or the *Oregon* or some other Pacific Mails steamer, and virtually the entire focus of San Francisco would revert to the incoming ship. The flurry of activity would keep merchants, bankers, hotels, restaurants, real estate agents, lawyers, and nearly everyone engaged in commerce, extremely busy. The excitement of news and mail from the Atlantic states, the arrival of cargo bearing the latest fashions or critically needed supplies, affected the entire population. Steamer day in San Francisco was imbued with a mixture of a festive holiday and a landmark commercial event. The excitement and bustle quickly spread through the population, even to the gamblers deeply ensconced in their lairs.

Mary Ellen doggedly attended the arrival of each ship hoping to find Thomas disembarking. She did not know when he would return. If only they had a telegraph, she mused, thinking of the news accounts about William Morse's recent invention and the installation of new telegraph lines in the east coast, Thomas could notify her upon his departure and she could plan for his imminent arrival. In the absence of any forewarning, and without any steamer due at this time of the month, the bark of the signal cannon from Telegraph Hill created a stir in the community and the flags raised on Telegraph Hill had most of the people baffled. Mary Ellen pressed through the crowd to catch a glimpse of a fast moving ship, raked with tall masts and a multitude of sails. The crowd gasped with wonderment at the sight of the beautiful ship. Unlike the lugubrious barques, schooners and brigs that plied the California coast, and which many in the crowd had experienced on long and tedious voyages to California, this ship moved astonishingly fast and gracefully as it rounded Clark's Point. One man in the crowd explained to his young son that they were looking at a new clipper ship designed for lightness and speed. Mary Ellen marveled at the beauty and symmetry of the long-armed, thin-waisted vessel as it glided through the choppy blue bay like a knife through soft butter.

The *Surprise* alertly dropped its sails and slowly hauled in at Cunningham's Wharf. Mary Ellen watched the passengers disembark and soon spied Thomas walking quickly down the gangplank. His face lit up when he saw her and he impulsively rushed toward her only to stop himself from throwing his arms around her at the last second.

"I've missed you so much, Thomas," Mary Ellen said softly as people jostled them in the mad rush on the wharf. Mary Ellen took this opportunity to put her head softly on Thomas's shoulder, then quickly pushed away.

His blue eyes danced in merriment and his broad smile spoke volumes about his feelings for her. "I've missed you, too, darling," he whispered close to her ear. "I'm not going to leave you alone this long again."

The porter brought Thomas's baggage and they hired a cab to take Thomas to the Tehama House. Thomas offered to drop Mary Ellen at the Excellent House. She smiled demurely and declined. They sat next to each other, their bodies touching innocently, but it aroused Mary Ellen, so she sidled up even closer and placed her hand on his leg.

Thomas stiffened and burst out laughing. "I'll have to remain in this cab for the next thirty minutes if you touch me like that again."

When they entered the lobby the porter nodded politely but with familiarity to Mary Ellen. She turned to Thomas. "Come to room 26. I have a surprise for you."

"Room 26? Whose room is it?" Thomas asked bewildered.

"Never mind. Just come as soon as you can. I'm sure you will enjoy it as much as I will," she said and left Thomas standing in the middle of the lobby, waiting for the porter to bring his baggage from the cab, a puzzled expression firmly etched on his face.

—~—

AS THE CONSTRUCTION OF THE *NIANTIC HOTEL* NEARED COMPLETION, Thomas received a notice from the city, signed by Assistant Alderman William Sharon, that required the owners of the lot to improve the property by grading the street and building a planked sidewalk directly in front of the *Niantic.* Thomas, not wishing to retard the progress of the hotel's construction, began grading the street. But he was incensed. He could not understand where the city had the power to compel him to spend money for such improvements, let alone present him with an unexpected bill toward the end of the project when projected funds had already been allocated and spent elsewhere. Mary Ellen agreed that the cost of any grading or planking should be undertaken by the city, not by them. They decided to discontinue making additional improvements until the matter could be cleared with the city.

They met with Assistant Alderman Sharon at the offices of the city council. Sharon, short, stiff, with a receding hairline, and a sharp glint in his eye, seemed affable. Thomas explained the situation, produced the invoices for the work already completed and handed the notice to Sharon who glanced at it briefly and then handed it back.

"I'm not aware of any ordinance that gives the city the right to require any owner to improve the road in front of his lot," Thomas said. "We've spent a great sum to build the hotel and to grade the street, but we can't afford to undertake such expensive improvements. Certainly not at this late stage of the project."

Sharon formed a little steeple with his hands and nodded in agreement. "I commiserate with your predicament. It seems harsh, but I'm only following the city council's instructions to give such notices to every project in town."

"But how do you expect us to pay for this? Look at how much the grading has already cost us. And as a practical matter how can we build a planked sidewalk just in front of our lot? Shouldn't the sidewalk be built at one time along the entire street front? What are the specifications or dimensions of the required planks for the street and the sidewalk? One inch thick? Three inches? And do we plank the street just for the width of our lot? Do we grade all the way across the street, or just to the middle? With all due respect Mr. Sharon, this notice makes no sense. Not only is it ambiguous, I believe it's unlawful."

Sharon barely blinked. He leaned across the desk and spoke in a low, almost conspiratorial tone. "I share your sentiments, Mr. Brand." He regarded Mary Ellen briefly, smiling charmingly, but directed his remarks at Thomas. "Frankly, I don't think the city can force you to make these improvements without recompense." He looked around as if someone might hear him. "Of course I can't impede the city council's action, but I have expressed my opposing view on this matter on more than one occasion. If you'll leave this in my hands I'll present it to the city council as a request on your behalf to be reimbursed for these costs. If you'd provide me with a written estimate for the balance of the work," he smiled, "a reasonable one prepared by someone whom the city council would consider credible, then perhaps we can resolve this problem. We are meeting tomorrow evening, so perhaps you could get it into my hands by this time tomorrow."

Sharon stood up. "This is the best I can do. I can't guarantee that the city council will agree, but I'll do my best." Sharon opened a desk drawer and pulled out a card which he handed to Thomas. "This attorney represents several clients with the same problem. He's highly knowledgeable. I'm certain he can prepare the necessary documents for submission to the city council. And his fees are quite reasonable."

Thomas looked at the card and gave it to Mary Ellen.

"I've never heard of him," Thomas said. "My lawyers are Halleck, Billings and Peachy."

Sharon flinched noticeably, but remained agreeable. "Yes, they're a fine firm. I'm sure they can achieve the same results, but I doubt they'd be able to do it as reasonably. But that's your choice. Now if you'll excuse me, I have an important engagement to attend."

Thomas began to remonstrate that he needed more information about what must be done, but Sharon simply reiterated that he would bring the issue to the attention of the full common council and that Thomas's best course of action would be to retain the attorney on the card. Mary Ellen prompted Thomas by tugging at his elbow. She thanked Sharon who stood up and bowed deeply.

Outside, Thomas remained tense, but Mary Ellen held tightly to him.

"Go to Peachy," she suggested. "He's a known commodity. I don't know who this other attorney is, and there's something about Mr. Sharon that makes my skin crawl."

"Mr. Sharon is a fine man, Mary Ellen. He has an excellent reputation. Look, he agreed to help us, didn't he?"

"Yes, but—"

"I don't think your instincts are quite on track with this one."

"Perhaps," Mary Ellen acknowledged, but her skin prickled and she felt uneasy about Sharon.

Chapter Nineteen

"Of course you're right about Peachy," Thomas agreed. "Why should we use a lawyer we don't know? It's bad enough when we use one we do know."

They both laughed, but Mary Ellen could not shake her feelings about Sharon. She tried to understand; Sharon had done nothing to make her so suspicious. Later that afternoon Peachy reviewed the notice and shook his head in amazement. "I'm not sure the city council ever sanctioned such a notice," he said. "And I wouldn't trust this lawyer. He's a shyster. The city will have to make these particular improvements. Of course they can direct you to make improvements on your lot in connection with your construction. But not the grading of the street or planking the walk. If you've done any work along these lines, submit the bill to the city. Let the city reimburse you. I'll take care of it."

A week later Thomas received a letter from the city confirming that the planking and grading of the street would be the responsibility of municipal officials. Peachy was able to get the city to repay Thomas for grading that had been done at the site, and presented Thomas with city scrip for the amount of $4,743.50, bearing interest at three percent per month. Thomas presented the city treasurer with the scrip, but the city would not honor it. The treasurer told Thomas the city's coffers were empty, and the city could not redeem any scrip. Thomas's efforts to discount the scrip with the banks met with equal failure. The banks were only willing to give him twenty-five cents on the dollar. Despite the accumulation of so much interest, and the city's obligation to redeem it, the scrip remained virtually worthless.

"I say scrap this damned scrip," Thomas told Mary Ellen. She could not argue, but the amount the city owed continued to increase. For once even the normally loquacious Peachy could not come up with a reasonable suggestion. An answer to their dilemma came from an unexpected source.

Gordon told Mary Ellen that Gibbs wanted to see her. She declined, using as many excuses as she could muster, but Gibbs sent her a short note through Gordon. She read it and her hand began to tremble. She read it again: "I would like to talk to you about the *Niantic*. It is important. W.G."

Gibbs, or perhaps Gordon, Mary Ellen could not tell which, used the only words which would compel her to meet someone against her own better judgment. They met at her Ecker Street laundry. Gibbs did not waste any time.

"I know you've been reluctant to talk to me . . . "

Mary Ellen started to rebut his statement, but he continued right through her words with a zeal and intensity she had not seen before.

"And I understand your concerns. I'm also reasonably sure, though Gordon denies it, that you've been the party behind some of his benevolent gifts to me."

Again Mary Ellen tried to rejoin, but stopped when Gibbs walked up to her and put his hands on her shoulders. She was stunned by his familiarity. A black man never touched a white woman, so his action subsumed some knowledge about her background. Her glare withered under his soft look. He dropped his arms.

"I'm truly appreciative of what you've done for me and for my cause."

Ah, she thought, *he said his, not our, cause.* She relaxed slightly.

"To show you my appreciation I have some words of wisdom for you. I know about your interest in the *Niantic*."

"I don't have the foggiest notion of what you're talking about," she said, an annoyed tone creeping into her voice.

"Please. Just listen. You don't have to acknowledge anything. I owe you a great deal and I hope this will be some recompense. I know about the scrip that you and Mr. Brand own. It's a great deal of money. You think it's worthless, but it isn't. Do you know Dr. Peter Smith?" he asked.

"No," Mary Ellen said hesitantly.

"He's been working for the city, taking care of the indigent. They paid him in scrip. They owe him a great deal of money, I think over twenty thousand dollars. He's come up with a very clever answer and expects to get all his money, and more."

"How?" Mary Ellen could not help herself.

"Some parties in the next legislature intend to introduce legislation which will allow the city to replace the scrip with new indebtedness that would be funded. The new debt would have a twenty-year maturity and bear interest at only ten percent per year. Because it's funded, with the legislature behind it, interest would be paid annually, and the principal when it matures. So it'll have some real value."

"That's a lot better than what we have now," Mary Ellen blurted out and immediately berated herself for getting drawn into any discussion.

Gibbs smiled broadly. "But Dr. Smith has a better idea."

Gibbs explained what Dr. Smith had in mind. When he finished he again thanked Mary Ellen and left so abruptly Mary Ellen hardly had a chance to thank him. He did not bother to explain how or where he got this information. Mary Ellen did not ask him. She just sat down and began to laugh. She laughed so hard she felt as if the whole city of San Francisco could hear her.

—w—

CATHERINE HAYES AND PROFESSOR BUSHNALL ARRIVED AT THE HOTEL at 9:00 P.M. The Monumental Engine Company, hosting the Grand Ball, arranged for two lines of uniformed men to form a cordon ushering the guests into the hotel. The great singer, walking on the arm of her manager, ignored the prying eyes of hungry men and jealous women. Though she was used to attention, the ardor of these men made her uncomfortable. Several hundred people had already gathered inside, and a large orchestra played a lively quadrille. Waiters wound their way through the throng offering cakes and ice cream.

"So typically California," Bushnall muttered contemptuously under his breath while maintaining a frozen smile as he greeted the people around them. Catherine knew his sentiments, but had a difficult time understanding just what prompted his strong views. Bushnall was not ambivalent about California and San Francisco. He hated the place. But he would not leave too soon, not while the money flooded into his pockets. They were becoming rich and this did not seem to offend Bushnall.

"Hello, Kate." Colbraith offered his hat and bowed formally.

Catherine turned around. "Hello, Colbraith. I thought you were in San José," she seemed startled and uncertain.

Bushnall removed his hat to acknowledge Colbraith. "Your eminence," he said sarcastically.

Colbraith ignored Bushnall. "Kate, may I have a word with you?"

"Unfortunately," Bushnall interjected, "we are about to have the next dance."

Catherine could not hide her surprise, both at seeing Colbraith and at Bushnall's demeanor. Bushnall offered his arm. Catherine took it hesitantly, but she continued to look at Colbraith, her eyes wistful and disconsolate.

"May I have the pleasure of the next dance?" Colbraith called out.

"Yes, you may," Catherine replied just as Bushnall was about to speak. Whatever he intended to say he stifled with a clearing of his throat as he led her away to the dance floor.

Colbraith retreated toward a group of his men, including Yankee Sullivan and Dutch Charlie. Colbraith looked over his shoulder as Bushnall boldly spun Catherine around, looking smug and self-assured. Catherine looked in Colbraith's direction and Colbraith felt a strange, haunting feeling, a stirring he had not felt in years. But just as quickly Bushnall whirled Catherine around and led her deeper into the middle of the dance floor. Colbraith bumped into someone.

"I'm sorry," he said as he turned and found himself face to face with Mary Ellen.

She rubbed her shoulder.

"Miss Price," Colbraith greeted her with his usual reserve. Selim Woodworth came up to them, "I see you know our lieutenant governor?"

"No, I mean yes," Mary Ellen found herself faltering under Colbraith's intense gaze.

"I mean yes I know Mr. O'Brien, but no, I didn't know he was our lieutenant governor."

"Not too many people know yet," Colbraith said.

"Come, come, Colbraith," Selim sounded caustic. "By the end of next week you might even be a U.S. Senator, if rumor has it right."

Colbraith flinched as if he had been struck. "I'm not sure I understand you, Selim," he said hesitantly.

"Of course you do," Selim replied tartly. "However, you might find it a difficult and bumpy road. Of course this isn't the time or place to discuss politics, is it? Please forgive me, Mary Ellen." Selim nodded to

Colbraith and walked off without waiting for Colbraith's remarks.

"I'm sorry, Mr. O'Brien," Mary Ellen said shocked by Selim's rude conduct.

"There's nothing to be sorry about," Colbraith said unabashedly. "We're on different sides of the aisle, you might say, in politics and in the senate chambers. And we know where we stand with each other."

Thomas joined them just as the quadrille ended. Colbraith's face darkened when he saw Thomas.

"Mr. O'Brien," Thomas offered his hand. Colbraith ignored him and turned to Mary Ellen.

"You know him?" he asked.

"Yes, she does," Thomas answered for her, clearly chagrined by Colbraith's cold shoulder.

"I wasn't speaking to you!" Colbraith snarled.

Mary Ellen moved closer to Thomas, as if she could protect him from an impending assault. Colbraith regarded her with deepening brows.

"Are you still riled up over the *Niantic*?" Thomas asked.

Colbraith did not answer. He appraised Thomas and Mary Ellen for a silent moment then walked away. Mary Ellen felt the chill of Colbraith's anger.

Colbraith, trying to regain some measure of composure, instinctively knew that Thomas and Mary Ellen had a close relationship and it set him to wonder whether she might have some involvement in the *Niantic*.. Unbeknownst to Thomas, his intervention in purchasing the Niantic prevented Colbraith from acquiring the entire block. It not only disrupted his plans but created an embarrassing problem for Colbraith's partners. Colbraith was furious and vowed that when given the opportunity he would pay Thomas back.

Mary Ellen intrigued him but now that he sensed her closeness to Thomas he would regard her as a friend of his enemy. Then he saw Catherine. She was engaged in a heated argument with Bushnall. But when Bushnall noticed Colbraith, he quickly broke off and walked away.

"Are you okay?" Colbraith asked.

"Yes," she dabbed at her eyes with her gloved hand. "Shall we dance?"

"I've never been much of a dancer," Colbraith confessed, "perhaps we could have some dessert on the balcony. It's beautiful outside, uncommonly warm for this time of year."

Catherine looked around uncertainly, then firmed her chin and accepted. Seated outside, overlooking the bay, the moonlight washing over the bay with streaks of sparkling silver, gave Colbraith the first opportunity to speak with Catherine. He sensed her hesitation to discuss the past so he steered around it. Colbraith desperately wanted to make Catherine comfortable, to hold her hand in his, and to explain what his old mentor Mike Walsh and her agent Bushnall had done to destroy the beauty they had shared. But he did not. She relaxed when they discussed her music and singing career. But as indulgent as she may have been about discussing her music, she seemed reticent to talk about him or any other subject. She continually looked about her as if someone, perhaps Bushnall, would join them unexpectedly. Colbraith could not calm the undercurrent of uncertainty that pervaded them like a frigid wind that chills the bones. Several times he pressed himself to take her hand but found it unnerving. So his hands stayed in his lap; two large but useless articles.

"Do you like San Francisco?" he asked.

"Oh, yes. This is a marvelous place," she replied without hesitation and looked past him at the bay. "There are so many ships," she laughed. "I never could have imagined a place like this."

Colbraith could feel his heart beating more rapidly. The past two years of separation had disintegrated as if they had never been apart.

"Perhaps you'll stay here for a while," he coaxed.

"For a while," her eyes had a distant look. Her face softened and she looked at Colbraith.

"In a few weeks we'll be leaving for Europe. Erik, I mean Professor Bushnall," she looked away, "has arranged for a major tour that will include special performances for European royalty. He believes that I have a real opportunity to become famous, to become internationally known."

Colbraith felt numb as if enshrouded in an icy wind. "But you've seen how this city has fallen in love with you. Perhaps you could delay your tour and give San Francisco a chance. You wouldn't regret it."

"Colbraith, you don't understand. All I have, all I crave, and all I want is to sing. You can't know what it feels like when you sing to an audience and strike a special chord, a special bond with them."

"I think I do understand, but . . . "

"No, Colbraith, you don't. Ever since you left New York I have devoted myself to singing. Without it I wouldn't have survived, not after the way you treated me as if I were dead. I owe my life to singing and to the people who are kind enough to appreciate my voice. I sing for the love of the music. People pay to hear me, but I'd sing for nothing. I suppose that's why someone like me needs a manager."

"Like Professor Bushnall," Colbraith said bitterly, unable to disguise his anger or loathing.

"Yes, like Mr. Bushnall," Catherine said firmly. "He stayed with me when I lost you. If it hadn't been for him I wouldn't have made it. And my success as a singer is all due to him."

"Why didn't you respond to my letter?" Colbraith asked.

"What letter?" She asked.

"The letter I left with Bushnall. After my brother died I discovered what Mike Walsh had done. I tried to reach you to apologize for my behavior. But you had moved and I couldn't locate you. I asked Bushnall for your address, but he wouldn't give it to me. I left the letter with him, explaining what had happened, how I learned that Walsh and Bushnall worked together to keep us apart. I hadn't heard a word from you during my entire election campaign. I needed you so badly. But not a word! I blamed you and ignored you at my brother's funeral. Then I learned how Walsh and Bushnall kept you away and destroyed my letters to you. I asked for you to contact me. I never heard from you so I assumed you had no interest in seeing me again. "

Catherine glared at Colbraith. Then she looked away slowly, as if she were looking back in time, and her face appeared hollow and ashen, even in the bright moonlight.

"I never got such a letter, any letter from you" she said dejectedly.

Colbraith began to explain, but Catherine did not appear to be paying much attention to his tale. He tried to hide his frustration as Catherine focused on something far away. Neither of them noticed Bushnall standing a few feet away. Colbraith saw him first and wondered how much he had heard.

Colbraith bristled. "Here, ask him yourself."

Catherine looked up and flashed an angry look when she saw Bushnall. Bushnall, holding a glass of champagne by the delicate stem, smiled benignly and approached them.

"Colbraith tells me he gave you a letter in New York which he asked you to deliver to me. Is that true?"

Bushnall looked appalled. "I don't recall anything like that, my dear. Of course if Mr. O'Brien had given me anything for you I would have made sure you received it. Catherine, you know I'm not given to fabrication or falsehood, characteristics which I personally find offensive."

Colbraith, seething, leaped up. "Are you calling me a liar?" he hissed and moved toward Bushnall.

"I'm not calling anyone a liar, Mr. O'Brien," Bushnall said mildly, disregarding Colbraith's belligerence. Instead Bushnall turned to Catherine. "You know that I've always had your interest at heart—I've placed your interests above everything and everyone else's including myself. If I had received any communication from Mr. O'Brien I would've delivered it to you."

"Well, I never received any letter from Colbraith after his brother died. How do you explain it," she asked.

"I can't speak for anyone else, only myself. I can only reiterate that I never received such a letter." Bushnall turned to Colbraith. "I don't know what you're trying to do, Mr. O'Brien, but fabricating such a monstrous story can only hurt Catherine. I demand . . . "

Bushnall never finished the sentence because Colbraith's ham-like fist smashed into his face with a force that sent Bushnall flying backwards, landing on a wooden table that split into two halves. Colbraith wanted to kick the lying son-of-a-bitch in the face, but several bystanders gripped his arms and Catherine quickly knelt at Bushnall's side.

"Oh my God, you've broken his nose," she wailed. "Someone, please help this man. Several men quickly moved to Bushnall's side and attended to the wounded man.

"You could've killed him," Catherine cried.

"If he doesn't die, it isn't because I didn't try," Colbraith growled. "That bastard is a liar."

"He's never lied to me before," Catherine responded. "Why would he lie now?"

Colbraith could have screamed in frustration. "Because he hated my guts and didn't want you to be with me."

"Of course he didn't want you to be with me. He made that patently clear to me. So he needn't have lied. He's always tried to protect me from the outside world."

Colbraith looked at Catherine disbelievingly. "Catherine," he pleaded. "I've told you the truth, so help me God!"

Catherine hesitated for a moment, then shook her head in disbelief and rushed back to Bushnall's side, tears streaming down her cheeks.

Some members of the Monumental Company arrived and now separated Colbraith from Bushnall, who sat up, blood flowing copiously from a gaping cut on the bridge of his broken nose. Bushnall's head swayed like a drunken sailor, and he tried unsuccessfully to blink the cobwebs away.

"Mr. O'Brien, you've worn out your welcome here," Captain Howard growled. "Please leave immediately."

Yankee Sullivan and Dutch Charlie appeared, taking a position on either side of Colbraith. The crowd quickly burgeoned as more members of Monumental rushed in. The tension became palpable.

"Should we throw these buggers out of here?" one of the Monumental shoulder-strikers asked Howard. Dutch Charlie, towering over everybody, stepped forward menacingly toward the speaker, a malignant smile forming on his lips as if to say, "Just give me a reason to beat the hell outta you."

"No." Howard turned to Colbraith. "This is our ball, Colbraith. You're here as a common courtesy between our fire companies. Please leave and take your men with you."

Colbraith looked at Catherine who still knelt next to Bushnall ministering to his broken nose. Bushnall, very groggy, looked up at Colbraith, and Colbraith could have sworn he saw a look of smug satisfaction in his bleary eyes.

Colbraith, the spark of resentment undiminished, left the hotel seething, followed by Yankee and Dutch Charlie. Catherine cast one sad look in his direction, but he did not see her. He also did not notice Mary Ellen and Thomas standing at the side of the crowd on the veranda, where they had been when Colbraith and Catherine first arrived. Although Mary Ellen and Thomas had not heard the entire conversation, they witnessed the event. Colbraith's intense feelings for Catherine Hayes. Mary Ellen had no doubt about the depth of his hatred for the man he struck. She found Colbraith's behavior both exciting and frightening, with a slight pinch of empathy thrown in for good measure. Instinctively she knew it had to do with love or jealousy.

"I'd hate to be the man who crosses O'Brien's bow," Mary Ellen said.

"Fortunately you can't be." Thomas smiled infectiously. "Though I'm afraid you're no longer on his list of friends now that he has seen us together. Obviously he has little love for me. Maybe we made a mistake buying the *Niantic* from under his nose."

Mary Ellen remained silent, but with a great sense of foreboding. She tried to break the spell. "He never exhibited these tendencies on board the *California*."

"Haven't you read about his involvement in politics?" Thomas asked.

"Yes, but why do men always resort to violence to resolve an issue?" She asked, though she thought she knew the answer.

"Not all men react like O'Brien," Thomas replied. "But something set him off tonight, because he had murder written all over his face."

"It has to do with his feelings for Catherine Hayes," Mary Ellen said. "I've met her before. She's beautiful."

"She has a beautiful voice," Thomas said.

Mary Ellen turned to him, her face questioning. "How do you know?"

"Oh, I don't know personally, it's just what I've heard from people who attended her concerts." He smiled, then turned and stared at Catherine.

"We better get you out of here before you become embroiled with her," she said.

"You mean broiled," he laughed and took Mary Ellen's arm. "I have no intention of getting anywhere close to that woman. O'Brien can be frightening," he repeated again as they left the veranda.

"Not to mention those two huge acolytes of his," Mary Ellen shivered.

—᠁—

ON MONDAY MARY ELLEN PICKED UP THE *DAILY ALTA CALIFORNIA* AND looked for an article about the events at the Monumental ball, about Colbraith and Hayes. Strangely not a word of the incident appeared in the paper. She looked in the editorial section, the "City Intelligence" column and the "Local Matters" column. Nothing. As if the fracas had never taken place. A paper that raked the courts, criminals, and anyone else displaying violent tendencies with a rabid pen, a paper that held itself as the public's guardian voice against crime, ignored an altercation involving the state's lieutenant governor. It dawned on Mary Ellen that Edward Kemble, the *Alta's* editor, was either a close friend of Colbraith, in his pocket, or simply intimidated.

After breakfast with Thomas at the Tehama House, they met with Peachy in his office. Peachy greeted them with an eagerness that foretold exciting news. He came right to the point.

"You're aware of Dr. Peter Smith, are you not?" he asked, as they sat in his office.

"Yes," Mary Ellen answered for both of them. "He's the one who has a small fortune in city scrip, isn't he?"

"Yes, that's the one." Peachy picked up a pipe which he filled with tobacco, relishing the elaborate ritual. He lit it and the sweet aroma wafted toward Mary Ellen. "He's brought suit against the city. He claims the city failed to pay or redeem his scrip and seeks monetary damages."

"Will he win?" Thomas asked.

"I think so," Peachy puffed on his pipe.

"But if the city doesn't have the money to pay the scrip, it won't have the money to pay the damages," Mary Ellen said though she knew the answer.

Peachy smiled as if he had just won a major judgment. "Exactly," he punctured the air with his pipe for emphasis. "That's what our Dr. Smith is expecting."

"Then I don't understand what he expects to gain."

Peachy put his pipe down. "He'll get his judgment and then ask Sheriff Hayes to execute on the judgment—seize and sell the city's assets to cover the judgment."

"What assets?" Thomas seemed confused.

"More city lots and possibly the wharves."

Thomas stared at Mary Ellen in stunned silence. "Will the city stand for it?" he asked.

"Aye, there's the rub, Thomas," Peachy kept them dangling like an old professor. "I suspect the city will claim that the sheriff doesn't have the authority to sell, but he does. In the process the city will issue a statement that warns any buyers of these 'assets' that they will not have legal title. And what do you think the result will be?" Peachy asked and waited. When Thomas just stared at him in confused silence, he continued, "There'll be fewer bidders at the sale, and the prices will suffer. Personally," he confided, "I plan to be there to buy at the auction because I know title will pass. But the prices will make the sale a steal."

"Should we join in the suit?" Thomas asked uncertainly.

"Yes, of course you should. Get cash for your scrip, and at the same time bid on the assets being sold. I hear O'Brien's people are buying the scrip from the banks at a discount of more than fifty percent of their face value. I plan to do the same thing, and I suggest that the two of you do the same."

"How does Mr. O'Brien know about this?" Mary Ellen asked and instantly regretted her question, which sounded so naive.

"Nothing happens in San Francisco that Mr. O'Brien doesn't know about. We're living under his regime, under a city charter that he drafted and that he personally walked though the state legislature when he was president of the Senate. I think he has a hand in manipulating the city into rejecting the scrip. Of course I wouldn't want this repeated outside of this office," Peachy, normally calm and collected, stirred nervously in his chair. "I don't have any evidence of this, you must understand, but it wouldn't be unreasonable to make the assumption . . . " he trailed off.

Mary Ellen and Thomas left Peachy's office and headed for the *Niantic* to monitor the ongoing construction. As they walked on the planked sidewalk, the boards creaking under their weight, they discussed Peachy's advice and Colbraith's ever-growing power. His tentacles now stretched throughout the city government and well into the state capital at San José. They agreed to invest in more city scrip, though Thomas vacillated about joining with Peter Smith in any legal action. Mary Ellen already knew of Smith's strategy from Gibbs and plotted to attend the auction through an intermediary. Unknown to Thomas she had purchased scrip from several sources at substantial discounts. She planned to surprise Thomas. They conferred about the merits of a lawsuit and decided to wait until the Peter Smith claims had wound their way through the courts.

At the *Niantic* they were relieved to find that the roof had been installed as planned and the glass windows mounted. They were cautiously optimistic that the grand opening would take place in less than two weeks, as planned, provided the merchants delivered all the furniture and furnishings in time. Painters were laying a final coat of paint on the building. The sight of the *Niantic* never failed to stir Mary Ellen, and as it took its final form it seemed like a dream come true.

"When we celebrate the grand opening, should we treat it as a launching of a ship or the opening of a hotel?" Thomas asked frivolously, though he tried vainly to keep a straight face.

"Let's do both," Mary Ellen said excitedly. "After all, we are launching both."

They toured the interior, which brought out groans of discontent from Mary Ellen. Despite all the assurances of the contractors, the core of the hotel still remained relatively incomplete. The floors and decks had been installed, and the room partitions completed. But the doors, molding, and carpets, remained in a warehouse on Montgomery street. The inner core looked like a series of narrow, barren hallways linked by empty cells, reminiscent, Mary Ellen thought, of a dormant bee hive—a hive that she would have buzzing with the energy of a frenetic swarm in less than a month. After giving the contractors final instructions, with words of vinegar and honey, they departed.

A gust of chilly wind greeted them as they walked back to the Tehama House.

"I can feel the change in seasons," Thomas remarked absently.

Mary Ellen felt the cutting wind in her bones, and clasped her coat tightly to her chest. The *Niantic* augured success. However, the roving black clouds moving rapidly over the city made her shudder as if a harbinger of darkness had just appeared on the horizon.

—~—

MARY ELLEN LISTENED AS SELIM WOODWORTH RAILED AT THE legislature's inability to elect a successor to John Fremont, whose seat in the U. S. Senate had expired. Although Fremont had declared his interest in reelection, he had little backing and virtually no public support.

"O'Brien had us completely hamstrung in the legislature," Woodworth explained to his guests, Brannan, William Howard, Isaac Bluxome, and William Coleman. They were seated in Selim's study for an after-dinner smoke.

"Over one hundred sixty ballots. Imagine! One hundred sixty ballots and no one could garner a majority vote." Selim inhaled the smoke from his Cuban cigar while Mary Ellen poured some more cognac into his glass.

"What was O'Brien's objective?" Bluxome, a lanky commission merchant, asked.

"Obviously to get elected as a U.S. Senator," Selim replied.

"Well, who did O'Brien vote for? Himself?" Brannan asked as he emptied his tumbler for the second time. Mary Ellen pour him a third.

"No. Geary!"

"Geary?" Bluxome looked stunned.

"That's right. Geary. Geary, like Fremont, never stood a chance, and O'Brien knew it. O'Brien refused to deal on votes. He played every imaginable trick of procedure. None of us were prepared for his antics, at least not in the last session."

Chapter Nineteen

"So it really came down to Heydenfeldt or King?" Brannan acted surprised, but despite the emerging alcoholic fog, Mary Ellen suspected Brannan knew the vote of each ballot cast as if he had attended the voting personally.

"Yes. Surprisingly King put up a good show. I voted for him, but we needed about ten more votes, and we couldn't swing it," Selim said.

"So California is without a U.S. Senator, all because of one man, one damned Irishman," Bluxome commented ruefully as Coleman shifted uncomfortably in his seat. "Colbraith O'Brien wants that spot for himself so badly it makes me sick!"

Coleman, a handsome man with delicate features and pale green eyes that belied his cold and analytical mind, listened, but said nothing.

"Colbraith O'Brien is a very dangerous man," Brannan said grudgingly. "He's wily, tough, and has the most powerful political organization in San Francisco, not to mention the largest fire company."

William Howard started to protest, but Brannan waved him off. "Don't misunderstand me, Bill. I know the Monumental is large, has far better equipment and an unmatchable esprit de corps, but Empire One is far more influential politically. That's a fact. Let's not argue about it. We should never underestimate O'Brien. I did it once. Never again."

"That son of a bitch has changed," Fred Woodworth, sitting next to his brother spoke for Selim. "Now he's colder than one of them northeasters in January. Nothing fazes him. He plays with the senate as if it's his little toy. Last year I could bear his company. He didn't let his ambition run ahead of his judgment. But now he's become intolerable."

"In the meantime San Francisco is bankrupt. Crime is rampant. And what has O'Brien done about it?" Brannan asked rhetorically.

But Coleman responded. "He got the legislature to pass the Water Lot Bill. California ceded the water lots to San Francisco for ninety-nine years, provided the city pays the state twenty-five percent of all the proceeds from the sale of the lots," Coleman recited what he read in the *Daily Alta*.

"That's true," Selim conceded, "and he fought like hell to remove the twenty-five percent payback provision. He argued rightly that the city would never accept the legislation."

"So he's not all bad?" Coleman asked, his eyes twinkling.

"Let's just say that in some ways he's very complicated, in others very simple and obvious," Brannan replied, recalling Colbraith's promise the previous year to take action on the water lots. *At least he kept his word,* Brannan thought, but kept his own counsel.

"I actually thanked him for that one," Selim blurted. "It helped confirm the legality of the water lots sold by the city. Hopefully it will give the courts some direction about the Colton Grants and the sale of land by the alcaldes and the ayuntamiento. But he wasn't doing it for us. He has more water lots than all of us combined. He did it for himself."

"Did he acknowledge your appreciation, Selim?" Brannan chortled and blew a perfect smoke ring.

"Actually, he invited me to dinner. Said he wanted to discuss how Democrats and Whigs could work together for the betterment of the state. What a bull-shitter. I know he has some Whigs working for him, telling him about the party. I won't be one of his spies."

"Did you go to dinner with him?" Coleman asked.

"No. He canceled at the last minute. The next time I saw him he was back to his normal blackhearted self and treated me like dirt."

Mary Ellen listened and pictured Colbraith standing on the deck of the *California,* staring out into the ocean, more often brooding and alone, but never bellicose. He kept to himself during the voyage, at least on the few occasions when she saw him, rarely socializing, except with two men she did not know. She also recalled his demeanor at the Monumental Ball—angry, contentious, and livid. She suspected that his fractiousness had something to do with that woman, Catherine Hayes. She made a mental note to find out more about O'Brien and Hayes, given the power that these men attributed to him. She excused herself and left for the kitchen. But, instead, she stopped briefly outside the study, listening.

Brannan mentioned the Sydney Ducks, the Australian immigrants behind the city's rampant crime. Many were former convicts from the penal colony. They lived together in a community at the base of Telegraph Hill. Brannan spoke in a hushed voice and, although Mary Ellen could not hear every word, she heard Brannan refer to the formation of some new organization. Suddenly Brannan stopped. She craned her neck, but remained a few feet away from the door. Mary Ellen held her breath to hear better. Then, without warning, Selim came out of the study and she found herself facing him, his face twisted in consternation.

"Why, Selim, you gave me the fright of my life," she clutched at her breast as if to still the beating of her heart and leaned against the wall.

"What are you doing here, Mary Ellen?" he asked solemnly.

"Oh, I was just coming back to find out if you men wished anything more from the kitchen, hot coffee or some tarts. You came through the door so quickly. I nearly fainted. Thank God I didn't have a tray in my hands." She exhaled and tried to still the beating of her heart.

"I see," Selim said, pondering her answer. Then, somewhat mollified he said: "No, we won't need anything. Please make sure the door to the study remains closed. We don't wish to be disturbed." Selim returned to the study, looked back at Mary Ellen one final time, then closed the door behind him. Such secrecy was contrary to the usual meetings and dinners Selim hosted.

Back at the Tehama Hotel, Mary Ellen and Thomas huddled on the sofa in his room. Thomas seemed laconic and Mary Ellen's heart still trembled at her encounter with Selim. She could not tell whether Selim had accepted her excuse or suspected her actions. She was angry with herself for being so careless. *The next day or two would tell,* she thought. Thomas seemed preoccupied and did not notice her agitation.

"I'm afraid of what may happen here," Thomas finally confided.

"Why? What could you possibly be afraid of?" Mary Ellen could not hide her surprise.

"Today several people mistook me for an Australian. Americans, you know, are not too discerning when they encounter different English accents; they can't distinguish a Scot from a Sydney Cove. One man actually spat at me and told me to get out of town while my hide remained intact. Such colorful language," he scoffed nervously, but Mary Ellen could see that he was troubled.

She stroked his flaxen hair. "Well, we may have to move into the *Niantic* and set sail."

"You really are such the romantic," he smiled sweetly and kissed her gently on the cheek. "Unfortunately, we, like the *Niantic,* are completely landlocked and at the mercy of angry and hostile citizens. Strangely, I'm in complete agreement with them. Mark my words, this city is in for some rough times, because the Sydney Ducks are a menace and sooner or later they'll have to be expelled, or executed!"

"Some people feel that we're in for another affair like the Hounds."

"Oh, my bonnie Mary Ellen," Thomas exaggerated his brogue, "you are so innocent. The Sydney Ducks are nothing at all like the Hounds. The Hounds were merely a tick on the hide of a stallion. The Sydney Ducks are not a tick on any hide. They're a large, dangerous pack of voracious wolves. They'll be exterminated, but it won't be easy and it won't be overnight."

Book Three

1851–1853

Chapter Twenty

The Secret Abolitionist

SAN FRANCISCO
APRIL AND MAY 1851

Mary Ellen kept her past to herself. Occasionally Gordon would mention Golden Oaks, but Mary Ellen did not invite such discussion, and her silence was an eloquent warning to drop the subject. Thomas never asked Mary Ellen about her childhood or where she had lived before coming to San Francisco. She suspected that Thomas wanted her to tell him, but she deftly managed to change the topic of conversation when the dreaded subject loomed. As time passed, and as their relationship grew closer, keeping such secrets became burdensome. At times Mary Ellen yearned to tell him, to open herself up to him, but inevitably she panicked and fled from the issue.

During the day, filled with its occupations, Mary Ellen lived a fairly comfortable life in San Francisco, comparatively free of worry or distractions. The nights were different. In the dark and foreboding stillness, after the day's hard labors, when the mind rummages through seldom used drawers, deep-rooted fears surfaced and became alive.

Late at night Mary Ellen lay awake, listening to the creaking walls or to the rustle of wind-blown leaves outside. Scared and confused she would pull the blankets close to her chin as if they would somehow protect her from the fears that plagued her. Despite the passage of time or her success in San Francisco, she could never eliminate the gnawing fear that her freedom was a sham or could somehow be voided by crafty lawyers. During the day she could easily suppress this concern and deal with it logically. Not in the depth of night.

The other fear was based on a solid foundation. One day Thomas would discover her origins, and she was certain he would drop her like a stone. These fears were never insignificant, but at night they magnified and Mary Ellen would huddle in a fetal position, and cry herself to sleep.

She had one more secret she did not share with Thomas—her involvement in the Underground Railroad. Thomas did not have an inkling of the part Mary Ellen played in bringing escaped slaves into California from New England—particularly Massachusetts. Openly, and with Thomas's lukewarm approval, Mary Ellen hired a few black women for their businesses. She explained her penchant for hiring these Negroes on economic terms: they would save money and get equal performance. Thomas did not object. This issue did not interest him much. They were doing well, unimaginably well. So he let Mary Ellen run this part of their business.

The former slaves would arrive in San Francisco scared witless. Those who had earlier survived the appalling conditions of the slave ships felt their terror anew upon boarding the ships bound for Panama, though their accommodations were vastly different. The majority of them were born as slaves on southern plantations. They did not fear the ships; they feared discovery and capture. Fugitive slave laws, uncertain legal issues, and ingrained hostility from whites stoked these fears like dry kindling on fire. Mary Ellen empathized with them. San Francisco was a new and unknown world. It disoriented them. Everything in San Francisco differed in almost every respect from anything they had ever seen or experienced. They entered a barren and hostile land. It bore nothing in common with their experience or expectations. There were no plantations, no green fields of cotton or tobacco or any other crop. A brash and aggressive population, composed of young males from every corner of the world, bent on making quick fortunes, inhabited the land. Neither did the strange city resemble any other in America. Not only did it not exist a few years earlier, major portions of the city had literally been raised in the last four months from the ashes of the Christmas fire. Everything was new: every store, every building, the wharves. Nothing was old. The city even had a different, though mercurial climate. It lacked the extremes of snow-racked blizzards or impossibly humid summers. San Francisco looked, felt, and smelled strange and forbidding to these hapless immigrants.

Upon their arrival Mary Ellen would have them taken to a small house she owned. She used the carrot and the stick. At a time when these homeless and frightened people needed to adjust to their new circumstances, she gave them the most comfortable lodgings and probably the best food they had ever had in their lives. She provided or arranged a job with low but decent pay. During their first week in California they remained in the house under strict orders not to venture out at night. They were not to gamble or drink. Each evening, when his work was finished, Gordon gathered the newcomers in one room and explained what Mary Ellen expected of them. He stressed the need to avoid trouble. He warned about getting involved with the authorities, particularly the police. Gordon did not hesitate to offer these scared souls his views on the probability that the California legislature would adopt a Fugitive Slave Law sometime soon. Silence, he advised, was their best friend. He also made it clear that Mary Ellen would instantly sack and send away anyone caught violating the rules. Gordon reminded them how fortunate they were to have someone like Mary Ellen supporting them, and how grateful they should be for her efforts. They were grateful.

They expressed their gratitude quietly and without fanfare. However, they also discovered good reasons to fear her. No one ever told the slaves whether Mary Ellen was white or not. Her speech, her dress, and her success, said white. Her appearance, the color of her skin, her coarse hair, the strange eyes, and her interest in their welfare, gave no inkling either way. If they were curious, or suspected that Mary Ellen was black or mulatto, or had been a slave, they remained mute. Usually on the third night they got a glimpse of another side of Mary Ellen which suggested more about her origin but left them wide-eyed and terrified. Mary Ellen conducted a voodoo ceremony, an initiation, virtually identical to the one her mother and Marie Laveau taught her. This ceremony, coupled with Gordon's injunctions about the legislature's anti-Negro bent, had its desired effect—scaring them into a fairly submissive state.

At the end of the week, Mary Ellen and Gordon would assess the newcomers. Anyone with the slightest possibility of being a troublemaker, or not being sufficiently subservient, would be placed on the first ship leaving California with a one-way ticket for any destination. Fortunately for Mary Ellen, the need for such strong redress had only come up once, and that stubborn man now lived somewhere in Oregon.

Mary Ellen showed great patience in giving the ex-slaves time to learn their new trades, mostly as servants, housekeepers and kitchen help. She hired some and arranged employment for others with such people as Selim and Fred Woodworth. Skeptical at first, the Woodworths quickly learned that their new employees were hard workers who never complained. Thomas was satisfied with the bottom line. Other employers were equally satisfied with their new employees. Through Gordon and other Negroes in her employ, others of color, men and women who came to California on their own, sought her out for employment.

The Negro community found that Mary Ellen was an enigma: on one hand a gracious benefactor with a strong and willing hand; On the other a mystical sorceress with powers of divination that filled them with terror. Whether through fear or gratitude the former slaves provided her with information, the only charge she ever made for her services.

She continued to send money back to John Brown and to other abolitionists to subsidize their work and to help defray the cost of transporting ex-slaves into California. At the beginning they came in a slow trickle. Mary Ellen diverted funds from the laundries and the livery stable to the Underground Railroad. Thomas never questioned any of these expenses because their businesses were doing so well. He left the operations in her hands.

Now Mary Ellen wanted to raise the ante, to increase the number of

Gambling Bar & Saloon

people she could bring to California and train for employment. The Negro community in San Francisco was growing slowly, but certainly not flourishing. Bringing more people required more money, and a new source of funds, a source which Thomas would be unable to discover. Mary Ellen found herself torn by three conflicting urges: the desire to be open and honest with Thomas, the desire for financial power, and a compulsive need to help her people. Something would have to give, but she rationalized the problems. Gordon accused her of living under an illusion: if she did not think about it, perhaps it would not happen.

James Ricker and Monroe Taylor, two recent emigres from the east coast, purchased the Atheneum Saloon at 273 Washington Street. Mary Ellen provided the funds. She had a good notion of how to make the business more profitable and create the income she needed to pursue her abolitionist interests. Women comprised less than one percent of the population of San Francisco. Men with money in their pockets, and successful businesses, sought to bring their families to California. This increased the number of wives, mothers, and daughters arriving each day, but the ratio of women to men did not change materially. The population was still essentially male, under the age of thirty. Consequently, men sought the companionship of women, any women, even those possessed of little or no moral virtue. Mary Ellen knew this from her own experiences, especially at the beginning at the Excellent House. She received more propositions, some lewd or indecent, others profoundly genuine for marriage or simple companionship. It took a great deal of courage to be a woman in San Francisco. It also required common sense. San Francisco would ultimately change. More women, more families, more children would turn San Francisco into a more normal city. Those women who wanted to make their future in San Francisco could not sell themselves or their reputations for quick money. Many women did not care. Mary Ellen did.

The Atheneum consisted of one large room in the front, and several smaller rooms in the rear. Although she wanted to furnish it elegantly to reach the highest clientele in the city, it was too dangerous. At least for the present. Only a few men knew of her ownership interest in the Atheneum, but anyone with sufficient effort and money, could have discovered her complicity.

Instead of making the Atheneum a club for the very rich, she opted for an operation that would woo lesser merchants, clerks, laborers and, of course—the best customers of all—miners. At one end of the room she built a podium for a small band. The piano, a battered honky-tonk upright, occupied center stage with several chairs for other musicians. The long rich brown mahogany bar with stools and a brass foot-rail occupied the entire length of the south wall. A huge mirror behind the bar made the room appear larger than it was. Simple wooden tables and chairs were set up near the walls, leaving a large open space in the middle. One large chandelier suspended over the middle of the dance floor; a second hung directly over the bar. Bottles of liquor, from bright reds and yellows, to deep ambers, sapphire blues, and rich scarlets, adorned the shelf along the mirror. Tumblers and glasses in assorted shapes and sizes accompanied the bottles. The reflection of the liquor and glasses in the mirror, heightened by rays of light thrown from the chandelier, blazed like a wild display of jewels.

One evening, while Thomas met with Peachy and Halleck on some of

Chapter Twenty

Eustace Barron's business matters, Mary Ellen joined the Atheneum's employees to review its operation before the grand opening a week hence. Ricker and Taylor were behind the bar, the pianist and a fiddler on stage. Ten women, dressed in long flowing dresses and boots, stood at the bar. Gordon and William Willmore, another transplanted slave, were also present. Like Gordon, Willmore displayed uncommon intelligence; unlike the diminutive Gordon, he stood more than six and a half feet tall.

Mary Ellen surveyed the premises. "I want to go over the rules again," she said. "After the director, Mr. Lacroix," she nodded to the fiddler who raised his fiddle to his shoulder, "calls out 'Gents, take your partners for a dance,' you'll have about one minute before the music begins. Is that correct, Mr. Lacroix?"

"Yessum. One minute exactly."

"You girls will take your men, or any man who is unattended, to the dance floor. You're to dance with gay abandon." Mary Ellen could see some of the women frown. "Lessette," she called out to one small, rather thin and shy girl with thick golden locks and large blue eyes.

"Yes, ma'am," Lessette stepped forward demurely.

"Why are we dancing briskly and with cheerfulness?"

"To make the men sweaty and thirsty?" she replied hesitantly.

"That's right. What else?"

"It gives the men less chance to grope," another woman, taller and heavier, laughed.

"Exactly. The faster you move, the less chance any man has of becoming too familiar. Most of these men are clumsy and awkward. That's why you're wearing boots, to protect your feet from their accidental kicking and stepping. Remember, we, and this means you, make money from the drinks. The more the men drink, the more money we all make. Get the men sweaty. This will make them thirsty. Let them have fun. We want our customers to be happy. But we do not want the men to attach themselves to anyone, and we'll not allow the men to 'grope' as Sarah said."

The women laughed nervously.

"After five minutes, Mr. Lacroix will stop the music and call out: 'Gents, take your partners to the bar, please!'"

Lacroix put his fiddle back down and looked at the piano player who remained impassive, probably wondering why he was just sitting at the piano and doing nothing.

"Mr. Ricker and Mr. Taylor will tend the drinks. You girls will take your dance partner to the bar and ask him to buy you a drink. The bar attendants will serve you sweet, colored water. You're not to drink real liquor! Is that understood?"

The women nodded their understanding.

"If your partner refuses to buy a drink let Mr. Ricker or Mr. Taylor know. You know how. Tell either bartender you've had enough for the evening. They'll escort the man out of the saloon. And let me remind you of one more thing. We're a hurdy-gurdy house, not a brothel. You ladies are not fallen angels, at least not in here. What you do on your own time is your business." Mary Ellen looked at the women her face severe and unbending. "That is, until your business interferes with ours. Then you're out."

Mr. Ricker cleared his throat. "The men will pay you a dollar a dance. You keep half, and give us half." He looked sternly at the women. "And no skimming! We'll pay fifteen percent of all drinks your partner orders."

"This means you can earn twenty-five to fifty dollars per night, and have fun, too," Mr. Taylor announced. "That ain't too shabby."

"I know Mr. Lacroix has been teaching you all the dances," Mary Ellen said. "Is there anyone who doesn't know the *Varsovienne* or waltz or quadrille?"

The girls shook their heads. Mary Ellen regarded them. Most of the girls were young, though two of the women were over thirty, too old under normal circumstances, but San Francisco was far from normal. Two girls had just arrived from Baltimore, care of John Brown, both light-skinned mulattos who still resided in Mary Ellen's house. The others had either been working in other saloons in San Francisco, or had just arrived. Only one held Mary Ellen's special interest, Lessette Flohr, and she was white as alabaster.

Lessette arrived alone in San Francisco a few weeks earlier on board a packet bound from Mazatlan. Her husband, a young architect, con-

Chapter Twenty

Tehama House

tracted cholera after leaving Panama City and died on board ship. Because of the cholera, the port authorities refused to allow the ship to land in Mazatlan. The ship remained at anchor, conditions worsening by the minute. Lessette, a strong swimmer, and a few others, quietly abandoned the ship one night and arrived in the village wet, hungry and without any money. Lessette hocked her wedding ring and used the proceeds to buy clothes and food. She did not have enough money left to buy a ticket on a steamer bound for California. A well-dressed American noticed Lessette and introduced himself. He seemed genuinely concerned with her predicament. With no one else to turn to she confided about the loss of her husband and her lack of funds. He expressed his sympathy and offered to pay for the balance of the ticket. She confessed that she did not have the money to pay him back or any prospects in California. He consoled her and offered to give her a job as a pretty waiter girl in his saloon in San Francisco. To allay any uncertainty about what she would have to do, the man described waiting on tables, serving drinks. Nothing more.

Lessette landed in San Francisco, still in shock over her husband's death. Without any family or friends to turn to, she found herself in a tawdry saloon where the pretty waiter girls wore dresses with the top unbuttoned, revealing all for the male customers to see and feel. She refused to dress up and told the owner she would not work like that. She cried and accused him of misleading her. He hotly denied her charges, grabbed her roughly by the arm and warned her that he would sue her for breaching a contract of employment. Then he punched her in the face and threw her out the back, leaving one puffy eye completely black and closed. The damaged face had its effect. Lessette could not land a job, at least not a decent one.

Finally, after two days without food or money, Lessette read an ad for a job and applied for an opening in one of Mary Ellen's laundries. Gordon interviewed Lessette and realized she was different from most of the women in San Francisco. So he brought the matter to Mary Ellen's attention, and Mary Ellen found herself taking Lessette under her wing. She settled with the insolent owner of the other saloon, sending an attorney with Willmore to make her point clear. Mary Ellen tried to understand her inclination to help Lessette. In many ways the reserved girl reminded Mary Ellen of her own arrival in San Francisco—young, innocent, out of place, and convalescing from an unprovoked beating. Lessette, like Mary Ellen, needed time to heal from the physical and psychological scars inflicted by others. Each day Mary Ellen found herself drawn closer and becoming more protective of Lessette.

"Let's have a toast! On the house! Come on girls," Mary Ellen coaxed them. "Here is to our grand opening tomorrow night." The girls sidled up to the bar giggling like little school girls, as Ricker and Taylor poured the drinks.

Mary Ellen remembered one more thing. She went behind the bar and whispered to Ricker.

He listened, nodded seriously and looked up. "Ladies, before the toast let me remind you of one more thing," he said in his deep resonant voice. "Anyone caught stealing, rolling, pickpocketing, or doing anything else illegal will go directly to the police. You'll bear the full force of the law." He paused for a second. "That is, after Mr. Willmore here breaks the offending arm."

The women involuntarily glanced at the large black man whose look made it clear that he would do whatever Ricker, Taylor, or Mary Ellen commanded him to do. After the toast, Mary Ellen and her partners made one more pass through their establishment in preparation for the gala opening. Mr. Lacroix standing next to the piano whispered to the pianist who finally smiled and turned to the keyboard. Mr. Lacroix raised the fiddle to his shoulder, stamped his foot three times, and brought his bow across the strings. The two musicians started a fast dance. The women rushed to the open floor, prancing and whirling each other around to the fast beat of the music. Ricker and Taylor soon joined them.

Months earlier some of San Francisco's leading icons attended the grand opening of the *Niantic* Hotel. O'Brien and all the members of his volunteer fire company, Empire One, were notable exceptions. That gala occasion was a great success. Less than twenty-four hours after its opening, the *Niantic* Hotel did not have a single vacancy left. Now Mary Ellen wanted the Atheneum's grand opening to be as successful. She spent part of every day at the *Niantic,* her pride and joy. The newest and most unconventional hotel in San Francisco buzzed with the efficiency of a well-oiled machine. Unlike the *Niantic,* the Atheneum held no special meaning for Mary Ellen. It was a source of funds and, to a lesser extent, due to its clientele, a possible but limited source of information; not, however, the kind that Mary Ellen normally sought—confidential communications about the czars of business and politics.

Lessette was Mary Ellen's only personal interest in the hurdy-gurdy house. Mary Ellen decided to find some way of making Lessette's life more tolerable.

At the end of April, Mary Ellen received a long letter from John Brown. He thanked her for the money and her help with the underground. A small, yellowed clipping from *The New York Herald* accompanied the letter. When she finished reading it she immediately left for her laundry to find Gordon. She took him upstairs to an empty room and gave him the clipping. He read it quietly but intently.

> Boston—Deputy Marshal Riley and assistants arrested at Cornhill Coffee-House to-day one Frederic Wilkins, a negro waiter, on a warrant issued by the United States Commissioner on a complaint that said Wilkins was a fugitive slave. He was taken without opposition and carried immediately to the United States Courtroom.
>
> The news of the arrest spread rapidly, and soon the courtroom was filled by a large crowd of rather excited spectators. The examination, however, went off quietly.
>
> From the documents offered by the claimant it appeared that the accused was the property of John Debree, Purser in the United States Navy, of Virginia, and that he escaped in May, 1850. The deposition was to the effect that the claimant had seen the prisoner in Boston and conversed with him, when the prisoner acknowledged that he had escaped from Norfolk.
>
> While the mob was in the court room, the sword of the marshal, hanging in its sheath over his desk, was drawn by one of them and flourished over the head of the officers. It was afterwards found in the street. The mob showed no weapons, though a number of negroes boasted of having revolvers in their possessions. One negro, in his flight, dropped his knife.
>
> There were several white persons in the mob, but they did not appear to act in the rescue. The rescue, of course, caused great excitement throughout the city, as one of the most daring outrages upon law and order ever enacted. It is thought impossible to re-arrest the fugitive, as his friends have no doubt buried him off ere this to the Canadian border. U.S. Marshal Devens is absent in Washington.

When he finished he looked up at her. "Was Mr. Brown involved?"

"He doesn't say in his letter," Mary Ellen took the clipping. "But he says this is only a small portent of larger things to come."

"Should we tell anyone about this?" he asked, uncertain why Mary Ellen decided to share it with him.

"No," she responded. "Well, tell Mifflin Gibbs. It'll make his day if he hasn't heard about it." She looked at Gordon. "This is really to allay some of your fears. Even if California enacts a Fugitive Slave Law, I don't think it'll be enforced."

Gordon regarded Mary Ellen. "I don't know. There aren't too many southerners in Boston. There are lots of them in California. Who knows? Maybe they'll gain power here. Then things could be different."

As Mary Ellen headed for the *Niantic* to join Thomas she thought about Gordon's comments, then dismissed them. She did not think the southerners in California, especially in San Francisco, the largest city, would ever gain control. It was more a case of Gordon always finding reason to fear the future. It was May 3, 1851. Her future seemed robust and she smiled to herself as she walked along the crowded planked streets, wading through the hustle and bustle of booming San Francisco.

Chapter Twenty-One

From The Ashes

SAN FRANCISCO
MAY 3, 1851

IT ALWAYS FELT STRANGE TO BE STANDING ON THE DECK OF A SHIP, PEERING over the gunwales at planked sidewalks where blue ocean had once been. A ship in the middle of the city, perched between ramshackle clapboard stores, its bow facing the street. Two portholes on either side of a missing bowsprit and figurehead gave the appearance of a weathered prizefighter with a broken nose and two puffy eyes peering out at the crowded sidewalks.

Thomas stood next to Mary Ellen on the deck as she gazed at the green hills, sparkling and fresh after the rain, dotted with recently constructed buildings of all shapes and sizes and huge open scars, where excavators had been at work. She absentmindedly ran her long fingers slowly back and forth along the polished mahogany handrail.

Thomas looked out at the bay and shook his head in amazement. "It's a remarkable sight," he said in a deep Scottish brogue, his blue eyes dancing. "It thrills me every time I see it."

More than five hundred ships lay at anchor or were moored alongside wharves extending into the bay from each of the city's main streets, from California Street on the south to Broadway on the north. In a mad rush to create more usable land in a city tucked among steep hills, San Franciscans, flush with gold, set out to reclaim Yerba Buena Cove, where the city was founded. Every day sand- and dirt-laden carts rushed from the hills toward the bay, sloshing through muddy streets in the winter or trailing choking clouds of dust in the summer, to empty their loads into the water.

Slowly, wharves built on piles and sitting high above the waterline became ordinary streets. Inexorably, as if pushed back by some incomprehensible force, the water's edge receded farther into the bay, replaced by land and then by streets such as Sansome and Battery. Even Montgomery Street, which only three years earlier lay only a few yards from the lapping water, sometimes submerged by high tides, now served as one of the city's central arteries, far removed from the shore.

In this rush to fill the bay, hundreds of laborers worked feverishly. They were paid handsomely to unload the dirt into the bay, not to remove large obstacles in their path—such as ships that had been abandoned by passengers, crew, and officers, bolting for the gold fields. These stranded vessels lay rotting, their masts swaying with the rolling seas as if dancing to a silent dirge. A thousand masts, bearing torn rigging, resembling a winter forest of tall bare trees, branches, and trailing vines growing in the middle of a bay, created a bizarre image.

As newcomers arrived, at the rate of a thousand or more each week, the demand for land escalated. With every able-bodied man scampering to the gold fields, the owners of the marooned ships were unable to hire crews to man the ships. The *Apollo,* the *General Harrison* and the *Niantic,* only three among the ships closest to shore, were ignored and soon found themselves landlocked, standing proudly on the streets as if hauled into dry dock only to be forgotten or forsaken by the sea. The *General Harrison,* on the corner of Clay and Battery streets, became a storehouse with a large hand-painted sign offering storage and goods. The *Apollo,* on Sansome Street, was turned into a store and a saloon. Other ships might have suffered the same fate, but were saved by economic circumstances.

Conditions changed in 1850. many disillusioned miners returned to San Francisco and sought employment, happy to have a roof over their heads, three square meals a day and regular wages. Shipmasters refitted their ships and found sailors willing to crew for them. On May 3, 1851, the ships that swayed and rolled with the waves and the gusty drafts were trim and fit for sailing. The forest of masts bristled with new rigging and colorful pennants.

The strong wind rippled through the flag on the *Niantic,* causing it to snap loudly, like a gunshot. Mary Ellen looked up. "I still get chills every time I see the *Niantic.* I can't believe it's ours."

Thomas smiled. "I don't know why you feel it's so special."

"I don't know how to explain it," she said. The *Niantic* provided Thomas and Mary Ellen with a steady flow of cash. Their portfolio of investments was growing. But of all their assets the *Niantic* was clearly Mary Ellen's favorite. It represented something so different, so unique, so out of character that she embraced the hotel with devotion, attending to its every need. She regarded the ship as a sister, one with the same forces, sharing the same painful experiences, marooned in a strange land only to be reawakened with a new life.

"I'm glad it stopped raining," Mary Ellen said as she looked up and watched the dark clouds, fringed with silver from the full moon, race across the mauve sky.

Thomas sniffed the air. "I think the storm has passed us, though it may drizzle some more tonight."

Mary Ellen regarded Thomas with an affectionate grin. "Let me guess," she said as the wind tugged at her cotton dress. "It will be a wee bit windy for the next twenty-four hours," she exaggerated his Scottish brogue.

"Am I that predictable, my bonny?" he laughed.

"Yes, my darling, you are," she whispered close to his ear.

Thomas instinctively reached for her arm and drew her closer, but caught himself quickly.

Feeling somewhat awkward, Mary Ellen said, "Let's take a walk."

"Why don't we go to the Plaza," Thomas offered.

"Is anything happening over there?" she asked.

"I don't think so, but you never know. Maybe another indignation meeting. These Sydney Ducks are really riling the population. People frequently mistake my accent. They think I'm from Australia and tell me to push off." He swore under his breath and looked around to see if anyone heard him.

Only a month earlier, at a large rally held in the Plaza, speaker after speaker denounced the Ducks and called for their expulsion. Others called for their execution, no matter how trifling the offense. Like so many others in the city, Mary Ellen detested the Ducks. But she was worried that Thomas would somehow be mistaken for one of them when the people of San Francisco finally took action; something she was certain would happen sooner than later.

They took the exterior staircase of the *Niantic* to the ground and headed toward the Plaza, as Portsmouth Square was known. Mary Ellen looked over her shoulder at the *Niantic* and suddenly felt cold as the blustery wind gusted at her feet. A piece of wood, dislodged from the wall of the adjacent building by the wind, crashed into the side of the *Niantic's* dark hull with a jarring sound. It startled Mary Ellen and she felt a strong sense of foreboding. She moved closer to Thomas as they headed to the Square, passing Jansen & Co., Dry Goods Store on Montgomery.

—∾—

C.J. Jansen, the proprietor of Jansen & Co, sat in the back of his store staring intently at the two pans on the balance scale. Working by the light of a single oil lamp, he toiled slowly and carefully; the slightest puff of wind or jarring of the scale could send gold dust worth hundreds of dollars vanishing into the air. The pans were still out of kilter, the lower, heavier one bearing the mound of gold dust that shimmered in the muted light. The other pan held several small cylindrical brass weights of different sizes. He picked up another quarter ounce brass weight by its little nib, placed it carefully on the measuring pan and watched it drift slowly downwards until the two sides of the scale were in balance: nineteen and one-half ounces of pure gold. He paused for a moment, a fleeting smile crossing his gaunt face, and went on with his business. He removed a well-worn buckskin pouch from his desk and carefully poured the gold dust into it, drawing the leather thong tightly around its neck. Then he recorded the weight into his leather-bound accounting journal. Although most of his customers now paid him in specie, some miners, especially the old-timers—those who had been in California more than one year—still paid in gold dust; an inconvenience, but a profitable one.

When he finished, he stood, stretched his wiry frame, and peered across the length of his store to the front door. It was ajar. A light drizzle fell outside and the dank air filled the shop. The oil lamp flickered and he looked up to see if it needed some adjustment. Like most of the merchants of San Francisco, Jack Jansen kept his store open until nine or ten o'clock at night, though in recent times fewer customers shopped so late into the evening, drawn instead to the games and other diversions offered by the city's notorious gambling halls and crowded saloons. He checked the lamp and adjusted the small knob; the oil reservoir was nearly full. Jansen returned to his desk, took a sip from his cup of tea, and continued with his accounting chores.

The front door opened and a man entered the store. Jansen could see the outline of the man against the bright blaze of the chandeliers from the saloon across the street. Dressed in a long gray coat and a black, broad-brimmed hat, the customer looked around and began to inspect the merchandise. He looked at the hats briefly, then at the shirts, picking up some red flannel ones so popular with the miners and held them up to his chest, to estimate their size and fit. He moved slowly from one bin to the next, examining the overalls and then some cooking gear. A thick mustache and grimy beard covered his face.

"Can I help you?" Jansen inquired.

"Yep. Need a dozen blankets," the man replied tersely.

Jansen put down his pen, secured the Colt navy revolver in his belt, and attended to his customer. The customer noticed the revolver, but did not react. In San Francisco everyone carried a weapon; gamblers preferred the derringer while miners armed themselves with revolvers and Bowie knives.

The weapons were displayed openly. It was de rigueur—fashionable, necessary, and expected. Only a few immigrants fresh off the boat would arrive in San Francisco unarmed. It did not take them long to discover their shortcomings and the reason why weapons had to be brandished in full view of the public.

Jansen approached the customer whose breath and clothes reeked of stale alcohol.

"This way." Jansen led him to the display of colored blankets. "You a miner?"

"Yep," the man replied, but his manner did not invite any further conversation.

The man seemed to stagger slightly, but steadied himself. Jansen smiled knowingly.

The merchants of San Francisco treated all their customers well, many of whom were miners. Miners were not neat or well groomed, and not too particular about their appearance. Various stages of intoxication were common. Miners came to San Francisco for only three reasons: to get provisions not available in towns near the mine fields; to gamble and drink to their good fortune; because they were completely spent, exhausted, and hopelessly broke. Those who found gold spent their time and their gold in the city until one or the other ran out. Merchants rarely turned away any customer, no matter how dirty, sweaty, ragged, and sometimes drunk, as all the miners were, because underneath the coarse woolen shirts and their filthy pants they would carry hundreds or thousands of dollars in gold dust or nuggets. Miners and their gold parted company easily and quickly to the delight of San Francisco's merchants, casinos, and brothels.

Jansen stopped before a large table with stacks of colorful blankets, placed his hand on one of the piles and asked, "How about these?"

The man shook his head. "No, white."

Jansen kept the white blankets in a separate bin, mostly to keep them from getting dirty or soiled by the unwashed hands of his customers.

"Right here." He brought out one white blanket and held it at arm's length, far enough away from the man to protect his goods from damage.

Chapter Twenty-One

Another man entered the store, saw Jansen displaying the blanket and approached.

"These here is fine. Gimme twelve," the first man said.

"That'll be forty-eight dollars," Jansen said.

The customer simply shrugged his shoulders, grumbled his approval and reached into his coat pocket.

Jansen regarded the second man for an instant. Tall, wearing a cloak and a hat with a pointed crown, the second man stopped to examine some merchandise only a few feet away.

"Where's the shirts?" he asked with a pronounced Australian accent.

Jansen hesitated. The first customer turned to Jansen and whispered: "I don't trust no Sydney Duck!"

"Over there." Jansen pointed to the shelves and placed his hand on the butt of his revolver. The tall man smirked and sauntered slowly to the shirts. The first customer glared at the tall man.

Jansen stooped down to retrieve the rest of the white blankets while keeping his eye on the tall man.

"Now!" the tall man yelled gruffly.

Jansen, startled, started to stand up, but the first man acted quickly. He pulled a short club with a molten lead head from his coat and with calculated steps, his drunken gait gone, he approached Jansen and brought the club crashing down on Jansen's head. Jansen fell roughly to the ground as the man continued to whip him on the head, grunting with each strike; the other man kicked Jansen in the rib cage with his mud-caked boots. Jansen groaned and tried to shield his head with his arms to ward off the persistent blows.

"Move over!" The tall man shoved the other roughly aside and delivered a powerful kick directly to the back of Jansen's head. Jansen's feeble resistance ended. He lay still, a small scarlet pool forming and slowly spreading.

"Help me drag him to the back," the tall man commanded. He pulled on Jansen's limp arms while the other grabbed the legs and hauled the slack body toward the rear of the store, leaving long crimson streaks on the planked floor, marred only by the shorter man's foot prints. They dumped the body in a dimly lit corner and covered it with some of Jansen's new blankets. The tall man went directly to Jansen's desk while his accomplice retrieved Jansen's pistol which had fallen to the floor during the assault. He inspected the weapon with a pleased expression.

The tall man looked at the desk and quickly spied the buckskin pouch. He lifted it up, opened the collar, noted the contents and smiled wickedly.

"Not bad! Eh?" he said. The other man placed Jansen's gun into his coat and reached for the pouch, but the tall man declined.

"Nah," he said and placed the bag into his own pocket. "Let's wait, mate. We'll divvy it up later." The shorter man did not argue. They turned to the desk, rifling through the drawers, throwing the contents carelessly to the floor, stopping now and then, like two nervous squirrels, to listen or look at the front door. Finding nothing of value they stopped.

"It's got to be around here. Every store has one." The tall man looked around. "Check the front door."

The shorter man stumbled over some of the spilled merchandise and went to the front, peering furtively into the darkness. "Nothin'. Just some people standing in front of the hotel."

"Look in the back." The tall man waved to the rear of the store.

The shorter man headed to the rear of the store, shoving tables and bins aside, as if insulted by their presence. The tall man joined him and looked carefully at the walls and the floorboards. Some of the wallboards in the corner were slightly off color. It was hardly noticeable in the pale glow of the single lamp. He stopped, knelt next to one of the overturned bins in the corner and touched its surface softly, almost sensuously, with his long fingers.

"Not much imagination," he said to no one in particular as he pulled a Bowie knife from his belt and pried at one of the oak panels next to the floor. In a few minutes he had found Jansen's secret locker and the small iron safe where Jansen kept his receipts and gold.

"Look for the key!" he ordered the shorter man who, with some difficulty, went down on all fours and rummaged through the spilled contents of the desk, looking through piles of papers, nails, cards and other articles strewn all over the floor.

Chapter Twenty-One

"Can't find it," he said.

"Keep looking," the tall man charged and joined in the search.

"It ain't here I tell ya," the shorter one replied with some annoyance.

The tall man slapped him hard on the back of his head with his open hand, knocking his hat off. "I said keep looking!"

The shorter man stifled his rage, quickly recovered his hat and continued to search silently.

The tall man went to Jansen's body, checked the pockets, roughly tearing Jansen's clothes and getting his hands stained from the blood-soaked garments.

"Damn!" The tall man pursed his lips and clenched his jaws.

"We could bust it open," the shorter man offered uncertainly.

"No! No time. We'll take it with us," the tall man disregarded his associate's suggestion.

They wrapped the safe in some blankets. The tall man managed to lift the heavy bundle and throw it over his shoulder like a sack of coal. At the front door they glanced outside. A few people milled around the Verandah, the gambling house across the street. From inside music blared, winners yelled, men argued over politics, losers groaned and swore. Those standing in front, talking to each other, occasionally turned their heads to look inside the gambling house; no one paid any attention to Jansen's side of the street. When the planked sidewalk was clear from the front of the store to the corner of Washington and Montgomery Streets, the tall Australian left the store and walked slowly, carrying the heavy safe over his shoulder. He kept his head low and walked with measured steps until he disappeared around Washington Street. The shorter man muttered "son of a bitch" in some anger and punctuated his feelings by spitting into the store. He delayed for a moment and watched to see if anyone displayed any curiosity or paid any attention to his Australian companion. No one did, so he walked back into the store and surveyed the damage. He noticed his own footprints on the bloody floor and frowned. The flickering light from the oil lamp caught his attention. He went over to it and pushed it off its base, sending the lantern crashing to the floor, glass breaking into flying splinters, oil seeping across the floor. The instantaneous flash as the burning

May 1851 Fire

wick made contact with the oil momentarily blinded him. He stumbled back towards the front door, his arm shielding his face from the blazing fire, looked behind him for a last glimpse of the spreading inferno, and walked out into the night.

—⁓—

HEAR THE LOUD ALARM BELLS—BRAZEN BELLS, WHAT A TALE OF TERROR, NOW their turbulency tells! In the startled ear of night how they scream out their affright! Out of time . . . mercy of the fire . . . the deaf and frantic fire, leaping higher, higher, higher! The bells! The bells! The ringing of the bells! Mary Ellen woke up with a start. Drenched in perspiration, her heart thumping rapidly, she was terrified by the dream; the nightmare. She had just finished reading Poe's poem the evening before after returning from her walk with Thomas, but the clanging of the bells continued unabated, sending a shudder down her spine and raising the hair on the nape of her sweaty neck.

Unsure if she were asleep or awake, and completely disoriented, she

Chapter Twenty-One

took a deep breath and nearly gagged on the acrid smoke. Something was burning. She coughed to clear her throat, wrinkled her nose and with a sudden terrified awareness, leaped out of her bed and ran to the shuttered window. Even before she flung the window open she could see the flames through the cracks in the shutter, sending their dancing images into her dark room.

"Oh, god! Not another fire," she screamed as she frantically tried to raise her window, tearing her fingernails in the futile effort. *The latch. The latch,* she remembered, and finally opened the window. Bedlam reigned in the street below. Shouting, wailing, shrieking, every imaginable sound, from terrorized animals to the din of the fire itself, merged into one horrifying howl. People were running in every direction, many yelling "Fire! Fire!" as if raising the alarm for the first time, but their shouts were lost in the fury of the panic. Crazed horses, released from burning liveries, ears quivering, eyes bright with fright, bolted down California Street trampling those unable to move out of their way quickly enough.

A fire engine, pulled by two horses, headed north through people milling in the crowded street. It was followed by a squad of firemen on foot, some wearing their hats and shirts, emblazoned with the insignia of their fire company, others only half dressed, a few in their undergarments, but all wearing their boots. The alarm bells rang from every quarter of the city and now Mary Ellen could see the flames leaping higher only a few blocks away. A strong gust of wind blew smoke and small red cinders into her room.

Mary Ellen quickly closed the window and stamped out the hot flames with a blanket.

"Mary Ellen, Mary Ellen!" someone pounded on her door. "Are you all right? Mary Ellen!"

"Thomas!" she yelled back and rushed for the locked door. Mary Ellen tried to turn the key, but her hands were trembling and she found it difficult to grip the key clasp.

"Open the door!" Thomas yelled and she could feel the door handle move up and down as Thomas tried to open the door from the outside.

"I'm coming!" She willed herself to calm down. Finally she managed to turn the key and unlock the door.

"Thank heaven you're okay!" Thomas said as he rushed in and hugged her. "I was worried. I thought you might be at the *Niantic*."

At the mention of that name Mary Ellen pushed away from Thomas. "We've got to go there, Thomas. We mustn't lose her." She found her shoes and put them on while Thomas ran to the window and looked out.

"It looks like its getting bigger," he said. "It must be around Montgomery and Jackson."

Mary Ellen wrapped a shawl around her flannel night clothes. "Let's go!" she said and both of them rushed down the stairs and onto the crowded plank sidewalks. They pushed through the throng and headed towards the *Niantic.* Manners were cast aside as people collided with one another, pushing and shoving in a mad effort to move somewhere. An elbow caught Mary Ellen on the mouth, splitting her lip, but she barely noticed it as shoulders crashed into her and people stepped on her feet.

"Don't fall down!" Thomas yelled. "You'll get trampled!"

They ran past Starr & Minturn, the shipping line and Mary Ellen's best customer. It was one of the newer buildings, made of solid brick and iron. She remembered their agent, Pettigrew, confidently declaring it to be completely "fire proof." Next door the terrified owners of Jones Hotel, an old wooden building, were already lining up buckets of water in dreaded anticipation of the rapidly moving fire.

Mary Ellen and Thomas fought their way onto Sansome. Suddenly Mary Ellen's feet gave way and she slipped to her knees on the slick mud directly in the path of a horse drawn wagon laden with barrels and merchandise. The driver whipped his horse, either not seeing the woman or not caring. Thomas waved his hands frantically, causing the horse to turn just enough for Mary Ellen to roll out of the way as the large wheels went by. Thomas pulled her up. She was covered with mud and soot. Both were shaken, but they continued pushing their way up the street. Suddenly they stopped in their tracks. The immense fire not only blocked the street ahead, but was heading their way.

"I don't think we can get there," Thomas said, squinting into the bright furnace before him.

"We've got to, Thomas." Mary Ellen's eyes felt as if they had been pricked by sharp needles. Her throat was raw and dry as she gulped for air. Determined to get to the *Niantic* she forged ahead, followed hesitantly by Thomas. The crowds thinned as they neared the fire. They ran against the people fleeing the inferno, avoiding the approaching fire engines, keeping their stinging eyes on the massive fire. They managed to get a short block from the *Niantic* before they were impeded by a squad of firemen. Wearing the Empire One Fire Company insignias, the men pumped furiously and sent a stream of water into the flames licking upwards from the windows of a large building.

"You can't go any farther!" One of the firemen yelled and blocked their way, trying to be heard over the din of the fire. Before Mary Ellen or Thomas could answer, a thundering explosion shook the ground, its concussion slamming into their bodies. Mary Ellen keeled over, her ears ringing. The explosion sucked away her breath. Her throat was on fire, as if the blaze had sucked all the fluids from her body. Thomas tried to speak but ended up coughing.

The fireman brought his face close so they could hear him. He held onto his hat. "Look," he yelled "you've got to get back." He rubbed his red eyes and coughed. Although he was yelling into their ears, his voice was carried away by the overpowering tumult. "We've brought in gunpowder!" he tried to explain, his voice hoarse. "We're blowing up buildings. Making a fire break. It's extremely dangerous up ahead." Another explosion rocked them and they all cowered.

"Mr. Brand owns the *Niantic*," Mary Ellen recovered. "We've got to get there."

"And do what?" the fireman asked nonplused.

"Save it!" she yelled back as the noise around them reached a crescendo.

"You can't, I tell you. It's too late. The fire's probably there. Look." He pointed toward Clay Street. The wind screamed. Clouds of red smoke billowed toward them. They could barely see a hundred yards. The heat was intense. Another explosion. This one closer. Burning splinters showered them.

"I'm going to the hotel," Mary Ellen declared defiantly and started past the fireman.

A strong hand grabbed her roughly by the arm and a voice growled, "You're going to do exactly what you're told to do!"

Mary Ellen turned around and came face to face with Colbraith, his massive hulk standing between her and Thomas. His grip tightening painfully around her arm. His face and his clothes were covered with grime. He held an ax in one hand and tightly gripped Mary Ellen's arm with the other.

"Let go of her!" Thomas demanded, but Colbraith ignored him and continued to glare at Mary Ellen with dark, brooding eyes.

"Please, Mr. O'Brien. Let me go," she said and their eyes locked. People rarely stared at her so intently, partly because the strange color of her eyes made people hesitant to stare. But Colbraith did not flinch. Colbraith now controlled nearly everything in San Francisco, from the city's elections to its elected officials. Everyone was in his pocket. He even controlled the California State Senate and the volunteer firemen who were fighting the conflagration. They risked their lives at his command without hesitation. He was accustomed to control.

"Please, Mr. O'Brien. You're hurting my arm." Mary Ellen pulled at her arm.

He looked at her and suddenly let go. "For your own safety, Miss Price, listen to the fireman."

"But we need to get to the *Niantic,*" she pleaded.

O'Brien frowned impatiently and regarded her cooly. "I'm glad you're so interested in *Mr. Brand's* hotel." She feared Colbraith knew of her involvement, and this remark affirmed it, which scared her. *How much more did he know,* she wondered.

"Now *don't* go past this intersection! Do what these firemen tell you! I don't want to repeat this warning again." He turned abruptly and called out to a group of firemen.

"I want you men over at Naglee's building now!" he commanded.

The men obeyed and disappeared into the billowing smoke. Thomas went to Colbraith. "Mr. O'Brien," he implored "could you please get some of your firemen over to the *Niantic?*"

"I'm sorry, Mr. Brand," Colbraith replied reprovingly, "but I'm afraid we have larger matters at hand." Colbraith watched in fascination as orange and red flames lashed out at the sky from the burning rooftops and disappeared into the massive cloud of gray smoke hanging low over the city. Another shuddering explosion made Thomas wince, but Colbraith ignored it. Scowling he turned back to Thomas. "I told you when you bought the *Niantic* not to cross me." He looked a the fire. "I don't have enough men. We can't protect your building. It's not a priority." Colbraith stopped. Even Colbraith, Mary Ellen could see, had difficulty breathing. She watched his bear-like chest expand and contract deeply as he sought to catch his breath. "We have to prevent the fire from consuming this whole goddamned city," he finally said through gritted teeth and walked to another group of firemen, as if he were impervious to the raging inferno about him.

Mary Ellen clutched her shawl tightly around her arms and glared at Colbraith's receding figure. "What a bastard," she screamed. "Naglee's a banker. His 'building,'" she imitated his pedantic manner, "must be protected. Our hotel doesn't count."

"Darling," Thomas coughed, "he's right. The *Niantic* is not a big deal for the city. Naglee's bank is. Let's get out of here." But Mary Ellen did not move. Thomas looked at the terrifying flames. Cracking timbers and the crash of a tumbling wall sent firemen scurrying past them.

Marry Ellen tried to be resolute. "Let's go down to Battery, then up Clay Street. Maybe that'll get us there." Mary Ellen suggested. But she was scared. As scared as she had ever been, even on that dreadful night in Cincinnati. She knew her obsession with the *Niantic* and her dangerous desire to get to the ship were irrational, but she kept pushing.

"Didn't you hear what the fireman said?" Thomas yelled at her.

"He's just covering up for O'Brien." She would not relent. "Probably stealing something from an abandoned building." She could feel her hatred and anger consuming her as if it were the fire itself. Thomas grabbed her arm and tried to pull her back. Mary Ellen started to cry but no tears came. Thomas did not notice. He looked at the massive wall of fire slowly moving toward them. "This one's the worst. Worse than the others."

"I know." Mary Ellen's voice seemed distant, almost remote. "But what if we lose the *Niantic?*" She looked plaintively at Thomas.

"We've got enough gold. Good investments. Please," he pleaded, "let's get away before its too late!"

"No!" Mary Ellen responded vehemently. She knew so many people who had been destroyed financially by previous fires. She also knew that the *Niantic* did not represent a large portion of their holdings in San Francisco. But her overwhelming urge to go to the *Niantic* seemed implacable.

Thomas looked at her and rasped from his scorched lungs. "Okay. Let's try it. But if Clay Street is just as bad, we're getting out."

They turned and headed east on Commercial Street, past small nondescript one-story ramshackle buildings, hastily constructed in the past six months on reclaimed land. Soot and ash fell like flakes of snow, covering everything with a suffocating gray mantle. Only a few people remained in the desolate streets. A few firemen and merchants with enough courage or lack of sense made a last ditch effort to protect some of the stores. At the intersection of Clay and Battery Streets Mary Ellen and Thomas came to an abrupt halt. The immense fire had gotten there first. Hot sparks and glowing ash rained, burning their flesh. They could barely breath. Then they saw the *General Harrison* in flames.

They watched in dismay. The old masts of the *General Harrison* turned into huge torches. Flames licked at the large signs, rolling and turning them to ashes as if they were pieces of thin paper. Only a few die-hard firemen remained, trying vainly to stop or slow down the onslaught. It was too late to save whatever was left of the goods stored on the ship. Houses along Commercial Street began to explode, one after the other, fueling the fire and feeding the flames.

"It's no use," Thomas gasped. He bent over, placed his hands on his knees and retched. Nothing came out. He held his stomach and panted: "We can't go farther. The *Niantic* is gone! This is hell!"

Mary Ellen's face dropped. Her burned hands balled up into fists, as she realized the truth of Thomas's words. Breathing had become intolerable. Thomas tore off a strip of his shirt and gave it to Mary Ellen for her nose and mouth. Mary Ellen held it tightly to her nose, her eyes dry and painful from the stinging smoke. Finally, she let Thomas take her by the hand and they started to back up, watching in horrid fascination as the *General Harrison* collapsed upon itself in a shower of sparks. The whoosh of another building exploding into flames nearby shocked them into sensibility. They turned and started to run from the fire. Mary Ellen's heart pounded. She tried to run faster but her legs, feeling heavy and lethargic, refused to follow instructions.

As they ran Thomas looked at the direction the flames and smoke were moving. "If we head back west, maybe up California with its brick buildings, we might be safer." Thomas yelled and pulled Mary Ellen by her hand when she started to falter.

They turned right on California, heading west and to the shelter of the newer, fire-safe buildings, but found themselves once again in the midst of the moving sea of people, all heading in the same direction, all trying to escape the advancing catastrophe. All around them flames leaped higher while weary firefighters and others tried to fend off the ensuing devastation. Suddenly, the planked sidewalks across the street started to explode as the fire found the cooler air cavities below the planks and sought this rich oxygen with a devilish thirst. One after the other, the planks exploded like a line of synchronized cannons. People screamed. Some were on fire. Others trapped by the igniting boards leaped high and twisted in strange, dance-like steps, further panicking the fleeing throng. Everyone now ran in the middle of the thoroughfare, packed together like sardines, trying to avoid the dangerous sidewalks.

They ran past Starr & Minturn. A fire engine, parked directly in front of the brick building, sent a stream of water shooting to the upper stories. But the heat was so intense, the water turned into steam and evaporated. The ironwork, on which Pettigrew had placed so much faith, glowed red hot. In some places it was melting.

"Can we get them out?" one of the firemen yelled.

"No. The iron's expanded and them doors is shut tight," another responded. Several exhausted firefighters were trying to break through the front door with axes but the iron cross-ties hampered their efforts. The iron work on the windows now served as an impenetrable barrier. No one could get in or out.

"We need some help!" came a shout from the front of another two-story brick building. The crowd continued right by, but Thomas suddenly swerved and, using his arms like paddle wheels, pushed toward the building. Mary Ellen tried to keep up with him, pushing and grunting as she shoved people aside, worried that she would be swept away.

"It's Dewitt & Harrison, Mary Ellen. I've got to help them."

"What can you possibly do?" Mary Ellen asked. "Nobody has any water left. All the buildings are on fire. We've got to get out of the city."

"I know. Look. You go on ahead. The fire is heading with the wind to the east. Just go up California Hill and you'll be safe."

"I won't leave you, Thomas."

But Thomas had already turned into Dewitt & Harrison's building. Mary Ellen remained outside.

"Let's get these buckets in line," Sanger Dewitt yelled.

"What are we going to use for water?" someone offered needlessly.

Because of the absence of reservoirs or assured sources of water, most buildings had large, water-filled barrels on their roofs in the event of fire. Dewitt's building had twelve barrels, but with a fire of this intensity, the water would not last more than a few minutes.

"We ain't got much water," Dewitt responded, "but we got over eighty thousand gallons of vinegar in store. Let's use it."

Soon a long line of men and women passed buckets to Dewitt inside the building. Dewitt cracked open barrels of vinegar and sloshed the contents into the pails. The filled buckets were handed on ladders to men who poured the smelly liquid on the roof and walls of the building. Embers hissed as they hit the vinegar, but the bucket brigade kept the vinegar coming, tossing the liquid at every small fire that flared.

The acrid smell of the steaming vinegar made Mary Ellen's eyes tear and burned her nose and throat. Her mouth felt as if it were filled with ashes, but she remained in the bucket line alongside Thomas until the flames slackened. Deep exhaustion started to set in and she felt weak and faint.

Thomas noticed and shouted, "Are you all right?"

"I feel dizzy."

Thomas put his arm around her waist and helped her to a building whose brick facade was untouched; others were also sitting or lying down, all exhausted.

"Stay with these people," he said, "I'll get you something to drink."

"No vinegar, please." Mary Ellen tried to laugh but instead a cough seized her.

Thomas had only gone a few steps when he heard a rumble and screams of terror caused him to turn back. The wall where Mary Ellen sat was collapsing on its helpless victims. She had already disappeared under a mound of debris.

"Oh my god!" he screamed as dust and debris clouded the air, limiting visibility to a few feet. Shocked onlookers were stunned into immobility until screams of agony jolted them into action. Thomas, blinded by dust and smoke, frantically sought the spot where he had last seen Mary Ellen. He stumbled through debris on his knees, over sharp broken bricks that ripped through his skin, but he paid no attention. A huge wooden beam poked up through the rubble directly where Mary Ellen had been. Thomas, screaming Mary Ellen's name, grabbed at arms, legs and hands reaching out from the debris. But Mary Ellen had disappeared in the carnage.

HALF A BLOCK AWAY FROM DEWITT & HARRISON'S BUILDING, TWO MEN were pulling on a horse hooked to a wagon that was stuck tightly in a muddy rut. The wagon was filled with supplies needed at the makeshift hospital on the hill above California Street. The exhausted and terrified horse was too numb to feel the sting of the whip. The driver put down the useless reins and whip, grabbed the horse's halter and yanked hard. The animal barely protested and tried to walk, but the wagon remained rooted to the ground.

Doc Ashe, former sheriff of Stockton and Terry Davis, his close friend from their days as Texas Rangers, stood next to the cart.

"I could sure use some water," Terry said.

"I think the fire's moving off, Terry," Doc responded.

"Can't really tell, Doc, not with a fire this big. What's that smell?

Vinegar?" He looked down the street and saw the bucket brigade pouring liquid on the roof of a brick building.

Just then the wall across the street from the bucket brigade collapsed. A mass of bricks toppled on a score or more of the people nearby. Terry did not hesitate. He immediately rushed through the choking dust with Doc, hanging onto his small black medical bag.

People were already digging, throwing bricks aside, trying to reach the injured. Removing the bricks was no problem; the wall had disintegrated into a heap of broken, bricks. The problem was the massive pine beam. A man bending over the beam yelled, "I need help over here! Please help me!" Terry and a couple of other men rushed to help. One of the men asked, "What happened, Thomas?"

"I don't know." Thomas seemed confused. "Please," he pleaded, "Mary Ellen's underneath. She was right here." Thomas continued to dig frantically through the rubble, bricks tearing at his fingers.

Terry took measure, "Doc, get the men over here on the double!" he shouted as he helped Thomas move bricks. Soon about a dozen men surrounded Thomas and Terry. "We've got to move this beam," Terry told them. "There are people trapped underneath. Hurry!"

In a few minutes the beam was exposed enough to grab. Terry positioned himself near the splintered end. He looked at the sharp slivers, some more than a foot long, as spiked and dangerous as the halberds he faced in Mexico. "Let's see if we can lift it up and move it there." He pointed to the muddy street.

The men grabbed the huge rafter and waited for a signal.

"Okay. Lift!" Terry yelled and struggled to raise his end of the beam. It barely moved, sending a few broken bricks tumbling to the side.

"Try again! Give it everything you've got!" he shouted. "Now!"

Again the men struggled and strained and finally the beam gave way. They lifted it about a foot above the ground and started to haul it to the street. Stumbling and sliding over loose bricks and debris, the men carried, dragged and pushed the beam out of the way. When they reached the road, they dropped the beam, most of the men bent over, hands on knees, chests heaving from the effort and the smoke and ash.

Chapter Twenty-One

Terry and Doc headed back to help Thomas clear the bricks. They lifted some smaller wooden joists and cross girders and found Mary Ellen, covered by a layer of dust and dirt, completely still.

"Oh my god!" Thomas exclaimed.

"This man is a doctor," Terry consoled Thomas. "Let him take a look at her."

Thomas reluctantly moved aside and Doc started his examination. After a few minutes, he turned to Terry. "I think this beam and girders saved her life. If her bones are broken I can't see it. Doesn't mean there aren't any or that she doesn't have internal injuries. We should get her out of here and to the hospital on the hill."

"Which hospital?" Thomas asked uncertainly. "St. Vincent's must have burned down."

"We've set up a tent hospital up on California Hill," Doc replied as he continued to examine Mary Ellen. "There's nothing more I can do for her, just get her to the tents." He rushed off to attend to others who were being brought out of the rubble, some able to sit up, others lying down, all covered with blood, dust, and ash.

"How can we get her to the hospital?" Thomas asked, panic creeping into his voice.

"We'll manage," Terry responded.

—~—

MARY ELLEN STRUGGLED TO REGAIN CONSCIOUSNESS. SHE THOUGHT she remembered being carried. Her throbbing head seemed heavy, her thoughts muddled and confused. She tried to open her eyes but the bright piercing light pained her. She floated in and out of sleep, dreaming strange dreams, hearing bells, smelling fire, smoke, and burning all around her. She heard voices, at first indistinct, unfathomable, but slowly coming into focus. She tried to sit up but could not move. Her limbs seemed to be frozen. Sharp pains seized her body almost everywhere. Only her ears seemed to work, so she just lay there and listened, trying to remember what happened.

"There's going to be hell to pay." She heard Thomas's voice.

"O'Brien claims the fire started at some furniture store," a stranger spoke with a pronounced southern accent.

"Not likely," Thomas said. "Five fires in eighteen months? I doubt it was just an accident."

"Looks like the whole city's been destroyed," a second stranger spoke, also with a southern accent.

Mary Ellen became alarmed and wondered if she had been taken back to the South. She did not recognize the voices; one voice seemed familiar, a strong voice with an unmistakable southern drawl.

"Let me tell you. I think it's those criminals. They commit a burglary, then cover it up with a fire," Thomas said. "But it won't last long. There's talk about forming a vigilance committee. They'll hang these bastards if the sheriff doesn't."

"I've heard about it. Read Brannan's speech. Can't say that I agree with people taking the law into their own hands. That's anarchy. How're they any different from anyone else who breaks the law?" the second stranger remarked.

"Terry, this city won't do anything. The sheriff and O'Brien are in cahoots with these criminals," the first stranger said.

"That's right, Doc. We've never hung anyone. The only jail is the brig *Euphemia* lying there in the harbor among all those ships. And it's always empty. We have so many robberies, assaults, and murders, but nobody ever gets convicted. You'll see. The vigilance committee will get rid of all the Ducks. The people are ready for some hangings," Thomas said heatedly.

"What about O'Brien. He controls the city and the sheriff. How will he react?" Doc asked.

"I suppose he'll fight back with all his Tammany b'hoys. If enough men join the vigilance committee it'll be a tough go for O'Brien. Especially if powerful people like Brannan take the reins."

Terry looked out at the harbor. "Look there. Must be at least a thousand masts."

"An amazing sight," Thomas concurred. "Looks like most of the ships were saved."

Chapter Twenty-One

The Brig Euphemia

The reference to an amazing sight impelled Mary Ellen to look, so she tried to open her eyes again. This time the light did not seem so piercing. At first she could not focus well. She looked up. The sky had a diffused yellow-white tint. No clouds. As her focus improved she realized that she was not looking at sky but at the top of a canvas tent, the front open, facing the bay. Thomas and the other two men were seated on the ground near the opening, gazing at the city and bay below them.

"I'll be darned. This is some city. Too bad its all burned down." Terry laughed. "I'll be happy to get back to the slower ways of Stockton."

Mary Ellen looked at the man speaking. Although he looked like Colbraith from the back, towering over Thomas and the other man, his voice seemed softer and more gentle. He had a simple manner about him and he spoke with a heavy Southern drawl. Thick brown hair lay matted on his large head. Mary Ellen could not see his face. At first she thought all the men were dressed alike. Then she realized that the soot and ash covering them made them look as if they wore dark gray clothes. The third man was built like Thomas, but instead of flaxen hair, he was bald. He was the one Thomas called Doc.

"Don't sell this city short just yet," Doc replied. "My guess is San Francisco will be rebuilt in less than two months. And better than before. That's what happened after each fire. Maybe now O'Brien will let the aldermen enact some building ordinances with teeth. Even if he doesn't get his usual tribute."

"You raise the specter of a vigilance committee running this city and hanging all sorts of people. O'Brien and his men, you tell me, now run the city. The problem, gentlemen, is fairly obvious. There is nothing left to run. The whole place is burned out. And what you had before was too much money, too much gambling, too many criminals. I don't know." Terry shook his head ruefully.

Mary Ellen tried to sit up and finally managed to prop herself on her elbows. She could barely make out the city below California Hill. She could barely recognize the scene. The whole section of town where the *Niantic* had been lay in waste. The area between Portsmouth Square on the west, Battery Street on the east, Pacific on the north, and Pine Street on the south, had disappeared. Black and gray skeletons remained. It looked like *Niantic* was gone. She lay back and started to cry, but no tears would come. She was too dehydrated.

"Doc's right, Mr. Davis. Don't sell us short. We'll have civil disorder. Lots of midnight hangings. But in a few years this will be one of the greatest, most sophisticated cities in the world," Thomas argued vehemently. "We'll continue to reclaim the bay. More gold flows through this city now than in any other city in the world, including New York. There are great fortunes to be made here. Why, when I arrived in early 1849, the population was about a thousand souls. Now it's well over twenty thousand and will probably double by next year."

"Maybe," Terry Davis said softly, "but it'll cost you. There'll be a war between O'Brien and the vigilantes. More gold will give rise to more fraud. You'll have more crime. I don't know if what you describe is Nirvana or the Tower of Babel. It sounds more like Babel to me."

The men looked down the hill at the charred ruins. Here and there a solitary building remained standing, unbowed by the enormous fire, but virtually the entire city had been razed to the ground. Smoldering skeletons of large and small buildings sent funnels of smoke into the brown sky.

"Terry, this isn't your kind of place. Maybe Stockton is. But I agree with Thomas. This will become a great city, and as with all great cities, we'll have our problems." Doc put his hand on Terry's shoulder. "Still you're welcome to visit any time."

Terry laughed heartily. "No thanks. I'll stick to Stockton and Sacramento. This city is too rough for me."

CHAPTER TWENTY-TWO

Temporary Reprieve

SAN FRANCISCO AND BENICIA
MAY-JUNE 1851

SELIM WOODWORTH'S HOUSE, AS IF PROTECTED BY A BENEVOLENT deity, stood firm and whole like a defiant sentinal surrounded by blackened skeletons of destroyed buildings, an oasis in a bleak and charred desert. Flames had lapped at the new paint, peeling and turning it brown; the back fence and front planked sidewalk were only ashes and soot; only one grizzled oak tree, its leaves scorched, was all that remained of the garden. Inside the house reeked of smoke that had penetrated every crack.

After fighting the fire through the night, Selim returned home and headed for bed. Utterly exhausted, he did not have the strength to remove his clothes. He lay back and was asleep instantly. He awoke in the afternoon, seized with a violent coughing fit, his throat parched dry. A large black shadow was left on the white bedspread where he had slept. Selim grabbed a pitcher of water from the vestibule. Despite the thin film of ashes floating on top, and the somewhat rancid smell, he drained most of it in a few gulps, letting the cool liquid quench his dust-filled throat. He splashed water on his face leaving tiny little black trails trickling down his neck. Ignoring his dry, stinging eyes, he went outside. The acrid smell of the fire hung in the air like a thick blanket. Selim's reddened eyes stung, and a hacking cough seized him every few minutes. No matter how much water he drank he could not get rid of the scorched feeling in his throat. People were slowly wandering the streets, many walking mindlessly, in shock. Others hurried over the rubble carting planks and lumber to their burned buildings. Despite Selim's and his brother's efforts, the fire was simply too much and too powerful. Their warehouse was destroyed along with hundreds of other buildings—homes, businesses, hotels, stores, and anything else in the way.

Fortunately, a ship laden with supplies for the Woodworth warehouse had arrived at the wharf shortly before the fire started. It was too dark to unload, so the captain waited until dawn. When the fire's orange flames shot into the sky, sending burning cinders over the wharves, the captain gathered a skeleton crew and took the ship to deep water anchorage. Fate not only spared Selim's house, it also prevented a major supply of Woodworth inventory from turning into ashes.

Selim did not have much time to think about his losses. A veteran of prior fires in San Francisco he immediately began the task of rebuilding his business. He had plenty of money, mostly gold stored in fireproof safes. The ship would return to the wharf with supplies. The new inventory would command high prices. All he needed was labor, labor to rebuild and to staff his business. He had no doubt that the fire created a huge supply of labor since many San Franciscans were now unemployed.

As Selim walked through the plaza, a small cloth over his mouth, he saw gun barrels lying near the old adobe, twisted and knotted like snakes from the intense heat. An iron house, supposed by its owners to be impervious to fire—"After all, iron doesn't burn," they said—had collapsed, the corrugated iron melting, leaving a deformed and undulating sheet of gray metal hovering a few feet above the ground. Small streams of smoke rose from the burned remains. Small lakes formed of molten glass in the colors of the rainbow. Implements of every kind—spoons, knives and other utensils—were scattered around or had melted in heaps. A mound of

After the Fire

nails, welded together from the intense heat in the shape of the keg that contained them, stood in the open, the only evidence of what had been Mellus and Kemp's store. The nail sculpture even retained the metal bands of the keg; only the wood was missing.

When Selim arrived at his warehouse he found Frederick already giving directions to a master carpenter. The pace at which everyone set about rebuilding no longer amazed him. San Francisco had already suffered through four major fires, each one ravaging a major portion of the city. Each time the merchants and residents rebuilt the city within a few months. A wagon filled with wood and building materials stood nearby with four men waiting quietly, leaning nonchalantly on the sideboard as if unaware of the devastation surrounding them.

"How long before you can finish the job?" Frederick asked.

"I can have the building ready in two days," the carpenter replied firmly, "supposing I get the rest of the materials. My crew's signed up," he pointed to the men and the wagon.

"Selim, should we put up a tent in the interim?" Frederick asked.

A forest of canvas tents had already sprung up, giving San Francisco the appearance of a new settlement, not the city it had been a day earlier.

"Nah," Selim dismissed the suggestion with a wave of his hand. "I'll see if Captain Shiller can keep the merchandise on board for a day or two. Then we can off-load it and leave it on the wharf until the building is finished. Only two days you say?"

The carpenter nodded his assent. After they finished with the carpenters Selim and Frederick decided to wander around and check on the welfare of some of their friends. They paused at the corner of Clay and Sansome Streets.

"Well look at that?" Selim said, pointing to the hulk of a ship standing bruised, but not battered by the fire. "The *Niantic* survived. I'll be damned."

"The ship survived, but the hotel's gone!"

Several men carefully made their way along the deck. Selim spotted Thomas descending a ladder. "Hey, Thomas!" he called out.

Thomas turned toward them. Although covered with grime he had washed his face; it looked like a bright full moon against a blackened sky.

"Selim, Frederick," he greeted them. "How did you fare?"

"Warehouse burnt out!" Frederick replied, "but our house is intact."

"Good, good."

"Looks like your ship weathered the storm," Selim said.

Thomas looked back at the *Niantic.* "She sure looks like she's been beached and dismasted by a storm, doesn't she? We tried to get here to help save the hotel. O'Brien stopped us. Said it was too dangerous to proceed. He actually threatened us."

"That bastard," Frederick remarked as Selim listened silently.

"It looked as if the fire was engulfing this area," Thomas tried to explain Colbraith's action. "Still, he had no right to speak to us the way he did. Then he and some of his Empire One volunteers headed elsewhere to protect another building."

"Probably one that belonged to one of his political cronies," Selim said softly. "I wouldn't put it past him. That son-of-a-bitch would let his mother go up in ashes for one damned vote."

"At least he didn't blow up your ship," Frederick tried some levity.

Thomas laughed. "I heard plenty of explosions. Fortunately it wasn't the *Niantic.* I don't know how this ship survived. It'll make Mary Ellen happy."

"By the way, where is Mary Ellen?" Selim asked as he looked around. "We need her help at the house."

"She's up at the makeshift hospital on California Hill," Thomas said.

Selim drew a sharp breath. "Is she okay? What happened?"

"A wall collapsed on her. We had to dig her out. But she's just shaken up and bruised. Nothing broken as we can see. She'll be all right."

"Thank God!" Selim said in relief. "I don't know what I'd do without her."

Selim did not notice Thomas flinch as if he had been struck. That very thought had been foremost in his mind. What would he do without Mary Ellen? Fortunately she survived, but it made him feel vulnerable and, for the first time in his life, very mortal.

"When can she go home?" Selim asked.

"She could go back now, but the Tehama was destroyed by the fire, so she needs to find a new place.

"Why doesn't she move into our house?" Selim suggested and Frederick nodded his agreement.

"That's very kind of you, but . . . "

"No buts. She's like a daughter to me. Bring her down. We can get someone to take care of her until she recovers."

"Right now Mary Ellen is being tended by a friend, Lessette Flohr," Thomas said. "Miss Flohr is doing a marvelous job. There's a strong bond between them."

"Good. Then tell both of them to come to my house."

Thomas felt a sense of gratitude to Selim, and a sense of separation from Mary Ellen. He would lodge aboard Eustace Barron's boat until the hotels were restored and he could get a room.

Later that afternoon Thomas arranged for an ambulance wagon to take Mary Ellen and Lessette Flohr from the temporary hospital on California Hill to Selim Woodworth's house. He thanked Doc Ashe and Terry Davis for their aid. The two men helped load Mary Ellen on the wagon and wished her well. Despite a pounding headache, one so severe she could hardly manage the slightest movement, Mary Ellen also thanked them. As the crude ambulance bounced down the hill, shock waves and flashes of light filled her head. She closed her eyes and fought the pain. Mary Ellen did not remember arriving at the Woodworth house. Selim gave her his bedroom, a large, airy room on the second floor, while he moved into a room with his brother. She did not even remember how the sight of the bedspread with its black angel silhouetted on the white cloth brought peals of laughter to the two women until another violent throb struck her.

"It reminds me of making angels in the snow as a child," Lessette wiped away her tears.

"At least there's a bed to sleep on," was all Mary Ellen could mumble drunkenly as Lessette pulled away the black and white bedspread.

Lessette moved in with Mary Ellen. Selim did not object. On the contrary, he took one look at the lovely young girl and melted. Even Mary Ellen, still nursing that terrible headache, noticed Selim's reaction. He

Chapter Twenty-Two

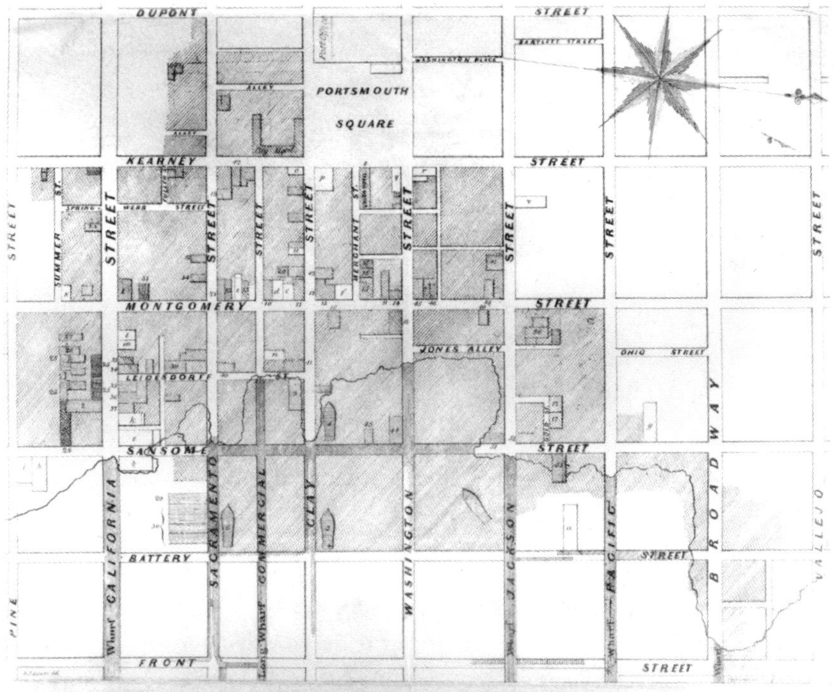

MAP of the BURNT DISTRICT of SAN FRANCISCO, SHOWING the EXTENT of the FIRE.

Map of Burnt District

could not take his eyes off Lessette. Usually staid and confident, ripping off commands with eloquence, Selim seemed a bit confused if not uncomfortable, stuttering uncharacteristically and unable to stay focused.

The fire destroyed the Atheneum Saloon, although Riker and Taylor quickly erected a canvas tent on the site after Gordon and Willmore cleared off the debris. They posted a large hand-painted sign announcing the opening of the New Atheneum. Overnight a contractor installed a new dance floor and Mr. Lacroix brought his fiddle. But replacing the liquor and the piano was another matter. Few saloons remained in business after the fire. Those that did, made a fortune until the competition rebuilt. Under the flimsy canvas roof the New Atheneum resumed its operations, but without liquor. However, the room filled with men eager to dance away the nightmare of the fire and the massive destruction. Despite the absence of liquor, the chief financial force in a hurdy-gurdy operation, the dancing re-established a much needed source of cash flow.

The livery was gutted as were two of the laundries but the building on Ecker remained intact, though it needed a complete cleaning before starting up operations. All in all, Mary Ellen and Thomas fared well.

Lessette not only took care of Mary Ellen, bringing meals to her room, helping her dress and wash herself, she also took over Mary Ellen's chores in Selim's house. As Mary Ellen regained her strength and the sharp pain in her temples lessened, the two women began working together. Slowly they put the Woodworth house back in order. They washed and scrubbed the walls and floors, sending buckets of black water into the street. Each cleaning revealed another thin layer of fine ash. It was arduous work, but within two weeks they had banished the ash, soot, and nearly all the odor.

Selim and Frederick also resumed entertaining their friends and customers. But the gaiety and warmth that had been so characteristic of the Woodworth brothers seemed absent, except when Lessette was around. Selim would find any excuse to be with her, lavishing his attention and care, almost doting on her. For the first time Lessette seemed to be happy, not just grateful to Mary Ellen for saving her, but happy to be attending to the two bachelors and making them laugh. One evening, Brannan and a few other men Mary Ellen recognized but whose names she did not know, arrived unexpectedly. Selim offered them some food and asked Mary Ellen and Lessette to serve the visitors.

In the kitchen Lessette mentioned how the men in the dining room seemed to cast a pall on the house. Selim became very serious and tight-lipped. The conversations died to a word or two when the two women and the servants entered the room, only to become heated as soon as they left. After her last close call in eavesdropping, Mary Ellen decided not to take any chances. Despite Selim's renewed amity, she remained extremely cautious, making sure he would not have any cause to question her conduct. Instead she sent Lessette to serve the refreshments. Lessette, who apparently could do no wrong in Selim's eyes, returned and told Mary Ellen what she heard.

Chapter Twenty-Two

"They're really burned up," Lessette put the dirty dishes on the kitchen table.

"About what?" Mary Ellen asked innocently.

"About the Sydney Ducks and crime. You should hear that man Brannan. He wants to hang every one of them Sydney Ducks. Says the faster San Francisco is rid of the scum, the better."

Mary Ellen thought about Thomas and his fears of being mistaken for someone from Australia. "What are they so upset about?"

"They said a thief started the fire to cover his theft, and they're sick of fighting fires. Have there been a lot of fires in San Francisco?"

"Yes, this is the fifth major fire. Each time the city burns down it gets rebuilt. The people don't get angry or depressed. They just rebuild everything in a few weeks. Each time the buildings get bigger and better," Mary Ellen replied as she rinsed the dishes.

"You're wrong, Mary Ellen," Lessette said timidly. "They're very angry. Brannan is leaving for Benicia. Says as soon as he gets back they'll do something."

"What's in Benicia?"

"The State Democratic Party meeting."

"You mean the convention?"

"I think that's it."

"And what does Mr. Brannan propose when he gets back?"

"I don't know," Lessette said firmly. "But I think it'll be something terrible. He scares me. You should see how the other men nod in agreement, their faces grim and angry. I bet it'll be something big."

"Well, something must be done. How much longer are the public officials going to abuse our patience?"

Chapter Twenty-Three

The Committee of Vigilance of 1851

SAN FRANCISCO
JUNE 1851

Sunday, June 8, 1851

SAM BRANNAN'S OFFICE BUILDING, A TWO-STORY CLAPBOARD STRUCTURE, survived the May fire. Located on the northeast corner of Bush and Sansome Streets, it stood amid similar newly built two-story frame houses. Only the lot directly opposite, on Sansome Street, remained vacant and ungraded. Huge hillocks of undisturbed sand rolled off toward the southwest. Brannan's building had three low-ceiling storerooms on the ground floor, each lined with white cotton cloth, dingy with dust and stained from the winter rain. The three stores, each fronting about twenty feet on Bush Street, and fifty feet deep, were vacant; Brannan had them on the market for rent.

The entrance to Brannan's office on Bush Street led up a narrow flight of steep stairs. His personal office, a little room partitioned by canvas from the loft at the Bush-Street side, belied the extensive business affairs that Brannan controlled. Brannan owned vast holdings of real estate, stores, farms, ranches, and mines; not that anyone could glean such wealth from his Spartan and modest office.

Late Sunday afternoon, under cloudless skies, with a gentle warm breeze of early summer caressing the golden hills, and the setting sun casting long shadows, Brannan sat at his desk reviewing some accounts with his clerk, Arbry Wardwell. Wardwell, a combination secretary, bookkeeper, and apprentice, was explaining why he allowed some of their customers more time to pay up their accounts. Brannan listened, made some notes, and asked some questions. Wardwell justified his stand on the effect of the fire and Brannan appeared satisfied with Wardwell's explanation. Brannan had Wardwell go through each file; the only way Brannan could keep his fingers on the pulse of his business. Many of San Francisco's merchants worked on Sunday, the only day of pensive solitude. The streets remained quiet; the usual clatter and noise from hucksters and traffic was noticeably absent.

As Wardwell retrieved another file, the tread of several men climbing the creaky stairs broke the stillness. Not expecting any visitors, Brannan's hand instantly reached for the loaded revolver he kept in the front desk drawer. Wardwell, who also carried a gun, placed it on his lap, under the table. A knock on the door echoed through the silent room.

"Who is it?" Brannan called out, his back ramrod straight, his hand clutching the gun and his eyes bored on the door.

"Sam, its George Oakes and James Neal."

Brannan's sigh of relief was audible, but a puzzled expression crossed his face. Usually he did not receive visitors on Sunday, especially not Oakes and Neal, two men with whom he had little personal business or social contact. Brannan closed the drawer as Wardwell put away his gun.

Wardwell unlocked the door and Brannan greeted the two men. "Come on in. Have a seat. Care for some coffee?"

Oakes and Neal sat while Wardwell produced two black tin cups and poured some coffee from the iron potbellied stove in the corner. The two men seemed taciturn and serious, so Brannan decided to forego any banal pleasantries.

"What can I do for you?" he asked, intrigued by their visit.

Chapter Twenty-Three

"Sam," George Oakes began, "have you seen this morning's *Alta*?"

"Haven't had the chance, George. Why?"

Oakes unfolded the paper he carried and pushed it across the desk. "Did you write this?" he looked intently, searchingly, at Brannan.

Brannan picked up the paper. An editorial entitled "Propositions for the Public Safety" was circled in ink. Someone who called himself "Justice," and identified by the paper as a respectable merchant, signed it. Brannan read it slowly, his interest piqued. When he finished, he handed the paper back to Oakes. "I didn't write this, but I sure as hell wish I did. It says it all, doesn't it?"

"We feel the same way," Neal said. "We need to form a committee of safety. We're sick and tired of having to jump at every sound, day or night."

Brannan and Wardwell exchanged glances, and Brannan absentmindedly touched the handle on his desk drawer.

Oakes read the paper aloud. "I like his idea of having the committee 'board, or cause to be boarded, every vessel coming in from Sydney, and inform the passengers that they will not be allowed to land unless they can satisfy this committee that they are respectable and honest men.'"

"Look at his next line," Brannan said, as if he had just memorized the article.

Oakes looked. "You mean the proposal to appoint a committee of vigilance, say twenty men in each ward?"

"That, and his view of shooting the criminals 'like dogs.'"

"What do you think of his view that an accusation by a policeman would be equivalent to a conviction?" Neal asked.

"Well, I don't know about that," Brannan mulled the question. "I'd prefer to have the facts laid out for the committee and let them decide guilt or innocence. But I tell you this—I'd hang anyone committing a crime—even stealing!"

"James and I've been discussing all the robberies and killings," Oakes said. "We think it's time to take some action, to take our city back from the Sydney Ducks. They live in their little community, free of the law. They commit most of the crimes and get off scot free. This can't go on any longer. Justice, whoever he is, is right."

Neal, also a prominent merchant, agreed. "It's going to get a lot worse, and it's bad enough already. No one's safe any more. We need to organize."

"That's why we're here," Oakes pleaded. "Will you help us? No one took on the Hounds until you spoke up. You were instrumental in ridding us of those dogs!"

"I'd be happy to help. It's every citizen's duty to take some action. Of course I'll help, but this'll require the action of a lot of folks. The Ducks aren't going to leave without some hard inducements. Just like the Hounds, only worse. There are too many of them as it is, and until Justice has his way," Brannan did not catch his own pun, "every ship from Australia brings in more pestilence. Let's make a list of the citizens we can count on, those who'd be willing to work hard, do whatever's necessary, and have the courage of their convictions. We could all meet and organize once and for all. Mr. Wardwell can take the list, prepare invitations and deliver them. What do you think?"

Oakes nodded his head. "I'm all for it. How 'bout you?" he turned to Neal.

"That's what I'm here for."

"Good. Then let's set up a meeting for tomorrow, say at noon, and see who comes."

"Where should we meet?" Wardwell asked.

"California Engine House," Oakes, foreman of that volunteer company, offered.

"Good. Tomorrow at noon. We need strong, discreet men," Brannan slapped the table. "Let's put the list together."

The four men exchanged names, debated the merits of each nominee, and kept Wardwell busy scribbling names and addresses. In less than thirty minutes they agreed on a list, headed by Selim and Frederick Woodworth. Brannan and Oakes agreed to get together in the morning to make arrangements for the meeting. After Oakes and Neal left, Brannan sent Wardwell to deliver all the invitations.

On Monday, June 9, Brannan, Oakes, Neal, and Wardwell arrived early and set up the room at the California Engine House, situated at the junction of Market and Bush Streets, opposite the Oriental Hotel. Their

Chapter Twenty-Three

Sam Brannan

guests began arriving shortly before noon. Instead of the small group Brannan expected, nearly forty men showed up. Brannan, standing near a table at the front of the room, welcomed each man, even though some of the people were not on the Wardwell list of the previous night. Selim and Frederick Woodworth arrived early and made their way to Brannan.

"This room is too damned small," Selim whispered to Brannan as more men flooded the narrow chamber. "We need a bigger place."

Brannan had already come to the same conclusion. It was fairly obvious that the rooms of the California Engine House were not large enough to accommodate forty people, let alone more. People were spilling out into the hallway. Those in the room pressed against each other like steers being led to the slaughter house; there was not enough room to turn. The air grew warm and stale, as the smell of perspiration mingled with cigar and cigarette smoke. Brannan could hear rumblings of discontent about the oppressive conditions and realized that some of the people would have to remain in the halls, unable to participate in the ensuing discussions.

As if reading Brannan's mind Oakes suggested they move to the plaza, but Selim and Brannan rejected the idea. First, it was too far—about a half a mile away, and they did not want to bring attention to themselves as forty or so men marched through the streets. More importantly, the plaza was not exactly the best place to conduct a secret meeting.

Brannan checked his gold watch. It was exactly noon, so he called the meeting to order. "Did you read this morning's *Alta*?" he asked, shaking the newspaper in his hand for emphasis. Dozens of sullen faces stared at him, listening intently. "The editorial is entitled '*Quousque Abater, Cairina, Patentee Nostra!*' Do you know what it means?"

Most of the men shrugged their shoulders and looked at each other as if Brannan had lost his mind.

"It's Latin. And it means," Brannan continued, "'how long will you abuse our patience?' How long will we endure all the crime and fires, all the curs who infest our city? How long will we endanger our citizens?" He looked at the men and repeated. "How long will you abuse our patience?" Brannan hesitated for a moment, letting the thought sink in. Again he brandished the paper, shaking it violently over his head. "There's more. Much more. Last Friday, our beloved Judge Parsons decided to disband the grand jury. He says it isn't properly constituted. Did he ask anyone? Did he seek the advice of other officials? The mayor? Aldermen? Anyone? No! He acted like a monarch with divine power. With a stroke of his judicial sword he cut off their heads. Now we don't have a grand jury until July 1. In the meantime who's going to indict the criminals? How long will you abuse our patience?" Brannan could feel the crowd stirring, a seething anger rising from the ashes.

"Hang the bastard!" someone called out to a thunderous ovation.

"Wait!" Brannan held his hands up. "That's not all. He also quashed the indictment of Benjamin Lewis on some technicality. Remember Lewis? He's the man who torched Colonel Stevenson's rooms. Claimed he was drunk and accidentally tipped over a candle. Mayor Brenham promised a fair trial. Told us he wouldn't fail us. He had faith in the courts, he said. Well, so much for those ill-kept promises. Lewis is free. He's a Sydney Duck. Free to start more fires, to rob. What lesson has Lewis learned?" Brannan paused for effect. "He can commit a crime, confess to it, have his indictment quashed and continue to commit crime with impunity. How long will you abuse our patience?"

"Damn that son-of-a-bitch!" Selim hissed.

"Hang the judge and hang Lewis," one man stood and called out. The crowd pressed forward as one, fists raised and shaking with anger. For a moment Selim felt they would be overwhelmed by the mob. The din was so intense it made him wince, but he felt exactly as the others.

"I'll supply the rope," he finally shouted, his voice trembling with indignation.

Brannan waited for the uproar to end. Slowly the shouting and cursing diminished and a temporary calm prevailed. Brannan and Selim alternated in addressing the assembled men. They agreed to continue to organize a committee, to invite more men, men of stock and standing in the community, and to consider the proposals Justice laid out in the Sunday *Alta* editorial. They organized themselves into committees, with Brannan, Oakes, Isaac Bluxome, and the Woodworth brothers on the committee to draft a constitution. Brannan proposed that all those present reconvene later that night at his store. There would be enough room for everyone, he swore. Before they adjourned, Brannan cautioned everyone about the need for secrecy. The city was already rife with rumors about secret meetings; news traveled fast in the crowded city. Brannan and Selim agreed that it was imperative to complete the committee's organization before any of the Ducks consolidated and took action against them. Or the police. Brannan and Selim had little doubt that O'Brien, the only man with a strong, well-organized, and well-armed presence, would find the existence of some new organization threatening. The Australians had no political power or ambition. But an organization of the city's merchants would present O'Brien with a potentially lethal adversary, one unlikely to dismiss the political implications.

Brannan, the Woodworths, Oakes, and Bluxome returned to Brannan's office to help organize the affair and prepare a draft of the constitution for the committee to review in the evening. It was evident to all of them that they needed to have more precise plans drawn for the conduct of the night's meeting where, Brannan hoped, the vigilance committee would be born.

That night, as the crowd pressed into the middle store of Brannan's building where Wardwell had set up tables and chairs, it became apparent that more room would be needed to hold such a large throng, nearly double the size of the group that flooded the California Engine House earlier in the day. Brannan grabbed a small knife and immediately cut away the canvas partitions to the other two stores, slitting the thin material between the studding, giving the men more room to congregate. Brannan, Selim, Frederick, Oakes, Colonel Stevenson, Isaac Bluxome, Stephen Payran, and Gerritt Ryckman sat at a center table.

Brannan called the meeting to order. "Men, although I see a lot of new faces among you I don't think I need to explain the purpose of our meeting. We all know why we're here. Our real purpose tonight it to discuss the best way to accomplish our goals." Again Brannan lashed out at Judge Parsons and gave a short chronology of recent crimes, underscoring the previous night's robbery of a jewelry store on Clay street and the bold daylight attack on Robbins's shop. Finally, Brannan eviscerated the Sydney Ducks for torching the building on Kearny and California Streets. Fortunately, he told the gathering, the neighbors found enough water on hand to extinguish the flames.

"We could've had another catastrophic fire!" Brannan railed and slowly built himself up into a lather. An eerie hush fell on the room as Brannan gesticulated wildly, ranted, threatened, prayed, and argued like a preacher bent on purging his flock from all sins. Even the remnants of the cut canvas partitions, hanging like tattered cotton curtains, remained absolutely still. Like an erupting volcano Brannan worked the congregation to a fever pitch.

"We must organize. We must forge a committee to expel and punish the bandits. A committee made of unyielding iron. Several of us met earlier this afternoon to discuss the organization. We recommend that we form an executive committee, selected by all of us, to carry out the day-to-day functions, and a general committee made up of all members to deal with extraordinary issues and to confirm the actions of the executive committee. We must elect officers for each committee and adopt a constitution that lays all this out. There's no doubt we're going to have to take the law into our own hands. If anyone feels that he doesn't belong with us, that our proposed actions are inappropriate or violate some higher law, let him speak up or leave now."

Brannan looked around at the expectant faces. Heads swiveled but no one moved, and the silence was unbroken.

"Good. We're about to take the first steps, no matter how drastic, to liberate this city once and for all. San Francisco is our city. If we have to hang every thief, every burglar, and every murderer, so be it!"

"What are we going to call ourselves?" someone shouted as if on cue.

"Secret Committee!" another voice yelled.

"Committee of Public Safety!" someone else offered the name suggested by Justice. Nearly every citizen of San Francisco by now had read the *Alta* editorial.

"Regulators!" a voice enjoined weakly, only to be showered with catcalls of derision.

Selim stood and raised his hands for silence. "How about Committee of Vigilance?" he offered.

Brannan looked at Selim and nodded his head in agreement. "Yes, that's a good name. It signifies being watchful and circumspect."

"But doesn't it smack of the Lynch law?" Colonel Stevenson inquired. The grumble emanating from the agitated crowd was like the drone from a swarm of bees.

"That's not our intention, Colonel," Brannan shot back, "but if that's the perception, so be it. Maybe it'll induce our friends from Sydney Town to beat a hasty retreat before the heat of Mr. Lynch scorches that trash and rends it asunder."

"Hang the bastards!" Bluxome yelled, and received a resounding ovation, though a few men remained mute and unenthusiastic.

After some more discussion they agreed upon "Committee of Vigilance" and the men quickly got to work on adopting the constitution and electing officers. Brannan nominated Selim as president of the general committee.

Selim became the general committee's first president for a term of three months. Selim then nominated Brannan as president of the executive committee, something both men had planned weeks earlier in the hours spent at Selim's house, huddled in secret meetings and conversations. Even most of the elements of the constitution had been well planned in advance. Selim thought how serendipitous for Oakes and Neal to serve as the catalysts for what he, Brannan, and their few friends, had been planning since the Jansen affair.

Near midnight the exhausted architects of the Committee of Vigilance had completed the constitution and decided to adjourn. Selim thought Brannan's use of the *Alta*'s editorial a masterstroke. Brannan suggested that the committee reconvene the following evening and offered the use of the three stores, for a nominal charge. As the bleary-eyed men filed out of the building, stunning by sheer number those bystanders still in the street so late at night, Selim and Frederick went to Robert Watson's side. Watson, a taciturn merchant with thin lips and aquiline nose, stood next to Brannan as the last of the organizers left.

"Thanks for getting that editorial published," Brannan whispered. "I didn't think it would work this quickly or effectively. It certainly moved Oakes and Neal. The word will get out that they started the ball rolling and that we were brought in."

"It couldn't have gone better," Frederick remarked.

"Where did you come up with Justice?" Selim laughed. "That was brilliant."

"It just seemed right at the time," Watson replied sardonically.

The four men bid each other adieu and left for their residences. Selim and Frederick agreed that the spark had been set, and now the fuse would burn brightly and quickly. They had no idea just how fast events would proceed.

—⁓—

THAT NIGHT COLBRAITH WAITED IMPATIENTLY IN COLONEL STEVENSON'S office. They had agreed the previous week to meet for a late dinner, but Stevenson was uncharacteristically late and his discomfited clerk could not tell Colbraith anything about the Colonel's whereabouts. The more Colbraith pressed, the more the clerk fidgeted and dissembled, giving Colbraith inconsistent answers that piqued Colbraith's interest while setting off an alarm bell. A rash of rumors about the formation of some secret society intent on taking the law into its own hands had spread throughout San Francisco as rapidly as the great May fire spread through the city. Colbraith read the editorials and had little doubt that they were coded calls for the formation of this furtive society. Colonel Stevenson had railed, during the past three months, about the city's inability to control what he called rather melodramatically "the runaway steam engine of crime." He became particularly strident after the Benjamin Lewis affair, aligning himself with Brannan on the city hall steps and calling for Lewis to be hung.

Still, Colbraith could not believe that Colonel Stevenson, or anyone else with his stature in the community, could be drawn into a society intent on breaking the law. Colbraith understood Stevenson's frustration with the old Hounds, since many of its members had mustered in his regiments, the old volunteers he brought to California in 1847. Highly respected and a prominent member of the city's elite, Stevenson's sensitivity, embarrassment, and subsequent anger over the Hounds affair was understandable, but the current lawlessness had nothing to do with him. Like everyone else in the city, Colbraith knew that Australian immigrants committed a disproportionate number of crimes. Many of them had been sent to Australia for committing crimes. They were criminals. At the end of their sentences they could return to England, but the trip from Australia to California was far shorter. And California had gold. But this had little to do with Stevenson. Other than the Lewis affair, Colbraith could not see why Stevenson seemed to get so worked up on the crime issue, taking it so personally.

Colbraith had no doubt that if a clandestine organization existed, Brannan and the Woodworths would be found right in the middle of it. But he did not have any first-hand information. He could not get it no matter how hard he tried. Usually his sources were reliable, at least with respect to anything taking place in San Francisco. But for some unfathomable reason, at this vital time when he needed it most, his wellhead came up dry; he had learned earlier in the afternoon that a large number of people attended a meeting at the California Engine House. An aide to foreman Oakes slipped up and mentioned the meeting to a friend, who passed the juicy gossip on to an Empire One volunteer. As soon as Kohler, foreman of Empire One, learned of this bit of information he immediately contacted Colbraith's key aides, George Wilkes and Yankee Sullivan, and they sent huge Dutch Charlie to investigate. By the time Colbraith learned about the meeting it had already adjourned.

Colbraith placed Yankee Sullivan and Dutch Charlie in charge of infiltrating the society. Wilkes, Colbraith's political mentor, seemed the most bothered by the turn of events. He always stressed the need to be in complete command of anything that happened in San Francisco. So far they had been very successful. But their inability to garner any information about what was happening right under their noses greatly disturbed Wilkes and Colbraith.

After Colbraith waited nearly an hour, and consumed several cups of coffee, Colonel Stevenson appeared. He walked into the antechamber of his office, lost in thought, when he spied Colbraith sitting with a china cup in his hand. Stevenson seemed genuinely shocked to see Colbraith, as if a ghost had suddenly materialized.

"Colbraith, what are you doing here?" he asked.

"Colonel, we had a dinner engagement tonight," Colbraith reminded him.

Stevenson placed his hand on his forehead. "Dammit, I completely forgot. Sorry, Colbraith, but something urgent came up. Could we reschedule for some other time?" he asked uncertainly, trying to avoid any eye contact with Colbraith.

Colbraith regarded his old friend who now seemed so distant and cold.

"What's going on Colonel?" Colbraith asked. "Are you embroiled in this safety committee business or whatever you call it?"

"I don't know what you're talking about," Stevenson stammered, his face turning red.

"You've never lied to me before," Colbraith clenched his jaw. "My question, Colonel, is what is going on here? Why all this secrecy? Why can't people work through the proper channels?"

"What proper channels?" Stevenson retorted harshly. "The courts? The law?" He glared at Colbraith. "You mean like Lewis?"

"I'm not here to discuss Lewis with you."

Stevenson regarded Colbraith, then turned away. "Do you realize what's going on? You've been in the legislature too long and out of touch. There's crime everywhere. San Francisco is riddled with it! This city is in jeopardy! No one is immune from it."

Colbraith felt his dander climbing. "That's why we have laws. To take care of these matters. Work through the legal system to address the problems that obviously upset you."

"Upset me?" Stevenson laughed abruptly. "My god, man, are you so far removed from the people, sitting on your political throne in San José, that you can't see what's happening right before your eyes. Upset me? Every man, woman and child in this city is upset, except for the criminals. But they won't be around much longer."

"Why haven't you come to me?" Colbraith asked heatedly. "I could take action if action is needed."

"Come to you? You're far too busy and you've been away too long. And maybe you're part of the problem."

"What do you mean?" Colbraith advanced toward Stevenson, whose face had turned crimson in anger, appearing burnt against his pure white hair. "What do you mean I may be part of the problem?"

"You're so intent on buying your way to become a U.S. Senator, selling patronage to fill your coffers. Why should the Sydney Ducks feel any different? Why shouldn't they steal and rob when the elected leaders of the community do so with impunity?"

Colbraith could hardly believe his ears. He advanced another step toward Stevenson who held his position. "Are you suggesting that I've been stealing?"

"No, I suppose not. You aren't a thief. Thieves work under cover of darkness, lurking in the shadows. Not you. But you sell patronage. If someone wants a state job you sell it to them, keeping half of their income for yourself and forcing them to do as you please," Stevenson firmed up. "And your b'hoys, Ira Cole, Dutch Charlie, and Yankee Sullivan, can beat a man senseless in public, and walk away knowing they won't be prosecuted because the police and the judges are in your pocket. What does that say about our legal system?"

Colbraith wanted to strike at the older man, but held himself in check. He owed Stevenson a great deal and he respected the older man. "We planned to have dinner tonight to iron out some of our differences," Colbraith said coldly, menacingly, "but it appears the gulf between us has become too great. All you care about is money and status. So you have both. But let me tell you something," Colbraith shook his finger at the Colonel. Less than a foot separated the two men. Stevenson thrust his chin defiantly at Colbraith. "I'll fight lawlessness whatever its form, from the Sydney Ducks to this so-called secret society," Colbraith growled.

Stevenson started to shake his head in denial, but Colbraith cut him off.

"No, don't demean yourself by denying it. Just remember, if you engage in any unlawful act, either alone or with others, I'll see to it that the law gives you everything but mercy. You better tell your friends. Tell Brannan. And the Woodworths. Tell all of them. So long as they act within the law they will find no obstacle in me. But if they cross the line they will have me to contend with."

Stevenson smiled, a snide and irksome smile. "You give yourself too much credit, Colbraith. Maybe Tammany Hall was right when they snuffed out your political career. You push too hard. You're so preoccupied with your desire to get even with the men of Tammany that you'll walk over your grandmother's body to get into the senate." Colbraith's nostrils flared like a wild horse, but he remained mute. Stevenson had just thrown his own words back at him. He was alone in this world, without any kin and committed to his quest for the senatorship. Yes, he would get even with the men in Albany.

"And don't tell me what I care about." Stevenson continued, "All you've ever sought is raw power. God help anyone who dares to cross you. But you better watch out as well. You aren't very popular with most of this city's merchants. And even with all your political power and Machiavellian schemes, you aren't big enough to take them all on. Now please leave my office."

Chapter Twenty-Three

Colbraith regarded his old benefactor with a mixture of rage and anguish, but mostly bitterness. He pointed his finger at Stevenson threateningly, but no words came out. Finally, he wheeled around in disgust and left.

—w—

Tuesday, June 10, 1851

ON TUESDAY EVENING, BRANNAN, SELIM, AND FREDERICK WELCOMED their guests. Even Brannan's old friend, Talbot Greene, a penniless victim of the May fire, came. The large turnout brought a smile to their faces. Nearly a hundred men, all respected and highly regarded by the community, entered Brannan's building. Having covered most of the preliminaries the previous evening, the committee quickly went about its business. First, those present approved a constitution for the Committee of Vigilance without a single dissenting vote. Bluxome, the newly elected secretary, copied the constitution onto the first two pages of a cap half-bound record. Selim, president of the general committee, read several editorials, including the Sunday and Monday *Alta* editions. He also recited portions of the Tuesday *Courier* whose editor went even farther than Justice had on Sunday. Selim cleared his throat: "Where the guilt of the criminal is clear and unquestionable, the first law of nature demands that they be instantly shot, hung, or burned alive." The popularity of these words with the members of the committee was quite evident; the wild cheering and chorus of support did not abate for over a minute.

The constitution was a relatively short document. Brannan, Selim and the others did not solicit the attendance of lawyers. Lawyers, they felt, were part of the problem. The first two paragraphs of the constitution dealt with the name and place of meetings for the committee. The third paragraph addressed how the general committee would be called. A bell would be struck twice, followed by a one minute pause, continuing until a quorum was present. The fourth paragraph stated their avowed purpose, to "bind themselves to defend and sustain each other in carrying out the determined action of this committee at the hazard of their lives and their fortunes." The final paragraph dealt with organizational matters. Loosely drawn, vague in places, and glaring in its omissions, the constitution would serve as a statement of their intentions as much as of their actual activities.

When all the matters before the general committee ended, Selim and Brannan asked the members present to sign Bluxome's binder. Selim signed first, followed by Brannan. Frederick signed fourth. To insure secrecy, the number appearing in the margin next to the signature became that man's code, and from thereon the committee members agreed to refer to each other by number instead of by name.

Before they adjourned, Selim announced that the executive committee would remain to discuss some urgent business. Again, he cautioned the members not to discuss any of the committee's matters or affairs with anyone else, and not to divulge any member's name, under the strictest of penalties, which everyone understood to mean at least ostracism, and possibly something much more sinister.

WHILE THE EXECUTIVE COMMITTEE WAS MEETING, GEORGE VIRGIN, A shipping and commission agent returned to his office from the copper festooned schooner *Warsaw* docked at Long Wharf. Smiling to himself after negotiating a good deal for his clients and for himself, he carried $1,500 in a small satchel, a good faith deposit which the *Warsaw's* buyer gave him to hold pending the preparation and execution of all legal documents. The buyer and his representative had inspected the boat from stem to stern. The survey revealed no major flaws, only a slew of minor, but reparable, conditions. The prospect of a large commission, $17,500, turned Virgin's inward smile into an outlandish grin.

His office, on the second floor of a building in the Washington block just at the end of Long Wharf, contained a small iron safe bolted to the floor and Virgin headed there to place the deposit in safe keeping. As he took the stairs two at a time, he did not notice a broad-shouldered man lurking in the shadows cast by the full moon overhead. Since a large saloon occupied the ground floor immediately below Virgin's office, customers of the saloon frequently milled outside. Virgin would not have noticed the stout man even if he stood directly under the street lamp. As he fumbled for the key to his door Virgin noticed the light in the office adjacent to his, a bookseller, and wondered how long it took the bookseller to earn $17,500.

Inside his office he lit a small oil lamp and opened his safe, a large cash drawer about fifteen inches cubed, made of thick iron. But the safe was full, so he locked it back up and went downstairs to the saloon, where the owner let him place the $1,500 in a much larger and heavier strongbox. After a few minutes with the owner, Virgin headed back to the wharf. He forgot to lock his office, not too unusual since he left his office unlocked most of the time.

Earlier in the afternoon, before the buyer had arrived to inspect the ship, the captain and Virgin had huddled over the cargo hold, checking the condition of different goods. The buyer's arrival interrupted their work and Virgin agreed to return to help the captain sort the merchandise for unloading. Virgin also wanted to remind the captain to keep the ship in Bristol condition for the pending sale. He did not want the buyer to have any excuse to cancel or reject the deal, though he had to admit to himself that this was a seller's market, and the buyer was unlikely to withdraw.

The broad-shouldered man watched Virgin head back up the wharf. Once Virgin disappeared behind a crowd of people the tall man walked slowly toward the stairway, his head bent, his features well hidden by a wide-brimmed hat. He could not do anything about his size. Taking three steps at a time he tried Virgin's door, found it unlocked and stepped in, closing the door quietly behind him. He knew where Virgin kept his safe. Two weeks earlier he pretended to be a customer looking for an agent and plied Virgin with questions, though his English accent and the cut of his clothes obviously made Virgin suspicious. Still, it gave him a good opportunity to case the office and he noticed the small safe.

The tall man tried to open the safe but the door would not budge. Virgin had locked it. So the tall man took out a crow bar and began ripping up the bolts. After a few minutes he managed to pry all the bolts loose. He pulled open a large sack that he had brought with him and reinforced it with a blanket filched from the corner of Virgin's office. Then he placed the safe, weighing about seventy pounds, in the sack, hoisting it as if it were a light load of laundry, and left quickly. As he descended the stairs he was startled to find Virgin coming up the stairs. They passed each other, Virgin looking at him long and hard, but the thief looked straight ahead, kept his gait even, as steady as his beating heart would allow. He did not look back, expecting Virgin to accost him at any moment or to question his reason for being there, but nothing happened. He headed to the far end of the wharf, about a quarter of a mile away, where he had tied his boat next to one of the pylons.

Virgin noticed the man. He looked familiar but said nothing, so Virgin assumed the man had come from the bookseller. But at the top of the stairs he noted that the bookseller's office was closed and dark. Virgin darted into his own office and immediately looked for his safe. It was gone.

He rushed back down the stairs, tripping at the bottom and slightly twisting his ankle. In the bluish moonlit night Virgin saw the man heading away, the large sack slung over his shoulder.

"Stop! Thief! Stop!" he yelled and started to run after the man who had just disappeared over the side of the wharf. "Stop that man! He stole my safe!" Virgin yelled and soon had about a dozen men running with him to the spot where the tall man disappeared. Other men rushed in his direction and soon the cry of alarm sounded up and down the wharf. Virgin arrived just in time to see the man jump into a small skiff and row toward Sydney Town, not toward the forest of ships in the harbor.

A few lighters headed for a steamer nearby heard the shouting and veered toward the commotion. The sailors could see a large crowd standing on the side of the wharf, jeering and gesticulating wildly.

"That man in the skiff, he's a thief," Virgin yelled down to them. "He stole my safe. Get him!"

The word spread over the water like wildfire as men yelled from boat to boat. About a dozen boats entered the chase. Several gunshots were fired into the air to serve as a warning to the man in the skiff and to get the attention of other boats.

The man rowed furiously, with long practiced strokes. But as he saw the other boats converging, he felt that empty feeling in his stomach, the same feeling he got when the police in London caught up with him after his first robbery. He knew exactly what to expect. He could out-row most men, but he did not have a chance against so many boats, many manned by sailors. He brought his oars up and stopped rowing, watching the boats encircle him and tighten the noose. Without hesitation he lifted the sack and dropped it softly over the side, letting the safe sink with only a line of tiny sparkling bubbles flowing up through the black waters. He did it carefully, without a splash, hoping it would not be noticed. At least he would not be caught with any evidence on him. The closest boat, probably satisfied that he had no means of escape, now headed directly for him, several men standing with guns pointed at him. Soon other boats clustered around him and he met grim faces and even more grim guns. He rested on his oars and smiled benignly at his captors.

A short, stocky, man, rowing alone in the first boat to reach him told him to put his arms up. He appeared unarmed, so the tall man stood up and said: "Drop dead! Get any closer and I'll break your neck."

The short man either did not hear him or completely disregarded his threat. Instead he picked up a small harpoon and smiled menacingly at the tall man.

"You're a lot smaller than the whales I've skewered. So you shut the fuck up and put your hands up. Or so help me God I'll put a hole the size of my fist where your knee is."

Strangely, although the threat of a gun would not have been intimidating, the sight of the barbed harpoon had an immediate effect. He blanched and sullenly did as he was told.

As Virgin watched from the wharf several men in the crowd behind him sidled up to him.

"What happened?" one of the men asked.

"That man in the skiff over there," he pointed to the shadowy boats without realizing that a single man on a skiff could barely be made out on the silver-streaked black waters, despite a full moon. "That man stole my safe when I was out of my office."

The two well-dressed men looked at each other knowingly, their faces taut. One of the men, George Schenk, #72, the other David Arrowsmith,

#25, had just left the committee meeting and decided to stroll along the wharf when they saw the commotion. Several policemen now appeared and made their way through the milling men.

The thief was brought up to the side of the wharf. His arms pinioned tightly behind him, and as he strained and spit at his captors, a few of the boatmen returned the favor by punching and kicking him. He staggered under the onslaught, but started to kick back. They quickly overwhelmed him and continued to punch and kick him as he tucked into a defensive ball.

"Now hold it," one of the policemen intervened. "Let the law take care of him."

A few jeered at this remark, but the police acted as if they had not heard anything. Several boatmen grabbed the broad-shouldered man, bleeding from several cuts on his face and a brutally split lip, and began to lead him toward the police station, as the policemen led the way. But Schenk and Arrowsmith had a different idea. Arrowsmith knew the boatmen. He walked hurriedly until he caught up with them.

"John," he spoke to the short man who still carried his harpoon. "We've got a better place for him! Follow Mr. Arrowsmith!"

John Silvane, the boatman, knew Arrowsmith and had also heard about the vigilance committee. In a flash of a second he put two and two together and guessed what Arrowsmith had in mind. He quickly whispered to the other boatmen and they turned with the prisoner and followed Arrowsmith. They did this without question or hesitation. The police of San Francisco had a dismal reputation. If the boatmen had any qualms about taking the prisoner elsewhere, they did not show it. Schenk rounded a few men and placed them as a barrier between the fast moving group following Arrowsmith toward Bush and Sansome Streets, to impede any attempt by the police to retake the tall man; and the police headed unawares toward the plaza.

—ɷ—

OAKES, WITH A BILLET OF WOOD IN HIS HANDS, CONTINUED TO STRIKE the bell of the California Engine Company as dictated by the rules of the

Chapter Twenty-Three

Selim Woodworth

Committee of Vigilance. Only a few minutes earlier, while the executive committee debated the need for acquiring weapons, Arrowsmith arrived with his prisoner in tow. Brannan, Selim, Frederick Woodworth, Oakes, and the others rushed outside to see the tall, ruggedly built man, standing defiantly among a dozen men with cocked pistols in their hands. When Brannan and Selim discovered what the man had done, they told Oakes to sound the alarm for the general committee and took the prisoner inside. Brannan ordered the guards to take the thief to his office and watched them hustle the prisoner up the stairs.

"You're not going to hold me here," the man shouted at his captors. "I'll be out of here by daybreak."

Brannan followed the men up the stairs and watched the guards restrain the squirming man by tying him to a chair.

"What's your name?" Brannan asked.

The man regarded Brannan with a hostile glare. "What business is it of yours?"

"You're charged with committing a crime. We're going to give you a trial. If you have any witnesses who could shed light on this, on who you are, and why we should be lenient, we need their names and we need yours."

"I want a lawyer."

"Lawyers can't help you. Rest assured that the trial will be conducted fairly. If you're guilty, you'll suffer the punishment. For your sake, and for the last time, what's your name?"

The man hesitated again, smiled benignly as if he did not have a care in the world. "John Jenkins, what's yours?"

Brannan ignored the question. "Mr. Jenkins, do you have any witnesses who can testify as to your good character, or who might shed light on what happened?"

Jenkins mulled the question. "I don't suppose you'd listen to Ben Lewis?" He laughed, but one of the guards slapped him hard across the face, opening the split lip wider.

"Don't do that!" Brannan commanded angrily. The guard and Jenkins looked at each other, Jenkins smiling, the guard holding his temper in check.

"This isn't a game," Brannan told Jenkins. "If you don't have witnesses, just say so. No one will touch you," Brannan glared at the guards, "unless you try to escape. Then they'll simply shoot you like a dog."

"John Bride and Will Blander. Those are my witnesses. They'll vouch for me and tell you what a good man I am."

"Give me the addresses and Mr. Ryckman will have the witnesses brought here right away."

Jenkins complied and as Brannan descended the stairs he heard the guards lock the door to his office.

The brazen alarm bell tolled at least twenty times. Many residents of the city thought the deep-throated clanging heralded another fire. Those who signed Isaac Bluxome's binder knew better; they recognized the signal instantly. It did not take long for most of the members of the general committee to arrive, curious to find out what prompted the call. They were not disappointed. A large crowd had already gathered at the corner of Sansome and Bush, where the committee's sergeant-at-arms, backed by two armed guards, refused admission to anyone who did not know his countersign. Men lined up at the door, and when their turn came up whispered their number, which the sergeant-at-arms checked against the roster. Those who could not gain entry remained outside, charged by the ominous portent of things to come.

Colbraith, fearing another fire and puzzled by the strange tempo of the alarm bell, headed in the direction of the California Engine House with Dutch Charlie and Ira Cole, as a stream of people rushed along in the same direction. Fred Kohler, Empire One's chief foreman, remained at the engine house to muster the volunteers into action if needed. At the California Engine House several firemen, wearing their hats, directed the traffic toward Sansome and Bush Streets. Colbraith instantly knew that something was taking place at Sam Brannan's office, and it probably involved the new secret society.

A huge throng milled in front of Brannan's building, obscuring the entry. But Dutch Charlie, Ira Cole, and Colbraith cleaved through the crowd to where a line of men wound around the building and several armed guards stood at the entrance to Brannan's offices. Colbraith saw Hal McAllister, one of the city's most prominent lawyers, arguing heatedly with the guards at the door, trying to gain entry and peer inside, but the guards, looking bleak and tense, would not budge. They blocked McAllister from entering. McAllister finally quit in disgust and stepped aside as more men whispered to the sergeant-at-arms and entered Brannan's building.

"Hal," Colbraith called out. "What's going on?"

"I heard they have a prisoner, and they intend to put him on trial," McAllister looked back at the entrance.

"Who are they?" Colbraith asked uncertainly, though he suspected the answer.

"I've been told," Hal turned closer to Colbraith, "that it's the Committee of Vigilance. They'll put on some mock trial, then hang the poor bastard."

"Who is it and what did he do?"

"His name is John Jenkins, though I understand his real name is Simpton. He's a Sydney Duck. Robbed some merchant and stole his safe. Open and shut case, they claim."

"Where did you hear this?" Colbraith asked.

"I can't say, Colbraith. All I know is I tried to go inside. I told them I was this man's lawyer. They asked me for my number, and when I asked what they meant they turned me away. They said I had no business inside."

A slight commotion at the front entrance drew Colbraith's attention. He saw a uniformed policeman pounding on the front door. "This is Captain Ray, of the Second District Police," the man shouted with authority. "Open this door now!" He pounded on the door again. "This is a police matter. Open the door!"

The door opened slightly and Sam Brannan thrust his head out. "What can I do for you, Captain Ray?"

"I am here to arrest Mr. Jenkins. I demand that you release him to my custody immediately!"

"Jenkins, you say?" Brannan looked puzzled.

"Mr. Brannan, don't trifle with me," Captain Ray sounded cross, but his hands balled into fists. "You know damned well who I am talking about."

"Yes, of course I do," Brannan said evenly. "But what does that have to do with me?"

"Mr. Brannan, for the last time, I want you to hand that man to me. I can't make that any more clear now, can I?"

Brannan seemed genuinely shocked. "Oh, I see. You think we have Mr. Jenkins here. I'm sorry Captain Ray, he was here a while ago, but he's not here any longer. If you'll wait a minute or two I'll try to find out where he is."

"Fine, please get on with it. I don't want any games here!"

"Just hold on," Brannan said, "I'll see what I can find out," then disappeared behind the closed door.

Captain Ray turned away from the door and paced back and forth. Several of his men stood idly by, nervously waiting for direction from their captain.

Chapter Twenty-Three

Colbraith and McAllister, followed by Dutch Charlie and Ira Cole, approached Captain Ray.

"Good evening, sir," Captain Ray saluted Colbraith.

"Wish it were so, Captain," Colbraith replied. "What have we got here?"

"I was told by two constables that a man by the name of Jenkins, who allegedly stole Virgin's safe, was brought here. I've come to take Jenkins away from this mob and lock him up before they lynch him."

"But I heard Brannan tell you he isn't here. Is that true?" McAllister asked.

"I don't know, Mr. McAllister," Captain Ray answered hesitantly. "All I can go by is what my men told me."

"Well, we've got to do something and do it quickly," Colbraith enjoined. "We can't allow a lynching in our city. We have a judiciary and police. These people can't flout the state's and city's laws."

"I agree," McAllister said. "But it may be a case of too little, too late. Look around you. There are hundreds, if not a thousand people here. What are you going to do?"

The men surveyed the scene. "I'll get the b'hoys out," Colbraith offered. "Captain Ray, I suggest you bring in reinforcements. Perhaps someone should go and get Captain Harding of the Third District. You need more men."

"I've already sent for help but, Mr. O'Brien, this is a large mob and I'm not sure we can handle it," he confided. "We'll do our best. I'm not prepared to let this rabble walk over us and take the law into their own hands. Not so long as I have a say in it."

"Good. Of course you're right. You can rely on my men to help you. I'll send for more help myself."

Colbraith turned to McAllister. "They have Jenkins inside. I can smell it."

"Then Captain Ray should push his way in. They won't dare interfere with the police," McAllister sounded less than convinced by his own argument.

"Hal, what do you think they've already done? There's no walking away from this. Not for either side. But I can't blame Captain Ray for not rushing in so fast. He doesn't have enough men and he doesn't know the layout. He could be easily ambushed. Better to wait outside until they produce Jenkins, dead or alive. Frankly I don't care one whit about Jenkins. But that's the only chance we have."

McAllister reflected for a moment. "They're going to hang Jenkins. I just know it."

"Not if I can do anything about it," Colbraith growled, but he knew his chances were slim, at least with such a large mob present.

The men stood silently, looking at the growing crowd—in numbers as well as in temper.

McAllister turned to Colbraith. "Let me ask you a question, if you don't mind? I'm a defense attorney. I defend criminals. These people may not like it, but they'll understand what I'm trying to do. But what about you? This city is ready to boil over. The sentiment of this crowd represents a large segment of our population. But you? What's your interest? Why jeopardize your political career?"

Colbraith was not sure how to answer the question. As he gained more power and prominence, people attributed his actions entirely to self-aggrandizement. No one seemed to give him any credit for having honest views or ethics. "It's fairly simple," he finally answered. "We can have law and order, or we can have anarchy. Those are the only two choices, and they are mutually exclusive. I believe in our constitution and in our laws. I've taken an oath to protect and defend the laws of this state and of this nation. How else can a city like San Francisco grow and prosper? Imagine a group of citizens taking the law into their own hands. Where will it lead? I intend to stop this madness!" Colbraith looked one final time at the endless stream of people congregating in front of Brannan's store, then left abruptly as Hal McAllister watched.

Colbraith told Dutch Charlie to stay there and help rescue Jenkins if it appeared possible. Colbraith grabbed Ira Cole by the arm and set off for Empire One. Colbraith knew one thing with astonishing clarity. If the committee intended to hang Jenkins, it would occur in one of two places—Brannan's building or at the plaza, and he banked on the plaza. Brannan liked the public light. He fed on it. Colbraith decided to assemble his men and wait for Brannan's committee at the plaza. If the hanging takes place inside Brannan's building or from his window, no one but God could save Jenkins.

—~—

"Do not let Captain Ray enter the premises," Brannan ordered the sergeant-at-arms. "The next time he tries to come in have him wait for me. Use your guile. Tell him you can't find me. Do whatever it takes, short of armed force, to keep him out. We need to buy time and keep him off balance."

Brannan returned to the room where the general committee had assembled and asked Selim to call it to order. The noisy throng became silent. Brannan briefed the members about Jenkins and the crime and explained that the executive committee would be organized as a court, with Brannan as chief judge. The rest of the executive committee would serve as associate judges. The trial of Jenkins would commence immediately and, if found guilty, his sentence would be carried out instantly. The judges would hear testimony and had already secured a score of eyewitnesses who saw Jenkins at Long Wharf. A jury made up from the general membership would listen to the testimony and render a verdict.

Selim ordered the sergeant-at-arms to clear the rooms of anyone not involved in the trial. About seventy men remained, making up the tribunal, the jury, and the guards. Brannan asked several witnesses to relate what they saw. Virgin testified. A sailor who managed to fish the safe out of the harbor testified. In less than thirty minutes Brannan was satisfied that Jenkins committed the crime for which he was charged. He directed the sergeant-at-arms to produce the defendant. Jenkins was brought down and told to sit in the witness chair. He chafed at the order and the burly guard shoved him roughly, forcing Jenkins to fall into the chair.

"Damn you!" he shouted.

"Keep quiet!" Brannan looked as if he would explode. "Such language will not be tolerated. Do you understand? I have no compunction about muzzling you."

Jenkins remained mute and just stared blankly at Brannan.

"Mr. Jenkins, you've been charged with stealing Mr. Virgin's safe. What have you got to say?"

"Not a goddamned word," Jenkins responded. "This is a turkey trial and I don't recognize the lot of you."

Gerrit Ryckman, his thick crop of shaggy hair flopping over his forehead, the only lawyer admitted as a member of the committee, whispered to Brannan and smiled confidently at Jenkins. Brannan nodded in acknowledgment.

"Mr. Ryckman has told us about this man's record. Perhaps he would share what he knows with Mr. Jenkins?"

"I don't know this man!" Jenkins yelled. "Where're my witnesses; they know me, not some idiot!"

Ryckman's face flushed beet red and Brannan put an arm to restrain Ryckman from going after the defendant. "Mr. Jenkins," Brannan said quickly, "your witnesses were brought here. They did not wish to come in. They said they did not know anyone by the name of John Jenkins. So much for your character witnesses."

"I didn't steal any safe!" Jenkins spoke calmly. Where's the safe I was supposed to have stolen?"

Ryckman smiled and pointed next to one of the tables. "Right there!"

Jenkins looked and saw the safe standing on the floor, a small puddle of water still leaking from it. A look of alarm briefly crossed his face.

"It was fished out just where you dropped it," Brannan told him, "in view of many witnesses."

"I don't know anything about that safe. And I don't care what you decide. I'll be going home tonight, or you'll all hang. I've got friends."

"That counts for absolutely nothing, here, Mr. Jenkins. If you don't have anything else to say, you're excused."

The guard grabbed Jenkins roughly and shoved him back toward the stairs. Jenkins uttered one profanity after another until someone or something smothered his voice. Only the muffled sounds of a shout remained.

By eleven o'clock the jury returned with the verdict: "Guilty as charged!" During the trial Selim doubled the guards and then redoubled them, especially after Captain Ray's second effort to enter the building. Unaccountably, Captain Ray had waited thirty minutes before trying to come in, and seemed reconciled to waiting longer as an effort to locate a missing Sam Brannan began again.

"What's your judgment on punishment?" Brannan asked. The judges hesitated, unable to come to grips with the inevitable sentence. Even Sam Brannan sat quietly thinking about it, his usual brusque and aggressive manner gone. The executive committee, finding itself face to face with exactly what they had set out to do, faltered for a moment. Suddenly William Howard rose, laid his revolver on the table, looked over the assembly and slowly said: "Gentlemen, as I understand it, we're here to hang somebody!"

Howard's statement served as an immediate catalyst. All indecision evaporated. The judges quickly agreed: "The prisoner should be hanged."

"When will we hang him?" Oakes asked.

"Right now!" Brannan growled. "The sooner the better. Let's get rid of him once and for all."

"I don't agree!" William Coleman's strong voice echoed through the chamber and all eyes turned to him. "To hang him at night, in such hot haste, would be to lay at our door an undeserved imputation of cowardice. Our judgments may be in secret, but our deeds should be visible in the broad light of day. Let this unfortunate man be held till morning, then hang him by the light of the rising sun in full view of our people."

"Good point," Selim said.

"No. It'd be too dangerous," Brannan interrupted. "It'll give his friends in Sydney Town too much time to organize his rescue."

"I agree with Sam," Ryckman said. "The sooner the better."

The judges agreed with Brannan and overruled Coleman's objections.

"Mr. Ryckman, would you inform Mr. Jenkins of our decision?"

Ryckman went into Brannan's office, where Jenkins sat on a chair, sporting a few new red marks on the side of his face. "The jury is in and the decision is final. You are to be hanged!"

"Bosh!" Jenkins said.

"Tell me truly, what is your name?" Ryckman asked.

"John Jenkins."

"Mr. Jenkins, so be it. You will die before daybreak."

"Go screw yourself and all these dung-eating judges. No, I'm not going to die," Jenkins laughed.

Ryckman ignored the remark and the laughter. "Have you any money or message to send your friends?"

"No."

"Do you wish me to write to anyone for you?"

"No."

"Can I do anything for you?"

"Sure. Bring me some brandy and a cigar."

Ryckman sent one of the guards to bring the brandy and cigar, which the man delivered shortly. While Ryckman waited Jenkins continued to look relaxed and carefree. He drank the brandy and asked for more, while he smoked the cigar with the air of a connoisseur and watched the blue smoke rise.

"Would you like a clergyman? And what denomination?"

"I don't need one," Jenkins puffed away.

"Mr. Jenkins," Ryckman spoke softly and deliberately. "Let me assure you, you're going to die in a few hours. Don't you want a chance to set things right with the Lord? You don't have much time."

"Well, if you insist," Jenkins laughed, "bring me an Episcopalian."

The Reverend Mr. Mines came immediately. Ryckman and the guards left the two men alone, but remained next to the door which they barred.

Nearly an hour passed and Brannan became impatient. "Where is the prisoner?" he demanded.

"Still with the good Reverend," Selim told him.

"Get Ryckman over here," Brannan called out.

Brannan, Ryckman, Selim and the other judges conferred and discussed their fear of a police rally. Brannan mentioned the possibility that Colbraith might come out as well, and Colonel Stevenson agreed completely with that assessment. Ryckman went back to the prisoner's room.

"Mr. Mines, you've now consumed three quarters of an hour, and I want you to bring this prayer business to a close. I'm going to hang this man in fifteen minutes."

Chapter Twenty-Three

In the meantime at Selim's suggestion Brannan and James Wadsworth went outside, and the crowd opened a passageway for them. Brannan ascended the mound of sand opposite the old Rassette House and explained to the large crowd how the courts and the law had failed the people of San Francisco. He warned the crowd about submission to such oppression and criminal rule. Brannan explained about the trial, the decision, and the clergyman's presence.

"Everything has been done according to the solemnity of this occasion. And now, tell me, does the action of the Committee of Vigilance meet with your approval?"

The response from the crowd was boisterous and mingled. Most agreed, others disagreed, a few asked who made up the committee while others shouted, "No names!" Brannan listened for a moment, then turned without further word and headed back into the building. Inside he told the executive committee that in his estimation most of the people agreed with their action—there were more ayes than nos. The next step, everyone in the room knew, was to hang Jenkins. But no one had ever hung a man before. They were merchants, not executioners. Brannan appointed William Coleman, Frederick Woodworth, and Gerrit Ryckman as a committee to determine the location and means of execution. The tenor had changed from seething anger, especially when Jenkins cussed and abused them, to one of resigned determination. William Howard's words remained: "We're here to hang somebody."

CHAPTER TWENTY-FOUR

The First Execution

SAN FRANCISCO
JUNE, 1851

Wednesday, June 11, 1851

AT HALF PAST ONE O'CLOCK IN THE MORNING, THE DOORS TO BRANNAN'S building burst open and a phalanx of armed men came out, marching four abreast. The men on the outside formed two lines, each holding long ropes. The two inner columns guarded the prisoner. Jenkins, his arms pinioned by two men nearly as large as him, a red handkerchief wrapped around his neck, walked calmly in the middle of the cavalcade. The diminutive George Ward, whose head barely reached Jenkins's chest, stood behind Jenkins, brandishing a revolver.

"If the police attempt to seize you, we'll blow your head off, sir!" Ward warned the prisoner and waved the gun. Jenkins ignored the smaller man.

Captain Ned Wakeman, placed in charge of the proceedings by Brannan and Selim, overheard Ward's remark. "Take that pistol away from that boy, or he'll hurt somebody!" he commented to no one in particular.

Bluxome tapped Jenkins on the shoulder and reiterated Ward's remarks. "If any attempt is made to take you out of our hands, at the first movement you make to escape, you die. That's my part of this night's program."

Ward chimed in: "if the police attempt to seize you, sir, we'll blow your head off, sir!"

Wakeman shook his head in dismay and moved the column forward. The California Engine Company bell tolled in the stillness of the night, joined by the Monumental Company bell, both maintaining the same tempo, tolling twice followed by a minute of silence. The column wound its way north on Sansome Street for two blocks, on to California, then Montgomery, moving like a mammoth centipede. The solemn death-knell of the California and Monumental Company bells continued, a mournful dirge echoing through the night. Room lights went on as drowsy men and women awoke, wondering, fearing, and uncertain about the meaning of the alarm. The trickle of people coming out of their lodgings became a torrent as more people poured into the streets and were swallowed by the tide.

As the committee's procession turned uphill on Clay, having covered the half mile to the plaza, it encountered its first opposition. Captain Ray and a squad of policemen stood at the corner of Clay and Kearney Streets. Ray walked into the middle of the intersection with his hand held high.

"Stop!" he yelled. "Give us the prisoner!"

"Keep marching, lads," Captain Wakemen enjoined his men. "Show your arms! Show them your damned weapons! Forward march!"

"I want my prisoner!" Captain Ray warned and leveled his revolver at the approaching column. His policemen formed a fan-like cordon around Ray, their weapons ready.

Some of the men in the column faltered, looking uncertainly at the police, forcing those behind them to slow down. Others marched ahead uncertainly, bumping or tripping into the men directly ahead of them. Wakeman turned and saw his stumbling cavalcade.

"I said keep your eyes forward and march!" Wakeman barked viciously.

Suddenly Captain Ray bolted toward the center of the stalling column in a frenzied effort to seize Jenkins. Thomas McCahill, a friend of Ray's, anticipated the charge and intercepted the police officer just as Ray reached the outside line. McCahill placed his gun to Ray's temple at about the same time six other men converged on Ray.

"Damn it, Ben, let it go," he whispered, then yelled: "Don't take another step or I'll blow your head off."

Ray grabbed hold of the rope, his dark eyes bound on Jenkins, who stood stone still.

"Ben, what the hell are you doing?" McCahill yelled into Ray's ears, his mouth only a few inches away. "They'll kill you!"

Another man now leveled a slingshot at Ray. "Give me the word," the man threatened, "and I'll drop him like a stone."

McCahill yanked Ray back. Ray's eyes blinked rapidly, beads of perspiration dripped down his forehead. He appeared bewildered by the mob's indifference to his rank or station. "I'll deal with him," McCahill told the others as he pulled Ray aside.

Other policemen made halfhearted efforts to secure the prisoner. One constable, Brian Blitz, lunged for Jenkins but someone struck his arm with a club, dislocating his shoulder. He fell back moaning, holding his useless arm. Hampton North, another constable tried to rescue Jenkins, but little Ward leveled a pistol at him. "I'll shoot you if you interfere!" North, too, withdrew. The other police officers appeared reluctant to enter the fray and the column regained some composure and marched clumsily into the plaza.

Colbraith, Dutch Charlie, Ira Cole, and a dozen other shoulder strikers, congregated near the liberty pole, a perfectly straight 110-foot Oregon fir donated by the people of Oregon to San Francisco in honor of California's statehood. A huge American flag and the California bear flag normally fluttered and snapped in the wind during the daylight hours. Not at two o'clock in the morning. Now the pole stood barren, ominously reaching upwards into the darkness, illuminated at the bottom by swaying and flickering light from hundreds of lanterns and torches. Colbraith and several other men placed a small cart near the post to give themselves a better vantage point. Since the liberty pole was the centerpiece and the highest point in the plaza, Colbraith reasoned the committee would try to hang Jenkins there. Colbraith could not have known that Coleman and Ryckman, sent by Brannan to select the execution site, had already dispensed with that notion. They did not want to despoil a monument to California's statehood by converting the liberty pole into a gallows. Still, the procession seemed headed toward it.

Colbraith saw the huge column bog down as the surging crowd of nearly two thousand, many carrying torches, screaming and jeering, pressed closer to get a better look at the condemned man.

"Ira," Colbraith commanded over the uproar. "They're almost at a standstill. Take some men and help Captain Harding over there," he pointed to a group of police officers slowly winding their way through the angry crowd toward Jenkins. "Officers Noyce and North are with him. There's Ray with some more men. Help them get Jenkins." From Colbraith's vantage point it almost looked like the police were swimming, their arms wheeling as they pulled themselves through the densely packed throng. Cole jumped off the cart and with about six shoulder-strikers waded into the crowd, pushing, shoving, and throwing fists and elbows to clear the way.

The vigilance committee's column had mired down. Its discipline had cracked, and it no longer resembled four rows of men marching in a Sunday parade. Instead it looked like a large misshapen herd of animals with no defined boundary. Colbraith saw Cole conferring with Harding. Then the men plunged ahead toward Jenkins.

Noyce and North got there first, ducked under the rope and thrust themselves into the thick of the armed men. Noyce reached and grabbed Jenkins, twisting the handcuffed man to the side. Suddenly someone jammed a pistol into Noyce's breast with enough force to crack one of his ribs. Stunned, Noyce shrank back.

"For God's sake, stop! Are you a Christian?" he cried out.

"I'll blow your heart out! Let go of the man!"

Noyce felt two more pistols thrust against him, one pressed at his temple, the other digging into the small of his back. He let Jenkins go. Colbraith could see Jenkins, in the hands of about thirty men, being rushed in the direction of the old adobe. He saw a group of men hold

North, but Cole and Harding pushed on, trying to keep up with Jenkins.

"They're heading for the adobe," Colbraith yelled to Dutch Charlie. Colbraith tried to figure out where they could hang the man in the old adobe. One of the last buildings from the days of Yerba Buena to survive the fires, it was a long, one-story structure built of adobe and roofed with tiles. Resting on a foundation four or five feet high, the building was surrounded by a wide porch or portico about three feet high, guarded by railings, and stretched around three sides of the building. The eaves projected as far as the outer edge of the portico forming a complete covering from the weather. Colbraith saw that a block and tackle was placed in the middle of the cross-beam that braced the porch roof. A group of men stood next to the rope which had been fed through the block and tackle. Colbraith instantly knew Jenkins's destination. They had little time remaining. Colbraith plunged into the crowd, followed by Dutch Charlie and the remainder of their men. Using their size the men bulled and pummeled their way through the crowd, knocking people aside or onto the ground. Colbraith kept his eye on Jenkins. The distance from the liberty pole to the adobe was only about forty yards and Captain Wakeman, at the lead of the committee's armed guards had reached the south porch. Colbraith doubled his efforts, ignoring the arms and fists hurled in his direction. Dutch Charlie smashed one man so hard the shattering jaw could be heard above the racket. Colbraith arrived at the adobe just as Captain Wakeman placed a noose around Jenkins's neck. Captain Ray, his spirits rekindled, had also blustered his way next to Jenkins. As Wakeman threw the noose over Jenkins's head, Ray leaped up in a desperate effort to intercept it. Half a dozen men wrestled him to the ground. Someone in the crowd with a booming voice incongruously yelled, "Napolean, come here, Napolean." Ira Cole and Captain Harding both reached Jenkins and despite all the threats and guns, inched closer to the prisoner.

"For God's sake," Jenkins was yelling, "take off my handkerchief."

Captain Harding started to untie the handkerchief as Cole struggled with the rope, but Jenkins's guards tugged the prisoner away, leaving the bright red handkerchief hanging loosely on his shoulders. The noose tightened around Jenkins's neck.

"Pull him up men!" Brannan called out.

Captain Wakeman also railed at his men: "String him up. Pull! Pull!"

"Heave it on!" Brannan exhorted the men.

About twenty-five men, led by Captain Wakeman and Frederick Woodworth, grabbed the rope and pulled as if they were engaged in tug-of-war or raising the mainsail on a schooner. The first wrench caused Jenkins to fall roughly to the ground. As the men pulled the rope Jenkins was dragged a few feet until he was directly under the beam. Then the pulley creaked loudly, almost like the crack of a gun, and his body leaped off the ground, kicking and squirming, until he was nearly fifteen feet in the air. His eyes bulged open in shock, his tongue protruded from his mouth. "You're committing murder!" someone yelled, but most of the people cheered as Jenkins kicked reflexively, at first large, awkward jerking kicks, as if his feet sought purchase, but after a minute the kicking subsided. The force of his exertions now caused his body to twist, first in one direction, until the rope groaned in protest, then back in the other direction.

"Get me a belaying pin," Captain Wakeman demanded, holding the end of the rope, but either no one around him knew what it was, or none could be produced. Instead Wakeman tied the rope to a nearby railing. The crowd fell silent as Jenkins continued to swing and turn slowly.

Colbraith watched in horrified amazement. Captains Harding and Ray tried to cut the rope, but several men, including the diminutive Ward, brandished their weapons and warned them not to do it. It was just a few minutes after two o'clock in the morning and the huge crowd, its blood-lust spent, watched in silence, then slowly began to disperse. Colbraith and his men huddled with the police.

"They won't even let us cut down the body," Captain Harding lamented while wiping a trickle of blood from his cut lip. "They want the body on public view as a warning to other criminals, Wakeman told me."

"That's a damned outrage!" Hal McAllister joined them. "They've hung the man, at least let him rest in peace."

"There'll be a coroner's inquest," Colbraith said. "Ned McGowan will be the judge. Brannan, Wakeman, Woodworth, and the others are going to pay for this." Ned McGowan was one of Colbraith's closest friends.

Chapter Twenty-Four

Jenkins's Hanging

"I don't know, Colbraith. I'd say most of the people out here supported them." Dutch Charlie rarely argued or disagreed with Colbraith. He was fearless. So his words had an ironic twist that caught Colbraith by surprise. But the others nodded their agreement.

"The most you can hope for, "McAllister offered, "is an inquest in which the truth is brought out. It may put pressure on your secret friends if they're publicly identified. After all, this was murder."

"Let's get the coroner out here at daybreak," Colbraith suggested. Although Captain Ray, as the most senior police officer served as chief of San Francisco's police, and already planned to do so, Colbraith took charge. No one, not even the chief of the city's police, questioned his authority. "He can start his investigation first thing," Colbraith continued. "I'll have a word with McGowan and make sure the inquest proceeds in absolute conformance with the letter of the law." Colbraith turned to Ray. "The police will have to provide the necessary protection for the court and the witnesses, with orders to shoot anyone who disrupts or interferes with the lawful process."

"What about Geary?" McAllister asked.

"What about him?" Colbraith barked. "You didn't see him around here tonight, did you? He'll take the easy way out and claim that he didn't know anything about the execution. He slept through the whole thing. Never heard the damned bells. I fear he has too many friends on the committee. It isn't politically advisable for him to act."

"What about you?" McAllister asked the same point Colbraith had briefly mulled while standing on the cart next to the liberty pole.

"I'll take my chances," Colbraith answered gruffly, and walked away.

DURING THE SECOND WEEK OF JUNE, MARY ELLEN, STILL LIVING IN Selim's house, felt the winds of change. Selim and Frederick, normally sanguine and cheerful, were tense, almost inhospitable. They came and went at all hours of the day and night, brought visitors for long discussions behind closed doors, and kept their own counsel. Mary Ellen made no effort to eavesdrop. She knew better. All the callers at Selim's house had that same determined and truculent manner. At mealtime Selim and Frederick ate sullenly, barely exchanging words with Mary Ellen, unlike their normal chats about social and political events. Selim even ignored Lessette upon whom he normally doted.

On Tuesday evening, before he left, Selim took Mary Ellen aside and gave her a stern warning. If she ever heard the bell from the California Engine Company or the Monumental Company ring twice, followed by a minute of silence, she and Lessette should remain inside the house and not venture outside—it was not a fire.

A few hours later the first bells sounded, followed an hour later by the second bell. Mary Ellen peeked out of the second floor window, looking into the darkness for some faint sign of a fire, flames, or even a distant glow. She could see people in the street below rushing in the direction of Bush and Sansome Streets where Selim told her he would be that evening. By midnight she heard the muffled sound of a mob, rising and falling like waves breaking on the sandy beach. Heeding Selim's advice Mary Ellen nestled with Lessette Flohr in the main salon, wondering what on earth could be taking place so late into the night.

Mary Ellen had little doubt that whatever was taking place in San Francisco involved the Sydney Ducks. She knew enough from Selim's previous meetings to understand the urgency many of the city's merchants attached to declaring war on these criminals. She also suspected that the secret society she heard about in Selim's meetings had to do with this war. She suddenly longed for Thomas and thought of rushing into the night to find him. He was not an Australian, but for the majority of Americans his Scottish accent would be enough to indict him; in the hands and minds of a mob, it could be fatal. Thomas, too, feared a mindless mob mistaking him for a Sydney Duck, fearing it more than anything else. Mary Ellen silently prayed that Thomas was safe.

Unable to sleep the two women kept each other company, trying to make sense of the growing roar, still garbled and dampened, but definitely ominous and frightening. The clamor seemed to shift its location, coming now from the direction of the plaza, where a faint glow appeared. Lessette seemed on the verge of panic protesting that another fire had started, but Mary Ellen did not think so. Cool and collected she told Lessette that something big was taking place at the plaza and the glow probably came from hundreds of torches, perhaps even bonfires. Still, Mary Ellen shuddered at the menacing drone. At a quarter past two o'clock in the morning, the sound suddenly subsided. The two looked at each other questioningly, relieved, yet alarmed by the abrupt stillness.

"Can I sleep in your bed tonight?" Lessette asked timorously.

"Of course you can," Mary Ellen answered, thankful for the company. The two women headed to Mary Ellen's room and lay quietly on top of the bedspread trying to sort things out, Lessette curled in a fetal position. After a few minutes Mary Ellen felt sleep coming and was about to doze off when she heard the front door open. She sat up, completely alert, her heart racing. Lessette, remained curled, but started to sob quietly. Mary Ellen put her arms around her.

"Be quiet, Lessette," she whispered. "Stay here a moment."

"Don't leave me," Lessette reached out and held Mary Ellen's hand tightly.

"Shush," Mary Ellen said gently. "I'm just going to the door to listen."

Mary Ellen pulled her hand away and tiptoed over the creaky floorboards to the door. She opened it just a bit and listened. She recognized Selim's voice; normally it would have been comforting, this time it had the opposite effect.

The men settled in the main salon. She could hear the clink of crystal and assumed that Selim or Frederick was pouring drinks.

"Well, we've gone and done it," Selim said.

"About time!" Brannan's thick voice chimed in. "I propose a toast. Here's to taking our city back!"

"Hear, hear," Frederick and several other men said.

A short pause ensued, and Mary Ellen strained even harder to hear.

"You know they're going to bring in the coroner in the morning," a familiar voice said, but Mary Ellen could not place it.

"Are we going to give the body to him?" Frederick asked.

"Why not? He's dead, isn't he?" Brannan replied.

"Don't we want him to hang there for a day as a lesson to the others?" the familiar voice went on.

"Colonel Stevenson, you were there. There must have been two, maybe three thousand people in the plaza. I think by now the word's out, and everyone in San Francisco knows what happened," Brannan said abruptly, somewhat impatiently.

"He's right, Jon," Selim agreed. "There's no need to keep him dangling any longer. Let's give up the body."

"What about an inquest?" another voice, a complete stranger to Mary Ellen, asked. "You realize, of course, that one will be held."

"So? What's your point?" Brannan snapped.

"O'Brien . . ."

Chapter Twenty-Four

"Did you see that bastard? His men almost got Jenkins," Frederick interrupted.

"O'Brien," the voice continued firmly, "will work with the police and with the courts. You can be sure an inquisition will be held, and names will be mentioned."

"I don't think so," Brannan replied heatedly. "No one will dare mention names. Or so help me . . . "

"Or so help you what? Hang somebody who's a witness? Is that where we are going?"

"No, George," Selim tried to conciliate Oakes. "We aren't going to hang anyone who hasn't committed a crime."

"George is right," Colonel Stevenson intoned. "What are we going to say at the inquest? Ned McGowan will be the judge. He's O'Brien's man. Witnesses will be called. Does anyone here think O'Brien will have any hesitation saying what he saw, or naming names?"

The room grew silent.

"So what do we do?" Selim raised the question.

"If one person is named, let's go to the *Alta* and name everyone in the committee," the unfamiliar voice suggested. "We could give them over 150 names. Think about it. What would O'Brien do? What would the courts do? What could they do? Arrest every respectable merchant in the city? I think not. Let's go public. Let's publicize our constitution, our bylaws and our actions. In numbers we have protection."

"I think Ryckman is right," Frederick said. "If anyone's named, let's put out a list that'll give them more than a slight pause. It'll blow them right out of the coroner's court. Mayor Geary won't do anything. The aldermen will remain silent."

"I'll call for the general committee to convene tomorrow evening," Selim told the men. "We'll put it to a vote. We need everyone's approval. Anyone who doesn't want his name in the paper should be allowed to withdraw."

Mary Ellen listened intently as the men spoke of the trial and the execution. Some of the men, she heard, thought Jenkins died like a man, and respected his courage. Others thought he died like the vermin he was, and should receive no further thought. She closed the door carefully and returned to her bed. Lessette looked up and Mary Ellen smiled back comfortingly. She thought of Thomas and a pang of fear pierced her racing heart.

—~—

AT SEVEN O'CLOCK IN THE MORNING THE CORONER ARRIVED AT THE plaza with several policemen. Jenkins's body remained perfectly still in the early morning calm. A few men lingered near the adobe, looking silently at the corpse. Several Committee of Vigilance guards squatted on the ground near the porch. They still carried their revolvers, but looked at ease and relaxed, not as tense or high-strung as the night before. Apparently no longer feeling physically threatened, they remained on duty to prevent Jenkins's family or friends from removing the body. Ward, one of the guards, saw the coroner and sprang to his feet.

"Hold on, now, sir. If you try to remove the body I'll shoot you."

Captain Harding ignored the threat. He walked up to Ward and without a single word shoved the small man aside. Ward's revolver went spinning into the dirt. "If you point that gun at me once more I'm going to shove it up your ass, you little shit," Wakeman snapped.

Ward hesitated, but there were now more policemen than guards, so Ward sullenly dusted himself off and backed away.

"Let's get the body down and take it to the city hall yard," the coroner intoned.

The men unfastened the rope and brought the body down carefully. The coroner removed the noose and examined the neck.

"His neck doesn't appear to be broken. Probably died of strangulation."

Captain Ray checked Jenkins's coat and found $218 in one pocket. The coroner's wagon arrived and carted the corpse away, letting the plaza return to a semblance of normalcy. Someone had already raised the American and California flags on the liberty pole.

Colbraith, worked through the night and into the morning to get the authorities to convene the coroner's inquest. He prodded and cajoled, and

Chapter Twenty-Four

by one o'clock in the afternoon the coroner's inquest began in Judge McGowan's court. After McGowan impaneled a jury, the twelve men went to the dead-house in the city hall yard, where the coroner explained his findings, examining the body in front of the curious men. When the coroner finished, the jury returned to the courtroom to hear testimony about the execution. Using a list compiled by Colbraith, his men, and by the police, the coroner called Colbraith, Ira Cole, Hal McAllister, Brannan, Frederick Woodworth, and other witnesses to the stand. Captains Harding and Ray testified. Officers Noyce, North, and Blitz told their stories reluctantly.

Jenkins's execution had a sobering effect on the witnesses. Almost every witness seemed disinclined to name names or to state exactly what he saw. Even the police appeared reticent, unsure just how far the committee would go to exact vengeance from hostile witnesses. Those who participated in the execution, including Frederick Woodworth, Captain Wakeman, James Ward and other committee members who were prominent in the plaza, testified tersely, giving the court little relevant information. Even Mayor Geary tried to weasel his way out of controversy. He testified that he heard the Monumental bell ringing, and as foreman of Monumental, went to the engine house and when he learned there was no fire simply told the man ringing the bell to stop. Then he went back to bed, he said.

Frederick Woodworth testified honestly. He admitted that the witnesses named by the coroner constituted a small segment of the Committee of Vigilance and that Jenkins died at the hands of the committee. But he took exception to the charge of murder, arguing heatedly that Jenkins had a full and fair trial, as fair as any he had ever seen, and that Jenkins was tried, condemned, and executed for burglary. Judge McGowan, asked Frederick whether he saw the execution.

"Your honor," Frederick said proudly, "I was present during the whole proceeding."

Unlike Frederick Woodworth, Brannan danced and skirted the damning questions. Judge McGowan slammed his gavel several times trying to rein in Brannan's testimony. It did not work. But when the judge asked Brannan about the committee's goals, Brannan suddenly became loquacious. He smiled for the first time. "The declared object of our committee," he told the judge, "is to be constantly on duty to protect the lives and property of our fellow citizens, to see that they are not troubled by burglars, incendiaries, and murderers, and to arrest and punish promptly parties caught in the act."

Brannan continued to use the courtroom as a forum to espouse his view of the committee and its actions. Colbraith listened to Brannan's testimony from McGowan's chamber with Wilkes and Sullivan. As a witness Colbraith was not allowed to sit in the inquest, but McGowan's clerk arranged for Colbraith's group to remain in the judge's chamber, next door to the courtroom. Colbraith wanted McGowan to get Brannan off the witness stand. Brannan knew how to stir emotions. The newspapers would give a word-for-word account of his testimony and by the end of the week, Colbraith imagined, the ranks of this secret organization would swell into the high hundreds, if not thousands. For the first time his confidence flagged a bit as he realized how much power Brannan and the committee wielded. It would get worse before it got better. Above all else he had to weather the storm.

While Colbraith and McGowan conferred through the night, Selim met with the editors of the city's three leading newspapers. The next morning's editorials called for a public meeting to be held at one o'clock in the afternoon in the plaza. The papers suggested that such a meeting would help the people of San Francisco understand what had happened and what course of action should be taken. At breakfast, Selim and Frederick ate heartily, their spirits light for the first time in weeks. They acknowledged Mary Ellen and Lessette and even engaged in some banalities. They did not discuss the night's events, but Selim noted Mary Ellen's uneasiness. As if to allay her concerns, Selim suggested that she might attend the afternoon's meeting at the plaza, where many of her questions would be answered.

Thomas arrived at Selim's house shortly before noon, excited and nervous. Mary Ellen was relieved to see him. He told Mary Ellen and Lessette about Jenkins's execution. The two women were fascinated and scared. Lessette fired question after question at Thomas who answered as well as he could. Finally, exhausted, he suggested they have lunch at the Union Hotel. As they walked to the hotel they could see and feel the air of disquietude and agitation. The city was abuzz with rumors about the previous night's events. Everyone seemed preoccupied with the execution. People talked about it on the streets, in stores, and in the restaurants. Throughout lunch Mary Ellen could hear snippets of conversation at the other tables—all relating to Jenkins or the committee. Newspapers carried articles about the hanging, applauding the action of the committee and calling for public support. After lunch Mary Ellen, Lessette, and Thomas walked to the plaza where a large crowd had already gathered.

Captain John Hutton stood at a table and chaired the public meeting. He thanked those assembled for coming, and without any preamble launched into a speech about the execution: "Normally I am a law-abiding citizen, but I consider the Lynch law as the only law adequate to protect our lives in this city." Hutton was interrupted by loud cheering and applause. He continued with his speech, detailing Jenkins's history of crime and the efforts the committee made to provide him with a fair trial. A man standing near Hutton offered a motion to sanction the action of the Committee of Vigilance and the people who participated in hanging Jenkins. Hutton asked the crowd to vote. First, those supporting the motion. A unanimous shout of "yes" echoed through the plaza, as people laughed and hooted; it had all the earmarks of a festival. Hutton smiled, nodded to the man who made the motion, and asked if anyone opposed the motion.

"No!" a single voice rang out.

"That's Howard Clarke," Thomas whispered to Mary Ellen. "He's a good man. I've done business with him."

This lone "no" stunned the crowd into a momentary silence. Mary Ellen could feel the stir of anger and hostility. It extinguished the flames of festivity like a blanket thrown over a fire. Then the indignant crowd turned surly, hissing and groaning. "Put him out!" one person yelled. Unfazed, Clarke mounted the balcony and said: "Almost alone I said 'no'! This meeting was called to sanction cold-blooded murder . . . "

The yelling and shouting forced Clarke to stop. He tried several times to continue, but finally gave up in disgust.

"Lynch him!" voices rang out in the crowd. A few people closest to Clarke seized him and hustled him into the midst of the unruly mob. Someone held a noose in the air, the other end of the rope disappearing in a wall of people. Clarke went sprawling to the ground as a number of men punched and kicked him. Others intervened and hauled him to his feet. The two groups began to argue, while Captain Hutton, losing control of the mob, declared the meeting adjourned. He announced hastily that the Committee of Vigilance would meet that evening and anyone interested in joining should apply.

But part of the crowd hovered around Clarke who was bleeding, his coat torn to shreds. Thomas started to go to the aid of his friend, but Mary Ellen held him back. Clarke brushed himself off, pulling his arms free. He straightened and walked slowly out of the plaza to his room, followed by several dozen men cursing and spitting at him. He barely managed to enter his building and close the door behind him.

Thomas, Mary Ellen, and Lessette followed the crowd and felt relieved when Clarke disappeared behind the closed door.

"Oh, my God!" Thomas said, and pointed to the second story, where Clarke now stood near his window, staring truculently at the boisterous crowd.

"What is he thinking? He could be shot," Thomas lamented.

But the unruly crowd satisfied itself by yelling and jeering, ignoring the isolated calls to lynch him. Clarke remained at the window looking scared but defiant, almost recklessly daring the mob to attack.

"I'm really frightened about the future," Thomas said softly to the two women. "Look what they did to Clarke, an innocent man simply expressing his opinion, an inalienable right under our Constitution. He's not a criminal but the mob almost tore him to pieces. Where were the authorities? Who's next? How many people will die, lynched by this secret society, before this is over?"

Mary Ellen leaned into Thomas. She lightly pressed her lips against his ear.

"It isn't safe for you right now. I think you should go away until things settle down."

He whipped around to face her. "That's what I feared." Thomas took her hand. "Oh, my bonnie." But his words were barely audible.

Book Four

1853

Chapter Twenty-Five

The Secret Revealed

San Francisco
1853

Selim Woodworth, returning to his house for lunch, brought Mary Ellen news of the arrival of the *Eustace.* It meant Thomas had finally returned from his voyage to Santa Barbara and Santa Cruz Island. Mary Ellen dabbed at her food with her fork, moving some rice from one side of her plate to another, and engaged in light conversation with Lessette and Selim, but she was not hungry. She had not been hungry for more than a week. Nothing looked appetizing. She attributed her aversion to food, even foods she normally craved, to the distance between her and Thomas. She missed him terribly. The prospect of seeing Thomas, though, made her smile inwardly but raised some troubling questions. He would undoubtedly be waiting for her at the *Niantic* once he finished his ship-board duties.

They had converted the old captain's cabin in the hull into a small office. She could picture Thomas reviewing his correspondence, writing letters, checking his gold watch for the time, then impatiently pacing back and forth, waiting for her to arrive. This was their ritual whenever

Thomas returned from one of his lengthy trips. But this time Mary Ellen felt a shudder of trepidation at the thought of seeing Thomas.

She glanced at her reflection in the oval mirror as she brushed her hair. Her face appeared more mature, but she could not tell why. Perhaps her cheeks had filled out a bit, enough to give her face a softer, more rounded appearance. Her eyes, one green, the other brown, stared back at her, as if the image in the mirror was a stranger. She regarded herself uneasily, and almost turned away. Even after so many years an awkward feeling would ripple down her spine every time she saw her eyes. As a child Mary Ellen supposed that people who refused to look you in the eye had something to hide, as if the eyes were a gateway, two round and distinct portals, to the soul. She believed that even a stranger peering into one's eyes, might catch a glimpse of some hidden secret, so the inclination to look away seemed reasonable. As she turned away from her own image she wondered if her eyes reflected two different souls, each discrete, each contrasting. Maybe that was why people were so afraid to look her in the eye; they had never been confronted with a window to two different souls, and this terrified them.

She still lived in Selim's house, though she no longer shared a room with Lessette. The temporary accommodations provided by Selim after the fire in 1851 turned into a permanent arrangement, which suited Mary Ellen quite well. She ran the household, but as time passed Lessette took over more of the chores and responsibilities, leaving Mary Ellen with more time to attend to her burgeoning business ventures and the Underground Railroad. Lessette was Mary Ellen's best friend outside of Thomas. Lessette regarded Mary Ellen as an angel; someone who saved her life when it was at its lowest ebb. Her sense of gratitude for all that Mary Ellen had done did not abate with the passage of time. Their friendship blossomed. Lessette became the only woman Mary Ellen trusted completely. Other than Thomas, Gordon, William Widmore, and to a lesser extent the Woodworth brothers, Mary Ellen kept her distance from others and her trust to herself. Mary Ellen kept her own counsel. She knew one thing with an uncanny certainty: even the best-intentioned people, warm and generous friends in good times, changed under stress and failure. The extent of change, Mary Ellen knew, was directly proportional to fear and suffering.

Chapter Twenty-Five

She recalled Mr. Williams in Cincinnati gracious and compassionate at the beginning, turning viciously against her when it affected his business. She did not want to place her life or her future in anyone else's hands so she worked hard to make herself independent, financially and socially.

Her confidence was briefly shaken by the fires of 1851 and the Vigilance Committee. But her worst fears, that the flames would leave her destitute, never materialized. On the contrary, 1851 produced some of her greatest successes, milestones toward a small but secure financial domain. The cash flowed in a steady and rising stream. The value of her holdings from the rebuilt laundries and livery, to the new Atheneum and other investments, continued to grow and multiply to the point where she could now sit back, even retire if she wished, and not have a financial worry for the rest of her life. She knew people in similar circumstances who did just that—rested on their laurels, content with the financial comfort that good times brought them. But Mary Ellen did not indulge herself. She did not intend to trust her future to good times, any more than she would place her future into anyone's hands. Optimistic by nature, she was absolutely pragmatic. Life, she knew, was made of cycles in which good periods alternated with bad ones. Anyone who failed to understand this basic premise, this circle of life, was doomed to failure. She knew how quickly one could fall from grace. She remembered Cincinnati as if it were yesterday. No, Mary Ellen did not feel all that sanguine despite her good fortunes.

After lunch she returned to her room feeling a bit nauseous. She sat down, brushed her hair back, tied it ponytail fashion, and used the special pomade that Gordon taught her to use so many years ago. Satisfied with her appearance, she donned a hat to make sure her hair was well-hidden from view. It was an obsession, born of fear of being discovered, a fear that hovered only skin deep. Her eyes were unusual, but revealed nothing about her past. The texture of her hair, a trifle crinkly for her taste, might reveal her breeding. With success came exposure, and with exposure the possibility of being recognized by someone hailing from the South. It was not a rational fear, she knew, but she was scared nonetheless. The fear caused her to undergo a daily self-examination to make sure she could pass. Even in Thomas's absence, she was resolute in her efforts to look and appear "proper."

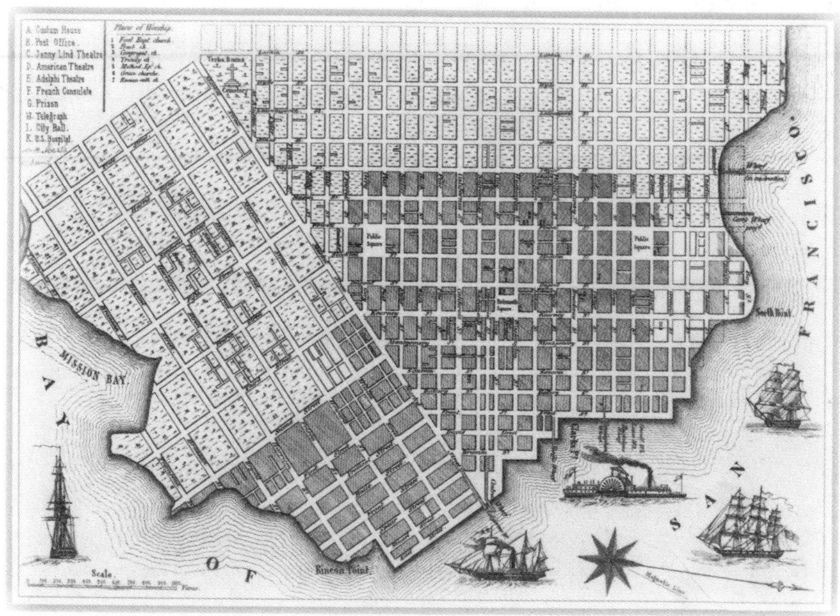

Streets of San Francisco

~1853~

Thomas's involvement with Alexander Forbes and the Barrons, Eustace and William, overseeing their holdings, especially Santa Cruz Island, and supervising the operations of New Almadein, their quicksilver mine, forced him to leave San Francisco for extended trips. He traveled to Santa Barbara to help the Forbes and Barrons build a house and other facilities on Santa Cruz Island. During his absence, and particularly in the previous week, Mary Ellen arrived at a critical decision: to tell him the truth about herself. It was a monumental gamble. And once she made up her mind she remained steadfast in her determination to be completely open and honest with him. But as the time for his anticipated return to San Francisco neared, she wavered. She was so nervous, so apprehensive, that not only could she not eat, she broke into a terrible rash on her face and her stomach. The blisters itched constantly and would not go away until Norman Ah-sing sent her a Chinese doctor who prescribed some herbal unguent that cleared the rash in one day.

Prior to his departure, Thomas bought a new house at 606 Stockton Street from an estate being administered by his attorney, Henry Halleck. It was a lovely cottage on a large one-hundred-vara lot. A few days before his departure, Thomas asked Mary Ellen to join him and live in the house. She declined. Thomas was disappointed, but not overly so. He misunderstood her reticence and assumed that it arose mostly from her sense of propriety and to a lesser extent her loyalty to the Woodworths. But her rebuff had nothing to do with either, not social decorum or her relationship with the Woodworths. Although she cared deeply for the Woodworths, she would have accepted Thomas's invitation in an instant. Mary Ellen's reservations arose from several sources. The ever-present dread, those fears that the baggage she carried from her past would be opened unexpectedly, remained deeply rooted. Thomas did not have a clue about her antecedents and Mary Ellen did not know how he would react if he learned she was not completely white. She was not prepared emotionally for a rejection and did not want to be living with Thomas if he chose to spurn her.

But she also had another reason, one less certain but possibly more suffocating, depending on the outcome. She had missed her last two menstrual cycles. Mary Ellen had little doubt Thomas loved her. It was evident in everything he did for her, the way he touched her, the softness with which he regarded her. He was a sensitive and caring man. But she constantly asked herself if his love was strong enough to endure, to overcome the enormous mantle of prejudice which society had ingrained in him or, if her truth were discovered, would place on both of them. It would destroy many of his social and business relationships, most importantly the ones he had forged over the years with Forbes and Barron. Word would spread like wildfire through San Francisco, and she could not be certain how even her closest associates, like the Woodworths, would react. And the possibility that she was carrying his child complicated everything.

Mary Ellen was financially secure. After all, she and Thomas had amassed enough assets to assure both of them a comfortable life, though many of their assets were in his name. But she did not know if she could survive a rejection emotionally. Moreover, the political climate of 1849 and 1850, when the population was in a state of flux with people deserting for the gold fields, and survival was the order of the day, had changed dramatically. San Francisco had matured with a more stable, cosmopolitan, and biased population. Control of the legislature by Chivalry, the pro-Southern wing of the Democratic Party, brought about a hardening of anti-black sentiments throughout the state. San Francisco was no exception. The national debate on slavery, the influx of so many Chinese, the ongoing battles with Indian tribes, all contributed to higher levels of bigotry in San Francisco's society. The sanguine and laissez-faire attitudes of the city's population in 1849 and 1850 had been replaced by a more structured, socially conscious, prejudiced and wealthier society.

Mary Ellen shuddered involuntarily at the prospect of presenting Thomas with his child. What color would the child be? Raven black like her own mother, or white with reddish hair like her father? Perhaps something in between. How would Thomas react if he peeked into the tiny blanketed bundle and found a baby with dark skin? These thoughts swirled through her mind like a series of unrelenting squalls. And the possibility that she was carrying Thomas's child compelled her to do the one thing she dreaded the most.

It was a windy day with heavy gray clouds scudding rapidly across the sky. Although Mary Ellen wanted to go directly to the *Niantic,* she first had an appointment with an attorney. She held her hat in place as she walked the few blocks to his office. It had not rained in weeks so the wind swirled little eddies of dust and Mary Ellen closed her eyes to avoid the annoying particles. Her attorney had some legal documents for her to sign. The New Atheneum, her hurdy-gurdy saloon, was so successful she now embarked upon a bolder venture, one she would not have dared attempt or even consider just a year earlier. The cold wind chilled her as she turned on Montgomery Street. Small whitecaps dotted the gray water in the bay. Ships with tall masts swayed back and forth and rocked up and down on the billowing sea. Mary Ellen tucked her chin and walked more briskly. Her clever attorney made sure her name would not appear on any document relating to the new business. At her urging he set up several layers of nominee holdings. He issued stock to these nominees who endorsed the certificates in blank, and without any dates. Mary Ellen would hold these certificates in safekeeping and, when necessary, transfer ownership by simply filling in a new name in the blank endorsement. Her attorney even arranged for title to the property to be held by a third party. These arrangements involved some risk, but it was worth it. Such elaborate measures were necessary to protect her and Thomas.

"Good day, Mis' Price," a colored person doffed his hat as he went by. It startled her. She turned around as the man continued down the street. She did not recognize him, but that did not matter. She smuggled so many Negroes to San Francisco from the eastern states that she could no longer keep track of all of them. Gordon and Widmore did it for her. They all knew who she was. She wanted to do more, to smuggle more men and women out of the South, but the enactment of the Fugitive Slave Law by the California Legislature in 1852, brought her operations to a halt.

Sponsored by Chivalry the act sailed through the senate and the assembly almost unopposed. Only Colbraith, fighting with a lion's heart, voted against it. Standing like a lone sentinel, unwilling to give up, Colbraith used every parliamentary ruse to table the law or send it from one committee to the next. In the end he was overwhelmed by its supporters. Strange, Mary Ellen thought, that such a cold and rough fish like Colbraith, would end up being the only man with enough guts to fight for the rights of all men. It gave her another view of the man she had grown to detest. But in the end he failed and the law came into being.

It was a frightening law. Under it a colored man or woman could be brought before a magistrate, claimed by someone as a fugitive slave, and not be allowed to testify in their own defense. Even their Negro friends could not testify on their behalf since Negroes had no right to testify in California's courts of law. Unless a white person could be found to help the alleged fugitive, the man was sunk. In the absence of any testimony to the contrary, the magistrate would be left with no alternative but to issue a certificate to the claimant confirming his right of ownership. Anyone assisting the fugitive was liable to the claimant for $500 or imprisonment for two months. All the slaves who escaped and came to California before it was admitted as a state, were automatically fugitives under this law. Even Mary Ellen had good reason to be afraid of this legislation. At the same time it steeled her, and made her more determined to fight for the rights of her people. One of her first acts was to double the amount of money she sent to her eastern abolitionist friends. She and John Brown corresponded irregularly, but she offered to supply him with more funds and to support all his efforts.

At the lawyer's office she reviewed the documents he drafted. They were in order as far as she could tell. After approving the final documentation she thanked her counsel, then headed directly to James King of Wm. & Co., a small, but discreet, banking house, owned jointly by Jacob Snyder and James King of William. And they were discreet. She did not explain what she had purchased, only how they were to dispense the funds.

Part of the money was dedicated to the purchase of a house on Washington Street. Mary Ellen had grand plans to remodel the exterior in the style of New Orleans, with wrought iron balconies, shutters, and brick siding. Thoughts of Marie Laveau's house in New Orleans were never far off. Lush tropical foliage in the grand fashion of Louisiana would carry visitors to a different place and time. Inside, the house would be sumptuously and elegantly furnished, with the best money could buy. Mary Ellen had no intention of rushing the construction. It had to be perfect in every detail. The house would only cater to the finest clientele—the most powerful and richest men in California. But until it opened for business, its use would be a closely kept secret. Even the laborers employed in the renovation would remain ignorant. Everything had to be discreet, with as little publicity as possible. Mary Ellen incorporated a hidden closet into the design, with a built-in sofa. She decided to have Gordon hire Mifflin Gibbs to build the closet. As Snyder completed the necessary bank drafts and made the final arrangement to transfer funds, the whole enterprise struck Mary Ellen as audacious but exciting. She shuddered in anticipation, for it was one very risky undertaking. The rewards were well worth the risk, or so she thought.

Finished with the bank she headed down the planked sidewalk straight for the *Niantic,* her heart beating furiously. The flag atop the tall pole cracked in the wind. It towered over all the adjacent buildings, even the new brick structures built after the last fire. The *Niantic* had not changed. Still in Bristol condition, the white hotel stood out against the gray sky, and the dark, newly painted hull looked durable and solid.

Mary Ellen climbed the stairway and wound her way through the corridors of the hotel down to the office. She knocked on the cabin door and entered. Thomas was sitting at the table poring over some letters, his jacket thrown carelessly over the back of his chair. He glanced up and broke into a broad smile. "Mary Ellen," he leaped up and hugged her, sweeping her off her feet. "Where have you been? I was getting worried."

"I'm sorry darling," she said, "but I was attending to some business. It took longer than I expected." He felt and smelled good.

"I thought you might not have gotten word about my arrival," he kissed her cheek and brushed the side of his face against hers. He put her down gently and rushed over to his coat. He fumbled through the pockets and produced a small black-lacquered box with intricate inlaid shells and handed it to her, his face beaming.

"What's this?" she asked.

"Go ahead, open it!" he said anxiously.

She opened the box carefully and gasped at its contents. Two dazzling diamond earrings sparkled in the light. The diamonds were oval-shaped and set in an intricate silver base.

"Oh, my God," she said. "These are beautiful."

"I tried to find something I thought would compete with your beauty, but now I see that they're flawed when compared to you," he said.

"Bosh," she replied. "This is exquisite." She put the earrings on, using a small mirror on the vestibule behind the desk. She turned her head from side to side, admiring the gleaming gems. "Thank you so much," she whispered. Thomas came behind her and hugged her as she continued to gaze into the mirror. Slowly Thomas moved his hand and cupped her breast softly. Mary Ellen twisted slightly as a shot of lightning ran through her body.

She turned and kissed him fully on the lips, her tongue playing softly with his, touching, twisting, pressing. He returned her kiss with unexpected hunger and passion. She felt exhilarated and aroused. Then her decision to talk about her past crept into the back of her mind. Reluctantly she gently pushed away from him. Thomas was puzzled by the sudden change. Mary Ellen gathered herself and stepped away from him.

"Tell me about your trip," she said lightly, unable to meet his gaze.

Thomas arched his brow and went back to the desk. "It was fine. Eustace wants to start a winery on the island. You should see how beautiful it is. Whales and dolphins frolic in the blue waters. The ocean teems with life. The weather is much milder than here. Still, all in all, I'd rather be stuck in the desert or at the equator with you."

"No you wouldn't," she smiled, a painful, shy smile. "I mean it may be a better place to live," she forced a laugh.

"There are worse places," Thomas admitted, but looked at her curiously, as if seeing her for the first time and sensing that not all was well.

"Thomas," she said reticently, "we need to talk."

Thomas looked surprised and apprehensive. "That sounds very ominous," he said.

"I'm serious," she said and absentmindedly touched the new earrings. "I love you more than anything on earth. We have a lovely relationship . . . "

"Oh, that sounds even more portentous," he sounded lighthearted, but Mary Ellen could see that he was trying to cover up his uneasiness at the turn of their conversation.

"I don't know how to tell you this, but I feel as if our relationship, as wonderful as it is, is not based on complete honesty between us. We must be brutally honest with each other if our relationship is to grow as I want it to grow. Don't you agree?"

"I guess so, but what is it you're concerned about?"

"Neither of us has spoken of our past, as if we had to hide something from each other. I've known you for more than three years. Do you understand?"

Thomas stiffened noticeably and started to pace back and forth nervously.

"I would like to share with you, to be open and forthcoming. Our bond would be that much stronger."

"I see," he finally said. "You're right," he wiped his sweaty forehead and walked back to Mary Ellen. He held her hands and his eyes looked sorrowful. "I'm really sorry I haven't told you. I should have, but I was afraid. I hope you'll forgive me," he looked at her, his eyes pleading.

"No, you don't understand," Mary Ellen began to protest, trying to explain that she had something to tell him, that she wanted to unburden herself.

"Please, Mary Ellen," he put his finger against her lips. "Don't say another word. Hear me out. You've always been the stronger of the two of us, and I thank you for forcing me to do what I should have done long ago. Please sit down, and let me tell you." Thomas guided Mary Ellen to the chair. She sat down uncertainly and listened to Thomas.

"This is my story . . . " Thomas began awkwardly, fumbling for words. "I left Scotland under a cloud," his jaw tightened as if he was in an inner struggle with himself. "I first came to San Francisco in 1845," he continued slowly, hesitantly, clearly uncomfortable. "Of course it was known, then, as Yerba Buena."

Mary Ellen could barely keep the astonishment from her face.

"It was a small pueblo. Just a few hundred people. But it was far enough from Scotland to suit my purposes." Thomas looked at Mary Ellen questioningly then lowered his gaze. She had a thousand questions, but she wanted to encourage him to continue, so she smiled benignly and remained quiet.

"A few months after I arrived we heard that the United States intended to seize California. You can't imagine the agitation, the consternation of the people. We also heard that Castro was organizing an army in Mexico to expel all foreigners and execute anyone who resisted. I was scared. So I hopped a whaler, disembarked in Mazatlan and made my way to Mexico City. I didn't speak Spanish very well, but I found employment with a British company at Tepic. It was owned by Eustace Barron and Alexander Forbes. They manufactured cotton goods. I got along splendidly with Alexander. They never questioned why I left Scotland. I also became good friends with William Barron, Eustace's nephew, and James Bolton. I spent most of my time in Mazatlan where Bolton happened to be the acting consul. Up to this point Forbes and Barron owned cotton mills, a plant, and engaged in trading goods.

"One day Bolton, acting for his employer, offered to sell Forbes part of a quicksilver mine . . . "

"New Almadein?" Mary Ellen found herself drawn into his story.

"Yes. Forbes already owned four shares which he bought from Castro himself who gave up the plan to defend California and sought to unload his California interests. Anyway, Forbes bought Castro's interest more out of political necessity, to appease Castro, than for investment. Bolton, who worked for a chap called de la Torre, went to California to study the mine. Forbes knew about quicksilver from his experiences in Peru where it was used in gold recovery. But Forbes had ideas on how to use it more efficiently and make it more valuable. So Forbes paid Bolton under the table to prepare a report favorable to his position and ended up buying de la Torre's interest in New Almadein."

Thomas stopped for a moment, walked to the window and looked outside as if he could see the past. Mary Ellen poured both of them some coffee and took the cup to Thomas. She wanted to know what Thomas had done in Scotland that found him half way around the globe and afraid to return, but he still did not seem inclined to tell her. Thomas thanked her for the coffee, absentmindedly nodding, but kept his gaze on the blue sky and the deep past. He took a sip and continued.

"I thought Forbes knew about my problems in Scotland, but he didn't. He hired me because I was close-mouthed and discreet. It turns out Forbes had lived in Peru in the early twenties, when Simon Bolivar led a successful revolution in Venezuela. The Spanish knew it was just a matter of time before Peru would fall. Then Ecuador fell. Panic struck the wealthy families. They had millions in gold and silver. Rumors about pillaging in Ecuador spread through Lima. These rumors were unfounded, but the wealthy families, including French and British merchants decided to leave. They loaded ships with bullion and sent them off. Unfortunately they employed ships manned by captains and crews who could not resist temptation. Avarice took over. The captains turned into pirates and stole the treasures from their owners."

Thomas started to laugh, a dark, mirthless laugh, then shook his head in dismay. He turned to Mary Ellen. "I can't believe I'm telling you all this. But you should know it. I'm revealing to you what few people in this world know. I shouldn't laugh. I was no better than they were." He stopped and looked at her with moist eyes. "God, I hope you'll forgive me for not telling you sooner."

Mary Ellen was torn between conflicting emotions. She wanted to know more about his past. She was frightened by what he would tell her. And she wanted to tell her story, unburden herself. She would tell him everything, everything, that is, except about the possibility that she was pregnant. But Thomas did not seem to be aware of her presence. He just continued with his story as if he were an explorer returning from an adventure and regaling the Royal Geographic Society with his tale.

"Forbes decided to leave until peaceful times returned, so he shipped off on a whaler destined for Vancouver. Instead, the old ship struck for the Galapagos Islands, where it ran into a severe storm near Chatham Island. The crew attempted to abandon the ship. As they descended into the long boats musket fire from the shore raked them to pieces. Only Forbes survived. The others, trying to get to shore, were either picked off one by one or drowned. Forbes went the opposite way. He swam out to sea, found some driftwood and held on until he was picked up by a passing ship. He warned the captain about the pirates on Chatham Island for which the captain was grateful.

"Forbes found himself on a ship carrying bullion from Peru, a large fortune of gold pesos and silver bars owned by a French merchant. It turned out that the captain of this brig, like the ones before him, had confiscated the fortune for himself and his crew. They were bound for Cocos Island. The crew removed the treasure and buried it on the island. The captain, finding that Forbes was the only man who could read or write, asked him to draw a map showing the location of the treasure. Forbes made two maps. One accurately depicted the shape of the island, the location of trees, and in all other respects appeared authentic, but he intentionally confused the directions to the treasure. He gave this map to the captain. The other he kept for himself. For nearly a quarter of a century Forbes kept the map and his secret.

"After I had been with Forbes for nearly a year he called me in and told me the story. It turns out another captain, Thompson, also stole a treasure which he hid in Cocos Island. It was known as the 'Loot of Lima.'

Many people went in search of Thompson's loot but never found it. Forbes's map was for a different treasure. Can you imagine that? Two treasures buried on the same island?

"Forbes and Barron finally outfitted a schooner and told everyone it would engage in coastal trade with South America. But we went to the Cocos instead. We spent weeks trying to locate the treasure, but to no avail. I was promised a partner's share, not as large as Forbes's or Barron's, but substantial enough. I always thought Forbes trusted me because he knew my secret, my past in Scotland, but that was not the case. He believed I could be fully trusted and I honored his trust."

"So what happened?" Mary Ellen found herself captivated by the tale of treasure and pirates. "Did you ever find it?"

"We kept on searching. Trees had fallen. The landscape had changed. Rivers had moved or disappeared altogether. At times Forbes thought he had accidentally given the good map to the captain. We began to think that perhaps the treasure had already been found by others or never existed in the first place. Forbes, though, was resolute. You should've seen him drive us, push us to the brink. Finally, when our spirits flagged, when the heat, the rains, the insects, and the exhausting work became insufferable, just when we were ready to quit, my spade struck something hard. I had found one of the crates. We found the treasure. We were delirious. It was really strange because we couldn't believe we actually found it. I, for one, was certain it was a delusion; the gods were playing with our imagination. We looked at the glittering coins and the bars of silver. We sprinkled the coins over each other, hurled the silver ingots into the air like stones. One of the crewmen broke his cheek bone in the frolic. We were in a dream, all of us. We wanted to look for more treasure, for the 'Loot of Lima,' but Forbes would have none of it. We headed back to Mazatlan with our treasure. Forbes insisted that if anyone found out about the treasure we were to say it was Captain Thompson's 'Loot of Lima' we found. Forbes didn't want anyone to know about the maps or his role in the incident.

"I returned to California in 1848 to attend to business at the New Almadein mine. When gold was discovered, quicksilver came into great demand. Quicksilver adheres to gold. It's called amalgam. Other useless substances are washed away and later the gold is easily recovered from the amalgam. In some ways quicksilver was even more valuable than gold. At first the miners didn't need it because they could find nuggets. After the nuggets had been plucked, miners looked for rock-bearing gold and the extraction required quicksilver." He stopped and sipped the coffee. The silence was overbearing. He turned to Mary Ellen, his voice faltering.

"So everything I had, all the money I told you I had borrowed from investors, was my own. All the wealth behind Forbes and Barron came from the treasure: Santa Cruz Island, the *Eustace*, everything. And the treasure was stolen! The only people who know the whole story are Forbes, Barron, Bolton, me, and now you. Even Halleck and Peachy don't know the whole story. They think Forbes and Barron gained their wealth from cotton. Not bloody likely."

Mary Ellen's eyes narrowed. "So everything you told me about the Rothschilds, our investors, was a lie?"

Thomas looked crestfallen, his face ashen. "No, not everything, Mary Ellen. Please try to understand. Yes, I have contacts with the Rothschilds. Ever since we found the treasure we've been able to circulate in the best financial circles in Europe. I still don't have any desire to go to England and I can't go to Scotland. And everything I've said to you about my feelings for you, about our amazing investments, the *Niantic*, why I would trade all the Cocos treasure for what we have, what we've built together. That's why I've been so afraid to tell you about my past and why every time I thought we were heading down that path I would change directions."

"I can't believe we've been together for so long and that I could've missed so much," Mary Ellen said, pushing his hand away. "What we've built together has been built on . . . ." She was about to say "lies" but her hands were equally dirty.

Thomas rushed to her, but Mary Ellen broke into tears.

"I love you with all my heart," Thomas tried to console her. "Please, don't be so angry and hurt. Can't you see this is why I never wanted to tell you? This all happened before we ever met."

Mary Ellen whirled around, her face contorted in anguish. "It's not just you, Thomas. It's me. It's both of us," she sobbed. "I haven't been honest with you either. And it's also in the past. But in my case it's also in the present."

Thomas looked confused. "What . . . what do you mean?" he stammered.

Mary Ellen turned away and dabbed at her face with a small white handkerchief. "Do you really love me, Thomas?" she asked, completely confused and uncertain.

"Of course I do," he said and tried to hold her face in his hands.

"Please don't," she said. "Wait until you hear me out."

"I'll do as you please," he said crestfallen. "I'm sorry."

Mary Ellen inhaled deeply and held her head up. She turned to him. "I was born at Golden Oaks in Georgia. It was a beautiful plantation not far from Augusta. I didn't know my father. My mother's name was Delila," Mary Ellen stopped. Her hands trembled.

Thomas's brow was furrowed. He looked uneasy and squirmed as if his clothes did not fit.

"My mother came from the islands. I'm not even sure which ones. My father was English and owned some plantations. But I was raised by Abigail Saunders." Mary Ellen stopped again and realized that tears were still streaming down her cheeks. She had not thought of either woman for a long time and suddenly it seemed as if it was just yesterday when they died.

Thomas remained still, afraid to interrupt what he realized was a very emotional moment for Mary Ellen.

Mary Ellen collected herself and continued. "Abigail and her husband owned Golden Oaks. My mother died when I was a small child, and Abigail cared for me as if I were her own. Abigail also died when I was about thirteen and then I was sold to Mr. Americus Price."

Thomas did not understand. "Sold? What do you mean sold?" he asked.

"Exactly that. I was sold to Mr. Price of Missouri. I was sold by Abigail and Carlyle. They owned me."

"I don't understand. How could they own you?" Thomas asked and then it dawned on him. "Why that can't be," he looked astonished.

Chapter Twenty-Five

"Yes it can; it was," Mary Ellen felt a strange sense of relief. Whatever was to happen she had finally unburdened herself. She felt as if a huge load had been lifted from her shoulders, except that the possible life of a child was also at stake. "Mr. Price gave me my freedom when I was eighteen. I was educated in New Orleans, at the Ursaline Convent.

"But you, you don't look . . . " he stumbled over the words.

"I am, in part. And proud of it."

They remained quiet as Thomas let the bombshell sink in. Then his face fell as if life had been fully drained from him.

Mary Ellen stifled a sob. Thomas remained mute, the blinking of his eyes the only testament to his being alive. "I can't believe it," he finally muttered softly to himself.

"I should've told you a long, long time ago and not let things get this far," Mary Ellen said, hoping he would snap out of it and take her in his arms and tell her it did not matter. That he would marry her, and be delighted by the prospects of having a son or daughter. But Thomas remained still, looking solemnly at the floor, his shoulders sagging.

"I hope you aren't too angry with me," Mary Ellen said.

"No, of course not," Thomas whispered, showing no emotion.

"And I hope we can remain friends," she said dejectedly as her stomach pitched upwards causing her to stifle the gag.

"Of course," he answered slowly, again without feeling.

"I'll keep your secret with me," Mary Ellen whispered as she steeled herself for his rejection. "I'm truly sorry," she began to cry again.

Thomas did not move; he appeared gaunt as if he had aged twenty years. "I'll keep your secret as well," he answered through gritted teeth.

Mary Ellen wanted to grab him by the shoulder, to shake him, to get some reaction, any reaction out of him. She wanted him to be contemptuous, mad, negative, angry, or supportive, though she now knew this was not realistic. He looked like a corpse, completely devoid of life. She never anticipated such a quiet, remote, and icy reception or rejection.

She removed the diamond earrings and put them on the small table before him. He looked at the sparkling stones without any show of sentiment. He could not or would not look at her. Mary Ellen raised her hand to stroke his face, to tell him how much she loved him and would always love him. She touched his face, but he stiffened at her touch and pulled back. Mary Ellen rushed out of the office, Thomas disconsolately closed the door behind her.

—∞—

MARY ELLEN WALLOWED IN HER MISERY FOR A WEEK, UNABLE TO FUNCTION or perform the most menial tasks. Lessette took over and nursed her friend, but Mary Ellen would not eat. Lessette could not pull Mary Ellen out of her abject despair. Mary Ellen lost weight, cried herself to sleep or stayed awake night after night. Lessette would not give up. She cajoled, implored, pleaded with Mary Ellen, but always with a loving hand. Their roles were reversed. Lessette now tried to help Mary Ellen as Mary Ellen had once helped her. But Mary Ellen kept sinking.

"You're going to have to eat," Lessette tried to spoon feed some porridge to Mary Ellen.

"I can't," she replied weakly. "It'll make me vomit."

Lessette regarded her friend quietly. Mary Ellen looked at the floor, defeated and dejected, her skin sallow, black bags under her red-rimmed eyes.

"If you don't eat you're going to die, Mary Ellen," Lessette was frustrated, angry and very afraid. "Why are you doing this?"

Mary Ellen looked into her friend's soft, tear-stained eyes. "I was once a slave. I grew up on a plantation. My mother was black, my father white."

Lessette had a faint smile on her face. "I suspected as much," she told Mary Ellen gently.

"How? Why?" Mary Ellen was surprised.

"I'm not really sure. Perhaps because of all the work you've done with Negroes in our city. You always seem to take them under your wing and help them. You have an uncommon fondness for them. More so than Selim or Frederick, and they're ardent foes of slavery."

"But I treated you the same way," Mary Ellen remonstrated. "I did that for a lot of people."

Chapter Twenty-Five

"Yes, dear Mary Ellen. You did that for me, and much more. As I said, I don't know what made me suspect it, but it's of no importance to me. It changes nothing between us. But is that why you're so forlorn? Does Thomas know about you?"

"He does now," Mary Ellen answered dejectedly.

"Aha," Lessette nodded in understanding. "How did he respond?"

"He shunned me as if I didn't exist." Mary Ellen began to cry, dropping her head on the pillow.

Lessette cupped Mary Ellen's hand in hers. "Is that why you haven't had a bite to eat for the past four week?"

"I've eaten some," Mary Ellen spoke into the pillow between sobs.

"Mary Ellen, are you pregnant?"

"I think so," Mary Ellen's sobbing began in earnest. "What am I going to do? Oh, my God, what can I do?" she wailed and Lessette quickly hugged her friend.

"Shush," she comforted Mary Ellen. "Have the baby."

"But I can't," Mary Ellen almost shrieked. "How can I? What'll happen? Selim will kick me out. No one will deal with me. It'll destroy me. And the child won't have a father."

"Selim won't kick you out," Lessette said. "You have many real friends, even if Thomas is a weak, heartless idiot. They'll stand by you. I'll be with you."

Mary Ellen hugged Lessette and held on to her friend as Lessette had once held on to her.

The following day Mary Ellen, accompanied by Lessette, went to Dr. Birch, one of San Francisco's finest physicians. After a complete and uncomfortable examination he advised her that she was, indeed, pregnant, the child due in about six months. Mary Ellen felt a sense of relief, perhaps most of all because she could share her fears, sorrows, and expectations with Lessette. Mary Ellen even felt some excitement at becoming a mother and began planning the event. She and Lessette decided that they could hide the pregnancy from Selim and the others only for so long. They would have to find some surrogate mother who would really serve in the role of a nanny. Mary Ellen would take a trip to Oregon, have the baby, and return with the baby and the nanny acting as its mother. They had plenty of time to plan the details and work out all the necessary arrangements. Lessette and Mary Ellen convinced themselves that it would work.

It was the salve that Mary Ellen needed. Even her morning sickness disappeared. Although thoughts of Thomas entered her mind frequently, Mary Ellen became upbeat and optimistic, forcing her energy and thoughts upon her baby. Selim, who worried about Mary Ellen, was delighted to see her about and active again. Lessette made up a story that Selim swallowed like a snake gorging on its prey.

On a balmy Friday night Mary Ellen turned in early, her window open to the breeze. She wore a white sleeping gown. She wanted to get up early and go to the market on Saturday morning. She had not felt that good in nearly two months. She fell asleep but woke up several hours later with a start. Something was wrong. She felt a sharp pain in her stomach, as if the muscles had knotted up. She pulled her blanket off and felt something wet in her bed. Mary Ellen bit her lip nervously and lit the lamp next to her bed. She looked down and shrieked like she had never shrieked in her life. The bed and her night clothes were soaked in blood.

MARY ELLEN LOST THE BABY. SHE ALMOST DIED FROM THE LOSS of blood. In the following weeks she wished that she had died, for the dead child, a boy, was only part of the bad news. Dr. Birch informed Mary Ellen that it was unlikely she would ever be able to bear children again.

Lessette pressed on, never judging, always supportive, emphasizing the very same things Mary Ellen had used with her. Mary Ellen did not know when she made up her mind to get back on her feet, to her business interests, but one night she had a strange, gentle dream, of living with Thomas in a huge mansion, surrounded by tall trees, attended by servants, and with several children running around. Then Abigail walked in and told the family about the loss of her infant daughter Eleanor, and how, despite that dreadful loss, Mary Ellen came into her life and brought her so much happiness. She kissed Mary Ellen on the cheek before leaving and whispered: "You'll find your happiness, too." Mary Ellen did not want to wake up from that dream. Lessette noticed that morning how Mary Ellen's listless gait and slumped posture of the past weeks had disappeared, replaced by a more determined, though not necessarily happy, woman.

During her convalescence a letter from Thomas arrived. It was brief and to the point. He apologized for putting Mary Ellen through so much pain and anguish. There was no hint that he knew anything about the pregnancy or loss of the baby. He suggested that they remain friends and business partners. Mary Ellen looked for some sign of affection, something on which to draw strength, but the letter had an austere, sterile quality—a business proposition, nothing more. Lessette worried about the letter's effect on Mary Ellen, fearing it would cause a relapse. Instead the letter served as further inducement for Mary Ellen to recover.

One evening the Woodworths held a small party for Frederick who was leaving for a trip to visit their relatives in the east. Mary Ellen, forcing herself back into the kitchen, arranged a lavish meal, with steamed crab, the finest cuts of beef, freshly baked breads, and some recently imported French wines. During dinner Mary Ellen was startled to see a greater intimacy between Selim and Lessette. Strange, she thought, that she had not noticed how much Selim doted on her friend. He sat near Lessette, laughing at her jokes, paying her a great deal of attention, as if she were the only person present. His lack of attentiveness was not lost on Frederick who seemed irritated by Selim's actions. Selim was preoccupied with one person.

After dinner, when the men withdrew into the study for their drinks and cigars, Mary Ellen approached Lessette. "I think Selim is smitten with you," she said.

Lessette blushed coyly, but did not deny it.

Mary Ellen regarded her friend. "You're not in love with him, are you?"

Lessette hesitated, and Mary Ellen had her answer.

"Does he know?" Mary Ellen asked.

"I don't think so, at least I haven't said anything to him. Do you really think he cares for me?" Lessette grabbed Mary Ellen's hand.

"More than that," Mary Ellen responded, shaking Lessette's hand briskly. "I think he's in love with you."

"I think I've known, but I kept telling myself it can't be true. Why should someone as important as Selim be interested in me?"

Mary Ellen wanted to scream, "Are you crazy? Look at him. He's middle-aged, not particularly handsome with his long, dark beard! And look at you, as beautiful and breathtaking as the loveliest dawn." But she knew better. "Lessette, he's a very good man, highly respected in the community. You've been here how long? More than a year, nearly two. This isn't some sort of infatuation. Why don't you marry the man?"

"He never asked," Lessette responded.

"So what?" Mary Ellen sighed. "It's your job to move him, to put the words in his mouth. What kind of a woman are you?"

"Well, certainly not that kind," Lessette laughed. "I'm not going to throw myself at him, if that's what you mean."

Mary Ellen shook her head in mock dismay. "I guess I'll have to take care of things as I always do." She prepared to leave.

Lessette, horrified, grabbed Mary Ellen's arm. "What are you planning? Whatever it is, please don't. I'll never be able to look him in the eye again."

"Oh, we'll see about that," Mary Ellen scoffed. "Just so long as you make me the godmother of your first child."

Lessette burst out laughing, her face a dark shade of red.

LESSETTE AND SELIM, IN A FAIRY-TALE WEDDING ATTENDED BY EVERY person of prominence in San Francisco or California, became husband and wife only a few months later. Mary Ellen, returning to a stiffer, colder, and even more serious semblance of her former self, felt like a mother who had given her child's hand in marriage, though the difference in age between her and Lessette was less than five years. As a wedding gift Selim purchased a new fashionable house at 36 Minna Street in Pleasant Valley, near the shore. They invited Mary Ellen to live with them. At first Mary Ellen declined, but both Lessette and Selim pleaded with her to give it a try. They would not take no for an answer and, finally, Mary Ellen moved into her new accommodations, a large, airy room with a beautiful view of the bay. She helped manage the household and put new energy into her business ventures, though she avoided unnecessary contact with Thomas. Except for those occasions when Thomas traveled on business for Forbes or Barron, Mary Ellen refrained from visiting the *Niantic*, which appeared in her eyes, to have a sad and forlorn aspect, with two teary eyes facing the cold and forbidding street.

Selim, Lessette, and Mary Ellen settled into their new home. Not much changed. Selim continued to dote on Lessette as he had before. Lessette took to domestic life like a fish to water. Her influence on Selim was unmistakable. It was a happy house on Minna Street, with the exception of Mary Ellen who could not free herself from the deep shadow the loss of Thomas produced. It left a bitter scar, a hollow in her soul, and every night she lay awake, staring at the dark ceiling, wondering what could have been. Lessette's friendship was the only redemption she could find, the only salve for her wounds. With the new Mrs. Woodworth, Mary Ellen now had a powerful friend and ally.

SEATED ON THE PORCH OF SELIM'S HOUSE ON A QUIET SUNDAY AFTERNOON, Mary Ellen closed her eyes and rocked back and forth. She pushed the chair with both feet firmly upon the ground. She inhaled. Exhaled. She felt the wind pick up and heard the leaves rustle. Although the city had sprouted up like an ever-growing patch of weeds, the land was still breathtakingly beautiful. Thomas entered her mind but she quickly tossed his image aside. She opened her eyes to see a painfully familiar face coming up the walkway.

"Good afternoon, Miss Price."

"Good afternoon, Mr. O'Brien," Mary Ellen responded tensely.

"I am here to see Mr. Woodworth. Is he in?"

Mary Ellen clutched both armrests and began to rise. Woodworth appeared at the door. To her surprise, he acted as if he had been expecting Colbraith.

"Mr. O'Brien." He nodded and stepped aside for Colbraith to enter. Woodworth did not even look at Mary Ellen. A sharpened machete could not have cut through the tension that thickened about the porch and entryway. She leaned back into the rocking chair.

Mary Ellen's composure dissolved instantly, sucked from her by Colbraith's sudden arrival, as an inferno draws oxygen from the surrounding air. Unprepared for his looming, hulking presence, standing before her like a frightful apparition, Mary Ellen sat stiffly in her chair unable to see the panorama before her. She clutched the armrests and felt pounding in her chest and ears, like a powerful steam engine pumping at full-throttle.

A flood of memories rushed through her mind, from their first meeting in Panama near Chagres, the celebration of Statehood, his ominous presence at the May 1851 fire, and his heroic rescue efforts after the *Sagamore* blew up. After all these years she realized that she really did not know anything about the man. He was a complete enigma.

She willed herself to sit patiently outside the house though she wanted to go inside and find out what the meeting was all about. After some time passed, she did not know how long, Colbraith came out, his hat crumpled under his arm. Mary Ellen tried to avoid eye contact and appear relaxed. Colbraith walked hurriedly past her, paused, as if he had forgotten something, and did the strangest thing. He turned to her and smiled.

"You know, Miss Price, perhaps you could do a better job of convincing the Woodworth brothers to support some of my legislative efforts. I don't seem to be getting anywhere."

Dumbfounded, Mary Ellen said, "I don't have the faintest notion of what you're talking about."

Chapter Twenty-Five

Colbraith's smile widened. "Well, if you give me an hour of your time, perhaps I could explain."

Mary Ellen squirmed in her chair under Colbraith's impenetrable gaze. "I don't know if . . ."

"Miss Price," Colbraith interrupted and stepped closer. "I understand you and Mr. Brand are not as close as you once were."

Mary Ellen could feel the blood draining from her face. "That, sir, is none of your business." She stood up abruptly. Colbraith's gaze remained unchanged.

"If you give me an hour of your time," he repeated more softly, "I'll show you that it is my business. Our business. And if I'm correct, I think you and I have had a mutual goal for several years. One we should work on together."

Despite her instinct to leave without further ado Mary Ellen found herself torn between her fear of Colbraith and interest in his baffling remarks. Perhaps it was his demeanor that finally settled her mind. He looked at her with an open, candid expression, as if he already knew her next move. He offered the crook of his arm and Mary Ellen, like a bee drawn to nectar, took his arm and they walked down the path. "Do you know," he said while looking straight ahead, "that I was the only one in the senate to fight the Fugitive Slave Law?"

Afterword

~ OR ~

THERE IS A TIME MACHINE

PALE TRUTH IS THE FIRST OF THREE NOVELS IN THE CALIFORNIA Chronicles. This effort did not begin with my thinking I was going to write three novels. The presumption of talent or time was outside my bounds. Like most paths that take us someplace we never expected, my first steps had humbler beginnings.

This adventure in story-telling began a decade ago on a trip overseas. I sat jet-lagged, unable to sleep, on a third-floor balcony overlooking a narrow winding street in an ancient city on the Mediterranean. It was three o'clock in the morning. With the exception of a scooter or solitary car darting through the deserted street below all was quiet. Bathed in the orange glow of a street lamp I began to write. That first story now fills three volumes. Such is life. If I had known that it would take me ten years to finish my story, undoubtedly I would have put away the yellow legal tablet, picked up someone else's novel, and read myself to sleep. If I had known how much sleep I would not get in the process of writing these chronicles I would not have undertaken the difficult journey. As in all voyages, there were big waves and bigger ones, times when I could write with abandon and times when I was sure I would drown in the effort. And still I rowed on toward a light that sometimes only my soul could see.

It would have been a great loss in my life if I had not embarked on this journey, dared to sail in these seas. I had many harbors in those ten years: the Research Library at UCLA, the Bancroft at Berkeley and the Davidson Library at the University of California at Santa Barbara. I visited bookstores that specialize in used or rare books, read and digested old newspapers, pamphlets, reminiscences of pioneers, countless books, and historical treatises. Looking at illustrations of people and places, I was literally transported back in time. It got to the point where I could envision San Francisco in 1849 as if I were there. I could see people slogging through muddy streets, old barks and schooners dotting the bay, men wearing vivid red-flannel shirts in stark contrast to the gray skies and brown hills. Even the major players in California history became personalized and familiar. Some disturbingly clear. I became a time traveler who sometimes forgets what time he was in, where he was drinking his morning coffee, having his late night reflection. At one point my wife was reading a draft of a chapter I had just finished and asked me what was fact and what was fiction. I confessed that I was no longer sure.

Others now ask this same question, for it is a question that readers of historical fiction often wonder, a reasonable question that demands a reasonable answer. First, let me say that California's tumultuous growth between 1848 and the Civil War involved more incredible events than one's wildest imagination could ever conceive. What purpose would be served by creating other fictional events or substantially altering actual ones, when so many wonderful tales sit there waiting to be told: spectacular crimes, unmitigated greed and corruption, conflagrations that destroyed entire cities, vigilantes, thousands of them, milling in the streets, publicly lynching criminals, disarming state militias, or placing a supreme court justice on trial for attempted murder of their executioner? The Hounds and Regulators terrorized the people of San Francisco. Jury tampering was routine. Judges were bought and sold like a commodity.

Fortunes were made and lost in the blink of an eye. So much gold flowed through the streets of San Francisco that in fifteen years it grew from a sleepy town of several hundred to one of America's most prosperous cities with a population approaching 100,000.

Of course the flow of my story, the story of Mary Ellen, Colbraith O'Brien, Thomas Brand and others, dictated the timing of sequences and events. In some cases dates were changed and events omitted. San Francisco was consumed by six fires over eighteen months. The telling of one fire was enough, and it was an important adjunct to the story, especially as it related to Mary Ellen's concern for the *Niantic*—a concern and involvement that was purely fictional. Even some of the dialogue, for example Brannan's oratory in Portsmouth Square excoriating the Sydney Ducks, is reasonably true to the mark.

Most of the characters in *Pale Truth* are real. They are portrayed as they lived, influencing the course of historical events, engaged in politics, and always attentive to commerce.

Colbraith O'Brien is patterned on David Broderick. I remain true to his personae. He was hell-bent on becoming a Senator from California and swore nothing would stand in his way. His relationship with J.D. Stevenson, minting gold coins with Kohler, forming the Tammany democracy in San Francisco, presenting the first city charter to the legislature, his virulent opposition to the Committee of Vigilance, involvement in the Democratic Party, and his ascension in state politics and government, are accurately portrayed. He was intriguing as he was puzzling. His interest in the *Niantic* is fiction. He did not arrive on the *California*. Neither did Mary Ellen, Stephen Field or Thomas Brand. Broderick came to San Francisco on June 13, 1849, aboard the *Stella*. Field came on the *California* but later that year. Subsequently Mary Ellen and Thomas Brand arrived together on the *Bolivia*. But I could not resist the temptation to place my leading friends on the first steamship to enter San Francisco, and portraying the obstacles they faced in their journey, beginning in Panama—all frighteningly real and accurate.

Colbraith's involvement with Catherine Hayes is also purely fictional. She was real, came to San Francisco as described, but there is nothing to suggest that they even knew each other. I have remained true to Colbraith's politics and commerce. He purchased water lots, became wealthy and politically powerful. He was corrupt, determined, stubborn, clever, ruthless and a staunch defender of civil rights. Colbraith is a principal character in the next two novels.

Mary Ellen is patterned on Mammy Pleasants. I have taken the most liberties with her, especially her early years, but I have been determined to remain true to her spirit, for it was a wonderful spirit of a most unusual woman. She was born as a slave, emancipated in her early years, met Americus Price, attended the Ursuline Convent, lived for a time in Cincinnati, and ultimately arrived in San Francisco after rounding the Horn. She and Thomas Bell, the Thomas Brand of *Pale Truth* were on the same ship, but no one knows if she really met him aboard. If, how much, or how long, she attempted to pass as white in San Francisco is uncertain. At some point in her life she not only acknowledged her origins publicly, she brought the first civil rights lawsuit in California. She amassed a fortune. She did so in league with Thomas Bell. With the exception of the *Niantic,* the assets she acquired—from the laundries, liveries, properties, and bordello—are described in this novel as reported in other writings. Despite my casual revisionism for the sake of a story, I am certain that Mary Ellen would not only forgive me, but smile approvingly for making her and the *Niantic* soul-sisters, metaphorically sharing so many traits in common—both ladies arrived in San Francisco alone, out of their element, far from their place of origin. They were vastly different from everyone else. Yet, they survived despite imposing obstacles and overwhelming odds. And here is an unsung heroism.

Thomas Brand is Thomas Bell's pseudonym. Not much of a change, and for most part, his life in the novel does not change much from his real life, at least as it was told in Helen Holdredge's excellent book *Mammy Pleasant's Partner*. However, there is nothing written to suggest whether Thomas knew of Mary Ellen's background in their early years. Moreover, the entire episode of her pregnancy and Thomas's rejection are fictional.

Terry Davis is one character who plays a minor role in Pale Truth, but who is a dominant and central figure in the California Chronicles. You will meet him in *Measured Swords* (due for publication in 2001).

Afterword

The Hounds or Regulators, the Vigilante Committee of 1851, the May 1851 fire, the execution of Jenkins, the arrival of the *Oregon* bearing news of statehood, the explosion of the *Sagamore* on the day of celebration, the political maneuverings, corruption, voting, ballot stuffing, and other events are accurately portrayed. So are the many individuals involved including Sam Brannan, Selim and Frederick Woodworth, Talbot Green, WDM Howard, A. A. Selover, Dutch Charley Duane, Yankee Sullivan, George Wilkes, Frederick Kohler, J.D. Stevenson, C. J. Jansen, John Jenkins, and Sam Roberts,

Finally, there is the haunting image of the *Niantic,* sitting stolidly on solid ground between two clapboard buildings, a hotel on its decks, on Clay Street. Like Mary Ellen, the *Niantic* survived the fires, earthquakes, floods, vigilantes and nearly every other conceivable disaster until it was torn down in the 1870s to make room for a larger building.

John Jakes, in *California Gold,* said it best: "To close, I present this novel to the diverse people of modern California, a gift in appreciation of what has been a wonderful learning experience." Here is real gold. Here is a story that enriches history. And hopefully the reader.

Daniel Alef

APPENDIX

California Timeline

JUNE 1846 TO DECEMBER 1852

June 1846	*U.S.S. Portsmouth* enters Yerba Buena Cove.
July 8, 1846	Captain Montgomery receives dispatch from Commodore Sloat. Sloat had taken possession of Monterey and orders Montgomery to occupy Yerba Buena.
July 9, 1846	Montgomery, with 70 soldiers and marines, takes control of Yerba Buena and announces Sloat's manifesto. Watson named military commander of the port.
July 31, 1846	The *Brooklyn* arrives in Yerba Buena with Sam Brannan and his party of 200 Mormons.
Aug. 15, 1846	The *Californian* is first published in Monterey.
Aug. 26, 1846	Lieutenant Washington A. Bartlett appointed to serve as first American alcalde of Yerba Buena, George Hyde as second alcalde.

Sept. 13, 1846	Election held in Yerba Buena and Bartlett confirmed.
Jan. 1847	Alcalde Bartlett, acting as chief magistrate, changes name from Yerba Buena to San Francisco. He is recalled a few days later after Sam Brannan accuses him of being influenced by Captain Montgomery (Bartlett was selling 50-vara lots to many sailors, including Captain Montgomery). Hyde becomes alcalde.
Jan. 9, 1847	*California Star* publishes first edition.
Jan. 19, 1847	Stockton appoints Fremont as governor and William H. Russel as Secretary of State, and appoints a legislative council for California consisting of Bandini, Alvarado, Spence, Grimes, Arguello, Vallejo and Larkin.
Feb. 22, 1847	Edwin Bryant replaces Hyde as chief magistrate and alcalde of San Francisco.
March 1, 1847	First meeting of legislative council is delayed.
March 6, 1847	*Thomas H. Perkins* arrives in San Francisco with Colonel Stevenson and first detachment of his New York volunteer regiment. Brannan and volunteer Sam Roberts exchange words at the long bar of the City Hotel.
March 19, 1847	*Susan Drew* arrives with more of Stevenson's First Regiment of volunteers.
March 26, 1847	*Loo Choo* arrives in San Francisco with the balance of Stevenson's regiment.
March 1847	Washington orders Fremont to return and gives Kearny

	executive powers in California. Monterey is designated as the capital.
Summer 1847	Census reports that San Francisco has 469 inhabitants and 147 houses, 50 of them made of adobe.
June 1847	*Californian* moves to San Francisco and begins publishing.
July 1847	Stockton departs, replaced by Colonel Mason, the military governor, who instructs Bartlett to call a town meeting for the election of a town council to serve to the end of 1848.
Sept. 13, 1847	Election for City Council of San Francisco takes place. A committee is formed to draft "The Laws of the Town of San Francisco." George Hyde is elected as alcalde, followed by Leavenworth.
Jan. 1848	Gold discovered by Marshall at the Coloma sawmill at Sutter's Creek
Jan. 24, 1848	Gold first reported at Sutter's Fort.
Feb. 2, 1848	Treaty of Guadalupe Hidalgo signed.
Feb. 1848	*Isabella* and *Sweden* arrive with more contingents of Stevenson's volunteers.
March 15, 1848	*Californian* announces the discovery of gold.
March 24, 1848	Edward Kemble, editor of *California Star*, Brannan's newspaper, calls the discovery "humbug".
Mid-May 1848	Brannan heads for gold fields and returns with gold!

May 27, 1848	San Francisco's population dwindles as its residents head to the gold fields.
Aug. 15, 1848	Companies C and K of Stevenson's Regiment are mustered out in San Francisco; Company H a few days later.
Sept. 1848	*Californian* and *California Star* merge and become the *Star and Californian,* edited by Frank Soulé, later to become author of *The Annals of San Francisco.*
Sept. 18, 1848	Companies E and G of Stevenson's Regiment mustered out in Los Angeles.
Oct. 3, 1848	Elections are held in San Francisco. Leavenworth becomes the alcalde (158 votes are cast).
Oct. 23, 24, 1848	Companies A, B and C of Stevenson's Regiment are mustered out in Monterey.
Nov. 1848	Governor Mason issues his official report of the discovery of gold.
Dec. 2, 1848	President Polk's address to Congress confirms discovery of gold in California.
Dec. 11, 1848	First meeting for the formation of civil government is held in San Jose.
Dec. 21, 1848	Second meeting for formation of civil government is held in San Francisco.
Dec. 27, 1848	A new election for Town Council of San Francisco takes place (347 votes are cast). The original council declares

the election to be a fraud. Another election is held and a third council chosen.

Dec. 28-30,1848 Meeting of old Town Council is held. Councilmen claim that the election of December 27 is invalid, and call for new elections on January 15, 1849.

Jan. 6, 8, 1849 Meetings for civil government held in Sacramento.

Jan. 15, 1849 New election for Town Council of San Francisco is held. The first council declares this election legitimate and rules itself out of existence.

Feb. 12, 1849 Public meetings are held in Portsmouth Square to consider anomalous situation of two city councils acting simultaneously. Myron Norton is called upon to preside. George Hyde presents a plan of municipal organization which is adopted. Resolutions are adopted for both councils to resign, to abolish the post of alcalde, and to hold elections for three justices and 15 town councilors on February 21.

Feb. 21, 1849 San Francisco election is held. Both councils resign. Fifteen members to a legislative assembly are elected and the office of alcalde is abolished. But alcalde Leavenworth refuses to relinquish the town records to the new chief magistrate, Myron Norton, as directed. Leavenworth resuscitates the old Town Council of 1848.

Feb. 26, 1849 General Persifor Smith arrives in San Francisco aboard the *California* to succeed Colonel/Governor Mason.

March 31, 1849 Pacific steamer *Oregon* arrives with Colonel John Geary and 350 passengers. Geary is the newly appointed U.S. postmaster and carries dispatches for the military.

April 12, 1849 Transport ship *Iowa* lands at Monterey with brevet Brigadier-general Bennett Riley and his brigade, with instructions to assume the administration of civil affairs in California—not as a military governor.

April 13, 1849 Riley announces he has assumed command of tenth military department of the United States and the administration of civil affairs for California.

Spring 1849 Australian criminals, commonly known as the Sydney Ducks, begin to arrive in San Francisco.

May 1, 1849 Mason leaves California.

May 1849 Wharf association for Central Wharf forms, raises capital and begins operations. Construction begins.

June 3, 1849 Riley issues a proclamation for elimination of military government and enforcement of the laws of California to extent not inconsistent with the U.S. Constitution. He orders an election to be held August 1 for the selection of delegates to a Constitutional Convention to be held September 1. Thirty-seven delegates are to be elected. San Diego (2), Los Angeles (4), Santa Barbara (2), San Luis Obispo (2), Monterey (5), San Francisco (5), Sonoma (4), San Jose (5), Sacramento (4), and San Joaquin (4).

June 4, 1849 Riley issues proclamation to San Francisco (received in the city on June 9) declaring the "legislative assembly of San Francisco" has usurped the powers of the Congress of the United States. He recognizes the office of alcalde Leavenworth.

June 4, 1849 Mail steamer arrives with news that Congress has failed to provide a formal government for California and has extended the revenue laws over California. The appointment of a tax collector is also announced (James Collier had been appointed in March 1849, but traveled overland and didn't arrive until late Autumn).

June 9, 1849 Public meeting held in San Francisco with an address by the committee of the legislative assembly, of which Peter Burnett is chairman. It proclaimed: "The legislative assembly of the district of San Francisco have believed it to be their duty to earnestly recommend to their fellow citizens the propriety of electing twelve delegates from each district to attend a general convention to be held at the pueblo de San Jose on the third day of Monday of August next for the purpose of organizing a government for the whole territory of California."

June 12, 1849 Mass meeting is held in Portsmouth Square, William Steuart presiding, in support of a convention to form a State Constitution. Resolutions are passed rejecting Riley's June 4 proclamation and declaring the right of the people to organize themselves since Congress failed to do so. A committee consisting of Burnett, Howard, Norton, Buffum and Gilbert is appointed to correspond with other districts. Thomas Butler King and William Gwin address the meeting.

June 14, 1849 Riley's proclamation is published in the *Alta.*

June 18, 1849	Committee issues an address recommending adoption of Riley's terms but claiming his proclamation to be discourteous and unbinding. They declare their intention to hold office.
June 22, 1849	First formal entertainment in San Francisco—a concert of vocal music, held in the schoolhouse on Portsmouth Square. Stephen C. Masset, a native of New York conducts the entire program. The program includes "Yankee Town Meeting" during which Masset gives imitations of seven different persons. Tickets are $3. The room is packed, and the "artist" makes $500. A piano borrowed from Collector of the Port cost $16 to move across the Square from the Custom House.
July 1849	Thomas Butler King, presidential confidant, makes extended tour of the mining districts accompanied by General Smith, Commodore Jones, Dr. Tyson and a cavalry detachment under Lieutenant Stoneman.
July 4, 1849	Thomas Butler King addresses the people of Sacramento.
July 4, 1849	Meeting held at Mormon Island with W.C. Bigelow in the chair and James Queen as secretary attacking the lack of Congressional support and urging the formation of a state government or, if need be, an "independent" government.
July 5, 1849	Mass meeting at Fowler's Hotel in Sacramento. King again addresses the people who adopt resolutions calling for cooperation with San Francisco and other districts for the purpose of forming a civil government.

July 9, 1849	Election is held in San Francisco supporting the Committee (the vote is 167 for and 7 against). But the turnout is so anemic the Committee dissolves and Leavenworth prevails.
July 15, 1849	Sunday, George Frank, a merchant, seeks payment of a debt from Pedro Cueto, a Chileno. The debt is handed for collection to the Regulators/Hounds. Later that evening, after holding a parade, the Regulators, led by Sam Roberts, under the guise of collecting the debt attack the Chilenos at their encampment near Telegraph Hill. Several are killed and many wounded.
July 16, 1849	After learning of the devastation suffered by the Chilenos, an incensed Sam Brannan makes his first speech calling for public action. In the afternoon, after a mass meeting, volunteer policemen form into four companies and round up the Hounds.
July 18, 1849	The criminals are tried and found guilty, but San Francisco has no jail facilities. The guilty men are banished from California under penalty of death.
July 31, 1849	Talbot Green, Robert Price and Sam Brannan meet in Brannan's office to discuss the elections for city councilmen. They are candidates for the next day's election.
Aug. 1, 1849	Elections for temporary officers and delegates to the constitutional convention takes place in each district.
Aug. 13, 1849	Riley appoints Peter Burnett, later to become first governor of California, as superior court judge.
Aug. 27, 1849	First edition of the *Pacific News,* a four-page tri-weekly

owned and edited by William Falkner and Warren Leland, is published.

Sept. 1, 1849 Constitutional Convention convenes in Monterey, but due to lack of necessary facilities, the delegates postpone their meetings.

Sept. 3, 1849 Constitutional Convention begins in earnest.

Oct. 3, 1849 San Francisco's ayuntamiento passes a resolution for the sale of 434 water lots pursuant to General Kearny's proclamation.

Oct. 13, 1849 Delegates approve and sign California's new Constitution.

Oct. 25, 1849 First Democratic Meeting held in California at Dennison's Exchange.

Meeting moves to Portsmouth Square with alcalde Geary as chair. Nominations for state senate and assembly are made.

Oct. 28, 1849 Start of the rainy season. (36" fell by March 22, 1850)

Oct. 29-30, 1849 Rowe's Olympic Circus opens to the public. It is the first "dramatic" event held in San Francisco.

Mass meeting held in Sacramento. Two tickets of nominations are elected for state senate and assembly.

Nov. 5, 1849 San Francisco resolves to sell 150 lots of 50-varas, and 20 lots of 100- varas at a public auction to be held on November 19.

Nov. 13, 1849 Elections are held in San Francisco. California's

	Constitution is adopted by a vote of 2,051 in favor, five against. Burnett is elected governor, and McDougal the lieutenant governor. Fremont and Gwin are the first U.S. Senators from California.
Nov. 19, 1849	Public auction for sale of water lots is to begin, but is delayed.
Nov. 22, 1849	Brannan moves to have city surveyor survey the balance of water property granted by Kearny to a depth of 12 feet at low water.
Dec. 1, 1849	Brannan resolves to sell 200 more 50-vara lots on December 10.
Dec. 10, 1849	Public auction for the sale of San Francisco water lots is to be held. The alcalde is authorized to grant 100-vara lots at $500 each and 50-vara lots at $200 a piece.
Dec. 13, 1849	Riley proclaims that the constitution of California has been duly adopted and ordained.
Dec. 15, 1849	First Legislature, "the Legislature of a Thousand Drinks," convenes. at San Jose.
Dec. 20, 1849	Burnett installed as governor and Riley withdraws.
Dec. 24, 1849	First major fire in San Francisco begins at Dennison's Exchange.
Dec. 25, 1849	San Francisco presents Riley with a gold snuff box.
Dec. 1849	Nearly 800 feet of Central wharf is completed.

Jan. 3, 1850	San Francisco municipal authorities sell 434 water lots for $635,130.
Jan. 8, 1850	An election is held for the state legislature, alcalde and the ayuntamiento. Polls close in the evening. Geary wins the post of alcalde, receiving 3,425 votes. Broderick is elected as a state senator. San Francisco's first plays are produced by Atwater and Anderson in the second floor of the building in the rear of the *Alta California* on Washington Street. Staged melodrama called *The Wife* and Shakespeare's *Richard III.*
Jan. 22, 1850	The *Alta California* becomes a daily. The weekly issue is retained.
Jan. 23, 1850	The *Journal of Commerce,* another daily, is launched, edited by Washington Bartlett.
Feb. 13, 1850	A draft of the San Francisco City Charter is amended and approved by the ayuntamiento. Messrs. Hagan and Talbot Green are instructed to present it to the representatives of the city for adoption by the state legislature.[1]
March 9, 1850	A mass meeting at Portsmouth Square, called by the Democrats, is attended by over 1,000 people. The Whigs also attend and fighting ensues between the two groups.
March 29, 1850	Friends of Col. John C. Hayes, a former Texas Ranger, hold a mass meeting on the plaza in anticipation of county elections for sheriff. The festivities include bands, demonstrations of horsemanship and parades. It is well attended.

Democrats assemble in the square that evening, with men, horses and wagons illuminated by flaming torches.

April 1850 — San Francisco's first theater is built.

April 1, 1850 — First election is held for San Francisco County officers. The principal office in contention is the sheriff. There are three candidates (Col H. Townes, Col. J.J. Bryant, a rich democrat and owner of the "Bryant House," and the Texas Ranger, Col. John Coffee Hayes, an independent). Hayes wins. Other offices filled are county judge, recorder, surveyor, treasurer, district attorney, county attorney, clerk, coroner and assessor.

April 15, 1850 — Legislature approves San Francisco's City charter. The city is divided into eight wards to be managed by two boards of aldermen, called the Common Council.

April 17, 1850 — Governor Burnett's bill to exclude free blacks from California is indefinitely tabled in the legislature through the acts of David Broderick.

May 1, 1850 — The San Francisco City Charter is submitted to residents for approval. It is adopted and the first elections are held. Geary is elected as Mayor.

May 4, 1850 — Second great fire begins at 4:00 A.M. in a building on the east side of the United States Exchange. Three blocks between Kearny, Clay, Montgomery and Washington, and two blocks between Dupont, Montgomery, Washington and Jackson are destroyed.

May 9, 1850 — Two boards of Aldermen meet at the new city hall (Kearny and Pacific Streets) to organize committees and receive a message from the mayor. One ordinance is adopted: fine anyone failing to aid during a conflagration.

June 1, 1850 — *San Francisco Daily Herald* comes into existence.

June 5, 1850 — One of the largest "indignation meetings" is held in Portsmouth Square, attended by 4,000 people reviling excessive salaries and taxation in city. The newly elected aldermen reject the resolutions adopted at this meeting.

June 7, 1850 — Flagpole on which Mexican flag flew before the American flag had been hoisted is removed from the Plaza and erected in front of the Custom-House at the corner of Montgomery and California streets.

June 12, 1850 — Another mass indignation meeting is called and highly attended, repeating its call for the presentation of resolutions to the aldermen. Geary supports lower salaries for aldermen.

June 14, 1850 — Third major fire destroys large sections of San Francisco.

July 1850 — 526 vessels are moored in San Francisco bay. Most of them are barques, the remainder brigs and schooners. There are at least one hundred large square-rigged vessels at Benicia, Sacramento and Stockton.

July 15, 1850 — Riley leaves after a farewell banquet given at the Pacific House at Monterey, 200 "covers were laid" and Major P. A. Roach presented to him a gold chain and medal weighing one pound.

July 4, 1850 — Grand celebration of "independence-day" is held in San

	Francisco's Portsmouth Square. The people of Portland, Oregon, present a magnificent flagstaff, or liberty-pole to San Francisco. It is erected in the Plaza. (111' tall and 1' in diameter at the bottom)
Aug. 1850	The Jenny Lind, the first of several theaters of that name, opens. (It subsequently burns down three times, the last on May 3, 1851. Owner, Tom Maguire builds a handsome stone building that becomes one of the chief architectural monuments in San Francisco, and becomes the City Hall.)
Aug. 14 1850	Squatters occupy lands owned by others in Sacramento. Officials attempt to remove the squatters and a serious riot ensues. Several officials are shot to death.
Aug. 15, 1850	News of the riots reach San Francisco and volunteers are sent to aid the authorities in Sacramento.
Sept. 5, 1850	First run on banks takes place and a monetary crisis ensues. Messrs. Burgoyne & Co., James King of William and Wells & Co. keep their doors open.
Sept. 9, 1850	Congress votes to admit California into statehood.
Sept. 17, 1850	Fourth great fire in San Francisco starts in Philadelphia House on north side of Jackson, near Washington market.
Oct. 18, 1850	Mail Steamer *Oregon* enters San Francisco harbor with news that California has been admitted as a state.
Oct. 29, 1850	Special procession and parade in San Francisco celebrates California's admission to the Union.

Oct. 29, 1850 Steamer *Sagamore* explodes in San Francisco Bay as it leaves the wharf for Stockton. Nearly forty persons are killed.

Oct. 31, 1850 Dr. Peter Smith's San Francisco City Hospital is destroyed by fire, but firemen and citizens prevent conflagration from spreading. Several patients are burned but no deaths occur.

Nov. 20, 1850 Catherine Hayes arrives on steamer *Oregon*. Ship also brings first reports of Daniel Webster's death.

Dec. 14, 1850 Fire breaks out in an old iron building on Sacramento Street, below Montgomery. Several large stores and substantial merchandise are destroyed, causing $1 million of damage. It is not considered one of the "great fires."

Jan. 6, 1851 Legislature convenes. There are no funds. State owes over $485,000 and expenditures exceed receipts by $122,180

Jan. 1851 The Pacific mining Company claims a major gold find at "Gold Bluffs" on the Klamath River at the coast. It reports that beaches are covered with pure gold. Normally any reasonable person would have discounted the story, but not in those days.

Feb. 18, 1851 At a joint session of the state legislature the first of 141 votes to elect a U.S. senator to fill the seat occupied by Fremont takes place. But after 141 votes no candidate receives a majority, and the legislature votes to postpone the election until January 1852.

Feb. 19, 1851 C. J. Jansen & Company robbed and Jansen is seriously injured.

Feb. 20, 1851 Wildred is arrested and charged with the Jansen crime.

Feb. 21, 1851 Thomas Burdue, alias James Stuart, is arrested and charged with the Jansen crime.

Feb. 22, 1851 Mass protests begin after attempts to rush the prisoners in court fail. Washington Guards are called upon to quell the mob. Handbills, probably made by Sam Brannan, are handed out demanding action to rid the city of its criminal element.

That evening a committee forms. Brannan calls for the execution of Jansen's attackers. Others disagree.

Feb. 23, 1851 On Sunday nearly six to seven thousand people attend a meeting in the plaza to denounce the courts and the mayor. Mayor Geary calls on them to remain calm and allow a jury trial to take place. Coleman and others disagree and decide to try the men themselves. Stuart is found not guilty.

Feb. 25, 1851 Dr. Peter Smith recovers judgment against San Francisco for $19,239. This is the beginning of the famous Peter Smith sales.

March 4, 1851 Dr. Peter Smith wins a second lawsuit relating to the failure of San Francisco to honor its scrip.

March 9, 1851 Another indignation meeting is held in San Francisco, relating to Judge Levi Parsons attempt to convict Walker, a *Daily Herald* journalist who blasted the judge for being too lenient on criminals. Several thousand people call for Parsons' resignation.

March 10, 1851 Nearly 4,000 people pay a visit to Walker in prison.

Walker is released on *habeas corpus* by the superior court confirms that Parsons abused his authority.

March 26, 1851 Legislature calls for Parsons' impeachment.

State cedes all rights to those parts of the city called Beach and Water Lots in exchange for 25% of all future payments received by the city for such lots.

Early 1851 First issue of the *Daily Herald* is published in San Francisco.

April 15, 1851 State legislature passes act re-incorporating San Francisco and enlarging its limits.

April 28, 1851 First election of municipal officers under the amended city charter takes place. 6,000 votes are cast. Charles Brenham is elected mayor. One of assistant aldermen is Henry A. Meiggs.

April 29, 1851 State legislature authorizes funding the floating debt of San Francisco, and the issuance of up to $700,000 in bonds to be issued in lieu of other scrip or obligations held by parties against the state. One half to be paid in New York on March 1, 1855, and other half in 1861, with interest at 7% per annum. Interest on San Francisco's scrip was accruing at the rate of three percent per month.

May 1, 1851 State legislature cedes all rights to Beach and Water Lots to San Francisco (not limited to 99 years as under prior legislation). State also agrees to fund a floating debt to San Francisco.

May 3-4, 1851 Fifth and largest fire destroys San Francisco.

May 19, 1851	First state convention of the Democratic Party assembles at Benicia to form the state and congressional ticket and the state central committee.
June 3, 1851	Primary examination of Benjamin Lewis for arson begins. Colonel Stevenson urges the crowd towards violence. Mayor Brenham seeks order.[2] San Francisco Common Council passes ordinance to import fresh water into the city by a system of pipes. One plan is to bring water from Mountain Lake, about four miles west of the plaza.
June 9, 1851	Brannan, Oakes, Neal and Wardwell call for the formation of a vigilance committee to deal with crime and the Sidney Ducks in San Francisco.
June 10, 1851	John Jenkins steals a safe from the Virgin & Company shipping office on Long Wharf. Jenkins is captured by vigilance committee members, tried and sentenced to hang. Brannan addresses the crowd from a sandbank in front of Monumental Engine House. Mayor Brenham is shouted down.
June 11, 1851	Jenkins is hanged by the Vigilance Committee despite the efforts of San Francisco police and other political forces to save him
June 22, 1851	Sixth great fire engulfs San Francisco.
July 3, 1851	The real James Stuart is arrested by the vigilance committee and tried for the attempted murder of Jansen.
July 8, 1851	The sheriff proceeds to sell city properties, including wharves and water lots, to satisfy the Dr. Peter Smith judgment.

July 11, 1851	Vigilance committee hangs James Stuart in San Francisco.
Sept. 16, 1851	Vigilance committee suspends its activities.
Sept. 17, 1851	Sheriff sells a hundred 100-vara lots, fifty-five 50-vara lots, and one water lot to satisfy the Dr. Peter Smith judgment. Sales are at nominal prices due to uncertainties of title. Buyers ultimately reap fortunes.
Oct. 3, 1851	Wells & Co. bankers suspend payment.
Oct. 4, 1851	New Jenny Lind Theater opens on the plaza. It seats over two thousand patrons. A year later it is purchased by San Francisco and becomes the new city hall. The transaction is the source of considerable speculation on political graft and fraud.
Oct. 20, 1851	American Theater, another large theater, opens its doors in San Francisco.
Feb. 4, 1852	Bill enacted by legislature making Vallejo California's permanent capital.
March 4, 1852	Sheriff sells additional water lots owned by San Francisco, with a value in excess of $500,000, at nominal prices in further satisfaction of the Dr. Peter Smith claims.
April 1852	On the first Monday of April San Francisco county elections are held.
June 1, 1852	State archives are returned to Vallejo.

June 4, 1852 — San Francisco purchases Jenny Lind Theater to serve as its new city hall.

July 14, 1852 — San Francisco's council adopts ordinance granting additional rights for water to the Mountain Lake Water Company, but reserves the right to determine prices.

Aug. 2, 1852 — Edward Gilbert, senior editor of the *Alta California* is killed in a duel with General J. W. Denver, state senator (and subsequent founder of the City of Denver).

Oct. 22, 1852 — San Francisco adopts ordinance granting a right of way to the California Telegraph Company to allow the construction of posts for extending wires into the city.

Footnotes

1. Declared "the limits of the City of San Francisco shall be the same which bounded the pueblo lands and town of San Francisco; and its municipal jurisdiction shall extend to said limits, and over the waters of the Bay of San Francisco, for the space of one league from the shore, including the Islands of Yerba Buena, Los Angeles, and Alcantraz."
2. Lewis was subsequently tried but could not be convicted due to technical flaws. This is one of many cases that brought about the Vigilance Committee of 1851.

Bibliography

This bibiliography covers research completed for all three novels of the *California Chronicles*: *Pale Truth*, *Measured Swords* (to be published in 2001) and *Honor Unto Death* (expected publication 2002).

Newspapers and Periodicals

Daily-Alta California, San Francisco
Daily California Chronicle, San Francisco
Daily Herald, San Francisco
Evening Bulletin, San Francisco
The Argonaut, San Francisco.
Union, Sacramento.

Published Books and Articles

Adams, Edgar. "Private Gold Coinage: Various Californian Private Mints, 1849-55," *American Journal of Numismatics* XLV (1911): 173-91.

Altrocchi, Julia C. *The Spectacular San Franciscans.* New York: E. P Dutton & Company, Inc. 1949.

Alverson, Margaret Blake. *Sixty Years of California Song.* San Francisco: Sunset Publishing House, 1913.

Asbury, Herbert. *The Barbary Coast.* New York: Alfred A. Knopf, 1933.

Atherton, Gertrude. *My San Francisco: A Wayward Biography.* The Bobbs-Merrill Company, New York, 1946

———*Golden Gate Country.* Duell, Sloan & Pearce, New York, 1945.

———*California: An Intimate History.* Blue Ribbon Books, Inc., New York, 1935.

Bailey, Paul. *Sam Brannan and the California Mormons.* Los Angeles: Westernlore Press, 1943.

Bancroft, Hubert Howe. *California Inter Pocula.* San Francisco: History Co., 1888.

———*History of California.* 7 vols. San Francisco: History Co Publishers., 1886. Reprint. Santa Barbara: Wallace Hebbard, 1963.

———*Popular Tribunals.* 2 vols. San Francisco: History Co. Publishers, 1887.

Barnhart, Jacqueline B. *The Fair but Frail: Prostitution in San Francisco 1849 - 1900.* Reno: University of Nevada Press, 1986.

Barry, T. A., and B. A. Patten. *Men and Memories of 1850.* San Francisco, 1873. Reprint. Oakland, Calif.: Biobooks, 1947.

Barth, Gunther. *Bitter Strength: A History of the Chinese in the United States, 1850-1870.* Cambridge: Harvard University Press, 1964.

Bates, Mrs. D. B. *Incidents on Land and Water, or Four Years on the Pacific Coast.* Boston: E. O. Libby & Co., 1858. Reprint. New York: Arno Press, 1974.

Bean, Walton. *California: an Interpretive History.* New York: McGraw-Hill Book Company, 1968.

Beasley, Delilah L. *The Negro Trail-Blazers of California.* Los Angeles, 1919. Reprint. San Francisco: R and E Research Associates, 1968.

Behrins, Harriet Frances. "Reminiscences of California in 1851." In *Let Them Speak for Themselves: Women in the American West, 1849-1900,* edited by Christiane Fischer. Hamden, Conn.: Shoe String Press, 1977.

Beilharz, Edwin A., and Carlos U. Lopez. *We Were 49ers! Chilean Accounts of the*

California Gold Rush. Pasadena, Calif.: Ward Ritchie Press, 1976.

Belden, L. Burr. *Death Valley Heroine: And Source Accounts of the 1849 Travelers.* San Bernardino, Calif.: Inland Printing & Engraving Co., 1954.

Belden, Josiah. *Josiah Belden, 1841 California Overland Pioneer: His Memoir and Early Letters.* Edited by Doyce B. Nunis. Georgetown, Calif.: Talisman Press, 1962.

Bell, Katherine. *Swinging the Censer: Reminiscences of Old Santa Barbara.* Santa Barbara: Katherine Bell Cheney, 1931.

Benard de Russailh, Albert. *Last Adventure: San Francisco in 1851.* Translated by Clarkson Crane. San Francisco: Westgate Press, 1931.

Berry, Mrs. John. "A Letter from the Mines." *California Historical Society Quarterly* 5 (1927): 293-295.

Berthold, Victor M. *The Pioneer Steamer California, 1848-49.* Boston: Houghton Mifflin Co., 1932.

Bidwell, John. *Echoes of the Past About California.* Chicago: Lakeside Press, 1928.

.*Life in California Before the Gold Discovery.* Palo Alto, Calif.: Lewis Osborne, 1966.

Black Angelenos: The Afro-American in Los Angeles, 1850-1950. Los Angeles: California Afro-American Museum, 1988.

Biggs, Donald. *Conquer and Colonize: Stevenson's Regiment and California.* San Rafael, 1977.

Binder, Frederick M. *James Buchanan and the American Empire.* Selinsgrove [PA]: Susquehanna University Press, 1994.

Bodeen, DeWitt. *Ladies of the Footlights.* Pasadena, Calif.: Pasadena Playhouse Association, n.d.

Bolton, Herbert E. *Outpost of Empire: The Story of the Founding of San Francisco.* New York: Alfred A. Knopf, 1931.

Book Club of California. *Early California Firehouses & Equipment.* [Edited by Albert Shumate] San Francisco, 1961.

Booth, Anne Willson. "Journal of a Voyage from Baltimore to San Francisco . . . , 1849." The Bancroft Library, University of California, Berkeley.

Borthwick, J. D. *Three Years in California.* Edinburgh: William Blackford & Sons, 1857. Reprint. Oakland, Calif.: Biobooks, 1948.

Bowman, Alan P, ed. *Index to the 1850 Census of the State of California.* Baltimore:

Genealogical Publishing Co., 1972.

Bowman, Mary M. "California's First American School and Its Teacher." *Historical Society of Southern California 10* (1915-1916): 86-94.

Bristow, Gwen. *Golden Dreams.* New York: Lippincott & Crowell, 1980.

Brooks, Sarah Merriam. *Across the Isthmus to California in '52.* San Francisco, 1894.

Brown, J. Ross. *Report of the Debates in the Convention of California on the Formation of the State Constitution* (Washington, D.C., 1850).

Brown, Dee. *The Gentle Tamers.* New York: G. P Putnam's Sons, 1958. Reprint. Lincoln: University of Nebraska Press, 1981.

Brown, John H. *Early Days of San Franicsco.* San Francisco, 1933.

Brown, Lucilla Linn. "Pioneer Letters." Edited by Gaylord A. Beaman. *Historical Society of Southern California Quarterly* (March 1939): 18-26.

Bruff, J. Goldsborough. *Gold Rush: The Journals, Drawings, and Other Papers of J. Goldsborough Bruff, April 2, 1849-July 20, 1851.* Edited by Georgia Willis Read and Ruth Gaines. New York: Columbia University Press, 1949.

Bryant, Edwin. *What I Saw in California.* New York: D. Appleton & Co., 1848. Reprint. Lincoln: University of Nebraska Press, 1985.

Buchanan, A. Russel. *David Terry: Dueling Judge.* San Marino: The Huntington Library , 1956.

Buck, Franklin A. *A Yankee Trader in the Gold Rush.* Boston: Houghton Mifflin Co., 1930.

Burchell, R. A. *The San Francisco Irish 1848-1880.* Berkeley and Los Angeles: University of California Press, 1980.

Burnett, Peter H. *Recollections and Opinions of an Old Pioneer.* New York: D. Appleton & Co., 1880. Reprint. New York: Da Capo Press, 1969.

Calhoon, F D. *49er Irish* New York: Exposition Press, 1977.

"California Emigrant Letters." *California Historical Society Quarterly* 24 (December 1945): 347.

California Reports, Vols. 1-14, San Francisco: Bancroft-Whitney Company, 1906.

Camp, William Martin. *San Francisco: Port of Gold.* Doubleday & Company, Inc., Garden City, 1948.

Bibliography

Caples, Mrs. James. *Reminiscence.* California State Library, Sacramento.

Caughey, John W *Gold Is the Cornerstone.* Berkeley and Los Angeles: University of California Press, 1948.

——— *Their Majesties the Mob.* Chicago: University of Chicago Press, 1967.

Chinn, Thomas W., ed. *A History of the Chinese in California: A Syllabus.* San Francisco: Chinese Historical Society of America, 1969.

Christman, Enos. *One Man's Gold: The Letters & Journal of a Forty-Niner.* Edited by Florence Morrow Christman. New York: McGraw-Hill Book Co., 1930.

Claiborne, J.F.H. *Mississippi as a Province, Territory and State.* Jackson, 1880.

Clappe, Louise Amelia Knapp Smith. *The Shirley Letters from the California Mines, 1851-1852.* New York: Alfred A. Knopf, 1949.

Clark, Arthur H. *The Clipper Ship Era.* New York: G. P Putnam's Sons, 1911.

Clark, Hiram. *Reminiscences of Life and Adventure on the Pacific Coast Twenty-Five Years Ago.* Union City: By an old Californian [1 vol. Newspaper clippings], 1874-5

Clarke, Dwight. *William Tecumseh Sherman: Gold Rush Banker.* California Historical Society, San Francisco, 1969.

Cleland, Robert G. *A History of California: The American Period.* New York: Macmillan Co., 1926.

Clyman, James. *James Clyman, Frontiersman: Adventures of a Trapper and Covered-Wagon Emigrant.* Edited by Charles L. Camp. Portland, Ore.: Champoeg Press, 1960.

Coblenz, Stanton A. *Villains and Vigilantes.* New York: thomas Yoseloff, Inc. 1957.

Cogan, Sara G. *The Jews of San Francisco and the Greater Bay Area, 1849-1919.* Berkeley, Calif.: Western Jewish History Center, 1973.

Coleman, William T. "San Francisco Vigilance Committees: By the Chairman of the Committees of 1851, 1856, and 1877." *Century Magazine* 43 (November, 1891): 133-50.

Collins, Carvel, ed. *Sam Ward in the Gold Rush.* Stanford, Calif.: Stanford University Press, 1949.

Colton, Walter. *Three Years in California.* New York: A. S. Barnes & Co., 1850. Reprint. Oakland, Calif.: Biobooks, 1948.

Comstock, David A. *Brides of the Gold Rush: The Nevada County Chronicles 1851-1859.* Grass Valley, Calif.: Comstock Bonanza Press, 1987.

———*Gold Diggers & Camp Followers: The Nevada County Chronicles 18451851.* Grass Valley, Calif.: Comstock Bonanza Press, 1982.

Conlin, Joseph R. *Bacon, Beans, and Galantines: Food and Foodways on the Western Mining Frontier.* Reno: University of Nevada Press, 1986.

Cooke, Lucy Rutledge. *Covered Wagon Days: Crossing the Plains in 1852.* Edited by Frank W Cooke. Modesto, Calif., 1923. Reprint. Plumas County Historical Society, 1980. Reprint. Glendale, Calif.: Arthur H. Clark Co., 1985.

Crosby, Elisha Oscar. *Memoirs of Elisha Oscar Crosby, Reminiscences of California and Guatemala from 1849 to 1864.* San Marino: Huntington Library Publications, 1945.

Cummings, Mariett Foster. "Journal." In *The Foster Family, California Pioneers,* edited by Lucy Ann Sexton. Santa Barbara, Calif: Press of the Schouer Printing Studio, *1925.* Reprint. In *Covered Wagon Women, vol. 4.* Glendale, Calif.: Arthur H. Clark Co., *1983.*

Currey, John. *The Terry-Broderick Duel.* Washington, D.C.: Gibson Bros., 1896.

Dana, Julian. *The Sacramento-River of Gold.* New York: Farrar & Rinehart, *1939.*

Daniels, Roger. *Asian America: Chinese and Japanese in the United States Since 1850.* Seattle: University of Washington Press, 1991.

Davis, W N., Jr. "Research Uses of County Court Records, *1850-1879:* And Incidental Intimate Glimpses of California Life and Society." *California Historical Quarterly* 52 (Fall *1973): 241-266.*

Davis, William C. *The Civil War—Brother Against Brother.* Alexandria: Time-Life Books, 1983.

Davis, Winfield J. *History of Political Conventions in California, 1849-1892.* Sacramento: Publications of the California State Library, 1893.

Day, Emeline Hubbard. *Journal, 1853-1856.* The Bancroft Library, University of California, Berkeley.

de Graaf, Lawrence B. "Race, Sex, and Region: Black Women in the American West, *1850-1920.*" *Pacific Historical Review 49* (May *1980): 285-313.*

Bibliography

Decker, Peter. *Fortunes and Failures.* Cambridge, Mass. 1978.

Delano, Alonzo. *Across the Plains and Among the Diggings.* 1853. Reprint. New York: Wilson-Erickson, 1936.

Delavan, James. *Notes on California and the Placers.* New York: H. Long & Bro., 1850. Reprint. Oakland, Calif.: Biobooks, 1956.

Delmatier, Royce D., McIntosh, Clarence F., and Waters, Earl g. *The Rumble of California politics: 1848-1970.* New York: John wiley & sons, 1970.

De Quille, Dan [Wright, William]. *The Big Bonanza.* New York: Alfred A. Knopf, 1967.

Derbec, Etienne. *A French Journalist in the California Gold Rush: The Letters of Etienne Derbec.* Edited by A. P Nasatir. Georgetown, Calif.: Talisman Press, 1964.

DeVoto, Bernard. *The Year of Decision: 1846.* Boston: Little, Brown & Co., 1943.

De Witt, Margaret. Letters. De Witt Family Papers. The Bancroft Library, University of California, Berkeley.

Dickson, Samuel. *San Francisco Kaleidoscope.* Stanford University Press. Stanford, 1949.

———*Tales of San Francisco.* Stanford University Press, Stanford, 1947.

Dickenson, Luella. *Reminiscences of a Trip Across the Plains in 1846 and Early Days in California.* San Francisco: Whitaker & Ray Co., 1904. Reprint. Fairfield, Wash.: Ye Galleon Press, 1977.

Dillon, Richard H. *Embarcadero: Being a Chronicle of True Sea Adventure from the Port of San Francisco.* Coward-McCann, Inc., New York 1959.

———*Texas Argonauts: Isaac H. Duval and the California Gold Rush.* San Francisco: Book Club of California, 1987.

Dobie, Charles C. *San Francisco's Chinatown.* New York: D. Appleton-Century Co., 1936.

———*San Francisco: A Pageant.* D. Appleton-Century Co., New York, 1935.

Downie, Major William. *Hunting for Gold.* San Francisco: California Publishing Co., 1893. Reprint. Palo Alto: American West Publishing Co., 1971.

DuBois, Ellen Carol. *Feminism and Suffrage: the Emergence of an Indpendent Women's Movement in America, 1848-1869.* Ithaca N.Y.: Cornell University Press, 1900.

Duffus, R.L. *The Tower of Jewels: Memories of San Francisco.* W. W. Norton & Company, Inc., New York, 1960.

Durant, Mary. Letter of 24 December 1853. Durant Family Letters. The Bancroft Library, University of California, Berkeley.

Eastman, Sophia A. Letters. Maria M. Eastman Child Collection. The Bancroft Library, University of California, Berkeley.

Eaves, Lucille. *A History of California Labor Legislation with an Introductory Sketch of the San Francisco Labor Movement.* Berkeley: University of California Press, 1910.

Egan, Ferol. *The El Dorado Trail: The Story of the Gold Rush Routes Across Mexico.* New York: McGraw-Hill, 1970. Reprint. Lincoln: University of Nebraska Press, 1984.

Eldridge, Zoeth S. *The Beginnings of San Francisco.* San Francisco: published by the author, 1912.

Elliot, Mary Ann. Letter, January 1850. Van Ness Family Papers. The Bancroft Library, University of California, Berkeley.

Ely, Edward. *The Wanderings of Edward Ely, a Mid-19th Century Seafarer's Diary.* Edited by Anthony and Allison Sima. New York: Hastings House Publishers, 1954.

Ernst, Robert. "The One and Only Mike Walsh," *New York Historical Society Quarterly* 26 (1952): 43-65.

Ethington, Philip J. *The Public City: The Political Construction of Urban Life in San Francisco, 1850-1900.* Cambridge: Cambridge University Press, 1994.

Faragher, John M. *Women and Men on the Overland Trail.* New Haven, Conn.: Yale University Press, 1979.

Farnham, Eliza W *California, In-Doors and Out; or, How we Farm, Mine, and Live Generally in the Golden State.* New York: Dix, Edwards & Co., 1856. Reprint. Nieuwkoop, The Netherlands: B. DeGraaf, 1972.

Faust, Drew. *James Henry Hammond and the Old South.* Baton Rouge: , 1982.

Ferguson, Charles D. *California Gold Fields.* Cleveland, Ohio: Williams Publishing Co., 1888. Reprint. Oakland, Calif.: Biobooks, 1948.

———*First Steamship Pioneers.* San Francisco: H. S. Crocker & Co., 1874.

Field, Stephen J. *California Alcalde.* Oakland: Biobooks, 1950.

Bibliography

Fremont, Jessie Benton. *A Year of American Travel: Narrative of Personal Experience.* New York: Harper & Bros., 1878. Reprint. San Francisco: Book Club of San Francisco, 1960.

Fritz, Christian G. "Politics and the Courts: The Struggle over Land in San Francisco 1846-1866." *Santa Clara Law Review* 26:1 (Winter 1986): 127-64.

Fritzche, Bruno. "San Francisco 1846-1848: the Coming of the Land Speculator." *California Historical Quarterly* 51:1 (Spring 1972): 17-34

Frizzell, Lodisa. *Across the Plains to California in 1852.* Edited by Victor H. Paltsits. New York: New York Public Library, 1915.

Gagey, Edmond M. *The San Francisco Stage: A History.* New York: Columbia University Press, 1950.

Gardiner, Howard C. *In Pursuit of the Golden Dream: Reminiscences . . . 1849-1857.* Edited by Dale L. Morgan. Stoughton, Mass.: Western Hemisphere, Inc., 1970.

Gentry, Curt. *The Madams of San Francisco.* New York: Doubleday & Co., 1964.

Giffen, Helen. *Trail-Blazing Pioneer: Colonel Joseph Ballinger Chiles.* San Francisco: John Howell-Books, 1969.

Gilliam, Harold. *San Francisco Bay.* Doubleday & Company, Inc., Garden City, 1957.

Goode, Kenneth G. *California's Black Pioneers.* Santa Barbara, Calif.: McNally & Loftin, 1974.

Goodwin, Cardinal. *The Establishment of State Government in California,* 1846-50. New York, 1914.

Gray, Charles G. *Off at Sunrise: The Overland Journal of Charles Glass Gray.* Edited by Thomas D. Clark. San Marino, Calif.: Huntington Library, 1976.

Griswold, Robert L. *Family and Divorce in California, 1850-1890: Victorian Illusions and Everyday Realities.* Albany: State University of New York Press, 1982.

Grivas, Theodore. *Military Governments in California 1846-50.* Glendale, 1963.

Groh, George W. *Gold Fever.* New York: William Morrow & Co., 1966.

Gudde, Erwin G. *Bigler's Chronicle of the West.* Berkeley and Los Angeles: University of California Press, 1962.

———*California Gold Camps: A Geographical and Historical Dictionary*. Berkeley and Los Angeles: University of California Press, 1975.

Hall, Carroll Douglas. *The Terry-Broderick Duel.* San Francisco: , 1939.

Hamilton, Holman. *Prologue to Conflict.* Lexington, 1964.

Hammond, George P *The Weber Era in Stockton History.* Berkeley, Calif.: Friends of the The Bancroft Library, 1982.

Hansen, Woodrow J. *The Search for Authority in California.* Oakland, Calif.: Biobooks, 1960.

Hardeman, Nicholas P. *Harbor of the Heartlands: A History of the Inland Seaport of Stockton, California, From the Gold Rush to 1985.* Stockton: Holt-Atherton Center for Western Studies, 1986.

Hargis, Donald E. "Women's Rights: California 1849." *Historical Society of Southern California* 37 (December 1955): 320-334.

Harris, Benjamin Butler. *The Gila Trail: The Texas Argonauts and the California Gold Rush.* Norman: University of Oklahoma Press, 1960.

Harlow, Neal. *California Conquered.* Berkeley, 1982

Harpending, Asbury. *The Great Diamond Hoax and Other Stirring Incidents in the Life of Asbury Harpending.* [Ed. by Wilkins, James], Norman: University of Oklahoma Press, 1958.

Hart, B. H. Liddell. *Sherman - Soldier-Realist-American.* Dodd, Mead & Company, New York, 1929.

Hawgood, John A. *America's Western Frontiers: The Explorations and the Settlement of the Trans-Mississippi West.* New York: Alfred A. Knopf, 1967.

Heintz, William. *San Francisco Mayors, 1850-80.* Woodside, 1975.

Herr, Pamela. *Jessie Benton Fremont: A Biography.* New York: Franklin Watts, 1987.

Hittell, John S. *A History of the City of San Francisco and Incidentally of the State of California.* San Francisco: A. L. Bancroft and Co., 1878.

Hittell, Theodore H. *Codes and Statutes of California.* 2 vols. San Francisco: A. L. Bancroft and Co., 1876.

———*History of California.* 4 vols. San Francisco, 1885-1897.

Holdredge, Helen. *Mammy Pleasant.* New York: G. P Putnam's Sons, 1953.

———*Mammy Pleasant's Partner.* New York G.P. Putnam's Sons, 1954

Holliday, J. S. *The World Rushed in: The California Gold Rush Experience.* New York: Simon & Schuster, 1981.

Bibliography

Hulbert, Archer Butler. *Forty-Niners: A Chronicle of the California Trail.* Nevada Publications, Las Vegas, 1986.

Hutchings, James M. *Seeking the Elephant, 1849: James Mason Hutchings' Overland Journal.* Edited by Shirley Sargent. Glendale, Calif.: Arthur H. Clark Co., 1980.

Ide, Simeon. *A Biographical Sketch of the Life of William B. Ide.* 1888. Reprint. Glorieta, N.M.: Rio Grande Press, 1967.

Jackson, Joseph H. *Anybody's Gold: The Story of California's Mining Towns.* New York: D. Appleton-Century Co., 1941.

———Introduction to *The Life and Adventures of Joaquin Murieta,* by John Rollin Ridge. Norman: University of Oklahoma Press, 1955.

Jacobson, Pauline. *City of the Golden 'Fifties.* Berkeley and Los Angeles: University of California Press, 1941.

Jensen, Joan M., and Darlis Miller. "The Gentle Tamers Revisited: New Approaches to the History of Women in the American West." *Pacific Historical Review* 49 (May 1980): 173-212.

Johnston, Wm. G. *Overland to California.* 1892. Reprint. Oakland, Calif.: Biobooks, 1948.

Kagin, Donald H. *Private Gold Coins and Patterns of the United States.* New York: ARCO Publishing, Inc., 1981.

Kelly, William. *A Stroll Through the Diggings of California.* London, 1852. Reprint. Oakland, Calif.: Biobooks, 1950.

Kemble, Edward C. *A Kemble Reader: Stories of California, 1846-1848.* San Francisco: California Historical Society, 1963.

Kemble, John H. *The Panama Route, 1848-1869.* Berkeley and Los Angeles: University of California Press, 1943.

Kirsch, Robert and Murphy, William S. *West of the West.* New York: E. P. Dutton & Co., Inc., 1967.

Klein, Philip. *President James Buchanan.* University Park, , 1962.

Knower, Daniel. *Adventures of a Forty-niner.* San Francisco, 1894.

Langum, David. *Thomas O. Larkin.* Norman, 1990.

Lapp, Rudolph M. *Blacks in Gold Rush California.* New Haven, Conn.: Yale University Press, 1977.

Latta, Frank F *Death Valley '49ers.* Santa Cruz, Calif.: Bear State Books, 1979.

Lavender, David. *Nothing Seemed Impossible: William C. Ralston and Early San Francisco.* American West Publishing Company, Palo Alto, 1975.

———*California: Land of new Beginnings.* University of Nebraska Press, Lincoln, 1972.

Lee, W. Storrs. *California: A Literary Chronicle.* Funk & Wagnalls, New York, 1968.

Levy, JoAnn. *They Saw the Elephant: Women in the California Gold Rush.* Norman: University of Oklahoma Press, 1992.

Lewis, Oscar. *Lola Montez: The Mid-Victorian Bad Girl in California.* San Francisco: Colt Press, 1938.

———*Sea Routes to the Gold Fields: The Migration by Water to California in* 1849-1852. New York: Alfred A. Knopf, *1949.*

———*Sutter's Fort: Gateway to the Gold Fields.* Englewood Cliffs, N.J.: Prentice Hall, *1966.*

———*San Francisco: Mission to Metropolis.* Howell-North Books, San Diego, 1980.

Silver Kings: The Lives and Times of Mackay, Fair, Flood, and O''Brien, Lords of the Nevada Comstock Lode. New York: Alfred A. Knopf, 1947.

Lewis, Oscar and Hall, Carroll D. *Bonanza Inn: America's First Luxury Hotel.* New York: Alfred A. Knopf, 1939.

Lippit, Francis. "The Boundary Question," *Century* 11 (1890): 794-5.

Long, Margaret. *The Shadow of the Arrow.* Caldwell, Idaho: Caxton Printers, *1950.*

Lotchin, Roger. *San Francisco* 1846-1856: *From Hamlet to City.* New York: Oxford University Press, 1974.

Lothrop, Gloria. "True Grit and Triumph of Juliette Brier." *The Californians* 2 (November/December *1984): 31-35.*

Lyman, George D. *John Marsh, Pioneer.* New York: Charles Scribner's Sons, *1931.*

———*The Saga of the Comstock Lode*: Boom Days in Virginia City. New York: Charles Scriber's Sons, 1934.

———*Ralston's Ring: California Plunders the Comstock Lode.* New York: Charles Scribner's Sons, 1945.

Lynch, Alice Kennedy. "Memoirs." In *Notes on California and the Placers,* by

James Delavan. Oakland, Calif.: Biobooks, *1956.*

Lynch, Jeremiah. *A Senator of the Fifties: David C. Broderick of California.* A.M. Robertson, San Francisco, 1911.

McElroy, Robert McNutt. *The Winning of the Far West.* G. P. Putnam's Sons. New York, 1914.

McCrackan, John. *Letters to his Family, 1849-1853.* The Bancroft Library, University of California, Berkeley.

McGlashan, C. E *History of the Donner Party. 1880.* Reprint. Palo Alto, Calif.: Stanford University Press, *1940.*

McGowan, Edward. *Narrative of Edward McGowan: Including a Full Account of the Author's Adventures and Perils, While Being Persecuted by the San Francisco Vigilance Committee of 1856.* San Francisco: Published by the Author, 1857.

Manly, William Lewis. *Death Valley in* '49. San Jose, Calif.: Pacific Tree and Vine Co., *1894.* Reprint. n.p.: Readex Microprint Corporation, *1966.*

Mann, Ralph. *After the Gold Rush: Society in Grass Valley and Nevada City, California* 1849-1870. Palo Alto, Calif.: Stanford University Press, *1982.*

Margo, Elisabeth. *Taming the Forty-Niner.* New York: Rinehart & Co., *1955.*

Marryat, Frank. *Mountains and Molehills.* New York: Harper & Bros., *1855.* Reprint. Palo Alto, Calif.: Stanford University Press, *1952.*

Mattes, Merrill J. *The Great Platte River Road.* Nebraska State Historical Society, *1969.*

Miles, Edwin. *Jacksonian Democracy in Mississippi.* Chapel Hill, 1960.

Miller, Edward F. *Ned McGowan's War.* Don Mills [Ont]: Burns and MacEachern, 1968.

Monaghan, Jay. *Chile, Peru, and the California Gold Rush of* 1849. Berkeley and Los Angeles: University of California Press, *1973.*

Morgan, Martha M. *A Trip Across the Plains in the Year* 1849, *with Notes of a Voyage to California by Way of Panama.* San Francisco: Pioneer Press, *1864.* Reprint. Fairfield, Wash.: Ye Galleon Press, *1983.*

Moses, Bernard. "The Establishment of Municipal Government in San Francisco." In *Johns Hopkins Studies in Historical and Political Science,* edited by Herbert Baxter Adams, 7 ser., vols. 1-2 Baltimore, 1889.

Moulder, A.J. "Broderick's Moral Courage," *Argonaut* 3, no. 24 (1878): 9-12.

Mullen, Kevin. *Let Justice Be done.* Reno, 1989.

Muscatine, Doris. *Old San Francisco: The Biography of a City from Early Days to the Earthquake.* New York: G. P. Putnam's Sons, 1975.

Myers, James. *The United States Catholic Almanac or Laity's Directory for the Year 1836.* Baltimore: James Myres, 1836

Myers, John Myers. *San Francisco's Reign of Terror.* Doubleday & Company, Inc. Garden City, New York, 1966.

Myres, Sandra L. *Weltering Women and the Frontier Experience* 1800-1915. Albuquerque: University of New Mexico Press, *1982.*

Nevins, Allan. *Fremont, the West's Greatest Adventurer.* London: Harper & Bros., *1928.*

Nunis, Doyce. *The San Francisco Vigilance Committee of 1856*. Los Angeles, 1971.

O'Brien, Robert. *This Is San Francisco.* Whittlesey House, New York, 1948.

Older, Fremont. *My Own Story.* San Francisco: Call Publishing co., 1919.

Olmstead, Roger R. (ed.), *Scenes of Wonder & Curiosity: From Hutchings' California Magazine 1856-1861*. Howell-North, Berkeley, 1962.

O'Meara, James. *Broderick and Gwin. The Most Extraordinary Contest for a Seat in the Senate of the United States Ever Known: A Brief History of Early Politics in California.* San Francisco: Bacon & company, Printers, 1881.

Oyster, Mary. *Gwin in the Constitutional Convention of 1849.* (Unpub. Diss., Univ. of Calif. at Berkeley, 1938.

Parkinson, R. R. *Pen Portraits; autobiographies of state officers, legislators, prominent business and professional men of the capital of the State of California; also of newspaper proprietors, editors, and members of the corps reportorial.* Sacramento City: Alta California Print, 1878.

Perkins, William. *Three Years in California: William Perkins' Journal of Life at Sonora,* 1849-1852. Berkeley and Los Angeles: University of California Press, *1964.*

Perlot, Jean Nicolas. *Gold Seeker: Adventures of a Belgian Argonaut During the Gold Rush Years.* Edited by Howard R. Lamar. New Haven, Conn.: Yale University Press, *1985.*

Peters, Charles. *The Autobiography of Charles Peters.* Sacramento: LaGrave Co., *1915.*

Phillips, Catherine C. *Coulterville Chronicle: The Annals of a Mother Lode Town.* San Francisco: Grabhorn Press, *1942.*

———*Jessie Benton Fremont: A Woman Who Made Destiny.* San Francisco: John Henry Nash, *1935.*

Pomfret, John E., ed. *California Gold Rush Voyages,* 1848-1849: *Three Original Narratives.* San Marino, Calif.: Huntington Library, 1954.

Potter, David M. *The Impending Crisis, 1848-1861.* Edited by Don E. Fehrenbacher. New York: Harper and Row, 1976.

Pratt, Sarah. "Daily Notes." In *Covered Wagon Women, vol. 4,* edited by Kenneth L. Holmes. Glendale, Calif.: Arthur H. Clark Co., *1983.*

Quinn, Arthur. *The Rivals: William Gwin, David Broderick, and the Birth of California.* Lincoln: University of Nebraska Press, 1997.

Radcliffe, Zoe. "Robert Baylor Semple, Pioneer," CHSQ 6 (1927): 130-58.

Read, Georgia Willis. "Diseases, Drugs and Doctors on the Oregon-California Trail in the Gold-Rush Years." *Missouri Historical Review* (April 1944): 260276.

———"Women and Children on the Oregon-California Trail in the Gold Rush Years." *Missouri Historical Review* (October 1944): 1-23.

Riesenberg Jr., Felix. *Golden Gate: the Story of San Francisco Harbor.* Tudor Publishing Inc., New York, 1940.

Rix, Alfred. *Rix Family Letters.* The Bancroft Library, University of California, Berkeley.

Robinson, Fayette. *California and Its Gold Regions.* New York: Stringer & Townsend, 1849. Reprint. New York: Promontory Press, 1974.

Rodecape, Lois foster. "Tom Maguire, Napoleon of the State." *California Historical Society Quarterly* 20 (December 1841): 289-96, and 21 (September 1942): 239-75.

Rolle, Andrew. *John Charles Fremont: Character as Destiny.* Norman, 1991.

Root, Virginia V *Following the Pot of Gold at the Rainbow's End in the Days of 1850.* Edited by Leonore Rowland. Downey, Calif.: Elena Quinn, 1960.

Rosenberg, Charles E. *The Cholera Years.* Chicago: University of Chicago Press, 1962.

Rourke, Constance. *Troupers of the Gold Coast, or the Rise of Lotta Crabtree.* New York: Harcourt, Brace & Co., 1928.

Rowe, Joseph A. *California's Pioneer Circus: Memoirs and Personal Correspondence Relative to the Circus Business Through the Gold Country in the '50s.* Edited by Albert Dressier. San Francisco: H. S. Crocker Co., 1926.

Royce, Josiah. *California, from the Conquest in 1846 to the Second Vigilance Committee in San Francisco; a Study of American Character.* Boston: Houghton Miffin and Company, 1886.

Sanford, Mary Fetter Hite. "A Trip Across the Plains, March 28 - October 27, 1853." California State Library, Sacramento.

Sanger, William W , M.D. *The History of Prostitution.* New York: Eugenics Publishing Co., 1937.

Savage, W Sherman. "Mary Ellen Pleasant." In *Notable American Women 1607-1950: A Biographical Dictionary.* Cambridge: Harvard University Press, 1971.

Saxon, Lyle. *Fabulous New Orleans.* Robert L. Crager & Company, New Orleans, 1947.

Scamehorn, Howard L., ed. *The Buckeye Rovers in the Gold Rush.* Athens: Ohio University Press, *1965.*

Scherer, James. *The Lion of the Vigilantes.* Indianpolis, 1939.

———*Thirty-First Star.* G.T. Putnam's Sons, New York, 1942

Scott, Reva. *Samuel Brannan and the Golden Fleece.* New York: The Macmillan Company, 1944.

Secrest, William B. *Juanita.* Fresno, Calif.: Saga-West Publishing Co., 1967.

Senkewicz, Robert. *Vigilantes in Gold Rush San Francisco.* Stanford, 1985.

Severson, Thor. *Sacramento, an Illustrated History: 1839-1874.* San Francisco: California Historical Society, *1973.*

Seymour vs. Ridgeway and Lawrence. Case File *789,* California Sixth Judicial District Court, *1851.* Archives & Collections, Sacramento History Center.

Sherman, William Tecumseh. *Memoirs.* New York, 1892.

———"Sherman and the San Francisco Vigilantes: Unpublished Letters of General W. T. Sherman." *Century Magazine* 43 (December 1891): 296-309.

Shinn, Charles Howard. *Mining Camps: A Study in American Frontier Government.* New York: Charles Scribner's Sons, *1885.* Reprint. New York: Alfred A. Knopf, *1948.*

Bibliography

Shumate, Albert. "'A Lady is More Observed Here': Maria Tuttle of Birds Valley." *The Californians* 5 (March/April 1987): 6- 7.

Shutes, Milton, "Henry Wagner Halleck, Lincoln's Chief of Staff," CHSQ 16 (1937): 195-208.

Simmons, Marc. "The Old Santa Fe Trail." *Overland Journal* 4 (Summer 1986): 61-69.

Smith, Elbert B. *The Presidency of James Buchanan.* Lawrence: University of Kansas Press, 1975.

Snyder, David L. "Negro Civil Rights in California: 1850." Sacramento: Sacramento Book Collectors Club, 1969.

Soule, Frank, Gihon, John H., and Nisbet, James. *The Annals of San Francisco; Containing a Summary of the History of the First Discovery, Settlement, Progress, and Present Condition of California, and a Complete History of all the Important Events Connected with its Great city: to which are added, Biographical memoirs of some Prominent Citizens.* New York: D. Appleton & Co., 1855.

Stafford, Mallie. *The March of Empire.* San Francisco: Geo. Spaulding & Co., 1884.

Staples, Mary Pratt. Reminiscences and Related Papers, 1850-1862. The Bancroft Library, University of California, Berkeley.

Starr, Kevin. *Americans and the California Dream.* Oxford: Oxford University Press, 1973

Steel, Edward M. *T. Butler King of Georgia.* Athens, Georgia; 1964.

Steele, Rev. John. *In Camp and Cabin.* Lodi, Wis., 1901. Reprint. Chicago: Lakeside Press, 1928.

Stellman, Louis J. *Sam Brannan: Builder of San Francisco.* New York: Exposition Press, 1953.

Stern, Madeleine B. "Two Letters from the Sophisticates of Santa Cruz." *Book Club of California Quarterly News-Letter* 33 (Summer 1968): 51-62.

Stewart, George R. *The California Trail.* New York: McGraw-Hill, 1962. Reprint. Lincoln: University of Nebraska Press, 1962.

———*The Opening of the California Trail.* Berkeley and Los Angeles: University of California Press, 1953.

———*Ordeal By Hunger.* 1936. Reprint. New York: Washington Square Press, 1960.

Stillman, Dr. Jacob D. B. *Around the Horn to California in 1849.* San Francisco: A. Roman & Co., 1877. Reprint. Palo Alto, Calif.: Lewis Osborne, 1967.

Stone, Irving. *Men to Match my Mountains; The Opening of the Far West, 1840-1900.* Garden City: Doubleday & Company, Inc., 1956.

Stott, Richard. *Workers in the Metropolis.* Ithaca, 1990.

Stover, Jacob Y "The Jacob Y Stover Narrative." In *Journals of Forty-Niners, Salt Lake to Los Angeles,* edited by LeRoy R. and Ann W Hafen. Glendale, Calif.: Arthur H. Clark Co., 1954.

Street, Franklin. *California in 1850 . . . Also a Concise Description of the Overland Route . . . including a Table of Distances . . . . Cincinnati:* R. E. Edwards & Co., 1851. Reprint. New York: Promontory Press, 1974.

Stewart, George. *Committee of Vigilance: Revolution in San Francisco.* 1851 (Boston, 1964).

Taylor, Bayard. *Eldorado, or, Adventures in the Path of Empire.* New York: George P. Putnam, 1850. Reprint. Glorietta, N.M.: Rio Grande Press, 1967.

Taylor, Rev. William. *Seven Years' Street Preaching in San Francisco, California; Embracing Incidents, Triumphant Death Scenes, Etc.* New York: Carlton & Porter, 1856.

Tays, George. *The Niantic Hotel.* Berkeley: University of California Press, 1936.

The Old West, *The Forty-Niners.* Time-Life Books, Inc., Alexandria, VA, 1974

Thomas, Lately. *Between Two Empires.* Houghton Mifflin Company, Boston, 1969.

Thompson and West. *History of Nevada County, California.* Oakland, Calif., 1880. Reprint. Berkeley, Calif.: Howell North Books, 1970.

Tinkham, George H. *A History of Stockton From its Organization up to the Present Time, Including a Sketch of San Joaquin County: Comprising a History of the Government, Politics, State of Religion, Fire Department, Commerce, Secret Societies, Art, Science, Manufactures, Agriculture and Miscellaneous Events Within the Past Thirty Years.* San Francisco: W.M. Hinton, 1880.

Townsend, Susanna Roberts. *Correspondence,* 1838-1868. The Bancroft Library, University of California, Berkeley.

Truman, Major Ben C. *Duelling in America.* San Diego: Joseph Tabler Books, 1992.

Tuck, Abigail. Letters. Marsh Family Papers. The Bancroft Library, University of California, Berkeley.

Underhill, Reuben L. *From Cowhides to Golden Fleece: A Narrative of California, 1832-1858.* Palo Alto, Calif.: Stanford University Press, 1939.

Unruh, John D., Jr. *The Plains Across.* Urbana: University of Illinois Press, 1982.

Van Every, Edward. *Sins of New York as "Exposed" by the Police Gazette.* New York: Frederick A. Stokes Company, 1930.

Walker, Wyman D., ed. *California Emigrant Letters.* New York: AMS Press, 1971.

Wagstaff, A. E. *Life of David S. Terry: Presenting an Authentic, Impartial and Vivid History of His Eventful Life and Tragic Death.* San Francisco: Continental Pub. Co., 1892.

Ware, Joseph E. *The Emigrant's Guide to California.* St. Louis, Mo.: J. Halsall, 1849. Reprint. Princeton, N.J.: Princeton University Press, 1932.

Wells, Evelyn. *Champagne Days of San Francisco.* D. Appleton-Century, New York, 1939.

Wells, Evelyn, and Harry C. Peterson. *The '49ers.* New York: Doubleday & Co., 1949.

Whipple, A. B. C. *The Challenge.* New York: William Morrow & Co., 1987.

Wienpahl, Robert W , ed. *A Gold Rush Voyage on the Bark Orion.* Glendale, Calif.: Arthur H. Clark Co., 1978.

Williams, David A. *William C. Broderick: A Political Portrait.* San Marino, Calif.: The Huntington Library, 1969.

Williams, Mary Floyd. *History of the San Francisco Committee of Vigilance of 1851: A Study of Social Control on the California Frontier in the Days of the Gold Rush.* Berkeley: University of California Press, 1921.

Wilson, Neil C. *The Story of the Oldest Incorporated Commercial Bank in the West and its First 105 Years in the Financial Development of the Pacific Coast.* The Bank of California, 1969.

Wright, Doris Marion. "The Making of Cosmopolitan California: An Analysis of Immigration 1848-1870." *California Historical Society Quarterly* (December 1940): *323-338;* (March 1941): *65-79.*

Young, John P. *History of Journalism in San Francisco.* San Francisco: Chronicle Publishing Co., 1915.

THE GREAT SEAL OF THE STATE OF
EUREKA
CALIFORNIA

List of Illustrations

List of Illustrations

EASTMAN
LOOMIS-ARMSTRONG

Follow the continuing saga of Colbraith O'Brien, Mary Ellen, Terry Davis and Thomas Brand in the second novel of the California Chronicles:

MEASURED SWORDS

By Daniel Alef

Preview of Measured Swords
Chapter One

The Stonecutter

CITY OF NEW YORK
MARCH 1836

IT STARTED WITH A BURNING SENSATION IN HIS LEFT ARM, NEAR THE shoulder, and a heaviness in his breathing. The stonemason hesitated for a moment, then ignored the discomfort and continued to work on the tall Corinthian column. Using his chisel and mallet he chipped some flakes from the smooth surface of the marble and looked up, trying to imagine what the magnificent room would look like with the huge rotunda on top of the sixteen columns, each thirty feet high. He softly caressed the polished stone, feeling the cool finish, and felt a sense of strength and relief from the oppressive sultry air in which he worked. He wondered whether the customhouse, when completed, would give him the same satisfaction he got from his work on the Capitol Building in Washington a few years earlier. Moving to New York with his wife and kids was not the economic disaster his wife had foretold, since the city's phenomenal growth meant his livelihood would be assured for years to come. There were few stonemasons with his experience or his artistic touch. Perhaps in a few years he could save enough money to buy a lot and build a house. Not bad for an Irish immigrant. He smiled to himself.

Suddenly his chest felt as if compressed by a huge clamp, creating enormous pressure up to his neck. Then, slowly the pressure dissipated, like air seeping out of a punctured bladder. He leaned against the column, standing on the scaffolding about thirty feet above the ground and mopped his brow. He felt dizzy and nauseated. Without warning another crushing force seized his chest. The pain was so excruciating, so pervasive, he was unable to utter a single word. He clutched at his throat and gasped, trying to suck up air. But he could not. A black shroud enveloped him and all he could see was darkness. Then his legs gave way and he toppled to the street below.

His limp body slammed into the ground, raising a small cloud of dust. The force of the fall cracked his skull. He lay there on his back, his face lacking any expression of pain or surprise or agony or fear, while a pool of bright red blood spread out and formed a halo around his head.

Construction workers nearby began to shout and point in the direction of the fallen figure. One man, standing less than five feet from where the body fell was so stunned by the near miss he could not move a muscle. The men crowded around the fallen stonemason. The construction foreman, Sean O'Leary, rushed forward and elbowed his way through the somber men. He knelt next to the body, placed his hand over the man's mouth, but felt nothing. Then he leaned over, placed his head on the fallen man's chest and listened for a heart beat. He heard nothing. The open eyes stared vacantly to the side. O'Leary gazed at that dead man and time seemed to stand still.

Then he shook his head in sadness and stood up. "Shamus O'Brien is dead," he announced. "May God rest his soul." Hats and caps were instantly removed. O'Leary looked at Shamus and muttered under his breath to no one in particular: "Another unlucky Irishman, gone to meet his Maker!" Most of the men were of Irish descent, with a smattering of stout Germans. "Let's bow our heads and pray for the poor man's soul." After a minute O'Leary raised his head and looked around.

"Kelly!" he called out. "You know Shamus's family, don't you?"

"Yeah, boss," Kelly replied. Dan Kelly, his red hair pasted down from sweat and grit, stood next to Shamus's body. He was one of Shamus's closest friends.

"Who should we get?" O'Leary asked.

"Well, there's his wife Liza and two boys," Kelly murmured. "I'd get the older boy, Colbraith. Shamus's wife ain't well."

O'Leary thought for a moment. "And where would we find Colbraith?"

"He's a stonecutter at Williams's, on the corner of Washington and Barrow Streets. But I hear he's been working up at Croton," Kelly replied.

"Better go get him." O'Leary scanned the ground nearby, found a gunnysack, and placed it over the dead man's head. There was nothing he could do for Shamus now. Shamus was in the hands of the Almighty. O'Leary shook his head ruefully and thought about how Shamus had been so alive, so robust and vital only a few minutes earlier; how life could change with such cold-blooded finality. Snuffed out like a candle, he was. Probably the best stonemason O'Leary ever knew. He looked at the men. He could see the fear in their eyes. Each man, he surmised, was thinking how easily it could have been him instead of Shamus and each man felt some morbid sense of relief that it was Shamus and not himself.

Kelly headed for Williams's and discovered that Colbraith, as he suspected, was at the Croton Reservoir construction site on York Hill. The only way to cover the five-mile ride to the reservoir was by hackney coach or cab, an expensive ride, costing $2.00 each way, a steep price for any laborer. Fortunately for Kelly, as soon as Williams heard the news he arranged for one of their yard carriages. The carriage was a loading wagon used by Williams to haul blocks, stone, and sand to construction sites. Kelly was shortly on his way to Croton's, sitting silently on the hard wood bench next to the driver who made no effort to converse with his sullen passenger. It would take nearly an hour to get to Croton's under normal circumstances, but the driver put the whip to the horse and they cut the time in half. Kelly thought about Shamus's family and considered what he would say to Colbraith.

21
32
19
20
12
11
8
9
E
D
C